ALISTAIR MACLEAN

Alistair MacLean, the son of a Scots minister, was born in 1922 and brought up in the Scottish Highlands. In 1941 at the age of eighteen he joined the Royal Navy; two-and-a-half years spent aboard a cruiser was later to give him the background for HMS *Ulysses*, his first novel, the outstanding documentary novel on the war at sea. After the war, he gained an English Honours degree at Glasgow University, and became a school master. In 1983 he was awarded a D.Litt from the same university.

He is now recognized as one of the outstanding popular writers of the 20th century. By the early 1970s he was one of the top 10 bestselling authors in the world, and the biggest-selling Briton. He wrote twenty-nine worldwide bestsellers that have sold more than 30 million copies, and many of which have been filmed, including *The Guns of Navarone*, *Where Eagles Dare*, *Fear is the Key* and *Ice Station Zebra*. Alistair MacLean died in 1987 at his home in Switzerland.

SAM LLEWELLYN

Sam Llewellyn is the author of a number of hugely successful thrillers, including *Blood Knot, Clawhammer* and *The Shadow in the Sands,* the continuation of Erskine Childers' classic adventure, *The Riddle of the Sands*. An experienced sailor, he has sailed all over the world and now lives with his wife and family in Herefordshire.

By Alistair MacLean

ALISTAIR MACLEAN
SAM LLEWELLYN

The Complete Navarone

The Guns of Navarone
•
Force 10 from Navarone
•
Storm Force from Navarone
•
Thunderbolt from Navarone

HARPER

These novels are entirely works of fiction.
The names, characters and incidents portrayed in them are
the work of the authors' imagination. Any resemblance to
actual persons, living or dead, events or localities is
entirely coincidental.

Harper
An imprint of HarperCollins*Publishers*
77–85 Fulham Palace Road,
Hammersmith, London W6 8JB

www.harpercollins.co.uk

This paperback edition 2011
1

The Guns of Navarone and *Force 10 from Navarone*
by Alistair MacLean
first published in Great Britain by William Collins Sons & Co. Ltd. 1957, 1968
Storm Force from Navarone and *Thunderbolt from Navarone*
by Sam Llewellyn
first published in Great Britain by HarperCollins*Publishers* 1996, 1998

The Complete Navarone omnibus edition first published in Great Britain by
HarperCollins*Publishers* 2008

Alistair MacLean and Sam Llewellyn assert the moral right to
be identified as the authors of these works

ISBN: 978 0 00 741695 0

Typeset in Meridien by Palimpsest Book Production Limited,
Polmont, Stirlingshire

Printed and bound in Great Britain by
Clays Ltd, St Ives plc

Contents

Introduction

I wanted to write a war story – with the accent on the story. Only a fool would pretend that there is anything noble or splendid about modern warfare but there is no denying that it provides a great abundance of material for a writer, provided no attempt is made either to glorify it or exploit its worst aspects. I think war is a perfectly legitimate territory for a story-teller. Personal experience, I suppose, helped to play some part in the location of this story. I spent some wartime months in and around Greece and the Aegean islands, although at no time, I must add, did I run the risk of anything worse than a severe case of sunburn, far less find myself exposed to circumstances such as those in which the book's characters find themselves.

But I did come across and hear about, both in the Aegean and in Egypt, men to whom danger and the ever-present possibility of capture and death were the very stuff of existence: these were the highly trained specialists of Earl Jellicoe's Special Boat Service and the men of the Long Range Desert Group, who had turned their attention to the Aegean islands after the fall of North Africa. Regularly these men were parachuted into enemy-held islands or came there by sea in the stormy darkness of a wind- and rain-filled night and operated, sometimes for months on end, as spies, saboteurs and liaison officers with local resistance groups. Some even had their own boats, based on German islands, and operated throughout the Aegean with conspicuous success and an almost miraculous immunity to capture and sinking.

Here, obviously, was excellent material for a story and it had the added advantage for the writer that it was set in an archipelago: I had the best of both worlds, the land and the sea, always ready to hand. But the determining factor in the choice of location and plot was neither material nor the islands themselves: that lay in the highly complicated political situation that existed in the islands at the time, and in the nature of Navarone itself.

There is no such island as Navarone – but there were one or two islands remarkably like it, inasmuch as they were (a) German-held, (b) had large guns that dominated important channels and (c) had these guns so located as to be almost immune to destruction by the enemy. Again the situation in the Dodecanese islands was danger-ous and perplexing in the extreme, as it was difficult to know from one month to another whether Germans, Greeks, British or Italians were in power there – an excellent setting for a story. So I moved a Navarone-type island from the middle of the Aegean to the Dodecanese, close in to the coast of Turkey, placed another island, filled with trapped and apparently doomed British soldiers, just to the north of it, and took as much advantage as I could of what I had seen, what I had heard, the fictitious geographical situation I had arranged for my own benefit, and the very real political and mili-tary state of affairs that existed in the Dodecanese at that time.

ALISTAIR MACLEAN
Glasgow, 1958

ALISTAIR MACLEAN

The Guns
of Navarone

To my mother

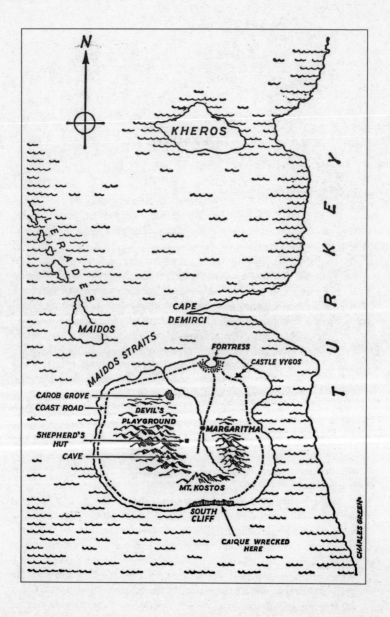

ONE

Prelude: Sunday
0100–0900

The match scratched noisily across the rusted metal of the corrugated iron shed, fizzled, then burst into a sputtering pool of light, the harsh sound and sudden brilliance alike strangely alien in the stillness of the desert night. Mechanically, Mallory's eyes followed the cupped sweep of the flaring match to the cigarette jutting out beneath the Group-Captain's clipped moustache, saw the light stop inches away from the face, saw too the sudden stillness of that face, the unfocused vacancy of the eyes of a man lost in listening. Then the match was gone, ground into the sand of the airfield perimeter.

'I can hear them,' the Group-Captain said softly. 'I can hear them coming in. Five minutes, no more. No wind tonight – they'll be coming in on Number Two. Come on, let's meet them in the interrogation room.' He paused, looked quizzically at Mallory and seemed to smile. But the darkness deceived, for there was no humour in his voice. 'Just curb your impatience, young man – just for a little longer. Things haven't gone too well tonight. You're going to have all your answers, I'm afraid, and have them all too soon.' He turned abruptly, strode off towards the squat buildings that loomed vaguely against the pale darkness that topped the level horizon.

Mallory shrugged, then followed on more slowly, step for step with the third member of the group, a broad, stocky figure with a very pronounced roll in his gait. Mallory wondered sourly just how much practice Jensen had required to achieve that sailorly effect. Thirty years at sea, of course – and Jensen had done exactly that – were sufficient warrant for a man to dance a hornpipe as he walked; but that wasn't the point. As the brilliantly successful Chief of Operations of the Subversive Operation Executive in Cairo, intrigue, deception, imitation and disguise were the breath of life to Captain James Jensen, DSO, RN. As a Levantine stevedore agitator, he had won the awed respect of the dock-labourers from Alexandretta to Alexandria: as a camel-driver, he had blasphemously out-camel-driven all available Bedouin competition: and no more pathetic beggar had ever exhibited such realistic sores in the bazaars and market-places of the East. Tonight, however, he was just the bluff and simple sailor. He was dressed in white from cap-cover to canvas shoes, the starlight glinted softly on the golden braid on epaulettes and cap peak.

Their footsteps crunched in companionable unison over the hard-packed sand, rang sharply as they moved on to the concrete of the runway. The hurrying figure of the Group-Captain was already almost lost to sight. Mallory took a deep breath and turned suddenly towards Jensen.

'Look, sir, just what *is* all this? What's all the flap, all the secrecy about? And why am *I* involved in it? Good lord, sir, it was only yesterday that I was pulled out of Crete, relieved at eight hours' notice. A month's leave, I was told. And what happens?'

'Well,' Jensen murmured, 'what did happen?'

'No leave,' Mallory said bitterly. 'Not even a night's sleep. Just hours and hours in the SOE Headquarters, answering a lot of silly, damnfool questions about climbing in the Southern Alps. Then hauled out of bed at midnight, told I was to meet you, and then driven for hours across the blasted desert by a mad Scotsman who sang drunken songs and asked hundreds of even more silly, damnfool questions!'

'One of my more effective disguises, I've always thought,' Jensen said smugly. 'Personally, I found the journey most entertaining!'

'One of your –' Mallory broke off, appalled at the memory of things he had said to the elderly bewhiskered Scots captain who had driven the command vehicle. 'I – I'm terribly sorry, sir. I never realised –'

'Of course you didn't!' Jensen cut in briskly. 'You weren't supposed to. Just wanted to find out if you were the man for the job. I'm sure you are – I was pretty sure you were before I pulled you out of Crete. But where you got the idea about leave I don't know. The sanity of the SOE has often been questioned, but even we aren't given to sending a flying-boat for the sole purpose of enabling junior officers to spend a month wasting their substance among the flesh-pots of Cairo,' he finished dryly.

'I still don't know –'

'Patience, laddie, patience – as our worthy Group-Captain has just advocated. Time is endless. To wait, and to keep on waiting – that is to be of the East.'

'To total four hours' sleep in three days is not,' Mallory said feelingly. 'And that's all I've had . . . Here they come!'

Both men screwed up their eyes in automatic reflex as the fierce glare of the landing lights struck at them, the flare path arrowing off into the outer darkness. In less than a minute the first bomber was down, heavily, awkwardly, taxiing to a standstill just beside them. The grey camouflage paint of the after fuselage and tail-planes was riddled with bullet and cannon shells, an aileron was shredded and the port outer engine out of commission, saturated in oil. The cabin Perspex was shattered and starred in a dozen places.

For a long time Jensen stared at the holes and scars of the damaged machine, then shook his head and looked away.

'Four hours' sleep, Captain Mallory,' he said quietly. 'Four hours. I'm beginning to think that you can count yourself damn lucky to have had even that much.'

The interrogation room, harshly lit by two powerful, unshaded lights, was uncomfortable and airless. The furniture consisted of some battered wall-maps and charts, a score or so of equally scuffed chairs and an unvarnished deal table. The Group-Captain, flanked by Jensen and Mallory, was sitting behind this when the door opened abruptly and the first of the flying crews entered, blinking rapidly in the fierceness of the unaccustomed light. They were led by a dark-haired, thick-set pilot, trailing helmet and flying-suit in his left hand. He had an Anzac bush helmet crushed on the back of his head, and the word 'Australia' emblazoned in white across each khaki shoulder. Scowling, wordlessly and without permission, he sat down in front of them, produced a pack of cigarettes and rasped a match across the surface of the table. Mallory looked furtively at the Group-Captain. The Group-Captain just looked resigned. He even sounded resigned.

'Gentlemen, this is Squadron Leader Torrance. Squadron Leader Torrance,' he added unnecessarily, 'is an Australian.' Mallory had the impression that the Group-Captain rather hoped this would explain some things, Squadron Leader Torrance among them. 'He led tonight's attack on Navarone. Bill, these gentlemen here – Captain Jensen of the Royal Navy, Captain Mallory of the Long

Range Desert Group – have a very special interest in Navarone. How did things go tonight?'

Navarone! So that's why I'm here tonight, Mallory thought. Navarone. He knew it well, rather, knew of it. So did everyone who had served any time at all in the Eastern Mediterranean: a grim, impregnable iron fortress off the coast of Turkey, heavily defended by – it was thought – a mixed garrison of Germans and Italians, one of the few Aegean islands on which the Allies had been unable to establish a mission, far less recapture, at some period of the war . . . He realised that Torrance was speaking, the slow drawl heavy with controlled anger.

'Bloody awful, sir. A fair cow, it was, a real suicide do.' He broke off abruptly, stared moodily with compressed lips through his own drifting tobacco smoke. 'But we'd like to go back again,' he went on. 'Me and the boys here. Just once. We were talking about it on the way home.' Mallory caught the deep murmur of voices in the background, a growl of agreement. 'We'd like to take with us the joker who thought this one up and shove him out at ten thousand over Navarone, without benefit of a parachute.'

'As bad as that, Bill?'

'As bad as that, sir. We hadn't a chance. Straight up, we really hadn't. First off, the weather was against us – the jokers in the Met. Office were about as right as they usually are.'

'They gave you clear weather?'

'Yeah. Clear weather. It was ten-tenths over the target,' Torrance said bitterly. 'We had to go down to fifteen hundred. Not that it made any difference. We would have to have gone down lower than that anyway – about three thousand feet below sea-level then fly up the way: that cliff overhang shuts the target clean off. Might as well have dropped a shower of leaflets asking them to spike their own bloody guns . . . Then they've got every second AA gun in the south of Europe concentrated along this narrow 50-degree vector – the only way you can approach the target, or anywhere near the target. Russ and Conroy were belted good and proper on the way in. Didn't even get half-way towards the harbour . . . They never had a chance.'

'I know, I know.' The Group-Captain nodded heavily. 'We heard. W/T reception was good . . . And McIlveen ditched just north of Alex?'

'Yeah. But he'll be all right. The old crate was still awash when we passed over, the big dinghy was out and it was as smooth as a millpond. He'll be all right,' Torrance repeated.

The Group-Captain nodded again, and Jensen touched his sleeve.

'May I have a word with the Squadron Leader?'

'Of course, Captain. You don't have to ask.'

'Thanks.' Jensen looked across at the burly Australian and smiled faintly.

'Just one little question, Squadron Leader. You don't fancy going back there again?'

'Too bloody right, I don't!' Torrance growled.

'Because?'

'Because I don't believe in suicide. Because I don't believe in sacrificing good blokes for nothing. Because I'm not God and I can't do the impossible.' There was a flat finality in Torrance's voice that carried conviction, that brooked no argument.

'It is impossible, you say?' Jensen persisted. 'This is terribly important.'

'So's my life. So are the lives of all these jokers.' Torrance jerked a big thumb over his shoulder. 'It's impossible, sir. At least, it's impossible for us.' He drew a weary hand down his face. 'Maybe a Dornier flying-boat with one of these new-fangled radio-controlled glider-bombs might do it and get off with it. I don't know. But I do know that nothing we've got has a snowball's chance in hell. Not,' he added bitterly, 'unless you cram a Mosquito full of TNT and order one of us to crash-dive it at four hundred into the mouth of the gun cave. That way there's always a chance.'

'Thank you, Squadron Leader – and all of you.' Jensen was on his feet. 'I know you've done your very best, no one could have done more. And I'm sorry . . . Group-Captain?'

'Right with you, gentlemen.' He nodded to the bespectacled Intelligence officer who had been sitting behind them to take his place, led the way out through a side door and into his own quarters.

'Well, that is that, I suppose.' He broke the seal of a bottle of Talisker, brought out some glasses. 'You'll have to accept it as final, Jensen. Bill Torrance's is the senior, most experienced squadron left in Africa today. Used to pound the Ploesti oil well and think it a helluva skylark. If anyone could have done tonight's job it was Bill Torrance, and if he says, it's impossible, believe me, Captain Jensen, it can't be done.'

'Yes.' Jensen looked down sombrely at the golden amber of the glass in his hand. 'Yes, I know now. I *almost* knew before, but I couldn't be sure, and I couldn't take the chance of being wrong . . .

A terrible pity that it took the lives of a dozen men to prove me right . . . There's just the one way left, now.'

'There's just the one,' the Group-Captain echoed. He lifted his glass, shook his head. 'Here's luck to Kheros!'

'Here's luck to Kheros!' Jensen echoed in turn. His face was grim.

'Look!' Mallory begged. 'I'm completely lost. Would somebody please tell me –'

'Kheros,' Jensen interrupted. 'That was your cue call, young man. All the world's a stage, laddie, etc., and this is where you tread the boards in this particular little comedy.' Jensen's smile was quite mirthless. 'Sorry you've missed the first two acts, but don't lose any sleep over that. This is no bit part: you're going to be the star, whether you like it or not. This is it. Kheros, Act 3, Scene 1. Enter Captain Keith Mallory.'

Neither of them had spoken in the last ten minutes. Jensen drove the big Humber command car with the same sureness, the same relaxed efficiency that hall-marked everything he did: Mallory still sat hunched over the map on his knees, a large-scale Admiralty chart of the Southern Aegean illuminated by the hooded dashboard light, studying an area of the Sporades and Northern Dodecanese heavily squared off in red pencil. Finally he straightened up and shivered. Even in Egypt these late November nights could be far too cold for comfort. He looked across at Jensen.

'I think I've got it now, sir.'

'Good!' Jensen gazed straight ahead along the winding grey ribbon of dusty road, along the white glare of the headlights that cleaved through the darkness of the desert. The beams lifted and dipped, constantly, hypnotically, to the cushioning of the springs on the rutted road. 'Good!' he repeated. 'Now, have another look at it and imagine yourself standing in the town of Navarone – that's on that almost circular bay on the north of the island. Tell me, what would you see from there?'

Mallory smiled.

'I don't have to look again, sir. Four miles or so away to the east I'd see the Turkish coast curving up north and west to a point almost due north of Navarone – a very sharp promontory, that, for the coastline above curves back almost due east. Then, about sixteen miles away, due north beyond this promontory – Cape Demirci, isn't it? – and practically in a line with it I'd see the island of Kheros.

Finally, six miles to the west is the island of Maidos, the first of the Lerades group. They stretch away in a north-westerly direction, maybe fifty miles.'

'Sixty.' Jensen nodded. 'You have the eye, my boy. You've got the guts and the experience – a man doesn't survive eighteen months in Crete without both. You've got one or two special qualifications I'll mention by and by.' He paused for a moment, shook his head slowly. 'I only hope you have the luck – all the luck. God alone knows you're going to need it.'

Mallory waited expectantly, but Jensen had sunk into some private reverie. Three minutes passed, perhaps five, and there was only the swish of the tyres, the subdued hum of the powerful engine. Presently Jensen stirred and spoke again, quietly, still without taking his eyes off the road.

'This is Saturday – rather, it's Sunday morning now. There are one thousand two hundred men on the island of Kheros – one thousand two hundred British soldiers – who will be dead, wounded or prisoner by next Saturday. Mostly they'll be dead.' For the first time he looked at Mallory and smiled, a brief smile, a crooked smile, and then it was gone. 'How does it feel to hold a thousand lives in your hands, Captain Mallory?'

For long seconds Mallory looked at the impassive face beside him, then looked away again. He stared down at the chart. Twelve hundred men on Kheros, twelve hundred men waiting to die. Kheros and Navarone, Kheros and Navarone. What was that poem again, that little jingle that he'd learnt all these long years ago in that little upland village in the sheeplands outside Queenstown? Chimborazo – that was it. 'Chimborazo and Cotopaxi, you have stolen my heart away.' Kheros and Navarone – they had the same ring, the same indefinable glamour, the same wonder of romance that took hold of a man and stayed with him. Kheros and – angrily, almost he shook his head, tried to concentrate. The pieces of the jigsaw were beginning to click into place, but slowly.

Jensen broke the silence.

'Eighteen months ago, you remember, after the fall of Greece, the Germans had taken over nearly all the islands of the Sporades: the Italians, of course, already held most of the Dodecanese. Then, gradually, we began to establish missions on these islands, usually spear-headed by your people, the Long Range Desert Group or the Special Boat Service. By last September we had retaken nearly all the larger islands except Navarone – it was too damned hard a nut, so we just by-passed it – and brought some of the garrisons up to, and beyond, battalion strength.' He grinned at Mallory. 'You were lurking in your cave somewhere in the White Mountains at the time, but you'll remember how the Germans reacted?'

'Violently?'

Jensen nodded.

'Exactly. Very violently indeed. The political importance of Turkey in this part of the world is impossible to over-estimate – and she's always been a potential partner for either Axis or Allies. Most of these islands are only a few miles off the Turkish coast. The question of prestige, of restoring confidence in Germany, was urgent.'

'So?'

'So they flung in everything – paratroopers, airborne troops, crack mountain brigades, hordes of Stukas – I'm told they stripped the Italian front of dive-bombers for these operations. Anyway, they flung everything in – the lot. In a few weeks we'd lost over ten thousand troops and every island we'd ever recaptured – except Kheros.'

'And now it's the turn of Kheros?'

'Yes.' Jensen shook out a pair of cigarettes, sat silently until Mallory had lit them and sent the match spinning through the window towards the pale gleam of the Mediterranean lying north below the coast road. 'Yes, Kheros is for the hammer. Nothing that we can do can save it. The Germans have absolute air superiority in the Aegean . . .'

'But – but how can you be so sure that it's this week?'

Jensen sighed.

'Laddie, Greece is fairly hotching with Allied agents. We have over two hundred in the Athens-Piraeus area alone and –'

'Two hundred!' Mallory interrupted incredulously. 'Did you say –'

'I did.' Jensen grinned. 'A mere bagatelle, I assure you, compared to the vast hordes of spies that circulate freely among our noble hosts in Cairo and Alexandria.' He was suddenly serious again. 'Anyway, our information is accurate. An armada of caiques will sail from the Piraeus on Thursday at dawn and island-hop across the Cyclades, holing up in the islands at night.' He smiled. 'An intriguing situation, don't you think? We daren't move in the Aegean in the daytime or we'd be bombed out of the water. The Germans don't dare move at night. Droves of our destroyers and MTBs and gun-boats move into the Aegean at dusk: the destroyers retire to the south before dawn, the small boats usually lie up in isolated island creeks. But we can't stop them from getting across. They'll be there Saturday or Sunday – and synchronise their landings with the first of the airborne troops: they've scores of Junkers 52s waiting just outside Athens. Kheros won't last a couple of days.' No one could have listened to Jensen's carefully casual voice, his abnormal matter-of-factness and not have believed him.

Mallory believed him. For almost a minute he stared down at the sheen of the sea, at the faerie tracery of the stars shimmering across its darkly placid surface. Suddenly he swung round on Jensen.

'But the Navy, sir! Evacuation! Surely the Navy –'

The Navy,' Jensen interrupted heavily, 'is not keen. The Navy is sick and tired of the Eastern Med and the Aegean, sick and tired of sticking out its long-suffering neck and having it regularly chopped off – and all for sweet damn all. We've had two battleships wrecked, eight cruisers out of commission – four of them sunk – and over a dozen destroyers gone . . . I couldn't even start to count the number of smaller vessels we've lost. And for what? I've told you – for sweet damn all! Just so's our High Command can play round-and-round-the-rugged-rocks and who's-the-king-of-the-castle with their opposite numbers in Berlin. Great fun for all concerned – except, of course, for the thousand or so sailors who've been drowned in the course of the game, the ten thousand or so Tommies and Anzacs and Indians who suffered and died on these same islands – and died without knowing why.'

Jensen's hands were white-knuckled on the wheel, his mouth tight-drawn and bitter. Mallory was surprised, shocked almost, by the vehemence, the depth of feeling; it was so completely out of character . . . Or perhaps it was in character, perhaps Jensen knew a very great deal indeed about what went on on the inside . . .

'Twelve hundred men, you said, sir?' Mallory asked quietly. 'You said there were twelve hundred men on Kheros?'

Jensen flickered a glance at him, looked away again.

'Yes. Twelve hundred men.' Jensen sighed. 'You're right, laddie, of course you're right. I'm just talking off the top of my head. Of course we can't leave them there. The Navy will do its damnedest. What's two or three more destroyers – sorry, boy, sorry, there I go again . . . Now listen, and listen carefully.

'Taking 'em off will have to be a night operation. There isn't a ghost of a chance in the daytime – not with two-three hundred

Stukas just begging for a glimpse of a Royal Naval destroyer. It'll have to be destroyers – transports and tenders are too slow by half. And they can't possibly go north about the northern tip of the Lerades – they'd never get back to safety before daylight. It's too long a trip by hours.'

'But the Lerades is a pretty long string of islands,' Mallory ventured. 'Couldn't the destroyers go through –'

'Between a couple of them? Impossible.' Jensen shook his head. 'Mined to hell and back again. Every single channel. You couldn't take a dinghy through.'

'And the Maidos-Navarone channel. Stiff with mines also, I suppose?'

'No, that's a clear channel. Deep water – you can't moor mines in deep water.'

'So that's the route you've got to take, isn't it, sir? I mean, they're Turkish territorial waters on the other side and we –'

'We'd go through Turkish territorial waters tomorrow, and in broad daylight, if it would do any good,' Jensen said flatly. 'The Turks know it and so do the Germans. But all other things being equal, the Western channel is the one we're taking. It's a clearer channel, a shorter route – and it doesn't involve any unnecessary international complications.'

'All other things being equal?'

The guns of Navarone.' Jensen paused for a long time, then repeated the words, slowly, expressionlessly, as one would repeat the name of some feared and ancient enemy. 'The guns of Navarone. They make everything equal. They cover the Northern entrances to both channels. We could take the twelve hundred men off Kheros tonight – if we could silence the guns of Navarone.'

Mallory sat silent, said nothing. He's coming to it now, he thought.

'These guns are no ordinary guns,' Jensen went on quietly. 'Our naval experts say they're about nine-inch rifle barrels. I think myself they're more likely a version of the 210 mm "crunch" guns that the Germans are using in Italy – our soldiers up there hate and fear those guns more than anything on earth. A dreadful weapon – shell extremely slow in flight and damnably accurate. Anyway,' he went on grimly, 'whatever they were they were good enough to dispose of the *Sybaris* in five minutes flat.'

Mallory nodded slowly.

'The *Sybaris*? I think I heard –'

'An eight-inch cruiser we sent up there about four months ago to try conclusions with the Hun. Just a formality, a routine exercise, we thought. The *Sybaris* was blasted out of the water. There were seventeen survivors.'

'Good God!' Mallory was shocked. 'I didn't know –'

'Two months ago we mounted a large-scale amphibious attack on Navarone.' Jensen hadn't even heard the interruption. 'Commandos, Royal Marine Commandos and Jellicoe's Special Boat Service. Less than an even chance, we knew – Navarone's practically solid cliff all the way round. But then these were very special men, probably the finest assault troops in the world today.' Jensen paused for almost a minute, then went on very quietly. 'They were cut to ribbons. They were massacred almost to a man.'

'Finally, twice in the past ten days – we've seen this attack on Kheros coming for a long time now – we sent in parachute saboteurs: Special Boat Service men.' He shrugged his shoulders helplessly. 'They just vanished.'

'Just like that?'

'Just like that. And then tonight – the last desperate fling of the gambler and what have you.' Jensen laughed, briefly and without humour. 'That interrogation hut – I kept pretty quiet in there tonight, I tell you. I was the "joker" that Torrance and his boys wanted to heave out over Navarone. I don't blame them. But I had to do it, I just had to do it. I knew it was hopeless – but it had to be done.'

The big Humber was beginning to slow down now, running silently between the tumble-down shacks and hovels that line the Western approach to Alexandria. The sky ahead was already beginning to streak in the first tenuous greys of the false dawn.

'I don't think I'd be much good with a parachute,' Mallory said doubtfully. 'In fact, quite frankly, I've never even *seen* a parachute.'

'Don't worry,' Jensen said briefly. 'You won't have to use one. You're going into Navarone the hard way.'

Mallory waited for more, but Jensen had fallen silent, intent on avoiding the large potholes that were beginning to pock the roadway. After a time Mallory asked:

'Why me, Captain Jensen?'

Jensen's smile was barely visible in the greying darkness. He swerved violently to avoid a gaping hole and straightened up again.

'Scared?'

'Certainly I'm scared. No offence intended, sir, but the way you talk you'd scare anyone . . . But that wasn't what I meant.'

'I know it wasn't. Just my twisted humour . . . Why you? Special qualifications, laddie, just like I told you. You speak Greek like a Greek. You speak German like a German. Skilled saboteur, first-class organiser and eighteen unscathed months in the White Mountains of Crete – a convincing demonstration of your ability to survive in enemy-held territory.' Jensen chuckled. 'You'd be surprised to know just how complete a dossier I have on you!'

'No, I wouldn't.' Mallory spoke with some feeling. 'And,' he added, 'I know of at least three other officers with the same qualifications.'

'There are others,' Jensen agreed. 'But there are no other Keith Mallorys. Keith Mallory,' Jensen repeated rhetorically. 'Who hadn't heard of Keith Mallory in the palmy, balmy days before the war? The finest mountaineer, the greatest rock climber New Zealand has ever produced – and by that, of course, New Zealanders mean the world. The human fly, the climber of the unclimbable, the scaler of vertical cliffs and impossible precipices. The entire south coast of Navarone,' said Jensen cheerfully, 'consists of one vast, impossible precipice. Nary a hand- or foot-hold in sight.'

'I see,' Mallory murmured. 'I see indeed. "Into Navarone the hard way." That was what you said.'

'That was,' Jensen acknowledged. 'You and your gang – just four others. Mallory's Merry Mountaineers. Hand-picked. Every man a specialist. You'll meet them all tomorrow – this afternoon, rather.'

They travelled in silence for the next ten minutes, turned up right from the dock area, jounced their uncomfortable way over the massive cobbles of the Rue Soeurs, slewed round into Mohammed Ali square, passed in front of the Bourse and turned right down the Sherif Pasha.

Mallory looked at the man behind the wheel. He could see his face quite clearly now in the gathering light.

'Where to, sir?'

'To see the only man in the Middle East who can give you any help now. Monsieur Eugene Vlachos of Navarone.'

'You are a brave man, Captain Mallory.' Nervously Eugene Vlachos twisted the long, pointed ends of his black moustache. 'A brave man and a foolish one, I would say – but I suppose we cannot call a man a fool when he only obeys his orders.' His eyes left the large drawing lying before him on the table and sought Jensen's impassive face.

'Is there no other way, Captain?' he pleaded.

Jensen shook his head slowly:

'There are. We've tried them all, sir. They all failed. This is the last.'

'He must go, then?'

'There are over a thousand men on Kheros, sir.'

Vlachos bowed his head in silent acceptance, then smiled faintly at Mallory.

'He calls me "sir". Me, a poor Greek hotel-keeper and Captain Jensen of the Royal Navy calls me "sir". It makes an old man feel good.' He stopped, gazed off vacantly into space, the faded eyes and tired, lined face soft with memory. 'An old man, Captain Mallory, an old man now, a poor man and a sad one. But I wasn't always, not always. Once I was just middle-aged, and rich and well content. Once I owned a lovely land, a hundred square miles of the most beautiful country God ever sent to delight the eyes of His creatures here below, and how well I loved that land!'

He laughed self-consciously and ran a hand through his thick, greying hair. 'Ah, well, as you people say, I suppose it's all in the eye of the beholder. "A lovely land," I say. "That blasted rock," as Captain Jensen has been heard to describe it out of my hearing.' He smiled at Jensen's sudden discomfiture. 'But we both give it the same name – Navarone.'

Startled, Mallory looked at Jensen. Jensen nodded.

'The Vlachos family has owned Navarone for generations. We had to remove Monsieur Vlachos in a great hurry eighteen months ago. The Germans didn't care overmuch for his kind of collaboration.'

'It was – how do you say – touch and go.' Vlachos nodded. 'They had reserved three very special places for my two sons and myself in the dungeons in Navarone . . . But enough of the Vlachos family. I just wanted you to know, young man, that I spent forty years on Navarone and almost four days' – he gestured to the table – 'on that map. My information and that map you can trust absolutely. Many things will have changed, of course, but some things never change. The mountains, the bays, the passes, the caves, the roads, the houses and, above all, the fortress itself – these have remained unchanged for centuries, Captain Mallory.'

'I understand, sir.' Mallory folded the map carefully, stowed it away in his tunic. 'With this, there's always a chance. Thank you very much.'

'It is little enough, God knows.' Vlachos's fingers drummed on the table for a moment, then he looked up at Mallory. 'Captain Jensen informs me that most of you speak Greek fluently, that you will be dressed as Greek peasants and will carry forged papers.

That is well. You will be – what is the word? – self-contained, will operate on your own.' He paused, then went on very earnestly.

'Please do not try to enlist the help of the people of Navarone. At all costs you must avoid that. The Germans are ruthless. I know. If a man helps you and is found out, they will destroy not only that man but his entire village – men, women and children. It has happened before. It will happen again.'

'It happened in Crete,' Mallory agreed quietly. 'I've seen it for myself.'

'Exactly.' Vlachos nodded. 'And the people of Navarone have neither the skill nor the experience for successful guerrilla operations. They have not had the chance – German surveillance has been especially severe in our island.'

'I promise you, sir –' Mallory began.

Vlachos held up his hand.

'Just a moment. If your need is desperate, really desperate, there are two men to whom you may turn. Under the first plane tree in the village square of Margaritha – at the mouth of the valley about three miles south of the fortress – you will find a man called Louki. He has been the steward of our family for many years. Louki has been of help to the British before – Captain Jensen will confirm that – and you can trust him with your life. He has a friend, Panayis: he, too, has been useful in the past.'

'Thank you, sir. I'll remember. Louki and Panayis and Margaritha – the first plane tree in the square.'

'And you will refuse all other aid, Captain?' Vlachos asked anxiously. 'Louki and Panayis – only these two,' he pleaded.

'You have my word, sir. Besides, the fewer the safer for us as well as your people.' Mallory was surprised at the old man's intensity.

'I hope so, I hope so.' Vlachos sighed heavily.

Mallory stood up, stretched out his hand to take his leave.

'You're worrying about nothing, sir. They'll never see us,' he promised confidently. 'Nobody will see us – and we'll see nobody. We're after only one thing – the guns.'

'Ay, the guns – those terrible guns.' Vlachos shook his head. 'But just suppose –'

'Please. It will be all right,' Mallory insisted quietly. 'We will bring harm to none – and least of all to your islanders.'

'God go with you tonight,' the old man whispered. 'God go with you tonight. I only wish that I could go too.'

TWO

Sunday Night
1900–0200

'Coffee, sir?'

Mallory stirred and groaned and fought his way up from the depths of exhausted sleep. Painfully he eased himself back on the metal-framed bucket-seat, wondering peevishly when the Air Force was going to get round to upholstering these fiendish contraptions. Then he was fully awake, tired, heavy eyes automatically focusing on the luminous dial of his wrist-watch. Seven o'clock. Just seven o'clock – he'd been asleep barely a couple of hours. Why hadn't they let him sleep on?

'Coffee, sir?' The young air-gunner was still standing patiently by his side, the inverted lid of an ammunition box serving as a tray for the cups he was carrying.

'Sorry, boy, sorry.' Mallory struggled upright in his seat, reached up for a cup of the steaming liquid, sniffed it appreciatively. 'Thank you. You know, this smells just like real coffee.'

'It is, sir.' The young gunner smiled proudly. 'We have a percolator in the galley.'

'He has a percolator in the galley.' Mallory shook his head in disbelief. 'Ye gods, the rigours of war in the Royal Air Force!' He leaned back, sipped the coffee luxuriously and sighed in contentment. Next moment he was on his feet, the hot coffee splashing unheeded on his bare knees as he stared out the window beside him. He looked at the gunner, gestured in disbelief at the mountainous landscape unrolling darkly beneath them.

'What the hell goes on here? We're not due till two hours after dark – and it's barely gone sunset! Has the pilot –?'

'That's Cyprus, sir.' The gunner grinned. 'You can just see Mount Olympus on the horizon. Nearly always, going to Castelrosso, we fly a big dog-leg over Cyprus. It's to escape observation, sir; and it takes us well clear of Rhodes.'

'To escape observation, he says!' The heavy transatlantic drawl came from the bucket-seat diagonally across the passage: the speaker was lying collapsed – there was no other word for it – in his seat, the bony knees topping the level of the chin by several inches. 'My Gawd! To escape observation!' he repeated in awed wonder. 'Dog-legs over Cyprus. Twenty miles out from Alex by launch so that nobody ashore can see us takin' off by plane. And then what?' He raised himself painfully in his seat, eased an eyebrow over the bottom of the window, then fell back again, visibly exhausted by the effort. 'And then what? Then they pack us into an old crate that's painted the whitest white you ever saw guaranteed visible to a blind man at a hundred miles – 'specially now that it's gettin' dark.'

'It keeps the heat out,' the young gunner said defensively.

'The heat doesn't worry me, son.' The drawl was tireder, more lugubrious than ever. 'I like the heat. What I don't like are them nasty cannon shells and bullets that can ventilate a man in all the wrong places.' He slid his spine another impossible inch down the seat, closed his eyes wearily and seemed asleep in a moment.

The young gunner shook his head admiringly and smiled at Mallory.

'Worried to hell, isn't he, sir?'

Mallory laughed and watched the boy disappear for'ard into the control cabin. He sipped his coffee slowly, looked again at the sleeping figure across the passage. The blissful unconcern was magnificent: Corporal Dusty Miller of the United States, and more recently of the Long Range Desert Force, would be a good man to have around.

He looked round at the others and nodded to himself in satisfaction. They would all be good men to have around. Eighteen months in Crete had developed in him an unerring sense for assessing a man's capacity for survival in the peculiar kind of irregular warfare in which he himself had been so long engaged. Offhand he'd have taken long odds on the capacity of these four to survive. In the matter of picking an outstanding team Captain Jensen, he reckoned, had done him proud. He didn't know them all yet – not personally. But he was intimately acquainted with the exhaustive dossier that Jensen held on each one of them. These were reassuring, to say the least.

Or was there perhaps a slight question mark against Stevens? Mallory wondered, looking across the passage at the fair-haired, boyish figure gazing out eagerly beneath the gleaming white wing of the Sunderland. Lieutenant Andy Stevens, RNVR, had been chosen for this assignment for three reasons. He would navigate the craft that was to take them to Navarone: he was a first-class Alpinist, with several outstanding climbs to his record: and, the product of the classical side of a red-brick university, he was an almost fanatical philhellene, fluent in both Ancient and Modern Greek, and had spent his last two long vacations before the war as a tourist courier in Athens. But he was young, absurdly young, Mallory thought as he looked at him, and youth could be dangerous. Too often, in that island guerrilla warfare, it had been fatal. The enthusiasm, the fire, the zeal of youth was not enough: rather, it was too much, a positive handicap. This was not a war of bugle calls and roaring engines and magnificent defiance in the clamour of battle: this was a war of patience and endurance and stability, of cunning and craft and stealth, and these were not commonly the attributes of youth . . . But he looked as if he might learn fast.

Mallory stole another glance at Miller. Dusty Miller, he decided, had learnt it all a long, long time ago. Dusty Miller on a white charger, the bugle to his lips – no, his mind just refused to encompass the incongruity of it. He just didn't look like Sir Lancelot. He just looked as if he had been around for a long, long time and had no illusions left.

Corporal Miller had, in fact, been around for exactly forty years. By birth a Californian, by descent three parts Irish and one part Central European, he had lived and fought and adventured more in the previous quarter of a century than most men would in a dozen lifetimes. Silver-miner in Nevada, tunneller in Canada and oil-fire shooter all over the globe, he had been in Saudi Arabia when Hitler attacked Poland. One of his more remote maternal ancestors, some time around the turn of the century, had lived in Warsaw, but that had been affront enough for Miller's Irish blood. He had taken the first available plane to Britain and lied his way into the Air Force, where, to his immense disgust, and because of his age, he was relegated to the rear turret of a Wellington.

His first operational flight had been his last. Within ten minutes of taking off from the Menidi airfield outside Athens on a January night in 1941, engine failure had brought them to an ignominious though well-cushioned end in a paddy field some miles north-west of the city. The rest of the winter he had spent seething with rage in a cookhouse back in Menidi. At the beginning of April he resigned from the Air Force without telling anyone and was making his way north towards the fighting and the Albanian frontier when he met the Germans coming south. As Miller afterwards told it, he reached Nauplion two blocks ahead of the nearest panzer division, was evacuated by the transport *Slamat*, sunk, picked up by the destroyer *Wryneck*, sunk, and finally arrived in Alexandria in an ancient Greek caique, with nothing left him in the world but a fixed determination never again to venture in the air or on the sea. Some months later he was operating with a long-range striking force behind the enemy lines in Libya.

He was, Mallory mused, the complete antithesis to Lieutenant Stevens. Stevens, young, fresh, enthusiastic, correct and immaculately dressed, and Miller, dried-up, lean, stringy, immensely tough and with an almost pathological aversion to spit and polish. How well the nickname 'Dusty' suited him: there could hardly have been a greater contrast. Again, unlike Stevens, Miller had never climbed a mountain in his life and the only Greek words he knew were invariably omitted from the dictionaries. And both these facts were of no importance at all. Miller had been picked for one reason only. A genius with explosives, resourceful and cool, precise and deadly in action, he was regarded by Middle East Intelligence in Cairo as the finest saboteur in southern Europe.

Behind Miller sat Casey Brown. Short, dark and compact, Petty Officer Telegraphist Brown was a Clydesider, in peace-time an installation and testing engineer in a famous yacht-builder's yard on the Gareloch. The fact that he was a born and ready-made engine-room artificer had been so blindingly obvious that the Navy had missed it altogether and stuck him in the Communications Branch. Brown's ill luck was Mallory's good fortune. Brown would act as the engineer of the boat taking them to Navarone and would maintain radio contact with base. He had also the further recommendation of being a first-class guerrilla fighter: a veteran of the Special Boat Service, he held the DCM and DSM for his exploits in the Aegean and off the coast of Libya.

The fifth and last member of the party sat directly behind Mallory. Mallory did not have to turn round to look at him. He already knew him, knew him better than he knew anyone else in the world, better even than he knew his own mother. Andrea, who had been his lieutenant for all these eighteen interminable months in Crete. Andrea of the vast bulk, the continual rumbling laughter and tragic past, with whom he had eaten, lived and slept in caves, rock-shelters and abandoned shepherd's huts while constantly harried by German patrols and aircraft – that Andrea had become his *alter ego*, his *doppelgänger*: to look at Andrea was to look in a mirror to remind himself what he was like . . . There was no question as to why Andrea had come along. He wasn't there primarily because he was a Greek himself, with an intimate knowledge of the islanders' language, thought and customs, nor even because of his perfect understanding with Mallory, although all these things helped. He was, instead, there exclusively for the protection and safety he afforded. Endlessly patient, quiet and deadly, tremendously fast in spite of his bulk, and with a feline stealth that exploded into berserker action, Andrea was the complete fighting machine. Andrea was their insurance policy against failure.

Mallory turned back to look out the window again, then nodded to himself in imperceptible satisfaction. Jensen probably couldn't have picked a better team if he'd scoured the whole Mediterranean theatre. It suddenly occurred to Mallory that Jensen probably had done just that. Miller and Brown had been recalled to Alexandria almost a month ago. It was almost as long since Stevens's relief had arrived aboard his cruiser in Malta. And if their battery-charging engine hadn't slipped down that ravine in the White Mountains, and if the sorely harassed runner from the nearest listening post hadn't taken a week to cover fifty miles of snowbound, enemy-patrolled mountains and another five days to find them, he and Andrea would have been in Alexandria almost a fortnight earlier. Mallory's opinion of Jensen, already high, rose another notch. A far-seeing man who planned accordingly, Jensen must have had all his preparations for this made even before the first of the two abortive parachute landings on Navarone.

It was eight o'clock and almost totally dark inside the plane when Mallory rose and made his way for'ard to the control cabin. The captain, face wreathed in tobacco smoke, was drinking coffee: the co-pilot waved a languid hand at his approach and resumed a bored scanning of the scene ahead.

'Good evening.' Mallory smiled. 'Mind if I come in?'

'Welcome in my office any time,' the pilot assured him. 'No need to ask.'

'I only thought you might be busy . . .' Mallory stopped and looked again at the scene of masterly inactivity. 'Just who is flying this plane?' he asked.

'George. The automatic pilot.' He waved a coffee-cup in the direction of a black, squat box, its blurred outlines just visible in the near darkness. 'An industrious character, and makes a damn sight fewer mistakes than that idle hound who's supposed to be on watch . . . Anything on your mind, Captain?'

'Yes. What were your instructions for tonight?'

'Just to set you blokes down in Castelrosso when it was good and dark.' The pilot paused, then said frankly, 'I don't get it. A ship this size for only five men and a couple of hundred odd pounds of equipment. Especially to Castelrosso. Especially after dark. Last plane that came down here after dark just kept on going down. Underwater obstruction – dunno what it was. Two survivors.'

'I know. I heard. I'm sorry, but I'm under orders too. As for the rest, forget it – and I mean forget. Impress on your crew that they mustn't talk. They've never seen us.'

The pilot nodded glumly. 'We've all been threatened with court-martial already. You'd think there was a ruddy war on.'

'There is . . . We'll be leaving a couple of cases behind. We're going ashore in different clothes. Somebody will be waiting for our old stuff when you get back.'

'Roger. And the best of luck, Captain. Official secrets, or no official secrets, I've got a hunch you're going to need it.'

'If we are, you can give us a good send-off.' Mallory grinned. 'Just set us down in one piece will you?'

'Reassure yourself, brother,' the pilot said firmly. 'Just set your mind at ease. Don't forget – I'm in this ruddy plane too.'

The clamour of the Sunderland's great engines was still echoing in their ears when the stubby little motor-boat chugged softly out of the darkness and nosed alongside the gleaming hull of the flying-boat. There was no time lost: there were no words spoken; within a minute the five men and all their gear had been embarked, within another the little boat was rubbing to a stop against the rough stone Navy jetty of Castelrosso. Two ropes were spinning up into the darkness, were caught and quickly secured by practised hands. Amidships, the rust-scaled iron ladder, recessed deep into the stone, stretched up into the star-dusted darkness above: as Mallory reached the top a figure stepped forward out of the gloom.

'Captain Mallory?'

'Yes.'

'Captain Briggs, Army. Have your men wait here, will you? The colonel would like to see you.' The nasal voice, peremptory in its clipped affectation, was far from cordial. Mallory stirred in slow anger, but said nothing. Briggs sounded like a man who might like his bed or his gin, and maybe their late visitation was keeping him from either or both. War was hell.

They were back in ten minutes, a third figure following behind them. Mallory peered at the three men standing on the edge of the jetty, identified them, then peered around again.

'Where's Miller got to?' he asked.

'Here, boss, here.' Miller groaned, eased his back off a big, wooden bollard, climbed wearily to his feet. 'Just restin', boss. Recuperatin', as you might say, from the nerve-rackin' rigours of the trip.'

'When you're all *quite* ready,' Briggs said acidly, 'Matthews here will take you to your quarters. You are to remain on call for the Captain, Matthews. Colonel's orders.' Briggs's tone left no doubt that he thought the colonel's orders a piece of arrant nonsense. 'And don't forget, Captain – two hours, the colonel said.'

'I know, I know,' Mallory said wearily. 'I was there when he said it. It was to me he was talking. Remember? All right, boys, if you're ready.'

'Our gear, sir?' Stevens ventured.

'Just leave it there. Right, Matthews, lead the way, will you?'

Matthews led the way along the jetty and up interminable flights of steep, worn steps, the others followed in Indian file, rubber soles noiseless on the stone. He turned sharply right at the top, went down a narrow, winding alley, into a passage, climbed a flight of creaking, wooden stairs, opened the first door in the corridor above.

'Here you are, sir. I'll just wait in the corridor outside.'

'Better wait downstairs,' Mallory advised. 'No offence, Matthews, but the less you know of this the better.'

He followed the others into the room, closing the door behind him. It was a small, bleak room, heavily curtained. A table and half a dozen chairs took up most of the space. Over in the far corner the springs of the single bed creaked as Corporal Miller stretched himself out luxuriously, hands clasped behind his head.

'Gee!' he murmured admiringly. 'A hotel room. Just like home. Kinda bare, though.' A thought occurred to him. 'Where are all you other guys gonna sleep?'

'We aren't,' Mallory said briefly. 'Neither are you. We're pulling out in less than two hours.' Miller groaned. 'Come on, soldier,' Mallory went on relentlessly. 'On your feet.'

Miller groaned again, swung his legs over the edge of the bed and looked curiously at Andrea. The big Greek was quartering the room methodically, pulling out lockers, turning pictures, peering behind curtains and under the bed.

'What's he doin'?' Miller asked. 'Lookin' for dust?'

'Testing for listening devices,' Mallory said curtly. 'One of the reasons why Andrea and I have lasted so long.' He dug into the inside pocket of his tunic, a dark naval battledress with neither badge nor insignia, pulled out a chart and the map Vlachos had given him, unfolded and spread them out. 'Round the table, all of you. I know you've been bursting with curiosity for the past couple of weeks, asking yourselves a hundred questions. Well, here are all the answers. I hope you like them . . . Let me introduce you to the island of Navarone.'

Mallory's watch showed exactly eleven o'clock when he finally sat back, folded away the map and chart. He looked quizzically at the four thoughtful faces round the table.

'Well, gentlemen, there you have it. A lovely set-up, isn't it?' He smiled wryly. 'If this was a film, my next line should be, "Any questions, men?" But we'll dispense with that because I just wouldn't have any of the answers. You all know as much as I do.'

'A quarter of a mile of sheer cliff, four hundred feet high, and he calls it the only break in the defences.' Miller, his head bent moodily over his tobacco tin, rolled a long, thin cigarette with one expert hand. This is just crazy, boss. Me, I can't even climb a bloody ladder without falling off.' He puffed strong, acrid clouds of smoke into the air. 'Suicidal. That's the word I was lookin' for. Suicidal. One buck gets a thousand we never get within five miles of them gawddamned guns!'

'One in a thousand, eh?' Mallory looked at him for a long time without speaking. 'Tell me, Miller, what odds are you offering on the boys on Kheros?'

'Yeah.' Miller nodded heavily. 'Yeah, the boys on Kheros. I'd forgotten about them. I just keep thinkin' about me and that damned cliff.' He looked hopefully across the table at the vast bulk of Andrea. 'Or maybe Andrea there would carry me up. He's big enough, anyway.'

Andrea made no reply. His eyes were half-closed, his thoughts could have been a thousand miles away.

'We'll tie you hand and foot and haul you up on the end of a rope,' Stevens said unkindly. 'We'll try to pick a fairly sound rope,' he added carelessly. The words, the tone, were jocular enough, but the worry on his face belied them. Mallory apart, only Stevens appreciated the almost insuperable technical difficulties of climbing a sheer, unknown cliff in the darkness. He looked at Mallory questioningly. 'Going up alone, sir, or –'

'Excuse me, please.' Andrea suddenly sat forward, his deep rumble of a voice rapid in the clear, idiomatic English he had learnt during his long association with Mallory. He was scribbling quickly on a piece of paper. 'I have a plan for climbing this cliff. Here is a diagram. Does the Captain think this is possible?'

He passed the paper across to Mallory. Mallory looked at it, checked, recovered, all in one instant. There was no diagram on it. There were only two large, printed words: 'Keep talking.'

'I see,' Mallory said thoughtfully. 'Very good indeed, Andrea. This has distinct possibilities.' He reversed the paper, held it up before him so that they could all see the words. Andrea had already risen to his feet, was padding cat-footed towards the door. 'Ingenious, isn't it, Corporal Miller,' he went on conversationally. 'Might solve quite a lot of our difficulties.'

'Yeah.' The expression on Miller's face hadn't altered a fraction, the eyes were still half-closed against the smoke drifting up from the cigarette dangling between his lips. 'Reckon that might solve the problem, Andrea – and get me up in one piece, too.' He laughed easily, concentrated on screwing a curiously-shaped cylinder on the barrel of an automatic that had magically appeared in his left hand. 'But I don't quite get that funny line and the dot at –'

It was all over in two seconds – literally. With a deceptive ease and nonchalance Andrea opened the door with one hand, reached out with the other, plucked a wildly-struggling figure through the gap, set him on the ground again and closed the door, all in one concerted movement. It had been as soundless as it had been swift. For a second the eavesdropper, a hatchet-faced, swarthy Levantine in badly-fitting white shirt and blue trousers, stood there in shocked immobility, blinking rapidly in the unaccustomed light. Then his hand dived in under his shirt.

'Look out!' Miller's voice was sharp, the automatic lining up as Mallory's hand closed over his.

'Watch!' Mallory said softly.

The men at the table caught only a flicker of blued steel as the knife arm jerked convulsively back and plunged down with vicious speed. And then, incredibly, hand and knife were stopped dead in mid-air, the gleaming point only two inches from Andrea's chest. There was a sudden scream of agony, the ominous cracking of wrist bones as the giant Greek tightened his grip, and then Andrea had the blade between finger and thumb, had removed the knife with the tender, reproving care of a parent saving a well-loved but irresponsible child from himself. Then the knife was reversed, the point was at the Levantine's throat and Andrea was smiling down pleasantly into the dark and terror-stricken eyes.

Miller let out a long breath, half-sigh, half-whistle.

'Well, now,' he murmured, 'I guess mebbe Andrea has done that sort of thing before?'

'I guess maybe he has,' Mallory mimicked. 'Let's have a closer look at exhibit A, Andrea.'

Andrea brought his prisoner close up to the table, well within the circle of light. He stood there sullenly before them, a thin, ferret-faced man, black eyes dulled in pain and fear, left hand cradling his crushed wrist.

'How long do you reckon this fellow's been outside, Andrea?' Mallory asked.

Andrea ran a massive hand through his thick, dark, curling hair, heavily streaked with grey above the temples.

'I cannot be sure, Captain. I imagined I heard a noise – a kind of shuffle – about ten minutes ago, but I thought my ears were playing tricks. Then I heard the same sound a minute ago. So I am afraid –'

'Ten minutes, eh?' Mallory nodded thoughtfully, then looked at the prisoner. 'What's your name?' he asked sharply. 'What are you doing here?'

There was no reply. There were only the sullen eyes, the sullen silence – a silence that gave way to a sudden yelp of pain as Andrea cuffed the side of his head.

'The Captain is asking you a question,' Andrea said reproachfully. He cuffed him again, harder this time. 'Answer the Captain.'

The stranger broke into rapid, excitable speech, gesticulating wildly with both hands. The words were quite unintelligible. Andrea sighed, shut off the torrent by the simple expedient of almost encircling the scrawny throat with his left hand.

Mallory looked questioningly at Andrea. The giant shook his head.

'Kurdistan or Armenian, Captain, I think. But I don't understand it.'

'I certainly don't,' Mallory admitted. 'Do you speak English?' he asked suddenly.

Black, hate-filled eyes glared back at him in silence. Andrea cuffed him again.

'Do you speak English?' Mallory repeated relentlessly.

'Eenglish? Eenglish?' Shoulders and upturned palms lifted in the age-old gesture of incomprehension. 'Ka Eenglish!'

'He says he don't speak English,' Miller drawled.

'Maybe he doesn't and maybe he does,' Mallory said evenly. 'All we know is that he *has* been listening and that we can't take any chances. There are far too many lives at stake.' His voice suddenly hardened, the eyes were grim and pitiless. 'Andrea!'

'Captain?'

'You have the knife. Make it clean and quick. Between the shoulder blades!'

Stevens cried out in horror, sent his chair crashing back as he leapt to his feet.

'Good God, sir, you can't –'

He broke off and stared in amazement at the sight of the prisoner catapulting himself bodily across the room to crash into a distant corner, one arm up-curved in rigid defence, stark, unreasoning panic lined in every feature of his face. Slowly Stevens looked away, saw the triumphant grin on Andrea's face, the dawning comprehension in Brown's and Miller's. Suddenly he felt a complete fool. Characteristically, Miller was the first to speak.

'Waal, waal, whaddya know! Mebbe he *does* speaka da Eenglish after all.'

'Maybe he does,' Mallory admitted. 'A man doesn't spend ten minutes with his ear glued to a keyhole if he doesn't understand a word that's being said . . . Give Matthews a call, will you, Brown?'

The sentry appeared in the doorway a few seconds later.

'Get Captain Briggs here, will you, Matthews?' he asked. 'At once please.'

The soldier hesitated.

'Captain Briggs has gone to bed, sir. He left strict orders that he wasn't to be disturbed.'

'My heart bleeds for Captain Briggs and his broken slumbers,' Mallory said acidly. 'He's had more sleep in a day than I've had in the past week.' He glanced at his watch and the heavy brows came down in a straight line over the tired, brown eyes. 'We've no time to waste. Get him here at once. Understand? At once!'

Matthews saluted and hurried away. Miller cleared his throat and clucked his tongue sadly.

'These hotels are all the same. The goin's-on – you'd never believe your eyes. Remember once I was at a convention in Cincinnati –'

Mallory shook his head wearily.

'You have a fixation about hotels, Corporal. This is a military establishment and these are army officers' billets.'

Miller made to speak but changed his mind. The American was a shrewd judge of people. There were those who could be ribbed and those who could not be ribbed. An almost hopeless mission, Miller was quietly aware, and as vital as it was, in his opinion, suicidal, but he was beginning to understand why they'd picked this tough, sunburnt New Zealander to lead it.

They sat in silence for the next five minutes, then looked up as the door opened. Captain Briggs was hatless and wore a white silk muffler round his throat in place of the usual collar and tie. The white contrasted oddly with the puffed red of the heavy neck and face above. These had been red enough when Mallory had first seen them in the colonel's office – high blood pressure and even higher living, Mallory had supposed: the extra deep shades of red and purple now present probably sprang from a misplaced sense of righteous indignation. A glance at the choleric eyes, gleaming light-blue prawns afloat in a sea of vermilion, was quite enough to confirm the obvious.

'I think this is a bit much, Captain Mallory!' The voice was high pitched in anger, more nasal than ever. I'm not the duty errand-boy, you know. I've had a damned hard day and –'

'Save it for your biography,' Mallory said curtly, 'and take a gander at this character in the corner.'

Briggs's face turned an even deeper hue. He stepped into the room, fists balled in anger, then stopped in his tracks as his eye lit on the crumpled, dishevelled figure still crouched in the corner of the room.

'Good God!' he ejaculated. 'Nicolai!'

'You know him.' It was a statement, not a question.

'Of course I know him!' Briggs snorted. 'Everybody knows him. Nicolai. Our laundry-boy.'

'Your laundry-boy! Do his duties entail snooping around the corridors at night, listening at keyholes?'

'What do you mean?'

'What I say.' Mallory was very patient. 'We caught him listening outside the door.'

'Nicolai? I don't believe it!'

'Watch it, mister,' Miller growled. 'Careful who you call a liar. We all saw him.'

Briggs stared in fascination at the black muzzle of the automatic waving negligently in his direction, gulped, looked hastily away.

'Well, what if you did?' He forced a smile. 'Nicolai can't speak a word of English.'

'Maybe not,' Mallory agreed dryly. 'But he understands it well enough.' He raised his hand. 'I've no desire to argue all night and I certainly haven't the time. Will you please have this man placed under arrest, kept in solitary confinement and incommunicado for the next week at least. It's vital. Whether he's a spy or just too damned nosy, he knows far too much. After that, do what you like. My advice is to kick him out of Castelrosso.'

'Your advice, indeed!' Briggs's colour returned, and with it his courage. 'Who the hell are you to give me advice or to give me orders, Captain Mallory?' There was a heavy emphasis on the word 'captain'.

'Then I'm asking it as a favour,' Mallory pleaded wearily. 'I can't explain, but it's terribly important. There are hundreds of lives –'

'Hundreds of lives!' Briggs sneered. 'Melodramatic stuff and nonsense!' He smiled unpleasantly. 'I suggest you keep that for *your* cloak-and-dagger biography, Captain Mallory.'

Mallory rose, walked round the table, stopped a foot away from Briggs. The brown eyes were still and very cold.

'I could go and see your colonel, I suppose. But I'm tired of arguing. You'll do exactly as I say or I'll go straight to Naval HQ and get on the radio-telephone to Cairo. And if I do,' Mallory went on, 'I swear to you that you'll be on the next ship home to England – and on the troop-deck, at that.'

His last words seemed to echo in the little room for an interminable time: the stillness was intense. And then, as suddenly as it had arisen, the tension was gone and Briggs's face, a now curiously mottled white and red, was slack and sullen in defeat.

'All right, all right,' he said. 'No need for all these damned stupid threats – not if it means all that much to you.' The attempt to bluster, to patch up the shredded rags of his dignity, was pathetic in its transparency. 'Matthews – call out the guard.'

The torpedo-boat, great aero engines throttled back half speed, pitched and lifted, pitched and lifted with monotonous regularity as it thrust its way into the long, gentle swell from the WNW. For the hundredth time that night Mallory looked at his watch.

'Running behind time, sir?' Stevens suggested.

Mallory nodded.

'We should have stepped straight into this thing from the Sunderland – there was a hold-up.'

Brown grunted. 'Engine trouble, for a fiver.' The Clydeside accent was very heavy.

'Yes, that's right.' Mallory looked up, surprised. 'How did you know?'

'Always the same with these blasted MTB engines,' Brown growled. 'Temperamental as a film star.'

There was silence for a time in the tiny blacked-out cabin, a silence broken only by the occasional clink of a glass. The Navy was living up to its traditional hospitality.

'If we're late,' Miller observed at last, 'why doesn't the skipper open her up? They tell me these crates can do forty to fifty knots.'

'You look green enough already,' Stevens said tactlessly. 'Obviously, you've never been in an MTB full out in a heavy sea.'

Miller fell silent a moment. Clearly, he was trying to take his mind off his internal troubles. 'Captain?'

'Yes, what is it?' Mallory answered sleepily. He was stretched full length on a narrow settee, an almost empty glass in his fingers.

'None of my business, I know, boss, but – would you have carried out that threat you made to Captain Briggs?'

Mallory laughed.

'It *is* none of your business, but – well, no, Corporal, I wouldn't. I wouldn't because I couldn't. I haven't all that much authority invested in me – and I didn't even know whether there was a radio-telephone in Castelrosso.'

'Yeah. Yeah, do you know, I kinda suspected that.' Corporal Miller rubbed a stubbled chin. 'If he'd called your bluff, what would you have done, boss?'

'I'd have shot Nicolai,' Mallory said quietly. 'If the colonel had failed me. I'd have had no choice left.'

'I knew that too. I really believe you would. For the first time I'm beginning to believe we've got a chance . . . But I kinda wish you *had* shot him – *and* little Lord Fauntleroy. I didn't like the expression on old Briggs's face when you went out that door. Mean wasn't the word. He coulda killed you then. You trampled right over his pride, boss – and to a phony like that nothin' else in the world matters.'

Mallory made no reply. He was already sound asleep, his empty glass fallen from his hand. Not even the banshee clamour of the great engines opening full out as they entered the sheltered calm of the Rhodes channel could plumb his bottomless abyss of sleep.

THREE

Monday
0700–1700

'My dear fellow, you make me feel dreadfully embarrassed.' Moodily the officer switched his ivory-handled flyswat against an immaculately trousered leg, pointed a contemptuous but gleaming toe-cap at the ancient caique, broad-beamed and two-masted, moored stern on to the even older and more dilapidated wooden pier on which they were standing. 'I am positively ashamed. The clients of Rutledge and Company, I assure you, are accustomed only to the best.'

Mallory smothered a smile. Major Rutledge of the Buffs, Eton and Sandhurst as to intonation, millimetrically tooth-brushed as to moustache, Savile Row as to the quite dazzling sartorial perfection of his khaki drill, was so magnificently out of place in the wild beauty of the rocky, tree-lined bluffs of that winding creek that his presence there seemed inevitable. Such was the major's casual assurance, so dominating his majestic unconcern, that it was the creek, if anything, that seemed slightly out of place.

'It *does* look as if it has seen better days,' Mallory admitted. 'Nevertheless, sir, it's exactly what we want.'

'Can't understand it, I really can't understand it.' With an irritable but well-timed swipe the major brought down a harmless passing fly. 'I've been providing chaps with everything during the past eight or nine months – caiques, launches, yachts, fishing boats, everything – but no one has ever yet specified the oldest, most dilapidated derelict I could lay hands on. Quite a job laying hands on it, too, I tell you.' A pained expression crossed his face. 'The chaps know I don't usually deal in this line of stuff.'

'What chaps?' Mallory asked curiously.

'Oh, up the islands; you know.' Rutledge gestured vaguely to the north and west.

'But – but those are enemy held –'

'So's this one. Chap's got to have his HQ somewhere,' Rutledge explained patiently. Suddenly his expression brightened. 'I say, old boy, I know just the thing for you. A boat to escape observation and investigation – that was what Cairo insisted I get. How about a German E-boat, absolutely perfect condition, one careful owner. Could get ten thou. for her at home. Thirty-six hours. Pal of mine over in Bodrum –'

'Bodrum?' Mallory questioned. 'Bodrum? But – but that's in Turkey, isn't it?'

'Turkey? Well, yes, actually, I believe it is,' Rutledge admitted. 'Chap has to get his supplies from somewhere, you know,' he added defensively.

'Thanks all the same' – Mallory smiled – 'but this is exactly what we want. We can't wait, anyway.'

'On your own heads be it!' Rutledge threw up his hands in admission of defeat. 'I'll have a couple of my men shove your stuff aboard.'

'I'd rather we did it ourselves, sir. It's – well, it's a very special cargo.'

'Right you are,' the major acknowledged. 'No questions Rutledge, they call me. Leaving soon?'

Mallory looked at his watch.

'Half an hour, sir.'

'Bacon, eggs and coffee in ten minutes?'

'Thanks very much.' Mallory grinned. 'That's one offer we'll be very glad to accept.'

He turned away, walked slowly down to the end of the pier. He breathed deeply, savouring the heady, herb-scented air of an Aegean dawn. The salt tang of the sea, the drowsily sweet perfume of honeysuckle, the more delicate, sharper fragrance of mint all subtly merged into an intoxicating whole, indefinable, unforgettable. On either side, the steep slopes, still brilliantly green with pine and walnut and holly, stretched far up to the moorland pastures above, and from these, faintly borne on the perfumed breeze, came the distant melodic tinkling of goats' bells, a haunting, a nostalgic music, true symbol of the leisured peace the Aegean no longer knew.

Unconsciously almost, Mallory shook his head and walked more quickly to the end of the pier. The others were still sitting where the torpedo boat had landed them just before dawn. Miller, inevitably, was stretched his full length, hat tilted against the golden, level rays of the rising sun.

'Sorry to disturb you and all that, but we're leaving in half an hour; breakfast in ten minutes. Let's get the stuff aboard.' He turned to Brown. 'Maybe you'd like to have a look at the engine?' he suggested.

Brown heaved himself to his feet, looked down unenthusiastically at the weather-beaten, paint-peeled caique.

'Right you are, sir. But if the engine is on a par with this bloody wreck . . .' He shook his head in prophetic gloom and swung nimbly over the side of the pier.

Mallory and Andrea followed him, reaching up for the equipment as the other two passed it down. First they stowed away a sackful of old clothes, then the food, pressure stove and fuel, the heavy boots, spikes, mallets, rock axes and coils of wire-centred rope to be used for climbing, then, more carefully, the combined radio receiver and transmitter and the firing generator fitted with the old-fashioned plunge handle. Next came the guns – two Schmeissers, two Brens, a Mauser and a Colt – then a case containing a weird but carefully selected hodge-podge of torches, mirrors, two sets of identity papers and, incredibly, bottles of Hock, Moselle, ouzo and retsina.

Finally, and with exaggerated care, they stowed away for'ard in the forepeak two wooden boxes, one green in colour, medium sized and bound in brass, the other small and black. The green box held high explosive – TNT., amatol and a few standard sticks of dynamite, together with grenades, gun-cotton primers and canvas hosing; in one corner of the box was a bag of emery dust, another of ground glass, and a sealed jar of potassium, these last three items having been included against the possibility of Dusty Miller's finding an opportunity to exercise his unique talents as a saboteur. The black box held only detonators, percussion and electrical, detonators with fulminates so unstable that their exposed powder could be triggered off by the impact of a falling feather.

The last box had been stowed away when Casey Brown's head appeared above the engine hatch. Slowly he examined the main-mast reaching up above his head, as slowly turned for'ard to look at the foremast. His face carefully expressionless, he looked at Mallory.

'Have we got sails for these things, sir?'

'I suppose so. Why?'

'Because God only knows we're going to need them!' Brown said bitterly. 'Have a look at the engine-room, you said. This isn't an engine-room. It's a bloody scrap-yard. And the biggest, most rusted bit of scrap down there is attached to the propeller shaft. And what do you think it is? An old Kelvin two-cylinder job built more or less on my own doorstep – about thirty years ago.' Brown shook his head in despair, his face as stricken as only a Clydeside engineer's can be at the abuse of a beloved machine. 'And it's been falling to bits for years, sir. Place is littered with discarded bits and spares. I've seen junk heaps off the Gallowgate that were palaces compared to this.'

'Major Rutledge said it was running only yesterday,' Mallory said mildly. 'Anyway, come on ashore. Breakfast. Remind me we're to pick up a few heavy stones on the way back, will you?'

'Stones!' Miller looked at him in horror. 'Aboard that thing?'

Mallory nodded, smiling.

'But that gawddamned ship is sinkin' already!' Miller protested. 'What do you want stones for?'

'Wait and see.'

Three hours later Miller saw. The caique was chugging steadily north over a glassy, windless sea, less than a mile off the coast of Turkey, when he mournfully finished lashing his blue battledress into a tight ball and heaved it regretfully over the side. Weighted by the heavy stone he had carried aboard, it was gone from sight in a second.

Morosely he surveyed himself in the mirror propped up against the for'ard end of the wheelhouse. Apart from a deep violet sash wrapped round his lean middle and a fancifully embroidered waist-coat with its former glory mercifully faded, he was dressed entire-ly in black. Black lacing jackboots, black baggy trousers, black shirt and black jacket: even his sandy hair had been dyed to the same colour.

He shuddered and turned away.

'Thank Gawd the boys back home can't see me now!' he said feelingly. He looked critically at the others, dressed, with some minor variations, like himself. 'Waal, mebbe I ain't quite so bad after all . . . Just what is all this quick-change business for, boss?'

'They tell me you've been behind the German lines twice, once as a peasant, once as a mechanic.' Mallory heaved his own ballasted uniform over the side. 'Well, now you see what the well-dressed Navaronian wears.'

'The double change, I meant. Once in the plane, and now.'

'Oh, I see. Army khaki and naval whites in Alex, blue battledress in Castelrosso and now Greek clothes? Could have been – almost certainly were – snoopers in Alex or Castelrosso or Major Rutledge's island. And we've changed from launch to plane to MTB to caique. Covering our tracks, Corporal. We just can't take any chances.'

Miller nodded, looked down at the clothes sack at his feet, wrinkled his brows in puzzlement, stooped and dragged out the white clothing that had caught his eye. He held up the long, voluminous clothes for inspection.

'To be used when passing through the local cemeteries, I suppose.' He was heavily ironic. 'Disguised as ghosts.'

'Camouflage,' Mallory explained succinctly. 'Snow-smocks.'

'What!'

'Snow. That white stuff. There are some pretty high mountains in Navarone, and we may have to take them. So – snow-smocks.'

Miller looked stunned. Wordlessly he stretched his length on the deck, pillowed his head and closed his eyes. Mallory grinned at Andrea.

'Picture of a man getting his full quota of sunshine before battling with the Arctic wastes . . . Not a bad idea. Maybe you should get some sleep, too. I'll keep watch for a couple of hours.'

For five hours the caique continued on its course parallel to the Turkish coast, slightly west of north and rarely more than two miles off-shore. Relaxed and warm in the still kindly November sun, Mallory sat wedged between the bulwarks of the blunt bows, his eyes ceaselessly quartering sky and horizon. Amidships, Andrea and Miller lay asleep. Casey Brown still defied all attempts to remove him from the engine-room. Occasionally – very occasionally – he came up for a breath of fresh air, but the intervals between his appearances steadily lengthened as he concentrated more and more on the aged Kelvin engine, regulating the erratic drip-fed lubrication, constantly adjusting the air intake: an engineer to his fingertips, he was unhappy about that engine: he was drowsy, too, and headachy – the narrow hatchway gave hardly any ventilation at all.

Alone in the wheelhouse – an unusual feature in so tiny a caique – Lieutenant Andy Stevens watched the Turkish coast slide slowly by. Like Mallory's, his eyes moved ceaselessly, but not with the same controlled wandering. They shifted from the coast to the chart:

from the chart to the islands up ahead off the port bow, islands whose position and relation to each other changed continually and deceptively, islands gradually lifting from the sea and hardening in definition through the haze of blue refraction: from the islands to the old alcohol compass swinging almost imperceptibly on corroded gimbals, and from the compass back to the coast again. Occasionally, he peered up into the sky, or swung a quick glance through a 180-degree sweep of the horizon. But one thing his eyes avoided all the time. The chipped, fly-blown mirror had been hung up in the wheelhouse again, but it was as if his eyes and the mirror were of opposite magnetic poles: he could not bring himself to look at it.

His forearms ached. He had been spelled at the wheel twice, but still they ached, abominably: his lean, tanned hands were ivory-knuckled on the cracked wheel. Repeatedly, consciously, he tried to relax, to ease the tension that was bunching up the muscles of his arms; but always, as if possessed of independent volition, his hands tightened their grip again. There was a funny taste in his mouth, too, a sour and salty taste in a dry, parched mouth, and no matter how often he swallowed, or drank from the sun-warmed pitcher at his side, the taste and the dryness remained. He could no more exorcise them than he could that twisting, cramping ball that was knotting up his insides, just above the solar plexus, or the queer, uncontrollable tremor that gripped his right leg from time to time.

Lieutenant Andy Stevens was afraid. He had never been in action before, but it wasn't that. This wasn't the first time he had been afraid. He had been afraid all his life, ever since he could remember: and he could remember a long way back, even to his early prep-school days when his famous father, Sir Cedric Stevens, the most celebrated explorer and mountaineer of his time, had thrown him bodily into the swimming pool at home, telling him that this was the only way he could learn to swim. He could remember still how he had fought and spluttered his way to the side of the pool, panic-stricken and desperate, his nose and mouth blocked with water, the pit of his stomach knotted and constricted in that nameless, terrifying ache he was to come to know so well: how his father and two elder brothers, big and jovial and nerveless like Sir Cedric himself, had wiped the tears of mirth from their eyes and pushed him in again . . .

His father and brothers . . . It had been like that all through his schooldays. Together, the three of them had made his life thoroughly miserable. Tough, hearty, open-air types who worshipped at the shrine of athleticism and physical fitness, they could not understand how anyone could fail to revel in diving from a five-metre spring-board or setting a hunter at a five-barred gate or climbing the crags of the Peak district or sailing a boat in a storm. All these things they had made him do and often he had failed in the doing, and neither his father nor his brothers could ever have understood how he had come to dread those violent sports in which they excelled, for they were not cruel men, nor even unkind, but simply stupid. And so to the simple physical fear he sometimes and naturally felt was added the fear of failure, the fear that he was bound to fail in whatever he had to do next, the fear of the inevitable mockery and ridicule: and because he had been a sensitive boy and feared the ridicule above all else, he had come to fear these things that provoked the ridicule. Finally, he had come to fear fear itself, and it was in a desperate attempt to overcome this double fear that he had devoted himself – this in his late teens – to crag and mountain climbing: in this he had ultimately become so proficient, developed such a reputation, that father and brothers had come to treat him with respect and as an equal, and the ridicule had ceased. But the fear had not ceased, rather it had grown by what it fed on, and often, on a particularly difficult climb, he had all but fall-en to his death, powerless in the grip of sheer, unreasoning terror. But this terror he had always sought, successfully so far, to conceal. As now. He was trying to overcome, to conceal that fear now. He was afraid of failing – in what he wasn't quite sure – of not measuring up to expectation: he was afraid of being afraid: and he was desperately afraid, above all things, of being seen, of being known to be afraid . . .

The startling, incredible blue of the Aegean; the soft, hazy sil-houette of the Anatolian mountains against the washed-out cerulean of the sky; the heart-catching, magical blending of the blues and violets and purples and indigoes of the sun-soaked islands drifting lazily by, almost on the beam now; the iridescent rippling of the water tanned by the gentle, scent-laden breeze newly sprung from the south-east; the peaceful scene on deck, the reassuring, interminable thump-thump thump-thump of the old Kelvin engine . . . All was peace and quiet and contentment and warmth and languor, and it seemed impossible that anyone could be afraid. The world and the war were very far away that afternoon.

Or perhaps, after all, the war wasn't so far away. There were occasional pin-pricks – and constant reminders. Twice a German

Arado seaplane had circled curiously overhead, and a Savoia and Fiat, flying in company, had altered course, dipped to have a look at them and flown off, apparently satisfied: Italian planes, these, and probably based on Rhodes, they were almost certainly piloted by Germans who had rounded up their erstwhile Rhodian allies and put them in prison camps after the surrender of the Italian Government. In the morning they had passed within half a mile of a big German caique – it flew a German flag and bristled with mounted machine-guns and a two-pounder far up in the bows; and in the early afternoon a high-speed German launch had roared by so closely that their caique had rolled wickedly in the wash of its passing: Mallory and Andrea had shaken their fists and cursed loudly and fluently at the grinning sailors on deck. But there had been no attempts to molest or detain them: neither British nor German hesitated at any time to violate the neutrality of Turkish territorial waters, but by the strange quixotry of a tacit gentlemen's agreement hostilities between passing vessels and planes were almost unknown. Like the envoys of warring countries in a neutral capital, their behaviour ranged from the impeccably and frigidly polite to a very pointed unawareness of one another's existence.

These, then, were the pin-pricks – the visitation and by-goings, harmless though they were, of the ships and planes of the enemy. The other reminders that this was no peace but an illusion, an ephemeral and a frangible thing, were more permanent. Slowly the minute hands of their watches circled, and every tick took them nearer to that great wall of cliff, barely eight hours away, that had to be climbed somehow: and almost dead ahead now, and less than fifty miles distant, they could see the grim, jagged peaks of Navarone topping the shimmering horizon and reaching up darkly against the sapphired sky, desolate and remote and strangely threatening.

At half-past two in the afternoon the engine stopped. There had been no warning coughs or splutters or missed strokes. One moment the regular, reassuring thump-thump: the next, sudden, completely unexpected silence, oppressive and foreboding in its absoluteness.

Mallory was the first to reach the engine hatch.

'What's up, Brown?' His voice was sharp with anxiety. 'Engine broken down?'

'Not quite, sir.' Brown was still bent over the engine, his voice muffled. 'I shut it off just now.' He straightened his back, hoisted himself wearily through the hatchway, sat on deck with his feet dangling, sucking in great draughts of fresh air. Beneath the heavy tan his face was very pale.

Mallory looked at him closely.

'You look as if you had the fright of your life.'

'Not that.' Brown shook his head. 'For the past two-three hours I've been slowly poisoned down that ruddy hole. Only now I realise it.' He passed a hand across his brow and groaned. 'Top of my blinkin' head just about lifting off, sir. Carbon monoxide ain't a very healthy thing.'

'Exhaust leak?'

'Aye. But it's more than a leak now.' He pointed down at the engine. 'See that stand-pipe supporting that big iron ball above the engine – the water-cooler? That pipe's as thin as paper, must have been leaking above the bottom flange for hours. Blew out a bloody great hole a minute ago. Sparks, smoke and flames six inches long. Had to shut the damned thing off at once, sir.'

Mallory nodded in slow understanding.

'And now what? Can you repair it, Brown?'

'Not a chance, sir.' The shake of the head was very definite. 'Would have to be brazed or welded. But there's a spare down there among the scrap. Rusted to hell and about as shaky as the one that's on . . . I'll have a go, sir.'

'I'll give him a hand,' Miller volunteered.

'Thanks, Corporal. How long, Brown, do you think?'

'Lord only knows, sir. Two hours, maybe four. Most of the nuts and bolts are locked solid with rust: have to shear or saw 'em – and then hunt for others.'

Mallory said nothing. He turned away heavily, brought up beside Stevens who had abandoned the wheelhouse and was now bent over the sail locker. He looked up questioningly as Mallory approached.

Mallory nodded. 'Just get them out and up. Maybe four hours, Brown says. Andrea and I will do our landlubbery best to help.'

Two hours later, with the engine still out of commission, they were well outside territorial waters, closing on a big island some eight miles away to the WNW. The wind, warm and oppressive now, had backed to a darkening and thundery east, and with only a lug and a jib – all the sails they had found – bent to the foremast, they could make no way at all into it. Mallory had decided to make for the island – the chances of being observed there were far less than in the open sea. Anxiously he looked at his watch then stared back moodily at the receding safety of the Turkish shore. Then he stiffened, peered closely at the dark line of sea, land and sky that lay to the east.

'Andrea! Do you see –'

'I see it, Captain.' Andrea was at his shoulder. 'Caique. Three miles. Coming straight towards us,' he added softly.

'Coming straight towards us,' Mallory acquiesced. 'Tell Miller and Brown. Have them come here.'

Mallory wasted no time when they were all assembled.

'We're going to be stopped and investigated,' he said quickly. 'Unless I'm much mistaken, it's that big caique that passed us this morning. Heaven only knows how, but they've been tipped off and they're going to be as suspicious as hell. This'll be no kid-glove, hands-in-the-pockets inspection. They'll be armed to the teeth and hunting trouble. There's going to be no half-measures. Let's be quite clear about that. Either they go under or we do: we can't possibly survive an inspection – not with all the gear *we've* got aboard. And,' he added softly, 'we're not going to dump that gear.' Rapidly he explained his plans. Stevens, leaning out from the wheelhouse window, felt the old sick ache in his stomach, felt the blood leaving his face. He was glad of the protection of the wheelhouse that hid the lower part of his body: that old familiar tremor in his leg was back again. Even his voice was unsteady.

'But, sir – sir –'

'Yes, yes, what is it, Stevens?' Even in his hurry Mallory paused at the sight of the pale, set face, the bloodless nails clenched over the sill of the window.

'You – you can't do *that,* sir!' The voice burred harshly under the sharp edge of strain. For a moment his mouth worked soundlessly, then he rushed on. 'It's massacre, sir, it's – it's just murder!'

'Shut up, kid!' Miller growled.

'That'll do, Corporal!' Mallory said sharply. He looked at the American for a long moment then turned to Stevens, his eyes cold. 'Lieutenant, the whole concept of directing a successful war is aimed at placing your enemy at a disadvantage, at *not* giving him an even chance. We kill them or they kill us. They go under or we do – and a thousand men on Kheros. It's just as simple as that, Lieutenant. It's not even a question of conscience.'

For several seconds Stevens stared at Mallory in complete silence. He was vaguely aware that everyone was looking at him. In that instant he hated Mallory, could have killed him. He hated him because – suddenly he was aware that he hated him only for the remorseless logic of what he said. He stared down at his clenched hands. Mallory, the idol of every young mountaineer and cragsman in pre-war England, whose fantastic climbing exploits had made world headlines, in '38 and '39: Mallory, who had twice been baulked by the most atrocious ill-fortune from surprising Rommel in his desert headquarters: Mallory, who had three times refused promotion in order to stay with his beloved Cretans who worshipped him the other side of idolatry. Confusedly these thoughts tumbled through his mind and he looked up slowly, looked at the lean, sunburnt face, the sensitive, chiselled mouth, the heavy, dark eyebrows bar-straight over the lined brown eyes that could be so cold or so compassionate, and suddenly he felt ashamed, knew that Captain Mallory lay beyond both his understanding and his judgment.

'I am very sorry, sir.' He smiled faintly. 'As Corporal Miller would say, I was talking out of turn.' He looked aft at the caique arrowing up from the south-east. Again he felt the sick fear, but his voice was steady enough as he spoke. 'I won't let you down, sir.'

'Good enough. I never thought you would.' Mallory smiled in turn, looked at Miller and Brown. 'Get the stuff ready and lay it out, will you? Casual, easy and keep it hidden. They'll have the glasses on you.'

He turned away, walked for'ard. Andrea followed him.

'You were very hard on the young man.' It was neither criticism nor reproach – merely statement of fact.

'I know.' Mallory shrugged. 'I didn't like it either . . . I had to do it.'

'I think you had,' Andrea said slowly. 'Yes, I think you had. But it was hard . . . Do you think they'll use the big guns in the bows to stop us?'

'Might – they haven't turned back after us unless they're pretty sure we're up to something fishy. But the warning shot across the bows – they don't go in for that Captain Teach stuff normally.'

Andrea wrinkled his brows.

'Captain Teach?'

'Never mind.' Mallory smiled. 'Time we were taking up position now. Remember, wait for me. You won't have any trouble in hearing my signal,' he finished dryly.

The creaming bow-wave died away to a gentle ripple, the throb of the heavy diesel muted to a distant murmur as the German boat slid alongside, barely six feet away. From where he sat on a fish-box on the port of the fo'c'sle, industriously sewing a button on to the old coat lying on the deck between his legs, Mallory could see six men, all dressed in the uniform of the regular Germany Navy – one crouched behind a belted Spandau mounted on its tripod just aft of the two-pounder, three others bunched amidships each armed with an automatic machine carbine – Schmeissers, he thought – the captain, a hard, cold-faced young lieutenant with the Iron Cross on his tunic, looking out the open door of the wheelhouse and, finally, a curious head peering over the edge of the engine-room hatch. From where he sat, Mallory couldn't see the poop-deck – the intermittent ballooning of the lug-sail in the uncertain wind blocked his vision; but from the restricted fore-and-aft lateral sweep of the Spandau, hungrily traversing only the for'ard half of their one caique, he was reasonably sure that there was another machine-gunner similarly engaged on the German's poop.

The hard-faced young lieutenant – a real product of the Hitler Jugend that one, Mallory thought – leaned out of the wheelhouse, cupped his hand to his mouth.

'Lower your sails!' he shouted.

Mallory stiffened, froze to immobility. The needle had jammed hard into the palm of his hand, but he didn't even notice it. The lieutenant had spoken in English! Stevens was so young, so inexperienced. He'd fall for it, Mallory thought with a sudden sick certainty, he's bound to fall for it.

But Stevens didn't fall for it. He opened the door, leaned out, cupped his hand to his ear and gazed vacantly up to the sky, his mouth wide open. It was so perfect an imitation of dull-witted failure to catch or comprehend a shouted message that it was almost a caricature. Mallory could have hugged him. Not in his actions alone, but in his dark, shabby clothes and hair as blackly counterfeit as Miller's, Stevens was the slow, suspicious island fisherman to the life.

'Eh?' he bawled.

'Lower your sails! We are coming aboard!' English again, Mallory noted; a persistent fellow this.

Stevens stared at him blankly, looked round helplessly at Andrea and Mallory: their faces registered a lack of comprehension as convincing as his own. He shrugged his shoulders in despair.

'I am sorry, I do not understand German,' he shouted. 'Can you not speak my language?' Stevens's Greek was perfect, fluent and idiomatic. It was also, the Greek of Attica, not of the islands; but Mallory felt sure that the lieutenant wouldn't know the difference.

He didn't. He shook his head in exasperation, called in slow, halting Greek: 'Stop your boat at once. We are coming aboard.'

'Stop my boat!' The indignation was so genuine, the accompanying flood of furious oaths so authentic, that even the lieutenant was momentarily taken aback. 'And why should I stop my boat for you, you – you –'

'You have ten seconds,' the lieutenant interrupted. He was on balance again, cold, precise. 'Then we will shoot.'

Stevens gestured in admission of defeat and turned to Andrea and Mallory.

'Our conquerors have spoken,' he said bitterly. 'Lower the sails.'

Quickly they loosened the sheets from the cleats at the foot of the mast. Mallory pulled the jib down, gathered the sail in his arms and squatted sullenly on the deck – he knew a dozen hostile eyes were watching him – close by the fish-box. The sail covering his knees and the old coat, his forearms on his thighs, he sat with head bowed and hands dangling between his knees, the picture of heart-struck dejection. The lug-sail, weighted by the boom at the top, came down with a rush. Andrea stepped over it, walked a couple of uncertain paces aft, then stopped, huge hands hanging emptily by his sides.

A sudden deepening of the muted throbbing of the diesel, a spin of the wheel and the big German caique was rubbing alongside. Quickly, but carefully enough to keep out of the line of fire of the mounted Spandaus – there was a second clearly visible now on the poop – the three men armed with the Schmeissers leapt aboard. Immediately one ran forward, whirled round level with the fore-mast, his automatic carbine circling gently to cover all of the crew. All except Mallory – and he was leaving Mallory in the safe hands of the Spandau gunner in the bows. Detachedly, Mallory admired the precision, the timing, the clockwork inevitability of an old routine.

He raised his head, looked around him with a slow, peasant indifference. Casey Brown was squatting on the deck abreast the engine-room, working on the big ball-silencer on top of the hatch-cover. Dusty Miller, two paces farther for'ard and with his brows furrowed in concentration, was laboriously cutting a section of metal from a little tin box, presumably to help in the engine repairs. He was holding the wire-cutting pliers in his left hand –

and Miller, Mallory knew, was right-handed. Neither Stevens nor Andrea had moved. The man beside the foremast still stood there, eyes unwinking. The other two were walking slowly aft, had just passed Andrea, their carriage relaxed and easy, the bearing of men who know they have everything so completely under control that even the idea of trouble is ridiculous.

Carefully, coldly and precisely, at point-blank range and through the folds of both coat and sail, Mallory shot the Spandau machine-gunner through the heart, swung the still chattering Bren round and saw the guard by the mast crumple and die, half his chest torn away by the tearing slugs of the machine-gun. But the dead man was still on his feet, still had not hit the deck, when four things happened simultaneously. Casey Brown had had his hand on Miller's silenced automatic, lying concealed beneath the ball-silencer, for over a minute. Now he squeezed the trigger four times, for he wanted to mak' siccar; the after machine-gunner leaned forward tiredly over his tripod, lifeless fingers locked on the firing-guard. Miller crimped the three-second chemical fuse with the pliers, lobbed the tin box into the enemy engine-room, Stevens spun the armed stick-grenade into the opposite wheelhouse and Andrea, his great arms reaching out with all the speed and precision of striking cobras, swept the Schmeisser gunners' heads together with sickening force. And then all five men had hurled themselves to the deck and the German caique was erupting in a roar of flame and smoke and flying débris: gradually the echoes faded away over the sea and there was left only the whining stammer of the Spandau, emptying itself uselessly skyward; and then the belt jammed and the Aegean was as silent as ever, more silent than it had ever been.

Slowly, painfully, dazed by the sheer physical shock and the ear-shattering proximity of the twin explosions, Mallory pushed himself off the wooden deck and stood shakily on his feet. His first conscious reaction was that of surprise, incredulity almost: the concussive blast of a grenade and a couple of lashed blocks of TNT, even at such close range, was far beyond anything he had expected.

The German boat was sinking, sinking fast. Miller's home-made bomb must have torn the bottom out of the engine-room. She was heavily on fire amidships, and for one dismayed instant Mallory had an apprehensive vision of towering black columns of smoke and enemy reconnaissance planes. But only for an instant:

timbers and planking, tinder-dry and resinous, were burning furiously with hardly a trace of smoke, and the flaming, crumpling deck was already canted over sharply to port: she would be gone in seconds.

His eyes wandered to the shattered skeleton of the wheelhouse, and he caught his breath suddenly when he saw the lieutenant impaled on the splintered wreck of the wheel, a ghastly, mangled caricature of what had once been a human being, decapitated and wholly horrible: vaguely, some part of Mallory's mind registered the harsh sound of retching, violent and convulsive, coming from the wheelhouse, and he knew Stevens must have seen it too. From deep within the sinking caique came the muffled roar of rupturing fuel tanks: a flame-veined gout of oily black smoke erupted from the engine-room and the caique miraculously struggled back on even keel, her gunwales almost awash, and then the hissing waters had overflowed and overcome the decks and the twisting flames, and the caique was gone, her slender masts sliding vertically down and vanishing in a turbulent welter of creaming foam and oil-filmed bubbles. And now the Aegean was calm and peaceful again, as placid as if the caique had never been, and almost as empty: a few charred planks and an inverted helmet drifted lazily on the surface of the shimmering sea.

With a conscious effort of will, Mallory turned slowly to look to his own ship and his own men. Brown and Miller were on their feet, staring down in fascination at where the caique had been. Stevens was standing at the wheelhouse door. He, too, was unhurt, but his face was ashen: during the brief action he had been a man above himself, but the aftermath, the brief glimpse he'd had of the dead lieutenant had hit him badly. Andrea, bleeding from a gash on the cheek, was looking down at the two Schmeisser gunners lying at his feet. His face was expressionless. For a long moment Mallory looked at him, looked in slow understanding.

'Dead?' he asked quietly.

Andrea inclined his head.

'Yes.' His voice was heavy. 'I hit them too hard.'

Mallory turned away. Of all the men he had ever known, Andrea, he thought, had the most call to hate and to kill his enemies. And kill them he did, with a ruthless efficiency appalling in its single-mindedness and thoroughness of execution. But he rarely killed without regret, without the most bitter self-condemnation, for he did not believe that the lives of his fellow-men were his to take. A destroyer of his fellow-man, he loved his fellow-man above all things. A simple man, a good man, a killer with a kindly heart, he was for ever troubled by his conscience, ill at ease with his inner self. But over and above the wonderings and the reproaches, he was informed by an honesty of thought, by a clear-sighted wisdom which sprang from and transcended his innate simplicity. Andrea killed neither for revenge, nor from hate, nor nationalism, nor for the sake of any of the other 'isms' which self-seekers and fools and knaves employ as beguilement to the battlefield and justification for the slaughter of millions too young and too unknowing to comprehend the dreadful futility of it all. Andrea killed simply that better men might live.

'Anybody else hurt?' Mallory's voice was deliberately brisk, cheerful. 'Nobody? Good! Right, let's get under way as fast as possible. The farther and the faster we leave this place behind, the better for all of us.' He looked at his watch. 'Almost four o'clock – time for our routine check with Cairo. Just leave that scrap-yard of yours for a couple of minutes, Chief. See if you can pick them up.' He looked at the sky to the east, a sky now purply livid and threatening, and shook his head. 'Could be that the weather forecast might be worth hearing.'

It was. Reception was very poor – Brown blamed the violent static on the dark, convoluted thunderheads steadily creeping up astern, now overspreading almost half the sky – but adequate. Adequate enough to hear information they had never expected to hear, information that left them silenced, eyes stilled in troubled speculation. The tiny loud-speaker boomed and faded, boomed and faded, against the scratchy background of static.

'Rhubarb calling Pimpernel! Rhubarb calling Pimpernel!' These were the respective code names for Cairo and Mallory. 'Are you receiving me?'

Brown tapped an acknowledgment. The speaker boomed again.

'Rhubarb calling Pimpernel. Now X minus one. Repeat, X minus one.' Mallory drew in his breath sharply. X – dawn on Saturday – had been the assumed date for the German attack on Kheros. It must have been advanced by one day – and Jensen was not the man to speak without certain knowledge. Friday, dawn – just over three days.

'Send "X minus one understood",' Mallory said quietly.

'Forecast, East Anglia,' the impersonal voice went on: the Northern Sporades, Mallory knew. 'Severe electrical storms probable this evening, with heavy rainfall. Visibility poor. Temperature falling, continuing to fall next twenty-four hours. Winds east to south-east, force six, locally eight, moderating early tomorrow.'

Mallory turned away, ducked under the billowing lugsail, walked slowly aft. What a set-up, he thought, what a bloody mess. Three days to go, engine u.s. and a first-class storm building up. He thought briefly, hopefully, of Squadron Leader Torrance's low opinion of the backroom boys of the Met. Office, but the hope was never really born. It couldn't be, not unless he was blind. The steep-piled buttresses of the thunderheads towered up darkly terrifying, now almost directly above.

'Looks pretty bad, huh?' The slow nasal drawl came from immediately behind him. There was something oddly reassuring about that measured voice, about the steadiness of the washed-out blue of the eyes enmeshed in a spider's web of fine wrinkles.

'It's not so good,' Mallory admitted.

'What's all this force eight business, boss?'

'A wind scale,' Mallory explained. 'If you're in a boat this size and you're good and tired of life, you can't beat a force eight wind.'

Miller nodded dolefully.

'I knew it. I might have known. And me swearing they'd never get me on a gawddamned boat again.' He brooded a while, sighed, slid his legs over the engine-room hatchway, jerked his thumb in the direction of the nearest island, now less than three miles away. 'That doesn't look so hot, either.'

'Not from here,' Mallory agreed. 'But the chart shows a creek with a right-angle bend. It'll break the sea and the wind.'

'Inhabited?'

'Probably.'

'Germans?'

'Probably.'

Miller shook his head in despair and descended to help Brown. Forty minutes later, in the semi-darkness of the overcast evening and in torrential rain, lance-straight and strangely chill, the anchor of the caique rattled down between the green walls of the forest, a dank and dripping forest, hostile in its silent indifference.

FOUR

Monday Evening
1700–2330

'Brilliant!' said Mallory bitterly. 'Ruddy well brilliant! "Come into my parlour said the spider to the fly."' He swore in chagrin and exasperated disgust, eased aside the edge of the tarpaulin that covered the for'ard hatchway, peered out through the slackening curtain of rain and took a second and longer look at the rocky bluff that elbowed out into the bend of the creek, shutting them off from the sea. There was no difficulty in seeing now, none at all: the drenching cloudburst had yielded to a gentle drizzle, and grey and white cloud streamers, shredding in the lifting wind, had already pursued the blackly towering cumulonimbus over the far horizon. In a clear band of sky far to the west, the sinking, flame-red sun was balanced on the rim of the sea. From the shadowed waters of the creek it was invisible, but its presence unmistakable from the gold-shot gauze of the falling rain, high above their heads.

The same golden rays highlighted the crumbling old watch-tower on the very point of the cliff, a hundred feet above the river. They burnished its fine-grained white Parian marble, mellowed it to a delicate rose: they gleamed on the glittering steel, the evil mouths of the Spandau machine-guns reaching out from the slotted embrasures in the massive walls, illumined the hooked cross of the swastika on the flag that streamed out stiffly from the staff above the parapet. Solid even in its decay, impregnable in its position, commanding in its lofty outlook, the tower completely dominated both waterborne approaches, from the sea and, upriver, down the narrow, winding channel that lay between the moored caique and the foot of the cliff.

Slowly, reluctantly almost, Mallory turned away and gently lowered the tarpaulin. His face was grim as he turned round to Andrea and Stevens, ill-defined shadows in the twilit gloom of the cabin.

'Brilliant!' he repeated. 'Sheer genius. Mastermind Mallory. Probably the only bloody creek within a hundred miles – and in a hundred islands – with a German guard post on it. And of course I had to go and pick it. Let's have another look at that chart, will you, Stevens?'

Stevens passed it across, watched Mallory study it in the pale light filtering in under the tarpaulin, leaned back against the bulkhead and drew heavily on his cigarette. It tasted foul, stale and acrid, but the tobacco was fresh enough, he knew. The old, sick fear was back again, as strongly as ever. He looked at the great bulk of Andrea across from him, felt an illogical resentment towards him for having spotted the emplacement a few minutes ago. They'll have cannon up there, he thought dully, they're bound to have cannon – couldn't control the creek otherwise. He gripped his thigh fiercely, just above the knee, but the tremor lay too deep to be controlled: he blessed the merciful darkness of the tiny cabin. But his voice was casual enough as he spoke.

'You're wasting your time, sir, looking at that chart and blaming yourself. This is the only possible anchorage within hours of sailing time from here. With that wind there was nowhere else we could have gone.'

'Exactly. That's just it.' Mallory folded the chart, handed it back. 'There was nowhere else we could have gone. There was nowhere else anyone could have gone. Must be a very popular port in a storm, this – a fact which must have become apparent to the Germans a long, long time ago. That's why I should have known they were almost bound to have a post here. However, spilt milk, as you say.' He raised his voice. 'Chief?'

'Hallo!' Brown's muffled voice carried faintly from the depths of the engine-room.

'How's it going?'

'Not too bad, sir. Assembling it now.'

Mallory nodded in relief.

'How long?' he called. 'An hour?'

'Aye, easy, sir.'

'An hour.' Again Mallory glanced through the tarpaulin, looked back at Andrea and Stevens. 'Just about right. We'll leave in an hour. Dark enough to give us some protection from our friends up top, but enough light left to navigate our way out of this damned corkscrew of a channel.'

'Do you think they'll try to stop us, sir?' Stevens's voice was just too casual, too matter of fact. He was pretty sure Mallory would notice.

'It's unlikely they'll line the banks and give us three hearty cheers,' Mallory said dryly. 'How many men do you reckon they'll have up there, Andrea?'

'I've seen two moving around,' Andrea said thoughtfully. 'Maybe three or four altogether, Captain. A small post. The Germans don't waste men on these.'

'I think you're about right,' Mallory agreed. 'Most of them'll be in the garrison in the village – about seven miles from here, according to the chart, and due west. It's not likely –'

He broke off sharply, stiffened in rigid attention. Again the call came, louder this time, imperative in its tone. Cursing himself for his negligence in not posting a guard – such carelessness would have cost him his life in Crete – Mallory pulled the tarpaulin aside, clambered slowly on to the deck. He carried no arms, but a half-empty bottle of Moselle dangled from his left hand; as part of a plan prepared before they had left Alexandria, he'd snatched it from a locker at the foot of the tiny companionway.

He lurched convincingly across the deck, grabbed at a stay in time to save himself from falling overboard. Insolently he stared down at the figure on the bank, less than ten yards away – it hadn't mattered about a guard, Mallory realised, for the soldier carried his automatic carbine slung over his shoulder – insolently he tilted the wine to his mouth and swallowed deeply before condescending to talk to him.

He could see the mounting anger in the lean, tanned face of the young German below him. Mallory ignored it. Slowly, an inherent contempt in the gesture, he dragged the frayed sleeve of his black jacket across his lips, looked the soldier even more slowly up and down in a minutely provocative inspection as disdainful as it was prolonged.

'Well?' he asked truculently in the slow speech of the islands. 'What the hell do you want?'

Even in the deepening dusk he could see the knuckles whitening on the stock of the carbine, and for an instant Mallory thought he had gone too far. He knew he was in no danger – all noise in the engine-room had ceased, and Dusty Miller's hand was never far from his silenced automatic – but he didn't want trouble. Not just yet.

Not while there were a couple of manned Spandaus in that watch-tower.

With an almost visible effort the young soldier regained his control. It needed little help from the imagination to see the draining anger, the first tentative stirrings of hesitation and bewilderment. It was the reaction Mallory had hoped for. Greeks – even half-drunk Greeks – didn't talk to their over-lords like that – not unless they had an overpoweringly good reason.

'What vessel is this?' The Greek was slow and halting but passable. 'Where are you bound for?'

Mallory tilted the bottle again, smacked his lips in noisy satisfaction. He held the bottle at arm's length, regarded it with a loving respect.

'One thing about you Germans,' he confided loudly. 'You do know how to make a fine wine. I'll wager *you* can't lay your hands on this stuff, eh? And the swill they're making up above' – the island term for the mainland – 'is so full of resin that it's only good for lighting fires.' He thought for a moment. 'Of course, if you know the right people in the islands, they *might* let you have some ouzo. But some of us can get ouzo *and* the best Hocks *and* the best Moselles.'

The soldier wrinkled his face in disgust. Like almost every fighting man he despised Quislings, even when they were on his side: in Greece they were very few indeed.

'I asked you a question,' he said coldly. 'What vessel, and where bound?'

'The caique *Aigion*,' Mallory replied loftily. 'In ballast, for Samos. Under orders,' he said significantly.

'Whose orders?' the soldier demanded. Shrewdly Mallory judged the confidence as superficial only. The guard was impressed in spite of himself.

'Herr Commandant in Vathy. General Graebel,' Mallory said softly. 'You will have heard of the Herr General before, yes?' He was on safe ground here, Mallory knew. The reputation of Graebel, both as a paratroop commander and an iron disciplinarian, had spread far beyond these islands.

Even in the half-light Mallory could have sworn that the guard's complexion turned paler. But he was dogged enough.

'You have papers? Letters of authority?'

Mallory sighed wearily, looked over his shoulder.

'Andrea!' he bawled.

'What do you want?' Andrea's great bulk loomed through the hatchway. He had heard every word that passed, had taken his cue from Mallory: a newly-opened wine bottle was almost engulfed in one vast hand and he was scowling hugely. 'Can't you see I'm busy?' he asked surlily. He stopped short at the sight of the German and scowled again, irritably. 'And what does this halfling want?'

'Our passes and letters of authority from Herr General. They're down below.'

Andrea disappeared, grumbling deep in his throat. A rope was thrown ashore, the stern pulled in against the sluggish current and the papers passed over. The papers – a set different from those to be used if emergency arose in Navarone – proved to be satisfactory, eminently so. Mallory would have been surprised had they been anything else. The preparation of these, even down to the photo-static facsimile of General Graebel's signature, was all in the day's work for Jensen's bureau in Cairo.

The soldier folded the papers, handed them back with a muttered word of thanks. He was only a kid, Mallory could see now – if he was more than nineteen his looks belied him. A pleasant, open-faced kid – of a different stamp altogether from the young fanatics of the SS Panzer Division – and far too thin. Mallory's chief reaction was one of relief: he would have hated to have to kill a boy like this. But he had to find out all he could. He signalled to Stevens to hand him up the almost empty crate of Moselle. Jensen, he mused, had been very thorough indeed: the man had literally thought of everything . . . Mallory gestured in the direction of the watch-tower.

'How many of you are up there?' he asked.

The boy was instantly suspicious. His face had tightened up, stilled in hostile surmise.

'Why do you want to know?' he asked stiffly.

Mallory groaned, lifted his hands in despair, turned sadly to Andrea.

'You see what it is to be one of them?' he asked in mournful complaint. 'Trust nobody. Think everyone is as twisted as . . .' He broke off hurriedly, turned to the soldier again. 'It's just that we don't want to have the same trouble every time we come in here,' he explained. 'We'll be back in Samos in a couple of days, and we've still another case of Moselle to work through. General Graebel keeps his – ah – special envoys well supplied . . . It must be thirsty work up there in the sun. Come on, now, a bottle each. How many bottles?'

The reassuring mention that they would be back again, the equally reassuring mention of Graebel's name, plus, probably, the attraction of the offer and his comrades' reaction if he told them he had refused it, tipped the balance, overcame scruples and suspicions.

'There are only three of us,' he said grudgingly.

'Three it is,' Mallory said cheerfully. 'We'll bring you some Hock next time we return.' He tilted his own bottle. '*Prosit!*' he said, an islander proud of airing his German, and then, more proudly still, '*Auf Wiedersehen!*'

The boy murmured something in return. He stood hesitating for a moment, slightly shame-faced, then wheeled abruptly, walked off slowly along the river bank, clutching his bottles of Moselle.

'So!' Mallory said thoughtfully. 'There are only three of them. That should make things easier –'

'Well done, sir!' It was Stevens who interrupted, his voice warm, his face alive with admiration. 'Jolly good show!'

'Jolly good show!' Miller mimicked. He heaved his lanky length over the coaming of the engine hatchway, '"Good" be damned! I couldn't understand a gawddamned word, but for my money that rates an Oscar. That was terrific, boss!'

'Thank you, one and all,' Mallory murmured. 'But I'm afraid the congratulations are a bit premature.' The sudden chill in his voice struck at them, so that their eyes aligned along his pointing finger even before he went on. 'Take a look,' he said quietly.

The young soldier had halted suddenly about two hundred yards along the bank, looked into the forest on his left in startled surprise, then dived in among the trees. For a moment the watchers on the boat could see another soldier, talking excitedly to the boy and gesticulating in the direction of their boat, and then both were gone, lost in the gloom of the forest.

'That's torn it!' Mallory said softly. He turned away. 'Right, that's enough. Back to where you were. It would look fishy if we ignored that incident altogether, but it would look a damned sight fishier if we paid too much attention to it. Don't let's appear to be holding a conference.'

Miller slipped down into the engine-room with Brown, and Stevens went back to the little for'ard cabin. Mallory and Andrea remained on deck, bottles in their hands. The rain had stopped now, completely, but the wind was still rising, climbing the scale with imperceptible steadiness, beginning to bend the tops of the tallest of the pines. Temporarily the bluff was affording them almost complete protection. Mallory deliberately shut his mind to what it must be like outside. They had to put out to sea – Spandaus permitting – and that was that.

'What do you think has happened, sir?' Stevens's voice carried up from the gloom of the cabin.

'Pretty obvious, isn't it?' Mallory asked. He spoke loudly enough for all to hear. 'They've been tipped off. Don't ask me how. This is the second time – and their suspicions are going to be considerably reinforced by the absence of a report from the caique that was sent to investigate us. She was carrying a wireless aerial, remember?'

'But why should they get so damned suspicious all of a sudden?' Miller asked. 'It doesn't make sense to me, boss.'

'Must be in radio contact with their HQ. Or a telephone – probably a telephone. They've just been given the old tic-tac. Consternation on all sides.'

'So mebbe they'll be sending a small army over from their HQ to deal with us,' Miller said lugubriously.

Mallory shook his head definitely. His mind was working quickly and well, and he felt oddly certain, confident of himself.

'No, not a chance. Seven miles as the crow flies. Ten, maybe twelve miles over rough hill and forest tracks – and in pitch darkness. They wouldn't think of it.' He waved his bottle in the direction of the watch-tower. 'Tonight's their big night.'

'So we can expect the Spandaus to open up any minute?' Again the abnormal matter-of-factness of Stevens's voice.

Mallory shook his head a second time.

'They won't. I'm positive of that. No matter how suspicious they may be, how certain they are that we're the big bad wolf, they are going to be shaken to the core when that kid tells them we're carrying papers and letters of authority signed by General Graebel himself. For all they know, curtains for us may be the firing squad for them. Unlikely, but you get the general idea. So they're going to contact HQ, and the commandant on a small island like this isn't going to take a chance on rubbing out a bunch of characters who may be the special envoys of the Herr General himself. So what? So he codes a message and radios it to Vathy in Samos and bites his nails off to the elbow till a message comes back saying Graebel has never heard of us and why the hell haven't we all been shot dead?'

Mallory looked at the luminous dial of his watch. 'I'd say we have at least half an hour.'

'And meantime we all sit around with our little bits of paper and pencil and write out our last wills and testaments.' Miller scowled. 'No percentage in that, boss. We gotta *do* somethin'.'

Mallory grinned.

'Don't worry, Corporal, we are going to do something. We're going to hold a nice little bottle party, right here on the poop.'

The last words of their song – a shockingly corrupted Grecian version of 'Lilli Marlene', and their third song in the past few minutes – died away in the evening air. Mallory doubted whether more than faint snatches of the singing would be carried to the watch-tower against the wind, but the rhythmical stamping of feet and waving of bottles were in themselves sufficient evidence of drunken musical hilarity to all but the totally blind and deaf. Mallory grinned to himself as he thought of the complete confusion and uncertainty the Germans in the tower must have been feeling then. This was not the behaviour of enemy spies, especially enemy spies who know that suspicions had been aroused and that their time was running out.

Mallory tilted the bottle to his mouth, held it there for several seconds, then set it down again, the wine untasted. He looked round slowly at the three men squatting there with him on the poop, Miller, Stevens and Brown. Andrea was not there, but he didn't have to turn his head to look for him. Andrea, he knew, was crouched in the shelter of the wheelhouse, a waterproof bag with grenades and a revolver strapped to his back.

'Right!' Mallory said crisply. 'Now's your big chance for *your* Oscar. Let's make this as convincing as we can.' He bent forward, jabbed his finger into Miller's chest and shouted angrily at him.

Miller shouted back. For a few moments they sat there, gesticulating angrily and, to all appearances, quarrelling furiously with each other. Then Miller was on his feet, swaying in drunken imbalance as he leaned threateningly over Mallory, clenched fists ready to strike. He stood back as Mallory struggled to his feet, and in a moment they were fighting fiercely, raining apparently heavy blows on each other. Then a haymaker from the American sent Mallory reeling back to crash convincingly against the wheelhouse.

'Right, Andrea.' He spoke quietly, without looking round. 'This is it. Five seconds. Good luck.' He scrambled to his feet, picked up a bottle by the neck and rushed at Miller, upraised arm and bludgeon swinging fiercely down. Miller dodged, swung a vicious foot, and Mallory roared in pain as his shins caught on the edge of the bulwarks. Silhouetted against the pale gleam of the creek, he stood poised for a second, arms flailing wildly, then plunged heavily, with a loud splash, into the waters of the creek.

For the next half-minute – it would take about that time for Andrea to swim underwater round the next upstream corner of the creek – everything was a confusion and a bedlam of noise. Mallory trod water as he tried to pull himself aboard: Miller had seized a boathook and was trying to smash it down on his head: and the others, on their feet now, had flung their arms round Miller, trying to restrain him: finally they managed to knock him off his feet, pin him to the deck and help the dripping Mallory aboard. A minute later, after the immemorial fashion of drunken men, the two combatants had shaken hands with one another and were sitting on the engine-room hatch, arms round each other's shoulders and drinking in perfect amity from the same freshly-opened bottle of wine.

'Very nicely done,' Mallory said approvingly. 'Very nicely indeed. An Oscar, definitely, for Corporal Miller.'

Dusty Miller said nothing. Taciturn and depressed, he looked moodily at the bottle in his hand. At last he stirred.

'I don't like it, boss,' he muttered unhappily. 'I don't like the set-up one little bit. You shoulda let me go with Andrea. It's three to one up there, and they're waiting and ready.' He looked accusingly at Mallory. 'Dammit to hell, boss, you're always telling us how desperately important this mission is!'

'I know,' Mallory said quietly. 'That's why I didn't send you with him. That's why none of us has gone with him. We'd only be a liability to him, get in his way.' Mallory shook his head. 'You don't know Andrea, Dusty.' It was the first time Mallory had called him that: Miller was warmed by the unexpected familiarity, secretly pleased. 'None of you know him. But I know him.' He gestured towards the watch-tower, its square-cut lines in sharp silhouette against the darkening sky. 'Just a big, fat, good-natured chap, always laughing and joking.' Mallory paused, shook his head again, went on slowly. 'He's up there now, padding through that forest like a cat, the biggest and most dangerous cat you'll ever see. Unless they offer no resistance – Andrea never kills unnecessarily – when I send him up there after these three poor bastards I'm executing them just as surely as if they were in the electric chair and I was pulling the switch.'

In spite of himself Miller was impressed, profoundly so.

'Known him a long time, boss, huh?' It was half question, half statement.

'A long time. Andrea was in the Albanian war – he was in the regular army. They tell me the Italians went in terror of him – his long-range patrols against the Iulia division, the Wolves of Tuscany, did more to wreck the Italian morale in Albania than any other single factor. I've heard a good many stories about them – not from Andrea – and they're all incredible. And they're all true. But it was afterwards I met him, when we were trying to hold the Servia Pass. I was a very junior liaison lieutenant in the Anzac brigade at the time. Andrea' – he paused deliberately for effect – 'Andrea was a lieutenant-colonel in the 19th Greek Motorised Division.'

'A *what*?' Miller demanded in astonishment. Stevens and Brown were equally incredulous.

'You heard me. Lieutenant-colonel. Outranks me by a fairish bit, you might say.' He smiled at them quizzically. 'Puts Andrea in rather a different light, doesn't it?'

They nodded silently but said nothing. The genial, hail-fellow Andrea – a good-natured, almost simpleminded buffoon – a senior army officer. The idea had come too suddenly, was too incongruous for easy assimilation and immediate comprehension. But, gradually, it began to make sense to them. It explained many things about Andrea to them – his repose, his confidence, the unerring sureness of his lightning reactions, and, above all, the implicit faith Mallory had in him, the respect he showed for Andrea's opinions whenever he consulted him, which was frequently. Without surprise now, Miller slowly recalled that he'd never yet heard Mallory give Andrea a direct order. And Mallory never hesitated to pull his rank, when necessary.

'After Servia,' Mallory went on, 'everything was pretty confused. Andrea had heard that Trikkala – a small country town where his wife and three daughters lived – had been flattened by the Stukas and Heinkels. He reached there all right, but there was nothing he could do. A land-mine had landed in the front garden and there wasn't even rubble left.'

Mallory paused, lit a cigarette. He stared through the drifting smoke at the fading outlines of the tower.

'The only person he found there was his brother-in-law, George. George was with us in Crete – he's still there. From George he heard for the first time of the Bulgarian atrocities in Thrace and

Macedonia – and his parents lived there. So they dressed in German uniforms – you can imagine how Andrea got those – commandeered a German army truck and drove to Protosami.' The cigarette in Mallory's hand snapped suddenly, was sent spinning over the side. Miller was vaguely surprised: emotion, or rather, emotional displays, were so completely foreign to that very tough New Zealander. But Mallory went on quietly enough.

'They arrived in the evening of the infamous Protosami massacre. George has told me how Andrea stood there, clad in his German uniform and laughing as he watched a party of nine or ten Bulgarian soldiers lash couples together and throw them into the river. The first couple in were his father and stepmother, both dead.'

'My Gawd above!' Even Miller was shocked out of his usual equanimity. 'It's just not possible –'

'You know nothing,' Mallory interrupted impatiently. 'Hundreds of Greeks in Macedonia died the same way – but usually alive when they were thrown in. Until you know how the Greeks hate the Bulgarians, you don't even begin to know what hate is . . . Andrea shared a couple of bottles of wine with the soldiers, found out that they had killed his parents earlier in the afternoon – they had been foolish enough to resist. After dusk he followed them up to an old corrugated-iron shed where they were billeted for the night. All he had was a knife. They left a guard outside. Andrea broke his neck, went inside, locked the door and smashed the oil lamp. George doesn't know what happened except that Andrea went berserk. He was back outside in two minutes, completely sodden, his uniform soaked in blood from head to foot. There wasn't a sound, not even a groan to be heard from the hut when they left, George says.'

He paused again, but this time there was no interruption, nothing said. Stevens shivered, drew his shabby jacket closer round his shoulders: the air seemed to have become suddenly chill. Mallory lit another cigarette, smiled faintly at Miller, nodded towards the watch-tower.

'See what I mean by saying we'd only be a liability to Andrea up there?'

'Yeah. Yeah, I guess I do,' Miller admitted. 'I had no idea, I had no idea . . . Not *all* of them, boss! He couldn't have killed –'

'He did,' Mallory interrupted flatly. 'After that he formed his own band, made life hell for the Bulgarian outposts in Thrace.

At one time there was almost an entire division chasing him through the Rhodope mountains. Finally he was betrayed and captured, and he, George and four others were shipped to Stavros – they were to go on to Salonika for trial. They overpowered their guards – Andrea got loose among them on deck at night – and sailed the boat to Turkey. The Turks tried to intern him – they might as well have tried to intern an earthquake. Finally he arrived in Palestine, tried to join the Greek Commando Battalion that was being formed in the Middle East – mainly veterans of the Albanian campaign, like himself.' Mallory laughed mirthlessly. 'He was arrested as a deserter. He was released eventually, but there was no place for him in the new Greek Army. But Jensen's bureau heard about him, knew he was a natural for Subversive Operations . . . And so we went to Crete together.'

Five minutes passed, perhaps ten, but nobody broke the silence. Occasionally, for the benefit of any watchers, they went through the motions of drinking; but even the half-light was fading now and Mallory knew they could only be half-seen blurs, shadowy and indistinct, from the heights of the watch-tower. The caique was beginning to rock in the surge from the open sea round the bluff. The tall, reaching pines, black now as midnight cypress and looming impossibly high against the star-dusted cloud wrack that scudded palely overhead, were closing in on them from either side, sombre, watchful and vaguely threatening, the wind moaning in lost and mournful requiem through their swaying topmost branches. A bad night, an eerie and an ominous night, pregnant with that indefinable foreboding that reaches down and touches the well-springs of the nameless fears, the dim and haunting memories of a million years ago, the ancient racial superstitions of mankind: a night that sloughed off the tissue veneer of civilisation and the shivering man complains that someone is walking over his grave.

Suddenly, incongruously, the spell was shattered and Andrea's cheerful hail from the bank had them all on their feet in a moment. They heard his booming laugh and even the forests seemed to shrink back in defeat. Without waiting for the stern to be pulled in, he plunged into the creek, reached the caique in half a dozen powerful strokes and hoisted himself easily aboard. Grinning down from his great height, he shook himself like some shaggy mastiff and reached out a hand for a convenient wine bottle.

'No need to ask how things went, eh?' Mallory asked, smiling.

'None at all. It was just too easy. They were only boys and they never even saw me.' Andrea took another long swig from the bottle and grinned in sheer delight. 'And I didn't lay a finger on them,' he went on triumphantly. 'Well, maybe a couple of little taps. They were all looking down here, staring out over the parapet when I arrived. Held them up, took their guns off them and locked them in a cellar. And then I bent their Spandaus – just a little bit.'

This is it, Mallory thought dully, this is the end. This is the finish of everything, the strivings, the hopes, the fears, the loves and laughter of each one of us. This is what it all comes to. This is the end, the end for us, the end for a thousand boys on Kheros. In unconscious futility his hand came up, slowly wiped lips salt from the spray bulleting off the wind-flattened wave-tops, then lifted farther to shade bloodshot eyes that peered out hopelessly into the storm-filled darkness ahead. For a moment the dullness lifted, and an almost intolerable bitterness welled through his mind. All gone, everything – everything except the guns of Navarone. The guns of Navarone. They would live on, they were indestructible. Damn them, damn them, damn them! Dear God, the blind waste, the terrible uselessness of it all!

The caique was dying, coming apart at the seams. She was literally being pounded to death, being shaken apart by the constant battering shocks of wind and sea. Time and time again the poop-deck dipped beneath the foam-streaked cauldron at the stern, the fo'c'sle rearing crazily into the air, dripping forefoot showing clear: then the plummeting drop, the shotgun, shuddering impact as broad-beamed bows crashed vertically down into the cliff-walled trough beyond, an explosive collision that threw so unendurable a strain on the ancient timbers and planks and gradually tore them apart.

It had been bad enough when they'd cleared the creek just as darkness fell, and plunged and wallowed their way through a quartering sea on a northward course for Navarone. Steering the unwieldy old caique had become difficult in the extreme: with the seas fine on the starboard quarter she had yawed wildly and unpredictably through a fifty degree arc, but at least her seams had been tight then, the rolling waves overtaking her in regular formation and the wind settled and steady somewhere east of south. But now all that was gone. With half a dozen planks sprung from the stem-post and working loose from the apron, and leaking heavily through the stuffing-gland of the propeller shaft, she was making water far faster than the ancient, vertical hand-pump could cope with: the wind-truncated seas were heavier, but broken and confused, sweeping down on them now from this quarter, now from that: and the wind itself, redoubled in its shrieking violence, veered and backed insanely from south-west to south-east. Just then it was steady from the south, driving the unmanageable craft blindly on to the closing iron cliffs of Navarone, cliffs that loomed invisibly ahead, somewhere in that all-encompassing darkness.

Momentarily Mallory straightened, tried to ease the agony of the pincers that were clawing into the muscles of the small of his back. For over two hours now he had been bending and straightening, bending and straightening, lifting a thousand buckets that Dusty Miller filled interminably from the well of the hold. God only knew how Miller felt. If anything, he had the harder job of the two and he had been violently and almost continuously sea-sick for hours on end. He looked ghastly, and he must have been feeling like death itself: the sustained effort, the sheer iron will-power to drive himself on in that condition reached beyond the limits of understanding. Mallory shook his head wonderingly. 'My God, but he's tough, that Yank.' Unbidden, the words framed themselves in his mind, and he shook his head in anger, vaguely conscious of the complete inadequacy of the words.

Fighting for his breath, he looked aft to see how the others were faring. Casey Brown, of course, he couldn't see. Bent double in the cramped confines of the engine-room, he, too, was constantly sick and suffering a blinding headache from the oil fumes and exhaust gases still filtering from the replacement stand-pipe, neither of which could find any escape in the unventilated engine-room: but, crouched over the engine, he had not once left his post since they had cleared the mouth of the creek, had nursed the straining, ancient Kelvin along with the loving care, the exquisite skill of a man born into a long and proud tradition of engineering. That engine had only to falter once, to break down for the time in which a man might draw a deep breath, and the end would be as immediate as it was violent. Their steerage way, their lives, depended entirely on the continuous thrust of that screw, the laboured thudding of that rusted old two-cylinder. It was the heart of the boat, and when that heart stopped beating the boat died too, slewed broadside on and foundering in the waiting chasms between the waves.

For'ard of the engine-room, straddle-legged and braced against the corner pillar of the splintered skeleton that was all that remained of the wheelhouse, Andrea laboured unceasingly at the pump, never once lifting his head, oblivious of the crazy lurching of the deck of the caique, oblivious, too, of the biting wind and stinging, sleet-cold spray that numbed bare arms and moulded the sodden shirt to the hunched and massive shoulders. Ceaselessly, tirelessly, his arm thrust up and down, up and down, with the metronomic regularity of a piston. He had been there for close on three hours now, and he looked as if he could go on for ever. Mallory, who had yielded him the pump in complete exhaustion after less than twenty minutes' cruel labour, wondered if there was any limit to the man's endurance.

He wondered, too, about Stevens. For four endless hours now Andy Stevens had fought and overcome a wheel that leapt and struggled in his hands as if possessed of a convulsive life and will of its own – the will to wrench itself out of exhausted hands and turn them into the troughs: he had done a superb job, Mallory thought, had handled the clumsy craft magnificently. He peered at him closely, but the spray lashed viciously across his eyes and blinded him with tears. All he could gather was a vague impression of a tightly-set mouth, sleepless, sunken eyes and little patches of skin unnaturally pale against the mask of blood that covered almost the entire face from hairline to throat. The twisting, towering comber that had stove in the planks of the wheelhouse and driven in the windows with such savage force had been completely unexpected: Stevens hadn't had a chance. The cut above the right temple was particularly bad, ugly and deep: the blood still pulsed over the ragged edge of the wound, dripped monotonously into the water that sloshed and gurgled about the floor of the wheelhouse.

Sick to his heart, Mallory turned away, reached down for another bucket of water. What a crew, he thought to himself, what a really terrific bunch of – of . . . He sought for words to describe them, even to himself, but he knew his mind was far too tired. It didn't matter anyway, for there were no words for men like that, nothing that could do them justice.

He could almost taste the bitterness in his mouth, the bitterness that washed in waves through his exhausted mind. God, how wrong it was, how terribly unfair! Why did such men have to die, he wondered savagely, why did they have to die so uselessly. Or maybe it wasn't necessary to justify dying, even dying ingloriously empty of achievement. Could one not die for intangibles, for the abstract and the ideal? What had the martyrs at the stake achieved?

Or what was the old tag – *dulce et decorum est pro patria mori*. If one lives well, what matter how one dies. Unconsciously his lips tightened in quick revulsion and he thought of Jensen's remarks about the High Command playing who's-the-king-of-the-castle. Well, they were right bang in the middle of their playground now, just a few more pawns sliding into the limbo. Not that it mattered – they had thousands more left to play with.

For the first time Mallory thought of himself. Not with bitterness or self-pity or regret that it was all over. He thought of himself only as the leader of this party, his responsibility for the present situation. It's my fault, he told himself over and over again, it's all my fault. I brought them here. I made them come. Even while one part of his mind was telling him that he'd had no option, that his hand had been forced, that if they had remained in the creek they would have been wiped out long before the dawn, irrationally he still blamed himself the more. Shackleton, of all the men that ever lived, maybe Ernest Shackleton could have helped them now. But not Keith Mallory. There was nothing he could do, no more than the others were doing, and they were just waiting for the end. But he was the leader, he thought dully, he should be planning something, he should be doing something . . . But there was nothing he could do. There was nothing anyone on God's earth could do. The sense of guilt, of utter inadequacy, settled and deepened with every shudder of the ancient timbers.

He dropped his bucket, grabbed for the security of the mast as a heavy wave swept over the deck, the breaking foam quicksilver in its seething phosphorescence. The waters swirled hungrily round his legs and feet, but he ignored them, stared out into the darkness. The darkness – that was the devil of it. The old caique rolled and pitched and staggered and plunged, but as if disembodied, in a vacuum. They could see nothing – not where the last wave had gone, nor where the next was coming from. A sea invisible and strangely remote, doubly frightening in its palpable immediacy.

Mallory stared down into the hold, was vaguely conscious of the white blur of Miller's face: he had swallowed some sea-water and was retching painfully, salt water laced with blood. But Mallory ignored it, involuntarily: all his mind was concentrated elsewhere, trying to reduce some fleeting impression, as vague as it had been evanescent, to a coherent realisation. It seemed desperately urgent that he should do so. Then another and still heavier wave broke over the side and all at once he had it.

The wind! The wind had dropped away, was lessening with every second that passed. Even as he stood there, arms locked round the mast as the second wave fought to carry him away, he remembered how often in the high hills at home he had stood at the foot of a precipice as an onrushing wind, seeking the path of least resistance, had curved and lifted up the sheer face, leaving him standing in a pocket of relative immunity. It was a common enough mountaineering phenomenon. And these two freak waves – the surging backwash! The significance struck at him like a blow. The cliffs! They were on the cliffs of Navarone!

With a hoarse, wordless cry of warning, reckless of his own safety, he flung himself aft, dived full length through the swirling waters for the engine-room hatchway.

'Full astern!' he shouted. The startled white smudge that was Casey Brown's face twisted up to his. 'For God's sake, man, full astern! We're heading for the cliffs!'

He scrambled to his feet, reached the wheelhouse in two strides, hand pawing frantically for the flare pocket.

'The cliffs, Stevens! We're almost on them! Andrea – Miller's still down below!'

He flicked a glance at Stevens, caught the slow nod of the set, blood-masked face, followed the line of sight of the expressionless eyes, saw the whitely phosphorescent line ahead, irregular but almost continuous, blooming and fading, blooming and fading, as the pounding seas smashed against and fell back from cliffs still invisible in the darkness. Desperately his hands fumbled with the flare.

And then, abruptly, it was gone, hissing and spluttering along the near-horizontal trajectory of its flight. For a moment, Mallory thought it had gone out, and he clenched his fists in impotent bitterness. Then it smashed against the rock face, fell back on to a ledge about a dozen feet above the water, and lay there smoking and intermittently burning in the driving rain, in the heavy spray that cascaded from the booming breakers.

The light was feeble, but it was enough. The cliffs were barely fifty yards away, black and wetly shining in the fitful radiance of the flare – a flare that illuminated a vertical circle of less than five yards in radius, and left the cliff below the ledge shrouded in the treacherous dark. And straight ahead, twenty, maybe fifteen yards from the shore, stretched the evil length of a reef, gap-toothed and needle-pointed, vanishing at either end into the outer darkness.

'Can you take her through?' he yelled at Stevens.

'God knows! I'll try!' He shouted something else about 'steerage way', but Mallory was already half-way to the for'ard cabin. As always in an emergency, his mind was racing ahead with that abnormal sureness and clarity of thought for which he could never afterwards account.

Grasping spikes, mallet and a wire-cored rope, he was back on deck in seconds. He stood stock still, rooted in an almost intolerable tension as he saw the towering, jagged rock bearing down upon them, fine on the starboard bow, a rock that reached half-way to the wheelhouse. It struck the boat with a crash that sent him to his knees, rasped and grated along half the length of the buckled, splintered gunwales: and then the caique had rolled over to port and she was through. Stevens frantically spinning the wheel and shouting for full astern.

Mallory's breath escaped in a long, heavy sigh of relief – he had been quite unaware that he had stopped breathing – and he hurriedly looped the coil of rope round his neck and under his left shoulder and stuck spikes and hammer in his belt. The caique was slewing heavily round now, port side to, plunging and corkscrewing violently as she began to fall broadside into the troughs of the waves, waves shorter and steeper than ever under the double thrust of the wind and the waves and the backwash recoiling from the cliffs: but she was still in the grip of the sea and her own momentum, and the distance was closing with frightening speed. It's a chance I have to take, Mallory repeated to himself over and over again; it's a chance I have to take. But that little ledge remote and just inaccessible, was fate's last refinement of cruelty, the salt in the wound of extinction, and he knew in his heart of hearts that it wasn't a chance at all, but just a suicidal gesture. And then Andrea had heaved the last of the tenders – worn truck tyres – outboard, and was towering above him, grinning down hugely into his face: and suddenly Mallory wasn't so sure any more.

'The ledge?' Andrea's vast, reassuring hand was on his shoulder.

Mallory nodded, knees bent in readiness, feet braced on the plunging, slippery deck.

'Jump for it,' Andrea boomed. 'Then keep your legs stiff.'

There was no time for any more. The caique was swinging in broadside to, teetering on the crest of a wave, as high up the cliff as she would ever be, and Mallory knew it was now or never. His hands swung back behind his body, his knees bent farther, and then, in one convulsive leap he had flung himself upwards, fingers scrabbling on the wet rock of the cliff, then hooking over the rim of the ledge. For an instant he hung there at the length of his arms, unable to move, wincing as he heard the foremast crash against the ledge and snap in two, then his fingers left the ledge without their own volition, and he was almost half-way over, propelled by one gigantic heave from below.

He was not up yet. He was held only by the buckle of his belt, caught on the edge of the rock, a buckle now dragged up to his breastbone by the weight of his body. But he did not paw frantically for a handhold, or wriggle his body or flail his legs in the air – and any of these actions would have sent him crashing down again. At last, and once again, he was a man utterly at home in his own element. The greatest rock climber of his time, men called him, and this was what he had been born for.

Slowly, methodically, he felt the surface of the ledge, and almost at once he discovered a crack running back from the face. It would have been better had it been parallel to the face – and more than the width of a match-stick. But it was enough for Mallory. With infinite care he eased the hammer and a couple of spikes from his belt, worked a spike into the crack to obtain a minimal purchase, slid the other in some inches nearer, hooked his left wrist round the first, held the second spike with the fingers of the same hand and brought up the hammer in his free hand. Fifteen seconds later he was standing on the ledge.

Working quickly and surely, catlike in his balance on the slippery, shelving rock, he hammered a spike into the face of the cliff, securely and at a downward angle, about three feet above the ledge, dropped a clove hitch over the top and kicked the rest of the coil over the ledge. Then, and only then, he turned round and looked below him.

Less than a minute had passed since the caique had struck, but already she was a broken-masted, splintered shambles, sides caving in and visibly disintegrating as he watched. Every seven or eight seconds a giant comber would pick her up and fling her bodily against the cliff, the heavy truck tyres taking up only a fraction of the impact that followed, the sickening, rending crash that reduced the gunwales to matchwood, holed and split the sides and cracked the oaken timbers: and then she would roll clear, port side showing, the hungry sea pouring in through the torn and ruptured planking.

Three men were standing by what was left of the wheelhouse. *Three* men – suddenly, he realised that Casey Brown was missing, realised, too, that the engine was still running, its clamour rising and falling then rising again, at irregular intervals. Brown was edging the caique backwards and forwards along the cliff, keeping her as nearly as humanly possible in the same position, for he knew their lives depended on Mallory – and on himself. 'The fool!' Mallory swore. 'The crazy fool!'

The caique surged back in a receding trough, steadied, then swept in against the cliff again, heeling over so wildly that the roof of the wheelhouse smashed and telescoped against the wall of the cliff. The impact was so fierce, the shock so sudden, that Stevens lost both handgrip and footing and was catapulted into the rock face, upflung arms raised for protection. For a moment he hung there, as if pinned against the wall, then fell back into the sea, limbs and head relaxed, lifeless in his limp acquiescence. He should have died then, drowned under the hammer-blows of the sea or crushed by the next battering-ram collision of caique and cliff. He should have died and he would have died but for the great arm that hooked down and plucked him out of the water like a limp and sodden rag doll and heaved him inboard a bare second before the next bludgeoning impact of the boat against the rock would have crushed the life out of him.

'Come on, for God's sake!' Mallory shouted desperately. 'She'll be gone in a minute! The rope – use the rope!' He saw Andrea and Miller exchange a few quick words, saw them shake and pummel Stevens and stand him on his feet, dazed and retching sea-water, but conscious. Andrea was speaking in his ear, emphasising something and guiding the rope into his hands, and then the caique was swinging in again, Stevens automatically shortening his grip on the rope. A tremendous boost from below by Andrea, Mallory's long arm reaching out and Stevens was on the ledge, sitting with his back to the cliff and hanging on to the spike, dazed still and shaking a muzzy head, but safe.

'You're next, Miller!' Mallory called. 'Hurry up, man – jump for it!'

Miller looked at him and Mallory could have sworn that he was grinning. Instead of taking the rope from Andrea, he ran for'ard to the cabin.

'Just a minute, boss!' he bawled. 'I've forgotten my toothbrush.'

He reappeared in a few seconds, but without the toothbrush. He was carrying the big, green box of explosives, and before Mallory had appreciated what was happening the box, all fifty pounds of it, was curving up into the air, upthrust by the Greek's tireless arms. Automatically Mallory's hands reached for and caught it. He over-balanced, stumbled and toppled forward, still clutching the box, then was brought up with a jerk. Stevens, still clutching the spike, was on his feet now, free hand hooked in Mallory's belt: he was shivering violently, with cold and exhaustion and an oddly fear-laced excite-ment. But, like Mallory, he was a hillman at home again.

Mallory was just straightening up when the waterproofed radio set came soaring up. He caught it, placed it down, looked over the side.

'Leave that bloody stuff alone!' he shouted furiously. 'Get up here yourselves – now!'

Two coils of rope landed on the ledge beside him, then the first of the rucksacks with the food and clothing. He was vaguely aware that Stevens was trying to stack the equipment in some sort of order.

'Do you hear me?' Mallory roared. 'Get up here at once! That's an order. The boat's sinking, you bloody idiots!'

The caique *was* sinking. She was filling up quickly and Casey Brown had abandoned the flooded Kelvin. But she was a far steadier platform now, rolling through a much shorter arc, less violent in her soggy, yielding collisions with the cliff wall. For a moment Mallory thought the sea was dropping away, then he realised that the tons of water in the caique's hold had drastically lowered her centre of gravity, were acting as a counter-balancing weight.

Miller cupped a hand to his ear. Even in the near darkness of the sinking flare his face had an oddly greenish pallor.

'Can't hear a word you say, boss. Besides, she ain't sinkin' yet.' Once again he disappeared into the for'ard cabin.

Within thirty seconds, with all five men working furiously, the remainder of the equipment was on the ledge. The caique was down by the stern, the poop-deck covered and water pouring down the engine-room hatch-way as Brown struggled up the rope, the fo'c'sle awash as Miller grabbed the rope and started after him, and as Andrea reached up and swung in against the cliff his legs dangled over an empty sea. The caique had foundered, completely gone from sight: no drifting flotsam, not even an air bubble marked where she had so lately been.

The ledge was narrow, not three feet wide at its broadest, taper-ing off into the gloom on either side. Worse still, apart from the few square feet where Stevens had piled the gear, it shelved sharply outwards, the rock underfoot treacherous and slippery. Backs to the wall, Andrea and Miller had to stand on their heels, hands outspread and palms inward against the cliff, pressing in to it as closely as possible to maintain their balance. But in less than a minute Mallory had another two spikes hammered in about twenty inches above the ledge, ten feet apart and joined with a rope, a secure lifeline for all of them.

Wearily Miller slid down to a sitting position, leaned his chest in heartfelt thankfulness against the safe barrier of the rope. He fumbled in his breast pocket, produced a pack of cigarettes and handed them round, oblivious to the rain that soaked them in an instant. He was soaking wet from the waist downwards and both his knees had been badly bruised against the cliff wall: he was bitterly cold, drenched by heavy rain and the sheets of spray that broke continually over the ledge: the sharp edge of the rock bit cruelly into the calves of his legs, the tight rope constricted his breathing and he was still ashen-faced and exhausted from long hours of labour and sea-sickness: but when he spoke, it was with a voice of utter sincerity.

'My Gawd!' he said reverently. 'Ain't this wonderful!'

FIVE

Monday Night
0100–0200

Ninety minutes later Mallory wedged himself into a natural rock chimney on the cliff face, drove in a spike beneath his feet and tried to rest his aching, exhausted body. Two minutes' rest he told himself, only two minutes while Andrea comes up: the rope was quivering and he could just hear, above the shrieking of the wind that fought to pluck him off the cliff face, the metallic scraping as Andrea's boots struggled for a foothold on that wicked overhang immediately beneath him, the overhang that had all but defeated him, the obstacle that he had impossibly overcome only at the expense of torn hands and body completely spent, of shoulder muscles afire with agony and breath that rasped in great gulping inhalations into his starving lungs. Deliberately he forced his mind away from the pains that racked his body, from its insistent demands for rest, and listened again to the ringing of steel against rock, louder this time, carrying clearly even in the gale . . . He would have to tell Andrea to be more careful on the remaining twenty feet or so that separated them from the top.

At least, Mallory thought wryly, no one would have to tell him to be quiet. He couldn't have made any noise with his feet if he'd tried – not with only a pair of torn socks as cover for his bruised and bleeding feet. He'd hardly covered his first twenty feet of the climb when he'd discovered that his climbing boots were quite useless, had robbed his feet of all sensitivity, the ability to locate and engage the tiny toe-holds which afforded the only sources of purchase. He had removed them with great difficulty, tied them to his belt by the laces – and lost them, had them torn off, when forcing his way under a projecting spur of rock.

73

The climb itself had been a nightmare, a brutal, gasping agony in the wind and the rain and the darkness, an agony that had eventually dulled the danger and masked the suicidal risks in climbing that sheer unknown face, in interminable agony of hanging on by fingertips and toes, of driving in a hundred spikes, of securing ropes then inching on again up into the darkness. It was a climb such as he had not ever made before, such as he knew he would not ever make again, for this was insanity. It was a climb that had extended him to the utmost of his great skill, his courage and his strength, and then far beyond that again, and he had not known that such reserves, such limitless resources, lay within him or any man. Nor did he know the well-spring, the source of that power that had driven him to where he was, within easy climbing reach of the top. The challenge to a mountaineer, personal danger, pride in the fact that he was probably the only man in southern Europe who could have made the climb, even the sure knowledge that time was running out for the men on Kheros – it was none of these things, he knew that: in the last twenty minutes it had taken him to negotiate that overhang beneath his feet his mind had been drained of all thought and all emotion, and he had climbed only as a machine.

Hand over hand up the rope, easily, powerfully, Andrea hauled himself over the smoothly swelling convexity of the overhang, legs dangling in midair. He was festooned with heavy coils of rope, girdled with spikes that protruded from his belt at every angle and lent him the incongruous appearance of a comic-opera Corsican bandit. Quickly he hauled himself up beside Mallory, wedged himself in the chimney and mopped his sweating forehead. As always, he was grinning hugely.

Mallory looked at him, smiled back. Andrea, he reflected, had no right to be there. It was Stevens's place, but Stevens had still been suffering from shock, had lost much blood: besides, it required a first-class climber to bring up the rear, to coil up the ropes as he came and to remove the spikes – there must be no trace left of the ascent: or so Mallory had told him, and Stevens had reluctantly agreed, although the hurt in his face had been easy to see. More than ever now Mallory was glad he had resisted the quiet plea in Stevens's face: Stevens was undoubtedly a fine climber, but what Mallory had required that night was not another mountaineer but a human ladder. Time and time again during the ascent he had stood on Andrea's back, his shoulders, his upturned palm and once – for at least ten seconds and while he was still wearing his steel-shod boots – on his head. And not once had Andrea protested or stumbled or yielded an inch. The man was indestructible, as tough and enduring as the rock on which he stood. Since dusk had fallen that evening, Andrea had laboured unceasingly, done enough work to kill two ordinary men, and, looking at him then, Mallory realised, almost with despair, that even now he didn't look particularly tired.

Mallory gestured at the rock chimney, then upwards at its shadowy mouth limned in blurred rectangular outline against the pale glimmer of the sky. He leant forward, mouth close to Andrea's ear.

'Twenty feet, Andrea,' he said softly. His breath was still coming in painful gasps. 'It'll be no bother – it's fissured on my side and the chances are that it goes up to the top.'

Andrea looked up the chimney speculatively, nodded in silence.

'Better with your boots off,' Mallory went on. 'And any spikes we use we'll work in by hand.'

'Even on a night like this – high winds and rain, cold and black as a pig's inside – and on a cliff like this?' There was neither doubt nor question in Andrea's voice: rather it was acquiescence, unspoken confirmation of an unspoken thought. They had been so long together, had reached such a depth of understanding that words between them were largely superfluous.

Mallory nodded, waited while Andrea worked home a spike, looped his ropes over it and secured what was left of the long ball of twine that stretched four hundred feet below to the ledge where the others waited. Andrea then removed boots and spikes, fastening them to the ropes, eased the slender, double-edged throwing-knife in its leather shoulder scabbard, looked across at Mallory and nodded in turn.

The first ten feet were easy. Palms and back against one side of the chimney and stocking-soled feet against the other, Mallory jack-knifed his way upwards until the widening sheer of the walls defeated him. Legs braced against the far wall, he worked in a spike as far up as he could reach, grasped it with both hands, dropped his legs across and found a toe-hold in the crevice. Two minutes later his hands hooked over the crumbling edge of the precipice.

Noiselessly and with an infinite caution he fingered aside earth and grass and tiny pebbles until his hands were locked on the solid rock itself, bent his knee to seek lodgment for the final toehold, then eased a wary head above the cliff-top, a movement imperceptible in its slow-motion, millimetric stealth. He stopped moving altogether as soon as his eyes had cleared the level of the cliff, stared out into the unfamiliar darkness, his whole being, the entire field of consciousness, concentrated into his eyes and his ears. Illogically, and for the first time in all that terrifying ascent, he became acutely aware of his own danger and helplessness, and he cursed himself for his folly in not borrowing Miller's silenced automatic.

The darkness below the high horizon of the lifting hills beyond was just one degree less than absolute: shapes and angles, heights and depressions were resolving themselves in nebulous silhouette, contours and shadowy profiles emerging reluctantly from the darkness, a darkness suddenly no longer vague and unfamiliar but disturbingly reminiscent in what it revealed, clamouring for recognition. And then abruptly, almost with a sense of shock, Mallory had it. The cliff-top before his eyes was exactly as Monsieur Vlachos had drawn and described it – the narrow, bare strip of ground running parallel to the cliff, the jumble of huge boulders behind them and then, beyond these, the steep scree-strewn lower slopes of the mountains. The first break they'd had yet, Mallory thought exultantly – but what a break! The sketchiest navigation but the most incredible luck, right bang on the nose of the target – the highest point of the highest, most precipitous cliffs in Navarone: the one place where the Germans never mounted a guard, because the climb was impossible! Mallory felt the relief, the high elation wash through him in waves. Jubilantly he straightened his leg, hoisted himself half-way over the edge, arms straight, palms down on the top of the cliff. And then he froze into immobility, petrified as the solid rock beneath his hands, his heart thudding painfully in his throat.

One of the boulders had moved. Seven, maybe eight yards away, a shadow had gradually straightened, detached itself stealthily from the surrounding rock, was advancing slowly towards the edge of the cliff. And then the shadow was no longer 'it'. There could be no mistake now – the long jack-boots, the long greatcoat beneath the waterproof cape, the close-fitting helmet were all too familiar. Damn Vlachos! Damn Jensen! Damn all the know-alls who sat at home, the pundits of Intelligence who gave a man wrong information and sent him out to die. And in the same instant Mallory damned himself for his own carelessness, for he had been expecting this all along.

For the first two or three seconds Mallory had lain rigid and unmoving, temporarily paralysed in mind and body: already the guard had advanced four or five steps, carbine held in readiness before him, head turned sideways as he listened into the high, thin whine of the wind and the deep and distant booming of the surf below, trying to isolate the sound that had aroused his suspicions. But now the first shock was over and Mallory's mind was working again. To go up on to the top of the cliff would be suicidal: ten to one the guard would hear him scrambling over the edge and shoot him out of hand: and if he did get up he had neither the weapons nor, after the exhausting climb, the strength to tackle an armed, fresh man. He would have to go back down. But he would have to slide down slowly, an inch at a time. At night, Mallory knew, side vision is even more acute than direct, and the guard might catch a sudden movement out of the corner of his eye. And then he would only have to turn his head and that would be the end: even in that darkness, Mallory realised, there could be no mistaking the bulk of his silhouette against the sharp line of the edge of the cliff.

Gradually, every movement as smooth and controlled as possible, every soft and soundless breath a silent prayer, Mallory slipped gradually back over the edge of the cliff. Still the guard advanced, making for a point about five yards to Mallory's left, but still he looked away, his ear turned into the wind. And then Mallory was down, only his finger-tips over the top, and Andrea's great bulk was beside him, his mouth to his ear.

'What is it? Somebody there?'

'A sentry,' Mallory whispered back. His arms were beginning to ache from the strain. 'He's heard something and he's looking for us.'

Suddenly he shrank away from Andrea, pressed himself as closely as possible to the face of the cliff, was vaguely aware of Andrea doing the same thing. A beam of light, hurtful and dazzling to eyes so long accustomed to the dark, had suddenly stabbed out at an angle over the edge of the cliff, was moving slowly along towards them. The German had his torch out, was methodically examining the rim of the cliff. From the angle of the beam, Mallory judged that he was walking along about a couple of feet from the edge. On that wild and gusty night he was taking no chances on the crumbly, treacherous top-soil of the cliff: even more likely, he was taking no chances on a pair of sudden hands reaching out for his ankles and jerking him to a mangled death on the rocks and reefs four hundred feet below.

Slowly, inexorably, the beam approached. Even at that slant, it was bound to catch them. With a sudden sick certainty Mallory realised that the German wasn't just suspicious: he *knew* there was someone there, and he wouldn't stop looking until he found them. And there was nothing they could do, just nothing at all . . . Then Andrea's head was close to his again.

'A stone,' Andrea whispered. 'Over there, behind him.'

Cautiously at first, then frantically, Mallory pawed the cliff-top with his right hand. Earth, only earth, grass roots and tiny pebbles – there was nothing even half the size of a marble. And then Andrea was thrusting something against him and his hand closed over the metallic smoothness of a spike: even in that moment of desperate urgency, with the slender, searching beam only feet away, Mallory was conscious of a sudden brief anger with himself – he had still a couple of spikes stuck in his belt and had forgotten all about them.

His arm swung back, jerked convulsively forward, sent the spike spinning away into the darkness. One second passed, then another, he knew he had missed, the beam was only inches from Andrea's shoulders, and then the metallic clatter of the spike striking a boulder fell upon his ear like a benison. The beam wavered for a second, stabbed out aimlessly into the darkness and then whipped round, probing into the boulders to the left. And then the sentry was running towards them, slipping and stumbling in his haste, the barrel of the carbine gleaming in the light of the torch held clamped to it. He'd gone less than ten yards when Andrea was over the top of the cliff like a great, black cat, was padding noiselessly across the ground to the shelter of the nearest boulder. Wraith-like, he flitted in behind it and was gone, a shadow long among shadows.

The sentry was about twenty yards away now, the beam of his torch darting fearfully from boulder to boulder when Andrea struck the haft of his knife against a rock, twice. The sentry whirled round, torch shining along the line of the boulders, then started to run clumsily back again, the skirts of the greatcoat fluttering grotesquely in the wind. The torch was swinging wildly now, and Mallory caught a glimpse of a white, straining face, wide-eyed and fearful, incongruously at variance with the gladiatorial strength of the steel helmet above. God only knew, Mallory thought, what wild and panic-stricken thoughts were passing through his confused mind: noises from the cliff-top, metallic sound from either side among the boulders, the long, eerie vigil, afraid and companionless, on a deserted cliff edge on a dark and tempest-filled night in a hostile land – suddenly Mallory felt a deep stab of compassion for this man, a man like himself, someone's well-loved husband or brother or son who was only doing a dirty and dangerous job as best he could and because he was told to, compassion for his loneliness and his anxieties and his fears, for the sure knowledge that before he had drawn breath another three times he would be dead . . . Slowly, gauging his time and distance, Mallory raised his head.

'Help!' he shouted. 'Help me! I'm falling!'

The soldier checked in mid-stride and spun round, less than five feet from the rock that hid Andrea. For a second the beam of his torch waved wildly around, then settled on Mallory's head. For another moment he stood stock still then the carbine in his right hand swung up, the left hand reached down for the barrel. Then he grunted once, a violent and convulsive exhalation of breath, and the thud of the hilt of Andrea's knife striking home against the ribs carried clearly to Mallory's ears, even against the wind . . .

Mallory stared down at the dead man, at Andrea's impassive face as he wiped the blade of his knife on the greatcoat, rose slowly to his feet, sighed and slid the knife back in its scabbard.

'So, my Keith!' Andrea reserved the punctilious 'Captain' for company only. 'This is why our young lieutenant eats his heart out down below.'

'That is why,' Mallory acknowledged. 'I knew it – or I almost knew it. So did you. Too many coincidences – the German caique investigating, the trouble at the watchtower – and now this.' Mallory swore, softly and bitterly. 'This is the end for our friend Captain Briggs of Castelrosso. He'll be cashiered within the month. Jensen will make certain of that.'

Andrea nodded.

'He let Nicolai go?'

'Who else could have known that we were to have landed here, tipped off everyone along the line?' Mallory paused, dismissed the thought, caught Andrea by the arm. 'The Germans are thorough. Even although they must know it's almost an impossibility to land on a night like this, they'll have a dozen sentries scattered along the cliffs.' Unconsciously Mallory had lowered his voice. 'But they wouldn't depend on one man to cope with five. So –'

'Signals,' Andrea finished for him. 'They must have some way of letting the others know. Perhaps flares –'

'No, not that,' Mallory disagreed. 'Give their position away. Telephone. It has to be that. Remember how they were in Crete – miles of field telephone wire all over the shop?'

Andrea nodded, picked up the dead man's torch, hooded it in his huge hand and started searching. He returned in less than a minute.

'Telephone it is,' he announced softly. 'Over there, under the rocks.'

'Nothing we can do about it,' Mallory said. 'If it does ring, I'll have to answer or they'll come hot-footing along. I only hope to heaven they haven't got a bloody password. It would be just like them.'

He turned away, stopped suddenly.

'But someone's got to come sometime – a relief, sergeant of the guard, something like that. Probably he's supposed to make an hourly report. Someone's bound to come – and come soon. My God, Andrea, we'll have to make it fast!'

'And this poor devil?' Andrea gestured to the huddled shadow at his feet.

'Over the side with him.' Mallory grimaced in distaste. 'Won't make any difference to the poor bastard now, and we can't leave any traces. The odds are they'll think he's gone over the edge – this top soil's as crumbly and treacherous as hell . . . You might see if he's any papers on him – never know how useful they might be.'

'Not half as useful as these boots on his feet.' Andrea waved a large hand towards the scree-strewn slopes. 'You are not going to walk very far there in your stocking soles.'

Five minutes later Mallory tugged three times on the string that stretched down into the darkness below. Three answering tugs came from the ledge, and then the cord vanished rapidly down over the edge of the overhang, drawing with it the long, steel-cored rope that Mallory paid out from the coil on the top of the cliff.

The box of explosives was the first of the gear to come up. The weighted rope plummeted straight down from the point of the overhang, and padded though the box was on every side with lashed rucksacks and sleeping-bags it still crashed terrifyingly against the cliff on the inner arc of every wind-driven swing of the pendulum. But there was no time for finesse, to wait for the diminishing swing of the pendulum after each tug. Securely anchored to a rope that stretched around the base of a great boulder, Andrea leaned far out over the edge of the precipice and reeled in the seventy-pound deadweight as another man would a trout. In less than three minutes the ammunition box lay beside him on the cliff-top; five minutes later the firing generator, guns and pistols, wrapped in a couple of other sleeping-bags and their lightweight, reversible tent – white on one side, brown and green camouflage on the other – lay beside the explosives.

A third time the rope went down into the rain and the darkness, a third time the tireless Andrea hauled it in, hand over hand. Mallory was behind him, coiling in the slack of the rope, when he heard Andrea's sudden exclamation: two quick strides and he was at the edge of the cliff, his hand on the big Greek's arm.

'What's up, Andrea? Why have you stopped –?'

He broke off, peered through the gloom at the rope in Andrea's hand, saw that it was being held between only finger and thumb. Twice Andrea jerked the rope up a foot or two, let it fall again: the weightless rope swayed wildly in the wind.

'Gone?' Mallory asked quietly.

Andrea nodded without speaking.

'Broken?' Mallory was incredulous. 'A wire-cored rope?'

'I don't think so.' Quickly Andrea reeled in the remaining forty feet. The twine was still attached to the same place, about a fathom from the end. The rope was intact.

'Somebody tied a knot.' Just for a moment the giant's voice sounded tired. 'They didn't tie it too well.'

Mallory made to speak, then flung up an instinctive arm as a great, forked tongue of flame streaked between the cliff-top and unseen clouds above. Their cringing eyes were still screwed tight shut, their nostrils full of the acrid, sulphurous smell of burning, when the first volley of thunder crashed in Titan fury almost directly overhead, a deafening artillery to mock the pitiful efforts of embattled man, doubly terrifying in the total darkness that followed that searing flash. Gradually the echoes pealed and faded inland in diminishing reverberations, were lost among the valleys of the hills.

'My God!' Mallory murmured. 'That was close. We'd better make it fast, Andrea – this cliff is liable to be lit up like a fairground any minute . . . What was in that last load you were bringing up?' He didn't really have to ask – he himself had arranged for the breaking up of the equipment into three separate loads before he'd left the ledge. It wasn't even that he suspected his tired mind of playing tricks on him; but it was tired enough, too tired, to probe the hidden compulsion, the nameless hope that prompted him to grasp at nameless straws that didn't even exist.

'The food,' Andrea said gently. '*All* the food, the stove, the fuel – and the compasses.'

For five, perhaps ten seconds, Mallory stood motionless. One half of his mind, conscious of the urgency, the desperate need for haste, was jabbing him mercilessly: the other half held him momentarily in a vast irresolution, an irresolution of coldness and numbness that came not from the lashing wind and sleety rain but from his own mind, from the bleak and comfortless imaginings of lost wanderings on that harsh and hostile island, with neither food nor fire . . . And then Andrea's great hand was on his shoulder, and he was laughing softly.

'Just so much less to carry, my Keith. Think how grateful our tired friend Corporal Miller is going to be . . . This is only a little thing.'

'Yes,' Mallory said. 'Yes, of course. A little thing.' He turned abruptly, tugged the cord, watched the rope disappear over the edge.

Fifteen minutes later, in drenching, torrential rain, a great, sheeting downpour almost constantly illuminated by the jagged, branching stilettos of the forked lightning, Casey Brown's bedraggled head came into view over the edge of the cliff. The thunder, too, emptily cavernous in that flat and explosive intensity of sound that lies at the heart of a thunderstorm, was almost continuous: but in the brief intervals, Casey's voice, rich in his native Clydeside accent, carried clearly. He was expressing himself fluently in basic Anglo-Saxon, and with cause. He had had the assistance of two ropes on the way up – the one stretched from spike to spike and the one used for raising supplies, which Andrea had kept pulling in as he made the ascent. Casey Brown had secured the end of this round his waist with a bowline, but the bowline had proved to be nothing of the sort but a slip-knot, and Andrea's enthusiastic help had almost cut him in half. He was still sitting on the cliff-top, exhausted head between his knees, the radio still strapped to his back, when two tugs on Andrea's rope announced that Dusty Miller was on his way up.

Another quarter of an hour elapsed, an interminable fifteen minutes when, in the lulls between the thunder-claps, every slightest sound was an approaching enemy patrol, before Miller materialised slowly out of the darkness, halfway down the rock chimney. He was climbing steadily and methodically, then checked abruptly at the cliff-top, groping hands pawing uncertainly on the top-soil of the cliff. Puzzled, Mallory bent down, peered into the lean face: both the eyes were clamped tightly shut.

'Relax, Corporal,' Mallory advised kindly. 'You have arrived.'

Dusty Miller slowly opened his eyes, peered round at the edge of the cliff, shuddered and crawled quickly on hands and knees to the shelter of the nearest boulders. Mallory followed and looked down at him curiously.

'What was the idea of closing your eyes coming over the top?'

'I did not,' Miller protested.

Mallory said nothing.

'I closed them at the bottom,' Miller explained wearily. 'I opened them at the top.'

Mallory looked at him incredulously.

'What! All the way?'

'It's like I told you, boss,' Miller complained. 'Back in Castelrosso. When I cross a street and step up on to the sidewalk I gotta hang on to the nearest lamp-post. More or less.' He broke off, looked at Andrea leaning far out over the side of the cliff, and shivered again. 'Brother! Oh, brother! Was I scared!'

Fear. Terror. Panic. Do the thing you fear and the death of fear is certain. Do the thing you fear and the death of fear is certain. Once, twice, a hundred times, Andy Stevens repeated the words to himself, over and over again, like a litany. A psychiatrist had told him that once and he'd read it a dozen times since. Do the thing you fear and the death of fear is certain. The mind is a limited thing, they had said. It can only hold one thought at a time, one impulse to action. Say to yourself, I am brave, I am overcoming this fear, this stupid, unreasoning panic which has no origin except in my own mind, and because the mind *can* only hold one thought at a time, and because thinking and feeling are one, then you *will* be brave, you *will* overcome and the fear will vanish like a shadow in the night. And so Andy Stevens said these things to himself, and the shadows only lengthened and deepened, lengthened and deepened, and the icy claws of fear dug ever more savagely into his dull exhausted mind, into his twisted, knotted stomach.

His stomach. That knotted ball of jangled, writhing nerve-ends beneath the solar plexus. No one could ever know how it was, how it felt, except those whose shredded minds were going, collapsing into complete and final breakdown. The waves of panic and nausea and faintness that flooded up through a suffocating throat to a mind dark and spent and sinewless, a mind fighting with woollen fingers to cling on to the edge of the abyss, a tired and lacerated mind, only momentarily in control, wildly rejecting the clamorous demands of a nervous system, which had already taken far too much, that he should let go, open the torn fingers that were clenched so tightly round the rope. It was just that easy. 'Rest after toil, port after stormy seas.' What was that famous stanza of Spenser's? Sobbing aloud, Stevens wrenched out another spike, sent it spinning into the waiting sea three hundred long feet below, pressed himself closely into the face and inched his way despairingly upwards.

Fear. Fear had been at his elbow all his life, his constant companion, his *alter ego*, at his elbow, or in close prospect or immediate recall. He had become accustomed to that fear, at times almost reconciled, but the sick agony of this night lay far beyond either tolerance or familiarity. He had never known anything like this before, and even in his terror and confusion he was dimly aware that the fear did not spring from the climb itself. True, the cliff was sheer and almost vertical, and the lightning, the ice-cold rain, the darkness and the bellowing thunder were a waking nightmare. But the climb, technically, was simple: the rope stretched all the way to the top and all he had to do was to follow it and dispose of the spikes as he went. He was sick and bruised and terribly tired, his head ached abominably and he had lost a great deal of blood: but then, more often than not, it is in the darkness of agony and exhaustion that the spirit of man burns most brightly.

Andy Stevens was afraid because his self-respect was gone. Always before, that had been his sheet anchor, had tipped the balance against his ancient enemy – the respect in which other men had held him, the respect he had had for himself. But now these were gone, for his two greatest fears had been realised – he was known to be afraid, he had failed his fellow-man. Both in the fight with the German caique and when anchored above the watch-tower in the creek, he had known that Mallory and Andrea knew. He had never met such men before, and he had known all along that he could never hide his secrets from such men. He should have gone up that cliff with Mallory, but Mallory had made excuses and taken Andrea instead – Mallory *knew* he was afraid. And twice before, in Castelrosso and when the German boat had closed in on them, he had almost failed his friends – and tonight he had failed them terribly. He had not been thought fit to lead the way with Mallory – and it was he, the sailor of the party, who had made such a botch of tying that last knot, had lost all the food and the fuel that had plummeted into the sea a bare ten feet from where he had stood on the ledge . . . and a thousand men on Kheros were depending on a failure so abject as himself. Sick and spent, spent in mind and body and spirit, moaning aloud in his anguish of fear and self-loathing, and not knowing where one finished and the other began, Andy Stevens climbed blindly on.

The sharp, high-pitched call-up buzz of the telephone cut abruptly through the darkness on the cliff-top. Mallory stiffened and half-turned, hands clenching involuntarily. Again it buzzed, the jarring stridency carrying clearly above the bass rumble of the thunder, fell silent again. And then it buzzed again and kept on buzzing, peremptory in its harsh insistence.

Mallory was half-way towards it when he checked in mid-step, turned slowly round and walked back towards Andrea. The big Greek looked at him curiously.

'You have changed your mind?'

Mallory nodded but said nothing.

'They will keep on ringing until they get an answer,' Andrea murmured. 'And when they get no answer, they will come. They will come quickly and soon.'

'I know, I know.' Mallory shrugged. 'We have to take that chance – certainty rather. The question is – how long will it be before anyone turns up.' Instinctively he looked both ways along the windswept cliff-top: Miller and Brown were posted one on either side about fifty yards away, lost in the darkness. 'It's not worth the risk. The more I think of it, the poorer I think my chances would be of getting away with it. In matters of routine the old Hun tends to be an inflexible sort of character. There's probably a set way of answering the phone, or the sentry has to identify himself by name, or there's a password – or maybe my voice would give me away. On the other hand the sentry's gone without trace, all our gear is up and so's everyone except Stevens. In other words, we've practically made it. We've landed – and nobody knows we're here.'

'Yes.' Andrea nodded slowly. 'Yes, you are right – and Stevens should be up in two or three minutes. It would be foolish to throw away everything we've gained.' He paused, then went on quietly: 'But they are going to come running.' The phone stopped ringing as suddenly as it had started. 'They are going to come now.'

'I know. I hope to hell Stevens . . .' Mallory broke off, spun on his heel, said over his shoulder, 'Keep your eye open for him, will you? I'll warn the others we're expecting company.'

Mallory moved quickly along the cliff-top, keeping well away from the edge. He hobbled rather than walked – the sentry's boots were too small for him and chafed his toes cruelly. Deliberately he closed his mind to the thought of how his feet would be after a few hours' walking over rough territory in these boots: time enough for the reality, he thought grimly, without the added burden of anticipation . . . He stopped abruptly as something hard and metallic pushed into the small of his back.

'Surrender or die!' The drawling, nasal voice was positively cheerful: after what he had been through on the caique and the cliff face, just to set feet on solid ground again was heaven enough for Dusty Miller.

'Very funny,' Mallory growled. 'Very funny indeed.' He looked curiously at Miller. The American had removed his oilskin cape – the rain had ceased as abruptly as it had come – to reveal a jacket and braided waistcoat even more sodden and saturated than his trousers. It didn't make sense. But there was no time for questions.

'Did you hear the phone ringing just now?' he asked.

'Was that what it was? Yeah, I heard it.'

'The sentry's phone. His hourly report, or whatever it was, must have been overdue. We didn't answer it. They'll be hot-footing along any minute now, suspicious as hell and looking for trouble. Maybe your side, maybe Brown's. Can't approach any other way unless they break their necks climbing over these boulders.' Mallory gestured at the shapeless jumble of rocks behind them. 'So keep your eyes skinned.'

'I'll do that, boss. No shootin', huh?'

'No shooting. Just get back as quickly and quietly as you can and let us know. Come back in five minutes anyway.'

Mallory hurried away, retracing his steps. Andrea was stretched full length on the cliff-top, peering over the edge. He twisted his head round as Mallory approached.

'I can hear him. He's just at the overhang.'

'Good.' Mallory moved on without breaking step. 'Tell him to hurry, please.'

Ten yards farther on Mallory checked, peered into the gloom ahead. Somebody was coming along the cliff-top at a dead run, stumbling and slipping on the loose gravelly soil.

'Brown?' Mallory called softly.

'Yes, sir. It's me.' Brown was up to him now, breathing heavily, pointing back in the direction he had just come. 'Somebody's coming, and coming fast! Torches waving and jumping all over the place – must be running.'

'How many?' Mallory asked quickly.

'Four or five at least.' Brown was still gasping for breath. 'Maybe more – four or five torches, anyway. You can see them for yourself.' Again he pointed backwards, then blinked in puzzlement. 'That's bloody funny! They're all gone.' He turned back swiftly to Mallory. 'But I can swear –'

'Don't worry,' Mallory said grimly. 'You saw them all right. I've been expecting visitors. They're getting close now and taking no chances . . . How far away?'

'Hundred yards – not more than a hundred and fifty.'

'Go and get Miller. Tell him to get back here fast.'

Mallory ran back along the cliff edge and knelt beside the huge length of Andrea.

'They're coming, Andrea,' he said quickly. 'From the left. At least five, probably more. Two minutes at the most. Where's Stevens? Can you see him?'

'I can see him.' Andrea was magnificently unperturbed. 'He is just past the overhang . . .' The rest of his words were lost, drowned in a sudden, violent thunderclap, but there was no need for more. Mallory could see Stevens now, climbing up the rope, strangely old and enfeebled in action, hand over hand in paralysing slowness, half-way now between the overhang and the foot of the chimney.

'Good God!' Mallory swore. 'What's the matter with him? He's going to take all day . . .' He checked himself, cupped his hands to his mouth. 'Stevens! Stevens!' But there was no sign that Stevens had heard. He still kept climbing with the same unnatural over-deliberation, a robot in slow motion.

'He is very near the end,' Andrea said quietly. 'You see he does not even lift his head. When a climber does not lift his head, he is finished.' He stirred. 'I will go down for him.'

'No.' Mallory's hand was on his shoulder. 'Stay here. I can't risk you both . . . Yes, what is it?' He was aware that Brown was back, bending over him, his breath coming in great heaving gasps.

'Hurry, sir; hurry, for God's sake!' A few brief words but he had to suck in two huge gulps of air to get them out. 'They're on top of us!'

'Get back to the rocks with Miller,' Mallory said urgently. 'Cover us . . . Stevens! Stevens!' But again the wind swept up the face of the cliff, carried his words away.

'Stevens! For God's sake, man! Stevens!' His voice was low-pitched, desperate, but this time some quality in it must have reached through Stevens's fog of exhaustion and touched his consciousness, for he stopped climbing and lifted his head, hand cupped to his ear.

'Some Germans coming!' Mallory called through funnelled hands, as loudly as he dared. 'Get to the foot of the chimney and stay there. Don't make a sound. Understand?'

Stevens lifted his hand, gestured in tired acknowledgment, lowered his head, started to climb up again. He was going even more slowly now, his movements fumbling and clumsy.

'Do you think he understands?' Andrea was troubled.

'I think so. I don't know.' Mallory stiffened and caught Andrea's arm. It was beginning to rain again, not heavily yet, and through the drizzle he'd caught sight of a hooded torch beam probing among the rocks thirty yards away to his left. 'Over the edge with the rope,' he whispered. 'The spike at the bottom of the chimney will hold it. Come on – let's get out of here!'

Gradually, meticulous in their care not to dislodge the smallest pebble, Mallory and Andrea inched back from the edge, squirmed round and headed back for the rocks, pulling themselves along on their elbows and knees. The few yards were interminable and without even a gun in his hand Mallory felt defenceless, completely exposed. An illogical feeling, he knew, for the first beam of light to fall on them meant the end not for them but for the man who held the torch. Mallory had complete faith in Brown and Miller . . . That wasn't important. What mattered was the complete escape from detection. Twice during the last endless few feet a wandering beam reached out towards them, the second a bare arm's length away: both times they pressed their faces into the sodden earth, lest the pale blur of their faces betray them, and lay very still. And then, all at once it seemed, they were among the rocks and safe.

In a moment Miller was beside them, a half-seen shadow against the darker dusk of the rocks around them.

'Plenty of time, plenty of time,' he whispered sarcastically. 'Why didn't you wait another half-hour?' He gestured to the left, where the flickering of torches, the now clearly audible murmur of guttural voices, were scarcely twenty yards away. 'We'd better move farther back. They're looking for him among the rocks.'

'For him or for his telephone,' Mallory murmured in agreement. 'You're right anyway. Watch your guns on these rocks. Take the gear with you . . . And if they look over and find Stevens we'll have to take the lot. No time for fancy work and to hell with the noise. Use the automatic carbines.'

Andy Stevens had heard, but he had not understood. It was not that he panicked, was too terrified to understand, for he was no longer afraid. Fear is of the mind, but his mind had ceased to function, drugged by the last stages of exhaustion, crushed by the utter, damnable tiredness that held his limbs, his whole body, in leaden thrall. He did not know it, but fifty feet below he had struck his head against a spur of rock, a sharp, wicked projection that had torn his gaping temple wound open to the bone. His strength drained out with the pulsing blood.

He had heard Mallory, had heard something about the chimney he had now reached, but his mind had failed to register the meaning of the words. All that Stevens knew was that he was climbing, and that one always kept on climbing until one reached the top. That was what his father had always impressed upon him, his brothers too. You must reach the top.

He was half-way up the chimney now, resting on the spike that Mallory had driven into the fissure. He hooked his fingers in the crack, bent back his head and stared up towards the mouth of the chimney. Ten feet away, no more. He was conscious of neither surprise nor elation. It was just there: he had to reach it. He could hear voices, carrying clearly from the top. He was vaguely surprised that his friends were making no attempt to help him, that they had thrown away the rope that would have made those last few feet so easy, but he felt no bitterness, no emotion at all: perhaps they were trying to test him. What did it matter anyway – he had to reach the top.

He reached the top. Carefully, as Mallory had done before him, he pushed aside the earth and tiny pebbles, hooked his fingers over the edge, found the same toe-hold as Mallory had and levered himself upwards. He saw the flickering torches, heard the excited voices, and then for an instant the curtain of fog in his mind lifted and a last tidal wave of fear washed over him and he knew that the voices were the voices of the enemy and that they had destroyed his friends. He knew now that he was alone, that he had failed, that this was the end, one way or another, and that it had all been for nothing. And then the fog closed over him again, and there was nothing but the emptiness of it all, the emptiness and the futility, the overwhelming lassitude and despair and his body slowly sinking down the face of the cliff. And then the hooked fingers – they, too, were slipping away, opening gradually, reluctantly as the fingers of a drowning man releasing their final hold on a spar of wood. There was no fear now, only a vast and heedless indifference as his hands slipped away and he fell like a stone, twenty vertical feet into the cradling bottle-neck at the foot of the chimney.

He himself made no sound, none at all: the soundless scream of agony never passed his lips, for the blackness came with the pain: but the straining ears of the men crouching in the rocks above caught clearly the dull, sickening crack as his right leg fractured cleanly in two, snapping like a rotten bough.

SIX

Monday Night
0200–0600

The German patrol was everything that Mallory had feared – efficient, thorough and very, very painstaking. It even had imagination, in the person of its young and competent sergeant, and that was more dangerous still.

There were only four of them, in high boots, helmets and green, grey and brown mottled capes. First of all they located the telephone and reported to base. Then the young sergeant sent two men to search another hundred yards or so along the cliff, while he and the fourth soldier probed among the rocks that paralleled the cliff. The search was slow and careful, but the two men did not penetrate very far into the rocks. To Mallory, the sergeant's reasoning was obvious and logical. If the sentry had gone to sleep or taken ill, it was unlikely that he would have gone far in among that confused jumble of boulders. Mallory and the others were safely back beyond their reach.

And then came what Mallory had feared – an organised, methodical inspection of the cliff-top itself: worse still, it began with a search along the very edge. Securely held by his three men with interlinked arms – the last with a hand hooked round his belt – the sergeant walked slowly along the rim, probing every inch with the spot-lit beam of a powerful torch. Suddenly he stopped short, exclaimed suddenly and stooped, torch and face only inches from the ground. There was no question as to what he had found – the deep gouge made in the soft, crumbling soil by the climbing rope that had been belayed round the boulder and gone over the edge of the cliff . . . Softly, silently, Mallory and his three companions straightened to their knees or to their feet, gun barrels lining along the tops of boulders or peering out between cracks in the rocks. There was no doubt in any of their minds that Stevens was lying there helplessly in the crutch of the chimney, seriously injured or dead. It needed only one German carbine to point down that cliff face, however carelessly, and these four men would die. They would have to die.

The sergeant was stretched out his length now, two men holding his legs. His head and shoulders were over the edge of the cliff, the beam from his torch stabbing down the chimney. For ten, perhaps fifteen seconds, there was no sound on the cliff-top, no sound at all, only the high, keening moan of the wind and the swish of the rain in the stunted grass. And then the sergeant had wriggled back and risen to his feet, slowly shaking his head. Mallory gestured to the others to sink down behind the boulders again, but even so the sergeant's soft Bavarian voice carried clearly in the wind.

'It's Ehrich all right, poor fellow.' Compassion and anger blended curiously in the voice. 'I warned him often enough about his carelessness, about going too near the edge of that cliff. It is very treacherous.' Instinctively the sergeant stepped back a couple of feet and looked again at the gouge in the soft earth. 'That's where his heel slipped – or maybe the butt of his carbine. Not that it matters now.'

'Is he dead, do you think, Sergeant?' The speaker was only a boy, nervous and unhappy.

'It's hard to say . . . Look for yourself.'

Gingerly the youth lay down on the cliff-top, peering cautiously over the lip of the rock. The other soldiers were talking among themselves, in short staccato sentences when Mallory turned to Miller, cupped his hands to his mouth and the American's ear. He could contain his puzzlement no longer.

'Was Stevens wearing his dark suit when you left him?' he whispered.

'Yeah,' Miller whispered back. 'Yeah, I think he was.' A pause. 'No dammit, I'm wrong. We both put on our rubber camouflage capes about the same time.'

Mallory nodded. The waterproofs of the Germans were almost identical with their own: and the sentry's hair, Mallory remembered had been jet black – the same colour as Stevens's dyed hair. Probably all that was visible from above was a crumpled, cape-shrouded figure and a dark head. The sergeant's mistake in identity was more than understandable: it was inevitable.

The young soldier eased himself back from the edge of the cliff and hoisted himself carefully to his feet.

'You're right, Sergeant. It *is* Ehrich.' The boy's voice was unsteady. 'He's alive, I think. I saw his cape move, just a little. It wasn't the wind, I'm sure of that.'

Mallory felt Andrea's massive hand squeezing his arm, felt the quick surge of relief, then elation, wash through him. So Stevens *was* alive! Thank God for that! They'd save the boy yet. He heard Andrea whispering the news to the others, then grinned wryly to himself, ironic at his own gladness. Jensen definitely would not have approved of this jubilation. Stevens had already done his part, navigated the boat to Navarone, and climbed the cliff: and now he was only a crippled liability, would be a drag on the whole party, reduce what pitiful chances of success remained to them. For a High Command who pushed the counters around crippled pawns slowed up the whole game, made the board so damnably untidy. It was most inconsiderate of Stevens not to have killed himself so that they could have disposed of him neatly and without trace in the deep and hungry waters that boomed around the foot of the cliff . . . Mallory clenched his hands in the darkness and swore to himself that the boy would live, come home again, and to hell with total war and all its inhuman demands . . . Just a kid, that was all, a scared and broken kid and the bravest of them all.

The young sergeant was issuing a string of orders to his men, his voice quick, crisp and confident. A doctor, splints, rescue stretcher, anchored sheer-legs, ropes, spikes – the trained, well-ordered mind missed nothing. Mallory waited tensely, wondering how many men, if any, would be left on guard, for the guards would have to go and that would inevitably betray them. The question of their quick and silent disposal never entered his mind – a whisper in Andrea's ear and the guards would have no more chance than penned lambs against a marauding wolf. Less chance even than that – the lambs could always run and cry out before the darkness closed over them.

The sergeant solved the problem for them. The assured competence, the tough unsentimental ruthlessness that made the German NCO the best in the world gave Mallory the chance he never expected to have. He had just finished giving his orders when the young soldier touched him on the arm, then pointed over the edge.

'How about poor Ehrich, Sergeant?' he asked uncertainly. 'Shouldn't – don't you think one of us ought to stay with him?'

'And what could you do if you did stay – hold his hand?' the sergeant asked acidly. 'If he stirs and falls, then he falls, that's all, and it doesn't matter then if a hundred of us are standing up here watching him. Off you go, and don't forget the mallets and pegs to stay the sheer-legs.'

The three men turned and went off quickly to the east without another word. The sergeant walked over to the phone, reported briefly to someone, then set off in the opposite direction – to check the next guard post, Mallory guessed. He was still in sight, a dwindling blur in the darkness, when Mallory whispered to Brown and Miller to post themselves on guard again: and they could still hear the measured crunch of his firm footfalls on a patch of distant gravel as their belayed rope went snaking over the edge of the cliff, Andrea and Mallory sliding swiftly down even before it had stopped quivering.

Stevens, a huddled, twisted heap with a gashed and bleeding cheek lying cruelly along a razor-sharp spur of rock, was still unconscious, breathing stertorously through his open mouth. Below the knee his right leg twisted upwards and outwards against the rock at an impossible angle. As gently as he could, braced against either side of the chimney and supported by Andrea, Mallory lifted and straightened the twisted limb. Twice, from the depths of the dark stupor of his unconsciousness, Stevens moaned in agony, but Mallory had no option but to carry on, his teeth clenched tight until his jaws ached. Then slowly, with infinite care, he rolled up the trouser leg, winced and screwed his eyes shut in momentary horror and nausea as he saw the dim whiteness of the shattered tibia sticking out through the torn and purply swollen flesh.

'Compound fracture, Andrea.' Gently his exploring fingers slid down the mangled leg, beneath the lip of the jackboot, stopped suddenly as something gave way beneath his feather touch. 'Oh, my God!' he murmured. 'Another break, just above the ankle. This boy is in a bad way. Andrea.'

'He is indeed,' Andrea said gravely. 'We can do nothing for him here?'

'Nothing. Just nothing. We'll have to get him up first.' Mallory straightened, gazed up bleakly at the perpendicular face of the chimney. 'Although how in the name of heaven –'

'I will take him up.' There was no suggestion in Andrea's voice either of desperate resolve or consciousness of the almost incredible effort involved. It was simply a statement of intention, the voice of a man who never questioned his ability to do what he said he would. 'If you will help me to raise him, to tie him to my back . . .'

'With his broken leg loose, dangling from a piece of skin and torn muscle?' Mallory protested. 'Stevens can't take much more. He'll die if we do this.'

'He'll die if we don't,' Andrea murmured.

Mallory stared down at Stevens for a long moment, then nodded heavily in the darkness.

'He'll die if we don't,' he echoed tiredly. 'Yes, we have to do this.' He pushed outwards from the rock, slid half a dozen feet down the rope and jammed a foot in the crutch of the chimney just below Stevens's body. He took a couple of turns of rope round his waist and looked up.

'Ready, Andrea?' he called softly.

'Ready.' Andrea stooped, hooked his great hands under Stevens's armpits and lifted slowly, powerfully, as Mallory pushed from below. Twice, three times before they had him up, the boy moaned deep down in his tortured throat, the long, quivering 'Aahs' of agony setting Mallory's teeth on edge: and then his dangling, twisted leg had passed from Mallory's reach and he was held close and cradled in Andrea's encircling arm, the rain-lashed, bleeding mask of a face lolling grotesquely backwards, forlorn and lifeless with the dead pathos of a broken doll. Seconds later Mallory was up beside them, expertly lashing Stevens's wrists together. He was swearing softly, as his numbed hands looped and tightened the rope, softly, bitterly, continuously, but he was quite unaware of this: he was aware only of the broken head that lolled stupidly against his shoulder, of the welling, rain-thinned blood that filmed the upturned face, of the hair above the gashed temple emerging darkly fair as the dye washed slowly out. Inferior bloody boot-blacking. Mallory thought savagely: Jensen shall know of this – it could cost a man's life. And then he became aware of his own thoughts and swore again, still more savagely and at himself this time, for the utter triviality of what he was thinking.

With both hands free – Stevens's bound arms were looped round his neck, his body lashed to his own – Andrea took less than thirty seconds to reach the top; if the dragging, one hundred and sixty pounds deadweight on his back made any difference to Andrea's climbing speed and power, Mallory couldn't detect it. The man's endurance was fantastic. Once, just once, as Andrea scrambled over the edge of the cliff, the broken leg caught on the rock, and the crucifying torture of it seared through the merciful shell of insensibility, forced a brief shriek of pain from his lips, a hoarse, bubbling whisper of sound all the more horrible for its muted agony. And then Andrea was standing upright and Mallory was behind him, cutting swiftly at the ropes that bound the two together.

'Straight into the rocks with him, Andrea, will you?' Mallory whispered. 'Wait for us at the first open space you come to.' Andrea nodded slowly and without raising his head, his hooded eyes bent over the boy in his arms, like a man sunk in thought. Sunk in thought or listening, and all unawares Mallory, too, found himself looking and listening into the thin, lost moaning of the wind, and there was nothing there, only the lifting, dying threnody and the chill of the rain hardening to an ice-cold sleet. He shivered, without knowing why, and listened again; then he shook himself angrily, turned abruptly towards the cliff face and started reeling in the rope. He had it all up, lying round his feet in a limp and rain-sodden tangle when he remembered about the spike still secured to the foot of the chimney, the hundreds of feet of rope suspended from it.

He was too tired and cold and depressed even to feel exasperated with himself. The sight of Stevens and the knowledge of how it was with the boy had affected him more than he knew. Moodily, almost, he kicked the rope over the side again, slid down the chimney, untied the second rope and sent the spike spinning out into the darkness. Less than ten minutes later, the wetly-coiled ropes over his shoulder, he led Miller and Brown into the dark confusion of the rocks.

They found Stevens lying under the lee of a huge boulder, less than a hundred yards inland, in a tiny, cleared space barely the size of a billiard table. An oilskin was spread beneath him on the sodden, gravelly earth, a camouflage cape covered most of his body: it was bitterly cold now, but the rock broke the force of the wind, sheltered the boy from the driving sleet. Andrea looked up as the three men dropped into the hollow and lowered their gear to the ground; already, Mallory could see, Andrea had rolled the trouser up beyond the knee and cut the heavy jackboot away from the mangled leg.

'Sufferin' Christ!' The words, half-oath, half-prayer, were torn involuntarily from Miller: even in the deep gloom the shattered leg looked ghastly. Now he dropped on one knee and stooped low over it. 'What a mess!' he murmured slowly. He looked up over his shoulder. 'We've gotta do something about that leg, boss, and we've no damned time to lose. This kid's a good candidate for the mortuary.'

'I know. We've got to save him, Dusty, we've just *got* to.' All at once this had become terribly important to Mallory. He dropped down on his knees. 'Let's have a look at him.'

Impatiently Miller waved him away.

'Leave this to me, boss.' There was a sureness, a sudden authority in his voice that held Mallory silent. 'The medicine pack, quick – and undo that tent.'

'You sure you can handle this?' God knew, Mallory thought, he didn't really doubt him – he was conscious only of gratitude, of a profound relief, but he felt he had to say something. 'How are you going –'

'Look, boss,' Miller said quietly. 'All my life I've worked with just three things – mines, tunnels and explosives. They're kinda tricky things, boss. I've seen hundreds of busted arms and legs – and fixed most of them myself.' He grinned wryly in the darkness. 'I was boss myself, then – just one of my privileges, I reckon.'

'Good enough!' Mallory clapped him on the shoulder. 'He's all yours, Dusty. But the tent!' Involuntarily he looked over his shoulder in the direction of the cliff. 'I mean –'

'You got me wrong, boss.' Miller's hands, steady and precise with the delicate certainty of a man who has spent a lifetime with high explosive, were busy with a swab and disinfectant. 'I wasn't fixin' on settin' up a base hospital. But we need tent-poles – splints for his legs.'

'Of course, of course. The poles. Never occurred to me for splints – and I've been thinking of nothing else for –'

'They're not too important, boss.' Miller had the medicine pack open now, rapidly selecting the items he wanted with the aid of a hooded torch. 'Morphine – that's the first thing, or this kid's goin' to die of shock. And then shelter, warmth, dry clothin' –'

'Warmth! Dry clothing!' Mallory interrupted incredulously. He looked down at the unconscious boy, remembering how Stevens had lost them the stove and all the fuel, and his mouth twisted in bitterness. His own executioner . . . 'Where in God's name are we going to find them?'

'I don't know, boss,' Miller said simply. 'But we gotta find them. And not just to lessen shock. With a leg like this and soaked to the skin, he's bound to get pneumonia. And then as much sulfa as that bloody great hole in his leg will take – one touch of sepsis in the state this kid's in . . .' His voice trailed away into silence.

Mallory rose to his feet.

'I reckon you're the boss.' It was a very creditable imitation of the American's drawl, and Miller looked up quickly, surprise melting into a tired smile, then looked away again. Mallory could hear the chatter of his teeth as he bent over Stevens, and sensed rather than saw that he was shivering violently, continuously, but oblivious to it all in his complete concentration on the job in hand. Miller's clothes, Mallory remembered again, were completely saturated: not for the first time, Mallory wondered how he had managed to get himself into such a state with a waterproof covering him.

'You fix him up. I'll find a place.' Mallory wasn't as confident as he felt: still, on the scree-strewn, volcanic slopes of these hills behind, there ought to be a fair chance of finding a rock shelter, if not a cave. Or there would have been in day-light: as it was they would just have to trust to luck to stumble on one . . . He saw that Casey Brown, grey-faced with exhaustion and illness – the after-effects of carbon monoxide poisoning are slow to disappear – had risen unsteadily to his feet and was making for a gap between the rocks.

'Where are you going, Chief?'

'Back for the rest of the stuff, sir.'

'Are you sure you can manage?' Mallory peered at him closely. 'You don't look any too fit to me.'

'I don't feel it either,' Brown said frankly. He looked at Mallory. 'But with all respects, sir, I don't think you've seen yourself recently.'

'You have a point,' Mallory acknowledged. 'All right then, come on. I'll go with you.'

For the next ten minutes there was silence in the tiny clearing, a silence broken only by the murmurs of Miller and Andrea working over the shattered leg, and the moans of the injured man as he twisted and struggled feebly in his dark abyss of pain: then gradually the morphine took effect and the struggling lessened and died away altogether, and Miller was able to work rapidly, without fear of interruption. Andrea had an oilskin outstretched above them. It served a double purpose – it curtained off the sleet that swept round them from time to time and blanketed the pinpoint light of the rubber torch he held in his free hand. And then the leg was set and bandaged and as heavily splinted as possible and Miller was on his feet, straightening his aching back.

'Thank Gawd that's done,' he said wearily. He gestured at Stevens. 'I feel just the way that kid looks.' Suddenly he stiffened, stretched out a warning arm. 'I can hear something, Andrea,' he whispered.

Andrea laughed. 'It's only Brown coming back, my friend. He's been coming this way for over a minute now.'

'How do you know it's Brown?' Miller challenged. He felt vaguely annoyed with himself and unobtrusively shoved his ready automatic back into his pocket.

'Brown is a good man among rocks,' Andrea said gently; 'but he is tired. But Captain Mallory . . .' He shrugged. 'People call me "the big cat" I know, but among the mountains and rocks the captain is more than a cat. He is a ghost, and that was how men called him in Crete. You will know he is here when he touches you on the shoulder.'

Miller shivered in a sudden icy gust of sleet.

'I wish you people wouldn't creep around so much,' he complained. He looked up as Brown came round the corner of a boulder, slow with the shambling, stumbling gait of an exhausted man. 'Hi, there, Casey. How are things goin'?'

'Not too bad.' Brown murmured his thanks as Andrea took the box of explosives off his shoulder and lowered it easily to the ground. 'This is the last of the gear. Captain sent me back with it. We heard voices some way along the cliff. He's staying behind to see what they say when they find Stevens gone.' Wearily he sat down on top of the box. 'Maybe he'll get some idea of what they're going to do next, if anything.'

'Seems to me he could have left you there and carried that damned box back himself,' Miller growled. Disappointment in Mallory made him more outspoken than he'd meant to be. 'He's much better off than you are right now, and I think it's a bit bloody much . . .' He broke off and gasped in pain as Andrea's fingers caught his arm like giant steel pincers.

'It is not fair to talk like that, my friend,' Andrea said reproachfully. 'You forget, perhaps, that Brown here cannot talk or understand a word of German?'

Miller rubbed his bruised arm tenderly, shaking his head in slow self-anger and condemnation.

'Me and my big mouth,' he said ruefully. 'Always talkin' outa turn Miller, they call me. Your pardon, one and all . . . And what is next on the agenda, gentlemen?'

'Captain says we're to go straight on into the rocks and up the right shoulder of this hill here.' Brown jerked a thumb in the direction of the vague mass, dark and strangely foreboding, that towered above and beyond them. 'He'll catch us up within fifteen minutes or so.' He grinned tiredly at Miller. 'And we're to leave this box and a rucksack for him to carry.'

'Spare me,' Miller pleaded. 'I feel only six inches tall as it is.' He looked down at Stevens, lying quietly under the darkly gleaming wetness of the oilskins, then up at Andrea. 'I'm afraid, Andrea –'

'Of course, of course!' Andrea stooped quickly, wrapped the oil-skins round the unconscious boy and rose to his feet, as effortlessly as if the oilskins had been empty.

'I'll lead the way,' Miller volunteered. 'Mebbe I can pick an easy path for you and young Stevens.' He swung generator and ruck-sacks on to his shoulder, staggering under the sudden weight; he hadn't realised he was so weak. 'At first, that is,' he amended. 'Later on, you'll have to carry us both.'

Mallory had badly miscalculated the time it would require to over-take the others; over an hour had elapsed since Brown had left him, and still there were no signs of the others. And with seventy pounds on his back, he wasn't making such good time himself.

It wasn't all his fault. The returning German patrol, after the first shock of discovery, had searched the cliff-top again, methodically and with exasperating slowness. Mallory had waited tensely for someone to suggest descending and examining the chimney – the gouge-marks of the spikes on the rock would have been a dead giveaway – but nobody even mentioned it. With the guard obvi-ously fallen to his death, it would have been a pointless thing to do anyway. After an unrewarding search, they had debated for an unconscionable time as to what they should do next. Finally they had done nothing. A replacement guard was left, and the rest made off along the cliff, carrying their rescue equipment with them.

The three men ahead had made surprisingly good time, although the conditions, admittedly, were now much easier. The heavy fall of boulders at the foot of the slope had petered out after another fifty yards, giving way to broken scree and rain-washed rubble. Possibly he had passed them, but it seemed unlikely: in the intervals between these driving sleet showers – it was more like hail now – he was able to scan the bare shoulder of the hill, and nothing moved. Besides, he knew that Andrea wouldn't stop until he reached what promised at least a bare minimum of shelter, and as yet these exposed windswept slopes had offered nothing that even remotely approached that.

In the end, Mallory almost literally stumbled upon both men and shelter. He was negotiating a narrow, longitudinal spine of rock, had just crossed its razor-back, when he heard the murmur of voices beneath him and saw a tiny glimmer of light behind the canvas stretching down from the overhang of the far wall of the tiny ravine at his feet.

Miller started violently and swung round as he felt the hand on his shoulder, the automatic was half-way out of his pocket before he saw who it was and sank back heavily on the rock behind him.

'Come, come, now! Trigger-happy.' Thankfully Mallory slid his burden from his aching shoulders and looked across at the softly laughing Andrea. 'What's so funny?'

'Our friend here.' Andrea grinned again. 'I told him that the first thing he would know of your arrival would be when you touched him on the shoulder. I don't think he believed me.'

'You might have coughed or somethin',' Miller said defensively. 'It's my nerves, boss,' he added plaintively. 'They're not what they were forty-eight hours ago.'

Mallory looked at him disbelievingly, made to speak, then stopped short as he caught sight of the pale blur of a face propped up against a rucksack. Beneath the white swathe of a bandaged forehead the eyes were open, looking steadily at him. Mallory took a step forward, sank down on one knee.

'So you've come round at last!' He smiled into the sunken parchment face and Stevens smiled back, the bloodless lips whiter than the face itself. He looked ghastly. 'How do you feel, Andy?'

'Not too bad, sir. Really I'm not.' The bloodshot eyes were dark and filled with pain. His gaze fell and he looked down vacantly at his bandaged leg, looked up again, smiled uncertainly at Mallory. 'I'm terribly sorry about all this, sir. What a bloody stupid thing to do.'

'It wasn't a stupid thing.' Mallory spoke with slow, heavy emphasis. 'It was criminal folly.' He knew everyone was watching them, but knew, also, that Stevens had eyes for him alone. 'Criminal, unforgivable folly,' he went on quietly, 'and I'm the man in the dock. I'd suspected you'd lost a lot of blood on the boat, but I didn't know you had these big gashes on your forehead. I should have made it my business to find out.' He smiled wryly. 'You should have heard what these two insubordinate characters had to say to me about it when they got to the top . . . And they were right. You should never had been asked to bring up the rear in the state you were in. It was madness.' He grinned again. 'You should have been hauled up like a sack of coals like the intrepid mountaineering team of Miller and Brown . . . God knows how you ever made it – I'm sure you'll never know.' He leaned forward, touched Stevens's sound knee. 'Forgive me, Andy. I honestly didn't realise how far through you were.'

Stevens stirred uncomfortably, but the dead pallor of the high-boned cheeks was stained with embarrassed pleasure.

'Please, sir,' he pleaded. 'Don't talk like that. It was just one of these things.' He paused, eyes screwed shut and indrawn breath hissing sharply through his teeth as a wave of pain washed up from his shattered leg. Then he looked at Mallory again. 'And there's no credit due to me for the climb,' he went on quietly. 'I hardly remember a thing about it.'

Mallory looked at him without speaking, eyebrows arched in mild interrogation.

'I was scared to death every step of the way up,' Stevens said simply. He was conscious of no surprise, no wonder that he was saying the thing he would have died rather than say. 'I've never been so scared in all my life.'

Mallory shook his head slowly from side to side, stubbled chin rasping in his cupped palm. He seemed genuinely puzzled. Then he looked down at Stevens and smiled quizzically.

'Now I know you *are* new to this game, Andy.' He smiled again. 'Maybe you think I was laughing and singing all the way up that cliff? Maybe you think *I* wasn't scared?' He lit a cigarette and gazed at Stevens through a cloud of drifting smoke. 'Well, I wasn't. "Scared" isn't the word – I was bloody well terrified. So was Andrea here. We knew too much not to be scared.'

'Andrea!' Stevens laughed, then cried out as the movement triggered off a crepitant agony in his bone-shattered leg. For a moment Mallory thought he had lost consciousness, but almost at once he spoke again, his voice husky with pain. 'Andrea!' he whispered. 'Scared! I don't believe it.'

'Andrea *was* afraid.' The big Greek's voice was very gentle. 'Andrea *is* afraid. Andrea is always afraid. That is why I have lived so long.' He stared down at his great hands. 'And why so many have died. They were not so afraid as I. They were not afraid of everything a man could be afraid of, there was always something they forgot to fear, to guard against. But Andrea was afraid of everything – and he forgot nothing. It is as simple as that.'

He looked across at Stevens and smiled.

'There are no brave men and cowardly men in the world, my son. There are only brave men. To be born, to live, to die – that takes courage enough in itself, and more than enough. We are all brave men and we are all afraid, and what the world calls a brave man, he, too, is brave and afraid like all the rest of us. Only he is brave for five minutes longer. Or sometimes ten minutes, or twenty minutes – or the time it takes a man sick and bleeding and afraid to climb a cliff.'

Stevens said nothing. His head was sunk on his chest, and his face was hidden. He had seldom felt so happy, seldom so at peace with himself. He had known that he could not hide things from men like Andrea and Mallory, but he had not known that it would not matter. He felt he should say something, but he could not think what and he was deathly tired. He knew, deep down, that Andrea was speaking the truth, but not the whole truth; but he was too tired to care, to try to work things out.

Miller cleared his throat noisily.

'No more talkin', Lieutenant,' he said firmly. 'You gotta lie down, get yourself some sleep.'

Stevens looked at him, then at Mallory in puzzled inquiry.

'Better do what you're told, Andy.' Mallory smiled. 'Your surgeon and medical adviser talking. He fixed your leg.'

'Oh! I didn't know. Thanks, Dusty. Was it very – difficult?'

Miller waved a deprecatory hand.

'Not for a man of my experience. Just a simple break,' he lied easily. 'Almost let one of the others do it . . . Give him a hand to lie down, will you, Andrea?' He jerked his head towards Mallory. 'Boss?'

The two men moved outside, turning their backs to the icy wind.

'We gotta get a fire, dry clothing, for that kid,' Miller said urgently. 'His pulse is about 140, temperature 103. He's runnin' a fever, and he's losin' ground all the time.'

'I know, I know,' Mallory said worriedly. 'And there's not a hope of getting any fuel on this damned mountain. Let's go in and see how much dried clothing we can muster between us.'

He lifted the edge of the canvas and stepped inside. Stevens was still awake, Brown and Andrea on either side of him. Miller was on his heels.

'We're going to stay here for the night,' Mallory announced, 'so let's make things as snug as possible. Mind you,' he admitted, 'we're a bit too near the cliff for comfort, but old Jerry hasn't a clue we're on the island, and we're out of sight of the coast. Might as well make ourselves comfortable.'

'Boss . . .' Miller made to speak, then fell silent again. Mallory looked at him in surprise, saw that he, Brown and Stevens were looking at one another, uncertainty, then doubt and a dawning, sick comprehension in their eyes. A sudden anxiety, the sure knowledge that something was far wrong, struck at Mallory like a blow.

'What's up?' he demanded, sharply. 'What is it?'

'We have bad news for you, boss,' Miller said carefully. 'We should have told you right away. Guess we all thought that one of the others would have told you . . . Remember that sentry you and Andrea shoved over the side?'

Mallory nodded, sombrely. He knew what was coming.

'He fell on top of that reef twenty-thirty feet or so from the cliff,' Miller went on. 'Wasn't much of him left, I guess, but what was was jammed between two rocks. He was really stuck good and fast.'

'I see,' Mallory murmured. 'I've been wondering all night how you managed to get so wet under your rubber cape.'

'I tried four times, boss,' Miller said quietly. 'The others had a rope round me.' He shrugged his shoulders. 'Not a chance. Them gawddamned waves just flung me back against the cliff every time.'

'It will be light in three or four hours,' Mallory murmured. 'In four hours they will know we are on the island. They will see him as soon as it's dawn and send a boat to investigate.'

'Does it really matter, sir,' Stevens suggested. 'He could still have fallen.'

Mallory eased the canvas aside and looked out into the night. It was bitterly cold and the snow was beginning to fall all around them. He dropped the canvas again.

'Five minutes,' he said absently. 'We will leave in five minutes.' He looked at Stevens and smiled faintly. 'We are forgetful too. We should have told you. Andrea stabbed the sentry through the heart.'

The hours that followed were hours plucked from the darkest nightmare, endless, numbing hours of stumbling and tripping and falling and getting up again, of racked bodies and aching, tortured muscles, of dropped loads and frantic pawing around in the deepening snow, of hunger and thirst and all-encompassing exhaustion.

They had retraced their steps now, were heading WNW back across the shoulder of the mountain – almost certainly the Germans would think they had gone due north, heading for the centre of the island. Without compass, stars or moon to guide, Mallory had nothing to orientate them but the feel of the slope of the mountain and the memory of the map Vlachos had shown them in Alexandria. But by and by he was reasonably certain that they had rounded the mountain and were pushing up some narrow gorge into the interior.

The snow was the deadly enemy. Heavy, wet and feathery, it swirled all around them in a blanketing curtain of grey, sifted down their necks and jackboots, worked its insidious way under their clothes and up their sleeves, blocked their eyes and ears and mouths, pierced and then anaesthetised exposed faces, and turned gloveless hands into leaden lumps of ice, benumbed and all but powerless. All suffered, and suffered badly, but Stevens most of all. He had lost consciousness again within minutes of leaving the cave and clad in clinging, sodden clothes as he was, he now lacked even the saving warmth generated by physical activity. Twice Andrea had stopped and felt for the beating of the heart, for he thought that the boy had died: but he could feel nothing for there was no feeling left in his hands, and he could only wonder and stumble on again.

About five in the morning, as they were climbing up the steep valley head above the gorge, a treacherous, slippery slope with only a few stunted carob trees for anchor in the sliding scree, Mallory decided that they must rope up for safety's sake. In single file they scrambled and struggled up the ever-steepening slope for the next twenty minutes: Mallory, in the lead, did not even dare to think how Andrea was getting on behind him. Suddenly the slope eased, flattened out completely, and almost before they realised what was happening they had crossed the high divide, still roped together and in driving, blinding snow with zero visibility, and were sliding down the valley on the other side.

They came to the cave at dawn, just as the first grey stirrings of a bleak and cheerless day struggled palely through the lowering, snow-filled sky to the east. Monsieur Vlachos had told them that the south of Navarone was honey-combed with caves, but this was the first they had seen, and even then it was no cave but a dark, narrow tunnel in a great heap of piled volcanic slabs, huge, twisted layers of rock precariously poised in a gully that threaded down the slope towards some broad and unknown valley a thousand, two thousand feet, beneath them, a valley still shrouded in the gloom of night.

It was no cave, but it was enough. For frozen, exhausted, sleep-haunted men, it was more than enough, it was more than they had ever hoped for. There was room for them all, the few cracks were quickly blocked against the drifting snow, the entrance curtained off by the boulder-weighted tent. Somehow, impossibly almost in the cramped darkness, they stripped Stevens of his sea- and rain-soaked clothes, eased him into a providentially zipped sleeping-bag, forced some brandy down his throat and cushioned the blood-stained head on some dry clothing. And then the four men, even the tireless Andrea, slumped down to the sodden, snow-chilled floor of the cave and slept like men already dead, oblivious alike of the rocks on the floor, the cold, their hunger and their clammy, sat-urated clothing, oblivious even to the agony of returning circula-tion in their frozen hands and faces.

SEVEN

Tuesday
1500–1900

The sun, rime-ringed and palely luminous behind the drifting cloud-wrack, was far beyond its zenith and dipping swiftly westwards to the snow-limned shoulder of the mountain when Andrea lifted the edge of the tent, pushed it gently aside and peered out warily down the smooth sweep of the mountainside. For a few moments he remained almost motionless behind the canvas, automatically easing cramped and aching leg muscles, narrowed, roving eyes gradually accustoming themselves to the white glare of the glistening, crystalline snow. And then he had flitted noiselessly out of the mouth of the tunnel and reached far up the bank of the gully in half a dozen steps; stretched full length against the snow, he eased himself smoothly up the slope, lifted a cautious eye over the top.

Far below him stretched the great, curved sweep of an almost perfectly symmetrical valley – a valley born abruptly in the cradling embrace of steep-walled mountains and falling away gently to the north. That towering, buttressed giant on his right that brooded darkly over the head of the valley, its peak hidden in the snow clouds – there could be no doubt about that, Andrea thought. Mt Kostos, the highest mountain in Navarone: they had crossed its western flank during the darkness of the night. Due east and facing his own at perhaps five miles' distance, the third mountain was barely less high: but its northern flank fell away more quickly, debouching on to the plains that lay to the north-east of Navarone. And about four miles away to the north-north-east, far beneath the snowline and the isolated shepherds' huts, a tiny, flat-roofed township lay in a fold in the hills, along the bank of the little stream that wound its way through the valley. That could only be the village of Margaritha.

Even as he absorbed the topography of the valley, his eyes probing every dip and cranny in the hills for a possible source of danger, Andrea's mind was racing back over the last two minutes of time, trying to isolate, to remember the nature of the alien sound that had cut through the cocoon of sleep and brought him instantly to his feet, alert and completely awake, even before his conscious mind had time to register the memory of the sound. And then he heard it again, three times in as many seconds, the high-pitched, lonely wheep of a whistle, shrill peremptory blasts that echoed briefly and died along the lower slopes of Mt Kostos: the final echo still hung faintly on the air as Andrea pushed himself backwards and slid down to the floor of the gully.

He was back on the bank within thirty seconds, cheek muscles contracting involuntarily as the ice-chill eyepieces of Mallory's Zeiss-Ikon binoculars screwed into his face. There was no mistaking them now, he thought grimly, his first, fleeting impression had been all too accurate. Twenty-five, perhaps thirty soldiers in all, strung out in a long, irregular line, they were advancing slowly across the flank of Kostos, combing every gully, each jumbled confusion of boulders that lay in their path. Every man was clad in a snow-suit, but even at a distance of two miles they were easy to locate: the arrow-heads of their strapped skis angled up above shoulders and hooded heads: startlingly black against the sheer whiteness of the snow, the skis bobbed and weaved in disembodied drunkenness as the men slipped and stumbled along the scree-strewn slopes of the mountain. From time to time a man near the centre of the line pointed and gestured with an alpenstock, as if co-ordinating the efforts of the search party. The man with the whistle, Andrea guessed.

'Andrea!' The call from the cave mouth was very soft. 'Anything wrong?'

Finger to his lips, Andrea twisted round in the snow. Mallory was standing by the canvas screen. Dark-jowled and crumple-clothed, he held up one hand against the glare of the snow while the other rubbed the sleep from his blood-shot eyes. And then he was limping forward in obedience to the crooking of Andrea's finger, wincing in pain at every step he took. His toes were swollen and skinned, gummed together with congealed blood. He had not had his boots off since he had taken them from the feet of the dead

German sentry: and now he was almost afraid to remove them, afraid of what he would find . . . He clambered slowly up the bank of the gully and sank down in the snow beside Andrea.

'Company?'

'The very worst of company,' Andrea murmured. 'Take a look, my Keith.' He handed over the binoculars, pointed down to the lower slopes of Mt Kostos. 'Your friend Jensen never told us that they were here.'

Slowly, Mallory quartered the slopes with the binoculars. Suddenly the line of searchers moved into his field of vision. He raised his head, adjusted the focus impatiently, looked briefly once more, then lowered the binoculars with a restrained deliberation of gesture that held a wealth of bitter comment.

'The WGB,' he said softly.

'A Jaeger battalion,' Andrea conceded. 'Alpine Corps – their finest mountain troops. This is most inconvenient, my Keith.'

Mallory nodded, rubbed his stubbled chin.

'If anyone can find us, they can. And they'll find us.' He lifted the glasses to look again at the line of advancing men. The painstaking thoroughness of the search was disturbing enough: but even more threatening, more frightening, was the snail-like relentlessness, the inevitability of the approach of these tiny figures. 'God knows what the Alpenkorps is doing here,' Mallory went on. 'It's enough that they are here. They must know that we've landed and spent the morning searching the eastern saddle of Kostos – that was the obvious route for us to break into the interior. They've drawn a blank there, so now they're working their way over to the other saddle. They must be pretty nearly certain that we're carrying a wounded man with us and that we can't have got very far. It's only going to be a matter of time, Andrea.'

'A matter of time,' Andrea echoed. He glanced up at the sun, a sun all but invisible in the darkening sky. 'An hour, an hour and a half at the most. They'll be here before the sun goes down. And we'll still be here.' He glanced quizzically at Mallory. 'We cannot leave the boy. And we cannot get away if we take the boy – and then he would die anyway.'

'We will not be here,' Mallory said flatly. 'If we stay we all die. Or finish up in one of those nice little dungeons that Monsieur Vlachos told us about.'

'The greatest good of the greatest number,' Andrea nodded slowly. 'That's how it has to be, has it not, my Keith? The greatest number.

That is what Captain Jensen would say.' Mallory stirred uncomfortably, but his voice was steady enough when he spoke.

'That's how I see it, too, Andrea. Simple proportion – twelve hundred to one. You know it has to be this way.' Mallory sounded tired.

'Yes, I know. But you are worrying about nothing.' Andrea smiled. 'Come, my friend. Let us tell the others the good news.'

Miller looked up as the two men came in, letting the canvas screen fall shut behind them. He had unzipped the side of Stevens's sleeping-bag and was working on the mangled leg. A pencil flashlight was propped on a rucksack beside him.

'When are we goin' to do somethin' about this kid, boss?' The voice was abrupt, angry, like his gesture towards the sleep-drugged boy beside him. 'This damned waterproof sleeping-bag is soaked right through. So's the kid – and he's about frozen stiff: his leg feels like a side of chilled beef. He's gotta have heat, boss, a warm room and hot drinks – or he's finished. Twenty-four hours.' Miller shivered and looked slowly round the broken walls of the rock-shelter. 'I reckon he'd have less than an even chance in a first-class general hospital . . . He's just wastin' his time keepin' on breathin' in this gawddamned ice-box.'

Miller hardly exaggerated. Water from the melting snow above trickled continuously down the clammy, green-lichened walls of the cave or dripped directly on to the half-frozen gravelly slush on the floor of the cave. With no through ventilation and no escape for the water accumulating at the sides of the shelter, the whole place was dank and airless and terribly chill.

'Maybe he'll be hospitalised sooner than you think,' Mallory said dryly. 'How's his leg?'

'Worse.' Miller was blunt. 'A helluva sight worse. I've just chucked in another handful of sulpha and tied things up again. That's all I can do, boss, and it's just a waste of time anyway . . . What was that crack about a hospital?' he added suspiciously.

'That was no crack,' Mallory said soberly, 'but one of the more unpleasant facts of life. There's a German search party heading this way. They mean business. They'll find us, all right.'

Miller swore. 'That's handy, that's just wonderful,' he said bitterly. 'How far away, boss?'

'An hour, maybe a little more.'

'And what are we goin' to do with Junior, here? Leave him? It's his only chance, I reckon.'

'Stevens comes with us.' There was a flat finality in Mallory's voice. Miller looked at him for a long time in silence: his face was very cold.

'Stevens comes with us,' Miller repeated. 'We drag him along with us until he's dead – that won't take long – and then we leave him in the snow. Just like that, huh?'

'Just like that, Dusty.' Absently Mallory brushed some snow off his clothes, and looked up again at Miller. 'Stevens knows too much. The Germans will have guessed why we're on the island, but they don't know how we propose to get inside the fortress – and they don't know when the Navy's coming through. But Stevens does. They'll make him talk. Scopolamine will make anyone talk.'

'Scopolamine! On a dying man?' Miller was openly incredulous.

'Why not? I'd do the same myself. If you were the German commandant and you knew that your big guns and half the men in your fortress were liable to be blown to hell any moment, you'd do the same.'

Miller looked at him, grinned wryly, shook his head.

'Me and my –'

'I know. You and your big mouth.' Mallory smiled and clapped him on the shoulder. 'I don't like it one little bit more than you do, Dusty.' He turned away and crossed to the other side of the cave. 'How are you feeling, Chief?'

'Not too bad, sir.' Casey Brown was only just awake, numbed and shivering in sodden clothes. 'Anything wrong?'

'Plenty,' Mallory assured him. 'Search party moving this way. We'll have to pull out inside half an hour.' He looked at his watch. 'Just on four o'clock. Do you think you could raise Cairo on the set?'

'Lord only knows,' Brown said frankly. He rose stiffly to his feet. 'The radio didn't get just the best of treatment yesterday. I'll have a go.'

'Thanks, Chief. See that your aerial doesn't stick up above the sides of the gully.' Mallory turned to leave the cave, but halted abruptly at the sight of Andrea squatting on a boulder just beside the entrance. His head bent in concentration, the big Greek had just finished screwing telescopic sights on to the barrel of his 7.92 mm Mauser and was now deftly wrapping a sleeping-bag lining round its barrel and butt until the entire rifle was wrapped in a white cocoon.

Mallory watched him in silence. Andrea glanced up at him, smiled, rose to his feet and reached out for his rucksack. Within thirty seconds he was clad from head to toe in his mountain camouflage suit, was drawing tight the purse-strings of his snow-hood and easing his feet into the rucked elastic anklets of his canvas boots. Then he picked up the Mauser and smiled slightly.

'I thought I might be taking a little walk, Captain,' he said apologetically. 'With your permission, of course.'

Mallory nodded his head several times in slow recollection.

'You said I was worrying about nothing,' he murmured. 'I should have known. You might have told me, Andrea.' But the protest was automatic, without significance. Mallory felt neither anger nor even annoyance at this tacit arrogation of his authority. The habit of command died hard in Andrea: on such occasions as he ostensibly sought approval for or consulted about a proposed course of action it was generally as a matter of courtesy and to give information as to his intentions. Instead of resentment, Mallory could feel only an overwhelming relief and gratitude to the smiling giant who towered above him: he had talked casually to Miller about driving Stevens till he died and then abandoning him, talked with an indifference that masked a mind sombre with bitterness at what he must do, but even so he had not known how depressed, how sick at heart this decision had left him until he knew it was no longer necessary.

'I am sorry.' Andrea was half-contrite, half-smiling. 'I should have told you. I thought you understood . . . It is the best thing to do, yes?'

'It is the only thing to do,' Mallory said frankly. 'You're going to draw them off up the saddle?'

'There is no other way. With their skis they would overtake me in minutes if I went down into the valley. I cannot come back, of course, until it is dark. You will be here?'

'Some of us will.' Mallory glanced across the shelter where a waking Stevens was trying to sit up, heels of his palms screwing into his exhausted eyes. 'We must have food and fuel, Andrea,' he said softly. 'I am going down into the valley tonight.'

'Of course, of course. We must do what we can.' Andrea's face was grave, his voice only a murmur. 'As long as we can. He is only a boy, a child almost . . . Perhaps it will not be long.' He pulled back the curtain, looked out at the evening sky. 'I will be back by seven o'clock.'

'Seven o'clock,' Mallory repeated. The sky, he could see, was darkening already, darkening with the gloom of coming snow, and the lifting wind was beginning to puff little clouds of air-spun, flossy white into the little gully. Mallory shivered and caught hold of the massive arm. 'For God's sake, Andrea,' he urged quietly, 'look after yourself!'

'Myself?' Andrea smiled gently, no mirth in his eyes, and as gently he disengaged his arm. 'Do not think about me.' The voice was very quiet, with an utter lack of arrogance. 'If you must speak to God, speak to Him about these poor devils who are looking for us.' The canvas dropped behind him and he was gone.

For some moments Mallory stood irresolutely at the mouth of the cave, gazing out sightlessly through the gap in the curtain. Then he wheeled abruptly, crossed the floor of the shelter and knelt in front of Stevens. The boy was propped up against Miller's anxious arm, the eyes lack-lustre and expressionless, bloodless cheeks deep-sunken in a grey and parchment face. Mallory smiled at him: he hoped the shock didn't show in his face.

'Well, well, well. The sleeper awakes at last. Better late than never.' He opened his waterproof cigarette case, proffered it to Stevens. 'How are you feeling now, Andy?'

'Frozen, sir.' Stevens shook his head at the case and tried to grin back at Mallory, a feeble travesty of a smile that made Mallory wince.

'And the leg?'

'I think it must be frozen, too.' Stevens looked down incuriously at the sheathed whiteness of his shattered leg. 'Anyway, I can't feel a thing.'

'Frozen!' Miller's sniff was a masterpiece of injured pride. 'Frozen, he says! Gawddamned ingratitude. It's the first-class medical care, if I do say so myself!'

Stevens smiled, a fleeting, absent smile that flickered over his face and was gone. For long moments he kept staring down at his leg, then suddenly lifted his head and looked directly at Mallory.

'Look, sir, there's no good kidding ourselves.' The voice was soft, quite toneless. 'I don't want to seem ungrateful and I hate even the idea of cheap heroics, but – well, I'm just a damned great millstone round your necks and –'

'Leave you, eh?' Mallory interrupted. 'Leave you to die of the cold or be captured by the Germans. Forget it, laddie. We can look after you – and these ruddy guns – at the same time.'

'But, sir –'

'You insult us, Lootenant.' Miller sniffed again. 'Our feelings are hurt. Besides, as a professional man I gotta see my case through to convalescence, and if you think I'm goin' to do that in any gawd-damned dripping German dungeon, you can –'

'Enough!' Mallory held up his hand. 'The subject is closed!' He saw the stain high up on the thin cheeks, the glad light that touched the dulled eyes, and felt the self-loathing and the shame well up inside him, shame for the gratitude of a sick man who did not know that their concern stemmed not from solicitude but from fear that he might betray them . . . Mallory bent forward and began to unlace his high jackboots. He spoke without looking up.

'Dusty.'

'Yeah?'

'When you're finishing boasting about your medical prowess, maybe you'd care to use some of it. Come and have a look at these feet of mine, will you? I'm afraid the sentry's boots haven't done them a great deal of good.'

Fifteen painful minutes later Miller snipped off the rough edges of the adhesive bandage that bound Mallory's right foot, straightened up stiffly and contemplated his handiwork with pride.

'Beautiful, Miller, beautiful,' he murmured complacently. 'Not even in Johns Hopkins in the city of Baltimore . . .' He broke off suddenly, frowned down at the thickly bandaged feet and coughed apologetically. 'A small point has just occurred to me, boss.'

'I thought it might eventually,' Mallory said grimly. 'Just how do you propose to get my feet into these damned boots again?' He shivered involuntarily as he pulled on a pair of thick woollen socks, matted and sodden with melted snow, picked up the German sentry's boots, held them at arm's length and examined them in disgust. 'Sevens, at the most – and a darned small sevens at that!'

'Nines,' Stevens said laconically. He handed over his own jack-boots, one of them slit neatly down the sides where Andrea had cut it open. 'You can fix that tear easily enough, and they're no damned good to me now. No arguments, sir, please.' He began to laugh softly, broke off in a sharply indrawn hiss of pain as the movement jarred the broken bones, took a couple of deep, quivering breaths, then smiled whitely. 'My first – and probably my last – contribution to the expedition. What sort of medal do you reckon they'll give me for that, sir?'

Mallory took the boots, looked at Stevens a long moment in silence, then turned as the tarpaulin was pushed aside. Brown stumbled in, lowered the transmitter and telescopic aerial to the floor of the cave and pulled out a tin of cigarettes. They slipped from his frozen fingers, fell into the icy mud at his feet, became brown and sodden on the instant. He swore briefly, and without enthusiasm, beat his numbed hands across his chest, gave it up and sat down heavily on a convenient boulder. He looked tired and cold and thoroughly miserable.

Mallory lit a cigarette and passed it across to him.

'How did it go, Casey? Manage to raise them at all?'

'They managed to raise me – more or less. Reception was lousy.' Brown drew the grateful tobacco smoke deep down into his lungs. 'And I couldn't get through at all. Must be that damned great hill to the south there.'

'Probably,' Mallory nodded. 'And what news from our friends in Cairo? Exhorting us to greater efforts? Telling us to get on with the job?'

'No news at all. Too damn worried about the silence at this end. Said that from now on they were going to come through every four hours, acknowledgment or no. Repeated that about ten times, then signed off.'

'That'll be a great help,' Miller said acidly. 'Nice to know they're on our side. Nothin' like moral support.' He jerked his thumb towards the mouth of the cave. 'Reckon them bloodhounds would be scared to death if they knew . . . Did you take a gander at them before you came in?'

'I didn't have to,' Brown said morosely. 'I could hear them – sounded like the officer in charge shouting directions.' Mechanically, almost, he picked up his automatic rifle, eased the clip in the magazine. 'Must be less than a mile away now.'

The search party, more closely bunched by this time, was less than a mile, was barely half a mile distant from the cave when the Oberleutnant in charge saw that the right wing of his line, on the steeper slopes to the south, was lagging behind once more. Impatiently he lifted his whistle to his mouth for the three sharp peremptory blasts that would bring his weary men stumbling into line again. Twice the whistle shrilled out its imperative urgency, the piercing notes echoing flatly along the snowbound slopes and dying away in the valley below: but the third *wheep* died at birth, caught up again and tailed off in a wailing, eldritch diminuendo that merged with dreadful harmony into a long, bubbling scream of agony. For two or three seconds the Oberleutnant stood motionless in his tracks, his face shocked and contorted: then he jackknifed violently forward and pitched down into the crusted snow. The burly sergeant beside him stared down at the fallen officer, looked up in sudden horrified understanding, opened his mouth to shout, sighed and toppled wearily over the body at his feet, the evil, whip-lash crack of the Mauser in his ears as he died.

High up on the western slopes of Mount Kostos, wedged in the V between two great boulders, Andrea gazed down the darkening mountainside over the depressed telescopic sights of his rifle and pumped another three rounds into the wavering, disorganised line of searchers. His face was quite still, as immobile as the eyelids that never flickered to the regular crashing of his Mauser, and drained of all feeling. Even his eyes reflected the face, eyes neither hard nor pitiless, but simply empty and almost frighteningly remote, a remoteness that mirrored his mind, a mind armoured for the moment against all thought and sensation, for Andrea knew that he must not think about this thing. To kill, to take the life of his fellows, that was the supreme evil, for life was a gift that it was not his to take away. Not even in fair fight. And this was murder.

Slowly Andrea lowered the Mauser, peered through the drifting gun-smoke that hung heavily in the frosty evening air. The enemy had vanished, completely, rolled behind scattered boulders or burrowed frantically into the blanketing anonymity of the snow. But they were still there, still potentially as dangerous as ever. Andrea knew that they would recover fast from the death of their officer – there were no finer, no more tenacious fighters in Europe than the ski-troops of the Jaeger mountain battalion – and would come after him, catch him and kill him if humanly possible. That was why Andrea's first case had been to kill their officer – he might not have come after him, might have stopped to puzzle out the reason for this unprovoked flank attack.

Andrea ducked low in reflex instinct as a sudden burst of automatic fire whined in murderous ricochet off the boulders before him. He had expected this. It was the old classic infantry attack pattern – advance under covering fire, drop, cover your mate and come again. Swiftly Andrea rammed home another charge into the magazine of his Mauser, dropped flat on his face and inched his way along behind the low line of broken rock that extended fifteen or twenty yards to his right – he had chosen his ambush point with care – and then petered out. At the far end he pulled his snow hood down to the level of his brows and edged a wary eye round the corner of the rock.

Another heavy burst of automatic fire smashed into the boulders he had just left, and half a dozen men – three from either end of the line – broke cover, scurried along the slope in a stumbling, crouching run, then pitched forward into the snow again. *Along* the slope – the two parties had run in opposite directions. Andrea lowered his head and rubbed the back of a massive hand across the stubbled grizzle of his chin. Awkward, damned awkward. No frontal attack for the foxes of the WGB. They were extending their lines on either side, the points hooking around in a great, encircling half-moon. Bad enough for himself, but he could have coped with that – a carefully reconnoitred escape gully wound up the slope behind him. But he hadn't foreseen what was obviously going to happen: the curving crescent of line to the west was going to sweep across the rock-shelter where the others lay hidden.

Andrea twisted over on his back and looked up at the evening sky. It was darkening by the moment, darkening with the gloom of coming snow, and daylight was beginning to fail. He twisted again and looked across the great swelling shoulder of Mount Kostos, looked at the few scattered rocks and shallow depressions that barely dimpled the smooth convexity of the slope. He took a second quick look round the rock as the rifles of the WGB opened up once more, saw the same encircling manoeuvre being executed again, and waited no longer. Firing blindly downhill, he half-rose to his feet and flung himself out into the open, finger squeezing on the trigger, feet driving desperately into the frozen snow as he launched himself towards the nearest rock-cover, forty yards away if an inch. Thirty-five yards to go, thirty, twenty and still not a shot fired, a slip, a stumble on the sliding scree, a catlike recovery, ten yards, still miraculously immune, and then he had dived into shelter to land on chest and stomach with a sickening impact that struck cruelly into his ribs and emptied his lungs with an explosive gasp.

Fighting for breath, he struck the magazine cover, rammed home another charge, risked a quick peep over the top of the rock and catapulted himself to his feet again, all inside ten seconds. The Mauser held across his body opened up again, firing downhill at vicious random, for Andrea had eyes only for the smoothly-treacherous ground at his feet, for the scree-lined depression so impossibly far ahead. And then the Mauser was empty, useless in his hand, and every gun far below had opened up, the shells whistling above his head or blinding him with spurting gouts of snow as they ricocheted off the solid rock. But twilight was touching the hills, Andrea was only a blur, a swiftly-flitting blur against a ghostly background, and uphill accuracy was notoriously difficult at any time. Even so, the massed fire from below was steadying and converging, and Andrea waited no longer. Unseen hands plucking wickedly at the flying tails of his snow-smock, he flung himself almost horizontally forward and slid the last ten feet face down into the waiting depression.

Stretched full length on his back in the hollow, Andrea fished out a steel mirror from his breast pocket and held it gingerly above his head. At first he could see nothing, for the darkness was deeper below and the mirror misted from the warmth of his body. And then the film vanished in the chill mountain air and he could see two, three and then half a dozen men breaking cover, heading at a clumsy run straight up the face of the hill – and two of them had come from the extreme right of the line. Andrea lowered the mirror and relaxed with a long sigh of relief, eyes crinkling in a smile. He looked up at the sky, blinked as the first feathery flakes of falling snow melted on his eyelids and smiled again. Almost lazily he brought out another charger for the Mauser, fed more shells into the magazine.

'Boss?' Miller's voice was plaintive.

'Yes? What is it?' Mallory brushed some snow off his face and the collar of his smock and peered into the white darkness ahead.

'Boss, when you were in school did you ever read any stories about folks gettin' lost in a snowstorm and wanderin' round and round in circles for days?'

'We had exactly the same book in Queenstown,' Mallory conceded.

'Wanderin' round and round until they died?' Miller persisted.

'Oh, for heaven's sake!' Mallory said impatiently. His feet, even in Stevens's roomy boots, hurt abominably. 'How can we be wandering in circles if we're going downhill all the time? What do you think we're on – a bloody spiral staircase?'

Miller walked on in hurt silence, Mallory beside him, both men ankle-deep in the wet, clinging snow that had been falling so silently, so persistently, for the past three hours since Andrea had drawn off the Jaeger search party. Even in midwinter in the White

Mountains in Crete Mallory could recall no snowfall so heavy and continuous. So much for the Isles of Greece and the eternal sunshine that gilds them yet, he thought bitterly. He hadn't reckoned on this when he'd planned on going down to Margaritha for food and fuel, but even so it wouldn't have made any difference to his decision. Although in less pain now, Stevens was becoming steadily weaker, and the need was desperate.

With moon and stars blanketed by the heavy snow-clouds – visibility, indeed, was hardly more than ten feet in any direction – the loss of their compasses had assumed a crippling importance. He didn't doubt his ability to find the village – it was simply a matter of walking downhill till they came to the stream that ran through the valley, then following that north till they came to Margaritha – but if the snow didn't let up their chances of locating that tiny cave again in the vast sweep of the hillsides . . .

Mallory smothered an exclamation as Miller's hand closed round his upper arm, dragged him down to his knees in the snow. Even in that moment of unknown danger he could feel a slow stirring of anger against himself, for his attention had been wandering along with his thoughts . . . He lifted his hand as vizor against the snow, peered out narrowly through the wet, velvety curtain of white that swirled and eddied out of the darkness before him. Suddenly he had it – a dark, squat shape only feet away. They had all but walked straight into it.

'It's the hut,' he said softly in Miller's ear. He had seen it early in the afternoon, half-way between their cave and Margaritha, and almost in line with both. He was conscious of relief, an increase in confidence: they would be in the village in less than half an hour. 'Elementary navigation, my dear Corporal,' he murmured. 'Lost and wandering in circles, my foot! Just put your faith . . .'

He broke off as Miller's fingers dug viciously into his arm, as Miller's head came close to his own.

'I heard voices, boss.' The words were a mere breath of sound.

'Are you sure?' Miller's silenced gun, Mallory noticed, was still in his pocket.

Miller hesitated.

'Dammit to hell, boss, I'm sure of nothin',' he whispered irritably. 'I've been imaginin' every damn thing possible in the past hour!' He pulled the snow-hood off his head, the better to listen, bent forward for a few seconds then sank back again. 'Anyway, I'm sure I *thought* I heard somethin'.'

'Come on. Let's take a look-see.' Mallory was on his feet again. 'I think you're mistaken. Can't be the Jaeger boys – they were half-way back across Mount Kostos when we saw them last. And the shepherds only use these places in the summer months.' He slipped the safety catch of his Colt .455, walked slowly, at a half-crouch, towards the nearest wall of the hut, Miller at his shoulder.

They reached the hut, put their ears against the frail, tar-paper walls. Ten seconds passed, twenty, half a minute, then Mallory relaxed.

'Nobody at home. Or if they are, they're keeping mighty quiet. But no chances, Dusty. You go that way, I'll go this. Meet at the door – that'll be on the opposite side, facing into the valley . . . Walk wide at the corners – never fails to baffle the unwary.'

A minute later both men were inside the hut, the door shut behind them. The hooded beam of Mallory's torch probed into every corner of the ramshackle cabin. It was quite empty – an earthen floor, a rough wooden bunk, a dilapidated stove with a rusty lantern standing on it, and that was all. No table, no chair, no chimney, not even a window.

Mallory walked over to the stove, picked up the lamp and sniffed it.

'Hasn't been used for weeks. Still full of kerosene, though. Very useful in that damn dungeon up there – if we can ever find the place . . .'

He froze into a sudden listening immobility, eyes unfocused and head cocked slightly to one side. Gently, ever so gently, he set the lamp down, walked leisurely across to Miller.

'Remind me to apologise at some future date,' he murmured. 'We have company. Give me your gun and keep talking.'

'Castelrosso again,' Miller complained loudly. He hadn't even raised an eyebrow. 'This is downright monotonous. A Chinaman – I'll bet it's a Chinaman this time.' But he was already talking to himself.

The silenced automatic balanced at his waist, Mallory walked noiselessly round the hut, four feet out from the walls. He had passed two corners, was just rounding the third when, out of the corner of his eye, he saw a vague figure behind him rising up swiftly from the ground and lunging out with upraised arm. Mallory stepped back quickly under the blow, spun round, swung his balled fist viciously and backwards into the stomach of his attacker. There was a sudden explosive gasp of agony as the man doubled up, moaned and crumpled silently to the ground. Barely in time Mallory arrested the downward, clubbing swipe of his reversed automatic.

Gun reversed again, the butt settled securely in his palm, Mallory stared down unblinkingly at the huddled figure, at the primitive wooden baton still clutched in the gloved right hand, at the unmilitary looking knapsack strapped to his back. He kept his gun lined up on the fallen body, waiting: this had been just too easy, too suspicious. Thirty seconds passed and still the figure on the ground hadn't stirred. Mallory took a short step forward and carefully, deliberately and none too gently kicked the man on the outside of the right knee. It was an old trick, and he'd never known it to fail – the pain was brief, but agonising. But there was no movement, no sound at all.

Quickly Mallory stooped, hooked his free hand round the knapsack shoulder straps, straightened and made for the door, half-carrying, half-dragging his captive. The man was no weight at all. With a proportionately much heavier garrison than ever in Crete, there would be that much less food for the islanders, Mallory mused compassionately. There would be very little indeed. He wished he hadn't hit him so hard.

Miller met him at the open door, stooped wordlessly, caught the unconscious man by the ankles and helped Mallory dump him unceremoniously on the bunk in the far corner of the hut.

'Nice goin', boss,' he complimented. 'Never heard a thing. Who's the heavyweight champ?'

'No idea.' Mallory shook his head in the darkness. 'Just skin and bones, that's all, just skin and bones. Shut the door, Dusty, and let's have a look at what we've got.'

EIGHT

Tuesday
1900–0015

A minute passed, two, then the little man stirred, moaned and pushed himself to a sitting position. Mallory held his arm to steady him, while he shook his bent head, eyes screwed tightly shut as he concentrated on clearing the muzziness away. Finally he looked up slowly, glanced from Mallory to Miller and back at Mallory again in the feeble light of the newly-lit shuttered lantern. Even as the men watched, they could see the colour returning to the swarthy cheeks, the indignant bristling of the heavy, dark moustache, the darkening anger in the eyes. Suddenly the man reached up, tore Mallory's hand away from his arm.

'Who are you?' He spoke in English, clear, precise, with hardly a trace of accent.

'Sorry, but the less you know the better.' Mallory smiled, deliberately to rob the words of offence. 'I mean that for your own sake. How are you feeling now?'

Tenderly the little man massaged his midriff, flexed his leg with a grimace of pain.

'You hit me very hard.'

'I had to.' Mallory reached behind him and picked up the cudgel the man had been carrying. 'You tried to hit me with this. What did you expect me to do – take my hat off so you could have a better swipe at me?'

'You are very amusing.' Again he bent his leg, experimentally, looking up at Mallory in hostile suspicion. 'My knee hurts me,' he said accusingly.

'First things first. Why the club?'

'I meant to knock you down and have a look at you,' he explained impatiently. 'It was the only safe way. You might have been one of the WGB . . . Why is my knee –?'

'You had an awkward fall,' Mallory said shamelessly. 'What are you doing here?'

'Who are you?' the little man countered.

Miller coughed, looked ostentatiously at his watch.

'This is all very entertainin', boss –'

'True for you, Dusty. We haven't all night.' Quickly Mallory reached behind him, picked up the man's rucksack, tossed it across to Miller. 'See what's in there, will you?' Strangely, the little man made no move to protest.

'Food!' Miller said reverently. 'Wonderful, wonderful food. Cooked meat, bread, cheese – and wine.' Reluctantly Miller closed the bag and looked curiously at their prisoner. 'Helluva funny time for a picnic.'

'So! An American, a Yankee.' The little man smiled to himself. 'Better and better!'

'What do you mean?' Miller asked suspiciously.

'See for yourself,' the man said pleasantly. He nodded casually to the far corner of the room. 'Look there.'

Mallory spun round, realised in a moment that he had been tricked, jerked back again. Carefully he leaned forward and touched Miller's arm.

'Don't look round too quickly, Dusty. And don't touch your gun. It seems our friend was not alone.' Mallory tightened his lips, mentally cursed himself for his obtuseness. Voices – Dusty had said there had been voices. Must be even more tired than he had thought . . .

A tall, lean man blocked the entrance to the doorway. His face was shadowed under an enveloping snow-hood, but there was no mistaking the gun in his hand. A short Lee Enfield rifle, Mallory noted dispassionately.

'Do not shoot!' The little man spoke rapidly in Greek. 'I am almost sure that they are those whom we seek, Panayis.'

Panayis! Mallory felt the wave of relief wash over him. That was one of the names Eugene Vlachos had given him, back in Alexandria.

'The tables turned, are they not?' The little man smiled at Mallory, the tired eyes crinkling, the heavy black moustache lifting engagingly at one corner. 'I ask you again, who are you?'

'SOE,' Mallory answered unhesitatingly.

The man nodded in satisfaction. 'Captain Jensen sent you?'

Mallory sank back on the bunk and sighed in long relief.

'We are among friends, Dusty.' He looked at the little man before him. 'You must be Louki – the first plane tree in the square in Margaritha?'

The little man beamed. He bowed, stretched out his hand.

'Louki. At your service, sir.'

'And this of course, is Panayis?'

The tall man in the doorway, dark, saturnine, unsmiling, inclined his head briefly but said nothing.

'You have us right!' The little man was beaming with delight. 'Louki and Panayis. They know about us in Alexandria and Cairo, then?' he asked proudly.

'Of course!' Mallory smothered a smile. 'They spoke highly of you. You have been of great help to the Allies before.'

'And we will again,' Louki said briskly. 'Come, we are wasting time. The Germans are on the hills. What help can we give you?'

'Food, Louki. We need food – we need it badly.'

'We have it!' Proudly, Louki gestured at the rucksacks. 'We were on our way up with it.'

'You were on your way . . .' Mallory was astonished. 'How did you know where we were – or even that we were on the island?'

Louki waved a deprecating hand.

'It was easy. Since first light German troops have been moving south through Margaritha up into the hills. All morning they combed the east col of Kostos. We knew someone must have landed, and that the Germans were looking for them. We heard, too, that the Germans had blocked the cliff path on the south coast, at both ends. So you must have come over the west col. They would not expect that – you fooled them. So we came to find you.'

'But you would never have found us –'

'We would have found you.' There was complete certainty in the voice. 'Panayis and I – we know every stone, every blade of grass in Navarone.' Louki shivered suddenly, stared out bleakly through the swirling snow. 'You couldn't have picked worse weather.'

'We couldn't have picked better,' Mallory said grimly.

'Last night, yes,' Louki agreed. 'No one would expect you in that wind and rain. No one would hear the aircraft or even dream that you would try to jump –'

'We came by sea,' Miller interrupted. He waved a negligent hand. 'We climbed the south cliff.'

'What? The south cliff!' Louki was frankly disbelieving. 'No one could climb the south cliff. It is impossible!'

'That's the way we felt when we were about half-way up,' Mallory said candidly. 'But Dusty, here, is right. That's how it was.'

Louki had taken a step back: his face was expressionless.

'I say it is impossible,' he repeated flatly.

'He is telling the truth, Louki,' Miller cut in quietly. 'Do you never read newspapers?'

'Of course I read newspapers!' Louki bristled with indignation. 'Do you think I am – how you say – illiterate?'

'Then think back to just before the war,' Miller advised. 'Think of mountaineerin' – and the Himalayas. You must have seen his picture in the papers – once, twice, a hundred times.' He looked at Mallory consideringly. 'Only he was a little prettier in those days. You must remember. This is Mallory, Keith Mallory of New Zealand.'

Mallory said nothing. He was watching Louki, the puzzlement, the comical screwing up of the eyes, head cocked to one side: then, all at once, something clicked in the little man's memory and his face lit up in a great, crinkling smile that swamped every last trace of suspicion. He stepped forward, hand outstretched in welcome.

'By heaven, you are right! Mallory! Of course I know Mallory!' He grabbed Mallory's hand, pumped it up and down with great enthusiasm. 'It is indeed as the American says. You need a shave . . . And you look older.'

'I feel older,' Mallory said gloomily. He nodded at Miller. 'This is Corporal Miller, an American citizen.'

'Another famous climber?' Louki asked eagerly. 'Another tiger of the hills, yes?'

'He climbed the south cliff as it has never been climbed before,' Mallory answered truthfully. He glanced at his watch, then looked directly at Louki. 'There are others up in the hills. We need help, Louki. We need it badly and we need it at once. You know the danger if you are caught helping us?'

'Danger?' Louki waved a contemptuous hand. 'Danger to Louki and Panayis, the foxes of Navarone? Impossible! We are the ghosts of the night.' He hitched his pack higher up on his shoulders. 'Come. Let us take this food to your friends.'

'Just a minute.' Mallory's restraining hand was on his arm. 'There are two other things. We need heat – a stove and fuel, and we need –'

'Heat! A stove!' Louki was incredulous. 'Your friends in the hills – what are they? A band of old women?'

'And we also need bandages and medicine,' Mallory went on patiently. 'One of our friends has been terribly injured. We are not sure, but we do not think that he will live.'

'Panayis!' Louki barked. 'Back to the village.' Louki was speaking in Greek now. Rapidly he issued his orders, had Mallory describe where the rock-shelter was, made sure that Panayis understood, then stood a moment in indecision, pulling at an end of his moustache. At length he looked up at Mallory.

'Could you find this cave again by yourself?'

'Lord only knows,' Mallory said frankly. 'I honestly don't think so.'

'Then I must come with you. I had hoped – you see, it will be a heavy load for Panayis – I have told him to bring bedding as well – and I don't think –'

'I'll go along with him,' Miller volunteered. He thought of his back-breaking labours on the caique, the climb up the cliff, their forced march through the mountains. 'The exercise will do me good.'

Louki translated his offer to Panayis – taciturn, apparently, only because of his complete lack of English – and was met by what appeared to be a torrent of protest. Miller looked at him in astonishment.

'What's the matter with old sunshine here?' he asked Mallory. 'Doesn't seem any too happy to me.'

'Says he can manage OK and wants to go by himself,' Mallory interpreted. 'Thinks you'll slow him up on the hills.' He shook his head in mock wonder. 'As if any man could slow Dusty Miller up!'

'Exactly!' Louki was bristling with anger. Again he turned to Panayis, fingers stabbing the empty air to emphasise his words. Miller turned, looked apprehensively at Mallory.

'What's he tellin' him now, boss?'

'Only the truth,' Mallory said solemnly. 'Saying he ought to be honoured at being given the opportunity of marching with Monsieur Miller, the world-famous American climber.' Mallory grinned. 'Panayis will be on his mettle tonight – determined to prove that a Navaronian can climb as well and as fast as any man.'

'Oh, my Gawd!' Miller moaned.

'And on the way back, don't forget to give Panayis a hand up the steeper bits.'

Miller's reply was luckily lost in a sudden flurry of snow-laden wind.

That wind was rising steadily now, a bitter wind that whipped the heavy snow into their bent faces and stung the tears from their blinking eyes. A heavy, wet snow that melted as it touched, and trickled down through every gap and chink in their clothing until they were wet and chilled and thoroughly miserable. A clammy, sticky snow that built up layer after energy-sapping layer under their leaden-footed boots, until they stumbled along inches above the ground, leg muscles aching from the sheer accumulated weight of snow. There was no visibility worthy of the name, not even of a matter of feet, they were blanketed, swallowed up by an impenetrable cocoon of swirling grey and white, unchanging, featureless: Louki strode on diagonally upwards across the slope with the untroubled certainty of a man walking up his own garden path.

Louki seemed as agile as a mountain goat, and as tireless. Nor was his tongue less nimble, less unwearied than his legs. He talked incessantly, a man overjoyed to be in action again, no matter what action so long as it was against the enemy. He told Mallory of the last three attacks on the island and how they had so bloodily failed – the Germans had been somehow forewarned of the seaborne assault, had been waiting for the Special Boat Service and the Commandos with everything they had and had cut them to pieces, while the two airborne groups had had the most evil luck, been delivered up to the enemy by misjudgment, by a series of unforeseeable coincidences; or how Panayis and himself had on both occasions narrowly escaped with their lives – Panayis had actually been captured the last time, had killed both his guards and escaped unrecognised; of the disposition of the German troops and check-points throughout the island, the location of the road blocks on the only two roads; and finally, of what little he himself knew of the layout of the fortress of Navarone itself. Panayis, the dark one, could tell him more of that, Louki said: twice Panayis had been inside the fortress, once for an entire night: the guns, the control rooms, the barracks, the officers' quarters, the magazine, the turbo rooms, the sentry points – he knew where each one lay, to the inch.

Mallory whistled softly to himself. This was more than he had ever dared hope for. They had still to escape the net of searchers, still to reach the fortress, still to get inside it. But once inside – and Panayis must know how to get inside . . . Unconsciously Mallory lengthened his stride, bent his back to the slope.

'Your friend Panayis must be quite something,' he said slowly. 'Tell me more about him, Louki.'

'What can I tell you?' Louki shook his head in a little flurry of snowflakes. 'What do I know of Panayis? What does anyone know of Panayis? That he has the luck of the devil, the courage of a mad-man and that sooner the lion will lie down with the lamb, the starving wolf spare the flock, than Panayis breathe the same air as the Germans? We all know that, and we know nothing of Panayis. All I know is that I thank God I am no German, with Panayis on the island. He strikes by stealth, by night, by knife and in the back.' Louki crossed himself. 'His hands are full of blood.'

Mallory shivered involuntarily. The dark, sombre figure of Panayis, the memory of the expressionless face, the hooded eyes, were beginning to fascinate him.

'There's more to him than that, surely,' Mallory argued 'After all, you are both Navaronians –'

'Yes yes, that is so.'

'This is a small island, you've lived together all your lives –'

'Ah, but that is where the major is wrong!' Mallory's promotion in rank was entirely Louki's own idea: despite Mallory's protests and explanations he seemed determined to stick to it. 'I, Louki, was for many years in foreign lands, helping Monsieur Vlachos. Monsieur Vlachos,' Louki said with pride, 'is a very important Government official.'

'I know,' Mallory nodded. 'A consul. I've met him. He is a very fine man.'

'You have met him! Monsieur Vlachos?' There was no mistaking the gladness, the delight in Louki's voice. 'That is good! That is won-derful! Later you must tell me more. He is a great man. Did I ever tell you –'

'We were speaking about Panayis,' Mallory reminded him gently.

'Ah, yes, Panayis. As I was saying, I was away for a long time. When I came back, Panayis was gone. His father had died, his mother had married again and Panayis had gone to live with his stepfather and two little stepsisters in Crete. His stepfather, half-fisherman, half-farmer, was killed in fighting the Germans near Candia – this was in the beginning. Panayis took over the boat of his father, helped many of the Allies to escape until he was caught

by the Germans, strung up by his wrists in the village square –
where his family lived – not far from Casteli. He was flogged till the
white of his ribs, of his backbone, was there for all to see, and left
for dead. Then they burnt the village and Panayis's family – disappeared. You understand, Major?'

'I understand,' Mallory said grimly. 'But Panayis –'

'He should have died. But he is tough, that one, tougher than a
knot in an old carob tree. Friends cut him down during the night,
took him away into the hills till he was well again. And then he
arrived back in Navarone, God knows how. I think he came from
island to island in a small rowing-boat. He never says why he
came back – I think it gives him greater pleasure to kill on his own
native island. I do not know, Major. All I know is that food and
sleep, the sunshine, women and wine – all these are nothing and
less than nothing to the dark one.' Again Louki crossed himself.
'He obeys me, for I am the steward of the Vlachos family, but even
I am afraid of him. To kill, to keep on killing, then kill again – that
is the very breath of his being.' Louki stopped momentarily,
sniffed the air like a hound seeking some fugitive scent, then
kicked the snow off his boots and struck off up the hill at a tan-
gent. The little man's unhesitating sureness of direction was
uncanny.

'How far to go now, Louki?'

'Two hundred yards, Major. No more.' Louki blew some snow off
his heavy, dark moustache and swore. 'I shall not be sorry to arrive.'

'Nor I.' Mallory thought of the miserable, draughty shelter in the
dripping rocks almost with affection. It was becoming steadily colder
as they climbed out of the valley, and the wind was rising, climbing up the register with a steady, moaning whine: they had to lean
into it now, push hard against it, to make any progress. Suddenly
both men stopped, listened, looked at each other, heads bent
against the driving snow. Around them there was only the white
emptiness and the silence: there was no sign of what had caused
the sudden sound.

'You heard something, too?' Mallory murmured.

'It is only I.' Mallory spun round as the deep voice boomed out
behind him and the bulky, white-smocked figure loomed out of the
snow. 'A milk wagon on a cobbled street is as nothing compared to
yourself and your friend here. But the snow muffled your voices
and I could not be sure.'

Mallory looked at him curiously. 'How come you're here, Andrea?'

'Wood,' Andrea explained. 'I was looking for firewood. I was
high up on Kostos at sunset when the snow lifted for a moment. I
could have sworn I saw an old hut in a gully not far from here – it
was dark and square against the snow. So I left –'

'You are right,' Louki interrupted. 'The hut of old Leri, the mad
one. Leri was a goatherd. We all warned him, but Leri would listen
and speak to no man, only to his goats. He died in his hut, in a
landslide.'

'It is an ill wind . . .' Andrea murmured. 'Old Leri will keep us
warm tonight.' He checked abruptly as the gully opened up at his
feet, then dropped quickly to the bottom, sure-footed as a mountain sheep. He whistled twice, a double high-pitched note, listening intently into the snow for the answering whistle, walked swiftly
up the gully. Casey Brown, gun lowered, met them at the entrance
to the cave and held back the canvas screen to let them pass inside.

The smoking tallow candle, guttering heavily to one side in the icy
draught, filled every corner of the cave with dark and flickering
shadows from its erratic flame. The candle itself was almost gone,
the dripping wick bending over tiredly till it touched the rock, and
Louki, snow-suit cast aside, was lighting another stump of candle
from the dying flame. For a moment, both candles flared up
together, and Mallory saw Louki clearly for the first time – a small,
compact figure in a dark-blue jacket black-braided at the seams and
flamboyantly frogged at the breast, the jacket tightly bound to his
body by the crimson *tsanta* or cummerbund, and, above, the
swarthy, smiling face, the magnificent moustache that he flaunted
like a banner. A Laughing Cavalier of a man, a miniature
d'Artagnan splendidly behung with weapons. And then Mallory's
gaze travelled up to the lined, liquid eyes, eyes dark and sad and
permanently tired, and his shock, a slow, uncomprehending shock,
had barely time to register before the stub of the candle had flared
up and died and Louki had sunk back into the shadows.

Stevens was stretched in a sleeping-bag, his breathing harsh and
shallow and quick. He had been awake when they had arrived but
had refused all food and drink, and turned away and drifted off into
an uneasy jerky sleep. He seemed to be suffering no pain at all
now: a bad sign, Mallory thought bleakly, the worst possible. He
wished Miller would return . . .

Casey Brown washed down the last few crumbs of bread with a
mouthful of wine, rose stiffly to his feet, pulled the screen aside and

peered out mournfully at the falling snow. He shuddered, let the canvas fall, lifted up his transmitter and shrugged into the shoulder straps, gathered up a coil of rope, a torch and a groundsheet. Mallory looked at his watch: it was fifteen minutes to midnight. The routine call from Cairo was almost due.

'Going to have another go, Casey? I wouldn't send a dog out on a night like this.'

'Neither would I,' Brown said morosely. 'But I think I'd better, sir. Reception is far better at night and I'm going to climb uphill a bit to get a clearance from that damned mountain there: I'd be spotted right away if I tried to do that in daylight.'

'Right you are, Casey. You know best.' Mallory looked at him curiously. 'What's all the extra gear for?'

'Putting the set under the groundsheet then getting below it myself with the torch,' Brown explained. 'And I'm pegging the rope here, going to pay it out on my way up. I'd like to be able to get back some time.'

'Good enough,' Mallory approved. 'Just watch it a bit higher up. This gully narrows and deepens into a regular ravine.'

'Don't you worry about me, sir,' Brown said firmly. 'Nothing's going to happen to Casey Brown.' A snow-laden gust of wind, the flap of the canvas and Brown was gone.

'Well, if Brown can do it . . .' Mallory was on his feet now, pulling his snow-smock over his head. 'Fuel, gentlemen – old Leri's hut. Who's for a midnight stroll?'

Andrea and Louki were on their feet together, but Mallory shook his head.

'One's enough. I think someone should stay to look after Stevens.'

'He's sound asleep,' Andrea murmured. 'He can come to no harm in the short time we are away.'

'I wasn't thinking of that. It's just that we can't take the chance of him falling into German hands. They'd make him talk, one way or another. It would be no fault of his – but they'd make him talk. It's too much of a risk.'

'Pouf!' Louki snapped his fingers. 'You worry about nothing, Major. There isn't a German within miles of here. You have my word.'

Mallory hesitated, then grinned. 'You're right. I'm getting the jumps.' He bent over Stevens, shook him gently. The boy stirred and moaned, opened his eyes slowly.

'We're going out for some firewood,' Mallory said. 'Back in a few minutes. You be OK?'

'Of course, sir. What can happen? Just leave a gun by my side – and blow out the candle.' He smiled. 'Be sure to call out before you come in!'

Mallory stooped, blew out the candle. For an instant the flame flared then died and every feature, every person in the cave was swallowed up in the thick darkness of a winter midnight. Abruptly Mallory turned on his heel and pushed out through the canvas into the drifting, windblown snow already filling up the floor of the gully, Andrea and Louki close behind.

It took them ten minutes to find the ruined hut of the old goatherd, another five for Andrea to wrench the door off its shattered hinges and smash it up to manageable lengths, along with the wood from the bunk and table, another ten to carry back with them to the rock-shelter as much wood as they could conveniently rope together and carry. The wind, blowing straight north off Kostos, was in their faces now – faces numbed with the chill, wet lash of the driving snow, and blowing almost at gale force: they were not sorry to reach the gully again, drop down gratefully between the sheltering walls.

Mallory called softly at the mouth of the cave. There was no reply, no movement from inside. He called again, listened intently as the silent seconds went by, turned his head and looked briefly at Andrea and Louki. Carefully, he laid his bundle of wood in the snow, pulled out his Colt and torch, eased aside the curtain, lamp switch and Colt safety-catch clicking as one.

The spotlight beam lit up the floor at the mouth of the cave, passed on, settled, wavered, probed into the farthest corner of the shelter, returned again to the middle of the cave and steadied there as if the torch were clamped in a vice. On the floor there was only a crumpled, empty sleeping-bag. Andy Stevens was gone.

NINE

Tuesday Night
0015–0200

'So I was wrong,' Andrea murmured. 'He wasn't asleep.'

'He certainly wasn't,' Mallory agreed grimly. 'He fooled me too – *and* he heard what I said.' His mouth twisted. 'He knows now why we're so anxious to look after him. He knows now that he was right when he spoke about a millstone. I should hate to feel the way he must be feeling right now.'

Andrea nodded. 'It is not difficult to guess why he has gone.'

Mallory looked quickly at his watch, pushed his way out of the cave.

'Twenty minutes – he can't have been gone more than twenty minutes. Probably a bit less to make sure we were well clear. He can only drag himself – fifty yards at the most. We'll find him in four minutes. Use your torches and take the hoods off – nobody will see us in this damn blizzard. Fan out uphill – I'll take the gully in the middle.'

'Uphill?' Louki's hand was on his arm, his voice puzzled. 'But his leg –'

'Uphill, I said,' Mallory broke in impatiently. 'Stevens has brains – and a damn sight more guts than he thinks we credit him with. He'll figure we'll think he's taken the easy way.' Mallory paused a moment then went on sombrely: 'Any dying man who drags himself out in this lot is going to do nothing the easy way. Come on!'

They found him in exactly three minutes. He must have suspected that Mallory wouldn't fall for the obvious, or he had heard them stumbling up the slope, for he had managed to burrow his way in behind the overhanging snowdrift that sealed off the space beneath a projecting ledge just above the rim of the gully. An almost perfect place of concealment, but his leg betrayed him: in the probing light of his torch Andrea's sharp eyes caught the tiny trickle of blood seeping darkly through the surface of the snow. He was already unconscious when they uncovered him, from cold or exhaustion or the agony of his shattered leg: probably from all three.

Back in the cave again, Mallory tried to pour some ouzo – the fiery, breath-catching local spirit – down Stevens's throat. He had a vague suspicion that this might be dangerous – or perhaps it was only dangerous in cases of shock, his memory was confused on that point – but it seemed better than nothing. Stevens gagged, spluttered and coughed most of it back up again, but some at least stayed down. With Andrea's help Mallory tightened the loosened splints on the leg, staunched the oozing blood, and spread below and above the boy every dry covering he could find in the cave. Then he sat back tiredly and fished out a cigarette from his water-proof case. There was nothing more he could do until Dusty Miller returned with Panayis from the village. He was pretty sure there was nothing that Dusty could do for Stevens either. There was nothing anybody could do for him.

Already Louki had a fire burning near the mouth of the cave, the old, tinder-dry wood blazing up in a fierce, crackling blaze with hardly a wisp of smoke. Almost at once its warmth began to spread throughout the cave, and the three men edged gratefully nearer. From half a dozen points in the roof, thin, steadily increasing streams of water from the melting snows above began to splash down on the gravelly floor beneath: with these and with the heat of the blaze, the ground was soon a quagmire. But, especially to Mallory and Andrea, these discomforts were a small price to pay for the privilege of being warm for the first time in over thirty hours. Mallory felt the glow seep through him like a benison, felt his entire body relax, his eyelids grow heavy and drowsy.

Back propped against the wall, he was just drifting off to sleep, still smoking that first cigarette, when there was a gust of wind, a sudden chilling flurry of snow and Brown was inside the cave, wearily slipping the transmitter straps from his shoulders. Lugubrious as ever, his tired eyes lit up momentarily at the sight of the fire. Blue-faced and shuddering with cold – no joke, Mallory thought grimly, squatting motionless for half an hour on that bleak and frozen hillside – he hunched down silently by the fire, dragged out the inevitable cigarette and gazed moodily into the flames, oblivious alike of the clouds of steam that almost immediately enveloped him, of the acrid smell of his singeing clothes. He looked utterly despondent. Mallory reached for a bottle, poured out some of the heated *retsina* – mainland wine heavily reinforced with resin – and passed it across to Brown.

'Chuck it straight down the hatch,' Mallory advised. 'That way you won't taste it.' He prodded the transmitter with his foot and looked up at Brown again. 'No dice this time either?'

'Raised them no bother, sir.' Brown grimaced at the sticky sweetness of the wine. 'Reception was first class – both here and in Cairo.'

'You got through!' Mallory sat up, leaned forward eagerly. 'And were they pleased to hear from their wandering boys tonight?'

'They didn't say. The first thing they told me was to shut up and stay that way.' Brown poked moodily at the fire with a steaming boot. 'Don't ask me how, sir, but they've been tipped off that enough equipment for two or three small monitoring stations has been sent here in the past fortnight.'

Mallory swore.

'Monitoring stations! That's damned handy, that is!' He thought briefly of the fugitive, nomad existence these same monitoring stations had compelled Andrea and himself to lead in the White Mountains of Crete. 'Dammit, Casey, on an island like this, the size of a soup plate, they can pin-point us with their eyes shut!'

'Aye, they can that, sir,' Brown nodded heavily.

'Have you heard anything of these stations, Louki?' Mallory asked.

'Nothing, Major, nothing.' Louki shrugged. 'I am afraid I do not even know what you are talking about.'

'I don't suppose so. Not that it matters – it's too late now. Let's have the rest of the good news, Casey.'

'That's about it, sir. No sending for me – by order. Restricted to code abbreviations – affirmative, negative, repetitive, wilco and such-like. Continuous sending only in emergency or when concealment's impossible anyway.'

'Like from the condemned cell in those ducky little dungeons in Navarone,' Mallory murmured. '"I died with my boots on, ma."'

'With all respects, sir, that's not funny,' Brown said morosely. 'Their invasion fleet – mainly caiques and E-boats – sailed this morning from the Piraeus,' he went on. 'About four o'clock this morning. Cairo expects they'll be holing up in the Cyclades somewhere tonight.'

'That's very clever of Cairo. Where the hell else could they hole up?' Mallory lit a fresh cigarette and looked bleakly into the fire. 'Anyway, it's nice to know they're on the way. That the lot, Casey?'

Brown nodded silently.

'Good enough, then. Thanks a lot for going out. Better turn in, catch up with some sleep while you can . . . Louki reckons we should be down in Margaritha before dawn, hole up there for the day – he's got some sort of abandoned well all lined up for us – and push on to the town of Navarone tomorrow night.'

'My God!' Brown moaned. 'Tonight a leaking cave. Tomorrow night an abandoned well – half-full of water probably. Where are we staying in Navarone, sir. The crypt in the local cemetery.'

'A singularly apt lodging, the way things are going,' Mallory said dryly. 'We'll hope for the best. We're leaving before five.' He watched Brown lie down beside Stevens and transferred his attention to Louki. The little man was seated on a box on the opposite side of the fire, occasionally turning a heavy stone to be wrapped in cloth and put to Stevens's numbed feet, and blissfully hugging the flames. By and by he became aware of Mallory's close scrutiny and looked up.

'You look worried, Major.' Louki seemed vexed. 'You look – what is the word? – concerned. You do not like my plan, no? I thought we had agreed –'

'I'm not worried about your plan,' Mallory said frankly. 'I'm not even worried, about you. It's that box you're sitting on. Enough HE in it to blow up a battleship – and you're only three feet from that fire. It's not just too healthy, Louki.'

Louki shifted uneasily on his seat, tugged at one end of his moustache.

'I have heard that you can throw this TNT into a fire and that it just burns up nicely, like a pine full of sap.'

'True enough,' Mallory acquiesced. 'You can also bend it, break it, file it, saw it, jump on it and hit it with a sledge-hammer, and all you'll get is the benefit of the exercise. But if it starts to sweat in a hot, humid atmosphere – and then the exudation crystallises. Oh, brother! And it's getting far too hot and sticky in this hole.'

'Outside with it!' Louki was on his feet, backing farther into the cave. 'Outside with it!' He hesitated. 'Unless the snow, the moisture –'

'You can also leave it immersed in salt water for ten years without doing it any harm,' Mallory interrupted didactically. 'But there are some primers there that might come to grief – not to mention that box of detonators beside Andrea. We'll just stick the lot outside, under a cape.'

'Pouf! Louki has a far better idea!' The little man was already slipping into his cloak. 'Old Leri's hut! The very place. Exactly! We can pick it up there whenever we want – and if you have to leave in a hurry you do not have to worry about it.' Before Mallory could protest, Louki had bent over the box lifted it with an effort, half-walked, half-staggered round the fire, making for the screen. He had hardly taken three steps when Andrea was by his side, had relieved him firmly of the box and tucked it under one arm.

'If you will permit me –'

'No, no!' Louki was affronted. 'I can manage easily. It is nothing.'

'I know, I know,' Andrea said pacifically. 'But these explosives – they must be carried a certain way. I have been trained,' he explained.

'So? I did not realise. Of course it must be as you say! I, then, will bring the detonators.' Honour satisfied, Louki thankfully gave up the argument, lifted the little box and scuttled out of the cave close on Andrea's heels.

Mallory looked at his watch. One o'clock exactly. Miller and Panayis should be back soon, he thought. The wind had passed its peak and the snow was almost gone: the going would be all that easier, but there would be tracks in the snow. Awkward, these tracks, but not fatal – they themselves would be gone before light, cutting straight downhill for the foot of the valley. The snow wouldn't lie there – and even if there were patches they could take to the stream that wound through the valley, leaving no trace behind.

The fire was sinking and the cold creeping in on them again. Mallory shivered in his still wet clothes, threw some more wood on the fire, watched it blaze up, and flood the cave with light. Brown, huddled on a groundsheet, was already asleep. Stevens, his back to him, was lying motionless, his breathing short and quick. God only knew how long the boy would stay alive: he was dying, Miller said, but 'dying' was a very indefinite term: when a man, a terribly injured, dying man, made up his mind not to die he became the toughest, most enduring creature on earth. Mallory had seen it happen before. But maybe Stevens didn't want to live. To live, to overcome these desperate injuries – that would be to prove himself to himself, and to others, and he was young enough, and sensitive enough and had been hurt and had suffered so much in the past that that could easily be the most important thing in the world to him: on the other hand, he knew what an appalling handicap he had become – he had heard Mallory say so; he knew, too, that Mallory's primary concern was not for his welfare but the fear that he would be captured, crack under pressure and tell everything – he had heard Mallory say so; and he knew that he had failed his friends. It was all very difficult, impossible to say how the balance of contending forces would work out eventually. Mallory shook his head, sighed, lit a fresh cigarette and moved closer to the fire.

Andrea and Louki returned less than five minutes later, and Miller and Panayis were almost at their heels. They could hear Miller coming some distance away, slipping, falling and swearing almost continuously as he struggled up the gully under a large and awkward load. He practically fell across the threshold of the cave and collapsed wearily by the fire. He gave the impression of a man who had been through a very great deal indeed. Mallory grinned sympathetically at him.

'Well, Dusty, how did it go? Hope Panayis here didn't slow you up too much.'

Miller didn't seem to hear him. He was gazing incredulously at the fire, lantern jaw drooping open as its significance slowly dawned on him.

'Hell's teeth! Would you look at that!' He swore bitterly. 'Here I spend half the gawddamned night climbing up a gawddamned mountain with a stove and enough kerosene to bath a bloody elephant. And what do I find?' He took a deep breath to tell them what he found, then subsided into a strangled, seething silence.

'A man your age should watch his blood pressure,' Mallory advised him. 'How did the rest of it go?'

'Okay, I guess.' Miller had a mug of ouzo in his hand and was beginning to brighten up again. 'We got the beddin', the medicine kit –'

'If you'll give me the bedding I will get our young friend into it now,' Andrea interrupted.

'And food?' Mallory asked.

'Yeah. We got the grub, boss. Stacks of it. This guy Panayis is a wonder. Bread, wine, goat-cheese, garlic sausages, rice – everything.'

'Rice?' It was Mallory's turn to be incredulous. 'But you can't get the stuff in the islands nowadays, Dusty.'

'Panayis can.' Miller was enjoying himself hugely now. 'He got it from the German commandant's kitchen. Guy by the name of Skoda.'

'The German commandant's – you're joking!'

'So help me, boss, that's Gospel truth.' Miller drained half the ouzo at a gulp and expelled his breath in a long, gusty sigh of satisfaction. 'Little ol' Miller hangs around the back door, knees knockin' like Carmen Miranda's castanets, ready for a smart take off in any direction while Junior here goes in and cracks the joint. Back home in the States he'd make a fortune as a cat-burglar. Comes back in about ten minutes, luggin' that damned suitcase there.' Miller indicated it with a casual wave of his hand. 'Not only cleans out the commandant's pantry, but also borrows his satchel to carry the stuff in. I tell you, boss, associatin' with this character gives me heart attacks.'

'But – but how about guards, about sentries?'

'Taken the night off, I guess, boss. Old Panayis is like a clam – never says a word, and even then I can't understand him. My guess is that everybody's out lookin' for us.'

'There and back and you didn't meet a soul.' Mallory filled him with a mug of wine. 'Nice going, Dusty.'

'Panayis's doin', not mine. I just tagged along. Besides, we did run into a couple of Panayis's pals – he hunted them up rather. Musta given him the tip-off about somethin'. He was hoppin' with excitement just afterwards, tried to tell me all about it.' Miller shrugged his shoulders sadly. 'We weren't operatin' on the same wave-length, boss.'

Mallory nodded across the cave. Louki and Panayis were close together, Louki doing all the listening, while Panayis talked rapidly in a low voice, gesticulating with both hands.

'He's still pretty worked up about something,' Mallory said thoughtfully. He raised his voice. 'What's the matter, Louki?'

'Matter enough, Major.' Louki tugged ferociously at the end of his moustache. 'We will have to be leaving soon – Panayis wants to go right away. He has heard that the German garrison is going to make a house-to-house check in our village during the night – about four o'clock, Panayis was told.'

'Not a routine check, I take it?' Mallory asked.

'This has not happened for many months. They must think that you have slipped their patrols and are hiding in the village.' Louki chuckled. 'If you ask me, I don't think they know *what* to think. It is nothing to you, of course. You will not be there – and even if you were they would not find you: and it will make it all the safer for you to come to Margaritha afterwards. But Panayis and I – we must not be found out of our beds. Things would go hard with us.'

'Of course, of course. We must take no risks. But there is plenty of time. You will go down in an hour. But first, the fortress.' He dug into his breast pocket, brought out the map Eugene Vlachos had drawn for him, turned to Panayis and slipped easily into the island Greek. 'Come, Panayis. I hear you know the fortress as Louki here knows his own vegetable patch. I already know much, but I want you to tell me everything about it – the layout, guns, magazines, power rooms, barracks, sentries, guard routine, exits, alarm systems, even where the shadows are deep and the others less deep – just everything. No matter how tiny and insignificant the details may seem to you, nevertheless you must tell me. If a door opens outwards instead of inwards, you must tell me: that could save a thousand lives.'

'And how does the Major mean to get inside?' Louki asked.

'I don't know yet. I cannot decide until I have seen the fortress.' Mallory was aware of Andrea looking sharply at him, then looking away. They had made their plans on the MTB for entering the fortress. But it was the keystone upon which everything depended, and Mallory felt that this knowledge should be confined to the fewest number possible.

For almost half an hour Mallory and the three Greeks huddled over the chart in the light of the flames, Mallory checking on what he had been told, meticulously pencilling in all the fresh information that Panayis had to give him – and Panayis had a very great deal to tell. It seemed almost impossible that a man could have assimilated so much in two brief visits to the fortress – and clandestine visits in the darkness, at that. He had an incredible eye and capacity for detail; and it was a burning hatred of the Germans, Mallory felt certain, that had imprinted these details on an all but photographic memory. Mallory could feel his hopes rising with every second that passed.

Casey Brown was awake again. Tired though he was, the babble of voices had cut through an uneasy sleep. He crossed over to where Andy Stevens, half-awake now, lay propped against the wall, talking rationally at times, incoherently at others. There was nothing for him to do there, Brown saw: Miller, cleaning, dusting and rebandaging the wounds had had all the help he needed – and very efficient help at that – from Andrea. He moved over to the mouth of the cave, listened blankly to the four men talking in

Greek, moved out past the screen for a breath of the cold, clean night air. With seven people inside the cave and the fire burning continuously, the lack of almost all ventilation had made it uncomfortably warm.

He was back in the cave in thirty seconds, drawing the screen tightly shut behind him.

'Quiet, everybody!' he whispered softly. He gestured behind him. 'There's something moving out there, down the slope a bit. I heard it twice, sir.'

Panayis swore softly, twisted to his feet like a wild cat. A footlong, two-edged throwing knife gleamed evilly in his hand and he had vanished through the canvas screen before anyone could speak. Andrea made to follow him, but Mallory stretched out his hand.

'Stay where you are, Andrea. Our friend Panayis is just that little bit too precipitate,' he said softly. 'There may be nothing – or it might be some diversionary move . . . Oh, damn!' Stevens had just started babbling to himself in a loud voice. 'He would start talking now. Can't you do something . . .'

But Andrea was already bent over the sick boy, holding his hand in his own, smoothing the hot forehead and hair with his free hand and talking to him soothingly, softly, continuously. At first he paid no attention, kept on talking in a rambling, inconsequential fashion about nothing in particular, gradually, however, the hypnotic effect of the stroking hand, the gentle caressing murmur took effect, and the babbling died away to a barely audible muttering, ceased altogether. Suddenly his eyes opened and he was awake and quite rational.

'What is it, Andrea? Why are you –?'

'Shh!' Mallory held up his hand. 'I can hear someone –'

'It's Panayis, sir.' Brown had his eye at a crack in the curtain. 'Just moving up the gully.'

Seconds later, Panayis was inside the cave, squatting down by the fire. He looked thoroughly disgusted.

'There is no one there,' he reported. 'Some goats I saw, down the hill, but that was all.' Mallory translated to the others.

'Didn't sound like goats to me,' Brown said doggedly. 'Different kind of sound altogether.'

'I will take a look,' Andrea volunteered. 'Just to make sure. But I do not think the dark one would make a mistake.' Before Mallory could say anything he was gone, as quickly and silently as Panayis.

He was back in three minutes, shaking his head. 'Panayis is right. There is no one. I did not even see the goats.'

'And that's what it must have been, Casey,' Mallory said. 'Still, I don't like it. Snow almost stopped, wind dropping and the valley probably swarming with German patrols – I think it's time you two were away. For God's sake, be careful. If anyone tries to stop you, shoot to kill. They'll blame it on us anyway.'

'Shoot to kill!' Louki laughed dryly. 'Unnecessary advice, Major, when the dark one is with us. He never shoots any other way.'

'Right, away you go. Damned sorry you've got yourselves mixed up in all this – but now that you are, a thousand thanks for all you've done. See you at half-past six.'

'Half-past six,' Louki echoed. 'The olive grove on the bank of the stream, south of the village. We will be waiting there.'

Two minutes later they were lost to sight and sound and all was still inside the cave again, except for the faint crackling of the embers of the dying fire. Brown had moved out on guard, and Stevens had already fallen into a restless, pain-filled sleep. Miller bent over him for a moment or two, then moved softly across the cave to Mallory. His right hand held a crumpled heap of blood-stained bandages. He held them out towards Mallory.

'Take a sniff at that, boss,' he asked quietly. 'Easy does it.'

Mallory bent forward, drew away sharply, his nose wrinkled in immediate disgust.

'Good lord, Dusty! That's vile!' He paused, paused in sure, sick certainty. He knew the answer before he spoke. 'What on earth is it?'

'Gangrene.' Miller sat down heavily by his side, threw the bandages into the fire. All at once he sounded tired, defeated. 'Gas gangrene. Spreadin' like a forest fire – and he would have died anyway. I'm just wastin' my time.'

TEN

Tuesday Night
0400–0600

The Germans took them just after four o'clock in the morning, while they were still asleep. Bonetired and deep-drugged with this sleep as they were, they had no chance, not the slightest hope of offering any resistance. The conception, timing and execution of the coup were immaculate. Surprise was complete.

Andrea was the first awake. Some alien whisper of sound had reached deep down to that part of him that never slept, and he twisted round and elbowed himself off the ground with the same noiseless speed as his hand reached out for his ready-cocked and loaded Mauser. But the white beam of the powerful torch lancing through the blackness of the cave had blinded him, frozen his stretching hand even before the clipped bite of command from the man who held the torch.

'Still! All of you!' Faultless English, with barely a trace of accent, and the voice glacial in its menace. 'You move, and you die!' Another torch switched on, a third, and the cave was flooded with light. Wide awake, now, and motionless Mallory squinted painfully into the dazzling beams: in the back-wash of reflected light, he could just discern the vague, formless shapes crouched in the mouth of the cave, bent over the dulled barrels of automatic rifles.

'Hands clasped above the heads and backs to the wall!' A certainty, an assured competence in the voice that made for instant obedience. 'Take a good look at them, Sergeant.' Almost conversational now, the tone, but neither torch nor gun barrel had wavered a fraction. 'No shadow of expression in their faces, not even a flicker of the eyes. Dangerous men, Sergeant. The English choose their killers well!'

Mallory felt the grey bitterness of defeat wash through him in an almost tangible wave, he could taste the sourness of it in the back of his mouth. For a brief, heart-sickening second he allowed himself to think of what must now inevitably happen and as soon as the thought had come he thrust it savagely away. Everything, every action, every thought, every breath must be on the present. Hope was gone, but not irrecoverably gone: not so long as Andrea lived. He wondered if Casey Brown had seen or heard them coming, and what had happened to him: he made to ask, checked himself just in time. Maybe he was still at large.

'How did you manage to find us?' Mallory asked quietly.

'Only fools burn juniper wood,' the officer said contemptuously. 'We have been on Kostos all day and most of the night. A dead man could have smelt it.'

'On Kostos?' Miller shook his head. 'How could –?'

'Enough!' The officer turned to someone behind him. 'Tear down that screen,' he ordered in German, 'and keep us covered on either side.' He looked back into the cave, gestured almost imperceptibly with his torch. 'All right, you three. Outside – and you had better be careful. Please believe me that my men are praying for an excuse to shoot you down, you murdering swine!' The venomous hatred in his voice carried utter conviction.

Slowly, hands still clasped above their heads, the three men stumbled to their feet. Mallory had taken only one step when the whip-lash of the German's voice brought him up short.

'Stop!' He stabbed the beam of his torch down at the unconscious Stevens, gestured abruptly at Andrea. 'One side, you! Who is this?'

'You need not fear from him,' Mallory said quietly. 'He is one of us but he is terribly injured. He is dying.'

'We will see,' the officer said tightly. 'Move to the back of the cave!' He waited until the three men had stepped over Stevens, changed his automatic rifle for a pistol, dropped to his knees and advanced slowly, torch in one hand, gun in the other, well below the line of fire of the two soldiers who advanced unbidden at his heels. There was an inevitability, a cold professionalism about it all that made Mallory's heart sink.

Abruptly the officer reached out his gun-hand, tore the covers off the boy. A shuddering tremor shook the whole body, his head rolled from side to side as he moaned in unconscious agony. The officer bent quickly over him, the hard, clean lines of the face, the fair hair beneath the hood high-lit in the beam of his own torch. A quick look at Stevens's pain-twisted, emaciated features, a glance at the shattered leg, a brief, distasteful wrinkling of the nose as he caught the foul stench of the gangrene, and he had hunched back on his heels, gently replacing the covers over the sick boy.

'You speak the truth,' he said softly. 'We are not barbarians. I have no quarrel with a dying man. Leave him there.' He rose to his feet, walked slowly backwards. 'The rest of you outside.'

The snow had stopped altogether, Mallory saw, and stars were beginning to twinkle in the clearing sky. The wind, too, had fallen away and was perceptibly warmer. Most of the snow would be gone by midday, Mallory guessed.

Carelessly, incuriously, he looked around him. There was no sign of Casey Brown. Inevitably Mallory's hopes began to rise. Petty Officer Brown's recommendation for this operation had come from the very top. Two rows of ribbons to which he was entitled but never wore bespoke his gallantry, he had a formidable reputation as a guerrilla fighter – and he had had an automatic rifle in his hand. If he were somewhere out there . . . Almost as if he had divined his hopes, the German smashed them at a word.

'You wonder where your sentry is, perhaps?' he asked mockingly. 'Never fear, Englishman, he is not far from here, asleep at his post. Very sound asleep, I'm afraid.'

'You've killed him?' Mallory's hands clenched until his palms ached.

The other shrugged his shoulder in vast indifference.

'I really couldn't say. It was all too easy. One of my men lay in the gully and moaned. A masterly performance – really pitiable – he almost had me convinced. Like a fool your man came to investigate. I had another man waiting above, the barrel of his rifle in his hand. A very effective club, I assure you . . .'

Slowly Mallory unclenched his fists and stared bleakly down the gully. Of course Casey would fall for that, he was bound to after what had happened earlier in the night. He wasn't going to make a fool of himself again, cry 'wolf' twice in succession: inevitably, he had gone to check first. Suddenly the thought occurred to Mallory that maybe Casey Brown *had* heard something earlier on, but the thought vanished as soon as it had come. Panayis did not look like the man to make a mistake: and Andrea never made a mistake; Mallory turned back to the officer again.

'Well, where do we go from here?'

'Margaritha, and very shortly. But one thing first.' The German, his own height to an inch, stood squarely in front of him, levelled revolver at waist height, switched-off torch dangling loosely from his right hand. 'Just a little thing, Englishman. Where are the explosives?' He almost spat the words out.

'Explosives?' Mallory furrowed his brows in perplexity. 'What explosives?' he asked blankly, then staggered and fell to the ground as the heavy torch swept round in a vicious half-circle, caught him flush on the side of the face. Dizzily he shook his head and climbed slowly to his feet again.

'The explosives.' The torch was balanced in the hand again, the voice silky and gentle. 'I asked you where they were.'

'I don't know what you are talking about.' Mallory spat out a broken tooth, wiped some blood off his smashed lips. 'Is this the way the Germans treat their prisoners?' he asked contemptuously.

'Shut up!'

Again the torch lashed out. Mallory was waiting for it, rode the blow as best he could: even so the torch caught him heavily high up on the cheek-bone, just below the temple, stunning him with its jarring impact. Seconds passed, then he pushed himself slowly off the snow, the whole side of his face afire with agony, his vision blurred and unfocused.

'We fight a clean war!' The officer was breathing heavily, in barely controlled fury. 'We fight by the Geneva Conventions. But these are for soldiers, not for murdering spies –'

'We are no spies!' Mallory interrupted. He felt as if his head was coming apart.

'Then where are your uniforms?' the officer demanded. 'Spies, I say – murdering spies who stab in the back and cut men's throats!' The voice was trembling with anger. Mallory was at a loss – nothing spurious about this indignation.

'Cut men's throats?' He shook his head in bewilderment. 'What the hell are you talking about?'

'My own batman. A harmless messenger, a boy only – and he wasn't even armed. We found him only an hour ago. Ach, I waste my time!' He broke off as he turned to watch two men coming up the gully. Mallory stood motionless for a moment, cursing the ill luck that had led the dead man across the path of Panayis – it could have been no one else – then turned to see what had caught the officer's attention. He focused his aching eyes with difficulty, looked at the bent figure struggling up the slope, urged on by the ungentle prodding of a bayoneted rifle. Mallory let go a long, silent breath of relief. The left side of Brown's face was caked with blood from a gash above the temple, but he was otherwise unharmed.

'Right! Sit down in the snow, all of you!' He gestured to several of his men. 'Bind their hands!'

'You are going to shoot us now, perhaps?' Mallory asked quietly. It was suddenly, desperately urgent that he should know: there was nothing they could do but die, but at least they could die on their feet, fighting; but if they weren't to die just yet, almost any later opportunity for resistance would be less suicidal than this.

'Not yet, unfortunately. My section commander in Margaritha, Hauptmann Skoda, wishes to see you first – maybe it would be better for you if I *did* shoot you now. Then the Herr Commandant in Navarone – Officer Commanding of the whole island.' The German smiled thinly. 'But only a postponement, Englishman. You will be kicking your heels before the sun sets. We have a short way with spies in Navarone.'

'But, sir! Captain!' Hands raised in appeal, Andrea took a step forward, brought up short as two rifle muzzles ground into his chest.

'Not Captain – Lieutenant,' the officer corrected him. 'Oberleutnant Turzig, at your service. What is it you want, fat one?' he asked contemptuously.

'Spies! You said spies! I am no spy!' The words rushed and tumbled over one another, as if he could not get them out fast enough. 'Before God, I am no spy! I am not one of them.' The eyes were wide and staring, the mouth working soundlessly between the gasped-out sentences. 'I am only a Greek, a poor Greek. They forced me to come along as an interpreter. I swear it, Lieutenant Turzig, I swear it!'

'You yellow bastard!' Miller ground out viciously, then grunted in agony as a rifle butt drove into the small of his back, just above the kidney. He stumbled, fell forward on his hands and knees, realised even as he fell that Andrea was only playing a part, that Mallory had only to speak half a dozen words in Greek to expose Andrea's lie. Miller twisted on his side in the snow, shook his fist weakly and hoped that the contorted pain on his face might be mistaken for fury. 'You two-faced, double-crossing dago! You gawddamned swine, I'll get you . . .' There was a hollow, sickening thud and Miller collapsed in the snow: the heavy ski-boot had caught him just behind the ear.

Mallory said nothing. He did not even glance at Miller. Fists balled helplessly at his sides and mouth compressed, he glared steadily at Andrea through narrowed slits of eyes. He knew the lieutenant was watching him, felt he must back Andrea up all the way. What Andrea intended he could not even begin to guess – but he would back him to the end of the world.

'So!' Turzig murmured thoughtfully. 'Thieves fall out, eh?' Mallory thought he detected the faintest overtones of doubt, of hesitancy, in his voice, but the lieutenant was taking no chances. 'No matter, fat one. You have cast your lot with these assassins. What is it the English say? "You have made your bed, you must lie on it."' He looked at Andrea's vast bulk dispassionately. 'We may need to strengthen a special gallows for you.'

'No, no, no!' Andrea's voice rose sharply, fearfully, on the last word. 'It is true what I tell you! I am not one of them, Lieutenant Turzig, before God I am not one of them!' He wrung his hands in distress, his great moonface contorted in anguish. 'Why must I die for no fault of my own? I didn't want to come. I am no fighting man, Lieutenant Turzig!'

'I can see that,' Turzig said dryly. 'A monstrous deal of skin to cover a quivering jelly-bag your size – and every inch of it precious to you.' He looked at Mallory, and at Miller, still lying face down in the snow. 'I cannot congratulate your friends on their choice of companion.'

'I can tell you everything, Lieutenant, I can tell you everything!' Andrea pressed forward excitedly, eager to consolidate his advantage, to reinforce the beginnings of doubt. 'I am no friend of the Allies – I will prove it to you – and then perhaps –'

'You damned Judas!' Mallory made to fling himself forward, but two burly soldiers caught him and pinioned his arms from behind. He struggled briefly, then relaxed, looked balefully at Andrea. 'If you dare to open your mouth, I promise you you'll never live to –'

'Be quiet!' Turzig's voice was very cold. 'I have had enough of recriminations, of cheap melodrama. Another word and you join your friend in the snow there.' He looked at him a moment in silence, then swung back to Andrea. 'I promise nothing. I will hear what you have to say.' He made no attempt to disguise the repugnance in his voice.

'You must judge for yourself.' A nice mixture of relief, earnestness and the dawn of hope, of returning confidence. Andrea paused a minute and gestured dramatically at Mallory, Miller and

Brown. 'These are no ordinary soldiers – they are Jellicoe's men, of the Special Boat Service!'

'Tell me something I couldn't have guessed myself,' Turzig growled. 'The English Earl has been a thorn in our flesh these many months past. If that is all you have to tell me, fat one –'

'Wait!' Andrea held up his hand. 'They are still no ordinary men but a specially picked force – an assault unit, they call themselves – flown last Sunday night from Alexandria to Castelrosso. They left that same night from Castelrosso in a motor-boat.'

'A torpedo boat,' Turzig nodded. 'So much we know already. Go on.'

'You know already! But how –?'

'Never mind how. Hurry up!'

'Of course, Lieutenant, of course.' Not a twitch in his face betrayed Andrea's relief. This had been the only dangerous point in his story. Nicolai, of course, had warned the Germans, but never thought it worth while mentioning the presence of a giant Greek in the party. No reason, of course, why he should have selected him for special mention – but if he had done, it would have been the end.

'The torpedo boat landed them somewhere in the islands, north of Rhodes. I do not know where. There they stole a caique, sailed it up through Turkish waters, met a big German patrol boat – and sunk it.' Andrea paused for effect. 'I was less than half a mile away at the time in my fishing boat.'

Turzig leaned forward. 'How did they manage to sink so big a boat?' Strangely, he didn't doubt that it had been sunk.

'They pretended to be harmless fishermen like myself. I had just been stopped, investigated and cleared,' Andrea said virtuously. 'Anyway, your patrol boat came alongside this old caique. Close alongside. Suddenly there were guns firing on both sides, two boxes went flying through the air – into the engine-room of your boat, I think. Pouf!' Andrea threw up his hands dramatically. 'That was the end of that!'

'We wondered . . .' Turzig said softly. 'Well, go on.'

'You wondered what, Lieutenant?' Turzig's eyes narrowed and Andrea hurried on.

'Their interpreter had been killed in the fight. They tricked me into speaking English – I spent many years in Cyprus – kidnapped me, let my sons sail the boat –'

'Why should they want an interpreter?' Turzig demanded suspiciously. 'There are many British officers who speak Greek.'

'I am coming to that,' Andrea said impatiently. 'How in God's name do you expect me to finish my story if you keep interrupting all the time? Where was I? Ah, yes. They forced me to come along, and their engine broke down. I don't know what happened – I was kept below. I think we were in a creek somewhere, repairing the engine, and then there was a wild bout of drinking – you will not believe this, Lieutenant Turzig, that men on so desperate a mission should get drunk – and then we sailed again.'

'On the contrary, I do believe you.' Turzig was nodding his head slowly, as if in secret understanding. 'I believe you indeed.'

'You do?' Andrea contrived to look disappointed. 'Well, we ran into a fearful storm, wrecked the boat on the south cliff of this island and climbed –'

'Stop!' Turzig had drawn back sharply, suspicion flaring in his eyes. 'Almost I believed you! I believed you because we know more than you think, and so far you have told the truth. But not now. You are clever, fat one, but not so clever as you think. One thing you have forgotten – or maybe you do not know. We are of the *Württembergische Gebirgsbataillon* – we *know* mountains, my friend, better than any troops in the world. I myself am a Prussian, but I have climbed everything worth climbing in the Alps and Transylvania – and I tell you that the south cliff cannot be climbed. It is impossible!'

'Impossible perhaps for you.' Andrea shook his head sadly. 'These cursed Allies will beat you yet. They are clever, Lieutenant Turzig, damnably clever!'

'Explain yourself,' Turzig ordered curtly.

'Just this. They knew men thought the south cliff could not be climbed. So they determined to climb it. You would never dream that this could be done, that an expedition could land on Navarone that way. But the Allies took a gamble, found a man to lead the expedition. He could not speak Greek, but that did not matter, for what they wanted was a man who could climb – and so they picked the greatest rock-climber in the world today.' Andrea paused for effect, flung out his arm dramatically. 'And this is the man they picked, Lieutenant Turzig! You are a mountaineer yourself and you are bound to know him. His name is Mallory – Keith Mallory of New Zealand!'

There was a sharp exclamation, the click of a switch, and Turzig had taken a couple of steps forward, thrust the torch almost into Mallory's eyes. For almost ten seconds he stared into the New

Zealander's averted, screwed-up face, then slowly lowered his arm, the harsh spotlight limning a dazzling white circle in the snow at his feet. Once, twice, half a dozen times Turzig nodded his head in slow understanding.

'Of course!' he murmured. 'Mallory – Keith Mallory! Of course I know him. There's not a man in my *Abteilung* but has heard of Keith Mallory.' He shook his head. 'I should have known him, I should have known him at once.' He stood for some time with his head bent, aimlessly screwing the toe of his right boot into the soft snow, then looked up abruptly. 'Before the war, even during it, I would have been proud to have known you, glad to have met you. But not here, not now. Not any more. I wish to God they had sent someone else.' He hesitated, made to carry on, then changed his mind, turned wearily to Andrea. 'My apologies, fat one. Indeed you speak the truth. Go on.'

'Certainly!' Andrea's round moon face was one vast smirk of satisfaction. 'We climbed the cliff as I said – although the boy in the cave there was badly hurt – and silenced the guard. Mallory killed him,' Andrea added unblushingly. 'It was a fair fight. We spent most of the night crossing the divide and found this cave before dawn. We were almost dead with hunger and cold. We have been here since.'

'And nothing has happened since?'

'On the contrary.' Andrea seemed to be enjoying himself hugely, revelling in being the focus of attention. 'Two people came up to see us. Who they were I do not know – they kept their faces hidden all the time – nor do I know where they came from.'

'It is as well that you admitted that,' Turzig said grimly. 'I knew someone had been here. I recognised the stove – it belongs to Hauptmann Skoda!'

'Indeed?' Andrea raised his eyebrows in polite surprise. 'I did not know. Well, they talked for some time and –'

'Did you manage to overhear anything they were talking about?' Turzig interrupted. The question came so naturally, so spontaneously, that Mallory held his breath. It was beautifully done. Andrea would walk into it – he couldn't help it. But Andrea was a man inspired that night.

'Overhear them!' Andrea clamped his lips shut in sorely-tried forbearance, gazed heavenwards in exasperated appeal. 'Lieutenant Turzig, how often must I tell you that I am the interpreter? They *could* only talk through me. Of course I know what they were talking about. They are going to blow up the big guns in the harbour.'

'I didn't think they had come here for their health!' Turzig said acidly.

'Ah, but you don't know that they have plans of the fortress. You don't know that Kheros is to be invaded on Saturday morning. You don't know that they are in radio contact with Cairo all the time. You don't know that destroyers of the British Navy are coming through the Maidos Straits on Friday night as soon as the big guns have been silenced. You don't know –'

'Enough!' Turzig clapped his hands together, his face alight with excitement. 'The Royal Navy, eh? Wonderful, wonderful! *That* is what we want to hear. But enough! Keep it for Hauptmann Skoda and the Kommandant in the fortress. We must be off. But first – one more thing. The explosives – where are they?'

'Alas, Lieutenant Turzig, I do not know. They took them out and hid them – some talk about the cave being too hot.' He waved a hand towards the western col, in the diametrically opposite direction to Leri's hut. 'That way, I think. But I cannot be sure, for they would not tell me.' He looked bitterly at Mallory. 'These Britishers are all the same. They trust nobody.'

'Heaven only knows that I don't blame them for that!' Turzig said feelingly. He looked at Andrea in disgust. 'More than ever I would like to see you dangling from the highest scaffold in Navarone. But Herr Kommandant in the town is a kindly man and rewards informers. You may yet live to betray some more comrades.'

'Thank you, thank you, thank you! I knew you were fair and just. I promise you, Lieutenant Turzig –'

'Shut up!' Turzig said contemptuously. He switched into German. 'Sergeant, have these men bound. And don't forget the fat one! Later we can untie him, and he can carry the sick man back to the post. Leave a man on guard. The rest of you come with me – we must find those explosives.'

'Could we not make one of them tell us, sir?' the sergeant ventured.

'The only man who would tell us, can't. He's already told us all he knows. As for the rest – well, I was mistaken about them, Sergeant.' He turned to Mallory, inclined his head briefly, spoke in English. 'An error of judgment, Herr Mallory. We are all very tired. I am almost sorry I struck you.' He wheeled abruptly, climbed swiftly up the bank. Two minutes later only a solitary soldier was left on guard.

*   *   *

For the tenth time Mallory shifted his position uncomfortably, strained at the cord that bound his hands together behind his back, for the tenth time recognised the futility of both these actions. No matter how he twisted and turned, the wet snow soaked icily through his clothes until he was chilled to the bone and shaking continually with the cold; and the man who had tied these knots had known his job all too well. Mallory wondered irritably if Turzig and his men meant to spend all night searching for the explosives: they had been gone for more than half an hour already.

He relaxed, lay back on his side in the cushioning snow of the gully bank, and looked thoughtfully at Andrea who was sitting upright just in front of him. He had watched Andrea, with bowed head and hunched and lifting shoulders, making one single, titanic effort to free himself seconds after the guard had gestured to them to sit down, had seen the cords bite and gouge until they had almost disappeared in his flesh, the fractional slump of his shoulders as he gave up. Since then the giant Greek had sat quite still and contented himself with scowling at the sentry in the injured fashion of one who has been grievously wronged. That solitary test of the strength of his bonds had been enough. Oberleutnant Turzig had keen eyes, and swollen, chafed and bleeding wrists would have accorded ill with the character Andrea had created for himself.

A masterly creation, Mallory mused, all the more remarkable for its spontaneity, its improvisation. Andrea had told so much of the truth, so much that was verifiable or could be verified, that belief in the rest of his story followed almost automatically. And at the same time he had told Turzig nothing of importance, nothing the Germans could not have found out for themselves – except the proposed evacuation of Kheros by the Navy. Wryly Mallory remembered his dismay, his shocked unbelief when he heard Andrea telling of it – but Andrea had been far ahead of him. There was a fair chance that the Germans might have guessed anyway – they would reason, perhaps, that an assault by the British on the guns of Navarone at the same time as the German assault on Kheros would be just that little bit too coincidental: again, escape for them all quite clearly depended upon how thoroughly Andrea managed to convince his captors that he was all he claimed, and the relative freedom of action that he could thereby gain – and there was no doubt at all that it was the news of the proposed evacuation that had tipped the scales with Turzig: and the fact that

Andrea had given Saturday as the invasion date would only carry all the more weight, as that had been Jensen's original date – obviously false information fed to his agents by German counter-intelligence, who had known it impossible to conceal the invasion preparations themselves; and finally, if Andrea hadn't told Turzig of the destroyers, he might have failed to carry conviction, they might all yet finish on the waiting gallows in the fortress, the guns would remain intact and destroy the naval ships anyway.

It was all very complicated, too complicated for the state his head was in. Mallory sighed and looked away from Andrea towards the other two. Brown and a now conscious Miller were both sitting upright, hands bound behind their backs, staring down into the snow, occasionally shaking muzzy heads from side to side. Mallory could appreciate all too easily how they felt – the whole right-hand side of his face ached cruelly, continuously. Nothing but aching, broken heads everywhere, Mallory thought bitterly. He wondered how Andy Stevens was feeling, glanced idly past the sentry towards the dark mouth of the cave, stiffened in sudden, almost uncomprehending shock.

Slowly, with an infinitely careful carelessness, he let his eyes wander away from the cave, let them light indifferently on the sentry who sat on Brown's transmitter, hunched watchfully over the Schmeisser cradled on his knees, finger crooked on the trigger. Pray God he doesn't turn round, Mallory said to himself over and over again, pray God he doesn't turn round. Let him sit like that just for a little while longer, only a little while longer . . . In spite of himself, Mallory felt his gaze shifting, being dragged back again towards that cave-mouth.

Andy Stevens was coming out of the cave. Even in the dim starlight every movement was terribly plain as he inched forward agonisingly on chest and belly, dragging his shattered leg behind him. He was placing his hands beneath his shoulders, levering himself upwards and forwards while his head dropped below his shoulders with pain and the exhaustion of the effort, lowering himself slowly on the soft and sodden snow, then repeating the same heart-sapping process over and over again. Exhausted and pain-filled as the boy might be, Mallory thought, his mind was still working: he had a white sheet over his shoulders and back as camouflage against the snow, and he carried a climbing spike in his right hand. He must have heard at least some of Turzig's conversation: there were two or three guns in the cave, he could easily have shot the guard without coming out at all – but he must have known that the sound of a shot would have brought the Germans running, had them back at the cave long before he could have crawled across the gully, far less cut loose any of his friends.

Five yards Stevens had to go, Mallory estimated, five yards at the most. Deep down in the gully where they were, the south wind passed them by, was no more than a muted whisper in the night; that apart, there was no sound at all, nothing but their own breathing, the occasional stirring as someone stretched a cramped or frozen leg. He's bound to hear him if he comes any closer, Mallory thought desperately, even in that soft snow he's bound to hear him.

Mallory bent his head, began to cough loudly, almost continuously. The sentry looked at him, in surprise first, then in irritation as the coughing continued.

'Be quiet!' the sentry ordered in German. 'Stop that coughing at once!'

'*Hüsten? Hüsten?* Coughing, is it? I can't help it,' Mallory protested in English. He coughed again, louder, more persistently than before. 'It is your Oberleutnant's fault,' he gasped. 'He has knocked out some of my teeth.' Mallory broke into a fresh paroxysm of coughing, recovering himself with an effort. 'Is it my fault that I'm choking on my own blood?' he demanded.

Stevens was less than ten feet away now, but his tiny reserves of strength were almost gone. He could no longer raise himself to the full stretch of his arms, was advancing only a few pitiful inches at a time. At length he stopped altogether, lay still for half a minute. Mallory thought he had lost consciousness, but by and by he raised himself up again, to the full stretch this time, had just begun to pivot himself forward when he collapsed, fell heavily in the snow. Mallory began to cough again, but he was too late. The sentry leapt off his box and whirled round all in one movement, the evil mouth of the Schmeisser lined up on the body almost at his feet. Then he relaxed as he realised who it was, lowered the barrel of his gun.

'So!' he said softly. 'The fledgling has left its nest. Poor little fledgling!' Mallory winced as he saw the back-swing of the gun ready to smash down on Stevens's defenceless head, but the sentry was a kindly enough man, his reaction had been purely automatic. He arrested the swinging butt inches above the tortured face, bent down and almost gently removed the spike from the feebly threatening hand, sent it spinning over the edge of the gully. Then he lifted

Stevens carefully by the shoulders, slid in the bunched-up sheet as pillow for the unconscious head against the bitter cold of the snow, shook his head wonderingly, sadly, went back to his seat on the ammunition box.

Hauptmann Skoda was a small, thin man in his late thirties, neat, dapper, debonair and wholly evil. There was something innately evil about the long, corded neck that stretched up scrawnily above his padded shoulders, something repellent about the incongruously small bullet head perched above. When the thin, bloodless lips parted in a smile, which was often, they revealed a perfect set of teeth: far from lighting his face, the smile only emphasised the sallow skin stretched abnormally taut across the sharp nose and high cheek-bones, puckered up the sabre scar that bisected the left cheek from eyebrow to chin: and whether he smiled or not, the pupils of the deep-set eyes remained always the same, still and black and empty. Even at that early hour – it was not yet six o'clock – he was immac-ulately dressed, freshly shaven, the wetly gleaming hair – thin, dark, heavily indented above the temples – brushed straight back across his head. Seated behind a flat-topped table, the sole article of furni-ture in the bench-lined guardroom, only the upper half of his body was visible: even so, one instinctively knew that the crease of the trousers, the polish of the jack-boots, would be beyond reproach.

He smiled often, and he was smiling now as Oberleutnant Turzig finished his report. Leaning far back in his chair, elbows on the arm-rests, Skoda steepled his lean fingers under his chin, smiled benignly round the guardroom. The lazy, empty eyes missed nothing – the guard at the door, the two guards behind the bound prisoner, Andrea sitting on the bench where he had just laid Stevens – one lazy sweep of those eyes encompassed them all.

'Excellently done, Oberleutnant Turzig!' he purred. 'Most effi-cient, really most efficient!' He looked speculatively at the three men standing before him, at their bruised and blood-caked faces, switched his glance to Stevens, lying barely conscious on the bench, smiled again and permitted himself a fractional lift of his eyebrows. 'A little trouble perhaps, Turzig? The prisoners were not too – ah – co-operative?'

'They offered no resistance, sir, no resistance at all,' Turzig said stiffly. The tone, the manner, were punctilious, correct, but the dis-taste, the latent hostility were mirrored in his eyes. 'My men were maybe a little enthusiastic. We wanted to make no mistake.'

'Quite right, Lieutenant, quite right,' Skoda murmured approvingly. 'These are dangerous men and one cannot take chances with dangerous men.' He pushed back his chair, rose easily to his feet, strolled round the table and stopped in front of Andrea. 'Except maybe this one, Lieutenant?'

'He is dangerous only to his friends,' Turzig said shortly. 'It is as I told you, sir. He would betray his mother to save his own skin.'

'And claiming friendship with us, eh?' Skoda asked musingly. 'One of our gallant allies, Lieutenant.' Skoda reached out a gentle hand, brought it viciously down and across Andrea's cheek, the heavy signet ring on his middle finger tearing skin and flesh. Andrea cried out in pain, capped one hand to his bleeding face and cowered away, his right arm raised above his head in blind defence.

'A notable addition to the armed forces of the Third Reich,' Skoda murmured. 'You were not mistaken, Lieutenant. A poltroon – the instinctive reaction of a hurt man is an infallible guide. It is curious,' he mused, 'how often very big men are thus. Part of nature's compensatory process, I suppose . . . What is your name, my brave friend?'

'Papagos,' Andrea muttered sullenly. 'Peter Papagos.' He took his hand away from his cheek, looked at it with eyes slowly widening with horror, began to rub it across his trouser leg with jerky, hurried movements, the repugnance on his face plain for every man to see. Skoda watched him with amusement.

'You do not like to see blood, Papagos, eh?' he suggested. 'Especially your own blood?'

A few seconds passed in silence, then Andrea lifted his head suddenly, his fat face screwed up in misery. He looked as if he were going to cry.

'I am only a poor fisherman, your Honour!' he burst out. 'You laugh at me and say I do not like blood, and it is true. Nor do I like suffering and war. I want no part of any of these things!' His great fists were clenched in futile appeal, his face puckered in woe, his voice risen an octave. It was a masterly exhibition of despair and even Mallory found himself almost believing in it. 'Why wasn't I left alone?' he went on pathetically. 'God only knows I am no fighting man –'

'A highly inaccurate statement,' Skoda interrupted dryly. 'That fact must be patently obvious to every person in the room by this time.' He tapped his teeth with a jade cigarette-holder, his eyes speculative. 'A fisherman you call yourself –'

'He's a damned traitor!' Mallory interrupted. The commandant was becoming just that little bit too interested in Andrea. At once Skoda wheeled round, stood in front of Mallory with his hands clasped behind his back, teetering on heels and toes, and looked him up and down in mocking inspection.

'So!' he said thoughtfully. 'The great Keith Mallory! A rather different proposition from our fat and fearful friend on the bench there, eh, Lieutenant?' He did not wait for an answer. 'What rank are you, Mallory?'

'Captain,' Mallory answered briefly.

'Captain Mallory, eh? Captain Keith Mallory, the greatest mountaineer of our time, the idol of pre-war Europe, the conqueror of the world's most impossible climbs.' Skoda shook his head sadly. 'And to think that it should all end like this . . . I doubt whether posterity will rank your last climb as among your greatest: there are only ten steps leading to the gallows in the fortress of Navarone.' Skoda smiled. 'Hardly a cheerful thought, is it, Captain Mallory?'

'I wasn't even thinking about it,' the New Zealander answered pleasantly. 'What worries me is your face.' He frowned. 'Somewhere or other I'm sure I've seen it or something like it before.' His voice trailed off into silence.

'Indeed?' Skoda was interested. 'In the Bernese Alps, perhaps? Often before the war –'

'I have it now!' Mallory's face cleared. He knew the risk he was taking, but anything that concentrated attention on himself to the exclusion of Andrea was justified. He beamed at Skoda. 'Three months ago, it was, in the zoo in Cairo. A plains buzzard that had been captured in the Sudan. A rather old and mangy buzzard, I'm afraid,' Mallory went on apologetically, 'but exactly the same scrawny neck, the same beaky face and bald head –'

Mallory broke off abruptly, swayed back out of reach as Skoda, his face livid and gleaming teeth bared in rage, swung at him with his fist. The blow carried with it all Skoda's wiry strength, but anger blurred his timing and the fist swung harmlessly by: he stumbled, recovered, then fell to the floor with a shout of pain as Mallory's heavy boot caught him flush on the thigh, just above the knee. He had barely touched the floor when he was up like a cat, took a pace forward and collapsed heavily again as his injured leg gave under him.

There was a moment's shocked stillness throughout the room, then Skoda rose painfully, supporting himself on the edge of the heavy table. He was breathing quickly, the thin mouth a hard, white line, the great sabre scar flaming redly in the sallow face drained now of all colour. He looked neither at Mallory nor anyone else, but slowly, deliberately, in an almost frightening silence, began to work his way round to the back of the table, the scuffling of his sliding palms on the leather top rasping edgily across over-tautened nerves.

Mallory stood quite still, watching him with expressionless face, cursing himself for his folly. He had overplayed his hand. There was no doubt in his mind – there could be no doubt in the mind of any-one in that room – that Skoda meant to kill him; and he, Mallory, would not die. Only Skoda and Andrea would die: Skoda from Andrea's throwing knife – Andrea was rubbing blood from his face with the inside of his sleeve, fingertips only inches from the sheath – and Andrea from the guns of the guards, for the knife was all he had. You fool, you fool, you bloody stupid fool, Mallory repeated to himself over and over again. He turned his head slightly and glanced out of the corner of his eye at the sentry nearest him. Nearest him – but still six or seven feet away. The sentry would get him, Mallory knew, the blast of the slugs from the Schmeisser would tear him in half before he could cover the distance. But he would try. He must try. It was the least he owed to Andrea.

Skoda reached the back of the table, opened a drawer and lifted out a gun. An automatic, Mallory noted with detachment – a little, blue-metal, snub-nosed toy – but a murderous toy, the kind of gun he would have expected Skoda to have. Unhurriedly Skoda pressed the release button, checked the magazine, snapped it home with the palm of his hand, flicked off the safety catch and looked up at Mallory. The eyes hadn't altered in the slightest – they were cold, dark and empty as ever. Mallory flicked a glance at Andrea and tensed himself for one convulsive fling backwards. Here it comes, he thought savagely, this is how bloody fools like Keith Mallory die – and then all of a sudden, and unknowingly, he relaxed, for his eyes were still on Andrea and he had seen Andrea doing the same, the huge hand slipping down unconcernedly from the neck, empty of any sign of knife.

There was a scuffle at the table and Mallory was just in time to see Turzig pin Skoda's gun-hand to the table-top.

'Not that, sir!' Turzig begged. 'For God's sake, not that way!'

'Take your hands away,' Skoda whispered. The staring, empty eyes never left Mallory's face. 'Take your hands away, I say – unless you want to go the same way as Captain Mallory.'

'You can't kill him, sir!' Turzig persisted doggedly. 'You just can't. Herr Kommandant's orders were very clear, Hauptmann Skoda. The leader must be brought to him alive.'

'He was shot while trying to escape,' Skoda said thickly.

'It's no good.' Turzig shook his head. 'We can't kill them all – and the other prisoners would talk.' He released his grip on Skoda's hands. 'Alive, Herr Kommandant said, but he didn't say how much alive.' He lowered his voice confidentially. 'Perhaps we may have some difficulty in making Captain Mallory talk,' he suggested.

'What! What did you say?' Abruptly the death's head smile flashed once more, and Skoda was completely on balance again. 'You are over-zealous, Lieutenant. Remind me to speak to you about it some time. You underestimate me: that was exactly what I was trying to do – frighten Mallory into talking. And now you've spoilt it all.' The smile was still on his face, the voice light, almost bantering, but Mallory was under no illusions. He owed his life to the young WGB lieutenant – how easily one could respect, form a friendship with a man like Turzig if it weren't for this damned, crazy war . . . Skoda was standing in front of him again: he had left his gun on the table.

'But enough of this fooling, eh, Captain Mallory?' The German's teeth fairly gleamed in the bright light from the naked lamps overhead. 'We haven't all night, have we?'

Mallory looked at him, then turned away in silence. It was warm enough, stuffy almost, in that little guardroom, but he was conscious of a sudden, nameless chill, he knew all at once, without knowing why, but with complete certainty, that this little man before him was utterly evil.

'Well, well, well, we are not quite so talkative now, are we, my friend?' He hummed a little to himself, looked up abruptly, the smile broader than ever. 'Where are the explosives, Captain Mallory?'

'Explosives?' Mallory lifted an interrogatory eyebrow. 'I don't know what you are talking about.'

'You don't remember, eh?'

'I don't know what you are talking about.'

'So.' Skoda hummed to himself again and walked over in front of Miller. 'And what about you, my friend?'

'Sure I remember,' Miller said easily. 'The captain's got it all wrong.'

'A sensible man!' Skoda purred – but Mallory could have sworn to an undertone of disappointment in the voice. 'Proceed, my friend.'

'Captain Mallory has no eye for detail,' Miller drawled. 'I was with him that day. He is malignin' a noble bird. It was a vulture, not a buzzard.'

Just for a second Skoda's smile slipped, then it was back again, as rigidly fixed and lifeless as if it had been painted on.

'Very, very witty men, don't you think, Turzig? What the British would call music-hall comedians. Let them laugh while they may, until the hangman's noose begins to tighten . . .' He looked at Casey Brown. 'Perhaps you –'

'Why don't you go and take a running jump to yourself?' Brown growled.

'A running jump? The idiom escapes me, but I fear it is hardly complimentary.' Skoda selected a cigarette from a thin case, tapped it thoughtfully on a thumb nail. 'Hmm. Not just what one might call too co-operative, Lieutenant Turzig.'

'You won't get these men to talk, sir.' There was a quiet finality in Turzig's voice.

'Possibly not, possibly not.' Skoda was quite unruffled. 'Nevertheless, I shall have the information I want, and within five minutes.' He walked unhurriedly across to his desk, pressed a button, screwed his cigarette into its jade holder, and leaned against the table, an arrogance, a careless contempt in every action, even to the leisurely crossing of the gleaming jack-boots.

Suddenly a side door was flung open and two men stumbled into the room, prodded by a rifle barrel. Mallory caught his breath, felt his nails dig savagely into the palms of his hands. Louki and Panayis! Louki and Panayis, bound and bleeding, Louki from a cut above the eye, Panayis from a scalp wound. So they'd got them too, and in spite of his warnings. Both men were shirt-sleeved; Louki, minus his magnificently frogged jacket, scarlet *stanta* and the small arsenal of weapons that he carried stuck beneath it, looked strangely pathetic and woebegone – strangely, for he was red-faced with anger, the moustache bristling more ferociously than ever. Mallory looked at him with eyes empty of all recognition, his face expressionless.

'Come now, Captain Mallory,' Skoda said reproachfully. 'Have you no word of greeting for two old friends? No? Or perhaps you are just overwhelmed?' he suggested smoothly. 'You had not expected to see them so soon again, eh, Captain Mallory?'

'What cheap trick is this?' Mallory asked contemptuously. 'I've never seen these men before in my life.' His eyes caught those of

Panayis, held there involuntarily: the black hate that stared out of those eyes, the feral malevolence – there was something appalling about it.

'Of course not,' Skoda sighed wearily. 'Oh, of course not. Human memory is so short, is it not, Captain Mallory.' The sigh was pure theatre – Skoda was enjoying himself immensely, the cat playing with the mouse. 'However, we will try again.' He swung round, crossed over to the bench where Stevens lay, pulled off the blanket and, before anyone could guess his intentions, chopped the outside of his right hand against Stevens's smashed leg, just below the knee . . . Stevens's entire body leapt in a convulsive spasm, but without even a whisper of a moan: he was still fully conscious, smiling at Skoda, blood trickling down his chin from where his teeth had gashed his lower lip.

'You shouldn't have done that, Hauptmann Skoda,' Mallory said. His voice was barely a whisper, but unnaturally loud in the frozen silence of the room. 'You are going to die for that, Hauptmann Skoda.'

'So? I am going to die, am I?' Again he chopped his hand against the fractured leg, again without reaction. 'Then I may as well die twice over – eh, Captain Mallory? This young man is very, very tough – but the British have soft hearts, have they not, my dear Captain?' Gently his hand slid down Stevens's leg, closed round the stockinged ankle. 'You have exactly five seconds to tell me the truth, Captain Mallory, and then I fear I will be compelled to rearrange these splints – *Gott in Himmel*! What's the matter with that great oaf?'

Andrea had taken a couple of steps forward, was standing only a yard away, swaying on his feet.

'Outside! Let me outside!' His breath came in short, fast gasps. He bowed his head, one hand to his throat, one over his stomach. 'I cannot stand it! Air! Air! I must have air!'

'Ah, no, my dear Papagos, you shall remain here and enjoy – Corporal! Quickly!' He had seen Andrea's eyes roll upwards until only the whites showed. 'The fool is going to faint! Take him away before he falls on top of us!'

Mallory had one fleeting glimpse of the two guards hurrying forwards, of the incredulous contempt on Louki's face, then he flicked a glance at Miller and Brown, caught the lazy droop of the American's eyelid in return, the millimetric inclination of Brown's head. Even as the two guards came up behind Andrea and lifted the flaccid arms across their shoulders, Mallory glanced half-left, saw the nearest sentry less than four feet away now, absorbed in the spectacle of the toppling giant. Easy, dead easy – the gun dangling by his side: he could hit him between wind and water before he knew what was happening . . .

Fascinated, Mallory watched Andrea's forearms slipping nervelessly down the shoulders of the supporting guards till his wrists rested loosely beside their necks, palms facing inwards. And then there was the sudden leap of the great shoulder muscles and Mallory had hurled himself convulsively sidewards and back, his shoulder socketing with vicious force into the guard's stomach, inches below the breastbone: an explosive *ouf!* of agony, the crash against the wooden walls of the room and Mallory knew the guard would be out of action for some time to come.

Even as he dived, Mallory had heard the sickening thud of heads being swept together. Now, as he twisted round on his side, he had a fleeting glimpse of another guard thrashing feebly on the floor under the combined weights of Miller and Brown, and then of Andrea tearing an automatic rifle from the guard who had been standing at his right shoulder: the Schmeisser was cradled in his great hands, lined up on Skoda's chest even before the unconscious man had hit the floor.

For one second, maybe two, all movement in the room ceased, every sound sheared off by a knife edge: the silence was abrupt, absolute – and infinitely more clamorous than the clamour that had gone before. No one moved, no one spoke, no one even breathed: the shock, the utter unexpectedness of what had happened held them all in thrall.

And then the silence erupted in a staccato crashing of sound, deafening in that confined space. Once, twice, three times, wordlessly, and with great care, Andrea shot Hauptmann Skoda through the heart. The blast of the shells lifted the little man off his feet, smashed him against the wall of the hut, pinned him there for one incredible second, arms outflung as though nailed against the rough planks in spread-eagle crucifixion; and then he collapsed, fell limply to the ground a grotesque and broken doll that struck its heedless head against the edge of the bench before coming to rest on its back on the floor. The eyes were still wide open, as cold, as dark, as empty in death as they had been in life.

His Schmeisser waving in a gentle arc that covered Turzig and the sergeant, Andrea picked up Skoda's sheath knife, sliced through the ropes that bound Mallory's wrists.

'Can you hold this gun, my Captain?'

Mallory flexed his stiffened hands once or twice, nodded, took the gun in silence. In three steps Andrea was behind the blind side of the door leading to the ante-room, pressed to the wall, waiting, gesturing to Mallory to move as far back as possible out of the line of sight.

Suddenly the door was flung open. Andrea could just see the tip of the rifle barrel projecting beyond it.

'Oberleutnant Turzig! *Was ist los? Wer schoss . . .*' The voice broke off in a coughing grunt of agony as Andrea smashed the sole of his foot against the door. He was round the outside of the door in a moment, caught the man as he fell, pulled him clear of the doorway and peered into the adjacent hut. A brief inspection, then he closed the door, bolted it from the inside.

'Nobody else there, my Captain,' Andrea reported. 'Just the one gaoler, it seems.'

'Fine! Cut the others loose, will you, Andrea?' He wheeled round towards Louki, smiled at the comical expression on the little man's face, the tentative, spreading, finally ear-to-ear grin that cut through the baffled incredulity.

'Where do the men sleep, Louki – the soldiers, I mean?'

'In a hut in the middle of the compound, Major. This is the officers' quarters.'

'Compound? You mean –?'

'Barbed wire,' Louki said succinctly. 'Ten feet high – and all the way round.'

'Exits?'

'One and one only. Two guards.'

'Good! Andrea – everybody into the side room. No, not you, Lieutenant. You sit down here.' He gestured to the chair behind the big desk. 'Somebody's bound to come. Tell him you killed one of us – trying to escape. Then send for the guards at the gate.'

For a moment Turzig didn't answer. He watched unseeingly as Andrea walked past him, dragging two unconscious soldiers by their collars. Then he smiled. It was a wry sort of smile.

'I am sorry to disappoint you, Captain Mallory. Too much has been lost already through my blind stupidity. I won't do it.'

'Andrea!' Mallory called softly.

'Yes?' Andrea stood in the ante-room doorway.

'I think I hear someone coming. Is there a way out of that side room?'.

Andrea nodded silently.

'Outside! The front door. Take your knife. If the Lieutenant . . .' But he was talking to himself, Andrea was already gone, slipping out through the back door, soundless as a ghost.

'You will do exactly as I say,' Mallory said softly. He took position himself in the doorway to the side room, where he could see the front entrance between door and jamb: his automatic rifle was trained on Turzig. 'If you don't, Andrea will kill the man at the door. Then we will kill you and the guards inside. Then we will knife the sentries at the gate. Nine dead men – and all for nothing, for we will escape anyway . . . Here he is now.' Mallory's voice was barely a whisper, eyes pitiless in a pitiless face. 'Nine dead men, Lieutenant – and just because your pride is hurt.' Deliberately, the last sentence was in German, fluent, colloquial, and Mallory's mouth twisted as he saw the almost imperceptible sag of Turzig's shoulders. He knew he had won, that Turzig had been going to take a last gamble on his ignorance of German, that this last hope was gone.

The door burst open and a soldier stood on the threshold, breathing heavily. He was armed, but clad only in a singlet and trousers, oblivious of the cold.

'Lieutenant! Lieutenant!' He spoke in German. 'We heard the shots –'

'It is nothing, Sergeant.' Turzig bent his head over an open drawer, pretended to be searching for something to account for his solitary presence in the room. 'One of our prisoners tried to escape . . . We stopped him.'

'Perhaps the medical orderly –'

'I'm afraid we stopped him rather permanently.' Turzig smiled tiredly. 'You can organise a burial detail in the morning. Meantime, you might tell the guards at the gate to come here for a minute. Then get to bed yourself – you'll catch your death of cold!'

'Shall I detail a relief guard –'

'Of course not!' Turzig said impatiently. 'It's just for a minute. Besides, the only people to guard against are already in here.' His lips tightened for a second as he realised what he had said, the unconscious irony of the words. 'Hurry up, man! We haven't got all night!' He waited till the sound of the running footsteps died away, then looked steadily at Mallory. 'Satisfied?'

'Perfectly. And my very sincere apologies,' Mallory said quietly. 'I hate to do a thing like this to a man like you.' He looked round the door as Andrea came into the room. 'Andrea, ask Louki and Panayis if there's a telephone switchboard in this block of huts. Tell them to smash it up and any receivers they can find.' He grinned. 'Then hurry back for our visitors from the gate. I'd be lost without you on the reception committee.'

Turzig's gaze followed the broad, retreating back.

'Captain Skoda was right. I still have much to learn.' There was neither bitterness nor rancour in his voice. 'He fooled me completely, that big one.'

'You're not the first,' Mallory reassured him. 'He's fooled more people than I'll ever know . . . You're not the first,' he repeated. 'But I think you must be just about the luckiest.'

'Because I'm still alive?'

'Because you're still alive,' Mallory echoed.

Less than ten minutes later the two guards at the gates had joined their comrades in the back room, captured, disarmed, bound and gagged with a speed and noiseless efficiency that excited Turzig's professional admiration, chagrined though he was. Securely tied hand and foot, he lay in a corner of the room, not yet gagged.

'I think I understand now why your High Command chose you for this task, Captain Mallory. If anyone could succeed, you would – but you must fail. The impossible must always remain so. Nevertheless, you have a great team.'

'We get by,' Mallory said modestly. He took a last look round the room, then grinned down at Stevens.

'Ready to take off on your travels again, young man, or do you find this becoming rather monotonous?'

'Ready when you are, sir.' Lying on a stretcher which Louki had miraculously procured, he sighed in bliss. 'First-class travel, this time, as befits an officer. Sheer luxury. I don't mind how far we go!'

'Speak for yourself,' Miller growled morosely. He had been allocated first stint at the front or heavy end of the stretcher. But the quirk of his eyebrows robbed the words of all offence.

'Right, then, we're off. One last thing. Where is the camp radio, Lieutenant Turzig?'

'So you can smash it up, I suppose?'

'Precisely.'

'I have no idea.'

'What if I threaten to blow your head off?'

'You won't.' Turzig smiled, though the smile was a trifle lop-sided. 'Given certain circumstances, you would kill me as you would a fly. But you wouldn't kill a man for refusing such information.'

'You haven't as much to learn as your late and unlamented captain thought,' Mallory admitted. 'It's not all that important . . . I regret we have to do all this. I trust we do not meet again – not at least, until the war is over. Who knows, some day we might even go climbing together.' He signed to Louki to fix Turzig's gag and walked quickly out of the room. Two minutes later they had cleared the barracks and were safely lost in the darkness and the olive groves that stretched to the south of Margaritha.

When they cleared the groves, a long time later, it was almost dawn. Already the black silhouette of Kostos was softening in the first feathery greyness of the coming day. The wind was from the south, and warm, and the snow was beginning to melt on the hills.

ELEVEN

Wednesday
1400–1600

All day long they lay hidden in the carob grove, a thick clump of
stunted, gnarled trees that clung grimly to the treacherous, scree-
strewn slope abutting what Louki called the 'Devil's Playground'. A
poor shelter and an uncomfortable one, but in every other way all
they could wish for: it offered concealment, a first-class defensive
position immediately behind, a gentle breeze drawn up from the
sea by the sun-baked rocks to the south, shade from the sun that
rode from dawn to dusk in a cloudless sky – and an incomparable
view of a sun-drenched, shimmering Aegean.

Away to their left, fading through diminishing shades of blue
and indigo and violet into faraway nothingness, stretched the
islands of the Lerades, the nearest of them, Maidos, so close that
they could see isolated fisher cottages sparkling whitely in the sun:
through that narrow, intervening gap of water would pass the ships
of the Royal Navy in just over a day's time. To the right, and even
farther away, remote, featureless, back-dropped by the towering
Anatolian mountains, the coast of Turkey hooked north and west
in a great curving scimitar: to the north itself, the thrusting spear
of Cape Demirci, rock-rimmed but dimpled with sandy coves of
white, reached far out into the placid blue of the Aegean: and north
again beyond the Cape, haze-blurred in the purple distance, the
island of Kheros lay dreaming on the surface of the sea.

It was a breath-taking panorama, a heart-catching beauty
sweeping majestically through a great semicircle over the sunlit
sea. But Mallory had no eyes for it, had spared it only a passing
glance when he had come on guard less than half an hour previously, just after two o'clock. He had dismissed it with one quick
glance, settled by the bole of a tree, gazed for endless minutes,

gazed until his eyes ached with strain at what he had so long waited to see. Had waited to see and come to destroy – the guns of the fortress of Navarone.

The town of Navarone – a town of from four to five thousand people, Mallory judged – lay sprawled round the deep, volcanic crescent of the harbour, a crescent so deep, so embracing, that it was almost a complete circle with only a narrow bottleneck of an entrance to the north-west, a gateway dominated by searchlights and mortar and machine-gun batteries on either side. Less than three miles distant to the north-east from the carob grove, every detail, every street, every building, every caique and launch in the harbour were clearly visible to Mallory and he studied them over and over again until he knew them by heart: the way the land to the west of the harbour sloped up gently to the olive groves, the dusty streets running down to the water's edge: the way the ground rose more sharply to the south, the streets now running parallel to the water down to the old town: the way the cliffs to the east – cliffs pock-marked by the bombs of Torrance's Liberator Squadron – stretched a hundred and fifty sheer feet above the water, then curved dizzily out over and above the harbour, and the great mound of volcanic rock towering above that again, a mound barricaded off from the town below by the high wall that ended flush with the cliff itself: and, finally, the way the twin rows of AA guns, the great radar scanners and the barracks of the fortress, squat, narrow-embrasured, built of big blocks of masonry, dominated everything in sight – including that great, black gash in the rock, below the fantastic overhang of the cliff.

Unconsciously, almost, Mallory nodded to himself in slow understanding. This was the fortress that had defied the Allies for eighteen long months, that had dominated the entire naval strategy in the Sporades since the Germans had reached out from the mainland into the isles, that had blocked all naval activity in that 2,000 square mile triangle between the Lerades and the Turkish coast. And now, when he saw it, it all made sense. Impregnable to land attack – the commanding fortress saw to that: impregnable to air attack – Mallory realised just how suicidal it had been to send out Torrance's squadron against the great guns protected by that jutting cliff, against those bristling rows of anti-aircraft guns: and impregnable to sea attack – the waiting squadrons of the Luftwaffe on Samos saw to that. Jensen had been right – only a guerrilla sabotage mission stood any chance at all: a remote chance, an all but suicidal chance, but still a chance, and Mallory knew he couldn't ask for more.

Thoughtfully he lowered the binoculars and rubbed the back of his hand across aching eyes. At last he felt he knew exactly what he was up against, was grateful for the knowledge, for the opportunity he'd been given of this long-range reconnaissance, this familiarising of himself with the terrain, the geography of the town. This was probably the one vantage point in the whole island that offered such an opportunity together with concealment and near immunity. No credit to himself, the leader of the mission, he reflected wryly, that they had found such a place: it had been Louki's idea entirely.

And he owed a great deal more than that to the sad-eyed little Greek. It had been Louki's idea that they first move up-valley from Margaritha, to give Andrea time to recover the explosives from old Leri's hut, and to make certain there was no immediate hue and cry and pursuit – they could have fought a rearguard action up through the olive groves, until they had lost themselves in the foothills of Kostos: it was he who had guided them back past Margaritha when they had doubled on their tracks, had halted them opposite the village while he and Panayis had slipped wraith-like through the lifting twilight, picked up outdoor clothes for themselves, and, on the return journey, slipped into the *Abteilung* garage, torn away the coil ignitions of the German command car and truck – the only transport in Margaritha – and smashed their distributors for good measure; it was Louki who had led them by a sunken ditch right up to the road-block guard post at the mouth of the valley – it had been almost ludicrously simple to disarm the sentries, only one of whom had been awake – and, finally, it was Louki who had insisted that they walk down the muddy centre of the valley track till they came to the metalled road, less than two miles from the town itself. A hundred yards down this they had branched off to the left across a long, sloping field of lava that left no trace behind, arrived in the carob copse just on sunrise.

And it had worked. All these carefully engineered pointers, pointers that not even the most sceptical could have ignored and denied, had worked magnificently. Miller and Andrea, who had shared the forenoon watch, had seen the Navarone garrison spending long hours making the most intensive house-to-house search of the town. That should make it doubly, trebly safe for them the following day, Mallory reckoned: it was unlikely that the search would be repeated,

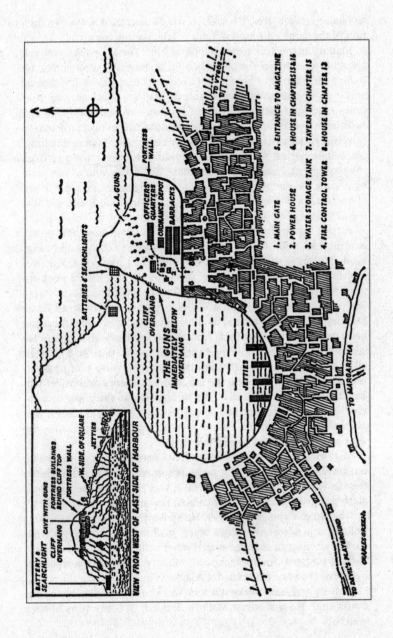

VIEW FROM WEST OF EAST SIDE OF HARBOUR

BATTERY & SEARCHLIGHT
CAVE WITH GUNS
CLIFF OVERHANG
FORTRESS BUILDINGS BEHIND CLIFF TOP
W. SIDE OF SQUARE
FORTRESS WALL
JETTIES

BATTERIES & SEARCHLIGHTS
A.A. GUNS
FORTRESS WALL
OFFICERS' QUARTERS
ORDNANCE DEPOT
BARRACKS
CLIFF OVERHANG
THE GUNS
IMMEDIATELY BELOW · OVERHANG
JETTIES
TO VYROS
TO MARGARITHA
TO DEVIL'S PLAYGROUND
CHARLES GREEN

1. MAIN GATE
2. POWER HOUSE
3. WATER STORAGE TANK
4. FIRE CONTROL TOWER
5. ENTRANCE TO MAGAZINE
6. HOUSE IN CHAPTERS 15 & 16
7. TAVERN IN CHAPTER 13
8.—HOUSE IN CHAPTER 13

still more unlikely that, if it were, it would be carried out with a fraction of the same enthusiasm. Louki had done his work well.

Mallory turned his head to look at him. The little man was still asleep – wedged on the slope behind a couple of tree-trunks, he hadn't stirred for five hours. Still dead tired himself, his legs aching and eyes smarting with sleeplessness, Mallory could not find it in him to grudge Louki a moment of his rest. He'd earned it all – and he'd been awake all through the previous night. So had Panayis, but Panayis was already awakening, Mallory saw, pushing the long, black hair out of his eyes: awake, rather, for his transition from sleep to full awareness was immediate, as fleeting and as complete as a cat's. A dangerous man, Mallory knew, a desperate man, almost, and a bitter enemy, but he knew nothing of Panayis, nothing at all. He doubted if he ever would.

Farther up on the slope, almost in the centre of the grove, Andrea had built a high platform of broken branches and twigs against a couple of carob poles maybe five feet apart, gradually filling up the space between slope and trees until he had a platform four feet in width, as nearly level as he could make it. Andy Stevens lay on this, still on his stretcher, still conscious. As far as Mallory could tell, Stevens hadn't closed his eyes since they had been marched away by Turzig from their cave in the mountains. He seemed to have passed beyond the need for sleep, or had crushed all desire for it. The stench from the gangrenous leg was nauseating, appalling, poisoned all the air around. Mallory and Miller had had a look at the leg shortly after their arrival in the copse, uncovered it, examined it, smiled at one another, tied it up again and assured Stevens that the wound was closing. Below the knee, the leg had turned almost completely black.

Mallory lifted his binoculars to have another look at the town, but lowered them almost at once as someone came sliding down the slope, touched him on the arm. It was Panayis, upset, anxious, almost angry looking. He gesticulated towards the westering sun.

'The time, Captain Mallory?' He spoke in Greek, his voice low, sibilant, urgent – an inevitable voice, Mallory thought, for the lean, dark mysteriousness of the man. 'What is the time?' he repeated.

'Half-past two, or thereabouts.' Mallory lifted an interrogatory eyebrow. 'You are concerned, Panayis. Why?'

'You should have wakened me. You should have wakened me hours ago!' He *was* angry, Mallory decided. 'It is my turn to keep watch.'

'But you had no sleep last night,' Mallory pointed out reasonably. 'It just didn't seem fair –'

'It is my turn to keep watch, I tell you!' Panayis insisted stub-
bornly.

'Very well, then. If you insist.' Mallory knew the high, fierce
pride of the islanders too well to attempt to argue. 'Heaven only
knows what we would have done without Louki and yourself . . .
I'll stay and keep you company for a while.'

'Ah, so that is why you let me sleep on!' There was no disguising the hurt in the eyes, the voice. 'You do not trust Panayis –'

'Oh, for heaven's sake!' Mallory began in exasperation, checked
himself and smiled. 'Of course we trust you. Maybe I should go and
get some more sleep anyway; you are kind to give me the chance.
You will shake me in two hours' time?'

'Certainly, certainly!' Panayis was almost beaming. 'I shall not
fail.'

Mallory scrambled up to the centre of the grove and stretched
out lazily along the ledge he had levelled out for himself. For a few
idle moments he watched Panayis pacing restlessly to and fro just
inside the perimeter of the grove, lost interest when he saw him
climbing swiftly up among the branches of a tree, seeking a high
lookout vantage point and decided he might as well follow his
advice and get some sleep while he could.

'Captain Mallory! Captain Mallory!' An urgent, heavy hand was
shaking his shoulder. 'Wake up! Wake up!'

Mallory stirred, rolled over on his back, sat up quickly, opening
his eyes as he did so. Panayis was stooped over him, the dark, saturnine face alive with anxiety. Mallory shook his head to clear away
the mists of sleep and was on his feet in one swift, easy movement.

'What's the matter, Panayis?'

'Planes!' he said quickly. 'There is a squadron of planes coming
our way!'

'Planes? What planes? Whose planes?'

'I do not know, Captain. They are yet far away. But –'

'What direction?' Mallory snapped.

'They come from the north.'

Together they ran down to the edge of the grove. Panayis gestured to the north, and Mallory caught sight of them at once, the
afternoon sun glinting off the sharp dihedral of the wings. Stukas,
all right, he thought grimly. Seven – no, eight of them – less than

three miles away, flying in two echelons of fours, two thousand, certainly not more than twenty-five hundred feet . . . He became aware that Panayis was tugging urgently at his arm.

'Come, Captain Mallory!' he said excitedly. 'We have no time to lose!' He pulled Mallory round, pointed with outstretched arm at the gaunt, shattered cliffs that rose steeply behind them, cliffs crazily riven by rock-jumbled ravines that wound their aimless way back into the interior – or stopped as abruptly as they had begun. 'The Devil's Playground! We must get in there at once! At once, Captain Mallory!'

'Why on earth should we?' Mallory looked at him in astonishment. 'There's no reason to suppose that they're after us. How can they be? No one knows we're here.'

'I do not care!' Panayis was stubborn in his conviction. 'I know. Do not ask me how I know, for I do not know that myself. Louki will tell you – Panayis knows these things. I know, Captain Mallory, I *know*!'

Just for a second Mallory stared at him, uncomprehending. There was no questioning the earnestness, the utter sincerity – but it was the machine-gun staccato of the words that tipped the balance of instinct against reason. Almost without realising it, certainly without realising why, Mallory found himself running uphill, slipping and stumbling in the scree. He found the others already on their feet, tense, expectant, shrugging on their packs, the guns already in their hands.

'Get to the edge of the trees up there!' Mallory shouted. 'Quickly! Stay there and stay under cover – we're going to have to break for that gap in the rocks.' He gestured through the trees at a jagged fissure in the cliff-side, barely forty yards from where he stood, blessed Louki for his foresight in choosing a hideout with so convenient a bolt-hole. 'Wait till I give the word. Andrea!' He turned round, then broke off, the words unneeded. Andrea had already scooped up the dying boy in his arms, just as he lay in stretcher and blankets and was weaving his way uphill in and out among the trees.

'What's up, boss?' Miller was by Mallory's side as he plunged up the slope. 'I don't see nothin'.'

'You can hear something if you'd just stop talking for a moment,' Mallory said grimly. 'Or just take a look up there.'

Miller, flat on his stomach now, and less than a dozen feet from the edge of the grove, twisted round and craned his neck upwards. He picked up the planes immediately.

'Stukas!' he said incredulously. 'A squadron of gawddamned Stukas! It can't be, boss!'

'It can and it is,' Mallory said grimly. 'Jensen told me that Jerry has stripped the Italian front of them – over two hundred pulled out in the last few weeks.' Mallory squinted up at the squadron, less than half a mile away now. 'And he's brought the whole damn issue down to the Aegean.'

'But they're not lookin' for us,' Miller protested.

'I'm afraid they are,' Mallory said grimly. The two bomber eche-lons had just dove-tailed into line-ahead formation. 'I'm afraid Panayis was right.'

'But – but they're passin' us by –'

'They aren't,' Mallory said flatly. 'They're here to stay. Just keep your eyes on that leading plane.'

Even as he spoke, the flight-commander tilted his gull-winged Junkers 87 sharply over to port, half-turned, fell straight out of the sky in a screaming power-dive, plummeting straight for the carob grove.

'Leave him alone!' Mallory shouted. 'Don't fire!' The Stukas, air-brakes at maximum depression, had steadied on the centre of the grove. Nothing could stop him now – but a chance shot might bring him down directly on top of them: the chances were poor enough as it was . . . 'Keep your hands over your heads – and your heads down!'

He ignored his own advice, his gaze following the bomber every foot of the way down. Five hundred, four hundred, three, the ris-ing crescendo of the heavy engine was beginning to hurt his ears, and the Stuka was pulling sharply out of its plunging fall, its bomb gone.

Bomb! Mallory sat up sharply, screwing up his eyes against the blue of the sky. Not one bomb but dozens of them, clustered so thickly that they appeared to be jostling each other as they arrowed into the centre of the grove, striking the gnarled and stunted trees, breaking off branches and burying themselves to their fins in the soft and shingled slope. Incendiaries! Mallory had barely time to realise that they had been spared the horror of a 500-kilo HE bomb when the incendiaries erupted into hissing, guttering life, into an incandescent magnesium whiteness that reached out and com-pletely destroyed the shadowed gloom of the carob grove. Within a matter of seconds the dazzling coruscation had given way to thick, evil-smelling clouds of acrid black smoke, smoke laced with flickering tongues of red, small at first then licking and twisting resinously upwards until entire trees were enveloped in a cocoon of flame. The Stuka was still pulling upwards out of its dive, had not yet levelled off when the heart of the grove, old and dry and tindery, was fiercely ablaze.

Miller twisted up and round, nudging Mallory to catch his attention through the crackling roar of the flames.

'Incendiaries, boss,' he announced.

'What did you think they were using?' Mallory asked shortly. 'Matches? They're trying to smoke us out, to burn us out, get us in the open. High explosive's not so good among trees. Ninety-nine times out of a hundred this would have worked.' He coughed as the acrid smoke bit into his lungs, peered up with watering eyes through the tree-tops. 'But not this time. Not if we're lucky. Not if they hold off another half-minute or so. Just look at that smoke!'

Miller looked. Thick, convoluted, shot through with fiery sparks, the rolling cloud was already a third of the way across the gap between grove and cliff, borne uphill by the wandering catspaws from the sea. It was the complete, the perfect smoke-screen. Miller nodded.

'Gonna make a break for it, huh, boss?'

'There's no choice – we either go, or we stay and get fried or blown into very little bits. Probably both.' He raised his voice. 'Anybody see what's happening up top?'

'Queuing up for another go at us, sir,' Brown said lugubriously. 'The first bloke's still circling around.'

'Waiting to see how we break cover. They won't wait long. This is where we take off.' He peered uphill through the rolling smoke, but it was too thick, laced his watering eyes until everything was blurred through a misted sheen of tears. There was no saying how far uphill the smoke-bank had reached, and they couldn't afford to wait until they were sure. Stuka pilots had never been renowned for their patience.

'Right, everybody!' he shouted. 'Fifteen yards along the tree-line to that wash, then straight up into the gorge. Don't stop till you're at least a hundred yards inside. Andrea, you lead the way. Off you go!' He peered through the blinding smoke. 'Where's Panayis?'

There was no reply.

'Panayis!' Mallory called. 'Panayis!'

'Perhaps he went back for somethin'.' Miller had stopped, half-turned. 'Shall I go –'

'Get on your way!' Mallory said savagely. 'And if anything happens to young Stevens I'll hold you –' But Miller, wisely, was already gone, Andrea stumbling and coughing by his side.

For a couple of seconds Mallory stood irresolute, then plunged back downhill towards the centre of the grove. Maybe Panayis had gone back for something – and he couldn't understand English. Mallory had hardly gone five yards when he was forced to halt and fling his arm up before his face: the heat was searing. Panayis couldn't be down there; no one could have been down there, could have lived for seconds in that furnace. Gasping for air, hair singeing and clothes smouldering with fire, Mallory clawed his way back up the slope, colliding with trees, slipping, falling, then stumbling desperately to his feet again.

He ran along to the east end of the wood. No one there. Back to the other end again, towards the wash, almost completely blind now, the superheated air searing viciously through throat and lungs till he was suffocating, till his breath was coming in great, whooping, agonised breaths. No sense in waiting longer, nothing he could do, nothing anyone could do except save himself. There was a noise in his ears, the roaring of the flames, the roaring of his own blood – and the screaming, heart-stopping roar of a Stuka in a power-dive. Desperately he flung himself forward over the sliding scree, stumbled and pitched headlong down to the floor of the wash.

Hurt or not, he did not know and he did not care. Sobbing aloud for breath, he rose to his feet, forced his aching legs to drive him somehow up the hill. The air was full of the thunder of engines, he knew the entire squadron was coming in to the attack, and then he had flung himself uncaringly to the ground as the first of the high explosive bombs erupted in its concussive blast of smoke and flame – erupted not forty yards away, to his left and ahead of him. *Ahead* of him! Even as he struggled upright again, lurched forward and upward once more, Mallory cursed himself again and again and again. You madman, he thought bitterly, confusedly, you damned crazy madman. Sending the others out to be killed. He should have thought of it – oh, God, he should have thought of it, a five-year-old could have thought of it. Of course Jerry wasn't going to bomb the grove: they had seen the obvious, the inevitable, as quickly as he had, were dive-bombing the pall of smoke between the grove and the cliff! A five-year-old – the earth exploded beneath his feet, a giant hand plucked him up and smashed him to the ground and the darkness closed over him.

TWELVE

Wednesday
1600–1800

Once, twice, half a dozen times, Mallory struggled up from the depths of a black, trance-like stupor and momentarily touched the surface of consciousness only to slide back into the darkness again. Desperately, each time, he tried to hang on to these fleeting moments of awareness, but his mind was like the void, dark and sinewless, and even as he knew that his mind was slipping backwards again, loosing its grip on reality, the knowledge was gone, and there was only the void once more. Nightmare, he thought vaguely during one of the longer glimmerings of comprehension, I'm having a nightmare, like when you know you are having a nightmare and that if you could open your eyes it would be gone, but you can't open your eyes. He tried it now, tried to open his eyes, but it was no good, it was still as dark as ever and he was still sunk in this evil dream, for the sun had been shining brightly in the sky. He shook his head in slow despair.

'Aha! Observe! Signs of life at last!' There was no mistaking the slow, nasal drawl. 'Ol' Medicine Man Miller triumphs again!' There was a moment's silence, a moment in which Mallory was increasingly aware of the diminishing thunder of aero engines, the acrid, resinous smoke that stung his nostrils and eyes, and then an arm had passed under his shoulders and Miller's persuasive voice was in his ear. 'Just try a little of this, boss. Ye olde vintage brandy. Nothin' like it anywhere.'

Mallory felt the cold neck of the bottle, tilted his head back, took a long pull. Almost immediately he had jerked himself upright and forward to a sitting position, gagging, spluttering and fighting for breath as the raw, fiery ouzo bit into the mucous membrane of cheeks and throat. He tried to speak but could do no more than croak, gasp for fresh air and stare indignantly at the shadowy figure that knelt by his side. Miller, for his part, looked at him with unconcealed admiration.

'See, boss? Just like I said – nothin' like it.' He shook his head admiringly. 'Wide awake in an instant, as the literary boys would say. Never saw a shock and concussion victim recover so fast!'

'What the hell are you trying to do?' Mallory demanded. The fire had died down in his throat, and he could breathe again. 'Poison me?' Angrily he shook his head, fighting off the pounding ache, the fog that still swirled round the fringes of his mind. 'Bloody fine physician you are! Shock, you say, yet the first thing you do is administer a dose of spirits –'

'Take your pick,' Miller interrupted grimly. 'Either that or a damned sight bigger shock in about fifteen minutes or so when brother Jerry gets here.'

'But they've gone away. I can't hear the Stukas any more.'

'This lot's comin' up from the town,' Miller said morosely. 'Louki's just reported them. Half a dozen armoured cars and a couple of trucks with field guns the length of a telegraph pole.'

'I see.' Mallory twisted round, saw a gleam of light at a bend in the wall. A cave – a tunnel, almost. Little Cyprus, Louki had said some of the older people had called it – the Devil's Playground was riddled with a honeycomb of caves. He grinned wryly at the memory of his momentary panic when he thought his eyes had gone and turned again to Miller. 'Trouble again, Dusty, nothing but trouble. Thanks for bringing me round.'

'Had to,' Miller said briefly. 'I guess we couldn't have carried you very far, boss.'

Mallory nodded. 'Not just the flattest of country hereabouts.'

'There's that, too,' Miller agreed. 'What I really meant is that there's hardly anyone left to carry you. Casey Brown and Panayis have both been hurt, boss.'

'What! Both of them?' Mallory screwed his eyes shut, shook his head in slow anger. 'My God, Dusty, I'd forgotten all about the bomb – the bombs.' He reached out his hand, caught Miller by the arm. 'How – how bad are they?' There was so little time left, so much to do.

'How bad?' Miller shook out a pack of cigarettes and offered one to Mallory. 'Not bad at all – if we could get them into hospital. But hellish painful and cripplin' if they gotta start hikin' up and down those gawddamned ravines hereabouts. First time I've seen canyon floors more nearly vertical than the walls themselves.'

'You still haven't told me –'

'Sorry, boss, sorry. Shrapnel wounds, both of them, in exactly the same place – left thigh, just above the knee. No bones gone, no tendons cut. I've just finished tying up Casey's leg – it's a pretty wicked-lookin' gash. He's gonna know all about it when he starts walkin'.'

'And Panayis?'

'Fixed his own leg,' Miller said briefly. 'A queer character. Wouldn't even let me look at it, far less bandage it. I reckon he'd have knifed me if I'd tried.'

'Better to leave him alone anyway,' Mallory advised. 'Some of these islanders have strange taboos and superstitions. Just as long as he's alive. Though I still don't see how the hell he managed to get here.'

'He was the first to leave,' Miller explained. 'Along with Casey. You must have missed him in the smoke. They were climbin' together when they got hit.'

'And how did I get here?'

'No prizes for the first correct answer.' Miller jerked a thumb over his shoulder at the huge form that blocked half the width of the cave. 'Junior here did his St Bernard act once again. I wanted to go with him, but he wasn't keen. Said he reckoned it would be difficult to carry both of us up the hill. My feelin's were hurt considerable.' Miller sighed. 'I guess I just wasn't born to be a hero, that's all.'

Mallory smiled. 'Thanks again, Andrea.'

'Thanks!' Miller was indignant. 'A guy saves your life and all you can say is "thanks"!'

'After the first dozen times or so you run out of suitable speeches,' Mallory said dryly. 'How's Stevens?'

'Breathin'.'

Mallory nodded forward towards the source of light, wrinkled his nose. 'Just round the corner, isn't he?'

'Yeah, it's pretty grim,' Miller admitted. 'The gangrene's spread up beyond the knee.'

Mallory rose groggily to his feet, picked up his gun. 'How is he really, Dusty?'

'He's dead, but he just won't die. He'll be gone by sundown. Gawd only knows what's kept him goin' so far.'

'It may sound presumptuous,' Mallory murmured; 'but I think I know too.'

'The first-class medical attention?' Miller said hopefully.

'Looks that way, doesn't it?' Mallory smiled down at the still kneeling Miller. 'But that wasn't what I meant at all. Come, gentlemen, we have some business to attend to.'

'Me, all I'm good for is blowin' up bridges and droppin' a handful of sand in engine bearin's,' Miller announced. 'Strategy and tactics are far beyond my simple mind. But I still think those characters down there are pickin' a very stupid way of committin' suicide. It would be a damned sight easier for all concerned if they just shot themselves.'

'I'm inclined to agree with you.' Mallory settled himself more firmly behind the jumbled rocks in the mouth of the ravine that opened on the charred and smoking remains of the carob grove directly below and took another look at the Alpenkorps troops advancing in extended order up the steep, shelterless slope. 'They're no children at this game. I bet they don't like it one little bit, either.'

'Then why the hell are they doin' it, boss?'

'No option, probably. First off, this place can only be attacked frontally.' Mallory smiled down at the little Greek lying between himself and Andrea. 'Louki here chose the place well. It would require a long detour to attack from the rear – and it would take them a week to advance through that devil's scrap-heap behind us. Secondly, it'll be sunset in a couple of hours, and they know they haven't a hope of getting us after it's dark. And finally – and I think this is more important than the other two reasons put together – it's a hundred to one that the commandant in the town is being pretty severely prodded by his High Command. There's too much at stake, even in the one in a thousand chance of us getting at the guns. They can't afford to have Kheros evacuated under their noses, to lose –'

'Why not?' Miller interrupted. He gestured largely with his hands. 'Just a lot of useless rocks –'

'They can't afford to lose face with the Turks,' Mallory went on patiently. 'The strategic importance of these islands in the Sporades is negligible, but their political importance is tremendous. Adolph badly needs another ally in these parts. So he flies in Alpenkorps troops by the thousand and the Stukas by the hundred, the best he has – and he needs them desperately on the Italian front.

But you've got to convince your potential ally that you're a pretty safe bet before you can persuade him to give up his nice, safe seat on the fence and jump down on your side.'

'Very interestin',' Miller observed. 'So?'

'So the Germans are going to have no compunction about thirty or forty of their best troops being cut into little pieces. It's no trouble at all when you're sitting behind a desk a thousand miles away . . . Let 'em come another hundred yards or so closer. Louki and I will start from the middle and work out: you and Andrea start from the outside.'

'I don't like it, boss,' Miller complained.

'Don't think that I do either,' Mallory said quietly. 'Slaughtering men forced to do a suicidal job like this is not my idea of fun – or even of war. But if we don't get them, they get us.' He broke off and pointed across the burnished sea to where Kheros lay peacefully on the hazed horizon, striking golden glints off the western sun. 'What do you think they would have us do, Dusty?'

'I know, I know, boss.' Miller stirred uncomfortably. 'Don't rub it in.' He pulled his woollen cap low over his forehead and stared bleakly down the slope. 'How soon do the mass executions begin?'

'Another hundred yards, I said.' Mallory looked down the slope again towards the coast road and grinned suddenly, glad to change the topic. 'Never saw telegraph poles shrink so suddenly before, Dusty.'

Miller studied the guns drawn up on the roads behind the two trucks and cleared his throat.

'I was only sayin' what Louki told me,' he said defensively.

'What Louki told you!' The little Greek was indignant. 'Before God, Major, the Americano is full of lies!'

'Ah, well, mebbe I was mistaken,' Miller said magnanimously. He squinted again at the guns, forehead lined in puzzlement. 'That first one's a mortar, I reckon. But what in the universe that other weird-looking contraption can be –'

'Also a mortar,' Mallory explained. 'A five-barrelled job, and very nasty. The *Nebelwerfer* or Moanin' Minnie. Howls like all the lost souls in hell. Guaranteed to turn the knees to jelly, especially after nightfall – but it's still the other one you have to watch. A six-inch mortar, almost certainly using fragmentation bombs – you use a brush and shovel for clearing up afterwards.'

That's right,' Miller growled. 'Cheer us all up.' But he was grateful to the New Zealander for trying to take their minds off what they had to do. 'Why don't they use them?'

'They will,' Mallory assured him. 'Just as soon as we fire and they find out where we are.'

'Gawd help us,' Miller muttered. 'Fragmentation bombs, you said!' He lapsed into gloomy silence.

'Any second now,' Mallory said softly. 'I only hope that our friend Turzig isn't among this lot.' He reached out for his field-glasses but stopped in surprise as Andrea leaned across Louki and caught him by the wrist before he could line the binoculars. 'What's the matter, Andrea?'

'I would not be using these, my Captain. They have betrayed us once already. I have been thinking, and it can be nothing else. The sunlight reflecting from the lenses . . .'

Mallory stared at him, slowly released his grip on the glasses, nodded several times in succession.

'Of course, of course! I had been wondering . . . Someone has been careless. There was no other way, there *could* have been no other way. It would only require a single flash to tip them off.' He paused, remembering, then grinned wryly. 'It could have been myself. All this started just after I had been on watch – and Panayis didn't have the glasses.' He shook his head in mortification. 'It must have been me, Andrea.'

'I do not believe it,' Andrea said flatly. 'You couldn't make a mistake like that, my Captain.'

'Not only could, but did, I'm afraid. But we'll worry about that afterwards.' The middle of the ragged line of advancing soldiers, slipping and stumbling on the treacherous scree, had almost reached the lower limits of the blackened, stunted remains of the copse. 'They've come far enough. I'll take the white helmet in the middle, Louki.' Even as he spoke he could hear the soft scrape as the three others slid their automatic barrels across and between the protective rocks in front of them, could feel the wave of revulsion that washed through his mind. But his voice was steady enough as he spoke, relaxed and almost casual. 'Right. Let them have it now!'

His last words were caught up and drowned in the tearing, rapid-fire crash of the automatic carbines. With four machine-guns in their hands – two Brens and two 9 mm Schmeissers – it was no war, as he had said, but sheer, pitiful massacre, with the defenceless figures on the slope below, figures still stunned and uncomprehending, jerking, spinning round and collapsing like marionettes in the hands of a mad puppeteer, some to lie where they fell, others to roll down the steep slope, legs and arms flailing in the grotesque disjointedness of death. Only a couple stood still where they had been hit, vacant surprise mirrored in their lifeless faces, then slipped down tiredly to the stony ground at their feet. Almost three seconds had passed before the handful of those who still lived – about a quarter of the way in from either end of the line where the converging streams of fire had not yet met – realised what was happening and flung themselves desperately to the ground in search of the cover that didn't exist.

The phrenetic stammering of the machine-guns stopped abruptly and in unison, the sound sheared off as by a guillotine. The sudden silence was curiously oppressive, louder, more obtrusive than the clamour that had gone before. The gravelly earth beneath his elbows grated harshly as Mallory shifted his weight slightly, looked at the two men to his right, Andrea with his impassive face empty of all expression, Louki with the sheen of tears in his eyes. Then he became aware of the low murmuring to his left, shifted round again. Bitter-mouthed, savage, the American was swearing softly and continuously, oblivious to the pain as he pounded his fist time and again into the sharp-edged gravel before him.

'Just one more, Gawd.' The quiet voice was almost a prayer. 'That's all I ask. Just one more.'

Mallory touched his arm. 'What is it, Dusty?'

Miller looked round at him, eyes cold and still and empty of all recognition, then he blinked several times and grinned, a cut and bruised hand automatically reaching for his cigarettes.

'Jus' daydreamin', boss,' he said easily. 'Jus' daydreamin'.' He shook out his pack of cigarettes. 'Have one?'

'That inhuman bastard that sent those poor devils up this hill,' Mallory said quietly. 'Make a wonderful picture seen over the sights of your rifle, wouldn't he?'

Abruptly Miller's smile vanished and he nodded.

'It would be all of that.' He risked a quick peep round one of the boulders, eased himself back again. 'Eight, mebbe ten of them still down there, boss,' he reported. 'The poor bastards are like ostriches – trying to take cover behind stones the size of an orange . . . We leave them be?'

'We leave them be!' Mallory echoed emphatically. The thought of any more slaughter made him feel almost physically sick. 'They won't try again.' He broke off suddenly, flattened himself in reflex instinct as a burst of machine-gun bullets struck the steep-walled rock above their heads and whined up the gorge in vicious ricochet.

'Won't try again, huh?' Miller was already sliding his gun around the rock in front of him when Mallory caught his arm and pulled him back.

'Not them? Listen!' Another burst of fire, then another, and now they could hear the savage chatter of the machine-gun, a chatter rhythmically interrupted by a weird, half-human sighing as its belt passed through the breech. Mallory could feel the prickling of the hairs on the nape of his neck.

'A Spandau. Once you've heard a Spandau you can never forget it. Leave it alone – it's probably fixed on the back of one of the trucks and can't do us any harm . . . I'm more worried about those damned mortars down there.'

'I'm not,' Miller said promptly. 'They're not firing at us.'

'That's why I'm worried . . . What do you think, Andrea.'

'The same as you, my Captain. They are waiting. This Devil's Playground, as Louki calls it, is a madman's maze, and they can only fire as blind men –'

'They won't be waiting much longer,' Mallory interrupted grimly. He pointed to the north. 'Here come their eyes.'

At first only specks above the promontory of Cape Demirci, the planes were soon recognisable for what they were, droning in slowly over the Aegean at about fifteen hundred feet. Mallory looked at them in astonishment, then turned to Andrea.

'Am I seeing things, Andrea?' He gestured at the first of the two planes, a high-winged little monoplane fighter. 'That can't be a PZL?'

'It can be and it is,' Andrea murmured. 'An old Polish plane we had before the war,' he explained to Miller. 'And the other is an old Belgian plane – Breguets, we called them.' Andrea shaded his eyes to look again at the two planes, now almost directly overhead. 'I thought they had all been lost during the invasion.'

'Me, too,' Mallory said. 'Must have patched up some bits and pieces. Ah, they've seen us – beginning to circle. But why on earth they use those obsolete death traps –'

'I don't know and I don't care,' Miller said rapidly. He had just taken a quick look round the boulder in front of him. 'Those damned guns down there are just linin' up on us, and muzzle-on they look a considerable sight bigger than telegraph poles.

Fragmentation bombs, you said! Come on, boss, let's get the hell outa here!'

Thus the pattern was set for the remainder of that brief November afternoon, for the grim game of tip-and-run, hide-and-seek among the ravines and shattered rocks of the Devil's Playground. The planes held the key to the game, cruised high overhead observing every move of the hunted group below, relaying the information to the guns on the coast road and the company of Alpenkorps that had moved up through the ravine above the carob grove soon after the planes reported that the positions there had been abandoned. The two ancient planes were soon replaced by a couple of modern Henschels – Andrea said that the PZL couldn't remain airborne for more than an hour anyway.

Mallory was between the devil and the deep sea. Inaccurate though the mortars were, some of the deadly fragmentation bombs found their way into the deep ravines where they took temporary shelter, the blast of metal lethal in the confined space between the sheering walls. Occasionally they came so close that Mallory was forced to take refuge in some of the deep caves that honeycombed the walls of the canyons. In these they were safe enough, but the safety was an illusion that could lead only to ultimate defeat and capture; in the lulls, the Alpenkorps, whom they had fought off in a series of brief, skirmishing rearguard actions during the afternoon, could approach closely enough to trap them inside. Time and time again Mallory and his men were forced to move on to widen the gap between themselves and their pursuers, following the indomitable Louki wherever he chose to lead them, and taking their chance, often a very slender and desperate chance, with the mortar bombs. One bomb arced into a ravine that led into the interior, burying itself in the gravelly ground not twenty yards ahead of them, by far the nearest anything had come during the afternoon. By one chance in a thousand, it didn't explode. They gave it as wide a berth as possible, almost holding their breaths until they were safely beyond.

About half an hour before sunset they struggled up the last few boulder-strewn yards of a steeply-shelving ravine floor, halted just beyond the shelter of the projecting wall where the ravine dipped again and turned sharply to the right and the north. There had been no more mortar bombs since the one that had failed to explode. The six-inch and the weirdly-howling *Nebelwerfer* had only a limited range, Mallory knew, and though the planes still cruised overhead, they cruised uselessly: the sun was dipping towards the horizon and the floors of the ravines were already deeply-sunk in shadowed gloom, invisible from above. But the Alpenkorps, tough, dogged, skilful soldiers, soldiers living only for the revenge of their massacred comrades, were very close behind. And they were highly-trained mountain troops, fresh, resilient, the reservoir of their energies barely tapped: whereas his own tiny band, worn out from continuous days and sleepless nights of labour and action . . .

Mallory sank to the ground near the angled turn of the ravine where he could keep lookout, glanced at the others with a deceptive casualness that marked his cheerless assessment of what he saw. As a fighting unit they were in a pretty bad way. Both Panayis and Brown were badly crippled, the latter's face grey with pain. For the first time since leaving Alexandria, Casey Brown was apathetic, listless and quite indifferent to everything: this Mallory took as a very bad sign. Nor was Brown helped by the heavy transmitter still strapped to his back – with point-blank truculence he had ignored Mallory's categorical order to abandon it. Louki was tired, and looked it: his physique, Mallory realised now, was no match for his spirit, for the infectious smile that never left his face, for the panache of that magnificently upswept moustache that contrasted so oddly with the sad, tired eyes above. Miller, like himself, was tired, but, like himself, could keep on being tired for a long time yet. And Stevens was still conscious, but even in the twilit gloom of the canyon floor his face looked curiously transparent, while the nails, lips and eyelids were drained of blood. And Andrea, who had carried him up and down all these killing canyon tracks – where there had been tracks – for almost two interminable hours, looked as he always did: immutable, indestructible.

Mallory shook his head, fished out a cigarette, made to strike a light, remembered the planes still cruising overhead and threw the match away. Idly his gaze travelled north along the canyon and he slowly stiffened, the unlit cigarette crumpling and shredding between his fingers. This ravine bore no resemblance to any of the others through which they had so far passed – it was broader, dead straight, at least three times as long – and, as far as he could see in the twilight, the far end was blocked off by an almost vertical wall.

'Louki!' Mallory was on his feet now, all weariness forgotten. 'Do you know where you are? Do you know this place?'

'But certainly, Major!' Louki was hurt. 'Have I not told you that Panayis and I, in the days of our youth –'

'But this is a cul-de-sac, a dead-end!' Mallory protested. 'We're boxed in, man, we're trapped!'

Louki grinned impudently and twirled a corner of his moustache. The little man was enjoying himself.

'So? The Major does not trust Louki, is that it?' He grinned again, relented, patted the wall by his side. 'Panayis and I, we have been working this way all afternoon. Along this wall there are many caves. One of them leads through to another valley that leads down to the coast road.'

'I see, I see.' Relief washing through his mind, Mallory sank down on the ground again. 'And where does this other valley come out?'

'Just across the strait from Maidos.'

'How far from the town?'

'About five miles, Major, maybe six. Not more.'

'Fine, fine! And you're sure you can find this cave?'

'A hundred years from now and my head in a goat-skin bag!' Louki boasted.

'Fair enough!' Even as he spoke, Mallory catapulted himself violently to one side, twisted in mid-air to avoid falling across Stevens and crashed heavily into the wall between Andrea and Miller. In a moment of unthinking carelessness he had exposed himself to view from the ravine they had just climbed: the burst of machine-gun fire from its lower end – a hundred and fifty yards away at the most – had almost blown his head off. Even as it was, the left shoulder of his jacket had been torn away, the shell just grazing his shoulder. Miller was already kneeling by his side, fingering the gash, running a gently exploratory hand across his back.

'Careless, damn careless,' Mallory murmured. 'But I didn't think they were so close.' He didn't feel as calm as he sounded. If the mouth of that Schmeisser had been another sixteenth of an inch to the right, he'd have had no head left now.

'Are you all right, boss?' Miller was puzzled. 'Did they –'

'Terrible shots,' Mallory assured him cheerfully. 'Couldn't hit a barn.' He twisted round to look at his shoulder. 'I hate to sound heroic, but this really is just a scratch . . .' He rose easily to his feet, and picked up his guns. 'Sorry and all that, gentlemen, but it's time we were on our way again. How far along is this cave, Louki?'

Louki rubbed his bristly chin, the smile suddenly gone. He looked quickly at Mallory, then away again.

'Louki!'

'Yes, yes, Major. The cave.' Louki rubbed his chin again. 'Well, it is a good way along. In fact, it is at the end,' he finished uncomfortably.

'The *very* end?' asked Mallory quietly.

Louki nodded miserably, stared down at the ground at his feet. Even the ends of his moustache seemed to droop.

'That's handy,' Mallory said heavily. 'Oh, that's very handy!' He sank down to the ground again. 'Helps us no end, that does.'

He bowed his head in thought and didn't even lift it as Andrea poked a Bren round the angle of the rock, and fired a short down-hill burst more in token of discouragement than in any hope of hitting anything. Another ten seconds passed, then Louki spoke again, his voice barely audible.

'I am very, very sorry. This is a terrible thing. Before God, Major, I would not have done it but that I thought they were still far behind.'

'It's not your fault, Louki.' Mallory was touched by the little man's obvious distress. He touched his ripped shoulder jacket. 'I thought the same thing.'

'Please!' Stevens put his hand on Mallory's arm. 'What's wrong? I don't understand.'

'Everybody else does, I'm afraid, Andy. It's very, very simple. We have half a mile to go along this valley here – and not a shred of cover. The Alpenkorps have less than two hundred yards to come up that ravine we've just left.' He paused while Andrea fired another retaliatory short burst, then continued. 'They'll do what they're doing now – keep probing to see if we're still here. The minute they judge we're gone, they'll be up here in a flash. They'll nail us before we're half-way, quarter-way to the cave – you know we can't travel fast. And they're carrying a couple of Spandaus – they'll cut us to ribbons.'

'I see,' Stevens murmured. 'You put it all so nicely, sir.'

'Sorry, Andy, but that's how it is.'

'But could you not leave two men as a rear-guard, while the rest –'

'And what happens to the rear-guard?' Mallory interrupted dryly.

'I see what you mean,' he said in a low voice. 'I hadn't thought of that.'

'No, but the rear-guard would. Quite a problem, isn't it?'

'There is no problem at all,' Louki announced. 'The Major is kind, but this is all my fault. I will –'

'You'll do damn all of the kind!' Miller said savagely. He tore Louki's Bren from his hand and laid it on the ground. 'You heard what the boss said – it wasn't your fault.' For a moment Louki stared at him in anger, then turned dejectedly away. He looked as if he were going to cry. Mallory, too, stared at the American, astonished at the sudden vehemence, so completely out of character. Now that he came to think of it, Dusty had been strangely taciturn and thoughtful during the past hour or so – Mallory couldn't recall his saying a word during all that time. But time enough to worry about that later on . . .

Casey Brown eased his injured leg, looking hopefully at Mallory. 'Couldn't we stay here till it's dark – real dark – then make our way –'

'No good. The moon's almost full tonight – and not a cloud in the sky. They'd get us. Even more important, we have to get into the town between sunset and curfew tonight. Our last chance. Sorry, Casey, but it's no go.'

Fifteen seconds, half a minute passed, and passed in silence, then they all started abruptly as Andy Stevens spoke.

'Louki *was* right, you know,' he said pleasantly. The voice was weak, but filled with a calm certainty that jerked every eye towards him. He was propped up on one elbow, Louki's Bren cradled in his hands. It was a measure of their concentration on the problem on hand that no one had heard or seen him reach out for the machine-gun. 'It's all very simple,' Stevens went on quietly. 'Just let's use our heads, that's all . . . The gangrene's right up past the knee, isn't it, sir?'

Mallory said nothing: he didn't know what to say, the complete unexpectedness had knocked him off balance. He was vaguely aware that Miller was looking at him, his eyes begging him to say 'No.'

'Is it or isn't it?' There was a patience, a curious understanding in the voice, and all of a sudden Mallory knew what to say.

'Yes,' he nodded. 'It is.' Miller was looking at him in horror.

'Thank you, sir.' Stevens was smiling in satisfaction. 'Thank you very much indeed. There's no need to point out all the advantages of my staying here.' There was an assurance in his voice no one had ever heard before, the unthinking authority of a man completely in charge of a situation. 'Time I did something for my living anyway. No fond farewells, please. Just leave me a couple of boxes of ammo, two or three thirty-six grenades and away you go.'

'I'll be darned if we will!' Miller was up on his feet making for the boy, then brought up abruptly as the Bren centred on his chest.

'One step nearer and I'll shoot you,' Stevens said calmly. Miller looked at him in long silence, sank slowly back to the ground.

'I would, you know,' Stevens assured him. 'Well good-bye, gentlemen. Thank you for all you've done for me.'

Twenty seconds, thirty, a whole minute passed in a queer, trance-like silence, then Miller heaved himself to his feet again, a tall, rangy figure with tattered clothes and a face curiously haggard in the gathering gloom.

'So long, kid. I guess – waal, mebbe I'm not so smart after all.' He took Stevens's hand, looked down at the wasted face for a long moment, made to say something else, then changed his mind. 'Be seein' you,' he said abruptly, turned and walked off heavily down the valley. One by one the others followed him, wordlessly, except for Andrea, who stopped and whispered in the boy's ear, a whisper that brought a smile and a nod of complete understanding, and then there was only Mallory left. Stevens grinned up at him.

'Thank you, sir. Thanks for not letting me down. You and Andrea – you understand. You always did understand.'

'You'll – you'll be all right, Andy?' God, Mallory thought, what a stupid, what an insane thing, to say.

'Honest, sir, I'm OK.' Stevens smiled contentedly. 'No pain left – I can't feel a thing. It's wonderful!'

'Andy, I don't –'

'It's time you were gone, sir. The others will be waiting. Now if you'll just light me a gasper and fire a few random shots down that ravine . . .'

Within five minutes Mallory had overtaken the others, and inside fifteen they had all reached the cave that led to the coast. For a moment they stood in the entrance, listening to the intermittent firing from the other end of the valley, then turned wordlessly and plunged into the cave. Back where they had left him, Andy Stevens was lying on his stomach, peering down into the now almost dark ravine. There was no pain left in his body, none at all. He drew deeply on a cupped cigarette, smiled as he pushed another clip home into the magazine of the Bren. For the first time in his life Andy Stevens was happy and content beyond his understanding, a man at last at peace with himself. He was no longer afraid.

THIRTEEN

Wednesday Evening
1800–1915

Exactly forty minutes later they were safely in the heart of the town of Navarone, within fifty yards of the great gates of the fortress itself.

Mallory, gazing out at the gates and the still more massive arch of stone that encased them, shook his head for the tenth time and tried to fight off the feeling of disbelief and wonder that they should have reached their goal at last – or as nearly as made no difference. They had been due a break some time, he thought, the law of averages had been overwhelmingly against the continuation of the evil fortune that had dogged them so incessantly since they had arrived on the island. It was only right, he kept telling himself, it was only just that this should be so: but even so, the transition from that dark valley where they had left Andy Stevens to die to this tumbledown old house on the east side of the town square of Navarone had been so quick, so easy, that it still lay beyond immediate understanding or unthinking acceptance.

Not that it had been too easy in the first fifteen minutes or so, he remembered. Panayis's wounded leg had given out on him immediately after they had entered the cave, and he had collapsed; he must have been in agony, Mallory had thought, with his torn, roughly-bandaged leg, but the failing light and the dark, bitter impassive face had masked the pain. He had begged Mallory to be allowed to remain where he was, to hold off the Alpenkorps when they had overcome Stevens and reached the end of the valley, but Mallory had roughly refused him permission. Brutally he had told Panayis that he was far too valuable to be left there – and that the chances of the Alpenkorps picking that cave out of a score of others were pretty remote. Mallory had hated having to talk to him like that, but there had been no time for gentle blandishments, and Panayis must have seen his point for he had made neither protest nor struggle when Miller and Andrea picked him up and helped him to limp through the cave. The limp, Mallory had noticed, had been much less noticeable then, perhaps because of the assistance, perhaps because now that he had been baulked of the chance of killing a few more Germans it had been pointless to exaggerate his hurt.

They had barely cleared the mouth of the cave on the other side and were making their way down the tree-tufted sloping valley side towards the sea, the dark sheen of the Aegean clearly visible in the gloom, when Louki, hearing something, had gestured them all to silence. Almost immediately Mallory, too, heard it, a soft guttural voice occasionally lost in the crunch of approaching feet on gravel. Mallory had seen that they were providentially screened by some stunted trees, given the order to stop and sworn in quick anger as he had heard the soft thud and barely muffled cry behind them. He had gone back to investigate and found Panayis stretched on the ground unconscious. Miller, who had been helping him along, had explained that Mallory had halted them so suddenly that he'd bumped into Panayis, that the Greek's bad leg had given beneath him, throwing him heavily, his head striking a stone as he had fallen. Mallory had stooped down in instantly renewed suspicion – Panayis was a throw-back, a natural-born killer, and he was quite capable of faking an accident if he thought he could turn it to his advantage, line a few more of the enemy up on the sights of his rifle . . . but there had been no fake about that: the bruised and bloodied gash above the temple was all too real.

The German patrol, having had no inkling of their presence, moved noisily up the valley till they had finally gone out of earshot. Louki had thought that the commandant in Navarone was becoming desperate, trying to seal off every available exit from the Devil's Playground. Mallory had thought it unlikely, but had not stayed to argue the point. Five minutes later they had cleared the mouth of the valley, and in another five had not only reached the coast road but silenced and bound two sentries – the drivers, probably – who had been guarding a truck and command car parked by the roadside, stripped them of denims and helmets and bundled them out of sight behind some bushes.

The trip into Navarone had been ridiculously simple, but the entire lack of opposition was easily understandable, because of the complete unexpectedness of it all. Seated beside Mallory on the front seat, clad, like Mallory, in captured clothes, Louki had driven the big car, and driven it magnificently, an accomplishment so unusual to find in a remote Aegean island that Mallory had been completely mystified until Louki had reminded him that he had been Eugene Vlachos's Consulate chauffeur for many years. The drive into town had taken less than twelve minutes – not only did the little man handle the car superbly, but he knew the road so well that he got the utmost possible out of the big machine, most of the time without benefit of any lights at all.

Not only a simple journey, but quite uneventful. They had passed several parked trucks at intervals along the road, and less than two miles from the town itself had met a group of about twenty soldiers marching in the opposite direction in column of twos. Louki had slowed down – it would have been highly suspicious had he accelerated, endangering the lives of the marching men – but had switched on the powerful headlights, blinding them, and blown raucously on the horn, while Mallory had leaned out of the right-hand window, sworn at them in perfect German and told them to get out of his damned way. This they had done, while the junior officer in charge had come smartly to attention, throwing up his hand in punctilious salute.

Immediately afterwards they had run through an area of high-walled, terraced market gardens, passed between a decaying Byzantine church and a whitewashed orthodox monastery that faced each other incongruously across the same dusty road, then almost at once were running through the lower part of the old town. Mallory had had a vague impression of narrow, winding, dim-lit streets only inches wider than the car itself, hugely cobbled and with almost knee-high pavements, then Louki was making his way up an arched lane, the car climbing steeply all the time. He had stopped abruptly and Mallory had followed his quick survey of the darkened lane; completely deserted though over an hour yet to curfew. Beside them had been a flight of white stone steps innocent of any hand-rail, running up parallel to the wall of a house, with a highly ornamented latticework grille protecting the outside landing at the top. A still groggy Panayis had led them up these stairs, through to a house – he had known exactly where he was – across a shallow roof, down some more steps, through a dark courtyard and into this ancient house where they were now. Louki had driven the car away even before they had reached the top of the stairs; it was only now that Mallory remembered that Louki hadn't thought it worth while to say what he intended to do with the car.

Still gazing out of the windowless hole in the wall at the fortress gate, Mallory found himself hoping intensely that nothing would happen to the sad-eyed little Greek, and not only because in his infinite resource and local knowledge he had been invaluable to them and was likely to prove so again; all these considerations apart, Mallory had formed the deepest affection for him, for his unvarying cheerfulness, his enthusiasm, his eagerness to help and to please, above all for his complete disregard of self. A thoroughly lovable little man, and Mallory's heart warmed to him. More than he could say for Panayis, he thought sourly, and then immediately regretted the thought; it was no fault of Panayis's that he was what he was, and in his own dark and bitter way he had done as much for them as Louki. But the fact remained that he was sadly lacking in Louki's warm humanity.

He lacked also Louki's quick intelligence, the calculated opportunism that amounted almost to genius. It had been a brilliant idea on Louki's part, Mallory mused, that they should take over this abandoned house: not that there had been any difficulty in finding an empty house – since the Germans had taken over the old castle the inhabitants of the town had left in their scores for Margaritha and other outlying villages, none more quickly than those who had lived in the town square itself; the nearness of the fortress wall that formed the north side of the square had been more than many of them could stomach, with the constant coming and going of their conquerors through the fortress gates, the sentries marching to and fro, the never-ceasing reminders that their freedom was a vanished thing. So many gone that more than half the houses on the west side of the square – those nearest the fortress – were now occupied by German officers. But this same enforced close observation of the fortress's activities had been exactly what Mallory had wanted. When the time came to strike they had only yards to go. And although any competent garrison commander would always be prepared against the unexpected, Mallory considered it unlikely indeed that any reasonable man could conceive of a sabotage group so suicidally minded as to spend an entire day within a literal stone's throw of the fortress wall.

Not that the house as such had much to recommend it. As a home, a dwelling place, it was just about as uncomfortable as

possible, as dilapidated as it could be without actually falling down.
The west side of the square – the side perched precariously on the
cliff-top – and the south side were made up of fairly modern buildings of whitewashed stone and Parian granite, huddled together in
the invariable fashion of houses in these island towns, flat-roofed
to catch as much as possible of the winter rains. But the east side
of the square, where they were, was made up of antiquated timber
and turf houses, of the kind much more often found in remote
mountain villages.

The beaten earth floor beneath his feet was hummocky, uneven,
and the previous occupants had used one corner of it – obviously –
for a variety of purposes, not least as a refuse dump. The ceiling
was of rough-hewn, blackened beams, more or less covered with
planks, these in turn being covered with a thick layer of trodden
earth: from previous experience of such houses in the White
Mountains, Mallory knew that the roof would leak like a sieve
whenever the rain came on. Across one end of the room was a
solid ledge some thirty inches high, a ledge that served, after the
fashion of similar structures in Eskimo igloos, as bed, tables or settee as the occasion demanded. The room was completely bare of
furniture.

Mallory started as someone touched him on the shoulder and
turned round. Miller was behind him munching away steadily, the
remains of a bottle of wine in his hand.

'Better get some chow, boss,' he advised. 'I'll take a gander
through this hole from time to time.'

'Right you are, Dusty. Thanks.' Mallory moved gingerly towards
the back of the room – it was almost pitch dark inside and they
dared not risk a light – and felt his way till he brought up against
the ledge. The tireless Andrea had gone through their provisions
and prepared a meal of sorts – dried figs, honey, cheese, garlic
sausages and pounded roast chestnuts. A horrible mixture, Mallory
thought, but the best Andrea could do: besides he was too hungry,
ravenously so, to worry about such niceties as the pleasing of his
palate. And by the time he had washed it down with some of the
local wine that Louki and Panayis had provided the previous day,
the sweetly-resinous rawness of the drink had obliterated every
other taste.

Carefully, shielding the match with his hand, Mallory lit a cigarette and began to explain for the first time his plan for entering the
fortress. He did not have to bother lowering his voice – a couple of

looms in the next house, one of the few occupied ones left on that side of the square, clacked incessantly throughout the evening. Mallory had a shrewd suspicion that this was more of Louki's doing although it was difficult to see how he could have got word through to any of his friends. But Mallory was content to accept the situation as it was, to concentrate on making sure that the others understood his instructions.

Apparently they did, for there were no questions. For a few minutes the talk became general, the usually taciturn Casey Brown having the most to say, complaining bitterly about the food, the drink, his injured leg and the hardness of the bench where he wouldn't be able to sleep a wink all night long. Mallory grinned to himself but said nothing; Casey Brown was definitely on the mend.

'I reckon we've talked enough, gentlemen.' Mallory slid off the bench and stretched himself. God, he was tired! 'Our first and last chance to get a decent night's sleep. Two hour watches – I'll take the first.'

'By yourself?' It was Miller calling softly from the other end of the room. 'Don't you think we should share watches, boss? One for the front, one for the back. Besides, you know we're all pretty well done up. One man by himself might fall asleep.' He sounded so anxious that Mallory laughed.

'Not a chance, Dusty. Each man will keep watch by the window there and if he falls asleep he'll damn soon wake up when he hits the floor. And it's because we're so darned bushed that we can't afford to have anyone lose sleep unnecessarily. Myself first, then you, then Panayis, then Casey, then Andrea.'

'Yeah, I suppose that'll be OK,' Miller conceded grudgingly.

He put something hard and cold into his hand. Mallory recognised it at once – it was Miller's most cherished possession, his silenced automatic.

'Just so's you can fill any nosy customers full of little holes without wakin' the whole town.' He ambled off to the back of the room, lit a cigarette, smoked it quietly for a few moments, then swung his legs up on the bench. Within five minutes everyone except the silently watchful man at the window was sound asleep.

Two or three minutes later Mallory jerked to unmoving attention as he heard a stealthy sound outside – from the back of the house, he thought. The clacking of the looms next door had stopped, and the house was very still. Again there came the noise, unmistakable this time, a gentle tapping at the door at the end of the passage that led from the back of the room.

'Remain there, my Captain.' It was Andrea's soft murmur, and Mallory marvelled for the hundredth time at Andrea's ability to rouse himself from the deepest of sleeps at the slightest alien sound: the violence of a thunderstorm would have left him undisturbed. 'I will see to it. It must be Louki.'

It was Louki. The little man was panting, near exhaustion, but extraordinarily pleased with himself. Gratefully he drank the cup of wine that Andrea poured for him.

'Damned glad to see you back again!' Mallory said sincerely. 'How did it go? Someone after you?'

Mallory could almost see him drawing himself up to his full height in the darkness.

'As if any of those clumsy fools could see Louki, even on a moonlit night, far less catch him,' he said indignantly. He paused to draw some deep breath. 'No, no, Major, I knew you would be worried about me so I ran back all the way. Well, nearly all the way,' he amended. 'I am not so young as I was, Major Mallory.'

'All the way from where?' Mallory asked. He was glad of the darkness that hid his smile.

'From Vygos. It is an old castle that the Franks built there many generations ago, about two miles from here along the coast road to the east.' He paused to drink another mouthful of wine. 'More than two miles, I would say – and I only walked twice, a minute at a time, on the way back.' Mallory had the impression that Louki already regretted his momentary weakness in admitting that he was no longer a young man.

'And what did you do there?' Mallory asked.

'I was thinking, after I left you,' Louki answered indirectly. 'Me, I am always thinking,' he explained. 'It is a habit of mine. I was thinking that when the soldiers who are looking for us out in the Devil's Playground find out that the car is gone, they will know that we are no longer in that accursed place.'

'Yes,' Mallory agreed carefully. 'Yes, they will know that.'

'Then they will say to themselves, "Ha, those *verdammt Englanders* have little time left." They will know that we will know that they have little hope of catching us in the island – Panayis and I, we know every rock and tree and path and cave. So all they can do is to make sure that we do not get into the town – they will block every road leading in, and tonight is our last chance to get in. You follow me?' he asked anxiously.

'I am trying very hard.'

'But first' – Louki spread his hands dramatically – 'but first they will make sure we are not in the town. They would be fools to block the roads if we were already in the town. They *must* make sure we are not in the town. And so – the search. The very great search. With – how do you say? – the teeth-comb!'

Mallory nodded his head in slow understanding.

'I'm afraid he's right, Andrea.'

'I, too, fear so,' Andrea said unhappily. 'We should have thought of this. But perhaps we could hide – the roof-tops or –'

'With a teeth-comb, I said!' Louki interrupted impatiently. 'But all is well. I, Louki, have thought it all out. I can smell rain. There will be clouds over the moon before long, and it will be safe to move . . . You do not want to know what I have done with the car, Major Mallory?' Louki was enjoying himself immensely.

'Forgotten all about it,' Mallory confessed. 'What *did* you do with the car?'

'I left it in the courtyard of Vygos castle. Then I emptied all the petrol from the tank and poured it over the car. Then I struck a match.'

'You did *what*?' Mallory was incredulous.

'I struck a match. I think I was standing too near the car, for I do not seem to have any eyebrows left.' Louki sighed. 'A pity – it was such a splendid machine.' Then he brightened. 'But before God, Major, it burned magnificently.'

Mallory stared at him.

'Why on earth –?'

It is simple,' Louki explained patiently. 'By this time the men out in the Devil's Playground must know that their car has been stolen. They see the fire. They hurry back to – how do you say?'

'Investigate?'

'So. Investigate. They wait till the fire dies down. They investigate again. No bodies, no bones in the car, so they search the castle. And what do they find?'

There was silence in the room.

'Nothing!' Louki said impatiently. 'They find nothing. And then they search the countryside for half a mile around. And what do they find? Again nothing. So then they know that they have been fooled, and that we are in the town, and will come to search the town.'

'With the teeth-comb,' Mallory murmured.

'With the teeth-comb. And what do they find?' Louki paused, then hurried on before anyone could steal his thunder. 'Once again, they will find nothing,' he said triumphantly. 'And why? For by then the rain will have come, the moon will have vanished, the explosives will be hidden – and we will be gone!'

'Gone where?' Mallory felt dazed.

'Where but to Vygos castle, Major Mallory. Never while night follows day will they think to look for us there!'

Mallory looked at him in silence for long seconds without speaking, then turned to Andrea.

'Captain Jensen's only made one mistake so far,' he murmured. 'He picked the wrong man to lead this expedition. Not that it matters anyway. With Louki here on our side, how can we lose?'

Mallory lowered his rucksack gently to the earthen roof, straightened and peered up into the darkness, both hands shielding his eyes from the first drizzle of rain. Even from where they stood – on the crumbling roof of the house nearest the fortress on the east side of the square – the walls stretched fifteen, perhaps twenty feet above their heads; the wickedly out- and down-curving spikes that topped the wall were all but lost in the darkness.

'There she is, Dusty,' Mallory murmured. 'Nothing to it.'

'Nothin' to it!' Miller was horrified. 'I've – I've gotta get over *that*?'

'You'd have a ruddy hard time going through it,' Mallory answered briefly. He grinned, clapped Miller on the back and prodded the rucksack at his feet. 'We chuck this rope up, the hook catches, you shin smartly up –'

'And bleed to death on those six strands of barbed wire,' Miller interrupted. 'Louki says they're the biggest barbs he's ever seen.'

'We'll use the tent for padding,' Mallory said soothingly.

'I have a very delicate skin, boss,' Miller complained. 'Nothin' short of a spring mattress –'

'Well, you've only an hour to find one,' Mallory said indifferently. Louki had estimated that it would be at least an hour before the search party would clear the northern part of the town, give himself and Andrea a chance to begin a diversion. 'Come on, let's cache this stuff and get out of here. We'll shove the rucksacks in this corner and cover 'em with earth. Take the rope out first, though; we'll have no time to start undoing the packs when we get here.'

Miller dropped to his knees, hands fumbling with straps, then exclaimed in sudden annoyance.

'This can't be the pack,' he muttered in disgust. Abruptly his voice changed. 'Here, wait a minute, though.'

'What's up, Dusty?'

Miller didn't answer immediately. For a few seconds his hands explored the contents of the pack, then he straightened.

'The slow-burnin' fuse, boss.' His voice was blurred with anger, with a vicious anger that astonished Mallory. 'It's gone!'

'What!' Mallory stooped, began to search through the pack. 'It can't be, Dusty, it just *can't*! Dammit to hell, man, you packed the stuff yourself!'

'Sure I did, boss,' Miller grated. 'And then some crawlin' bastard comes along behind my back and unpacks it again.'

'Impossible!' Mallory protested. 'It's just downright impossible, Dusty. You closed that rucksack – I saw you do it in the grove this morning – and Louki has had it all the time. And I'd trust Louki with my life.'

'So would I, boss.'

'Maybe we're both wrong,' Mallory went on quietly. 'Maybe you did miss it out. We're both helluva tired, Dusty.'

Miller looked at him queerly, said nothing for a moment, then began to swear again. 'It's my own fault, boss, my own damned fault.'

'What do you mean, your own fault? Heavens above, man, I was there when . . .' Mallory broke off, rose quickly to his feet and stared through the darkness at the south side of the square. A single shot had rung out there, the whiplash crack of a carbine followed the thin, high whine of a ricochet, and then silence.

Mallory stood quite still, hands clenched by his sides. Over ten minutes had passed since he and Miller had left Panayis to guide Andrea and Brown to the Castle Vygos – and they should have been well away from the square by this time. And almost certainly Louki wouldn't be down there, Mallory's instructions to him had been explicit – to hide the remainder of the TNT blocks in the roof and then wait there to lead himself and Miller to the keep. But something could have gone wrong, something could always go wrong. Or a trap, maybe a ruse. But what kind of trap?

The sudden off-beat stammering of a heavy machine-gun stilled his thoughts, and for a moment or two he was all eyes and straining ears. And then another, and lighter machine-gun, cut in, just for a few seconds: as abruptly as they had started, both guns died away, together. Mallory waited no longer.

'Get the stuff together again,' he whispered urgently. 'We're taking it with us. Something's gone wrong.' Within thirty seconds they had ropes and explosives back in their knapsacks, had strapped them on their backs and were on their way.

Bent almost double, careful to make no noise whatsoever they ran across the roof-tops towards the old house where they had hidden earlier in the evening, where they were now to rendezvous with Louki. Still running, they were only feet away from the house when they saw his shadowy figure rise up, only it wasn't Louki. Mallory realised at once, for it was too tall for Louki and without breaking step he catapulted the horizontal driving weight of his 180 pounds at the unknown figure in a homicidal tackle, his shoulder catching the man just below the breast-bone, emptying every last particle of air from the man's lungs with an explosive agonised *whoosh*. A second later both of Miller's sinewy hands were clamped round the man's neck, slowly choking him to death.

And he would have choked to death, neither of the two men were in any mind for half-measures, had not Mallory, prompted by some fugitive intuition, stooped low over the contorted face, the staring, protruding eyes, choked back a cry of sudden horror.

'Dusty!' he whispered hoarsely. 'For God's sake, stop! Let him go! It's Panayis!'

Miller didn't hear him. In the gloom his face was like stone, his head sunk farther and farther between hunching shoulders as he tightened his grip, strangling the Greek in a weird savage silence.

'It's Panayis, you bloody fool, Panayis!' Mallory's mouth was at the American's ear, his hands clamped round the other's wrists as he tried to drag him off Panayis's throat. He could hear the muffled drumming of Panayis's heels on the turf of the roof, tore at Miller's wrists with all his strength: twice before he had heard that sound as a man had died under Andrea's great hands, and he knew with sudden certainty that Panayis would go the same way, and soon, if he didn't make Miller understand. But all at once Miller understood, relaxed heavily, straightened up, still kneeling, hands hanging limply by his sides. Breathing deeply he stared down in silence at the man at his feet.

'What the hell's the matter with you?' Mallory demanded softly. 'Deaf or blind or both?'

'Just one of those things, I guess.' Miller rubbed the back of a hand across his forehead, his face empty of expression. 'Sorry, boss, sorry.'

'Why the hell apologise to me?' Mallory looked away from him, looked down at Panayis: the Greek was sitting up now, hands massaging his bruised throat, sucking in long draughts of air in great, whooping gasps. 'But maybe Panayis here might appreciate –'

'Apologies can wait,' Miller interrupted brusquely. 'Ask him what's happened to Louki.'

Mallory looked at him for a moment, made to reply, changed his mind, translated the question. He listened to Panayis's halting answer – it obviously hurt him even to try to speak – and his mouth tightened in a hard, bitter line. Miller watched the fractional slump of the New Zealander's shoulders, felt he could wait no longer.

'Well, what is it, boss? Somethin's happened to Louki, is that it?'

'Yes,' Mallory said tonelessly. 'They'd only got as far as the lane at the back when they found a small German patrol blocking their way. Louki tried to draw them off and the machine-gunner got him through the chest. Andrea got the machine-gunner and took Louki away. Panayis says he'll die for sure.'

FOURTEEN

Wednesday Night
1915–2000

The three men cleared the town without any difficulty, striking out directly across country for the castle Vygos and avoiding the main road. It was beginning to rain now, heavily, persistently, and the ground was mired and sodden, the few ploughed fields they crossed almost impassable. They had just struggled their way through one of these and could just see the dim outline of the keep – less than a cross-country mile from the town instead of Louki's exaggerated estimate – when they passed by an abandoned earthen house and Miller spoke for the first time since they had left the town square of Navarone.

'I'm bushed, boss.' His head was sunk on his chest, and his breathing was laboured. 'Ol' man Miller's on the downward path, I reckon, and the legs are gone. Couldn't we squat inside here for a couple of minutes, boss, and have a smoke?'

Mallory looked at him in surprise, thought how desperately weary his own legs felt and nodded in reluctant agreement. Miller wasn't the man to complain unless he was near exhaustion.

'Okay, Dusty, I don't suppose a minute or two will harm.' He translated quickly into Greek and led the way inside, Miller at his heels complaining at length about his advancing age. Once inside, Mallory felt his way across to the inevitable wooden bunk, sat down gratefully, lit a cigarette then looked up in puzzlement. Miller was still on his feet, walking slowly round the hut, tapping the walls as he went.

'Why don't you sit down?' Mallory asked irritably. 'That was why you came in here in the first place, wasn't it?'

'No, boss, not really.' The drawl was very pronounced. 'Just a low-down trick to get us inside. Two-three very special things I want to show you.'

'Very special? What the devil are you trying to tell me?'

'Bear with me, Captain Mallory,' Miller requested formally. 'Bear with me just a few minutes, I'm not wastin' your time. You have my word, Captain Mallory.'

'Very well.' Mallory was mystified, but his confidence in Miller remained unshaken. 'As you wish. Only don't be too long about it.'

'Thanks, boss.' The strain of formality was too much for Miller. 'It won't take long. There'll be a lamp or candles in here – you said the islanders never leave an abandoned house without 'em?'

'And a very useful superstition it's been to us, too.' Mallory reached under the bunk with his torch, straightened his back. 'Two or three candles here.'

'I want a light, boss. No windows – I checked. OK?'

'Light one and I'll go outside to see if there's anything showing.' Mallory was completely in the dark about the American's intentions. He felt Miller didn't want him to say anything, and there was a calm surety about him that precluded questioning. Mallory was back in less than a minute. 'Not a chink to be seen from the outside,' he reported.

'Fair enough. Thanks, boss.' Miller lit a second candle, then slipped the rucksack straps from his shoulders, laid the pack on the bunk and stood in silence for a moment.

Mallory looked at his watch, looked back at Miller.

'You were going to show me something,' he prompted.

'Yeah, that's right. Three things, I said.' He dug into the pack, brought out a little black box hardly bigger than a match-box. 'Exhibit A, boss.'

Mallory looked at it curiously. 'What's that?'

'Clockwork fuse.' Miller began to unscrew the back panel. 'Hate the damned things. Always make me feel like one of those Bolshevik characters with a dark cloak, a moustache like Louki's and carryin' one of those black cannon-ball things with a sputterin' fuse stickin' outa it. But it works.' He had the back off the box now, examining the mechanism in the light of his torch. 'But this one doesn't, not any more,' he added softly. 'Clock's OK, but the contact arm's been bent right back. This thing could tick till Kingdom Come and it couldn't even set off a firework.'

'But how on earth –?'

'Exhibit B.' Miller didn't seem to hear him. He opened the detonator box, gingerly lifted a fuse from its felt and cotton-wool bed and examined it closely under his torch. Then he looked at Mallory again. 'Fulminate of mercury, boss. Only seventy-seven grains, but enough to blow your fingers off. Unstable as hell, too – the littlest tap will set it off.' He let it fall to the ground, and Mallory winced and drew back involuntarily as the American smashed a heavy heel down on top of it. But there was no explosion, nothing at all.

'Ain't workin' so good either, is it, boss? A hundred to one the rest are all empty, too.' He fished out a pack of cigarettes, lit one, and watched the smoke eddy and whirl about the heat of the candles. He slid the cigarettes into his pocket.

'There was a third thing you were going to show me,' Mallory said quietly.

'Yeah, I was goin' to show you somethin' else.' The voice was very gentle and Mallory felt suddenly cold. 'I was goin' to show you a spy, a traitor, the most vicious, twistin', murderin', double-crossin' bastard I've ever known.' The American had his hand out of his pocket now, the silenced automatic sitting snugly against his palm, the muzzle trained over Panayis's heart. He went on, more gently than ever. 'Judas Iscariot had nothin' on the boy-friend here, boss . . . Take your coat off, Panayis.'

'What the devil are you doing? Are you crazy?' Mallory started forward, half-angry, half-amazed, but brought up sharply against Miller's extended arm, rigid as a bar of iron. 'What bloody non-sense is this? He doesn't understand English!'

'Don't he, though? Then why was he out of the cave like a flash when Casey reported hearin' sounds outside . . . and why was he the first to leave the carob grove this afternoon if he didn't under-stand your order? Take your coat off, Judas, or I'll shoot you through the arm. I'll give you two seconds.'

Mallory made to throw his arms round Miller and bring him to the ground, but halted in mid-step as he caught the look on Panayis's face – teeth bared, murder glaring out from the coal-black eyes. Never before had Mallory seen such malignity in a human face, a malignity that yielded abruptly to shocked pain and disbe-lief as the .32 bullet smashed into his upper arm, just below the shoulder.

'Two seconds and then the other arm,' Miller said woodenly. But Panayis was already tearing off his jacket, the dark, bestial eyes never leaving Miller's face. Mallory looked at him, shivered invol-untarily, looked at Miller. Indifference, he thought, that was the only word to describe the look on the American's face. Indifference. Unaccountably, Mallory felt colder than ever.

'Turn round!' The automatic never wavered.

Slowly Panayis turned round. Miller stepped forward, caught the black shirt by the collar, ripped it off his back with one convulsive jerk.

'Waal, waal, now, whoever woulda thought it?' Miller drawled. 'Surprise, surprise, surprise! Remember, boss, this was the character that was publicly flogged by the Germans in Crete, flogged until the white of his ribs showed through. His back's in a helluva state, isn't it?'

Mallory looked but said nothing. Completely off balance, his mind was in a kaleidoscopic whirl, his thoughts struggling to adjust themselves to a new set of circumstances, a complete reversal of all his previous thinking. Not a scar, not a single blemish, marked the dark smoothness of that skin.

'Just a natural quick healer,' Miller murmured. 'Only a nasty, twisted mind like mine would think that he had been a German agent in Crete, became known to the Allies as a fifth columnist, lost his usefulness to the Germans and was shipped back to Navarone by fast motor-launch under cover of night. Floggin'! Island-hoppin' his way back here in a row-boat! Just a lot of bloody eyewash!' Miller paused, and his mouth twisted. 'I wonder how many pieces of silver he made in Crete before they got wise to him?'

'But heavens above, man, you're not going to condemn someone just for shooting a line!' Mallory protested. Strangely he didn't feel nearly as vehement as he sounded. 'How many survivors would there be among the Allies if –?'

'Not convinced yet, huh?' Miller waved his automatic negligently at Panayis. 'Roll up the left trouser leg, Iscariot. Two seconds again.'

Panayis did as he was told. The black venomous eyes never looked away from Miller's. He rolled the dark cloth up to the knee.

'Farther yet? That's my little boy,' Miller encouraged him. 'And now take that bandage off – right off.' A few seconds passed, then Miller shook his head sadly. 'A ghastly wound, boss, a ghastly wound!'

'I'm beginning to see your point,' Mallory said thoughtfully. The dark sinewy leg wasn't even scratched. 'But why on earth –?'

'Simple. Four reasons at least Junior here is a treacherous, slimy bastard – no self-respectin' rattlesnake would come within a mile of him – but he's a clever bastard. He faked his leg so he could stay in the cave in the Devil's Playground when the four of us went back to stop the Alpenkorps from comin' up the slope below the carob grove.'

'Why? Frightened he'd stop something?'

Miller shook his head impatiently.

'Junior here's scared o' nothin'. He stayed behind to write a note. Later on he used his leg to drop behind us some place, and leave the note where it could be seen. Early on, this must have been. Note probably said that we would come out at such and such a place, and would they kindly send a welcomin' committee to meet us there. They sent it, remember: it was their car we swiped to get to town . . . That was the first time I got real suspicious of the boy-friend: after he'd dropped behind he made up on us again quick – too damn quick for a man with a game leg. But it wasn't till I opened that rucksack in the square this evenin' that I really knew.'

'You only mentioned two reasons,' Mallory prompted.

'Comin' to the others. Number three – he could fall behind when the welcomin' committee opened up in front – Iscariot here wasn't goin to get himself knocked off before he collected his salary. And number four – remember that real touchin' scene when he begged you to let him stay at the far end of the cave that led into the valley we came out? Goin' to do his Horatio-on-the-bridge act?'

'Going to show them the right cave to pick, you mean.'

'Check. After that he was gettin' pretty desperate. I still wasn't sure, but I was awful suspicious, boss. Didn't know what he might try next. So I clouted him good and hard when that last patrol came up the valley.'

'I see,' Mallory said quietly. 'I see indeed.' He looked sharply at Miller. 'You should have told me. You had no right –'

'I was goin' to, boss. But I hadn't a chance – Junior here was around all the time. I was just startin' to tell you half an hour back, when the guns started up.'

Mallory nodded in understanding. 'How did you happen on all this in the first place, Dusty?'

'Juniper,' Miller said succinctly. 'Remember that's how Turzig said he came to find us? He smelt the juniper.'

'That's right. We *were* burning juniper.'

'Sure we were. But he said he smelt it on Kostos – and the wind was blowin' off Kostos all day long.'

'My God,' Mallory whispered. 'Of course, of course! And I missed it completely.'

'But Jerry knew we were there. How? Waal, he ain't got second sight no more than I have. So he was tipped off – he was tipped of by the boy-friend here. Remember I said he'd talked to some of his pals in Margaritha when we went down there for the supplies?' Miller spat in disgust. 'Fooled me all along the line. Pals? I didn't know how right I was. Sure they were his pals – his German pals! And that food he said he got from the commandant's kitchen – he got it from the kitchen all right. Almost certainly he goes in and asks for it – and old Skoda hands him his own suitcase to stow it in.'

'But the German he killed on the way back to the village? Surely to God –'

'Panayis killed him.' There was a tired certainty in Miller's voice. 'What's another corpse to Sunshine here. Probably stumbled on the poor bastard in the dark and had to kill him. Local colour. Louki was there, remember, and he couldn't have Louki gettin' suspicious. He would have blamed it on Louki anyway. The guy ain't human . . . And remember when he was flung into Skoda's room in Margaritha along with Louki, blood pourin' from a wound in his head?'

Mallory nodded.

'High-grade ketchup. Probably also from the commandant's kitchen,' Miller said bitterly. 'If Skoda had failed by every other means, there would still have been the boy-friend here as a stool-pigeon. Why he never asked Louki where the explosives were I don't know.'

'Obviously he didn't know Louki knew.'

'Mebbe. But one thing the bastard did know – how to use a mirror. Musta heliographed the garrison from the carob grove and given our position. No other way, boss. Then sometime this morning he must have got hold of my rucksack, whipped out all the slow fuse and fixed the clock fuse and detonators. He should have had his hands blown off tamperin' with them fulminates. Lord only knows where he learnt to handle the damn things.'

'Crete.' Mallory said positively. 'The Germans would see to that. A spy who can't also double as a saboteur is no good to them.'

'And he was very good to them,' Miller said softly. 'Very, very good. They're gonna miss their little pal. Iscariot here was a very smart baby indeed.'

'He was. Except tonight. He should have been smart enough to know that at least one of us would be suspicious –'

'He probably was,' Miller interrupted. 'But he was misinformed. I think Louki's unhurt. I think Junior here talked Louki into letting him stay in his place – Louki was always a bit scared of him – then he strolled across to his pals at the gate, told 'em to send a strong-arm squad out to Vygos to pick up the others, asked them to fire a few shots – he was very strong on local colour, was our loyal little pal – then strolls back across the square, hoists himself up on the roof and waits to tip off his pals as soon as we came in the back door. But Louki forgot to tell him just one thing – that we were goin' to rendezvous on the roof of the house, not inside. So the boy-friend here lurks away for all he's worth up top, waiting to signal his friends. Ten to one that he's got a torch in his pocket.'

Mallory picked up Panayis's coat and examined it briefly. 'He has.'

'That's it, then.' Miller lit another cigarette, watched the match burn down slowly to his fingers, then looked up at Panayis. 'How does it feel to know that you're goin' to die, Panayis, to feel like all them poor bastards who've felt just as you're feeling now, just before they died – all the men in Crete, all the guys in the sea-borne and air landings on Navarone who died because they thought you were on their side? How does it feel, Panayis?'

Panayis said nothing. His left hand clutching his torn right arm, trying to stem the blood, he stood there motionless, the dark, evil face masked in hate, the lips still drawn back in that less than human snarl. There was no fear in him, none at all, and Mallory tensed himself for the last, despairing attempt for life that Panayis must surely make, and then he had looked at Miller and knew there would be no attempt, because there was a strange sureness and inevitability about the American, an utter immobility of hand and eye that somehow precluded even the thought, far less the possibility, of escape.

'The prisoner has nothin' to say.' Miller sounded very tired. 'I suppose I should say somethin'. I suppose I should give out with a long spiel about me bein' the judge, the jury and the executioner, but I don't think I'll bother myself. Dead men make poor witnesses . . . Mebbe it's not your fault, Panayis, mebbe there's an awful good reason why you came to be what you are. Gawd only knows. I don't, and I don't much care. There are too many dead men. I'm goin' to kill you, Panayis, and I'm goin' to kill you now.' Miller dropped his cigarette, ground it into the floor of the hut. 'Nothin' at all to say?'

And he had nothing at all to say, the hate, the malignity of the black eyes said it all for him and Miller nodded, just once, as if in secret understanding. Carefully, accurately, he shot Panayis through the heart, twice, blew out the candles, turned his back and was half-way towards the door before the dead man had crashed to the ground.

'I am afraid I cannot do it, Andrea.' Louki sat back wearily, shook his head in despair. 'I am very sorry, Andrea. The knots are too tight.'

'No matter.' Andrea rolled over from his side to a sitting position, tried to ease his tightly-bound legs and wrists. 'They are cunning, these Germans, and wet cords can only be cut.' Characteristically, he made no mention of the fact that only a couple of minutes previously he had twisted round to reach the cords on Louki's wrist and undone them with half a dozen tugs of his steel-trap fingers. 'We will think of something else.'

He looked away from Louki, glanced across the room in the faint light of the smoking oil-lamp that stood by the grille door, a light so yellow, so dim that Casey Brown, trussed like a barnyard fowl and loosely secured, like himself, by a length of rope to the iron hooks suspended from the roof, was no more than a shapeless blur in the opposite corner of the stone-flagged room. Andrea smiled to himself, without mirth. Taken prisoner again, and for the second time that day – and with the same ease and surprise that gave no chance at all of resistance: completely unsuspecting, they had been captured in an upper room, seconds after Casey had finished talking to Cairo. The patrol had known exactly where to find them – and with their leader's assurance that it was all over, with his gloating explanation of the part Panayis had played, the unexpectedness, the success of the coup was all too easy to understand. And it was difficult not to believe his assurance that neither Mallory nor Miller had a chance. But the thought of ultimate defeat never occurred to Andrea.

His gaze left Casey Brown, wandered round the room, took in what he could see of the stone walls and floor, the hooks, the ventilation ducts, the heavy grille door. A dungeon, a torture dungeon, one would have thought, but Andrea had seen such places before. A castle, they called this place, but it was really only an old keep, no more than a manor house built round the crenellated towers. And the long-dead Frankish nobles who had built these keeps had lived well. No dungeon this, Andrea knew, but simply the larder where they had hung their meat and game, and done without windows and light for the sake of . . .

The light! Andrea twisted round, looking at the smoking oil-lamp, his eyes narrowing.

'Louki!' he called softly. The little Greek turned round to look at him.

'Can you reach the lamp?'

'I think so . . . Yes, I can.'

'Take the glass off,' Andrea whispered. 'Use a cloth – it will be hot. Then wrap it in the cloth, hit it on the floor – gently. The glass is thick – you can cut me loose in a minute or two.'

Louki stared at him for an uncomprehending moment, then nodded in understanding. He shuffled across the floor – his legs were still bound – reached out, then halted his hand abruptly, only inches from the glass. The peremptory, metallic clang had been only feet away, and he raised his head slowly to see what had caused it.

He could have stretched out his hand, touched the barrel of the Mauser that protruded threateningly through the bars of the grille door. Again the guard rattled the rifle angrily between the bars, shouted something he didn't understand.

'Leave it alone, Louki,' Andrea said quietly. His voice was tranquil, unshadowed by disappointment. 'Come back here. Our friend outside is not too pleased.' Obediently Louki moved back, heard the guttural voice again, rapid and alarmed this time, the rattle as the guard withdrew his rifle quickly from the bars of the door, the urgent pounding of his feet on the flagstones outside as he raced up the passage.

'What's the matter with our little friend?' Casey Brown was as lugubrious, as weary as ever. 'He seems upset.'

'He is upset.' Andrea smiled. 'He's just realised that Louki's hands are untied.'

'Well, why doesn't he tie them up again?'

'Slow in the head he may be, but he is no fool,' Andrea explained. 'This could be a trap and he's gone for his friends.'

Almost at once they heard a thud, like the closing of a distant door, the sound of more than one pair of feet running down the passage, the tinny rattling of keys on a ring, the rasp of a key against the lock, a sharp click, the squeal of rusty hinges and then two soldiers were in the room, dark and menacing with their jack-boots and ready guns. Two or three seconds elapsed while they looked around them, accustoming their eyes to the gloom, then the man nearest the door spoke.

'A terrible thing, boss, nothin' short of deplorable! Leave 'em alone for a couple of minutes and see what happens? The whole damn bunch tied up like Houdini on an off night!'

There was a brief, incredulous silence, then all three were sitting upright, staring at them. Brown recovered first.

'High time, too,' he complained. 'Thought you were never going to get here.'

'What he means is that he thought we were never going to see you again,' Andrea said quietly. 'Neither did I. But here you are, safe and sound.'

'Yes,' Mallory nodded. 'Thanks to Dusty and his nasty suspicious mind that cottoned on to Panayis while all the rest of us were asleep.'

'Where is he?' Louki asked.

'Panayis?' Miller waved a negligent hand. 'We left him behind – he met with a sorta accident.' He was across at the other side of the room now, carefully cutting the cords that pinioned Brown's injured leg, whistling tunelessly as he sawed away with his sheath knife. Mallory, too, was busy, slicing through Andrea's bonds, explaining rapidly what had happened, listening to the big Greek's equally concise account of what had befallen the other in the keep. And then Andrea was on his feet, massaging his numbed hands, looking across at Miller.

'That whistling, my Captain. It sounds terrible and, what is worse, it is very loud. The guards –'

'No worry there,' Mallory said grimly. 'They never expected to see Dusty and myself again . . . They kept a poor watch.' He turned round to look at Brown, now hobbling across the floor.

'How's the leg, Casey?'

'Fine, sir.' Brown brushed it aside as of no importance. 'I got through to Cairo, tonight, sir. The report –'

'It'll have to wait, Casey. We must get out as fast as we can. You all right, Louki?'

'I am heart-broken, Major Mallory. That a countryman of mine – a trusted friend –'

'That too, will have to wait. Come on!'

'You are in a great hurry,' Andrea protested mildly. They were already out in the passage, stepping over the cell guard lying in a crumpled heap on the floor. 'Surely if they're all like our friend here –'

'No danger from this quarter,' Mallory interrupted impatiently. 'The soldiers in the town – they're bound to know by now that we've either missed Panayis or disposed of him. In either case they'll know that we're certain to come hot-footing out here. Work it out for yourself. They're probably half-way here already, and if they do come . . .' He broke off, stared at the smashed generator and the ruins of Casey Brown's transmitter set lying in one corner of the entrance hall. 'Done a pretty good job on those, haven't they?' he said bitterly.

'Thank the Lord,' Miller said piously. 'All the less to tote around, is what I say. If you could only see the state of my back with that damned generator –'

'Sir!' Brown had caught Mallory's arm, an action so foreign to the usually punctilious petty officer that Mallory halted in surprise. 'Sir, it's terribly important – the report, I mean. You *must* listen, sir!'

The action, the deadly earnestness, caught and held Mallory's full attention. He turned to face Brown with a smile.

'OK, Casey, let's have it,' he said quietly. 'Things can't possibly be any worse than they are now.'

'They can, sir.' There was something tired, defeated about Casey Brown, and the great, stone hall seemed strangely chill. 'I'm afraid they can, sir. I got through tonight. First-class reception. Captain Jensen himself, and he was hopping mad. Been waiting all day for us to come on the air. Asked how things were, and I told him that you were outside the fortress just then, and hoped to be inside the magazine in an hour or so.'

'Go on.'

'He said that was the best news he'd ever had. He said his information had been wrong, he'd been fooled, that the invasion fleet didn't hole up overnight in the Cyclades, that they had come straight through under the heaviest air and E-boat escort ever seen in the Med, and are due to hit the beaches on Kheros some time before dawn tomorrow. He said our destroyers had been waiting to the south all day, moved up at dusk and were waiting word from him to see whether they would attempt the passage of the Maidos Straits. I told him maybe something could go wrong, but he said not with Captain Mallory and Miller inside and besides he wasn't – he couldn't risk the lives of twelve hundred men on Kheros just on the off chance that he might be wrong.' Brown broke off suddenly and looked down miserably at his feet. No one else in the hall moved or made any sound at all.

'Go on,' Mallory repeated in a whisper. His face was very pale.

'That's all, sir. That's all there is. The destroyers are coming through the Straits at midnight.' Brown looked down at his luminous watch. 'Midnight. Four hours to go.'

'Oh, God! Midnight!' Mallory was stricken, his eyes for the moment unseeing, ivory-knuckled hands clenched in futility and despair. 'They're coming through at midnight! God help them! God help them all now!'

FIFTEEN

Wednesday Night
2000–2115

Eight-thirty, his watch said. Eight-thirty. Exactly half an hour to curfew. Mallory flattened himself on the roof, pressed himself as closely as possible against the low retaining wall that almost touched the great, sheering sides of the fortress, swore softly to himself. It only required one man with a torch in his hand to look over the top of the fortress wall – a cat-walk ran the whole length of the inside of the wall, four feet from the top – and it would be the end of them all. The wandering beam of a torch and they were bound to be seen, it was impossible not to be seen: he and Dusty Miller – the American was stretched out behind him and clutching the big truck battery in his arms – were wide open to the view of anyone who happened to glance down that way. Perhaps they should have stayed with the others a couple of roofs away, with Casey and Louki, the one busy tying spaced knots in a rope, the other busy splicing a bent wire hook on to a long bamboo they had torn from a bamboo hedge just outside the town, where they had hurriedly taken shelter as a convoy of three trucks had roared past them heading for the castle Vygos.

Eight thirty-two. What the devil was Andrea doing down there, Mallory wondered irritably and at once regretted his irritation. Andrea wouldn't waste an unnecessary second. Speed was vital, haste fatal. It seemed unlikely that there would be any officers inside – from what they had seen, practically half the garrison were combing either the town or the countryside out in the direction of Vygos – but if there were and even one gave a cry it would be the end.

Mallory stared down at the burn on the back of his hand, thought of the truck they had set on fire and grinned wryly to himself. Setting the truck on fire had been his only contribution to the night's performance so far. All the other credit went to either Andrea or Miller. It was Andrea who had seen in this house on the west side of the square – one of several adjoining houses used as officers' billets – the only possible answer to their problem. It was Miller, now lacking all time-fuses, clockwork, generator and every other source of electric power who had suddenly stated that he must have a battery, and again it was Andrea, hearing the distant approach of a truck, who had blocked the entrance to the long driveway to the keep with heavy stones from the flanking pillars, forcing the soldiers to abandon their truck at the gates and run up the drive towards their house. To overcome the driver and his mate and bundle them senseless into a ditch had taken seconds only, scarcely more time than it had taken Miller to unscrew the terminals of the heavy battery, find the inevitable jerry-can below the tailboard and pour the contents over engine, cab and body. The truck had gone up in a roar and *whoosh* of flames: as Louki had said earlier in the night, setting petrol-soaked vehicles on fire was not without its dangers – the charred patch on his hand stung painfully – but, again as Louki had said it had burned magnificently. A pity, in a way – it had attracted attention to their escape sooner than was necessary – but it had been vital to destroy the evidence, the fact that a battery was missing. Mallory had too much experience of and respect for the Germans ever to underrate them: they could put two and two together better than most.

He felt Miller tug at his ankle, started, twisted round quickly. The American was pointing beyond him, and he turned again and saw Andrea signalling to him from the raised trap in the far corner: he had been so engrossed in his thinking, the giant Greek so catlike in his silence, that he had completely failed to notice his arrival. Mallory shook his head, momentarily angered at his own abstraction, took the battery from Miller, whispered to him to get the others, then edged slowly across the roof, as noiselessly as possible. The sheer deadweight of the battery was astonishing, it felt as if it weighed a ton, but Andrea plucked it from his hands, lifted it over the trap coaming, tucked it under one arm and nimbly descended the stairs to the tiny hall-way as if it weighed nothing at all.

Andrea moved out through the open doorway to the covered balcony that overlooked the darkened harbour, almost a hundred vertical feet beneath, Mallory, following close behind, touched him on the shoulder as he lowered the battery gently to the ground.

'Any trouble?' he asked softly.

'None at all, my Keith.' Andrea straightened. 'The house is empty. I was so surprised that I went over it all, twice, just to make sure.'

'Fine! Wonderful! I suppose the whole bunch of them are out scouring the country for us – interesting to know what they would say if they were told we were sitting in their front parlour?'

'They would never believe it,' Andrea said without hesitation. 'This is the last place they would ever think to look for us.'

'I've never hoped so much that you're right!' Mallory murmured fervently. He moved across to the latticed railing that enclosed the balcony, gazed down into the blackness beneath his feet and shivered. A long, long drop and it was very cold, that sluicing, vertical rain chilled one to the bone . . . He stepped back, shook the railing.

'This thing strong enough, do you think?' he whispered.

'I don't know, my Keith. I don't know at all.' Andrea shrugged. 'I hope so.'

'I hope so,' Mallory echoed. 'It doesn't really matter. This is how it has to be.' Again he leaned far out over the railing, twisted his head to the right and upwards. In the rain-filled gloom of the night he could just faintly make out the still darker gloom of the mouth of the cave housing the two great guns, perhaps forty feet away from where he stood, at least thirty feet higher – and all vertical cliff-face between. As far as accessibility went, the cave mouth could have been on the moon.

He drew back, turned round as he heard Brown limping on to the balcony.

'Go to the front of the house and stay there, Casey, will you? Stay by the window. Leave the front door unlocked. If we have any visitors let them in.'

'Club 'em, knife 'em, no guns,' Brown murmured. 'Is that it, sir?'

'That's it, Casey.'

'Just leave this little thing to me,' Brown said grimly. He hobbled away through the doorway.

Mallory turned to Andrea. 'I make it twenty-three minutes.'

'I, too. Twenty-three minutes to nine.'

'Good luck,' Mallory murmured. He grinned at Miller. 'Come on, Dusty. Opening time.'

Five minutes later, Mallory and Miller were seated in a *taverna* just off the south side of the town square. Despite the garish blue paint with which the *tavernaris* had covered everything in sight – walls, tables, chairs, shelves all in the same execrably vivid colour (blue and red for the wine shops, green for the sweetmeat shops was the almost invariable rule throughout the islands) – it was a gloomy, ill-lit place, as gloomy almost as the stern, righteous, magnificently-moustached heroes of the Wars of Independence whose dark, burning eyes glared down at them from a dozen faded prints scattered at eye-level along the walls. Between each pair of portraits was a brightly-coloured wall advertisement for Fix's beer: the effect of the décor, taken as a whole, was indescribable, and Mallory shuddered to think what it would have been like had the *tavernaris* had at his disposal any illumination more powerful than the two smoking oil-lamps placed on the counter before him.

As it was, the gloom suited him well. Their dark clothes, braided jackets, *tsantas* and jack-boots looked genuine enough, Mallory knew, and the black-fringed turbans Louki had mysteriously obtained for them looked as they ought to look in a tavern where every islander there – about eight of them – wore nothing else on their heads. Their clothes had been good enough to pass muster with the *tavernaris* – but then even the keeper of a wine shop could hardly be expected to know every man in a town of five thousand, and a patriotic Greek, as Louki had declared this man to be, wasn't going to lift even a faintly suspicious eyebrow as long as there were German soldiers present. And there were Germans present – four of them, sitting round a table near the counter. Which was why Mallory had been glad of the semi-darkness. Not, he was certain, that he and Dusty Miller had any reason to be physically afraid of these men. Louki had dismissed them contemptuously as a bunch of old women – headquarters clerks, Mallory guessed – who came to this tavern every night of the week. But there was no point in sticking out their necks unnecessarily.

Miller lit one of the pungent, evil-smelling local cigarettes, wrinkling his nose in distaste.

'Damn funny smell in this joint, boss.'

'Put your cigarette out,' Mallory suggested.

'You wouldn't believe it, but the smell I'm smelling is a damn sight worse than that.'

'Hashish,' Mallory said briefly. 'The curse of these island ports.' He nodded over towards a dark corner. 'The lads of the village over there will be at it every night in life. It's all they live for.'

'Do they have to make that gawddamned awful racket when they're at it?' Miller asked peevishly. 'Toscanini should see this lot!'

Mallory looked at the small group in the corner, clustered round the young man playing a *bouzouko* – a long-necked mandolin – and singing the haunting, nostalgic *rembetika* songs of the hashish smokers of the Piraeus. He supposed the music did have a certain melancholy, lotus-land attraction, but right then it jarred on him. One had to be in a certain twilit, untroubled mood to appreciate that sort of thing; and he had never felt less untroubled in his life.

'I suppose it *is* a bit grim,' he admitted. 'But at least it lets us talk together, which we couldn't do if they all packed up and went home.'

'I wish to hell they would,' Miller said morosely. 'I'd gladly keep my mouth shut.' He picked distastefully at the *meze* – a mixture of chopped olives, liver, cheese and apples – on the plate before him: as a good American and a bourbon drinker of long standing he disapproved strongly of the invariable Greek custom of eating when drinking. Suddenly he looked up and crushed his cigarette against the table top. 'For Gawd's sake, boss, how much longer?'

Mallory looked at him, then looked away. He knew exactly how Dusty Miller felt, for he felt that way himself – tense, keyed-up, every nerve strung to the tautest pitch of efficiency. So much depended on the next few minutes; whether all their labour and their suffering had been necessary, whether the men on Kheros would live or die, whether Andy Stevens had lived and died in vain. Mallory looked at Miller again, saw the nervous hands, the deepened wrinkles round the eyes, the tightly compressed mouth, white at the outer corners, saw all these signs of strain, noted them and discounted them. Excepting Andrea alone, of all the men he had ever known he would have picked the lean, morose American to be his companion that night. Or maybe even including Andrea. 'The finest saboteur in southern Europe' Captain Jensen had called him back in Alexandria. Miller had come a long way from Alexandria, and he had come for this alone. Tonight was Miller's night.

Mallory looked at his watch.

'Curfew in fifteen minutes,' he said quietly. 'The balloon goes up in twelve minutes. For us, another four minutes to go.'

Miller nodded, but said nothing. He filled his glass again from the beaker in the middle of the table, lit a cigarette. Mallory could see a nerve twitching high up in his temple and wondered dryly how many twitching nerves Miller could see in his own face. He wondered, too, how the crippled Casey Brown was getting on in the house they had just left. In many ways he had the most responsible

job of all – and at the critical moment he would have to leave the
door unguarded, move back to the balcony. One slip up there . . .
He saw Miller look strangely at him and grinned crookedly. This had
to come off, it just had to: he thought of what must surely happen
if he failed, then shied away from the thought. It wasn't good to
think of these things, not now, not at this time.

He wondered if the other two were at their posts, unmolested;
they should be, the search party had long passed through the
upper part of the town; but you never knew what could go wrong,
there was so much that could go wrong, and so easily. Mallory
looked at his watch again: he had never seen a second hand move
so slowly. He lit a last cigarette, poured a final glass of wine, listened without really hearing to the weird, keening threnody of
the *rembetika* song in the corner. And then the song of the hashish
singers died plaintively away, the glasses were empty and Mallory
was on his feet.

'Time bringeth all things,' he murmured. 'Here we go again.'

He sauntered easily towards the door, calling good night to the
tavernaris. Just at the doorway he paused, began to search impatiently through his pockets as if he had lost something: it was a
windless night, and it was raining, he saw, raining heavily, the
lances of rain bouncing inches off the cobbled street – and the
street itself was deserted as far as he could see in either direction.
Satisfied, Mallory swung round with a curse, forehead furrowed in
exasperation, started to walk back towards the table he had just
left, right hand now delving into the capacious inner pocket of his
jacket. He saw without seeming to that Dusty Miller was pushing
his chair back, rising to his feet. And then Mallory had halted, his
face clearing and his hands no longer searching. He was exactly
three feet from the table where the four Germans were sitting.

'Keep quite still!' He spoke in German, his voice low but as
steady, as menacing, as the Navy Colt .455 balanced in his right
hand. 'We are desperate men. If you move we will kill you.'

For a full three seconds the soldiers sat immobile, expressionless
except for the shocked widening of their eyes. And then there was
a quick flicker of the eyelids from the man sitting nearest the
counter, a twitching of the shoulder and then a grunt of agony as
the .32 bullet smashed into his upper arm. The soft thud of Miller's
silenced automatic couldn't have been heard beyond the doorway.

'Sorry, boss,' Miller apologised. 'Mebbe he's only sufferin' from
St. Vitus' dance.' He looked with interest at the pain-twisted face,

the blood welling darkly between the fingers clasped tightly over the wound. 'But he looks kinda cured to me.'

'He is cured,' Mallory said grimly. He turned to the innkeeper, a tall, melancholy man with a thin face and mandarin moustache that drooped forlornly over either corner of his mouth, spoke to him in the quick, colloquial speech of the islands. 'Do these men speak Greek?'

The *tavernaris* shook his head. Completely unruffled and unimpressed, he seemed to regard armed hold-ups in his tavern as the rule rather than the exception.

'Not them!' he said contemptuously. 'English a little, I think – I am sure. But not our language. That I do know.'

'Good. I am a British Intelligence officer. Have you a place where I can hide these men?'

'You shouldn't have done this,' the *tavernaris* protested mildly. 'I will surely die for this.'

'Oh, no, you won't.' Mallory had slid across the counter, his pistol boring into the man's midriff. No one could doubt that the man was being threatened – and violently threatened – no one, that is, who couldn't see the broad wink that Mallory had given the innkeeper. 'I'm going to tie you up with them. All right?'

'All right. There is a trap-door at the end of the counter here. Steps lead down to the cellar.'

'Good enough. I'll find it by accident.' Mallory gave him a vicious and all too convincing shove that sent the man staggering, vaulted back across the counter, walked over to the *rembetika* singers at the far corner of the room.

'Go home,' he said quickly. 'It is almost curfew time anyway. Go out the back way, and remember – you have seen nothing, no one. You understand?'

'We understand.' It was the young *bouzouko* player who spoke. He jerked his thumb at his companions and grinned. 'Bad men – but good Greeks. Can we help you?'

'No!' Mallory was emphatic. 'Think of your families – these soldiers have recognised you. They must know you well – you and they are here most nights, is that not so?'

The young man nodded.

'Off you go, then. Thank you all the same.'

A minute later, in the dim, candle-lit cellar, Miller prodded the soldier nearest him – the one most like himself in height and build. 'Take your clothes off!' he ordered.

'English pig!' the German snarled.

'Not *English*,' Miller protested. 'I'll give you thirty seconds to get your coat and pants off.'

The man swore at him, viciously, but made no move to obey. Miller sighed. The German had guts, but time was running out. He took a careful bead on the soldier's hand and pulled the trigger. Again the soft *plop* and the man was staring down stupidly at the hole torn in the heel of his left hand.

'Mustn't spoil the nice uniforms, must we?' Miller asked conversationally. He lifted the automatic until the soldier was staring down the barrel of the gun. 'The next goes between the eyes.' The casual drawl carried complete conviction. 'It won't take me long to undress you, I guess.' But the man had already started to tear his uniform off, sobbing with anger and the pain of his wounded hand.

Less than another five minutes had passed when Mallory, clad like Miller in German uniform, unlocked the front door of the tavern and peered cautiously out. The rain, if anything, was heavier than ever – and there wasn't a soul in sight. Mallory beckoned Miller to follow and locked the door behind him. Together the two men walked up the middle of the street, making no attempt to seek either shelter or shadows. Fifty yards took them into the town square, where they turned right along the south side of the square, then left along the east side, not breaking step as they passed the old house where they had hidden earlier in the evening, not even as Louki's hand appeared mysteriously behind the partly opened door, a hand weighted down with two German Army rucksacks – rucksacks packed with rope, fuses, wire and high explosive. A few yards farther on they stopped suddenly, crouched down behind a couple of huge wine barrels outside a barber's shop, gazed at the two armed guards in the arched gateway, less than a hundred feet away, as they shrugged into their packs and waited for their cue.

They had only moments to wait – the timing had been split-second throughout. Mallory was just tightening the waist-belt of his rucksack when a series of explosions shook the centre of the town, not three hundred yards away, explosions followed by the vicious rattle of a machine-gun, then by further explosions. Andrea was doing his stuff magnificently with his grenades and homemade bombs.

Both men suddenly shrank back as a broad, white beam of light stabbed out from a platform high above the gateway, a beam that paralleled the top of the wall to the east, showed up every hooked spike and strand of barbed wire as clearly as sunlight. Mallory and Miller looked at each other for a fleeting moment, their faces grim. Panayis hadn't missed a thing: they would have been pinned on these strands like flies on fly-paper and cut to ribbons by machine-guns.

Mallory waited another half-minute, touched Miller's arm, rose to his feet and started running madly across the square, the long hooked bamboo pressed close to his side, the American pounding behind him. In a few seconds they had reached the gates of the fortress, the startled guards running the last few feet to meet them.

'Every man to the Street of Steps!' Mallory shouted. 'Those damned English saboteurs are trapped in a house down there! We've got to have some mortars. Hurry, man, hurry, in the name of God!'

'But the gate!' one of the two guards protested. 'We cannot leave the gate!' The man had no suspicions, none at all: in the circumstances – the near darkness, the pouring rain, the German-clad soldier speaking perfect German, the obvious truth that there was a gun-battle being fought near-at-hand – it would have been remarkable had he shown any signs of doubt.

'Idiot!' Mallory screamed at him. *'Dummkopf!* What is there to guard against here? The English swine are in the Street of Steps. They must be destroyed! For God's sake, hurry!' he shouted desperately. 'If they escape again it'll be the Russian Front for all of us!'

Mallory had his hand on the man's shoulder now, ready to push him on his way, but his hand fell to his side unneeded. The two men were already gone, running pell-mell across the square, had vanished into the rain and the darkness already. Seconds later Mallory and Miller were deep inside the fortress of Navarone.

Everywhere there was complete confusion – a bustling, purposeful confusion as one would expect with the seasoned troops of the Alpenkorps, but confusion nevertheless, with much shouting of orders, blowing of whistles, starting of truck engines, sergeants running to and fro chivvying their men into marching order or into the waiting transports. Mallory and Miller ran too, once or twice through groups of men milling round the tailboard of a truck. Not that they were in any desperate hurry for themselves, but nothing could have been more conspicuous – and suspicious – than the sight of a couple of men walking calmly along in the middle of all that urgent activity. And so they ran, heads down or averted whenever they passed through a pool of light, Miller cursing feelingly and often at the unaccustomed exercise.

They skirted two barrack blocks on their right, then the power-house on their left, then an ordnance depot on their right and then the *Abteilung* garage on their left. They were climbing, now, almost in darkness, but Mallory knew where he was to the inch: he had so thoroughly memorised the closely tallying descriptions given him by Vlachos and Panayis that he would have been confident of finding his way with complete accuracy, even if the darkness had been absolute.

'What's that, boss?' Miller had caught Mallory by the arm, was pointing to a large, uncompromisingly rectangular building that loomed gauntly against the horizon. 'The local hoosegow?'

'Water storage tank,' Mallory said briefly. 'Panayis estimates there's half a million gallons in there – magazine flooding in an emergency. The magazines are directly below.' He pointed to a squat, box-like, concrete structure a little farther on. 'The only entrance to the magazine. Locked and guarded.'

They were approaching the senior officers' quarters now – the commandant had his own flat on the second storey, directly over-looking the massive, reinforced ferro-concrete control tower that controlled the two great guns below. Mallory suddenly stopped, picked up a handful of dirt, rubbed it on his face and told Miller to do the same.

'Disguise,' he explained. 'The experts would consider it a bit on the elementary side, but it'll have to do. The lighting's apt to be a bit brighter inside this place.'

He went up the steps to the officers' quarters at a dead run, crashed through the swing doors with a force that almost took them off their hinges. The sentry at the keyboard looked at him in astonishment, the barrel of his sub-machine-gun lining up on the New Zealander's chest.

'Put that thing down, you damned idiot!' Mallory snapped furiously. 'Where's the commandant? Quickly, you oaf! It's life or death!'

'Herr – Herr Kommandant?' the sentry stuttered. 'He's left – they are all gone, just a minute ago.'

'What? All gone?' Mallory was staring at him with narrowed, dangerous eyes. 'Did you say "all gone"?' he asked softly.

'Yes. I – I'm sure they're . . .' He broke off abruptly as Mallory's eyes shifted to a point behind his shoulder.

'Then who the hell is that?' Mallory demanded savagely.

The sentry would have been less than human not to fall for it. Even as he was swinging round to look, the vicious judo cut took him just below the left ear. Mallory had smashed open the glass of the keyboard before the unfortunate guard had hit the floor, swept all the keys – about a dozen in all – off their rings and into his pocket. It took them another twenty seconds to tape the man's mouth and hands and lock him in a convenient cupboard; then they were on their way again, still running.

One more obstacle to overcome, Mallory thought as they pounded along in the darkness, the last of the triple defences. He did not know how many men would be guarding the locked door to the magazine, and in that moment of fierce exaltation he didn't particularly care. Neither, he felt sure, did Miller. There were no worries now, no taut-nerved tensions or nameless anxieties. Mallory would have been the last man in the world to admit it, or even believe it, but this was what men like Miller and himself had been born for.

They had their hand-torches out now, the powerful beams swinging in wild arcs as they plunged along, skirting the massed batteries of AA guns. To anyone observing their approach from the front, there could have been nothing more calculated to disarm suspicion than the sight and sound of the two men running towards them without any attempt at concealment, one of them shouting to the other in German, both with lit torches whose beams lifted and fell, lifted and fell as the men's arms windmilled by their sides. But these same torches were deeply hooded, and only a very alert observer indeed would have noticed that the downward arc of the light never passed backwards beyond the runners' feet.

Suddenly Mallory saw two shadows detaching themselves from the darker shadow of the magazine entrance, steadied his torch for a brief second to check. He slackened speed.

'Right!' he said softly. 'Here they come – only two of them. One each – get as close as possible first. Quick and quiet – a shout, a shot, and we're finished. And for God's sake don't start clubbing 'em with your torch. There'll be no lights on in that magazine and I'm not going to start crawling around there with a box of bloody matches in my hand!' He transferred his torch to his left hand, pulled out his Navy Colt, reversed it, caught it by the barrel, brought up sharply only inches away from the guards now running to meet them.

'Are you all right?' Mallory gasped. 'Anyone been here? Quickly, man, *quickly*!'

'Yes, yes, we're all right.' The man was off guard, apprehensive. 'What in the name of God is all that noise –'

'Those damned English saboteurs!' Mallory swore viciously. 'They've killed the guards and they're inside! Are you sure no one's been here? Come, let me see.'

He pushed his way past the guard, probed his torch at the massive padlock, then straightened his back.

'Thank heaven for that anyway!' He turned round, let the dazzling beam of his torch catch the man square in the eyes, muttered an apology and switched off the light, the sound of the sharp click lost in the hollow, soggy thud of the heel of his Colt catching the man behind the ear, just below the helmet. The sentry was still on his feet, just beginning to crumple, when Mallory staggered as the second guard reeled into him, staggered, recovered, clouted him with the Colt for good measure, then stiffened in sudden dismay as he heard the vicious hissing *plop* of Miller's automatic, twice in rapid succession.

'What the hell –'

'Wily birds, boss,' Miller murmured. 'Very wily indeed. There was a third character in the shadows at the side. Only way to stop him.' Automatic cocked in his ready hand, he stooped over the man for a moment, then straightened. 'Afraid he's been stopped kinda permanent, boss.' There was no expression in his voice.

'Tie up the others.' Mallory had only half heard him, he was already busy at the magazine door, trying a succession of keys in the lock. The third key fitted, the lock opened and the heavy steel door gave easily to his touch. He took a last swift look round, but there was no one in sight, no sound but the revving engine of the last of the trucks clearing the fortress gates, the distant rattle of machine-gun fire. Andrea was doing a magnificent job – if only he didn't overdo it, leave his withdrawal till it was too late . . . Mallory turned quickly, switched on his torch, stepped inside the door. Miller would follow when he was ready.

A vertical steel ladder fixed to the rock led down to the floor of the cave. On either side of the ladder were hollow lift-shafts, unprotected even by a cage, oiled wire ropes glistening in the middle, a polished metal runner at each side of the square to guide and steady the spring-loaded sidewheels of the lift itself. Spartan in their simplicity but wholly adequate, there was no mistaking these for anything but what they were – the shell hoist shafts going down to the magazine.

Mallory reached the solid floor of the cave and swept his torch round through a 180-degree arc. This was the very end of that great cave that opened out beneath the towering overhang of rock that dominated the entire harbour. Not the natural end, he saw after a moment's inspection, but a man-made addition: the volcanic rock around him had been drilled and blasted out. There was nothing here but the two shafts descending into the pitchy darkness and another steel ladder, also leading to the magazine. But the magazine could wait: to check that there were no more guards down here and to ensure an emergency escape route – these were the two vital needs of the moment.

Quickly Mallory ran along the tunnel, flipping his torch on and off. The Germans were past-masters of booby traps – explosive booby traps – for the protection of important installations, but the chances were that they had none in that tunnel – not with several hundred tons of high explosive stored only feet away.

The tunnel itself, dripping-damp and duck-board floored, was about seven feet high and even wider, but the central passage was very narrow – most of the space was taken up by the roller conveyors, one on either side, for the great cartridges and shells. Suddenly the conveyors curved away sharply to the left and right, the sharply-sheering tunnel roof climbed steeply up into the near-darkness of the vaulted dome above, and, almost at his feet, their burnished steel caught in the beam from his torch, twin sets of parallel rails, embedded in the solid stone and twenty feet apart, stretched forward into the lightened gloom ahead, the great, gaping mouth of the cave. And just before he switched off the torch – searchers returning from the Devil's Playground might easily catch the pin-point of light in the darkness – Mallory had a brief glimpse of the turn-tables that crowned the far end of these shining rails and, crouched massively above, like some nightmare monsters from an ancient and other world, the evil, the sinister silhouettes of the two great guns of Navarone.

Torch and revolver dangling loosely in his hands, only dimly aware of the curious tingling in the tips of his fingers, Mallory walked slowly forward. Slowly, but not with the stealthy slowness, the razor-drawn expectancy of a man momentarily anticipating trouble – there was no guard in the cave, Mallory was quite sure of that now – but with that strange, dream-like slowness, the half-belief of a man who has accomplished something he had known all along he could never accomplish, with the slowness of a man at last face to face with a feared but long-sought enemy. I'm here at last, Mallory said to himself over and over again. I'm here at last, I've made it, and these are the guns of Navarone: these are the guns I came to destroy, the guns of Navarone, and I have come at last. But somehow he couldn't quite believe it . . .

Slowly still Mallory approached the guns, walked half-way round the perimeter of the turn-table of the gun on the left, examined it as well as he could in the gloom. He was staggered by the sheer size of it, the tremendous girth and reach of the barrel that stretched far out into the night. He told himself that the experts thought it was only a nine-inch crunch gun, that the crowding confines of the caves were bound to exaggerate its size. He told himself these things, discounted them: twelve-inch bore if an inch, that gun was the biggest thing he had ever seen. Big? Heavens above, it was gigantic! The fools, the blind crazy fools who had sent the *Sybaris* out against these . . .

The train of thought was lost, abruptly. Mallory stood quite still, one hand resting against the massive gun carriage and tried to recall the sound that had jerked him back to the present. Immobile, he listened for it again, eyes closed the better to hear, but the sound did not come again, and suddenly he knew that it was no sound at all but the absence of sound that had cut through his thoughts, triggered off some unconscious warning bell. The night was suddenly very silent, very still: down in the heart of the town the guns had stopped firing.

Mallory swore softly to himself. He had already spent far too much time day-dreaming, and time was running short. It *must* be running short – Andrea had withdrawn, it was only a matter of time until the Germans discovered that they had been duped. And then they would come running – and there was no doubt where they would come. Swiftly Mallory shrugged out of his rucksack, pulled out the hundred-foot wire-cored rope coiled inside. Their emergency escape route – whatever else he did he must make sure of that.

The rope looped round his arm, he moved forward cautiously, seeking a belay, but had only taken three steps when his right knee-cap struck something hard and unyielding. He checked the exclamation of pain, investigated the obstacle with his free hand, realised immediately what it was – an iron railing stretched waist-high across the mouth of the cave. Of course! There had been bound to be something like that, some barrier to prevent people from falling over the edge, especially in the darkness of the night. He hadn't been able to pick it up with the binoculars from the carob grove that afternoon – close though it was to the entrance, it had been concealed in the gloom of the cave. But he should have thought of it.

Quickly Mallory felt his way along to the left, to the very end of the railing, crossed it, tied the rope securely to the base of the vertical stanchion next to the wall, paid out the rope as he moved gingerly to the lip of the cave mouth. And then, almost at once, he was there and there was nothing below his probing foot but a hundred and twenty feet of sheer drop to the land-locked harbour of Navarone.

Away to his right was a dark, formless blur lying on the water, a blur that might have been Cape Demirci: straight ahead, across the darkly velvet sheen of the Maidos Straits, he could see the twinkle of far-away lights – it was a measure of the enemy's confidence that they permitted these lights at all, or, more likely, these fisher cottages were useful as a bearing marker for the guns at night: and to the left, surprisingly near, barely thirty feet away in a horizontal plane, but far below the level where he was standing, he could see the jutting end of the outside wall of the fortress where it abutted on the cliff, the roofs of the houses on the west side of the square beyond that, and, beyond that again, the town itself curving sharply downwards and outwards, to the south first, then to the west, close-girdling and matching the curve of the crescent harbour. Above – but there was nothing to be seen above, that fantastic overhang above blotted out more than half the sky; and below the darkness was equally impenetrable, the surface of the harbour inky and black as night. There were vessels down there, he knew, Grecian caiques and German launches, but they might have been a thousand miles away for any sign he could see of them.

The brief, all encompassing glance had taken barely ten seconds, but Mallory waited no longer. Swiftly he bent down, tied a double bowline in the end of the rope and left it lying on the edge. In an emergency they could kick it out into the darkness. It would be thirty feet short of the water, he estimated – enough to clear any launch or masted caique that might be moving about the harbour. They could drop the rest of the way, maybe a bone-breaking fall on to the deck of a ship, but they would have to risk it. Mallory took one last look down into the Stygian blackness and shivered: he hoped to God that he and Miller wouldn't have to take that way out.

Dusty Miller was kneeling on the duck-boards by the top of the ladder leading down to the magazine as Mallory came running back up the tunnel, his hands busy with wires, fuses, detonators and explosives. He straightened up as Mallory approached.

'I reckon this stuff should keep 'em happy, boss.' He set the hands of the clockwork fuse, listened appreciatively to the barely audible hum, then eased himself down the ladder. 'In here among the top two rows of cartridges, I thought.'

'Wherever you say,' Mallory acquiesced. 'Only don't make it too obvious – or too difficult to find. Sure there's no chance of them suspecting that we knew the clock and fuses were dud?'

'None in the world,' Miller said confidently. 'When they find this here contraption they'll knock holes in each other's back congratulatin' themselves – and they'll never look any further.'

'Fair enough.' Mallory was satisfied. 'Lock the door up top?'

'Certainly I locked the door!' Miller looked at him reproachfully. 'Boss, sometimes I think . . .'

But Mallory never heard what he thought. A metallic, reverberating clangour echoed cavernously through the cave and magazine, blotting out Miller's words, then died away over the harbour. Again the sound came, while the two men stared bleakly at one another, then again and again, then escaped for a moment of time.

'Company,' Mallory murmured. 'Complete with sledge-hammers. Dear God, I only hope that door holds.' He was already running along the passage towards the guns, Miller close behind him.

'Company!' Miller was shaking his head as he ran. 'How in the hell did they get here so soon?'

'Our late lamented little pal,' Mallory said savagely. He vaulted over the railing, edged back to the mouth of the cave. 'And we were suckers enough to believe he told the whole truth. But he never told us that opening that door up top triggered off an alarm bell in the guard-room.'

SIXTEEN

Wednesday Night
2115–2345

Smoothly, skilfully, Miller paid out the wire-cored rope – double-turned round the top rail – as Mallory sank out of sight into the darkness. Fifty feet had gone, he estimated, fifty-five, sixty, then there came the awaited sharp double tug on the signal cord looped round his wrist and he at once checked the rope, stooped and tied it securely to the foot of the stanchion.

And then he had straightened again, belayed himself to the rail with the rope's end, leaned far out over the edge, caught hold of the rope with both hands as far down as he could reach and began slowly, almost imperceptibly at first, then with gradually increasing momentum, to swing man and rope from side to side, pendulum-wise. As the swings of the pendulum grew wider, the rope started to twist and jump in his hands, and Miller knew that Mallory must be striking outcrops of rock, spinning uncontrollably as he bounced off them. But Miller knew that he couldn't stop now, the clanging of the sledges behind him was almost continuous: he only stooped the lower over the rope, flung all the strength of his sinewy arms and shoulders into the effort of bringing Mallory nearer and still nearer to the rope that Brown would by now have thrown down from the balcony of the house where they had left him.

Far below, half-way between the cave mouth and the invisible waters of the harbour, Mallory swung in a great arc through the rain-filled darkness of the sky, forty rushing, bone-bruising feet between the extremities of the swings. Earlier he had struck his head heavily on an outcrop of rock, all but losing consciousness and his grip on the rope. But he knew where to expect that projection now and pushed himself clear each time as he approached it, even although this made him spin in a complete circle every time.

It was as well, he thought, that it was dark, that he was independent of sight anyway: the blow had reopened an old wound Turzig had given him, his whole upper face was masked with blood, both eyes completely gummed.

But he wasn't worried about the wound, about the blood in his eyes. The rope – that was all that mattered. Was the rope there? Had anything happened to Casey Brown? Had he been jumped before he could get the rope over the side? If he had, then all hope was gone and there was nothing they could do, no other way they could span the forty sheer feet between house and cave. It just *had* to be there. But if it were there, why couldn't he find it? Three times now, at the right extremity of a swing, he had reached out with his bamboo pole, heard the hook scrape emptily, frustratingly, against the bare rock.

And then, the fourth time, stretched out to the straining limit of both arms, he felt the hook catch on! Immediately he jerked the pole in, caught the rope before he dropped back on the downward swing, jerked the signal cord urgently, checked himself gradually as he fell back. Two minutes later, near exhaustion from the sixty-foot climb up the wet, slippery rope, he crawled blindly over the lip of the cave and flung himself to the ground, sobbing for breath.

Swiftly, without speaking, Miller bent down, slipped the twin loops of the double bowline from Mallory's legs, undid the knot, tied it to Brown's rope, gave the latter a tug and watched the joined ropes disappear into the darkness. Within two minutes the heavy battery was across, underslung from the two ropes, lowered so far by Casey Brown then hauled up by Mallory and Miller. Within another two minutes, but with infinitely more caution, this time, the canvas bag with the nitro, primers and detonators, had been pulled across, lay on the stone floor beside the battery.

All noise had ceased, the hammering of the sledges against the steel door had stopped completely. There was something threatening, foreboding about the stillness, the silence was more menacing than all the clamour that had gone before. Was the door down, the lock smashed, the Germans waiting for them in the gloom of the tunnel, waiting with cradled machine-carbines that would tear the life out of them? But there was no time to wonder, no time to wait, no time now to stop to weigh the chances. The time for caution was past, and whether they lived or died was of no account any more.

The heavy Colt .455 balanced at his waist, Mallory climbed over the safety barrier, padded silently past the great guns and through the passage, his torch clicking on half-way down its length. The place was deserted, the door above still intact. He climbed swiftly up the ladder, listened at the top. A subdued murmur of voices, he thought he heard, and a faint hissing sound on the other side of the heavy steel door, but he couldn't be sure. He leaned forward to hear better, the palm of his hand against the door, drew back with a muffled exclamation of pain. Just above the lock, the door was almost red-hot. Mallory dropped down to the floor of the tunnel just as Miller came staggering up with the battery.

'That door's as hot as blazes. They must be burning —'

'Did you hear anything?' Miller interrupted.

'There was a kind of hissing —'

'Oxy-acetylene torch,' Miller said briefly. 'They'll be burnin' out the lock. It'll take time — that door's made of armoured steel.'

'Why don't they blow it in — gelignite or whatever you use for that job?'

'Perish the thought,' Miller said hastily. 'Don't even *talk* about it, boss. Sympathetic detonation's a funny thing — there's an even chance that the whole damned lot would go up. Give me a hand with this thing, boss, will you?'

Within seconds Dusty Miller was again a man absorbed in his own element, the danger outside, the return trip he had yet to make across the face of the cliff, completely forgotten for a moment. The task took him four minutes from beginning to end. While Mallory was sliding the battery below the floored well of the lift, Miller squeezed in between the shining steel runners of the lift shaft itself, stooped to examine the rear one with his torch and establish, by the abrupt transition from polished to dull metal, exactly where the spring-loaded wheel of the shell-hoist came to rest. Satisfied, he pulled out a roll of sticky black tape, wound it a dozen times round the shaft, stepped back to look at it: it was quite invisible.

Quickly he taped the ends of two rubber-covered wires on the insulated strip, one at either side, taped these down also until nothing was visible but the bared steel cores at the tips, joined these to two four-inch strips of bared wire, taped these also, top and bottom, to the insulated shaft, vertically and less than half an inch apart. From the canvas bag he removed the TNT, the primer and the detonator — a bridge mercury detonator lugged and screwed to his own specification — fitted them together and connected one of the wires from the steel shaft to a lug on the detonator, screwing it firmly home. The other wire from the shaft he led to the positive terminal on the battery, and a third wire from the negative terminal to the detonator. It only required the ammunition hoist to sink down into the magazine – as it would do as soon as they began firing – and the spring-loaded wheel would short out the bare wires, completing the circuit and triggering off the detonator. A last check on the position of the bared vertical wires and he sat back satisfied. Mallory had just descended the ladder from the tunnel. Miller tapped him on the leg to draw his attention, negligently waving the steel blade of his knife within an inch of the exposed wires.

'Are you aware, boss,' he said conversationally, 'that if I touched this here blade across those terminals, the whole gawddamned place would go up in smithereens.' He shook his head musingly. 'Just one little slip of the hand, just one teeny little touch and Mallory and Miller are among the angels.'

'For God's sake put that thing away!' Mallory snapped nervously. 'And let's get the hell out of here. They've got a complete half-circle cut through that door already!'

Five minutes later Miller was safe – it had been a simple matter of sliding down a 45-degree tautened rope to where Brown waited. Mallory took a last look back into the cave, and his mouth twisted. He wondered how many soldiers manned the guns and magazine during action stations. One thing, he thought, they'll never know anything about it, the poor bastards. And then he thought, for the hundredth time, of all the men on Kheros and the destroyers, and his lips tightened and he looked away. Without another backward glance he slipped over the edge, dropped down into the night. He was half-way there, at the very lowest point of the curve and about to start climbing again, when he heard the vicious, staccato rattle of machine-gun fire directly overhead.

It was Miller who helped him over the balcony rail, an apprehensive-looking Miller who glanced often over his shoulder in the direction of the gun-fire – and the heaviest concentration of fire, Mallory realised with sudden dismay, was coming from their own, the west side of the square, only three or four houses away. Their escape route was cut off.

'Come on, boss!' Miller said urgently. 'Let's get away from this joint. Gettin' downright unhealthy round these parts.'

Mallory jerked his head in the direction of the fire. 'Who's down there?' he asked quickly.

'A German patrol.'

'Then how in the hell can we get away?' Mallory demanded. 'And where's Andrea?'

'Across the other side of the square, boss. That's who those birds along there are firing at.'

'The other side of the square!' He glanced at his watch. 'Heavens above, man, what's he doing there?' He was moving through the house now, speaking over his shoulder. 'Why did you let him go?'

'I didn't let him go, boss,' Miller said carefully. 'He was gone when I came. Seems that Brown here saw a big patrol start a house to house search of the square. Started on the other side and were doin' two or three houses at a time. Andrea – he'd come back by this time – thought it a sure bet that they'd work right round the square and get here in two or three minutes, so he took off like a bat across the roofs.'

'Going to draw them off?' Mallory was at Louki's side staring out of the window. 'The crazy fool! He'll get himself killed this time – get himself killed for sure! There are soldiers everywhere. Besides, they won't fall for it again. He tricked them once up in the hills, and the Germans –'

'I'm not so sure, sir,' Brown interrupted excitedly. 'Andrea's just shot out the searchlight on his side. They'll think for certain that we're going to break out over the wall and – look, sir, look! There they go!' Brown was almost dancing with excitement, the pain of his injured leg forgotten. 'He's done it, sir, he's done it!'

Sure enough, Mallory saw, the patrol had broken away from their shelter in the house to their right and were running across the square in extended formation, their heavy boots clattering on the cobbles, stumbling, falling, recovering again as they lost footing on the slippery wetness of the uneven stones. At the same time Mallory could see torches flickering on the roofs of the houses opposite, the vague forms of men crouching low to escape observation and making swiftly for the spot where Andrea had been when he had shot out the great Cyclops eye of the searchlight.

'They'll be on him from every side.' Mallory spoke quietly enough, but his fists clenched until the nails cut into the palms of his hands. He stood stock-still for some seconds, stooped quickly and gathered a Schmeisser up from the floor. 'He hasn't a chance. I'm going after him.' He turned abruptly, brought up with equal suddenness: Miller was blocking his way to the door.

'Andrea left word that we were to leave him be, that he'd find his own way out.' Miller was very calm, very respectful. 'Said that no one was to help him, not on any account.'

'Don't try to stop me, Dusty.' Mallory spoke evenly, mechanically almost. He was hardly aware that Dusty Miller was there. He only knew that he must get out at once, get to Andrea's side, give him what help he could. They had been together too long, he owed too much to the smiling giant to let him go so easily. He couldn't remember how often Andrea had come after *him*, more than once when he had thought hope was gone . . . He put his hand against Miller's chest.

'You'll only be in his way, boss,' Miller said urgently. 'That's what you said . . .'

Mallory pushed him aside, strode for the door, brought up his fist to strike as hands closed round his upper arm. He stopped just in time, looked down into Louki's worried face.

'The American is right,' Louki said insistently. 'You must not go. Andrea said you were to take us down to the harbour.'

'Go down yourselves,' Mallory said brusquely. 'You know the way, you know the plans.'

'You would let us all go, let us all –'

'I'd let the whole damn world go if I could help him.' There was an utter sincerity in the New Zealander's voice. 'Andrea would never let me down.'

'But you would let him down,' Louki said quietly. 'Is that it, Major Mallory?'

'What the devil do you mean?'

'By not doing as he wishes. He may be hurt, killed even, and if you go after him and are killed too, that makes it all useless. He would die for nothing. Is it thus you would repay your friend?'

'All right, all right, you win,' Mallory said irritably.

'That is how Andrea would want it,' Louki murmured. 'Any other way you would be –'

'Stop preaching at me! Right, gentlemen, let's be on our way.' He was back on balance again, easy, relaxed, the primeval urge to go out and kill well under control. 'We'll take the high road – over the roofs. Dig into that kitchen stove there, rub the ashes all over your hands and faces. See that there's nothing white on you anywhere. And no talking!'

The five-minute journey down to the harbour wall – a journey made in soft-footed silence with Mallory hushing even the beginnings of a whisper – was quite uneventful. Not only did they see no soldiers, they saw no one at all. The inhabitants of Navarone were wisely obeying the curfew, and the streets were completely deserted.

Andrea had drawn off pursuit with a vengeance. Mallory began to
fear that the Germans had taken him, but just as they reached the
water's edge he heard the gunfire again, a good deal farther away
this time, in the very north-east corner of the town, round the back
of the fortress.

Mallory stood on the low wall above the harbour, looked at his
companions, gazed out over the dark oiliness of the water. Through
the heavy rain he could just distinguish, to his right and left, the
vague blurs of caiques moored stern on to the wall. Beyond that he
could see nothing.

'Well, I don't suppose we can get much wetter than we are right
now,' he observed. He turned to Louki, checked something the little man was trying to say about Andrea. 'You sure you can find it
all right in the darkness?' 'It' was the commandant's personal
launch, a thirty-six-foot ten-tonner always kept moored to a buoy
a hundred feet offshore. The engineer, who doubled as guard, slept
aboard, Louki had said.

'I am already there,' Louki boasted. 'Blindfold me as you will
and I –'

'All right, all right,' Mallory said hastily. 'I'll take your word for
it. Lend me your hat, will you, Casey?' He jammed the automatic
into the crown of the hat, pulled it firmly on to his head, slid gently into the water and struck out by Louki's side.

'The engineer,' Louki said softly. 'I think he will be awake, Major.'

'I think so, too,' Mallory said grimly. Again there came the chatter of machine-carbines, the deeper whiplash of a Mauser. 'So will
everyone else in Navarone, unless they're deaf or dead. Drop
behind as soon as we see the boat. Come when I call.'

Ten seconds, fifteen passed, then Louki touched Mallory on the
arm.

'I see it,' Mallory whispered. The blurred silhouette was less than
fifteen yards away. He approached silently, neither legs nor arms
breaking water, until he saw the vague shape of a man standing on
the poop, just aft of the engine-room hatchway. He was immobile,
staring out in the direction of the fortress and the upper town:
Mallory slowly circled round the stern of the boat and came up
behind him, on the other side. Carefully he removed his hat, took
out the gun, caught the low gunwale with his left hand. At the
range of seven feet he knew he couldn't possibly miss, but he
couldn't shoot the man, not then. The guard-rails were token
affairs only, eighteen inches high at the most, and the splash of the

man falling into the water would almost certainly alert the guards at the harbour mouth emplacements.

'If you move I will kill you!' Mallory said softly in German. The man stiffened. He had a carbine in his hand, Mallory saw.

'Put the gun down. Don't turn round.' Again the man obeyed, and Mallory was out of the water and on to the deck, in seconds, neither eye nor automatic straying from the man's back. He stepped softly forward, reversed the automatic, struck, caught the man before he could fall overboard and lowered him quietly to the deck. Three minutes later all the others were safely aboard.

Mallory followed the limping Brown down to the engine room, watched him as he switched on his hooded torch, looked around with a professional eye, looked at the big, gleaming, six-cylinder in-line Diesel engine.

'This,' said Brown reverently, 'is an engine. What a beauty! Operates on any number of cylinders you like. I know the type, sir.'

'I never doubted but you would. Can you start her up, Casey?'

'Just a minute till I have a look round, sir.' Brown had all the unhurried patience of the born engineer. Slowly, methodically, he played the spotlight round the immaculate interior of the engine-room, switched on the fuel and turned to Mallory. 'A dual control job, sir. We can take her from up top.'

He carried out the same painstaking inspection in the wheel-house, while Mallory waited impatiently. The rain was easing off now, not much, but sufficiently to let him see the vague outlines of the harbour entrance. He wondered for the tenth time if the guards there had been alerted against the possibility of an attempted escape by boat. It seemed unlikely – from the racket Andrea was making, the Germans would think that escape was the last thing in their minds . . . He leaned forward, touched Brown on the shoulder.

'Twenty past eleven, Casey,' he murmured. 'If these destroyers come through early we're apt to have a thousand tons of rock falling on our heads.'

'Ready now, sir,' Brown announced. He gestured at the crowded dashboard beneath the screen. 'Nothing to it really.'

'I'm glad you think so,' Mallory murmured fervently. 'Start her moving, will you? Just keep it slow and easy.'

Brown coughed apologetically. 'We're still moored to the buoy. And it might be a good thing, sir, if we checked on the fixed guns, searchlights, signalling lamps, life-jackets and buoys. It's useful to know where these things are,' he finished deprecatingly.

Mallory laughed softly, clapped him on the shoulder.

'You'd make a great diplomat, Chief. We'll do that.' A landsman first and last, Mallory was none the less aware of the gulf that stretched between him and a man like Brown, made no bones about acknowledging it to himself. 'Will you take her out, Casey?'

'Right, sir. Would you ask Louki to come here – I think it's steep to both sides, but there may be snags or reefs. You never know.'

Three minutes later the launch was half-way to the harbour mouth, purring along softly on two cylinders, Mallory and Miller, still clad in German uniform, standing on the deck for'ard of the wheelhouse, Louki crouched low inside the wheelhouse itself. Suddenly, about sixty yards away, a signal lamp began to flash at them, its urgent clacking quite audible in the stillness of the night.

'Dan'l Boone Miller will now show how it's done,' Miller muttered. He edged closer to the machine-gun on the starboard bow. 'With my little gun I shall . . .'

He broke off sharply, his voice lost in the sudden clacking from the wheelhouse behind him, the staccato off-beat chattering of a signal shutter triggered by professional fingers. Brown had handed the wheel over to Louki, was morsing back to the harbour entrance, the cold rain lancing palely through the flickering beams of the lamp. The enemy lamp had stopped but now began again.

'My, they got a lot to say to each other,' Miller said admiringly. 'How long do the exchange of courtesies last, boss?'

'I should say they are just about finished.' Mallory moved back quickly to the wheelhouse. They were less than a hundred feet from the harbour entrance. Brown had confused the enemy, gained precious seconds, more time than Mallory had ever thought they could gain. But it couldn't last. He touched Brown on the arm.

'Give her everything you've got when the balloon goes up.' Two seconds later he was back in position in the bows, Schmeisser ready in his hands. 'Your big chance, Dan'l Boone. Don't give the search-lights a chance to line up – they'll blind you.'

Even as he spoke, the light from the signal lamp at the harbour mouth cut off abruptly and two dazzling white beams, one from either side of the harbour entrance, stabbed blindingly through the darkness, bathing the whole harbour in their savage glare – a glare that lasted for only a fleeting second of time, yielded to a contrastingly Stygian darkness as two brief bursts of machine-gun fire smashed them into uselessness. From such short range it had been almost impossible to miss.

'Get down, everyone!' Mallory shouted. 'Flat on the deck!'

The echoes of the gunfire were dying away, the reverberations fading along the great sea wall of the fortress when Casey Brown cut in all six cylinders of the engine and opened the throttle wide, the surging roar of the big Diesel blotting out all other sounds in the night. Five seconds, ten seconds, they were passing through the entrance, fifteen, twenty, still not a shot fired, half a minute and they were well clear, bows lifting high out of the water, the deep-dipped stern trailing its long, seething ribbon of phosphorescent white as the engine crescendoed to its clamorous maximum power and Brown pulled the heeling craft sharply round to starboard, seeking the protection of the steep-walled cliffs.

'A desperate battle, boss, but the better men won.' Miller was on his feet now, clinging to a mounted gun for support as the deck canted away beneath his feet. 'My grandchildren shall hear of this.'

'Guards probably all up searching the town. Or maybe there *were* some poor blokes behind those searchlights. Or maybe we just took 'em all by surprise.' Mallory shook his head. 'Anyway you take it, we're just plain damn lucky.'

He moved aft, into the wheelhouse. Brown was at the wheel, Louki almost crowing with delight.

'That was magnificent, Casey,' Mallory said sincerely. 'A first-class job of work. Cut the engine when we come to the end of the cliffs. Our job's done. I'm going ashore.'

'You don't have to, Major.'

Mallory turned. 'What's that?'

'You don't have to. I tried to tell you on the way down, but you kept telling me to be quiet.' Louki sounded injured, turned to Casey. 'Slow down, please. The last thing Andrea told me, Major, was that we were to come this way. Why do you think he let himself be trapped against the cliffs to the north instead of going out into the country, where he could have hidden easily?'

'Is this true, Casey?' Mallory asked.

'Don't ask me, sir. Those two – they always talk in Greek.'

'Of course, of course.' Mallory looked at the low cliffs close off the starboard beam, barely moving now with the engine shut right down, looked back at Louki. 'Are you quite sure . . .'

He stopped in mid-sentence, jumped out through the wheelhouse door. The splash – there had been no mistaking the noise – had come from almost directly ahead. Mallory, Miller by his side, peered into the darkness, saw a dark head surfacing above the water less than twenty feet away, leaned far over with outstretched arm as the launch slid slowly by. Five seconds later Andrea stood on the deck, dripping mightily and beaming all over his great moon face. Mallory led him straight into the wheelhouse, switched on the soft light of the shaded chart-lamp.

'By all that's wonderful, Andrea, I never thought to see you again. How did it go?'

'I will soon tell you,' Andrea laughed. 'Just after –'

'You've been wounded!' Miller interrupted. 'Your shoulder's kinda perforated.' He pointed to the red stain spreading down the sea-soaked jacket.

'Well, now, I believe I have.' Andrea affected vast surprise. 'Just a scratch, my friend.'

'Oh, sure, sure, just a scratch! It would be the same if your arm had been blown off. Come on down to the cabin – this is just a kindergarten exercise for a man of my medical skill.'

'But the captain –'

'Will have to wait. And your story. Ol' Medicine Man Miller permits no interference with his patients. Come on!'

'Very well, very well,' Andrea said docilely. He shook his head in mock resignation, followed Miller out of the cabin.

Brown opened up to full throttle again, took the launch north almost to Cape Demirci to avoid any hundred to one chance the harbour batteries might make, turned due east for a few miles then headed south into the Maidos Straits. Mallory stood by his side in the wheelhouse, gazing out over the dark, still waters. Suddenly he caught a gleam of white in the distance, touched Brown's arm and pointed for'ard.

'Breakers ahead, Casey, I think. Reefs perhaps?'

Casey looked in long silence, finally shook his head.

'Bow-wave,' he said unemotionally. 'It's the destroyers coming through.'

SEVENTEEN

Wednesday Night
Midnight

Commander Vincent Ryan, RN, Captain (Destroyers) and Commanding Officer of His Majesty's latest S-class destroyer *Sirdar*, looked round the cramped chart-room and tugged thoughtfully at his magnificent Captain Kettle beard. A scruffier, a more villainous, a more cut and battered-looking bunch of hard cases he had never seen, he reflected, with the possible exception of a Bias Bay pirate crew he had helped round up when a very junior officer on the China Station. He looked at them more closely, tugged his beard again, thought there was more to it than mere scruffiness. He wouldn't care to be given the task of rounding this lot up. Dangerous, highly dangerous, he mused, but impossible to say why, there was only this quietness, this relaxed watchfulness that made him feel vaguely uncomfortable. His 'hatchet-men', Jensen had called them: Captain Jensen picked his killers well.

'Any of you gentlemen care to go below,' he suggested. 'Plenty of hot water, dry clothes – and warm bunks. We won't be using them tonight.'

'Thank you very much, sir.' Mallory hesitated. 'But we'd like to see this through.'

'Right then, the bridge it is,' Ryan said cheerfully. The *Sirdar* was beginning to pick up speed again, the deck throbbing beneath their feet. 'It is at your own risk, of course.'

'We lead charmed lives,' Miller drawled. 'Nothin' ever happens to us.'

The rain had stopped and they could see the cold twinkling of stars through broadening rifts in the clouds. Mallory looked around him, could see Maidos broad off the port bow and the great bulk of Navarone slipping by to starboard. Aft, about a cable length away, he could just distinguish two other ships, high-curving bow-waves piled whitely against tenebrious silhouettes. Mallory turned to the captain.

'No transports, sir?'

'No transports.' Ryan felt a vague mixture of pleasure and embarrassment that this man should call him 'sir'. 'Destroyers only. This is going to be a smash-and-grab job. No time for dawdlers tonight – and we're behind schedule already.'

'How long to clear the beaches?'

'Half an hour.'

'What! Twelve hundred men?' Mallory was incredulous.

'More.' Ryan sighed. 'Half the ruddy inhabitants want to come with us, too. We could still do it in half an hour, but we'll probably take a bit longer. We'll embark all the mobile equipment we can.'

Mallory nodded, let his eye travel along the slender outlines of the *Sirdar*. 'Where are you going to put 'em all, sir.'

'A fair question,' Ryan admitted. 'Five p.m. on the London Underground will be nothing compared to this little lot. But we'll pack them in somehow.'

Mallory nodded again and looked across the dark waters at Navarone. Two minutes, now, three at the most, and the fortress would open behind that headland. He felt a hand touch his arm, half-turned and smiled down at the sad-eyed little Greek by his side.

'Not long now, Louki,' he said quietly.

'The people, Major,' he murmured. 'The people in the town. Will they be all right?'

'They'll be all right. Dusty says the roof of the cave will go straight up. Most of the stuff will fall into the harbour.'

'Yes, but the boats –?'

'Will you stop worrying! There's nobody aboard them – you know they have to leave at curfew time.' He looked round as someone touched his arm.

'Captain Mallory, this is Lieutenant Beeston, my gunnery officer.' There was a slight coolness in Ryan's voice that made Mallory think that he wasn't overfond of his gunnery officer. 'Lieutenant Beeston is worried.'

'I *am* worried!' The tone was cold, aloof, with an indefinable hint of condescension. 'I understand that you have advised the captain not to offer any resistance?'

'You sound like a BBC communiqué,' Mallory said shortly. 'But you're right, I did say that. You couldn't locate the guns except by searchlight and that would be fatal. Similarly with gunfire.'

'I'm afraid I don't understand.' One could almost see the lift of the eyebrows in the darkness.

'You'd give away your position,' Mallory said patiently. 'They'd nail you first time. Give 'em two minutes and they'd nail you anyway. I have good reason to believe that the accuracy of their gunners is quite fantastic'

'So has the Navy,' Ryan interjected quietly. 'Their third shell got the *Sybaris*'s B magazine.'

'Have you got any idea why this should be, Captain Mallory?' Beeston was quite unconvinced.

'Radar-controlled guns,' Mallory said briefly. 'They have two huge scanners atop the fortress.'

'The *Sirdar* had radar installed last month,' Beeston said stiffly. 'I imagine we could register some hits ourselves if –'

'You could hardly miss.' Miller drawled out the words, the tone dry and provocative. 'It's a helluva big island, Mac.'

'Who – who are you?' Beeston was rattled. 'What the devil do you mean?'

'Corporal Miller.' The American was unperturbed. 'Must be a very selective instrument, Lootenant, that can pick out a cave in a hundred square miles of rock.'

There was a moment's silence, then Beeston muttered something and turned away.

'You've hurt Guns's feelings, Corporal,' Ryan murmured. 'He's very keen to have a go – but we'll hold our fire . . . How long till we clear that point, Captain?'

'I'm not sure.' He turned. 'What do you say, Casey?'

'A minute, sir. No more.'

Ryan nodded, said nothing. There was a silence on the bridge, a silence only intensified by the sibilant rushing of the waters, the weird, lonesome pinging of the Asdic. Above, the sky was steadily clearing, and the moon, palely luminous, was struggling to appear through a patch of thinning cloud. Nobody spoke, nobody moved. Mallory was conscious of the great bulk of Andrea beside him, of Miller, Brown and Louki behind. Born in the heart of the country, brought up on the foothills of the Southern Alps, Mallory knew himself as a landsman first and last, an alien to the sea and ships: but he had never felt so much at home in his life, never really known till now what it was to belong. He was more than happy, Mallory thought vaguely to himself, he was content. Andrea and his new friends and the impossible well done – how could a man be but content? They weren't all going home, Andy Stevens wasn't coming with them, but strangely he could feel no sorrow, only a gentle melancholy . . . Almost as if he had divined what Mallory was thinking, Andrea leaned towards him, towering over him in the darkness.

'He should be here,' he murmured. 'Andy Stevens should be here. That is what you are thinking, is it not?'

Mallory nodded and smiled, and said nothing.

'It doesn't really matter, does it, my Keith?' No anxiety, no questioning, just a statement of fact. 'It doesn't really matter.'

'It doesn't matter at all.'

Even as he spoke, he looked up quickly. A light, a bright orange flame had lanced out from the sheering wall of the fortress; they had rounded the headland and he hadn't even noticed it. There was a whistling roar – Mallory thought incongruously of an express train emerging from a tunnel – directly overhead, and the great shell had crashed into the sea just beyond them. Mallory compressed his lips, unconsciously tightened his clenched fists. It was easy now to see how the *Sybaris* had died.

He could hear the gunnery officer saying something to the captain, but the words failed to register. They were looking at him and he at them and he did not see them. His mind was strangely detached. Another shell, would that be next? Or would the roar of the gunfire of that first shell come echoing across the sea? Or perhaps . . . Once again, he was back in that dark magazine entombed in the rocks, only now he could see men down there, doomed, unknowing men, could see the overhead pulleys swinging the great shells and cartridges towards the well of the lift, could see the shell hoist ascending slowly, the bared, waiting wires less than half an inch apart, the shining, spring-loaded wheel running smoothly down the gleaming rail, the gentle bump as the hoist . . .

A white pillar of flame streaked up hundreds of feet into the night sky as the tremendous detonation tore the heart out of the great fortress of Navarone. No after-fire of any kind, no dark, billowing clouds of smoke, only that one blinding white column that lit up the entire town for a single instant of time, reached up incredibly till it touched the clouds, vanished as if it had never been. And then, by and by, came the shock waves, the solitary thunderclap of the explosion, staggering even at that distance, and finally the deep-throated rumbling as thousands of tons of rock toppled majestically into the harbour – thousands of tons of rock and the two great guns of Navarone.

The rumbling was still in their ears, the echoes fading away far out across the Aegean, when the clouds parted and the moon broke through, a full moon silvering the darkly-rippling waters to starboard, shining iridescently through the spun phosphorescence of the *Sirdar*'s boiling wake. And dead ahead, bathed in the white moonlight, mysterious, remote, the island of Kheros lay sleeping on the surface of the sea.

ALISTAIR MACLEAN

Force 10
from Navarone

To Lewis and Caroline

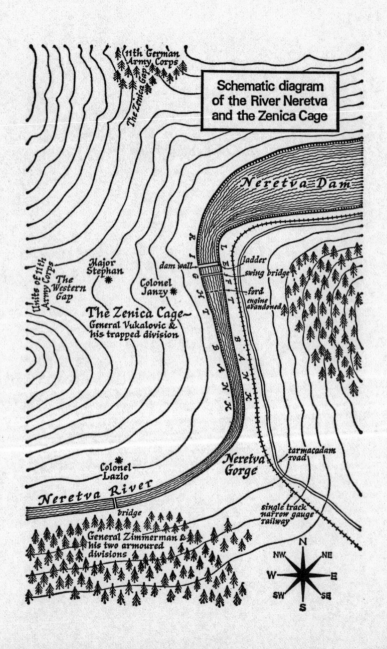

Schematic diagram of the River Neretva and the Zenica Cage

ONE

Prelude: Thursday
0000–0600

Commander Vincent Ryan, RN, Captain (Destroyers) and commanding officer of His Majesty's latest S-class destroyer *Sirdar*, leaned his elbows comfortably on the coaming of his bridge, brought up his night-glasses and gazed out thoughtfully over the calm and silvered waters of the moonlit Aegean.

He looked first of all due north, straight out over the huge and smoothly sculpted and whitely phosphorescent bow-wave thrown up by the knife-edged forefoot of his racing destroyer: four miles away, no more, framed in its backdrop of indigo sky and diamantine stars, lay the brooding mass of a darkly cliff-girt island: the island of Kheros, for months the remote and beleaguered outpost of two thousand British troops who had expected to die that night, and who would now not die.

Ryan swung his glasses through 180° and nodded approvingly. This was what he liked to see. The four destroyers to the south were in such perfect line astern that the hull of the leading vessel, a gleaming bone in its teeth, completely obscured the hulls of the three ships behind. Ryan turned his binoculars to the east.

It was odd, he thought inconsequentially, how unimpressive, even how disappointing, the aftermath of either natural or man-made disaster could be. Were it not for that dull red glow and wisping smoke that emanated from the upper part of the cliff and lent the scene a vaguely Dantean aura of primeval menace and foreboding, the precipitous far wall of the harbour looked as it might have done in the times of Homer. That great ledge of rock that looked from that distance so smooth and regular and somehow inevitable could have been carved out by the wind and weather of a hundred million years: it could equally well have been cut away fifty

centuries ago by the masons of Ancient Greece seeking marble for
the building of their Ionian temples: what was almost inconceivable, what almost passed rational comprehension, was the fact that
ten minutes ago that ledge had not been there at all, that there had
been in its place tens of thousands of tons of rock, the most impregnable German fortress in the Aegean and, above all, the two great
guns of Navarone, now all buried for ever three hundred feet
under the sea. With a slow shake of his head Commander Ryan
lowered his binoculars and turned to look at the men responsible
for achieving more in five minutes than nature could have done in
five million years.

Captain Mallory and Corporal Miller. That was all he knew of
them, that and the fact that they had been sent on this mission by
an old friend of his, a naval captain by the name of Jensen who, he
had learnt only twenty-four hours previously – and that to his total
astonishment – was the Head of Allied Intelligence in the
Mediterranean. But that was all he knew of them and maybe he
didn't even know that. Maybe their names weren't Mallory and
Miller. Maybe they weren't even a captain and a corporal. They
didn't look like any captain or corporal he'd ever seen. Come to
that, they didn't look like any soldiers he'd ever seen. Clad in salt-
water-and blood-stained German uniforms, filthy, unshaven, quiet
and watchful and remote, they belonged to no category of men
he'd ever encountered: all he could be certain of as he gazed at the
blurred and blood-shot sunken eyes, the gaunt and trenched and
stubbled-grey faces of two men no longer young, was that he had
never before seen human beings so far gone in total exhaustion.

'Well, that seems to be about it,' Ryan said. 'The troops on
Kheros waiting to be taken off, our flotilla going north to take them
off and the guns of Navarone no longer in any position to do anything about our flotilla. Satisfied, Captain Mallory?'

'That was the object of the exercise,' Mallory agreed.

Ryan lifted his glasses again. This time, almost at the range of
night vision, he focused on a rubber dinghy closing in on the rocky
shoreline to the west of Navarone harbour. The two figures seated
in the dinghy were just discernible, no more: Ryan lowered his
glasses and said thoughtfully:

'Your big friend – and the lady with him – doesn't believe in hanging about. You didn't – ah – introduce me to them, Captain Mallory.'

'I didn't get the chance to. Maria and Andrea. Andrea's a colonel
in the Greek army: 19th Motorized Division.'

'Andrea *was* a colonel in the Greek army,' Miller said. 'I think he's just retired.'

'I rather think he has. They were in a hurry, Commander, because they're both patriotic Greeks, they're both islanders and there is much for both to do in Navarone. Besides, I understand they have some urgent and very personal matters to attend to.'

'I see.' Ryan didn't press the matter, instead he looked out again over the smoking remains of the shattered fortress. 'Well, that seems to be that. Finished for the evening, gentlemen?'

Mallory smiled faintly. 'I think so.'

'Then I would suggest some sleep.'

'What a wonderful word that is.' Miller pushed himself wearily off the side of the bridge and stood there swaying as he drew an exhausted forearm over blood-shot, aching eyes. 'Wake me up in Alexandria.'

'Alexandria?' Ryan looked at him in amusement. 'We won't be there for thirty hours yet.'

'That's what I meant,' Miller said.

Miller didn't get his thirty hours. He had, in fact, been asleep for just over thirty minutes when he was wakened by the slow realization that something was hurting his eyes: after he had moaned and feebly protested for some time he managed to get one eye open and saw that that something was a bright overhead light let into the deckhead of the cabin that had been provided for Mallory and himself. Miller propped himself up on a groggy elbow, managed to get his second eye into commission and looked without enthusiasm at the other two occupants of the cabin: Mallory was seated by a table, apparently transcribing some kind of message, while Commander Ryan stood in the open doorway.

'This is outrageous,' Miller said bitterly. 'I haven't closed an eye all night.'

'You've been asleep for thirty-five minutes,' Ryan said. 'Sorry. But Cairo said this message for Captain Mallory was of the greatest urgency.'

'It is, is it?' Miller said suspiciously. He brightened. 'It's probably about promotions and medals and leave and so forth.' He looked hopefully at Mallory who had just straightened after decoding the message. 'Is it?'

'Well, no. It starts off promisingly enough, mind you, warmest congratulations and what-have-you, but after that the tone of the message deteriorates a bit.'

Mallory reread the message: SIGNAL RECEIVED WARMEST CONGRATU-LATIONS MAGNIFICENT ACHIEVEMENT. YOU BLOODY FOOLS WHY YOU LET ANDREA GET AWAY? ESSENTIAL CONTACT HIM IMMEDIATELY. WILL EVACUATE BEFORE DAWN UNDER DIVERSIONARY AIR ATTACK AIR STRIP ONE MILE SOUTH-EAST MANDRAKOS. SEND CE VIA SIRDAR. URGENT 3 REPEAT URGENT 3. BEST LUCK. JENSEN.

Miller took the message from Mallory's outstretched hand, moved the paper to and fro until he had brought his bleary eyes into focus, read the message in horrified silence, handed it back to Mallory and stretched out his full length on his bunk. He said, 'Oh, my God!' and relapsed into what appeared to be a state of shock.

'That about sums it up,' Mallory agreed. He shook his head wearily and turned to Ryan. 'I'm sorry, sir, but we must trouble you for three things. A rubber dinghy, a portable radio transmitter and an immediate return to Navarone. Please arrange to have the radio lined up on a pre-set frequency to be constantly monitored by your WT room. When you receive a CE signal, transmit it to Cairo.'

'CE?' Ryan asked.

'Uh-huh. Just that.'

'And that's all?'

'We could do with a bottle of brandy,' Miller said. 'Something – anything – to see us through the rigours of the long night that lies ahead.'

Ryan lifted an eyebrow. 'A bottle of five-star, no doubt, Corporal?'

'Would you,' Miller asked morosely, 'give a bottle of three-star to a man going to his death?'

As it happened, Miller's gloomy expectations of an early demise turned out to be baseless – for that night, at least. Even the expected fearful rigours of the long night ahead proved to be no more than minor physical inconveniences.

By the time the *Sirdar* had brought them back to Navarone and as close in to the rocky shores as was prudent, the sky had become darkly overcast, rain was falling and a swell was beginning to blow up from the south-west so that it was little wonder to either Mallory or Miller that by the time they had paddled their dinghy within strik-ing distance of the shore, they were in a very damp and miserable condition indeed: and it was even less wonder that by the time they had reached the boulder-strewn beach itself, they were soaked to the

skin, for a breaking wave flung their dinghy against a sloping shelf of
rock, overturning their rubber craft and precipitating them both into
the sea. But this was of little enough account in itself: their
Schmeisser machine-pistols, their radio, their torches were securely
wrapped in waterproof bags and all of those were safely salvaged. All
in all, Mallory reflected, an almost perfect three-point landing compared to the last time they had come to Navarone by boat, when
their Greek caique, caught in the teeth of a giant storm, had been
battered to pieces against the jaggedly vertical – and supposedly
unclimbable – South Cliff of Navarone.

Slipping, stumbling and with suitably sulphuric comments, they
made their way over the wet shingle and massively rounded boulders until their way was barred by a steeply-angled slope that
soared up into the near-darkness above. Mallory unwrapped a pencil torch and began to quarter the face of the slope with its narrow,
concentrated beam. Miller touched him on the arm.

'Taking a bit of a chance, aren't we? With that thing, I mean?'

'No chance,' Mallory said. 'There won't be a soldier left on guard
on the coasts tonight. They'll all be fighting the fires in the town.
Besides, who is left for them to guard against? We are the birds and
the birds, duty done, have flown. Only a madman would come
back to the island again.'

'I know what we are,' Miller said with feeling. 'You don't have
to tell me.'

Mallory smiled to himself in the darkness and continued his
search. Within a minute he had located what he had been hoping
to find – an angled gully in the slope. He and Miller scrambled up
the shale- and rock-strewn bed of the gully as fast as the treacherous footing and their encumbrances would permit: within fifteen-
minutes they had reached the plateau above and paused to take
their breath. Miller reached inside the depths of his tunic, a discreet
movement that was at once followed by a discreet gurgling.

'What are you doing?' Mallory enquired.

'I thought I heard my teeth chattering. What's all this "urgent 3
repeat urgent 3" business in the message, then?'

'I've never seen it before. But I know what it means. Some people, somewhere, are about to die.'

'I'll tell you two for a start. And what if Andrea won't come?
He's not a member of our armed forces. He doesn't have to come.
And he said he was getting married right away.'

Mallory said with certainty: 'He'll come.'

'What makes you so sure?'

'Because Andrea is the one completely responsible man I've ever met. He has two great responsibilities – one to others, one to himself. That's why he came back to Navarone – because he knew the people needed him. And that's why he'll leave Navarone when he sees this "urgent 3" signal, because he'll know that someone, in some other place, needs him even more.'

Miller retrieved the brandy bottle from Mallory and thrust it securely inside his tunic again. 'Well, I can tell you this. The future Mrs Andrea Stavros isn't going to be very happy about it.'

'Neither is Andrea Stavros and I'm not looking forward to telling him,' Mallory said candidly. He peered at his luminous watch and swung to his feet. 'Mandrakos in half an hour.'

In precisely thirty minutes, their Schmeissers removed from their waterproof bags and now shoulder-slung at hip level, Mallory and Miller moved swiftly but very quietly from shadow to shadow through the plantations of carob trees on the outskirts of the village of Mandrakos. Suddenly, from directly ahead, they heard the unmistakable clink of glasses and bottlenecks.

For the two men a potentially dangerous situation such as this was so routine as not even to warrant a glance at each other. They dropped silently to their hands and knees and crawled forward, Miller sniffing the air appreciatively as they advanced: the Greek resinous spirit *ouzo* has an extraordinary ability to permeate the atmosphere for a considerable distance around it. Mallory and Miller reached the edge of a clump of bushes, sank prone and looked ahead.

From their richly-befrogged waistcoats, cummerbunds and fancy headgear, the two characters propped against the bole of a plane tree in the clearing ahead were obviously men of the island: from the rifles across their knees, their role appeared to be that of guards of some kind: from the almost vertical angle at which they had to tip the *ouzo* bottle to get at what little was left of its contents, it was equally apparent that they weren't taking their duties too seriously, nor had been for some considerable time past.

Mallory and Miller withdrew somewhat less stealthily than they had advanced, rose and glanced at each other. Suitable comment seemed lacking. Mallory shrugged and moved on, circling around to his right. Twice more, as they moved swiftly into the centre of Mandrakos, flitting from the shadow of carob grove to carob grove, from the shadow of plane tree to plane tree, from the shadow of house to house, they came upon but easily avoided other ostensible sentries, all busy interpreting their duties in a very liberal fashion. Miller pulled Mallory into a doorway.

'Our friends back there,' he said. 'What were they celebrating?'

'Wouldn't you? Celebrate, I mean. Navarone is useless to the Germans now. A week from now and they'll all be gone.'

'All right. So why are they keeping a watch?' Miller nodded to a small, whitewashed Greek Orthodox church standing in the centre of the village square. From inside came a far from subdued murmur of voices. Also from inside came a great deal of light escaping through very imperfectly blacked-out windows. 'Could it be anything to do with that?'

Mallory said: 'Well, there's one sure way to find out.'

They moved quietly on, taking advantage of all available cover and shadow until they came to a still deeper shadow caused by two flying buttresses supporting the wall of the ancient church. Between the buttresses was one of the few more successfully blacked-out windows with only a tiny chink of light showing along the bottom edge. Both men stooped and peered through the narrow aperture.

The church appeared even more ancient inside than on the outside. The high unpainted wooden benches, adze-cut oak from centuries long gone, had been blackened and smoothed by untold generations of churchgoers, the wood itself cracked and splintered by the ravages of time: the whitewashed walls looked as if they required buttresses within as well as without, crumbling to an extinction that could not now be long delayed: the roof appeared to be in imminent danger of falling in at any moment.

The now even louder hum of sound came from islanders of almost every age and sex, many in ceremonial dress, who occupied nearly every available seat in the church: the light came from literally hundreds of guttering candles, many of them ancient and twisted and ornamented and evidently called out for this special occasion, that lined the walls, the central aisle and the altar: by the altar itself, a priest, a bearded patriarch in Greek Orthodox robes, waited impassively.

Mallory and Miller looked interrogatively at each other and were on the point of standing upright when a very deep and very quiet voice spoke behind them.

'Hands behind the necks,' it said pleasantly. 'And straighten very slowly. I have a Schmeisser machine-pistol in my hands.'

Slowly and carefully, just as the voice asked, Mallory and Miller did as they were told.

'Turn round. Carefully, now.'

So they turned round, carefully. Miller looked at the massive dark figure who indeed had, as he'd claimed, a machine-pistol in his hands, and said irritably: 'Do you mind? Point that damned thing somewhere else.'

The dark figure gave a startled exclamation, lowered the gun to his side and bent forward, the dark, craggy, lined face expressing no more than a passing flicker of surprise. Andrea Stavros didn't go in very much for registering unnecessary emotional displays and the recovery of his habitual composure was instantaneous.

'The German uniforms,' he explained apologetically. 'They had me fooled.'

'You could have fooled me, too,' Miller said. He looked incredulously at Andrea's clothes, at the unbelievably baggy black trousers, the black jackboots, the intricately ornamented black waistcoat and violently purple cummerbund, shuddered and closed his eyes in pain. 'Been visiting the Mandrakos pawn shop?'

'The ceremonial dress of my ancestors,' Andrea said mildly. 'You two fall overboard?'

'Not intentionally,' Mallory said. 'We came back to see you.'

'You could have chosen a more convenient time.' He hesitated, glanced at a small lighted building across the street and took their arms. 'We can talk in here.'

He ushered them in and closed the door behind him. The room was obviously, from its benches and Spartan furnishings, some sort of communal meeting-place, a village hall: illumination came from three rather smoky oil lamps, the light from which was most hospitably reflected by the scores of bottles of spirit and wine and beer and glasses that took up almost every available inch of two long trestle tables. The haphazardly unaesthetic layout of the refreshments bespoke a very impromptu and hastily improvised preparation for a celebration: the serried rows of bottles heralded the intention of compensating for lack of quality by an excess of quantity.

Andrea crossed to the nearest table, picked up three glasses and a bottle of *ouzo*, and began to pour drinks. Miller fished out his brandy and offered it, but Andrea was too preoccupied to notice. He handed them the *ouzo* glasses.

'Health.' Andrea drained his glass and went on thoughtfully: 'You did not return without a good reason, my Keith.'

Silently, Mallory removed the Cairo radio message from its waterproof oilskin wallet and handed it to Andrea, who took it half-unwillingly, then read it, scowling blackly.

He said: 'Urgent 3 means what I think it means?'

Again Mallory remained silent, merely nodding as he watched Andrea unwinkingly.

'This is most inconvenient for me.' The scowl deepened. *'Most* inconvenient. There are many things for me to do in Navarone. The people will miss me.'

'It's also inconvenient for me,' Miller said. 'There are many things I could profitably be doing in the West End of London. They miss me, too. Ask any barmaid. But that's hardly the point.'

Andrea regarded him for an impassive moment, then looked at Mallory. *'You* are saying nothing.'

'I've nothing to say.'

The scowl slowly left Andrea's face, though the brooding frown remained. He hesitated, then reached again for the bottle of *ouzo*. Miller shuddered delicately.

'Please.' He indicated the bottle of brandy.

Andrea smiled, briefly and for the first time, poured some of Miller's five-star into their glasses, reread the message and handed it back to Mallory. 'I must think it over. I have some business to attend to first.'

Mallory looked at him thoughtfully. 'Business?'

'I have to attend a wedding.'

'A wedding?' Miller said politely.

'Must you two repeat everything I say? A wedding.'

'But who do *you* know?' Miller asked. 'And at this hour of night.'

'For some people in Navarone,' Andrea said drily, 'the night is the only safe time.' He turned abruptly, walked away, opened the door and hesitated.

Mallory asked curiously: 'Who's getting married?'

Andrea made no reply. Instead he walked back to the nearest table, poured and drained a half-tumbler of the brandy, ran a hand through his thick dark hair, straightened his cummerbund, squared his shoulders and walked purposefully towards the door. Mallory and Miller stared after him, then at the door that closed behind him: then they stared at each other.

Some fifteen minutes later they were still staring at each other, this time with expressions which alternated between the merely bemused and slightly stunned.

They were seated in the back seat of the Greek Orthodox church – the only part of any pew in the entire church not now occupied by islanders. From where they sat, the altar was at least sixty feet away but as they were both tall men and sitting by the central aisle, they had a pretty fair view of what was going on up there.

There was, to be accurate, nothing going on up there any more. The ceremony was over. Gravely, the Orthodox priest bestowed his blessing and Andrea and Maria, the girl who had shown them the way into the fortress of Navarone, turned with the slow dignity becoming the occasion, and walked down the aisle. Andrea bent over, tenderness and solicitousness both in expression and manner, and whispered something in her ear, but his words, it would have seemed, bore little relation to the way in which they were expressed, for halfway down the aisle a furious altercation broke out between them. Between, perhaps, is not the right word: it was less an altercation than a very one-sided monologue. Maria, her face flushed and dark eyes flashing, gesticulating and clearly mad through, was addressing Andrea in far from low tones of not even barely-controlled fury: Andrea, for his part, was deprecatory, placatory, trying to hush her up with about the same amount of success as Canute had in holding back the tide, and looking apprehensively around. The reaction of the seated guests varied from disbelief through open-mouthed astonishment and bafflement to downright horror: clearly all regarded the spectacle as a highly unusual after-math to a wedding ceremony.

As the couple approached the end of the aisle opposite the pew where Mallory and Miller were seated, the argument, if such it could be called, raged more furiously than ever. As they passed by the end pew, Andrea, hand over his mouth, leaned over towards Mallory.

'This,' he said, *sotto voce*, 'is our first married quarrel.'

He was given time to say no more. An imperative hand seized his arm and almost literally dragged him through the church door-way. Even after they had disappeared from sight, Maria's voice, loud and clear, could still be heard by everyone within the church. Miller turned from surveying the empty doorway and looked thoughtfully at Mallory.

'Very high-spirited girl, that. I wish I understood Greek. What was she saying there?'

Mallory kept his face carefully expressionless. 'What about my honeymoon?'

'Ah!' Miller's face was equally dead-pan. 'Don't you think we'd better follow them?'

'Why?'

'Andrea can take care of most people.' It was the usual masterly Miller understatement. 'But he's stepped out of his class this time.'

Mallory smiled, rose and went to the door, followed by Miller, who was in turn followed by an eager press of guests understandably anxious to see the second act of this unscheduled entertainment: but the village square was empty of life.

Mallory did not hesitate. With the instinct born from the experience of long association with Andrea, he headed across the square to the communal hall where Andrea had made the earlier of his two dramatic statements. His instincts hadn't betrayed him. Andrea, with a large glass of brandy in his hand and moodily fingering a spreading patch of red on his cheek, looked up as Mallory and Miller entered.

He said moodily: 'She's gone home to her mother.'

Miller glanced at his watch. 'One minute and twenty-five seconds,' he said admiringly. 'A world record.'

Andrea glowered at him and Mallory moved in hastily.

'You're coming, then.'

'Of course I'm coming,' Andrea said irritably. He surveyed without enthusiasm the guests now swarming into the hall and brushing unceremoniously by as they headed, like the camel for the oasis, towards the bottle-laden tables. 'Somebody's got to look after you two.'

Mallory looked at his watch. 'Three and a half hours yet before that plane is due. We're dead on our feet, Andrea. Where can we sleep – a safe place to sleep. Your perimeter guards are drunk.'

'They've been that way ever since the fortress blew up,' Andrea said. 'Come, I'll show you.'

Miller looked around the islanders, who, amid a loud babel of cheerful voices, were already quite exceptionally busy with bottles and glasses. 'How about your guests?'

'How about them, then?' Andrea surveyed his compatriots morosely. 'Just look at that lot. Ever known a wedding reception yet where anybody paid any attention to the bride and groom? Come.'

They made their way southwards through the outskirts of Mandrakos to the open countryside beyond. Twice they were challenged by guards, twice a scowl and growl from Andrea sent them back hurriedly to their *ouzo* bottles. It was still raining heavily, but Mallory's and Miller's clothes were already so saturated that a little more rain could hardly make any appreciable difference to the way they felt, while Andrea, if anything, seemed even more oblivious of it. Andrea had the air of a man who had other things on his mind.

After fifteen minutes' walk, Andrea stopped before the swing doors of a small, dilapidated and obviously deserted roadside barn.

'There's hay inside,' he said. 'We'll be safe here.'

Mallory said: 'Fine. A radio message to the *Sirdar* to send her CE message to Cairo and –'

'CE?' Andrea asked. 'What's that?'

'To let Cairo know we've contacted you and are ready for pick-up . . . And after that, three lovely hours' sleep.'

Andrea nodded. 'Three hours it is.'

'Three *long* hours,' Mallory said meditatively.

A smile slowly broke on Andrea's craggy face as he clapped Mallory on the shoulder.

'In three long hours,' he said, 'a man like myself can accomplish a great deal.'

He turned and hurried off through the rain-filled night. Mallory and Miller looked after him with expressionless faces, looked at each other, still with the same expressionless faces, then pushed open the swing doors of the barn.

The Mandrakos airfield would not have received a licence from any Civil Air Board anywhere in the world. It was just over half a mile long, with hills rising steeply at both ends of the alleged runway, not more than forty yards wide and liberally besprinkled with a variety of bumps and potholes virtually guaranteed to wreck any undercarriage in the aviation business. But the RAF had used it before so it was not impossible that they might be able to use it at least once again.

To the south, the airstrip was lined with groves of carob trees. Under the pitiful shelter afforded by one of those, Mallory, Miller and Andrea sat waiting. At least Mallory and Miller did, hunched, miserable and shivering violently in their still sodden clothes. Andrea, however, was stretched out luxuriously with his hands behind his head, oblivious of the heavy drips of rain that fell on his upturned face. There was about him an air of satisfaction, of com-placency almost, as he gazed at the first greyish tinges appearing in the sky to the east over the black-walled massif of the Turkish coast.

Andrea said: 'They're coming now.'

Mallory and Miller listened for a few moments, then they too heard it – the distant, muted roar of heavy aircraft approaching. All three rose and moved out to the perimeter of the airstrip. Within a minute, descending rapidly after their climb over the mountains to the south and at a height of less than a thousand feet, a squadron of eighteen Wellingtons, as much heard as seen in the light of early dawn, passed directly over the airstrip, heading for the town of Navarone. Two minutes later, the three watchers both heard the detonations and saw the brilliant orange mushrooming of light as the Wellingtons unloaded their bombs over the shattered fortress to the north. Sporadic lines of upward-flying tracers, obviously exclusively small-arm, attested to the ineffectuality, the weakness of the ground defences. When the fortress had blown up, so had all the anti-aircraft batteries in the town. The attack was short and sharp: less than two minutes after the bombardment had started it ceased as abruptly as it had begun and then there was only the fading dying sound of desynchronized engines as the Wellingtons pulled away, first to the north and then the west, across the still-dark waters of the Aegean.

For perhaps a minute the three watchers stood silent on the perimeter of the Mandrakos airstrip, then Miller said wonderingly: 'What makes us so important?'

'I don't know,' Mallory said. 'But I don't think you're going to enjoy finding out.'

'And that won't be long now.' Andrea turned round and looked towards the mountains to the south. 'Hear it?'

Neither of the others heard it, but they did not doubt that, in fact, there was something to hear. Andrea's hearing was on a par with his phenomenal eyesight. Then, suddenly, they could hear it, too. A solitary bomber – also a Wellington – came sinking in from the south, circled the perimeter area once as Mallory blinked his torch upwards in rapidly successive flashes, lined up its approach, landed heavily at the far end of the airstrip and came taxiing towards them, bumping heavily across the atrocious surface of the airfield. It halted less than a hundred yards from where they stood: then a light started winking from the flight deck.

Andrea said: 'Now, don't forget. I've promised to be back in a week.'

'Never make promises,' Miller said severely. 'What if we aren't back in a week? What if they're sending us to the Pacific?'

'Then when we get back I'll send you in first to explain.'

Miller shook his head. 'I don't really think I'd like that.'

'We'll talk about your cowardice later on,' Mallory said. 'Come on. Hurry up.'

The three men broke into a run towards the waiting Wellington.

The Wellington was half an hour on the way to its destination, wherever its destination was, and Andrea and Miller, coffee mugs in hand, were trying, unsuccessfully, to attain a degree of comfort on the lumpy palliasses on the fuselage floor when Mallory returned from the flightdeck. Miller looked up at him in weary resignation, his expression characterized by an entire lack of enthusiasm and the spirit of adventure.

'Well, what did you find out?' His tone of voice made it abundantly clear that what he had expected Mallory to find out was nothing short of the very worst. 'Where to, now? Rhodes? Beirut? The flesh-pots of Cairo?'

'Termoli, the man says.'

'Termoli, is it? Place I've always wanted to see.' Miller paused. 'Where the hell's Termoli?'

'Italy, so I believe. Somewhere on the south Adriatic coast.'

'Oh, no!' Miller turned on his side and pulled a blanket over his head. 'I *hate* spaghetti.'

TWO

Thursday
1400–2330

The landing on Termoli airfield, on the Adriatic coast of Southern Italy, was every bit as bumpy as the harrowing take-off from the Mandrakos airstrip had been. The Termoli fighter airbase was officially and optimistically listed as newly-constructed but in point of fact was no more than half-finished and felt that way for every yard of the excruciating touchdown and the jack-rabbit run-up to the prefabricated control tower at the eastern end of the field. When Mallory and Andrea swung down to terra firma, neither of them looked particularly happy: Miller, who came a very shaky last, and who was widely known to have an almost pathological loathing and detestation of all conceivable forms of transport, looked very ill indeed.

Miller was given time neither to seek nor receive commiseration. A camouflaged British 5th Army jeep pulled up alongside the plane, and the sergeant at the wheel, having briefly established their identity, waved them inside in silence, a silence which he stonily maintained on their drive through the shambles of the war-torn streets of Termoli. Mallory was unperturbed by the apparent unfriendliness. The driver was obviously under the strictest instructions not to talk to them, a situation which Mallory had encountered all too often in the past. There were not, Mallory reflected, very many groups of untouchables, but his, he knew, was one of them: no one, with two or three rare exceptions, was ever permitted to talk to them. The process, Mallory knew, was perfectly understandable and justifiable, but it was an attitude that did tend to become increasingly wearing with the passing of the years. It tended to make for a certain lack of contact with one's fellow men.

After twenty minutes, the jeep stopped below the broad-flagged steps of a house on the outskirts of the town. The jeep driver gestured briefly to an armed sentry on the top of the steps who responded with a similarly perfunctory greeting. Mallory took this as a sign that they had arrived at their destination and, not wishing to violate the young sergeant's vow of silence, got out without being told. The others followed and the jeep at once drove off.

The house – it looked more like a modest palace – was a rather splendid example of late Renaissance architecture, all colonnades and columns and everything in veined marble, but Mallory was more interested in what was inside the house than what it was made of on the outside. At the head of the steps their path was barred by the young corporal sentry armed with a Lee-Enfield .303. He looked like a refugee from high school.

'Names, please.'

'Captain Mallory.'

'Identity papers? Pay-books?'

'Oh, my God,' Miller moaned. 'And me feeling so sick, too.'

'We have none,' Mallory said gently. 'Take us inside, please.'

'My instructions are –'

'I know, I know,' Andrea said soothingly. He leaned across, effortlessly removed the rifle from the corporal's desperate grasp, ejected and pocketed the magazine and returned the rifle. 'Please, now.'

Red-faced and furious, the youngster hesitated briefly, looked at the three men more carefully, turned, opened the door behind him and gestured for the three to follow him.

Before them stretched a long, marble-flagged corridor, tall leaded windows on one side, heavy oil paintings and the occasional set of double-leather doors on the other. Halfway down the passage Andrea tapped the corporal on the shoulder and handed the magazine back without a word. The corporal took it, smiling uncertainly, and inserted it into his rifle without a word. Another twenty paces and he stopped before the last pair of leather doors, knocked, heard a muffled acknowledgement and pushed open one of the doors, standing aside to let the three men pass him. Then he moved out again, closing the door behind him.

It was obviously the main drawing-room of the house – or palace – furnished in an almost medieval opulence, all dark oak, heavily brocaded silk curtains, leather upholstery, leather-bound books, what were undoubtedly a set of Old Masters on the walls and a flowing sea of dull bronze carpeting from wall to wall. Taken all in all, even a member of the old-pre-war Italian nobility wouldn't have turned up his nose at it.

The room was pleasantly redolent with the smell of burning pine, the source of which wasn't difficult to locate: one could have roasted a very large ox indeed in the vast and crackling fireplace at the far end of the room. Close by this fireplace stood three young men who bore no resemblance whatsoever to the rather ineffectual youngster who had so recently tried to prevent their entry. They were, to begin with, a good few years older, though still young men. They were heavily-built, broad-shouldered characters and had about them a look of tough and hard-bitten competence. They were dressed in the uniform of that élite of combat troops, the Marine Commandos, and they looked perfectly at home in those uniforms.

But what caught and held the unwavering attention of Mallory and his two companions was neither the rather splendidly effete decadence of the room and its furnishings nor the wholly unexpected presence of the three commandos: it was the fourth figure in the room, a tall, heavily built and commanding figure who leaned negligently against a table in the centre of the room. The deeply-trenched face, the authoritative expression, the splendid grey beard and the piercing blue eyes made him a prototype for the classic British naval captain, which, as the immaculate white uniform he wore indicated, was precisely what he was. With a collective sinking of their hearts, Mallory, Andrea and Miller gazed again, and with a marked lack of enthusiasm, upon the splendidly piratical figure of Captain Jensen, RN, Chief of Allied Intelligence, Mediterranean, and the man who had so recently sent them on their suicidal mission to the island of Navarone. All three looked at one another and shook their heads in slow despair.

Captain Jensen straightened, smiled his magnificent sabre-toothed tiger's smile and strode forward to greet them, his hand outstretched.

'Mallory! Andrea! Miller!' There was a dramatic five-second pause between the words. 'I don't know what to say! I just don't know what to say! A magnificent job, a magnificent –' He broke off and regarded them thoughtfully. 'You – um – don't seem at all surprised to see me, Captain Mallory?'

'I'm not. With respect, sir, whenever and wherever there's dirty work afoot, one looks to find –'

'Yes, yes, yes. Quite, quite. And how are you all?'

'Tired,' Miller said firmly. 'Terribly tired. We need a rest. At least, I do.'

Jensen said earnestly: 'And that's exactly what you're going to have, my boy. A rest. A long one. A *very* long one.'

'A *very* long one?' Miller looked at him in frank incredulity.

'You have my word.' Jensen stroked his beard in momentary diffidence. 'Just as soon, that is, as you get back from Yugoslavia.'

'Yugoslavia!' Miller stared at him.

'Tonight.'

'Tonight!'

'By parachute.'

'By *parachute!*'

Jensen said with forbearance: 'I am aware, Corporal Miller, that you have had a classical education and are, moreover, just returned from the Isles of Greece. But we'll do without the Ancient Greek Chorus bit, if you don't mind.'

Miller looked moodily at Andrea. 'Bang goes your honeymoon.'

'What was that?' Jensen asked sharply.

'Just a private joke, sir.'

Mallory said in mild protest: 'You're forgetting, sir, that none of us has ever made a parachute jump.'

'I'm forgetting nothing. There's a first time for everything. What do you gentlemen know about the war in Yugoslavia?'

'What war?' Andrea asked warily.

'Precisely.' There was satisfaction in Jensen's voice.

'I heard about it,' Miller volunteered. 'There's a bunch of what-do-you-call-'em – Partisans, isn't it – offering some kind of underground resistance to the German occupation troops.'

'It is probably as well for you,' Jensen said heavily, 'that the Partisans cannot hear you. They're not underground, they're very much over ground and at the last count there were 350,000 of them tying down twenty-eight German and Bulgarian divisions in Yugoslavia.' He paused briefly. 'More, in fact, than the combined Allied armies are tying down here in Italy.'

'Somebody should have told me,' Miller complained. He brightened. 'If there's 350,000 of them around, what would they want us for?'

Jensen said acidly: 'You must learn to curb your enthusiasm, Corporal. The fighting part of it you may leave to the Partisans – and they're fighting the cruellest, hardest, most brutal war in Europe today. A ruthless, vicious war with no quarter and no surrender on either side. Arms, munitions, food, clothes – the Partisans are desperately short of all of those. But they have those twenty-eight divisions pinned down.'

'I don't want any part of that,' Miller muttered.

Mallory said hastily: 'What do you want us to do, sir?'

'This.' Jensen removed his glacial stare from Miller. 'Nobody appreciates it yet, but the Yugoslavs are our most important Allies in Southern Europe. Their war is our war. And they're fighting a war they can never hope to win. Unless –'

Mallory nodded. 'The tools to finish the job.'

'Hardly original, but true. The tools to finish the job. We are the *only* people who are at present supplying them with rifles, machine-guns, ammunition, clothing and medical supplies. And those are not getting through.' He broke off, picking up a cane, walked almost angrily across the room to a large wall-map hanging between a couple of Old Masters and rapped the tip of the bamboo against it. 'Bosnia-Herzegovina, gentlemen. West-Central Yugoslavia. We've sent in four British Military Missions in the past two months to liaise with the Yugoslavs – the Partisan Yugoslavs. The leaders of all four missions have disappeared without trace. Ninety per cent of our recent airlift supplies have fallen into German hands. They have broken all our radio codes and have established a network of agents in Southern Italy here with whom they are apparently able to communicate as and when they wish. Perplexing questions, gentlemen. Vital questions. I want the answers. Force 10 will get me the answers.'

'Force 10?' Mallory said politely.

'The code name for your operation.'

'Why that particular name?' Andrea said.

'Why not? Ever heard of *any* code name that had *any* bearing on the operation on hand? It's the whole essence of it, man.'

'It wouldn't, of course,' Mallory said woodenly, 'have anything to do with a frontal attack on something, a storming of some vital place.' He observed Jensen's total lack of reaction and went on in the same tone: 'On the Beaufort Scale, Force 10 means a storm.'

'A storm!' It is very difficult to combine an exclamation and a moan of anguish in the same word, but Miller managed it without any difficulty. 'Oh, my God, and all I want is a flat calm, and that for the rest of my life.'

'There are limits to my patience, Corporal Miller,' Jensen said. 'I may – I say *may* – have to change my mind about a recommendation I made on your behalf this morning.'

'On my behalf?' Miller said guardedly.

'For the Distinguished Conduct Medal.'

'That should look nice on the lid of my coffin,' Miller muttered.

'What was that?'

'Corporal Miller was just expressing his appreciation.' Mallory moved closer to the wall-map and studied it briefly. 'Bosnia-Herzegovina – well, it's a fair-sized area, sir.'

'Agreed. But we can pinpoint the spot – the approximate location of the disappearances – to within twenty miles.'

Mallory turned from the map and said slowly: 'There's been a lot of homework on this one. That raid this morning on Navarone. The Wellington standing by to take us here. All preparations – I infer this from what you've said – laid on for tonight. Not to mention –'

'We've been working on this for almost two months. You three were supposed to have come here some days ago. But – ah – well, you know.'

'We know.' The threatened withholding of his DCM had left Miller unmoved. 'Something else came up. Look, sir, why us? We're saboteurs, explosives experts, combat troops – this is a job for undercover espionage agents who speak Serbo-Croat or whatever.'

'You must allow me to be the best judge of that,' Jensen gave them another flash of his sabre-toothed smile. 'Besides, you're lucky.'

'Luck deserts tired men,' Andrea said. 'And we are very tired.'

'Tired or not, I can't find another team in Southern Europe to match you for resource, experience and skill.' Jensen smiled again. 'And luck. I have to be ruthless, Andrea. I don't like it, but I have to. But I take the point about your exhaustion. That's why I have decided to send a back-up team with you.'

Mallory looked at the three young soldiers standing by the hearth, then back to Jensen, who nodded.

'They're young, fresh and just raring to go. Marine Commandos, the most highly trained combat troops we have today. Remarkable variety of skills, I assure you. Take Reynolds, here.' Jensen nodded to a very tall, dark sergeant in his late twenties, a man with a deeply-tanned aquiline face. 'He can do anything from underwater demolition to flying a plane. And he will be flying a plane tonight. And, as you can see, he'll come in handy for carrying any heavy cases you have.'

Mallory said mildly: 'I've always found that Andrea makes a pretty fair porter, sir.'

Jensen turned to Reynolds. 'They have their doubts. Show them you can be of some use.'

Reynolds hesitated, then stooped, picked up a heavy brass poker and proceeded to bend it between his hands. Obviously, it wasn't an easy poker to bend. His face turned red, the veins stood out on his forehead and the tendons in his neck, his arms quivered with the strain, but slowly, inexorably, the poker was bent into a figure 'U'. Smiling almost apologetically, Reynolds handed the poker over to Andrea. Andrea took it reluctantly. He hunched his shoulders, his knuckles gleamed white but the poker remained in its 'U' shape. Andrea looked up at Reynolds, his expression thoughtful, then quietly laid the poker down.

'See what I mean?' Jensen said. 'Tired. Or Sergeant Groves here. Hot-foot from London, via the Middle East. Ex-air navigator, with all the latest in sabotage, explosives and electrics. For booby-traps, time-bombs and concealed microphones, a human mine-detector. And Sergeant Saunders here – a top-flight radio operator.'

Miller said morosely to Mallory: 'You're a toothless old lion and you're over the hill.'

'Don't talk rubbish, Corporal!' Jensen's voice was sharp. 'Six is the ideal number. You'll be duplicated in every department, and those men are *good*. They'll be invaluable. If it's any salve to your pride, they weren't originally picked to go with you: they were picked as a reserve team in case you – um – well –'

'I see.' The lack of conviction in Miller's voice was total.

'All clear then?'

'Not quite,' Mallory said. 'Who's in charge?'

Jensen said in genuine surprise: 'You are, of course.'

'So.' Mallory spoke quietly and pleasantly. 'I understand the training emphasis today – especially in the Marine Commandos – is on initiative, self-reliance, independence in thought and action. Fine – if they happen to be caught out on their own.' He smiled, almost deprecatingly. 'Otherwise I shall expect immediate, unquestioning and total compliance with orders. My orders. Instant and total.'

'And if not?' Reynolds asked.

'A superfluous question, Sergeant. You know the wartime penalty for disobeying an officer in the field.'

'Does that apply to your friends, too?'

'No.'

Reynolds turned to Jensen. 'I don't think I like that, sir.'

Mallory sank wearily into a chair, lit a cigarette, nodded at Reynolds and said, 'Replace him.'

'What!' Jensen was incredulous.

'Replace him, I said. We haven't even left and already he's questioning my judgement. What's it going to be like in action? He's dangerous. I'd rather carry a ticking time-bomb with me.'

'Now, look here, Mallory –'

'Replace him or replace me.'

'And me,' Andrea said quietly.

'And me,' Miller added.

There was a brief and far from companionable silence in the room, then Reynolds approached Mallory's chair.

'Sir.'

Mallory looked at him without encouragement.

'I'm sorry,' Reynolds went on. 'I stepped out of line. I will never make the same mistake twice. I *want* to go on this trip, sir.'

Mallory glanced at Andrea and Miller. Miller's face registered only his shock at Reynolds's incredibly foolhardy enthusiasm for action. Andrea, impassive as ever, nodded almost imperceptibly. Mallory smiled and said: 'As Captain Jensen said, I'm sure you'll be a great asset.'

'Well, that's it, then.' Jensen affected not to notice the almost palpable relaxation of tension in the room. 'Sleep's the thing now. But first I'd like a few minutes – report on Navarone, you know.' He looked at the three sergeants. 'Confidential, I'm afraid.'

'Yes, sir,' Reynolds said. 'Shall we go down to the field, check flight plans, weather, parachutes and supplies?'

Jensen nodded. As the three sergeants closed the double doors behind them, Jensen crossed to a side door, opened it and said: 'Come in, General.'

The man who entered was very tall, very gaunt. He was probably about thirty-five, but looked a great deal older. The care, the exhaustion, the endless privations inseparable from too many years' ceaseless struggle for survival had heavily silvered the once-black hair and deeply etched into the swarthy, sunburnt face the lines of physical and mental suffering. The eyes were dark and glowing and intense, the hypnotic eyes of a man inspired by a fanatical dedication to some as yet unrealized ideal. He was dressed in a British Army officer's uniform, bereft of insignia and badges.

Jensen said: 'Gentlemen, General Vukalovic. The general is second-in-command of the Partisan forces in Bosnia-Herzegovina. The RAF flew him out yesterday. He is here as a Partisan doctor seeking medical supplies. His true identity is known only to us. General, those are your men.'

Vukalovic looked them over severally and steadily, his face expressionless. He said: 'Those are tired men, Captain Jensen. So much depends . . . too tired to do what has to be done.'

'He's right, you know,' Miller said earnestly.

'There's maybe a little mileage left in them yet,' Jensen said mildly. 'It's a long haul from Navarone. Now then –'

'Navarone?' Vukalovic interrupted. 'These – these are the men –'

'An unlikely-looking lot, I agree.'

'Perhaps I was wrong about them.'

'No, you weren't, General,' Miller said. 'We're exhausted. We're completely –'

'Do you mind?' Jensen said acidly. 'Captain Mallory, with two exceptions the general will be the only person in Bosnia who knows who you are and what you are doing. Whether the general reveals the identity of the others is entirely up to him. General Vukalovic will be accompanying you to Yugoslavia, but not in the same plane.'

'Why not?' Mallory asked.

'Because his plane will be returning. Yours won't.'

'Ah!' Mallory said. There was a brief silence while he, Andrea and Miller absorbed the significance behind Jensen's words. Abstractedly, Andrea threw some more wood on the sinking fire and looked around for a poker: but the only poker was the one that Reynolds had already bent into a 'U' shape. Andrea picked it up. Absent-mindedly, effortlessly, Andrea straightened it out, poked the fire into a blaze and laid the poker down, a performance Vukalovic watched with a very thoughtful expression on his face.

Jensen went on: 'Your plane, Captain Mallory, will not be returning because your plane is expendable in the interests of authenticity.'

'Us, too?' Miller asked.

'You won't be able to accomplish very much, Corporal Miller, without actually putting your feet on the ground. Where you're going, no plane can possibly land: so you jump – and the plane crashes.'

'That sounds very authentic,' Miller muttered.

Jensen ignored him. 'The realities of total war are harsh beyond belief. Which is why I sent those three youngsters on their way – I don't want to dampen their enthusiasm.'

'Mine's water-logged,' Miller said dolefully.

'Oh, do be quiet. Now, it would be fine if, by way of a bonus, you could discover why eighty per cent of our air-drops fall into German hands, fine if you could locate and rescue our captured mission leaders. But not important. Those supplies, those agents are militarily expendable. What are not expendable are the seven thousand men under the command of General Vukalovic here, seven thousand men trapped in an area called the Zenica Cage, seven thousand starving men with almost no ammunition left, seven thousand men with no future.'

'We can help them?' Andrea asked heavily. 'Six men?'

Jensen said candidly: 'I don't know.'

'But you have a plan?'

'Not yet. Not as such. The glimmerings of an idea. No more.' Jensen rubbed his forehead wearily. 'I myself arrived from Alexandria only six hours ago.' He hesitated, then shrugged. 'By tonight, who knows? A few hours' sleep this afternoon might transform us all. But, first, the report on Navarone. It would be pointless for you three other gentlemen to wait – there are sleeping quarters down the hall. I daresay Captain Mallory can tell me all I want to know.'

Mallory waited till the door closed behind Andrea, Miller and Vukalovic and said: 'Where shall I begin my report, sir?'

'What report?'

'Navarone, of course.'

'The hell with Navarone. That's over and done with.' He picked up his cane, crossed to the wall, pulled down two more maps. 'Now, then.'

'You – you *have* a plan,' Mallory said carefully.

'Of course I have a plan,' Jensen said coldly. He rapped the map in front of him. 'Ten miles north of here. The Gustav Line. Right across Italy along the line of the Sangro and Liri rivers. Here the Germans have the most impregnable defensive positions in the history of modern warfare. Monte Cassino here – our finest Allied divisions have broken on it, some for ever. And here – the Anzio beachhead. Fifty thousand Americans fighting for their lives. For five solid months now we've been battering our heads against the Gustav Line and the Anzio perimeter. Our losses in men and machines – incalculable. Our gains – not one solitary inch.'

Mallory said diffidently: 'You mentioned something about Yugoslavia, sir.'

'I'm coming to that,' Jensen said with restraint. 'Now, our only hope of breaching the Gustav Line is by weakening the German defensive forces and the only way we can do *that* is by persuading them to withdraw some of their front-line divisions. So we practise the Allenby technique.'

'I see.'

'You don't see at all. General Allenby, Palestine, 1918. He had an east-west line from the Jordan to the Mediterranean. He planned to attack from the west – so he convinced the Turks the attack was coming from the east. He did this by building up in the east a huge city of army tents occupied by only a few hundred men who came out and dashed around like beavers whenever enemy planes came over on reconnaissance. He did this by letting the same planes see large army truck convoys pouring to the east all day long – what the Turks didn't know was that the same convoys poured back to the west all night long. He even had fifteen thousand canvas dummies of horses built. Well, we're doing the same.'

'Fifteen thousand canvas horses?'

'Very, very amusing.' Jensen rapped the map again. 'Every airfield between here and Bari is jammed with dummy bombers and gliders. Outside Foggia is the biggest military encampment in Italy – occupied by two hundred men. The harbours of Bari and Taranto are crowded with assault landing craft, the whole lot made of plywood. All day long columns of trucks and tanks converge on the Adriatic coast. If you, Mallory, were in the German High Command, what would you make of this?'

'I'd suspect an airborne and sea invasion of Yugoslavia. But I wouldn't be sure.'

'The German reaction exactly,' Jensen said with some satisfaction. 'They're badly worried, worried to the extent that they have already transferred two divisions from Italy to Yugoslavia to meet the threat.'

'But they're not certain?'

'Not quite. But almost.' Jensen cleared his throat. 'You see, our four captured mission leaders were all carrying unmistakable evidence pointing to an invasion of Central Yugoslavia in early May.'

'They carried evidence –' Mallory broke off, looked at Jensen for a long and speculative moment, then went on quietly: 'And how *did* the Germans manage to capture them all?'

'We told them they were coming.'

'You did what!'

'Volunteers all, volunteers all,' Jensen said quickly. There were, apparently, some of the harsher realities of total war that even he didn't care to dwell on too long. 'And it will be your job, my boy, to turn near-conviction into absolute certainty.' Seemingly oblivious of the fact that Mallory was regarding him with a marked lack of enthusiasm, he wheeled round dramatically and stabbed his cane at a large-scale map of Central Yugoslavia.

'The valley of the Neretva,' Jensen said. 'The vital sector of the main north-south route through Yugoslavia. Whoever controls this valley controls Yugoslavia – and no one knows this better than the Germans. If the blow falls, they know it must fall here. They are fully aware that an invasion of Yugoslavia is on the cards, they are terrified of a link-up between the Allies and the Russians advancing from the east and they *know* that any such link-up must be along this valley. They already have two armoured divisions along the Neretva, two divisions that, in the event of invasion, could be wiped out in a night. From the north – here – they are trying to force their way south to the Neretva with a whole army corps – but the only way is through the Zenica Cage here. And Vukalovic and his seven thousand men block the way.'

'Vukalovic knows about this?' Mallory asked. 'About what you really have in mind, I mean?'

'Yes. And the Partisan command. They know the risks, the odds against them. They accept them.'

'Photographs?' Mallory asked.

'Here.' Jensen pulled some photographs from a desk drawer, selected one and smoothed it out on the table. 'This is the Zenica Cage. Well named: a perfect cage, a perfect trap. To the north and west, impassable mountains. To the east, the Neretva dam and the Neretva gorge. To the south, the Neretva river. To the north of the cage here, at the Zenica gap, the German 11th Army Corps is trying to break through. To the west here – they call it the West Gap – more units of the 11th trying to do the same. And to the south here, over the river and hidden in the trees, two armoured divisions under a General Zimmermann.'

'And this?' Mallory pointed to a thin black line spanning the river just north of the two armoured divisions.

'That,' Jensen said thoughtfully, 'is the bridge at Neretva.'

Close-up, the bridge at Neretva looked vastly more impressive than it had done in the large-scale photograph: it was a massively cantilevered structure in solid steel, with a black asphalt roadway laid on top. Below the bridge rushed the swiftly-flowing Neretva, greenish-white in colour and swollen with melting snow. To the south there was a narrow strip of green meadowland bordering the river and, to the south of this again, a dark and towering pine forest began. In the safe concealment of the forest's gloomy depths, General Zimmermann's two armoured divisions crouched waiting.

Parked close to the edge of the wood was the divisional command radio truck, a bulky and very long vehicle so beautifully camouflaged as to be invisible at more than twenty paces.

General Zimmermann and his ADC, Captain Warburg, were at that moment inside the truck. Their mood appeared to match the permanent twilight of the woods. Zimmermann had one of those high-foreheaded, lean and aquiline and intelligent faces which so rarely betray any emotion, but there was no lack of emotion now, no lack of anxiety and impatience as he removed his cap and ran his hand through his thinning grey hair. He said to the radio operator seated behind the big transceiver:

'No word yet? Nothing?'

'Nothing, sir.'

'You are in constant touch with Captain Neufeld's camp?'

'Every minute, sir.'

'And his operator is keeping a continuous radio watch?'

'All the time, sir. Nothing. Just nothing.'

Zimmermann turned and descended the steps, followed by Warburg. He walked, head down, until he was out of earshot of the truck, then said: 'Damn it! Damn it! God damn it all!'

'You're as sure as that, sir.' Warburg was tall, good-looking, flaxen-haired and thirty, and his face at the moment reflected a nice balance of apprehension and unhappiness. 'That they're coming?'

'It's in my bones, my boy. One way or another it's coming, coming for all of us.'

'You can't be *sure*, sir,' Warburg protested.

'True enough.' Zimmermann sighed. 'I can't be sure. But I'm sure of this. If they do come, if the 11th Army Group can't break through from the north, if we can't wipe out those damned Partisans in the Zenica Cage –'

Warburg waited for him to continue, but Zimmermann seemed lost in reverie. Apparently apropos of nothing, Warburg said: 'I'd like to see Germany again, sir. Just once more.'

'Wouldn't we all, my boy, wouldn't we all.' Zimmermann walked slowly to the edge of the wood and stopped. For a long time he gazed out over the bridge at Neretva. Then he shook his head, turned and was almost at once lost to sight in the dark depths of the forest.

The pine fire in the great fireplace in the drawing-room in Termoli was burning low. Jensen threw on some more logs, straightened, poured two drinks and handed one to Mallory.

Jensen said: 'Well?'

'That's the plan?' No hint of his incredulity, of his near-despair, showed in Mallory's impassive face. 'That's *all* of the plan?'

'Yes.'

'Your health.' Mallory paused. 'And mine.' After an even longer pause he said reflectively: 'It should be interesting to watch Dusty Miller's reactions when he hears this little lot this evening.'

As Mallory had said, Miller's reactions were interesting, even if wholly predictable. Some six hours later, clad now, like Mallory and Andrea, in British Army uniform, Miller listened in visibly growing horror as Jensen outlined what he considered should be their proposed course of action in the next twenty-four hours or so. When he had finished, Jensen looked directly at Miller and said: 'Well? Feasible?'

'Feasible?' Miller was aghast. 'It's suicidal!'

'Andrea?'

Andrea shrugged, lifted his hands palms upwards and said nothing.

Jensen nodded and said: 'I'm sorry, but I'm fresh out of options. We'd better go. The others are waiting at the airstrip.'

Andrea and Miller left the room, began to walk down the long passageway. Mallory hesitated in the doorway, momentarily blocking it, then turned to face Jensen who was watching him with a surprised lift of the eyebrows.

Mallory said in a low voice: 'Let me tell Andrea, at least.'

Jensen looked at him for a considering moment or two, shook his head briefly and brushed by into the corridor.

Twenty minutes later, without a further word being spoken, the four men arrived at the Termoli airstrip to find Vukalovic and two sergeants waiting for them: the third, Reynolds, was already at the controls of his Wellington, one of them standing at the end of the airstrip, propellers already turning. Ten minutes later both planes were airborne, Vukalovic in one, Mallory, Miller, Andrea, and the three sergeants in the other, each plane bound for its separate destination.

Jensen, alone on the tarmac, watched both planes climbing, his straining eyes following them until they disappeared into the overcast darkness of the moonless sky above. Then, just as General Zimmermann had done that afternoon, he shook his head in slow finality, turned and walked heavily away.

THREE

Friday
0030–0200

Sergeant Reynolds, Mallory reflected, certainly knew how to handle a plane, especially this one. Although his eyes showed him to be always watchful and alert, he was precise, competent, calm and relaxed in everything he did. No less competent was Groves: the poor light and cramped confines of his tiny plotting-table clearly didn't worry him at all and as an air navigator he was quite clearly as experienced as he was proficient. Mallory peered forward through the windscreen, saw the white-capped waters of the Adriatic rushing by less than a hundred feet beneath their fuselage, and turned to Groves.

'The flight plan calls for us to fly as low as this?'

'Yes. The Germans have radar installations on some of the outlying islands off the Yugoslav coast. We start climbing when we reach Dalmatia.'

Mallory nodded his thanks, turned to watch Reynolds again. He said, curiously: 'Captain Jensen was right about you. As a pilot. How on earth does a Marine Commando come to learn to drive one of those things?'

'I've had plenty of practice,' Reynolds said. 'Three years in the RAF, two of them as sergeant-pilot in a Wellington bomber squadron. One day in Egypt I took a Lysander up without permission. People did it all the time – but the crate I'd picked had a defective fuel gauge.'

'You were grounded?'

'With great speed.' He grinned. 'There were no objections when I applied for a service transfer. I think they felt I wasn't somehow quite right for the RAF.'

Mallory looked at Groves. 'And you?'

Groves smiled broadly. 'I was his navigator in that old crate. We were fired on the same day.'

Mallory said consideringly: 'Well, I should think that might be rather useful.'

'What's useful?' Reynolds asked.

'The fact that you're used to this feeling of disgrace. It'll enable you to act your part all the better when the time comes. If the time comes.'

Reynolds said carefully: 'I'm not quite sure –'

'Before we jump, I want you – all of you – to remove every dis-tinguishing badge or emblem of rank on your clothes.' He gestured to Andrea and Miller at the rear of the flight-deck to indicate that they were included as well, then looked at Reynolds again. 'Sergeants' stripes, regimental flashes, medal ribbons – the lot.'

'Why the hell should I?' Reynolds, Mallory thought, had the lowest boiling-point he'd come across in quite some time. 'I *earned* those stripes, those ribbons, that flash. I don't see –'

Mallory smiled. 'Disobeying an officer on active service?'

'Don't be so damned touchy,' Reynolds said.

'Don't be so damned touchy, *sir.*'

'Don't be so damned touchy, *sir.*' Reynolds suddenly grinned. 'OK, so who's got the scissors?'

'You see,' Mallory explained, 'the last thing we want to happen is to fall into enemy hands.'

'Amen,' Miller intoned.

'But if we're to get the information we want we're going to have to operate close to or even inside their lines. We might get caught. So we have our cover story.'

Groves said quietly: 'Are we permitted to know just what that cover story is, sir?'

'Of course you are,' Mallory said in exasperation. He went on earnestly: 'Don't you realize that, on a mission like this, survival depends on one thing and one thing only – complete and mutual trust? As soon as we start having secrets from each other – we're finished.'

In the deep gloom at the rear of the flight-deck, Andrea and Miller glanced at each other and exchanged their wearily cynical smiles.

As Mallory left the flight-deck for the fuselage, his right hand brushed Miller's shoulder. After about two minutes Miller yawned, stretched and made his way aft. Mallory was waiting towards the rear of the fuselage. He had two pieces of folded paper in his hand, one of which he opened and showed to Miller, snapping on a flash-light at the same time. Miller stared at it for some moments, then lifted an eyebrow.

'And what is this supposed to be?'

'It's the triggering mechanism for a 1,500-pound submersible mine. Learn it by heart.'

Miller looked at it without expression, then glanced at the other paper Mallory held.

'And what have you there?'

Mallory showed him. It was a large-scale map, the central fea-ture of which appeared to be a winding lake with a very long east-ern arm which bent abruptly at right-angles into a very short southern arm, which in turn ended abruptly at what appeared to be a dam wall. Beneath the dam, a river flowed away through a winding gorge.

Mallory said: 'What does it look like to you? Show them both to Andrea and tell him to destroy them.'

Mallory left Miller engrossed in his homework and moved for-ward again to the flight-deck. He bent over Groves's chart table.

'Still on course?'

'Yes, sir. We're just clearing the southern tip of the island of Hvar. You can see a few lights on the mainland ahead.' Mallory fol-lowed the pointing hand, located a few clusters of lights, then reached out a hand to steady himself as the Wellington started to climb sharply. He glanced at Reynolds.

'Climbing now, sir. There's some pretty lofty stuff ahead. We should pick up the Partisan landing lights in about half an hour.'

'Thirty-three minutes,' Groves said. 'One-twenty, near enough.'

For almost half an hour Mallory remained on a jump-seat in the flight-deck, just looking ahead. After a few minutes Andrea disap-peared and did not reappear. Miller did not return. Groves navigated, Reynolds flew, Saunders listened in to his portable transceiver and nobody talked at all. At one-fifteen Mallory rose, touched Saunders on the shoulders, told him to pack up his gear and headed aft. He found Andrea and a thoroughly miserable-looking Miller with their parachute snap-catches already clipped on to the jumping wire. Andrea had the door pulled back and was throwing out tiny pieces of shredded paper which swirled away in the slipstream. Mallory shivered in the suddenly intense cold. Andrea grinned, beckoned him to the open doorway and pointed downwards. He yelled in Mallory's ear: 'There's a lot of snow down there.'

There was indeed a lot of snow down there. Mallory understood now Jensen's insistence on not landing a plane in those parts. The terrain below was rugged in the extreme, consisting almost entirely of a succession of deep and winding valleys and steep-sided mountains. Maybe half of the landscape below was covered in dense forests of pine trees: all of it was covered in what appeared to be a very heavy blanket of snow. Mallory drew back into the comparative shelter of the Wellington's fuselage and glanced at his watch.

'One-sixteen.' Like Andrea, he had to shout.

'Your watch is a little fast, maybe?' Miller bawled unhappily. Mallory shook his head, Miller shook his. A bell rang and Mallory made his way to the flight-deck, passing Saunders going the other way. As Mallory entered, Reynolds looked briefly over his shoulder, then pointed directly ahead. Mallory bent over his shoulder and peered forwards and downwards. He nodded.

The three lights, in the form of an elongated V, were still some miles ahead, but quite unmistakable. Mallory turned, touched Groves on the shoulder and pointed aft. Groves rose and left. Mallory said to Reynolds: 'Where are the red and green jumping lights?'

Reynolds indicated them.

'Press the red light. How long?'

'Thirty seconds. About.'

Mallory looked ahead again. The lights were less than half as distant as they had been when first he'd looked. He said to Reynolds: 'Automatic pilot. Close the fuel switches.'

'Close the – for the petrol that's left –'

'Shut off the bloody tanks! And get aft. Five seconds.'

Reynolds did as he was told. Mallory waited, briefly made a last check of the landing lights ahead, pressed the green light button, rose and made his way swiftly aft. By the time he reached the jump door, even Reynolds, the last of the first five, was gone. Mallory clipped on his snap-catch, braced his hands round the edge of the doorway and launched himself out into the bitter Bosnian night.

The sudden jarring impact from the parachute harness made him look quickly upwards: the concave circle of a fully open parachute was a reassuring spectacle. He glanced downwards and saw the equally reassuring spectacle of another five open parachutes, two of which were swaying quite wildly across the sky – just as was his own. There were some things, he reflected, about which he,

Andrea and Miller had a great deal to learn. Controlling parachute descents was one of those things.

He looked up and to the east to see if he could locate the Wellington, but it was no longer visible. Suddenly, as he looked and listened, both engines, almost in perfect unison, cut out. Long seconds passed when the only sound was the rush of the wind in his ears, then there came an explosively metallic sound as the bomber crashed either into the ground or into some unseen mountainside ahead. There was no fire or none that he could see: just the crash, then silence. For the first time that night, the moon broke through.

Andrea landed heavily on an uneven piece of ground, rolled over twice, rose rather experimentally to his feet, discovered he was still intact, pressed the quick-release button of his parachute, then automatically, instinctively – Andrea had a built-in computer for assuring survival – swung through a complete 360° circle. But no immediate danger threatened, or none that he could see. Andrea made a more leisurely survey of their landing spot.

They had, he thought grimly, been most damnably lucky. Another hundred yards to the south and they'd have spent the rest of the night, and for all he knew, the rest of the war, clinging to the tops of the most impossibly tall pine trees he had ever seen. As it was, luck had been with them and they had landed in a narrow clearing which abutted closely on the rocky scarp of a mountainside.

Or rather, all but one. Perhaps fifty yards from where Andrea had landed, an apex of the forest elbowed its way into the clearing. The outermost tree in this apex had come between one of the parachutists and terra firma. Andrea's eyebrows lifted in quizzical astonishment, then he broke into an ambling run.

The parachutist who had come to grief was dangling from the lowermost bough of the pine. He had his hands twisted in the shrouds, his legs bent, knees and ankles close together in the classic landing position, his feet perhaps thirty inches from the ground. His eyes were screwed tightly shut. Corporal Miller seemed acutely unhappy.

Andrea came up and touched him on the shoulder, gently. Miller opened his eyes and glanced at Andrea, who pointed downwards. Miller followed his glance and lowered his legs, which were then four inches from the ground. Andrea produced a knife, sliced through the shrouds and Miller completed the remainder of his journey. He straightened his jacket, his face splendidly impassive, and lifted an enquiring elbow. Andrea, his face equally impassive, pointed down the clearing. Three of the other four parachutists had already landed safely: the fourth, Mallory, was just touching down.

Two minutes later, just as all six were coming together some little distance away from the most easterly landing flare, a shout announced the appearance of a young soldier running towards them from the edge of the forest. The parachutists' guns came up and were almost immediately lowered again: this was no occasion for guns. The soldier was trailing his by the barrel, excitedly waving his free hand in greeting. He was dressed in a faded and tattered near-uniform that had been pillaged from a variety of armies, had long flowing hair, a cast to his right eye and a straggling ginger beard. That he was welcoming them, was beyond doubt. Repeating some incomprehensible greeting over and over again, he shook hands all round and then a second time, the huge grin on his face reflecting his delight.

Within thirty seconds he'd been joined by at least a dozen others, all bearded, all dressed in the same nondescript uniforms, no two of which were alike, all in the same almost festive mood. Then, as at a signal almost, they fell silent and drew slightly apart as the man who was obviously their leader appeared from the edge of the forest. He bore little resemblance to his men. He differed in that he was completely shaven and wore a uniform, a British battledress, which appeared to be all of one piece. He differed in that he was not smiling: he had about him the air of one who was seldom if ever given to smiling. He also differed from the others in that he was a hawk-faced giant of a man, at least six feet four inches in height, carrying no fewer than four wicked-looking Bowie-type knives in his belt – an excess of armament that on another man might have looked incongruous or even comical but which on this man provoked no mirth at all. His face was dark and sombre and when he spoke it was in English, slow and stilted, but precise.

'Good evening.' He looked round questioningly. 'I am Captain Droshny.'

Mallory took a step forward. 'Captain Mallory.'

'Welcome to Yugoslavia, Captain Mallory – Partisan Yugoslavia.' Droshny nodded towards the dying flare, his face twitched in what may have been an attempt at a smile, but he made no move to shake hands. 'As you can see, we were expecting you.'

'Your lights were a great help,' Mallory acknowledged.

'Thank you.' Droshny stared away to the east, then back to Mallory, shaking his head. 'A pity about the plane.'

'All war is a pity.'

Droshny nodded. 'Come. Our headquarters is close by.'

No more was said. Droshny, leading, moved at once into the shelter of the forest. Mallory, behind him, was intrigued by the footprints, clearly visible in the now bright moonlight, left by Droshny in the deep snow. They were, thought Mallory, most peculiar. Each sole left three V-shaped marks, the heel one: the right-hand side of the leading V on the right sole had a clearly defined break in it. Unconsciously, Mallory filed away this little oddity in his mind. There was no reason why he should have done so other than that the Mallorys of this world always observe and record the unusual. It helps them to stay alive.

The slope steepened, the snow deepened and the pale moonlight filtered thinly down through the spreading, snow-laden branches of the pines. The light wind was from the east: the cold was intense. For almost ten minutes no voice was heard, then Droshny's came, softly but clearly and imperative in its staccato urgency.

'Be still.' He pointed dramatically upward. 'Be still! Listen!'

They stopped, looked upward and listened intently. At least, Mallory and his men looked upward and listened intently, but the Yugoslavs had other things on their minds: swiftly, efficiently and simultaneously, without either spoken or gestured command being given, they rammed the muzzles of their machine-guns and rifles into the sides and backs of the six parachutists with a force and uncompromising authority that rendered any accompanying orders quite superfluous.

The six men reacted as might have been expected. Reynolds, Groves and Saunders, who were rather less accustomed to the vicissitudes of fate than their three older companions, registered a very similar combination of startled anger and open-mouthed astonishment. Mallory looked thoughtful. Miller lifted a quizzical eyebrow. Andrea, predictably, registered nothing at all: he was too busy exhibiting his usual reaction to physical violence.

His right hand, which he had instantly lifted halfway to his shoulder in an apparent token of surrender, clamped down on the barrel of the rifle of the guard to his right, forcing it away from him, while his left elbow jabbed viciously into the solar plexus of the guard to his left, who gasped in pain and staggered back a couple of paces. Andrea, with both hands now on the rifle of the other guard, wrenched it effortlessly free, lifted it high and brought the barrel down in one continuous blur of movement. The guard collapsed as if a bridge had fallen on him. The winded guard to the left, still bent and whooping in agony, was trying to line up his rifle when the butt of Andrea's rifle struck him in the face: he made a brief coughing sound and fell senseless to the forest floor.

It took all of the three seconds that this action had lasted for the Yugoslavs to release themselves from their momentary thrall of incredulity. Half-a-dozen soldiers flung themselves on Andrea, bearing him to the ground. In the furious, rolling struggle that followed, Andrea laid about him in his usual willing fashion, but when one of the Yugoslavs started pounding him on the head with the barrel of a pistol, Andrea opted for discretion and lay still. With two guns in his back and four hands on either arm Andrea was dragged to his feet: two of his captors already looked very much the worse for wear.

Droshny, his eyes bleak and bitter, came up to Andrea, unsheathed one of his knives and thrust its point against Andrea's throat with a force savage enough to break the skin and draw blood that trickled on to the gleaming blade. For a moment it seemed that Droshny would push the knife home to the hilt, then his eyes moved sideways and downwards to look at the two huddled men lying in the snow. He nodded to the nearest man.

'How are they?'

A young Yugoslav dropped to his knees, looked first at the man who had been struck by the rifle-barrel, touched his head briefly, examined the second man, then stood up. In the filtered moonlight, his face was unnaturally pale.

'Josef is dead. I think his neck is broken. And his brother – he's breathing – but his jaw seems to be –' The voice trailed away uncertainly.

Droshny transferred his gaze back to Andrea. His lips drew back, he smiled the way a wolf smiles and leaned a little harder on the knife.

'I *should* kill you now. I *will* kill you later.' He sheathed his knife, held up his clawed hands in front of Andrea's face, and shouted: 'Personally. With those hands.'

'With those hands.' Slowly, meaningly, Andrea examined the four pairs of hands pinioning his arms, then looked contemptuously at Droshny. He said: 'Your courage terrifies me.'

There was a brief and unbelieving silence. The three young sergeants stared at the tableau before them with faces reflecting various degrees of consternation and incredulity. Mallory and Miller looked on impassively. For a moment or two, Droshny looked as if he hadn't heard aright, then his face twisted in savage anger as he struck Andrea backhanded across the face. Immediately a trickle of blood appeared at the right-hand corner of Andrea's mouth but Andrea himself remained unmoving, his face without expression.

Droshny's eyes narrowed. Andrea smiled again, briefly. Droshny struck again, this time with the back of the other hand. The effect was as before, with the exception that this time the trickle of blood came from the left-hand corner of the mouth. Andrea smiled again but to look into his eyes was to look into an open grave. Droshny wheeled and walked away, then halted as he approached Mallory.

'You *are* the leader of those men, Captain Mallory?'

'I am.'

'You're a very – *silent* leader, Captain?'

'What am I to say to a man who turns his guns on his friends and allies?' Mallory looked at him dispassionately. 'I'll talk to your commanding officer, not to a madman.'

Droshny's face darkened. He stepped forward, his arm lifted to strike. Very quickly, but so smoothly and calmly that the movement seemed unhurried, and totally ignoring the two rifle-muzzles pressing into his side, Mallory lifted his Luger and pointed it at Droshny's face. The click of the Luger safety-catch being released came like a hammer-blow in the suddenly unnatural intensity of silence.

And unnatural intensity of silence there was. Except for one little movement, so slow as to be almost imperceptible, both Partisans and parachutists had frozen into a tableau that would have done credit to the frieze on an Ionic temple. The three sergeants, like most of the Partisans, registered astonished incredulity. The two men guarding Mallory looked at Droshny with questioning eyes. Droshny looked at Mallory as if he were mad. Andrea wasn't looking at anyone, while Miller wore that look of world-weary detachment which only he could achieve. But it was Miller who made that one little movement, a movement that now came to an end with his thumb resting on his Schmeisser's safety-release. After a moment or two he removed his thumb: there would come a time for Schmeissers, but this wasn't it.

Droshny lowered his hand in a curious slow-motion gesture and took two paces backwards. His face was still dark with anger, the dark eyes cruel and unforgiving, but he had himself well in hand.

He said: 'Don't you know we have to take precautions? Till we are satisfied with your identity?'

'How should I know that?' Mallory nodded at Andrea. 'Next time you tell your men to take precautions with my friend here, you might warn them to stand a little farther back. He reacted the only way he knows how. And I know why.'

'You can explain later. Hand over your guns.'

'No.' Mallory returned the Luger to its holster.

'Are you mad? I can take them from you.'

That's so,' Mallory said reasonably. 'But you'd have to kill us first, wouldn't you? I don't think you'd remain a captain very long, my friend.'

Speculation replaced anger in Droshny's eyes. He gave a sharp order in Serbo-Croat and again his soldiers levelled their guns at Mallory and his five companions. But they made no attempt to remove the prisoners' guns. Droshny turned, gestured and started moving up the steeply-sloping forest floor again. Droshny wasn't, Mallory reflected, a man likely to be given to taking too many chances.

For twenty minutes they scrambled awkwardly up the slippery hillside. A voice called out from the darkness ahead and Droshny answered without breaking step. They passed by two sentries armed with machine-carbines and, within a minute, were in Droshny's HQ.

It was a moderately-sized military encampment – if a wide circle of rough-hewn adze-cut cabins could be called an encampment – set in one of those very deep hollows in the forest floor that Mallory was to find so characteristic of the Bosnian area. From the base of this hollow grew two concentric rings of pines far taller and more massive than anything to be found in western Europe, massive pines whose massive branches interlocked eighty to a hundred feet above the ground, forming a snow-shrouded canopy of such impenetrable density that there wasn't even a dusting of snow on the hard-packed earth of the camp compound: by the same token, the same canopy also effectively prevented any upward escape of light: there was no attempt at any black-out in several illuminated cabin windows and there were even some oil lamps suspended on outside hooks to illuminate the compound itself. Droshny stopped and said to Mallory:

'You come with me. The rest of you stay here.'

He led Mallory towards the door of the largest hut in the compound. Andrea, unbidden, slipped off his pack and sat on it, and the others, after various degrees of hesitation, did the same. Their guards looked them over uncertainly, then withdrew to form a ragged but watchful semi-circle. Reynolds turned to Andrea, the expression on his face registering a complete absence of admiration and goodwill.

'You're crazy.' Reynolds's voice came in a low, furious whisper. 'Crazy as a loon. You could have got yourself killed. You could have got all of us killed. What are you, shell-shocked or something?'

Andrea did not reply. He lit one of his obnoxious cigars and regarded Reynolds with mild speculation or as near an approach to mildness as it was possible for him to achieve.

'Crazy isn't half the word for it.' Groves, if anything, was even more heated than Reynolds. 'Or didn't you *know* that was a Partisan you killed? Don't you *know* what that means? Don't you *know* people like that must always take precautions?'

Whether he knew or not, Andrea wasn't saying. He puffed at his cigar and transferred his peaceable gaze from Reynolds to Groves.

Miller said soothingly: 'Now, now. Don't be like that. Maybe Andrea *was* a mite hasty but -'

'God help us all,' Reynolds said fervently. He looked at his fellow-sergeants in despair. 'A thousand miles from home and help and saddled with a trigger-happy bunch of has-beens.' He turned back to Miller and mimicked: '"Don't be like that."'

Miller assumed his wounded expression and looked away.

The room was large and bare and comfortless. The only concession to comfort was a pine fire crackling in a rough hearth-place. The only furniture consisted of a cracked deal table, two chairs and a bench.

Those things Mallory noted only subconsciously. He didn't even register when he heard Droshny say: 'Captain Mallory. This is my commanding officer.' He seemed to be too busy staring at the man seated behind the table.

The man was short, stocky and in his mid-thirties. The deep lines around eyes and mouth could have been caused by weather or humour or both: just at that moment he was smiling slightly. He was dressed in the uniform of a captain in the German Army and wore an Iron Cross at his throat.

FOUR

Friday
0200–0330

The German captain leaned back in his chair and steepled his fingers. He had the air of a man enjoying the passing moment.

'Hauptmann Neufeld, Captain Mallory.' He looked at the places on Mallory's uniform where the missing insignia should have been. 'Or so I assume. You are surprised to see me?'

'I am *delighted* to meet you, Hauptmann Neufeld.' Mallory's astonishment had given way to the beginnings of a long, slow smile and now he sighed in deep relief. 'You just can't imagine *how* delighted.' Still smiling, he turned to Droshny, and at once the smile gave way to an expression of consternation. 'But who *are* you? Who is this man, Hauptmann Neufeld? Who in the name of God are those men out there? They must be – they must be –'

Droshny interrupted heavily: 'One of his men killed one of my men tonight.'

'What!' Neufeld, the smile now in turn vanishing from his face, stood abruptly: the backs of his legs sent his chair crashing to the floor. Mallory ignored him, looked again at Droshny.

'*Who are you?* For God's sake, tell me!'

Droshny said slowly: 'They call us Cetniks.'

'Cetniks? Cetniks? What on earth are Cetniks?'

'You will forgive me, Captain, if I smile in weary disbelief.' Neufeld was back on balance again, and his face had assumed a curiously wary impassivity, an expression in which only the eyes were alive: things, Mallory reflected, unpleasant things could happen to people misguided enough to underrate Hauptmann Neufeld. 'You? The leader of a special mission to this country and you haven't been well enough briefed to know that the Cetniks are our Yugoslav allies?'

'Allies? Ah!' Mallory's face cleared in understanding. 'Traitors? Yugoslav Quislings? Is that it?'

A subterranean rumble came from Droshny's throat and he moved towards Mallory, his right hand closing round the haft of a knife. Neufeld halted him with a sharp word of command and a brief downward-chopping motion of his hand.

'And what do you mean by a special mission?' Mallory demanded. He looked at each man in turn and smiled in wry understanding. 'Oh, we're special mission all right, but not in the way you think. At least, not in the way I think you think.'

'No?' Neufeld's eyebrow-raising technique, Mallory reflected, was almost on a par with Miller's. 'Then why do you think we were expecting you?'

'God only knows,' Mallory said frankly. 'We thought the Partisans were. That's why Droshny's man was killed, I'm afraid.'

'That's why Droshny's man –' Neufeld regarded Mallory with his warily impassive eyes, picked up his chair and sat down thoughtfully. 'I think, perhaps, you had better explain yourself.'

As befitted a man who had adventured far and wide in the West End of London, Miller was in the habit of using a napkin when at meals, and he was using one now, tucked into the top of his tunic, as he sat on his rucksack in the compound of Neufeld's camp and fastidiously consumed some indeterminate goulash from a mess-tin. The three sergeants, seated nearby, briefly observed this spectacle with open disbelief, then resumed a low-voiced conversation. Andrea, puffing the inevitable nostril-wrinkling cigar and totally ignoring half-a-dozen watchful and understandably apprehensive guards, strolled unconcernedly about the compound, poisoning the air wherever he went. Clearly through the frozen night air came the distant sound of someone singing a low-voiced accompaniment to what appeared to be guitar music. As Andrea completed his circuit of the compound, Miller looked up and nodded in the direction of the music.

'Who's the soloist?'

Andrea shrugged. 'Radio, maybe.'

'They want to buy a new radio. My trained ear –'

'Listen.' Reynolds's interrupting whisper was tense and urgent. 'We've been talking.'

Miller performed some fancy work with his napkin and said kindly: 'Don't. Think of the grieving mothers and sweethearts you'd leave behind you.'

'What do you mean?'

'About making a break for it is what I mean,' Miller said. 'Some other time, perhaps?'

'Why not now?' Groves was belligerent. 'They're off guard –'

'Are they now.' Miller sighed. 'So young, so young. Take another look. You don't think Andrea *likes* exercise, do you?'

The three sergeants took another look, furtively, surreptitiously, then glanced interrogatively at Andrea.

'Five dark windows,' Andrea said. 'Behind them, five dark men. With five dark machine-guns.'

Reynolds nodded and looked away.

'Well, now.' Neufeld, Mallory noted, had a great propensity for steepling his fingers: Mallory had once known a hanging judge with exactly the same propensity. 'This *is* a most remarkably odd story you have to tell us, my dear Captain Mallory.'

'It is,' Mallory agreed. 'It would have to be, wouldn't it, to account for the remarkably odd position in which we find ourselves at this moment.'

'A point, a point.' Slowly, deliberately, Neufeld ticked off other points on his fingers. 'You have for some months, you claim, been running a penicillin and drug-running ring in the south of Italy. As an Allied liaison officer you found no difficulty in obtaining supplies from American Army and Air Force bases.'

'We found a little difficulty towards the end,' Mallory admitted.

'I'm coming to that. Those supplies, you also claim, were funnelled through to the Wehrmacht.'

'I wish you wouldn't keep using the word "claim" in that tone of voice,' Mallory said irritably. 'Check with Field-Marshal Kesselring's Chief of Military Intelligence in Padua.'

'With pleasure.' Neufeld picked up a phone, spoke briefly in German and replaced the receiver.

Mallory said in surprise: 'You have a direct line to the outside world? From *this* place?'

'I have a direct line to a hut fifty yards away where we have a very powerful radio transmitter. So. You further claim that you were caught, court-martialled and were awaiting the confirmation of your death sentence. Right?'

'If your espionage system in Italy is all we hear it is, you'll know about it tomorrow,' Mallory said drily.

'Quite, quite. You then broke free, killed your guards and over-heard agents in the briefing room being briefed on a mission to Bosnia.' He did some more finger-steepling. 'You may be telling the truth at that. What did you say their mission was?'

'I didn't say. I didn't really pay attention. It had something to do with locating missing British mission leaders and trying to break your espionage set-up. I'm not sure. We had more important things to think about.'

'I'm sure you had,' Neufeld said distastefully. 'Such as your skins. What happened to your epaulettes, Captain? The medal rib-bons? The buttons?'

'You've obviously never attended a British court-martial, Hauptmann Neufeld.'

Neufeld said mildly: 'You could have ripped them off yourself.'

'And then, I suppose, emptied three-quarters of the fuel from the tanks before we stole the plane?'

'Your tanks were only a quarter full?' Mallory nodded. 'And your plane crashed without catching fire?'

'We didn't mean to crash,' Mallory said in a weary patience. 'We meant to land. But we were out of fuel – and, as we know now, at the wrong place.'

Neufeld said absently: 'Whenever the Partisans put up landing flares we try a few ourselves – *and* we knew that you – or someone – were coming. No petrol, eh?' Again Neufeld spoke briefly on the tele-phone, then turned back to Mallory. 'All very satisfactory – if true. There just remains to explain the death of Captain Droshny's man here.'

'I'm sorry about that. It was a ghastly blunder. But surely you can understand. The last thing we wanted was to land among you, to make direct contact with you. We've heard what happens to British parachutists dropping over German territory.'

Neufeld steepled his fingers again. 'There is a state of war. Proceed.'

'Our intention was to land in Partisan territory, slip across the lines and give ourselves up. When Droshny turned his guns on us we thought the Partisans were on to us, that they had been notified that we'd stolen the plane. And that could mean only one thing for us.'

'Wait outside. Captain Droshny and I will join you in a moment.'

Mallory left. Andrea, Miller and the three sergeants were sitting patiently on their rucksacks. From the distance there still came the sound of distant music. For a moment Mallory cocked his head to listen to it, then walked across to join the others. Miller patted his lips delicately with his napkin and looked up at Mallory.

'Had a cosy chat?'

'I spun him a yarn. The one we talked about in the plane.' He looked at the three sergeants. 'Any of you speak German?'

All three shook their heads.

'Fine. Forget you speak English too. If you're questioned you know nothing.'

'If I'm not questioned,' Reynolds said bitterly, 'I still don't know anything.'

'All the better,' Mallory said encouragingly. 'Then you can never tell anything, can you?'

He broke off and turned round as Neufeld and Droshny appeared in the doorway. Neufeld advanced and said: 'While we're waiting for some confirmation, a little food and wine, perhaps.' As Mallory had done, he cocked his head and listened to the singing. 'But first of all, you must meet our minstrel boy.'

'We'll settle for just the food and wine,' Andrea said.

'Your priorities are wrong. You'll see. Come.'

The dining-hall, if it could be dignified by such a name, was about forty yards away. Neufeld opened the door to reveal a crude and makeshift hut with two rickety trestle tables and four benches set on the earthen floor. At the far end of the room the inevitable pine fire burnt in the inevitable stone hearth-place. Close to the fire, at the end of the farther table, three men – obviously, from their high-collared coats and guns propped by their sides, some kind of temporarily off-duty guards – were drinking coffee and listening to the quiet singing coming from a figure seated on the ground by the fire.

The singer was dressed in a tattered anorak type jacket, an even more incredibly tattered pair of trousers and a pair of knee boots that gaped open at almost every possible seam. There was little to be seen of his face other than a mass of dark hair and a large pair of rimmed dark spectacles.

Beside him, apparently asleep with her head on his shoulder, sat a girl. She was clad in a high-collared British Army greatcoat in an advanced state of dilapidation, so long that it completely covered her tucked-in legs. The uncombed platinum hair spread over her shoulders would have done justice to any Scandinavian, but the broad cheekbones, dark eyebrows and long dark lashes lowered over very pale cheeks were unmistakably Slavonic.

Neufeld advanced across the room and stopped by the fireside. He bent over the singer and said: 'Petar, I want you to meet some friends.'

Petar lowered his guitar, looked up, then turned and touched the girl on the arm. Instantly, the girl's head lifted and her eyes, great dark sooty eyes, opened wide. She had the look, almost, of a hunted animal. She glanced around her, almost wildly, then jumped quickly to her feet, dwarfed by the greatcoat which reached almost to her ankles, then reached down to help the guitarist to his feet. As he did so, he stumbled: he was obviously blind.

'This is Maria,' Neufeld said. 'Maria, this is Captain Mallory.'

'Captain Mallory.' Her voice was soft and a little husky: she spoke in almost accentless English. 'You are English, Captain Mallory?'

It was hardly, Mallory thought, the time or the place for proclaiming his New Zealand ancestry. He smiled. 'Well, sort of.'

Maria smiled in turn. 'I've always wanted to meet an Englishman.' She stepped forward towards Mallory's outstretched hand, brushed it aside and struck him, open-handed and with all her strength, across the face.

'Maria!' Neufeld stared at her. 'He's on our side.'

'An Englishman *and* a traitor!' She lifted her hand again but the swinging arm was suddenly arrested in Andrea's grip. She struggled briefly, futilely, then subsided, dark eyes glowing in an angry face. Andrea lifted his free hand and rubbed his own cheek in fond recollection.

He said admiringly: 'By heavens, she reminds me of my own Maria,' then grinned at Mallory. 'Very handy with their hands, those Yugoslavs.'

Mallory rubbed his cheek ruefully with his hand and turned to Neufeld. 'Perhaps Petar – that's his name –'

'No.' Neufeld shook his head definitely. 'Later. Let's eat now.' He led the way across to the table at the far end of the room, gestured the others to seats, sat down himself and went on: 'I'm sorry. That was my fault. I should have known better.'

Miller said delicately: 'Is she – um – all right?'

'A wild animal, you think?'

'She'd make a rather dangerous pet, wouldn't you say?'

'She's a graduate of the University of Belgrade. Languages. With honours, I'm told. Some time after graduation she returned to her home in the Bosnian mountains. She found her parents and two small brothers butchered. She – well, she's been like this ever since.'

Mallory shifted in his seat and looked at the girl. Her eyes, dark and unmoving and unwinking, were fixed on him and their expression was less than encouraging. Mallory turned back to Neufeld.

'Who did it? To her parents, I mean.'

'The Partisans,' Droshny said savagely. 'Damn their black souls, the Partisans. Maria's people were our people. Cetniks.'

'And the singer?' Mallory said.

'Her elder brother.' Neufeld shook his head. 'Blind from birth. Wherever she goes, she leads him by the hand. She is his eyes: she is his life.'

They sat in silence until food and wine were brought in. If an army marched on its stomach, Mallory thought, this one wasn't going to get very far: he had heard that the food situation with the Partisans was close to desperate, but, if this were a representative sample, the Cetniks and Germans appeared to be in little better case. Unenthusiastically, he spooned – it would have been impossible to use a fork – a little of the greyish stew, a stew in which little oddments of indefinable meat floated forlornly in a mushy gravy of obscure origin, glanced across at Andrea and marvelled at the gastronomic fortitude that lay behind the already almost empty plate. Miller averted his eyes from the plate before him and delicately sipped the rough red wine. The three sergeants, so far, hadn't even looked at their food: they were too occupied in looking at the girl by the fireside. Neufeld saw their interest, and smiled.

'I do agree, gentlemen, that I've never seen a more beautiful girl and heaven knows what she'd look like if she had a wash. But she's not for you, gentlemen. She's not for any man. She's wed already.' He looked at the questioning faces and shook his head. 'Not to any man. To an ideal – if you can call death an ideal. The death of the Partisans.'

'Charming,' Miller murmured. There was no other comment, for there was none to make. They ate in silence broken only by the soft singing from the fireside, the voice was melodious enough, but the guitar sounded sadly out of tune. Andrea pushed away his empty plate, looked irritably at the blind musician and turned to Neufeld.

'What's that he's singing?'

'An old Bosnian love song, I've been told. Very old and very sad. In English you have it too.' He snapped his fingers. 'Yes, that's it. "The girl I left behind me".'

'Tell him to sing something else,' Andrea muttered. Neufeld looked at him, puzzled, then looked away as a German sergeant entered and bent to whisper in his ear. Neufeld nodded and the sergeant left.

'So.' Neufeld was thoughtful. 'A radio report from the patrol that found your plane. The tanks *were* empty. I hardly think we need await confirmation from Padua, do you, Captain Mallory?'

'I don't understand.'

'No matter. Tell me, have you ever heard of a General Vukalovic?'

'General which?'

'Vukalovic.'

'He's not on our side,' Miller said positively. 'Not with a name like that.'

'You must be the only people in Yugoslavia who *don't* know him. Everybody else does. Partisans, Cetniks, Germans, Bulgarians, everyone. He is one of their national heroes.'

'Pass the wine,' Andrea said.

'You'd do better to listen.' Neufeld's tone was sharp. 'Vukalovic commands almost a division of Partisan infantry who have been trapped in a loop of the Neretva river for almost three months. Like the men he leads. Vukalovic is insane. They have no shelter, none. They are short of weapons, have almost no ammunition left and are close to starvation. Their army is dressed in rags. They are finished.'

'Then why don't they escape?' Mallory asked.

'Escape is impossible. The precipices of the Neretva cut them off to the east. To the north and west are impenetrable mountains. The only conceivable way out is to the south, over the bridge at Neretva. And we have two armoured divisions waiting there.'

'No gorges?' Mallory asked. 'No passes through the mountains?'

'Two. Blocked by our best combat troops.'

'Then why don't they give up?' Mallory asked reasonably. 'Has no one told them the rules of war?'

'They're insane, I tell you,' Neufeld said. 'Quite insane.'

At that precise moment in time, Vukalovic and his Partisans were proving to some other Germans just how extraordinary their degree of insanity was.

The Western Gap was a narrow, tortuous, boulder-strewn and precipitously walled gorge that afforded the only passage through the impassable mountains that shut off the Zenica Cage to the east.

For three months now German infantry units – units which had recently included an increasing number of highly-skilled Alpine troops – had been trying to force the pass: for three months they had been bloodily repulsed. But the Germans never gave up trying and on this intensely cold night of fitful moonlight and gently, intermittently falling snow, they were trying again.

The Germans carried out their attack with the coldly professional skill and economy of movement born of long and harsh experience. They advanced up the gorge in three fairly even and judiciously spaced lines: the combination of white snow suits, of the utilization of every scrap of cover and of confining their brief forward rushes to those moments when the moon was temporarily obscured made it almost impossible to see them. There was, however, no difficulty in locating them: they had obviously ammunition and to spare for machine-pistols and rifles alike and the fire-flashes from those muzzles were almost continuous. Almost as continuous, but some distance behind them, the sharp flat cracks of fixed mountain pieces pinpointed the source of the creeping artillery barrage that preceded the Germans up the boulder-strewn slope of that narrow defile.

The Yugoslav Partisans waited at the head of the gorge, entrenched behind a redoubt of boulders, hastily piled stones and splintered tree-trunks that had been shattered by German artillery fire. Although the snow was deep and the east wind full of little knives, few of the Partisans wore greatcoats. They were clad in an extraordinary variety of uniforms, uniforms that had belonged in the past to members of British, German, Italian, Bulgarian and Yugoslav armies: the one identifying feature that all had in common was a red star sewn on to the right-hand side of their forage caps. The uniforms, for the most part, were thin and tattered, offering little protection against the piercing cold, so that the men shivered almost continuously. An astonishing proportion of them appeared to be wounded: there were splinted legs, arms in slings and bandaged heads everywhere. But the most common characteristic among this rag-tag collection of defenders was their pinched and emaciated faces, faces where the deeply etched lines of starvation were matched only by the calm and absolute determination of men who have no longer anything to lose.

Near the centre of the group of defenders, two men stood in the shelter of the thick bole of one of the few pines still left standing. The silvered black hair, the deeply trenched – and now even more

exhausted – face of General Vukalovic was unmistakable. But the
dark eyes glowed as brightly as ever as he bent forward to accept a
cigarette and light from the officer sharing his shelter, a swarthy,
hook-nosed man with at least half of his black hair concealed
under a blood-stained bandage. Vukalovic smiled.

'Of course I'm insane, my dear Stephan. You're insane – or you
would have abandoned this position weeks ago. We're all insane.
Didn't you know?'

'I know this.' Major Stephan rubbed the back of his hand across
a week-old growth of beard. 'Your parachute landing, an hour ago.
That was insane. Why, you –' He broke off as a rifle fired only feet
away, moved to where a thin youngster, not more than seventeen
years of age, was peering down into the white gloom of the gorge
over the sights of a Lee-Enfield. 'Did you get him?'

The boy twisted and looked up. A child. Vukalovic thought
despairingly, no more than a child: he should still have been at
school. The boy said: 'I'm not sure, sir.'

'How many shells have you left? Count them.'

'I don't have to. Seven.'

'Don't fire till you are sure.' Stephan turned back to Vukalovic.
'God above, General, you were almost blown into German hands.'

'I'd have been worse off without the parachute,' Vukalovic said
mildly.

'There's so little time.' Stephan struck a clenched fist against a
palm. 'So little time left. You were crazy to come back. They need
you far more –' He stopped abruptly, listened for a fraction of a second, threw himself at Vukalovic and brought them both crashing
heavily to the ground as a whining mortar shell buried itself among
loose rocks a few feet away, exploding on impact. Close by, a man
screamed in agony. A second mortar shell landed, then a third and
a fourth, all within thirty feet of one another.

'They've got the range now, damn them.' Stephan rose quickly to
his feet and peered down the gorge. For long seconds he could see
nothing, for a band of dark cloud had crossed the face of the moon:
then the moon broke through and he could see the enemy all too
clearly. Because of some almost certainly prearranged signal, they
were no longer making any attempt to seek cover: they were
pounding straight up the slope with all the speed they could muster,
machine-carbines and rifles at the ready in their hands – and as
soon as the moon broke through they squeezed the triggers of those
guns. Stephan threw himself behind the shelter of a boulder.

'Now!' he shouted. 'Now!'

The first ragged Partisan fusillade lasted for only a few seconds, then a black shadow fell over the valley. The firing ceased.

'Keep firing,' Vukalovic shouted. 'Don't stop now. They're closing in.' He loosed off a burst from his own machine-pistol and said to Stephan, 'They know what they are about, our friends down there.'

'They should.' Stephan armed a stick grenade and spun it down the hill. 'Look at all the practice we've given them.'

The moon broke through again. The leading German infantry were no more than twenty-five yards away. Both sides exchanged hand-grenades, fired at point-blank range. Some German soldiers fell, but many more came on, flinging themselves on the redoubt. Matters became temporarily confused. Here and there bitter hand-to-hand fighting developed. Men shouted at each other, cursed each other, killed each other. But the redoubt remained unbroken. Suddenly, dark heavy clouds again rolled over the moon, darkness flooded the gorge and everything slowly fell quiet. In the distance the thunder of artillery and mortar fire fell away to a muted rumble, then finally died.

'A trap?' Vukalovic said softly to Stephan. 'You think they will come again?'

'Not tonight.' Stephan was positive. 'They're brave men, but –'

'But not insane?'

'But not insane.'

Blood poured down over Stephan's face from a reopened wound in his face, but he was smiling. He rose to his feet and turned as a burly sergeant came up and delivered a sketchy salute.

'They've gone, Major. We lost seven of ours this time, and fourteen wounded.'

'Set pickets two hundred metres down,' Stephan said. He turned to Vukalovic. 'You heard, sir? Seven dead. Fourteen hurt.'

'Leaving how many?'

'Two hundred. Perhaps two hundred and five.'

'Out of four hundred.' Vukalovic's mouth twisted. 'Dear God, out of four hundred.'

'And sixty of those are wounded.'

'At least you can get them down to the hospital now.'

'There is no hospital,' Stephan said heavily. 'I didn't have time to tell you. It was bombed this morning. Both doctors killed. All our medical supplies – poof! Like that.'

'Gone? All gone?' Vukalovic paused for a long moment. 'I'll have some sent up from HQ. The walking wounded can make their own way to HQ.'

'The wounded won't leave, sir. Not any more.'

Vukalovic nodded in understanding and went on: 'How much ammunition?'

'Two days. Three, if we're careful.'

'Sixty wounded.' Vukalovic shook his head in slow disbelief. 'No medical help whatsoever for them. Ammunition almost gone. No food. No shelter. And they won't leave. Are they insane, too?'

'Yes, sir.'

'I'm going down to the river,' Vukalovic said. 'To see Colonel Lazlo at HQ.'

'Yes, sir.' Stephan smiled faintly. 'I doubt if you'll find his mental equilibrium any better than mine.'

'I don't suppose I will,' Vukalovic said.

Stephan saluted and turned away, mopping blood from his face, walked a few short swaying steps then knelt down to comfort a badly wounded man. Vukalovic looked after him expressionlessly, shaking his head: then he, too, turned and left.

Mallory finished his meal and lit a cigarette. He said, 'So what's going to happen to the Partisans in the Zenica Cage, as you call it?'

'They're going to break out,' Neufeld said. 'At least, they're going to try to.'

'But you've said yourself that's impossible.'

'Nothing is too impossible for those mad Partisans to try. I wish to heaven,' Neufeld said bitterly, 'that we were fighting a normal war against normal people, like the British or Americans. Anyway, we've had information – reliable information – that an attempted break-out is imminent. Trouble is, there are those two passes – they might even try to force the bridge at Neretva – and we don't know where the break-out is coming.'

'This is very interesting.' Andrea looked sourly at the blind musician who was still giving his rendering of the same old Bosnian love-song. 'Can we get some sleep now?'

'Not tonight, I'm afraid.' Neufeld exchanged a smile with Droshny. '*You* are going to find out for us where this break-out is coming.'

'We are?' Miller drained his glass and reached for the bottle. 'Infectious stuff, this insanity.'

Neufeld might not have heard him. 'Partisan HQ is about ten kilometres from here. You are going to report there as the bona-fide British mission that has lost its way. Then, when you've found out their plans, you tell them that you are going to their main HQ at Drvar, which of course, you don't. You come back here instead. What could be simpler?'

'Miller's right,' Mallory said with conviction. 'You *are* mad.'

'I'm beginning to think there's altogether too much talk of this madness.' Neufeld smiled. 'You would prefer, perhaps, that Captain Droshny here turned you over to his men. I assure you, they are most unhappy about their – ah – late comrade.'

'You can't ask us to do this!' Mallory was hard-faced in anger. 'The Partisans are bound to get a radio message about us. Sooner or later. And then – well, you know what then. You just can't ask this of us.'

'I can and I will.' Neufeld looked at Mallory and his five companions without enthusiasm. 'It so happens that I don't care for dope-peddlers and drug-runners.'

'I don't think your opinion will carry much weight in certain circles,' Mallory said.

'And that means?'

'Kesselring's Director of Military Intelligence isn't going to like this at all.'

'If you don't come back, they'll never know. If you do –' Neufeld smiled and touched the Iron Cross at his throat – 'they'll probably give me an oak leaf to this.'

'Likeable type, isn't he?' Miller said to no one in particular.

'Come then.' Neufeld rose from the table. 'Petar?'

The blind singer nodded, slung his guitar over his shoulder and rose to his feet, his sister rising with him.

'What's this, then?' Mallory asked.

'Guides.'

'*Those* two?'

'Well,' Neufeld said reasonably, 'you can't very well find your own way there, can you? Petar and his sister – well, his sister – know Bosnia better than the foxes.'

'But won't the Partisans –' Mallory began, but Neufeld interrupted.

'You don't know your Bosnia. These two wander wherever they like and no one will turn them from their door. The Bosnians believe, and God knows with sufficient reason, that they are accursed and have the evil eye on them. This is a land of superstition, Captain Mallory.'

'But – but how will they know where to take us?'

'They'll know.' Neufeld nodded to Droshny, who talked rapidly to Maria in Serbo-Croat: she in turn spoke to Petar, who made some strange noises in his throat.

'That's an odd language,' Miller observed.

'He's got a speech impediment,' Neufeld said shortly. 'He was born with it. He can sing, but not talk – it's not unknown. Do you wonder people think they are cursed?' He turned to Mallory. 'Wait outside with your men.'

Mallory nodded, gestured to the others to precede him. Neufeld, he noted, was immediately engaged in a short, low-voiced discussion with Droshny, who nodded, summoned one of his Cetniks and dispatched him on some errand. Once outside, Mallory moved with Andrea slightly apart from the others and murmured something in his ear, inaudible to all but Andrea, whose nodded acquiescence was almost imperceptible.

Neufeld and Droshny emerged from the hut, followed by Maria who was leading Petar by the hand. As they approached Mallory's group, Andrea walked casually towards them, smoking the inevitable noxious cigar. He planted himself in front of a puzzled Neufeld and arrogantly blew smoke into his face.

'I don't think I care for you very much, Hauptmann Neufeld,' Andrea announced. He looked at Droshny. 'Nor for the cutlery salesman here.'

Neufeld's face immediately darkened, became tight in anger. But he brought himself quickly under control and said with restraint: 'Your opinion of me is of no concern to me.' He nodded to Droshny. 'But do not cross Captain Droshny's path, my friend. He is a Bosnian and a proud one – and the best man in the Balkans with a knife.'

'The best man –' Andrea broke off with a roar of laughter, and blew smoke into Droshny's face. 'A knife-grinder in a comic opera.'

Droshny's disbelief was total but of brief duration. He bared his teeth in a fashion that would have done justice to any Bosnian wolf, swept a wickedly-curved knife from his belt and threw himself on Andrea, the gleaming blade hooking viciously upwards, but Andrea, whose prudence was exceeded only by the extraordinary speed with which he could move his vast bulk, was no longer there when the knife arrived. But his hand was. It caught Droshny's knife wrist as it flashed upwards and almost at once the two big men crashed heavily to the ground, rolling over and over in the snow while they fought for possession of the knife.

So unexpectedly, so wholly incredible the speed with which the fight had developed from nowhere that, for a few seconds, no one moved. The three young sergeants, Neufeld and the Cetniks registered nothing but utter astonishment. Mallory, who was standing close behind the wide-eyed girl, rubbed his chin thoughtfully while Miller, delicately tapping the ash off the end of his cigarette, regarded the scene with a sort of weary interest.

Almost at the same instant, Reynolds, Groves and two Cetniks flung themselves upon the struggling pair on the ground and tried to pull them apart. Not until Saunders and Neufeld lent a hand did they succeed. Droshny and Andrea were pulled to their feet, the former with contorted face and hatred in his eyes, Andrea calmly resuming the smoking of the cigar which he'd somehow picked up after they had been separated.

'You madman!' Reynolds said savagely to Andrea. 'You crazy maniac. You – you're a bloody psychopath. You'll get us all killed.'

'That wouldn't surprise me at all,' Neufeld said thoughtfully. 'Come. Let us have no more of this foolishness.'

He led the way from the compound, and as he did so they were joined by a group of half-a-dozen Cetniks, whose apparent leader was the youth with the straggling ginger beard and cast to his eye, the first of the Cetniks to greet them when they had landed.

'Who are they and what are they for?' Mallory demanded of Neufeld. 'They're not coming with us.'

'Escort,' Neufeld explained. 'For the first seven kilometres only.'

'Escorts? What would we want with escorts? We're in no danger from you, nor, according to what you say, will we be from the Yugoslav Partisans.'

'We're not worried about you,' Neufeld said drily. 'We're worried about the vehicle that is going to take you most of the way there. Vehicles are very few and very precious in this part of Bosnia – and there are many Partisan patrols about.'

Twenty minutes later, in a now moonless night and with snow falling, they reached a road, a road which was little more than a winding track running through a forested valley floor. Waiting for them there was one of the strangest four-wheeled contraptions Mallory or his companions had ever seen, an incredibly ancient and battered truck which at first sight, from the vast clouds of smoke emanating from it, appeared to be on fire. It was, in fact, a very much pre-war wood-burning truck, of a type at one time common in the Balkans. Miller regarded the smoke-shrouded truck in astonishment and turned to Neufeld.

'You call this a vehicle?'

'You call it what you like. Unless you'd rather walk.'

'Ten kilometres? I'll take my chance on asphyxiation.' Miller climbed in, followed by the others, till only Neufeld and Droshny remained outside.

Neufeld said: 'I shall expect you back before noon.'

'If we ever come back,' Mallory said. 'If a radio message has come through –'

'You can't make an omelette without breaking eggs,' Neufeld said indifferently.

With a great rattling and shaking and emission of smoke and steam, all accompanied by much red-eyed coughing from the canvas-covered rear, the truck jerked uncertainly into motion and moved off slowly along the valley floor, Neufeld and Droshny gazing after it. Neufeld shook his head. 'Such clever little men.'

'Such *very* clever little men,' Droshny agreed. 'But I want the big one, Captain.'

Neufeld clapped him on the shoulder. 'You shall have him, my friend. Well, they're out of sight. Time for you to go.'

Droshny nodded and whistled shrilly between his fingers. There came the distant whirr of an engine starter, and soon an elderly Fiat emerged from behind a clump of pines and approached along the hard-packed snow of the road, its chains clanking violently, and stopped beside the two men. Droshny climbed into the front passenger seat and the Fiat moved off in the wake of the truck.

FIVE

Friday
0330–0500

For the fourteen people jammed on the narrow side benches under the canvas-hooped roof, the journey could hardly be called pleasurable. There were no cushions on the seats just as there appeared to be a total absence of springs on the vehicle, and the torn and badly fitting hood admitted large quantities of icy night air and eye-smarting smoke in about equal proportions. At least, Mallory thought, it all helped considerably to keep them awake.

Andrea was sitting directly opposite him, seemingly oblivious of the thick choking atmosphere inside the truck, a fact hardly surprising considering that the penetrating power and the pungency of the smoke from the truck was of a lower order altogether than that emanating from the black cheroot clamped between Andrea's teeth. Andrea glanced idly across and caught Mallory's eye. Mallory nodded once, a millimetric motion of the head that would have gone unremarked by even the most suspicious. Andrea dropped his eyes until his gaze rested on Mallory's right hand, lying loosely on his knee. Mallory sat back and sighed, and as he did his right hand slipped until his thumb was pointing directly at the floor. Andrea puffed out another Vesuvian cloud of acrid smoke and looked away indifferently.

For some kilometres the smoke-enshrouded truck clattered and screeched its way along the valley floor, then swung off to the left on to an even narrower track, and began to climb. Less than two minutes later, with Droshny sitting impassively in the front passenger seat, the pursuing Fiat made a similar turn off.

The slope was now so steep and the spinning driving wheels losing so much traction on the frozen surface of the track that the ancient wood-burning truck was reduced to little more than walking pace. Inside the truck, Andrea and Mallory were as watchful as ever, but Miller and the three sergeants seemed to be dozing off, whether through exhaustion or incipient asphyxiation it was difficult to say. Maria and Petar, hand in hand, appeared to be asleep. The Cetniks, on the other hand, could hardly have been more wide awake, and were making it clear for the first time that the rents and holes in the canvas cover had not been caused by accident: Droshny's six men were now kneeling on the benches with the muzzles of their machine-pistols thrust through the apertures in the canvas. It was clear that the truck was now moving into Partisan territory, or, at least, what passed for no-man's-land in that wild and rugged territory.

The Cetnik farthest forward in the truck suddenly withdrew his face from a gap in the canvas and rapped the butt of his gun against the driver's cab. The truck wheezed to a grateful halt, the ginger-bearded Cetnik jumped down, checked swiftly for any signs of ambush, then gestured the others to disembark, the repeatedly urgent movements of his hand making it clear that he was less than enamoured of the idea of hanging around that place for a moment longer than necessity demanded. One by one Mallory and his companions jumped down on to the frozen snow. Reynolds guided the blind singer down to the ground, then reached up a hand to help Maria as she clambered over the tailboard. Wordlessly, she struck his hand aside and leapt nimbly to the ground: Reynolds stared at her in hurt astonishment. The truck, Mallory observed, had stopped outside a small clearing in the forest. Backing and filling and issuing denser clouds of smoke than ever, it used this space to turn around in a remarkably short space of time and clanked its way off down the forest path at a considerably higher speed than it had made the ascent. The Cetniks gazed impassively from the back of the departing truck, made no gesture of farewell.

Maria took Petar's hand, looked coldly at Mallory, jerked her head and set off up a tiny footpath leading at right-angles from the track. Mallory shrugged and set off, followed by the three sergeants. For a moment or two, Andrea and Miller remained where they were, gazing thoughtfully at the corner round which the truck had just disappeared. Then they, too, set off, talking in low tones to each other.

The ancient wood-burning truck did not maintain its initial impetus for any lengthy period of time. Less than four hundred yards

after rounding the corner which blocked it from the view of
Mallory and his companions it braked to a halt. Two Cetniks, the
ginger-bearded leader of the escort and another black-bearded
man, jumped over the tailboard and moved at once into the protective covering of the forest. The truck rattled off once more, its
belching smoke hanging heavily in the freezing night air.

A kilometre farther down the track, an almost identical scene was
taking place. The Fiat slid to a halt, Droshny scrambled from the
passenger's seat and vanished among the pines. The Fiat reversed
quickly and moved off down the track.

The track up through the heavily wooded slope was very narrow,
very winding: the snow was no longer hard-packed, but soft and deep
and making for very hard going. The moon was quite gone now, the
snow, gusted into their faces by the east wind, was becoming steadily
heavier and the cold was intense. The path frequently arrived at a
V-shaped branch but Maria, in the lead with her brother, never hesitated: she knew, or appeared to know, exactly where she was going.
Several times she slipped in the deep snow, on the last occasion so
heavily that she brought her brother down with her. When it happened yet again, Reynolds moved forward and took the girl by the
arm to help her. She struck out savagely and drew her arm away.
Reynolds stared at her in astonishment, then turned to Mallory.

'What the devil's the matter with – I mean, I was only trying to
help –'

'Leave her alone,' Mallory said. 'You're one of them.'

'I'm one of –'

'You're wearing a British uniform. That's all the poor kid understands. Leave her be.'

Reynolds shook his head uncomprehendingly. He hitched his
pack more securely on his shoulders, glanced back down the trail,
made to move on, then glanced backwards again. He caught
Mallory by the arm and pointed.

Andrea had already fallen thirty yards behind. Weighed down by
his rucksack and Schmeisser and weight of years, he was very obviously making heavy weather of the climb and was falling steadily
behind by the second. At a gesture and word from Mallory the rest
of the party halted and peered back down through the driving
snow, waiting for Andrea to make up on them. By this time Andrea
was beginning to stumble almost drunkenly and clutched at his
right side as if in pain. Reynolds looked at Groves: they both looked

at Saunders: all three slowly shook their heads. Andrea came up with them and a spasm of pain flickered across his face.

'I'm sorry.' The voice was gasping and hoarse. 'I'll be all right in a moment.'

Saunders hesitated, then advanced towards Andrea. He smiled apologetically, then reached out a hand to indicate the rucksack and Schmeisser.

'Come on, Dad. Hand them over.'

For the minutest fraction of a second a flicker of menace, more imagined than seen, touched Andrea's face, then he shrugged off his rucksack and wearily handed it over. Saunders accepted it and tentatively indicated the Schmeisser.

'Thanks.' Andrea smiled wanly. 'But I'd feel lost without it.'

Uncertainly, they resumed their climb, looking back frequently to check on Andrea's progress. Their doubts were well-founded. Within thirty seconds Andrea had stopped, his eyes screwed up, and bent almost double in pain. He said, gaspingly: 'I must rest . . . Go on. I'll catch up with you.'

Miller said solicitously: 'I'll stay with you.'

'I don't need anybody to stay with me,' Andrea said surlily. 'I can look after myself.'

Miller said nothing. He looked at Mallory and jerked his head in an uphill direction. Mallory nodded, once, and gestured to the girl. Reluctantly, they moved off, leaving Andrea and Miller behind. Twice, Reynolds looked back over his shoulder, his expression an odd mixture of worry and exasperation: then he shrugged his shoulders and bent his back to the hill.

Andrea, scowling blackly and still clutching his ribs, remained bent double until the last of the party had rounded the nearest uphill corner, then straightened effortlessly, tested the wind with a wetted forefinger, established that it was moving up-trail, produced a cigar, lit it and puffed in deep and obvious contentment. His recovery was quite astonishing, but it didn't appear to astonish Miller, who grinned and nodded downhill. Andrea grinned in return, made a courteous gesture of precedence.

Thirty yards down-trail, at a position which gave them an uninterrupted view of almost a hundred yards of the track below them they moved into the cover of the bole of a giant pine. For about two minutes they stood there, staring downhill and listening intently, then suddenly Andrea nodded, stooped and carefully laid his cigar in a sheltered dried patch of ground behind the bole of the pine.

They exchanged no words: there was need of none. Miller crawled round to the downhill-facing front of the pine and carefully arranged himself in a spread-eagled position in the deep snow, both arms outflung, his apparently sightless face turned up to the falling snow. Behind the pine, Andrea reversed his grip on his Schmeisser, holding it by the barrel, produced a knife from the recesses of his clothing and stuck it in his belt. Both men remained as motionless as if they had died there and frozen solid over the long and bitter Yugoslav winter.

Probably because his spread-eagled form was sunk so deeply in the soft snow as to conceal most of his body, Miller saw the two Cetniks coming quite some time before they saw him. At first they were no more than two shapeless and vaguely ghostlike forms gradually materializing from the falling snow: as they drew nearer, he identified them as the Cetnik escort leader and one of his men.

They were less than thirty yards away before they saw Miller. They stopped, stared, remained motionless for at least five seconds, looked at each other, unslung their machine-pistols and broke into a stumbling uphill run. Miller closed his eyes. He didn't require them any more, his ears gave him all the information he wanted, the closing sound of crunching footsteps in the snow, the abrupt cessation of those, the heavy breathing as a man bent over him.

Miller waited until he could actually feel the man's breath in his face, then opened his eyes. Not twelve inches from his own were the eyes of the ginger-bearded Cetnik. Miller's outflung arms curved upwards and inwards, his sinewy fingers hooked deeply into the throat of the startled man above him.

Andrea's Schmeisser had already reached the limit of its back-swing as he stepped soundlessly round the bole of the pine. The black-bearded Cetnik was just beginning to move to help his friend when he caught sight of Andrea from the corner of one eye, and flung up both arms to protect himself. A pair of straws would have served him as well. Andrea grimaced at the sheer physical shock of the impact, dropped the Schmeisser, pulled out his knife and fell upon the other Cetnik still struggling desperately in Miller's stranglehold.

Miller rose to his feet and he and Andrea stared down at the two dead men. Miller looked in puzzlement at the ginger-bearded man, then suddenly stooped, caught the beard and tugged. It came away in his hand, revealing beneath it a clean-shaven face and a scar which ran from the corner of a lip to the chin.

Andrea and Miller exchanged speculative glances, but neither made comment. They dragged the dead men some little way off the path into the concealment of some undergrowth. Andrea picked up a dead branch and swept away the dragmarks in the snow and, by the base of the pine, all traces of the encounter: inside the hour, he knew, the brushmarks he had made would have vanished under a fresh covering of snow. He picked up his cigar and threw the branch deep into the woods. Without a backward glance, the two men began to walk briskly up the hill.

Had they given this backward glance, it was barely possible that they might have caught a glimpse of a face peering round the trunk of a tree farther downhill. Droshny had arrived at the bend in the track just in time to see Andrea complete his brushing operations and throw the branch away: what the meaning of this might be he couldn't guess.

He waited until Andrea and Miller had disappeared from his sight, waited another two minutes for good measure and safety, then hurried up the track, the expression on his swarthy brigand's face nicely balanced between puzzlement and suspicion. He reached the pine where the two Cetniks had been ambushed, briefly quartered the area, then followed the line of brushmarks leading into the woods, the puzzlement on his face giving way first to pure suspicion, then the suspicion to complete certainty.

He parted the bushes and peered down at the two Cetniks lying half-buried in a snow-filled gully with that curiously huddled shapelessness that only the dead can achieve. After a few moments he straightened, turned and looked uphill in the direction in which Andrea and Miller had vanished: his face was not pleasant to look upon.

Andrea and Miller made good time up the hill. As they approached one of the innumerable bends in the trail they heard up ahead the sound of a softly-played guitar, curiously muffled and softened in tone by the falling snow. Andrea slowed up, threw away his cigar, bent forward and clutched his ribs. Solicitously, Miller took his arm.

The main party, they saw, was less than thirty yards ahead. They, too, were making slow time: the depth of snow and the increasing slope of the track made any quicker movement impossible. Reynolds glanced back – Reynolds was spending a great deal of his time in looking over his shoulder, he appeared to be in a highly apprehensive state – caught sight of Andrea and Miller and called

out to Mallory who halted the party and waited for Andrea and
Miller to make up with them. Mallory looked worriedly at Andrea.

'Getting worse?'

'How far to go?' Andrea asked hoarsely.

'Must be less than a mile.'

Andrea said nothing, he just stood there breathing heavily and
wearing the stricken look of a sick man contemplating the prospect of
another upward mile through deep snow. Saunders, already carrying
two rucksacks, approached Andrea diffidently, tentatively. He said: 'It
would help, you know, if –'

'I know.' Andrea smiled painfully, unslung his Schmeisser and
handed it to Saunders. 'Thanks, son.'

Petar was still softly plucking the strings of his guitar, an indescrib-
ably eerie sound in those dark and ghostly pine woods. Miller looked
at him and said to Mallory: 'What's the music while we march for?'

'Petar's password, I should imagine.'

'Like Neufeld said? Nobody touches our singing Cetnik?'

'Something like that.'

They moved on up the trail. Mallory let the others pass by until
he and Andrea were bringing up the rear. Mallory glanced incuriously at Andrea, his face registering no more than a mild concern
for the condition of his friend. Andrea caught his glance and nodded fractionally: Mallory looked away.

Fifteen minutes later they were halted, at gunpoint, by three
men, all armed with machine-pistols, who simply appeared to have
materialized from nowhere, a surprise so complete that not even
Andrea could have done anything about it – even if he had had his
gun. Reynolds looked urgently at Mallory, who smiled and shook
his head.

'It's all right. Partisans – look at the red star on their forage caps.
Just outposts guarding one of the main trails.'

And so it proved. Maria talked briefly to one of the soldiers, who
listened, nodded and set off up the path, gesturing to the party to
follow him. The other two Partisans remained behind, both men
crossing themselves as Petar again strummed gently on his guitar.
Neufeld, Mallory reflected, hadn't exaggerated about the degree of
awed respect and fear in which the blind singer and his sister were
held.

They came to Partisan HQ inside another ten minutes, an HQ
curiously similar in appearance and choice of location to
Hauptmann Neufeld's camp: the same rough circle of crude huts set

deep in the same *jamba* – depression – with similar massive pines towering high above. The guide spoke to Maria and she turned coldly to Mallory, the disdain on her face making it very plain how much against the grain it went for her to speak to him at all.

'We are to go to the guest hut. You are to report to the commandant. This soldier will show you.'

The guide beckoned in confirmation. Mallory followed him across the compound to a fairly large, fairly well-lit hut. The guide knocked, opened the door and waved Mallory inside, he himself following.

The commandant was a tall, lean, dark man with that aquiline, aristocratic face so common among the Bosnian mountainmen. He advanced towards Mallory with outstretched hand and smiled.

'Major Broznik, and at your service. Late, late hours, but as you see we are still up and around. Although I must say I did expect you before this.'

'I don't know what you're talking about.'

'You don't know – you *are* Captain Mallory, are you not?'

'I've never heard of him.' Mallory gazed steadily at Broznik, glanced briefly sideways at the guide, then looked back to Broznik again. Broznik frowned for a moment, then his face cleared. He spoke to the guide, who turned and left. Mallory put out his hand.

'Captain Mallory, at your service. I'm sorry about that, Major Broznik, but I insist we must talk alone.'

'You trust no one? Not even in *my* camp?'

'No one.'

'Not even your own men?'

'I don't trust them not to make mistakes. I don't trust myself not to make mistakes. I don't trust you not to make mistakes.'

'Please?' Broznik's voice was as cold as his eyes.

'Did you ever have two of your men disappear, one with ginger hair, the other with black, the ginger-haired man with a cast to his eye and a scar running from mouth to chin?'

Broznik came closer. 'What do you know about those men?'

'Did you? Know them, I mean?'

Broznik nodded and said slowly: 'They were lost in action. Last month.'

'You found their bodies?'

'No.'

'There were no bodies to be found. They had deserted – gone over to the Cetniks.'

'But they *were* Cetniks – converted to our cause.'

'They'd been reconverted. They followed us tonight. On the orders of Captain Droshny. I had them killed.'

'You – had – them – killed?'

'Think, man,' Mallory said wearily. 'If they had arrived here – which they no doubt intended to do a discreet interval after our arrival – we wouldn't have recognized them and you'd have welcomed them back as escaped prisoners. They'd have reported our every movement. Even if we had recognized them after they had arrived here and done something about it, you may have *other* Cetniks here who would have reported back to their masters that we had done away with their watchdogs. So we disposed of them very quietly, no fuss, in a very remote place, then hid them.'

'There are no Cetniks in my command, Captain Mallory.'

Mallory said drily: 'It takes a very clever farmer, Major, to see two bad apples on the top of the barrel and be quite certain that there are none lower down. No chances. None. Ever.' Mallory smiled to remove any offence from his words and went on briskly: 'Now, Major, there's some information that Hauptmann Neufeld wants.'

To say that the guest hut hardly deserved so hospitable a title would have been a very considerable understatement. As a shelter for some of the less-regarded domesticated animals it might have been barely acceptable: as an overnight accommodation for human beings it was conspicuously lacking in what our modern effete European societies regard as the minimum essentials for civilized living. Even the Spartans of ancient Greece would have considered it as too much of a good thing. One rickety trestle table, one bench, a dying fire and lots of hard-packed earthen floor. It fell short of being a home from home.

There were six people in the hut, three standing, one sitting, two stretched out on the lumpy floor. Petar, for once without his sister, sat on the floor, silent guitar clasped in his hands, gazing sightlessly into the fading embers. Andrea, stretched in apparently luxurious ease in a sleeping-bag, peacefully puffed at what, judging from the frequent suffering glances cast in his direction, appeared to be a more than normally obnoxious cigar. Miller, similarly reclining, was reading what appeared to be a slender volume of poetry. Reynolds and Groves, unable to sleep, stood idly by the solitary window, gazing out abstractedly into the dimly-lit compound: they turned as

Saunders removed his radio transmitter from its casing and made for the door.

With some bitterness Saunders said: 'Sleep well.'

'Sleep well?' Reynolds raised an eyebrow. 'And where are you going?'

'Radio hut across there. Message to Termoli. Mustn't spoil your beauty sleep while I'm transmitting.'

Saunders left. Groves went and sat by the table, cradling a weary head in his hands. Reynolds remained by the window, watched Saunders cross the compound and enter a darkened hut on the far side. Soon a light appeared in the window as Saunders lit a lamp.

Reynolds's eyes moved in response to the sudden appearance of an oblong of light across the compound. The door to Major Broznik's hut had opened and Mallory stood momentarily framed there, carrying what appeared to be a sheet of paper in his hand. Then the door closed and Mallory moved off in the direction of the radio hut.

Reynolds suddenly became very watchful, very still. Mallory had taken less than a dozen steps when a dark figure detached itself from the even darker shadow of a hut and confronted him. Quite automatically, Reynolds's hand reached for the Luger at his belt, then slowly withdrew. Whatever this confrontation signified for Mallory it certainly wasn't danger, for Maria, Reynolds knew, did not carry a gun. And unquestionably it was Maria who was now in such apparent close conversation with Mallory.

Bewildered now, Reynolds pressed his face close against the glass. For almost two minutes he stared at this astonishing spectacle of the girl who had slapped Mallory with such venom, who had lost no opportunity of displaying an animosity bordering on hatred, now talking to him not only animatedly but also clearly very amicably. So total was Reynolds's baffled incomprehension at this inexplicable turn of events that his mind moved into a trance-like state, a spell that was abruptly snapped when he saw Mallory put a reassuring arm around her shoulder and pat her in a way that might have been comforting or affectionate or both but which in any event clearly evoked no resentment on the part of the girl. This was still inexplicable: but the only interpretation that could be put upon it was an uncompromisingly sinister one. Reynolds whirled round and silently and urgently beckoned Groves to the window. Groves rose quickly, moved to the window and looked out, but by the time he had done so there was no longer any sign of Maria: Mallory was alone, walking across the compound towards the radio hut, the paper still in his hand. Groves glanced questioningly at Reynolds.

'They were together,' Reynolds whispered. 'Mallory and Maria. I saw them! They were talking!'

'What? You sure?'

'God's my witness. I *saw* them, man. He even had his arm around – Get away from this window – Maria's coming.'

Without haste, so as to arouse no comment from Andrea or Miller, they turned and walked unconcernedly towards the table and sat down. Seconds later, Maria entered and, without looking at or speaking to anyone, crossed to the fire, sat by Petar and took his hand. A minute or so later Mallory entered, and sat on a palliasse beside Andrea, who removed his cigar and glanced at him in mild enquiry. Mallory casually checked to see that he wasn't under observation, then nodded. Andrea returned to the contemplation of his cigar.

Reynolds looked uncertainly at Groves, then said to Mallory, 'Shouldn't we be setting a guard, sir?'

'A guard?' Mallory was amused. 'Whatever for? This is a Partisan camp, Sergeant. Friends, you know. And, as you've seen, they have their own excellent guard system.'

'You never know –'

'*I* know. Get some sleep.'

Reynolds went on doggedly: 'Saunders is alone over there. I don't like –'

'He's coding and sending a short message for me. A few minutes, that's all.'

'But –'

'Shut up,' Andrea said. 'You heard the captain?'

Reynolds was by now thoroughly unhappy and uneasy, an unease which showed through in his instantly antagonistic irritation.

'Shut up? Why should I shut up? I don't take orders from you. And while we're telling each other what to do, you might put out that damned stinking cigar.'

Miller wearily lowered his book of verse.

'I quite agree about the damned cigar, young fellow. But do bear in mind that you are talking to a ranking colonel in the army.'

Miller reverted to his book. For a few moments Reynolds and Groves stared open-mouthed at each other, then Reynolds stood up and looked at Andrea.

'I'm extremely sorry, sir. I – I didn't realize –'

Andrea waved him to silence with a magnanimous hand and resumed his communion with his cigar. The minutes passed in silence. Maria, before the fire, had her head on Petar's shoulder, but otherwise had not moved: she appeared to be asleep. Miller shook his head in rapt admiration of what appeared to be one of the more esoteric manifestations of the poetic muse, closed his book reluctantly and slid down into his sleeping-bag. Andrea ground out his cigar and did the same. Mallory seemed to be already asleep. Groves lay down and Reynolds, leaning over the table, rested his forehead on his arms. For five minutes, perhaps longer, Reynolds remained like this, uneasily dozing off, then he lifted his head, sat up with a jerk, glanced at his watch, crossed to Mallory and shook him by the shoulder. Mallory stirred.

'Twenty minutes,' Reynolds said urgently. 'Twenty minutes and Saunders isn't back yet.'

'All right, so it's twenty minutes,' Mallory said patiently. 'He could take that long to make contact, far less transmit the message.'

'Yes, sir. Permission to check, sir?'

Mallory nodded wearily and closed his eyes. Reynolds picked up his Schmeisser, left the hut and closed the door softly behind him. He released the safety-catch on his gun and ran across the compound.

The light still burned in the radio hut. Reynolds tried to peer through the window but the frost of that bitter night had made it completely opaque. Reynolds moved around to the door. It was slightly ajar. He set his finger to the trigger and opened the door in the fashion in which all Commandos were trained to open doors – with a violent kick of his right foot.

There was no one in the radio hut, no one, that is, who could bring him to any harm. Slowly, Reynolds lowered his gun and walked in a hesitant, almost dreamlike fashion, his face masked in shock.

Saunders was leaning tiredly over the transmitting table, his head resting on it at an unnatural angle, both arms dangling limply towards the ground. The hilt of a knife protruded between his shoulderblades: Reynolds noted, almost subconsciously, that there was no trace of blood: death had been instantaneous. The transmitter itself lay on the floor, a twisted and mangled mass of metal that was obviously smashed beyond repair. Tentatively, not knowing why he did so, he reached out and touched the dead man on the shoulder: Saunders seemed to stir, his cheek slid along the table and he toppled to one side, falling heavily across the battered remains of the transmitter. Reynolds stooped low over him. Grey parchment now, where a bronzed tan had been, sightless, faded eyes uselessly guarding a mind now flown. Reynolds swore briefly, bitterly, straightened and ran from the hut.

Everyone in the guest hut was asleep, or appeared to be. Reynolds crossed to where Mallory lay, dropped to one knee and shook him roughly by the shoulder. Mallory stirred, opened weary eyes and propped himself up on one elbow. He gave Reynolds a look of unenthusiastic enquiry.

'Among friends, you said!' Reynolds's voice was low, vicious, almost a hissing sound. 'Safe, you said. Saunders will be all right, you said. You *knew*, you said. You bloody well knew.'

Mallory said nothing. He sat up abruptly on his palliasse, and the sleep was gone from his eyes. He said: 'Saunders?'

Reynolds said, 'I think you'd better come with me.'

In silence the two men left the hut, in silence they crossed the deserted compound and in silence they entered the radio hut. Mallory went no farther than the doorway. For what was probably no more than ten seconds but for what seemed to Reynolds to be an unconsciously long time, Mallory stared at the dead man and the smashed transmitter, his eyes bleak, his face registering no emotional reaction. Reynolds mistook the expression, or lack of it, for something else, and could suddenly no longer contain his pent-up fury.

'Well, aren't you bloody well going to do something about it instead of standing there all night?'

'Every dog's entitled to his one bite,' Mallory said mildly. 'But don't talk to me like that again. Do what, for instance?'

'Do what?' Reynolds visibly struggled for self-control. 'Find the nice gentleman who did this.'

'Finding him will be very difficult.' Mallory considered. 'Impossible, I should say. If the killer came from the camp here, then he'll have gone to earth in the camp here. If he came from outside, he'll be a mile away by this time and putting more distance between himself and us every second. Go and wake Andrea and Miller and Groves and tell them to come here. Then go and tell Major Broznik what's happened.'

'I'll tell them what's happened,' Reynolds said bitterly. 'And I'll also tell them it never *would* have happened if you'd listened to me. But oh no, you wouldn't listen, would you?'

'So you were right and I was wrong. Now do as I ask you.'

Reynolds hesitated, a man obviously on the brink of outright revolt. Suspicion and defiance alternated in the angry face. Then some strange quality in the expression in Mallory's face tipped the balance for sanity and compliance and he nodded in sullen antagonism, turned and walked away.

Mallory waited until he had rounded the corner of the hut, brought out his torch and started, not very hopefully, to quarter the hard-packed snow outside the door of the radio hut. But almost at once he stopped, stooped, and brought the head of the torch close to the surface of the ground.

It was a very small portion of footprint indeed, only the front half of the sole of a right foot. The pattern showed two V-shaped marks, the leading V with a cleanly-cut break in it. Mallory, moving more quickly now, followed the direction indicated by the pointed toeprint and came across two more similar indentations, faint but unmistakable, before the frozen snow gave way to the frozen earth of the compound, ground so hard as to be incapable of registering any footprints at all. Mallory retraced his steps, carefully erasing all three prints with the toe of his boot and reached the radio hut only seconds before he was joined by Reynolds, Andrea, Miller and Groves. Major Broznik and several of his men joined them soon after.

They searched the interior of the radio hut for clues as to the killer's identity, but clues there were none. Inch by inch they searched the hard-packed snow surrounding the hut, with the same completely negative results. Reinforced, by this time, by perhaps sixty or seventy sleepy-eyed Partisan soldiers, they carried out a simultaneous search of all the buildings and of the woods surrounding the encampment: but neither the encampment nor the surrounding woods had any secrets to yield.

'We may as well call it off,' Mallory said finally. 'He's got clean away.'

'It looks that way,' Major Broznik agreed. He was deeply troubled and bitterly angry that such a thing should have happened in his encampment. 'We'd better double the guards for the rest of the night.'

'There's no need for that,' Mallory said. 'Our friend won't be back.'

'There's no need for that,' Reynolds mimicked savagely. 'There was no need for that for poor Saunders, you said. And where's Saunders now? Sleeping comfortably in his bed? Is he hell! No need –'

Andrea muttered warningly and took a step nearer Reynolds, but Mallory made a brief conciliatory movement of his right hand. He said: 'It's entirely up to you, of course, Major. I'm sorry that we have been responsible for giving you and your men so sleepless a night. See you in the morning.' He smiled wryly. 'Not that that's so far away.' He turned to go, found his way blocked by Sergeant Groves, a Groves whose normally cheerful countenance now mirrored the tight hostility of Reynolds's.

'So he's got clear away, has he? Away to hell and gone. And that's the end of it, eh?'

Mallory looked at him consideringly. 'Well, no. I wouldn't quite say that. A little time. We'll find him.'

'A little time? Maybe even before he dies of old age?'

Andrea looked at Mallory. 'Twenty-four hours?'

'Less.'

Andrea nodded and he and Mallory turned and walked away towards the guest hut. Reynolds and Groves, with Miller slightly behind them, watched the two men as they went, then looked at each other, their faces still bleak and bitter.

'Aren't they a nice warm-hearted couple now? Completely broken up about old Saunders.' Groves shook his head. 'They don't care. They just don't care.'

'Oh, I wouldn't say that,' Miller said diffidently. 'It's just that they don't *seem* to care. Not at all the same thing.'

'Faces like wooden Indians,' Reynolds muttered. 'They never even said they were *sorry* that Saunders was killed.'

'Well,' Miller said patiently, 'it's a cliché, but different people react in different ways. Okay, so grief and anger is the natural reaction to this sort of thing, but if Mallory and Andrea spent their time in reacting in that fashion to all the things that have happened to *them* in their lifetimes, they'd have come apart at the seams years ago. So they don't react that way any more. They do things. Like they're going to do things to your friend's killer. Maybe you didn't get it, but you just heard a death sentence being passed.'

'How do *you* know?' Reynolds said uncertainly. He nodded in the direction of Mallory and Andrea who were just entering the guest hut. 'And how did *they* know? Without talking, I mean.'

'Telepathy.'

'What do you mean – "telepathy"?'

'It would take too long,' Miller said wearily. 'Ask me in the morning.'

SIX

Friday
0800–1000

Crowning the tops of the towering pines, the dense, interlocking snow-laden branches formed an almost impenetrable canopy that effectively screened Major Broznik's camp, huddled at the foot of the *jamba*, from all but the most fleeting glimpses of the sky above. Even at high noon on a summer's day, it was never more than a twilit dusk down below: on a morning such as this, an hour after dawn with snow falling gently from an overcast sky, the quality of light was such as to be hardly distinguishable from a starlit midnight. The interior of the dining hut, where Mallory and his company were at breakfast with Major Broznik, was gloomy in the extreme, the darkness emphasized rather than alleviated by the two smoking oil lamps which formed the only primitive means of illumination.

The atmosphere of gloom was significantly deepened by the behaviour and expression of those seated round the breakfast table. They ate in a moody silence, heads lowered, for the most part not looking at one another: the events of the previous night had clearly affected them all deeply but none so deeply as Reynolds and Groves in whose faces was still unmistakably reflected the shock caused by Saunders's murder. They left their food untouched.

To complete the atmosphere of quiet desperation, it was clear that the reservations held about the standard of the Partisan early-morning cuisine were of a profound and lasting nature. Served by two young *partisankas* – women members of Marshal Tito's army – it consisted of *polenta*, a highly unappetizing dish made from ground corn, and *raki*, a Yugoslav spirit of unparalleled fierceness. Miller spooned his breakfast with a marked lack of enthusiasm.

'Well,' he said to no one in particular, 'it makes a change, I'll say that.'

'It's all we have,' Broznik said apologetically. He laid down his spoon and pushed his plate away from him. 'And even that I can't eat. Not this morning. Every entrance to the *jamba* is guarded, yet there was a killer loose in my camp last night. But maybe he *didn't* come in past the guards, maybe he was already inside. Think of it – a traitor in my own camp. And if there is, I can't even find him. I can't even believe it!'

Comment was superfluous, nothing could be said that hadn't been said already, nobody as much as looked in Broznik's direction: his acute discomfort, embarrassment and anger were apparent to everyone in his tone of voice. Andrea, who had already emptied his plate with apparent relish, looked at the two untouched plates in front of Reynolds and Groves and then enquiringly at the two sergeants themselves, who shook their heads. Andrea reached out, brought their plates before him and set to with every sign of undiminished appetite. Reynolds and Groves looked at him in shocked disbelief, possibly awed by the catholicity of Andrea's taste, more probably astonished by the insensitivity of a man who could eat so heartily only a few hours after the death of one of his comrades. Miller, for his part, looked at Andrea in near horror, tried another tiny portion of his *polenta* and wrinkled his nose in delicate distaste. He laid down his spoon and looked morosely at Petar who, guitar slung over his shoulder, was awkwardly feeding himself.

Miller said irritably: 'Does he *always* wear that damned guitar?'

'Our lost one,' Broznik said softly. 'That's what we call him. Our poor blind lost one. Always he carries it or has it by his side. Always. Even when he sleeps – didn't you notice last night? That guitar means as much to him as life itself. Some weeks ago, one of our men, by way of a joke, tried to take it from him: Petar, blind though he is, almost killed him.'

'He must be stone tone deaf,' Miller said wonderingly. 'It's the most god-awful guitar I ever heard.'

Broznik smiled faintly. 'Agreed. But don't you understand? He can feel it. He can touch it. It's his own. It's the only thing left to him in the world, a dark and lonely and empty world. Our poor lost one.'

'He could at least tune it,' Miller muttered.

'You are a good man, my friend. You try to take our minds off what lies ahead this day. But no man can do that.' He turned to Mallory. 'Any more than you can hope to carry out your crazy scheme of rescuing your captured agents and breaking up the German counter-espionage network here. It is insanity. Insanity!'

Mallory waved a vague hand. 'Here you are. No food. No artillery. No transport. Hardly any guns – and practically no ammunition for those guns. No medical supplies. No tanks. No planes. No hope – and you keep on fighting. That makes you sane?'

'Touché.' Broznik smiled, pushed across the bottle of *raki*, waited until Mallory had filled his glass. 'To the madmen of this world.'

'I've just been talking to Major Stephan up at the Western Gap,' General Vukalovic said. 'He thinks we're all mad. Would you agree, Colonel Lazlo?'

The man lying prone beside Vukalovic lowered his binoculars. He was a burly, sun-tanned, thickset, middle-aged man with a magnificent black moustache that had every appearance of being waxed. After a moment's consideration, he said: 'Without a doubt, sir.'

'Even you?' Vukalovic said protestingly. 'With a Czech father?'

'He came from the High Tatra,' Lazlo explained. 'They're all mad there.'

Vukalovic smiled, settled himself more comfortably on his elbows, peered downhill through the gap between two rocks, raised his binoculars and scanned the scene to the south of him, slowly raising his glasses as he did so.

Immediately in front of where he lay was a bare, rocky hillside, dropping gently downhill for a distance of about two hundred feet. Beyond its base it merged gradually into a long flat grassy plateau, no more than two hundred yards wide at its maximum, but stretching almost as far as the eye could see on both sides, on the right-hand side stretching away to the west, on the left curving away to the east, north-east and finally north.

Beyond the edge of the plateau, the land dropped abruptly to form the bank of a wide and swiftly flowing river, a river of that peculiarly Alpine greenish-white colour, green from the melting ice-water of spring, white from where it foamed over jagged rocks and overfalls in the bed of the river. Directly to the south of where Vukalovic and Lazlo lay, the river was spanned by a green-and-white-painted and very solidly-constructed cantilevered steel bridge. Beyond the river, the grassy bank on the far side rose in a very easy slope for a distance of about a hundred yards to the very regularly defined limit of a forest of giant pines which stretched away into the southern distance. Scattered through the very outermost of the pines were a few dully metallic objects, unmistakably tanks. In the farthest distance, beyond the river and beyond the pines, towering, jagged mountains dazzled in their brilliant covering of snow and above that again, but more to the south-east, an equally white and dazzling sun shone from an incongruously blue patch in an otherwise snow-cloud-covered sky.

Vukalovic lowered his binoculars and sighed.

'No idea at all how many tanks are across in the woods there?'

'I wish to heaven I knew.' Lazlo lifted his arms in a small, helpless gesture. 'Could be ten. Could be two hundred. We've no idea. We've sent scouts, of course, but they never came back. Maybe they were swept away trying to cross the Neretva.' He looked at Vukalovic, speculation in his eyes. 'Through the Zenica Gap, through the Western Gap or across that bridge there – you don't know where the attack is coming from, do you, sir?'

Vukalovic shook his head.

'But you expect it soon?'

'Very soon.' Vukalovic struck the rocky ground with a clenched fist. 'Is there *no* way of destroying that damned bridge?'

'There have been five RAF attacks,' Lazlo said heavily. 'To date, twenty-seven planes lost – there are two hundred AA guns along the Neretva and the nearest Messerschmitt station is only ten minutes' flying time away. The German radar picks up the British bombers crossing our coast – and the Messerschmitts are here, waiting, by the time they arrive. And don't forget that the bridge is set in rock on either side.'

'A direct hit or nothing?'

'A direct hit on a target seven metres wide from three thousand metres. It is impossible. And a target so camouflaged that you can hardly see it five hundred metres away on land. Doubly impossible.'

'And impossible for us,' Vukalovic said bleakly.

'Impossible for us. We made our last attempt two nights ago.'

'You made – I told you not to.'

'You *asked* us not to. But of course I, Colonel Lazlo, knew better. They started firing star-shells when our troops were halfway across the plateau, God knows how they knew they were coming. Then the searchlights –'

'Then the shrapnel shells,' Vukalovic finished. 'And the Oerlikons. Casualties?'

'We lost half a battalion.'

'Half a battalion! And tell me, my dear Lazlo, what would have happened in the unlikely event of your men reaching the bridge?'

'They had some amatol blocks, some hand-grenades –'

'No fireworks?' Vukalovic asked in heavy sarcasm. 'That might have helped. That bridge is built of steel set in reinforced concrete, man! You were mad even to try.'

'Yes, sir.' Lazlo looked away. 'Perhaps you ought to relieve me.'

'I think I should.' Vukalovic looked closely at the exhausted face. 'In fact I would. But for one thing.'

'One thing?'

'All my other regimental commanders are as mad as you are. And if the Germans do attack – maybe even tonight?'

'We stand here. We are Yugoslavs and we have no place to go. What else can we do?'

'What else? Two thousand men with pop-guns, most of them weak and starving and lacking ammunition, against what may perhaps be two first-line German armoured divisions. And you stand there. You could always surrender, you know.'

Lazlo smiled. 'With respect, General, this is no time for facetiousness.'

Vukalovic clapped his shoulder. 'I didn't think it funny, either. I'm going up to the dam, to the northeastern redoubt. I'll see if Colonel Janzy is as mad as you are. And Colonel?'

'Sir?'

'If the attack comes, I may give the order to retreat.'

'Retreat!'

'Not surrender. Retreat. Retreat to what, one hopes, may be victory.'

'I am sure the General knows what he is talking about.'

'The General isn't.' Oblivious to possible sniper fire from across the Neretva, Vukalovic stood up in readiness to go. 'Ever heard of a man called Captain Mallory. Keith Mallory, a New Zealander?'

'No,' Lazlo said promptly. He paused, then went on: 'Wait a minute, though. Fellow who used to climb mountains?'

'That's the one. But he has also, I'm given to understand, other accomplishments.' Vukalovic rubbed a stubbly chin. 'If all I hear about him is true, I think you could quite fairly call him a rather gifted individual.'

'And what about this gifted individual?' Lazlo asked curiously.

'Just this.' Vukalovic was suddenly very serious, even sombre. 'When all things are lost and there is no hope left, there is always, somewhere in the world, one man you can turn to. There may be only that one man. More often than not there *is* only that one man. But that one man is always there.' He paused reflectively. 'Or so they say.'

'Yes, sir,' Lazlo said politely. 'But about this Keith Mallory –'

'Before you sleep tonight, pray for him. I will.'

'Yes, sir. And about us? Shall I pray for us, too?'

'That,' said Vukalovic, 'wouldn't be at all a bad idea.'

The sides of the *jamba* leading upwards from Major Broznik's camp were very steep and very slippery and the ascending cavalcade of men and ponies were making very heavy going of it. Or most of them were. The escort of dark stocky Bosnian Partisans, to whom such terrain was part and parcel of existence, appeared quite unaffected by the climb: and it in no way appeared to interfere with Andrea's rhythmic puffing of his usual vile-smelling cigar. Reynolds noticed this, a fact which fed fresh fuel to the already dark doubts and torments in his mind.

He said sourly: 'You seem to have made a remarkable recovery in the night-time, Colonel Stavros, sir.'

'Andrea.' The cigar was removed. 'I have a heart condition. It comes and goes.' The cigar was replaced.

'I'm sure it does,' Reynolds muttered. He glanced suspiciously, and for the twentieth time, over his shoulder. 'Where the hell is Mallory?'

'Where the hell is *Captain* Mallory,' Andrea chided.

'Well, where?'

'The leader of an expedition has many responsibilities,' Andrea said. 'Many things to attend to. Captain Mallory is probably attending to something at this very moment.'

'You can say that again,' Reynolds muttered.

'What was that?'

'Nothing.'

Captain Mallory was, as Andrea had so correctly guessed, attending to something at that precise moment. Back in Broznik's office, he and Broznik were bent over a map spread out on the trestle table. Broznik pointed to a spot near the northern limit of the map.

'I agree. This *is* the nearest possible landing strip for a plane. But it is very high up. At this time of year there will still be almost a metre of snow up there. There are other places, better places.'

'I don't doubt that for a moment,' Mallory said. 'Faraway fields are always greener, maybe even faraway airfields. But I haven't the time to go to them.' He stabbed his forefinger on the map. 'I want a landing-strip here and only here by night-fall. I'd be most grateful if you'd send a rider to Konjic within the hour and have my request radioed immediately to your Partisan HQ at Drvar.'

Broznik said drily: 'You are accustomed to asking for instant miracles, Captain Mallory?'

'This doesn't call for miracles. Just a thousand men. The feet of a thousand men. A small price for seven thousand lives?' He handed Broznik a slip of paper. 'Wavelength and code. Have Konjic transmit it as soon as possible.' Mallory glanced at his watch. 'They have twenty minutes on me already. I'd better hurry.'

'I suppose you'd better,' Broznik said hurriedly. He hesitated, at a momentary loss for words, then went on awkwardly: 'Captain Mallory, I – I –'

'I know. Don't worry. The Mallorys of this world never make old bones anyway. We're too stupid.'

'Aren't we all, aren't we all?' Broznik gripped Mallory's hand. 'Tonight, I make a prayer for you.'

Mallory remained silent for a moment, then nodded.

'Make it a long one.'

The Bosnian scouts, now, like the remainder of the party, mounted on ponies, led the winding way down through the gentle slope of the thickly-forested valley, followed by Andrea and Miller riding abreast, then by Petar, whose pony's bridle was in the hand of his sister. Reynolds and Groves, whether by accident or design, had fallen some little way behind and were talking in soft tones.

Groves said speculatively: 'I wonder what Mallory and the Major are talking about back there?'

Reynolds's mouth twisted in bitterness. 'It's perhaps as well we don't know.'

'You may be right at that. I just don't know.' Groves paused, went on almost pleadingly: 'Broznik is on the up-and-up. I'm sure of it. Being what he is, he *must* be.'

'That's as may be. Mallory too, eh?'

'*He* must be, too.'

'Must?' Reynolds was savage. 'God alive, man, I tell you I saw him with my own eyes.' He nodded towards Maria, some twenty yards ahead, and his face was cruel and hard. 'That girl hit him – and *how* she hit him – back in Neufeld's camp and the next thing I see is the two of them having a cosy little lovey-dovey chat outside Broznik's hut. Odd, isn't it? Soon after, Saunders was murdered. Coincidence, isn't it? I tell you, Groves, Mallory could have done it himself. The girl *could* have had time to do it before she met Mallory – except that it would have been physically impossible for her to drive a six-inch knife home to the hilt. But Mallory could have done it all right. He'd time enough – and opportunity enough – when he handed that damned message into the radio hut.'

Groves said protestingly: 'Why in God's name should he do that?'

'Because Broznik had given him some urgent information. Mallory *had* to make a show of passing this information back to Italy. But maybe sending that message was the last thing he wanted. Maybe he stopped it in the only way he knew how – and smashed the transmitter to make sure no one else could send a message. Maybe that's why he stopped me from mounting a guard or going to see Saunders – to prevent me from discovering the fact that Saunders was already dead – in which case, of course, because of the time factor, suspicion would have automatically fallen on him.'

'You're imagining things.' Despite his discomfort, Groves was reluctantly impressed by Reynolds's reasoning.

'You think so? That knife in Saunders's back – did I imagine that too?'

Within half an hour, Mallory had rejoined the party. He jogged past Reynolds and Groves, who studiously ignored him, past Maria and Petar, who did the same, and took up position behind Andrea and Miller.

It was in this order, for almost an hour, that they passed through the heavily-wooded Bosnian valleys. Occasionally, they came to clearings in the pines, clearings that had once been the site of human habitation, small villages or hamlets. But now there were no humans, no habitations, for the villages had ceased to exist. The clearings were all the same, chillingly and depressingly the same. Where the hard-working but happy Bosnians had once lived in their simple but sturdy homes, there were now only the charred and blackened remains of what had once been thriving communities, the air still heavy with the acrid smell of ancient smoke, the sweet-sour stench of corruption and death, mute testimony to the no-quarter viciousness and total ruthlessness of the war between the Germans and the Partisan Yugoslavs. Occasionally, here and there, still stood a few small, stone-built houses which had not been worth the expenditure of bombs or shells or mortars or petrol:

but few of the larger buildings had escaped complete destruction. Churches and schools appeared to have been the primary targets: on one occasion, as evidenced by some charred steel equipment that could have come only from an operating theatre, they passed by a small cottage hospital that had been so razed to the ground that no part of the resulting ruins was more than three feet high. Mallory wondered what would have happened to the patients occupying the hospital at the time: but he no longer wondered at the hundreds of thousands of Yugoslavs – 350,000 had been the figure quoted by Captain Jensen, but, taking women and children into account, the number must have been at least a million – who had rallied under the banner of Marshal Tito. Patriotism apart, the burning desire for liberation and revenge apart, there was no place else left for them to go. They were a people, Mallory realized, with literally nothing left, with nothing to lose but their lives which they apparently held of small account, but with everything to gain by the destruction of the enemy: were he a German soldier, Mallory reflected, he would not have felt particularly happy about the prospect of a posting to Yugoslavia. It was a war which the Wehrmacht could never win, which the soldiers of no Western European country could ever have won, for the peoples of the high mountains are virtually indestructible.

The Bosnian scouts, Mallory observed, looked neither to left nor right as they passed through the lifeless shattered villages of their countrymen, most of whom were now almost certainly dead. They didn't *have* to look, he realized: they had their memories, and even their memories would be too much for them. If it were possible to feel pity for an enemy, then Mallory at that moment felt pity for the Germans.

By and by they emerged from the narrow winding mountain track on to a narrow, but comparatively wide road, wide enough, at least, for single-file vehicular traffic. The Bosnian scout in the lead threw up his hand and halted his pony.

'Unofficial no-man's-land, it would seem.' Mallory said. 'I think this is where they turfed us off the truck this morning.'

Mallory's guess appeared to be correct. The Partisans wheeled their horses, smiled widely, waved, shouted some unintelligible words of farewell and urged their horses back the way they had come.

With Mallory and Andrea in the lead and the two sergeants bringing up the rear, the seven remaining members of the party moved off down the track. The snow had stopped now, the clouds above had cleared away and the sunlight was filtering down between the now thinning pines. Suddenly Andrea, who had been peering to his left, reached out and touched Mallory on the arm. Mallory followed the direction of Andrea's pointing hand. Downhill, the pines petered out less than a hundred yards away and through the trees could be glimpsed some distant object, a startling green in colour. Mallory swung round in his saddle.

'Down there. I want to take a look. *Don't* move below the tree-line.'

The ponies picked their delicate sure-footed way down the steep and slippery slope. About ten yards from the tree-line and at a signal from Mallory, the riders dismounted and advanced cautiously on foot, moving from the cover of one pine to the next. The last few feet they covered on hands and knees, then finally stretched out flat in the partial concealment of the boles of the lowermost pines. Mallory brought out his binoculars, cleared the cold-clouded lenses and brought them to his eyes.

The snow-line, he saw, petered out some three or four hundred yards below them. Below that again was a mixture of fissured and eroded rock-faces and brown earth and beyond that again a belt of sparse and discouraged-looking grass. Along the lower reaches of this belt of grass ran a tarmacadam road, a road which struck Mallory as being, for that area, in remarkably good condition: the road was more or less exactly paralleled, at a distance of about a hundred yards, by a single-track and extremely narrow-gauge railway: a grass-grown and rusted line that looked as if it hadn't been used for many years. Just beyond the line the land dropped in a precipitous cliff to a narrow winding lake, the farther margin of which was marked by far more towering precipices leading up without break and with hardly any variation in angle to rugged snow-capped mountains.

From where he lay Mallory was directly overlooking a right-angled bend in the lake, a lake which was almost incredibly beautiful. In the bright clear sparkling sunlight of that spring morning it glittered and gleamed like the purest of emeralds. The smooth surface was occasionally ruffled by errant catspaws of wind, catspaws which had the effect of deepening the emerald colour to an almost translucent aquamarine. The lake itself was nowhere much more than a quarter of a mile in width, but obviously miles in length: the long right-hand arm, twisting and turning between the mountains, stretched to the east almost as far as the eye could

see: to the left, the short southern arm, hemmed in by increasingly
vertical walls which finally appeared almost to meet overhead,
ended against the concrete ramparts of a dam. But what caught
and held the attention of the watchers was the incredible mirrored gleam of the far mountains in that equally incredible emerald mirror.

'Well, now,' Miller murmured, 'that *is* nice.' Andrea gave him a
long expressionless look, then turned his attention to the lake
again.

Groves's interest momentarily overcame his animosity.

'What lake is that, sir?'

Mallory lowered the binoculars. 'Haven't the faintest idea.
Maria?' She made no answer. 'Maria! What – lake – is – that?'

'That's the Neretva dam,' she said sullenly. 'The biggest in
Yugoslavia.'

'It's important, then?'

'It is important. Whoever controls that controls Central
Yugoslavia.'

'And the Germans control it, I suppose?'

'They control it. *We* control it.' There was more than a hint of tri-
umph in her smile. 'We – the Germans – have got it completely
sealed off. Cliffs on both sides. To the east there – the upper end –
they have a boom across a gorge only ten yards wide. And that
boom is patrolled night and day. So is the dam wall itself. The only
way in is by a set of steps – ladders, rather – fixed to the cliff-face
just below the dam.'

Mallory said drily: 'Very interesting information – for a parachute brigade. But we've other and more urgent fish to fry. Come
on.' He glanced at Miller, who nodded and began to ease his way
back up the slope, followed by the two sergeants, Maria and Petar.
Mallory and Andrea lingered for a few moments longer.

'I wonder what it's like,' Mallory murmured.

'What's what like?' Andrea said.

'The other side of the dam.'

'And the ladder let into the cliff?'

'And the ladder let into the cliff.'

From where General Vukalovic lay, high on a cliff-top on the right-
hand or western side of the Neretva gorge, he had an excellent
view of the ladder let into the cliff: he had, in fact, an excellent
view of the entire outer face of the dam wall and of the gorge

which began at the foot of the wall and extended southwards for almost a mile before vanishing from sight round an abrupt right-hand corner.

The dam wall itself was quite narrow, not much more than thirty yards in width, but very deep, stretching down in a slightly V-formation from between overhanging cliff-faces to the greenish-white torrent of water foaming from the outlet pipes at the base. On top of the dam, at the eastern end and on a slight eminence, were the control station and two small huts, one of which, judging from the clearly visible soldiers patrolling the top of the wall, was almost certainly a guard-room. Above those buildings the walls of the gorge rose quite vertically for about thirty feet, then jutted out in a terrifying overhang.

From the control-room, a zig-zag, green-painted iron ladder, secured by brackets to the rock-face, led down to the floor of the gorge. From the base of the ladder a narrow path extended down the gorge for a distance of about a hundred yards, ending abruptly at a spot where some ancient landslide had gouged a huge scar into the side of the gorge. From here a bridge spanned the river to another path on the right-hand bank.

As bridges go, it wasn't much, an obviously very elderly and rickety wooden swing bridge which looked as if its own weight would be enough to carry it into the torrent at any moment: what was even worse, it seemed, at first glance, as if its site had been deliberately picked by someone with an unhinged mind, for it lay directly below an enormous boulder some forty feet up the land-slide, a boulder so clearly in a highly precarious state of balance that none but the most foolhardy would have lingered in the cross-ing of the bridge. In point of fact, no other site would have been possible.

From the western edge of the bridge, the narrow, boulder-strewn path followed the line of the river, passing by what looked like an extremely hazardous ford, and finally curving away from sight with the river.

General Vukalovic lowered his binoculars, turned to the man at his side and smiled.

'All quiet on the eastern front, eh, Colonel Janzy?'

'All quiet on the eastern front,' Janzy agreed. He was a small, puckish, humorous-looking character with a youthful face and incongruous white hair. He twisted round and gazed to the north. 'But not so quiet on the northern front, I'm afraid.'

The smile faded from Vukalovic's face as he turned, lifted his binoculars again and gazed to the north. Less than three miles away and clearly visible in the morning sunlight, lay the heavily wooded Zenica Gap, for weeks a hotly contested strip of territory between Vukalovic's northern defensive forces, under the command of Colonel Janzy, and units of the invading German 11th Army Corps. At that moment frequent puffs of smoke could be seen, to the left a thick column of smoke spiralled up to form a dark pall against the now cloudless blue of the sky, while the distant rattle of small-arms fire, punctuated by the occasional heavier boom of artillery, was almost incessant. Vukalovic lowered his glasses and looked thoughtfully at Janzy.

'The softening-up before the main attack?'

'What else? The final assault.'

'How many tanks?'

'It's difficult to be sure. Collating reports, my staff estimate a hundred and fifty.'

'One hundred and fifty!'

'That's what they make it – and at least fifty of those are Tiger tanks.'

'Let's hope to heaven your staff can't count.' Vukalovic rubbed a weary hand across his bloodshot eyes: he'd had no sleep during the night just gone, no sleep during the night previous to that. 'Let's go and see how many *we* can count.'

Maria and Petar led the way now, with Reynolds and Groves, clearly in no mood for other company, bringing up the rear almost fifty yards behind. Mallory, Andrea and Miller rode abreast along the narrow road. Andrea looked at Mallory, his eyes speculative.

'Saunders's death? Any idea?'

Mallory shook his head. 'Ask me something else.'

'The message you'd given him to send. What was it?'

'A report of our safe arrival in Broznik's camp. Nothing more.'

'A psycho,' Miller announced. 'The handy man with the knife, I mean. Only a psycho would kill for that reason.'

'Maybe he didn't kill for that reason,' Mallory said mildly. 'Maybe he thought it was some other kind of message.'

'Some other kind of message?' Miller lifted an eyebrow in the way that only he knew how. 'Now what kind –' He caught Andrea's eye, broke off and changed his mind about saying anything more. Both he and Andrea gazed curiously at Mallory who seemed to have fallen into a mood of intense introspection.

Whatever its reason, the period of deep preoccupation did not last for long. With the air of a man who has just arrived at a conclusion about something, Mallory lifted his head and called to Maria to stop, at the same time reining in his own pony. Together they waited until Reynolds and Groves had made up on them.

'There are a good number of options open to us,' Mallory said, 'but for better or worse this is what I have decided to do.' He smiled faintly. 'For better, I think, if for no other reason than that this is the course of action that will get us out of here fastest. I've talked to Major Broznik and found out what I wanted. He tells me –'

'Got your information for Neufeld, then, have you?' If Reynolds was attempting to mask the contempt in his voice he made a singularly poor job of it.

'The hell with Neufeld,' Mallory said without heat. 'Partisan spies have discovered where the four captured Allied agents are being held.'

'They have?' Reynolds said. 'Then why don't the Partisans do something about it?'

'For a good enough reason. The agents are held deep in German territory. In an impregnable block-house high up in the mountains.'

'And what are *we* going to do about the Allied agents held in this impregnable block-house?'

'Simple.' Mallory corrected himself. 'Well, in theory it's simple. We take them out of there and make our break tonight.'

Reynolds and Groves stared at Mallory, then at each other in frank disbelief and consternation. Andrea and Miller carefully avoided looking at each other or at anyone else.

'You're mad!' Reynolds spoke with total conviction.

'You're mad, *sir,*' Andrea said reprovingly.

Reynolds looked uncomprehendingly at Andrea, then turned back to Mallory again.

'You must be!' he insisted. 'Break? Break for where, in heaven's name?'

'For home. For Italy.'

'Italy!' It took Reynolds all of ten seconds to digest this startling piece of information, then he went on sarcastically: 'We're going to fly there, I suppose?'

'Well, it's a long swim across the Adriatic, even for a fit youngster like you. How else?'

'Flying?' Groves seemed slightly dazed.

'Flying. Not ten kilometres from here is a high – a very high mountain plateau, mostly in Partisan hands. There'll be a plane there at nine o'clock tonight.'

In the fashion of people who have failed to grasp something they have just heard, Groves repeated the statement in the form of a question. 'There'll be a plane there at nine o'clock tonight? You've just arranged this?'

'How could I? We've no radio.'

Reynolds's distrustful face splendidly complemented the scepticism in his voice. 'But *how* can you be sure – well, at nine o'clock?'

'Because, starting at six o'clock this evening, there'll be a Wellington bomber over the airstrip every three hours for the next week if necessary.'

Mallory kneed his pony and the party moved on, Reynolds and Groves taking up their usual position well to the rear of the others. For some time Reynolds, his expression alternating between hostility and speculation, stared fixedly at Mallory's back: then he turned to Groves.

'Well, well, well. Isn't that very convenient indeed. We just *happen* to be sent to Broznik's camp. He just *happens* to know where the four agents are held. It just *happens* that an airplane will be over a certain airfield at a certain time – and it also so happens that I know for an absolute certainty that there are no airfields up in the high plateau. Still think everything clean and above-board?'

It was quite obvious from the unhappy expression on Groves's face that he thought nothing of the kind. He said: 'What in God's name are we going to do?'

'Watch our backs.'

Fifty yards ahead of them Miller cleared his throat and said delicately to Mallory: 'Reynolds seems to have lost some of his – um – earlier confidence in you, sir.'

Mallory said drily: 'It's not surprising. He thinks I stuck that knife in Saunders's back.'

This time Andrea and Miller did exchange glances, their faces registering expressions as close to pure consternation as either of those poker-faced individuals was capable of achieving.

SEVEN

Friday
1000–1200

Half a mile from Neufeld's camp they were met by Captain Droshny and some half-dozen of his Cetniks. Droshny's welcome was noticeably lacking in cordiality but at least he managed, at what unknown cost, to maintain some semblance of inoffensive neutrality.

'So you came back?'

'As you can see,' Mallory agreed.

Droshny looked at the ponies. 'And travelling in comfort.'

'A present from our good friend Major Broznik.' Mallory grinned. 'He thinks we're heading for Konjic on them.'

Droshny didn't appear to care very much what Major Broznik had thought. He jerked his head, wheeled his horse and set off at a fast trot for Neufeld's camp.

When they had dismounted inside the compound, Droshny immediately led Mallory into Neufeld's hut. Neufeld's welcome, like Droshny's, was something less than ecstatic, but at least he succeeded in imparting a shade more benevolence to his neutrality. His face held, also, just a hint of surprise, a reaction which he explained at once.

'Candidly, Captain, I did not expect to see you again. There were so many – ah – imponderables. However, I am delighted to see you – you would not have returned without the information I wanted. Now then, Captain Mallory, to business.'

Mallory eyed Neufeld without enthusiasm. 'You're not a very business-like partner, I'm afraid.'

'I'm not?' Neufeld said politely. 'In what way?'

'Business partners don't tell lies to each other. Sure you said Vukalovic's troops are massing. So they are indeed. But not, as you said, to break out. Instead, they're massing to defend themselves against the final German attack, the assault that is to crush them once and for all, and this assault they believe to be imminent.'

'Well, now, you surely didn't expect me to give away our military secrets – which you might, I say just might, have relayed to the enemy – before you had proved yourselves,' Neufeld said reasonably. 'You're not that naïve. About this proposed attack. Who gave you the information?'

'Major Broznik.' Mallory smiled in recollection. 'He was very expansive.'

Neufeld leaned forward, his tension reflected in the sudden stillness of his face, in the way his unblinking eyes held Mallory's. 'And did they say where they expected this attack to come?'

'I only know the name. The bridge at Neretva.'

Neufeld sank back into his chair, exhaled a long soundless sigh of relief and smiled to rob his next words of any offence. 'My friend, if you weren't British, a deserter, a renegade and a dope-peddler, you'd get the Iron Cross for this. By the way,' he went on, as if by casual afterthought, 'you've been cleared from Padua. The bridge at Neretva? You're sure of this?'

Mallory said irritably: 'If you doubt my word –'

'Of course not, of course not. Just a manner of speaking.' Neufeld paused for a few moments, then said softly: 'The bridge at Neretva.' The way he spoke them, the words sounded almost like a litany.

Droshny said softly: 'This fits in with all we suspected.'

'Never mind what you suspected,' Mallory said rudely. 'To *my* business now, if you don't mind. We have done well, you would say? We have fulfilled your request, got the precise information you wanted?' Neufeld nodded. 'Then get us the hell out of here. Fly us deep into some German-held territory. Into Austria or Germany itself, if you like – the farther away from here the better. You know what will happen to us if we ever again fall into British or Yugoslav hands?'

'It's not hard to guess,' Neufeld said almost cheerfully. 'But you misjudge us, my friend. Your departure to a place of safety has already been arranged. A certain Chief of Military Intelligence in northern Italy would very much like to make your personal acquaintance. He has reason to believe that you can be of great help to him.'

Mallory nodded his understanding.

General Vukalovic trained his binoculars on the Zenica Gap, a narrow and heavily-wooded valley floor lying between the bases of two high and steep-shouldered mountains, mountains almost identical in both shape and height.

The German 11th Army Corps tanks among the pines were not difficult to locate, for the Germans had made no attempt either to camouflage or conceal them, measure enough, Vukalovic thought grimly, of the Germans' total confidence in themselves and in the outcome of the battle that lay ahead. He could clearly see soldiers working on some stationary vehicles: other tanks were backing and filling and manoeuvring into position as if making ready to take up battle formation for the actual attack: the deep rumbling roar of the heavy engines of Tiger tanks was almost incessant.

Vukalovic lowered his glasses, jotted down a few more pencil marks on a sheet of paper already almost covered with similar pencil marks, performed a few exercises in addition, laid paper and pencil aside with a sigh and turned to Colonel Janzy, who was similarly engaged.

Vukalovic said wryly: 'My apologies to your staff, Colonel. They can count just as well as I can.'

For once, Captain Jensen's piratical swagger and flashing, confident smile were not very much in evidence: at that moment, in fact, they were totally absent. It would have been impossible for a face of Jensen's generous proportions ever to assume an actually haggard appearance, but the set, grim face displayed unmistakable signs of strain and anxiety and sleeplessness as he paced up and down the 5th Army Operations Headquarters in Termoli in Italy.

He did not pace alone. Beside him, matching him step for step, a burly grey-haired officer in the uniform of a lieutenant-general in the British Army accompanied him backwards and forwards, the expression on his face an exact replica of that on Jensen's. As they came to the farther end of the room, the General stopped and glanced interrogatively at a head-phone-wearing sergeant in front of a large RCA transceiver. The sergeant slowly shook his head. The two men resumed their pacing.

The General said abruptly: 'Time is running out. You do appreciate, Jensen, that once you launch a major offensive you can't possibly stop it?'

'I appreciate it,' Jensen said heavily. 'What are the latest reconnaissance reports, sir?'

'There is no shortage of reports, but God alone knows what to make of them all.' The General sounded bitter. 'There's intense activity all along the Gustav Line, involving – as far as we can make out – two Panzer divisions, one German infantry division, one Austrian infantry division and two Jaeger battalions – their crack Alpine troops. They're not mounting an offensive, that's for sure – in the first place, there's no possibility of their making an offensive from the areas in which they are manoeuvring and in the second place if they *were* contemplating an offensive they'd take damn good care to keep all their preparations secret.'

'All this activity, then? If they're not planning an attack.'

The General sighed. 'Informed opinion has it that they're making all preparations for a lightning pull-out. Informed opinion! All that concerns me is that those blasted divisions are still in the Gustav Line. Jensen, *what has gone wrong*?'

Jensen lifted his shoulders in a gesture of helplessness. 'It was arranged for a radio rendezvous every two hours from four a.m. –'

'There have been no contacts whatsoever.'

Jensen said nothing.

The General looked at him, almost speculatively. 'The best in Southern Europe, you said.'

'Yes, I did say that.'

The General's unspoken doubts as to the quality of the agents Jensen had selected for operation Force 10 would have been considerably heightened if he had been at that moment present with those agents in the guest hut in Hauptmann Neufeld's camp in Bosnia. They were exhibiting none of the harmony, understanding and implicit mutual trust which one would have expected to find among a team of agents rated as the best in the business. There was, instead, tension and anger in the air, an air of suspicion and mistrust so heavy as to be almost palpable. Reynolds, confronting Mallory, had his anger barely under control.

'I want to know now!' Reynolds almost shouted the words.

'Keep your voice down,' Andrea said sharply.

'I want to know now,' Reynolds repeated. This time his voice was little more than a whisper, but none the less demanding and insistent for that.

'You'll be told when the time comes.' As always, Mallory's voice was calm and neutral and devoid of heat. 'Not till then. What you don't know, you can't tell.'

Reynolds clenched his fists and advanced a step. 'Are you damn well insinuating that –'

Mallory said with restraint: 'I'm insinuating nothing. I was right, back in Termoli, Sergeant. You're no better than a ticking time-bomb.'

'Maybe.' Reynolds's fury was out of control now. 'But at least there's something honest about a bomb.'

'Repeat that remark,' Andrea said quietly.

'What?'

'Repeat it.'

'Look, Andrea –'

'Colonel Stavros, sonny.'

'Sir.'

'Repeat it and I'll guarantee you a minimum of five years for insubordination in the field.'

'Yes, sir.' Reynolds's physical effort to bring himself under control was apparent to everyone. 'But *why* should he *not* tell us his plans for this afternoon and at the same time let us all know that we'll be leaving from this Ivenici place tonight?'

'Because our plans are something the Germans can do something about,' Andrea said patiently. 'If they find out. If one of us talked under duress. But they can't do anything about Ivenici – that's in Partisan hands.'

Miller pacifically changed the subject. He said to Mallory: 'Seven thousand feet up, you say. The snow must be thigh-deep up there. How in God's name does anyone hope to clear all that lot away?'

'I don't know,' Mallory said vaguely. 'I suspect somebody will think of something.'

And seven thousand feet up on the Ivenici plateau, somebody had indeed thought of something.

The Ivenici plateau was a wilderness in white, a bleak and desolate and, for many months of the year, a bitterly cold and howling and hostile wilderness, totally inimical to human life, totally intolerant of human presence. The plateau was bounded to the west by a five-hundred-foot-high cliff-face, quite vertical in some parts, fractured and fissured in others. Scattered along its length were numerous frozen waterfalls and occasional lines of pine trees, impossibly growing on impossibly narrow ledges, their frozen branches drooped and laden with the frozen snow of six long months gone by. To the east the plateau was bounded by nothing but an abrupt and sharply defined line marking the top of another cliff-face which dropped away perpendicularly into the valleys below.

The plateau itself consisted of a smooth, absolutely level, unbroken expanse of snow, snow which at that height of 2,000 metres and in the brilliant sunshine gave off a glare and dazzling reflection which was positively hurtful to the eyes. In length, it was perhaps half a mile: in width, nowhere more than a hundred yards. At its southern end, the plateau rose sharply to merge with the cliff-face which here tailed off and ran into the ground.

On this prominence stood two tents, both white, one small, the other a large marquee. Outside the small tent stood two men, talking. The taller and older man, wearing a heavy greatcoat and a pair of smoked glasses, was Colonel Vis, the commandant of a Sarajevo-based brigade of Partisans: the younger, slighter figure was his adjutant, a Captain Vlanovich. Both men were gazing out over the length of the plateau.

Captain Vlanovich said unhappily: 'There must be easier ways of doing this, sir.'

'You name it, Boris, my boy, and I'll do it.' Both in appearance and voice Colonel Vis gave the impression of immense calm and competence. 'Bull-dozers, I agree, would help. So would snow-ploughs. But you will agree that to drive either of them up vertical cliff-faces in order to reach here would call for considerable skill on the part of the drivers. Besides, what's an army for, if not for marching?'

'Yes, sir,' Vlanovich said, dutifully and doubtfully.

Both men gazed out over the length of the plateau to the north.

To the north, and beyond, for all around a score of encircling mountain peaks, some dark and jagged and sombre, others rounded and snow-capped and rose-coloured, soared up into the cloudless washed-out pale blue of the sky. It was an immensely impressive sight.

Even more impressive was the spectacle taking place on the plateau itself. A solid phalanx of a thousand uniformed soldiers, perhaps half in the buff grey of the Yugoslav army, the rest in a motley array of other countries' uniforms, were moving, at a snail-pace, across the virgin snow.

The phalanx was fifty people wide but only twenty deep, each line of fifty linked arm-in-arm, heads and shoulders bowed forward as they laboriously trudged at a painfully slow pace through the snow. That the pace was so slow was no matter for wonder, the leading line of men were ploughing their way through waist-deep snow, and already the signs of strain and exhaustion were showing in their faces. It was killingly hard work, work which, at that altitude, doubled the pulse rate, made a man fight for every gasping breath, turned a man's legs into leaden and agonized limbs where only the pain could convince him that they were still part of him.

And not only men. After the first five lines of soldiers, there were almost as many women and girls in the remainder of the phalanx as there were men, although everyone was so muffled against the freezing cold and biting winds of those high altitudes that it was impossible almost to tell man from woman. The last two lines of the phalanx were composed entirely of *partisankas* and it was significantly ominous of the murderous labour still to come that even they were sinking knee-deep in the snow.

It was a fantastic sight, but a sight that was far from unique in wartime Yugoslavia. The airfields of the lowlands, completely dominated by the armoured divisions of the Wehrmacht, were permanently barred to the Yugoslavs and it was thus that the Partisans constructed many of their airstrips in the mountains. In snow of this depth and in areas completely inaccessible to powered mechanical aids, there was no other way open to them.

Colonel Vis looked away and turned to Captain Vlanovich.

'Well, Boris, my boy, do you think you're up here for the winter sports? Get the food and soup kitchens organized. We'll use up a whole week's rations of hot food and hot soup in this one day.'

'Yes, sir.' Vlanovich cocked his head, then removed his ear-flapped fur cap the better to listen to the newly-begun sound of distant explosions to the north. 'What on earth is that?'

Vis said musingly: 'Sound does carry far in our pure Yugoslavian mountain air, does it not?'

'Sir? Please?'

'That, my boy,' Vis said with considerable satisfaction, 'is the Messerschmitt fighter base at Novo Derventa getting the biggest plastering of its lifetime.'

'Sir?'

Vis sighed in long-suffering patience. 'I'll make a soldier of you some day. Messerschmitts, Boris, are fighters, carrying all sorts of nasty cannons and machine-guns. What, at this moment, is the finest fighter target in Yugoslavia?'

'What is –' Vlanovich broke off and looked again at the trudging phalanx. 'Oh!'

'"Oh," indeed. The British Air Force have diverted six of their best Lancaster heavy bomber squadrons from the Italian front just to attend to our friends at Novo Derventa.' He in turn removed his cap, the better to listen. 'Hard at work, aren't they? By the time they're finished there won't be a Messerschmitt able to take off from that field for a week. If, that is to say, there are any left to take off.'

'If I might venture a remark, sir?'

'You may so venture, Captain Vlanovich.'

'There are other fighter bases.'

'True.' Vis pointed upwards. 'See anything?'

Vlanovich craned his neck, shielded his eyes against the brilliant sun, gazed into the empty blue sky and shook his head.

'Neither do I,' Vis agreed. 'But at seven thousand metres – and with their crews even colder than we are – squadrons of Beaufighters will be keeping relief patrol up there until dark.'

'Who – who *is* he, sir? Who can ask for all our soldiers down here, for squadrons of bombers and fighters?'

'Fellow called Captain Mallory, I believe.'

'A *captain?* Like me?'

'A captain. I doubt, Boris,' Vis went on kindly, 'whether he's quite like you. But it's not the rank that counts. It's the name. Mallory.'

'Never heard of him.'

'You will, my boy, you will.'

'But – but this man Mallory. What does he want all this *for?'*

'Ask him when you see him tonight.'

'When I – he's coming here tonight?'

'Tonight. If,' Vis added sombrely, 'he lives that long.'

Neufeld, followed by Droshny, walked briskly and confidently into his radio hut, a bleak, ramshackle lean-to furnished with a table, two chairs, a large portable transceiver and nothing else. The German corporal seated before the radio looked up enquiringly at their entrance.

'The Seventh Armoured Corps HQ at the Neretva bridge,' Neufeld ordered. He seemed in excellent spirits. 'I wish to speak to General Zimmermann personally.'

The corporal nodded acknowledgment, put through the call-sign and was answered within seconds. He listened briefly, looked up at Neufeld. 'The General is coming now, sir.'

Neufeld reached out a hand for the ear-phones, took them and nodded towards the door. The corporal rose and left the hut while

Neufeld took the vacated seat and adjusted the head-phones to his satisfaction. After a few seconds he automatically straightened in his seat as a voice came crackling over the ear-phones.

'Hauptmann Neufeld here, Herr General. The Englishmen have returned. Their information is that the Partisan division in the Zenica Cage is expecting a full-scale attack from the south across the Neretva bridge.'

'Are they now?' General Zimmermann, comfortably seated in a swivel chair in the back of the radio truck parked on the tree-line due south of the Neretva bridge, made no attempt to conceal the satisfaction in his voice. The canvas hood of the truck was rolled back and he removed his peaked cap the better to enjoy the pale spring sunshine. 'Interesting, very interesting. Anything else?'

'Yes,' Neufeld's voice crackled metallically over the loudspeaker. 'They've asked to be flown to sanctuary. Deep behind our lines, even to Germany. They feel – ah – unsafe here.'

'Well, well, well. Is that how they feel.' Zimmermann paused, considered, then continued. 'You are fully informed of the situation, Hauptmann Neufeld? You are aware of the delicate balance of – um – niceties involved?'

'Yes, Herr General.'

'This calls for a moment's thought. Wait.'

Zimmermann swung idly to and fro in his swivel chair as he pondered his decision. He gazed thoughtfully but almost unseeingly to the north, across the meadows bordering the south bank of the Neretva, the river spanned by the iron bridge, then the meadows on the far side rising steeply to the rocky redoubt which served as the first line of defence for Colonel Lazlo's Partisan defenders. To the east, as he turned, he could look up the green-white rushing waters of the Neretva, the meadows on either side of it narrowing until, curving north, they disappeared suddenly at the mouth of the cliff-sided gorge from which the Neretva emerged. Another quarter turn and he was gazing into the pine forest to the south, a pine forest which at first seemed innocuous enough and empty of life – until, that was, one's eyes became accustomed to the gloom and scores of large rectangular shapes, effectively screened from both observation from the air and from the northern bank of the Neretva by camouflage canvas, camouflage nets and huge piles of dead branches. The sight of those camouflaged spearheads of his two Panzer divisions somehow helped Zimmermann to make up his mind. He picked up the microphone.

'Hauptmann Neufeld? I have decided on a course of action and you will please carry out the following instructions precisely . . .'

Droshny removed the duplicate pair of earphones that he had been wearing and said doubtfully to Neufeld: 'Isn't the general asking rather a lot of us?'

Neufeld shook his head reassuringly. 'General Zimmermann *always* knows what he is doing. His psychological assessment of the Captain Mallorys of this world is invariably a hundred per cent right.'

'I hope so.' Droshny was unconvinced. 'For our sakes, I hope so.'

They left the hut. Neufeld said to the radio operator: 'Captain Mallory in my office, please. And Sergeant Baer.'

Mallory arrived in the office to find Neufeld, Droshny and Baer already there. Neufeld was brief and businesslike.

'We've decided on a ski-plane to fly you out – they're the only planes that can land in those damned mountains. You'll have time for a few hours' sleep – we don't leave till four. Any questions?'

'Where's the landing-strip?'

'A clearing. A kilometre from here. Anything else?'

'Nothing. Just get us out of here, that's all.'

'You need have no worry on that score,' Neufeld said emphatically. 'My one ambition is to see you safely on your way. Frankly, Mallory, you're just an embarrassment to me and the sooner you're on your way the better.'

Mallory nodded and left. Neufeld turned to Baer and said: 'I have a little task for you, Sergeant Baer. Little but very important. Listen carefully.'

Mallory left Neufeld's hut, his face pensive, and walked slowly across the compound. As he approached the guest hut, Andrea emerged and passed wordlessly by, wreathed in cigar smoke and scowling. Mallory entered the hut where Petar was again playing the Yugoslavian version of 'The girl I left behind me'. It seemed to be his favourite song. Mallory glanced at Maria, Reynolds and Groves, all sitting silently by, then at Miller who was reclining in his sleeping-bag with his volume of poetry.

Mallory nodded towards the doorway. 'Something's upset our friend.'

Miller grinned and nodded in turn towards Petar. 'He's playing Andrea's tune again.'

Mallory smiled briefly and turned to Maria. 'Tell him to stop playing. We're pulling out late this afternoon and we all need all the sleep we can get.'

'We can sleep in the plane,' Reynolds said sullenly. 'We can sleep when we arrive at our destination – wherever that may be.'

'No, sleep now.'

'Why now?'

'Why now?' Mallory's unfocused eyes gazed into the far distance. He said in a quiet voice: 'For now is all the time there may be.'

Reynolds looked at him strangely. For the first time that day his face was empty of hostility and suspicion. There was puzzled speculation in his eyes, and wonder and the first faint beginnings of understanding.

On the Ivenici plateau, the phalanx moved on, but they moved no more like human beings. They stumbled along now in the advanced stages of exhaustion, automatons, no more, zombies resurrected from the dead, their faces twisted with pain and unimaginable fatigue, their limbs on fire and their minds benumbed. Every few seconds someone stumbled and fell and could not get up again and had to be carried to join scores of others already lying in an almost comatose condition by the side of the primitive runway, where *partisankas* did their best to revive their frozen and exhausted bodies with mugs of hot soup and liberal doses of *raki*.

Captain Vlanovich turned to Colonel Vis. His face was distressed, his voice low and deeply earnest.

'This is madness, Colonel, madness! It's – it's impossible, you can see it's impossible. We'll never – look, sir, two hundred and fifty dropped out in the first two hours. The altitude, the cold, sheer physical exhaustion. It's madness.'

'All war is madness,' Vis said calmly. 'Get on the radio. We require five hundred more men.'

EIGHT

Friday
1500–2115

Now it had come, Mallory knew. He looked at Andrea and Miller and Reynolds and Groves and knew that they knew it too. In their faces he could see very clearly reflected what lay at the very surface of his own mind, the explosive tension, the hair-trigger alertness straining to be translated into equally explosive action. Always it came, this moment of truth that stripped men bare and showed them for what they were. He wondered how Reynolds and Groves would be: he suspected they might acquit themselves well. It never occurred to him to wonder about Miller and Andrea, for he knew them too well: Miller, when all seemed lost, was a man above himself, while the normally easy-going, almost lethargic Andrea was transformed into an unrecognizable human being, an impossible combination of an icily calculating mind and berserker fighting machine entirely without the remotest parallel in Mallory's knowledge or experience. When Mallory spoke his voice was as calmly impersonal as ever.

'We're due to leave at four. It's now three. With any luck we'll catch them napping. Is everything clear?'

Reynolds said wonderingly, almost unbelievingly: 'You mean if anything goes wrong we're to shoot our way out?'

'You're to shoot and shoot to kill. That, Sergeant, is an order.'

'Honest to God,' Reynolds said, 'I just don't know what's going on.' The expression on his face clearly indicated that he had given up all attempts to understand what was going on.

Mallory and Andrea left the hut and walked casually across the compound towards Neufeld's hut. Mallory said: 'They're on to us, you know.'

'I know. Where are Petar and Maria?'

'Asleep, perhaps? They left the hut a couple of hours ago. We'll collect them later.'

'Later may be too late . . . They are in great peril, my Keith.'

'What can a man do, Andrea? I've thought of nothing else in the past ten hours. It's a crucifying risk to have to take, but I have to take it. They are expendable, Andrea. You know what it would mean if I showed my hand now.'

'I know what it would mean,' Andrea said heavily. 'The end of everything.'

They entered Neufeld's hut without benefit of knocking. Neufeld, sitting behind his desk with Droshny by his side, looked up in irritated surprise and glanced at his watch.

He said curtly: 'Four o'clock, I said, not three.'

'Our mistake,' Mallory apologized. He closed the door. 'Please do not be foolish.'

Neufeld and Droshny were not foolish, few people would have been while staring down the muzzles of two Lugers with perforated silencers screwed to the end: they just sat there, immobile, the shock slowly draining from their faces. There was a long pause then Neufeld spoke, the words coming almost haltingly.

'I have been seriously guilty of underestimating –'

'Be quiet. Broznik's spies have discovered the whereabouts of the four captured Allied agents. We know roughly where they are. You know precisely where they are. You will take us there. Now.'

'You're mad,' Neufeld said with conviction.

'We don't require you to tell us that.' Andrea walked round behind Neufeld and Droshny, removed their pistols from their holsters, ejected the shells and replaced the pistols. He then crossed to a corner of the hut, picked up two Schmeisser machine-pistols, emptied them, walked back round to the front of the table and placed the Schmeissers on its top, one in front of Neufeld, one in front of Droshny.

'There you are, gentlemen,' Andrea said affably. 'Armed to the teeth.'

Droshny said viciously: 'Suppose we decide not to come with you?'

Andrea's affability vanished. He walked unhurriedly round the table and rammed the Luger's silencer with such force against Droshny's teeth that he gasped in pain. 'Please –' Andrea's voice was almost beseeching – '*please* don't tempt me.'

Droshny didn't tempt him. Mallory moved to the window and peered out over the compound. There were, he saw, at least a dozen Cetniks within thirty feet of Neufeld's hut, all of them armed. Across the other side of the compound he could see that the door to the stables was open indicating that Miller and the two sergeants were in position.

'You will walk across the compound to the stables,' Mallory said. 'You will talk to nobody, warn nobody, make no signals. We will follow about ten yards behind.'

'Ten yards behind. What's to prevent us making a break for it? You wouldn't dare hold a gun on us out there.'

'That's so,' Mallory agreed. 'From the moment you open this door you'll be covered by three Schmeissers from the stables. If you try anything – *anything* – you'll be cut to pieces. That's why we're keeping well behind you – we don't want to be cut to pieces too.'

At a gesture from Andrea, Neufeld and Droshny slung their empty Schmeissers in angry silence. Mallory looked at them consideringly and said: 'I think you'd better do something about your expressions. They're a dead giveaway that something is wrong. If you open that door with faces like that, Miller will cut you down before you reach the bottom step. Please try to believe me.'

They believed him and by the time Mallory opened the door had managed to arrange their features into a near enough imitation of normality. They went down the steps and set off across the compound to the stables. When they had reached halfway Andrea and Mallory left Neufeld's hut and followed them. One or two glances of idle curiosity came their way, but clearly no one suspected that anything was amiss. The crossing to the stables was completely uneventful.

So also, two minutes later, was their departure from the camp. Neufeld and Droshny, as would have been proper and expected, rode together in the lead, Droshny in particular looking very warlike with his Schmeisser, pistol and the wickedly-curved knives at his waist. Behind them rode Andrea, who appeared to be having some trouble with the action of his Schmeisser, for he had it in his hands and was examining it closely: he certainly wasn't looking at either Droshny or Neufeld and the fact that the gun barrel, which Andrea had sensibly pointed towards the ground, had only to be lifted a foot and the trigger pressed to riddle the two men ahead was a preposterous idea that would not have occurred to even the most suspicious. Behind Andrea, Mallory and Miller rode abreast: like Andrea, they appeared unconcerned, even slightly bored. Reynolds and Groves brought up the rear, almost but not quite attaining the degree of nonchalance of the other three: their still faces and restlessly darting eyes betrayed the strain they were under. But their anxiety was needless for all seven passed from the camp not only unmolested but without as much as even an enquiring glance being cast in their direction.

They rode for over two and a half hours, climbing nearly all the time, and a blood-red sun was setting among the thinning pines to the west when they came across a clearing set on, for once, a level stretch of ground. Neufeld and Droshny halted their ponies and waited until the others came up with them. Mallory reined in and gazed at the building in the middle of the clearing, a low, squat, immensely strong-looking block-house, with narrow, heavily barred windows and two chimneys, from one of which smoke was coming.

'This is the place?' Mallory asked.

'Hardly a necessary question.' Neufeld's voice was dry, but the underlying resentment and anger unmistakable. 'You think I spent all this time leading you to the wrong place?'

'I wouldn't put it past you,' Mallory said. He examined the building more closely. 'A hospitable-looking place.'

'Yugoslav Army ammunition dumps were never intended as first-class hotels.'

'I dare say not,' Mallory agreed. At a signal from him they urged their ponies forward into the clearing, and as they did so two metal strips in the facing wall of the block-house slid back to reveal a pair of embrasures with machine-pistols protruding. Exposed as they were, the seven mounted men were completely at the mercy of those menacing muzzles.

'Your men keep a good watch,' Mallory acknowledged to Neufeld. 'You wouldn't require many men to guard and hold a place like this. How many are there?'

'Six,' Neufeld said reluctantly.

'Seven and you're a dead man,' Andrea warned.

'Six.'

As they approached, the guns – almost certainly because the men behind them had identified Neufeld and Droshny – were withdrawn, the embrasures closed, the heavy metal front door opened. A sergeant appeared in the doorway and saluted respectfully, his face registering a certain surprise.

'An unexpected pleasure, Hauptmann Neufeld,' the sergeant said. 'We had no radio message informing us of your arrival.'

'It's out of action for the moment.' Neufeld waved them inside but Andrea gallantly insisted on the German officer taking precedence, reinforcing his courtesy with a threatening hitch of his Schmeisser. Neufeld entered, followed by Droshny and the other five men.

The windows were so narrow that the burning oil lamps were obviously a necessity, the illumination they afforded being almost doubled by a large log fire blazing in the hearth. Nothing could ever overcome the bleakness created by four rough-cut stone walls, but the room itself was surprisingly well furnished with a table, chairs, two armchairs and a sofa: there were even some pieces of carpet. Three doors led off from the room, one heavily barred. Including the sergeant who had welcomed them, there were three armed soldiers in the room. Mallory glanced at Neufeld who nodded, his face tight in suppressed anger.

Neufeld said to one of the guards: 'Bring out the prisoners.' The guard nodded, lifted a heavy key from the wall and headed for the barred door. The sergeant and the other guard were sliding the metal screens back across the embrasures. Andrea walked casually towards the nearest guard, then suddenly and violently shoved him against the sergeant. Both men cannoned into the guard who had just inserted the key into the door. The third man fell heavily to the ground: the other two, though staggering wildly, managed to retain a semblance of balance or at least remain on their feet. All three twisted round to stare at Andrea, anger and startled incomprehension in their faces, and all three remained very still, and wisely so. Faced with a Schmeisser machine-pistol at three paces, the wise man always remains still.

Mallory said to the sergeant: 'There are three other men. Where are they?'

There was no reply: the guard glared at him in defiance. Mallory repeated the question, this time in fluent German: the guard ignored him and looked questioningly at Neufeld, whose lips were tight-shut in a mask of stone.

'Are you mad?' Neufeld demanded of the sergeant. 'Can't you see those men are killers? Tell him.'

'The night guards. They're asleep.' The sergeant pointed to a door. 'That one.'

'Open it. Tell them to walk out. Backwards and with their hands clasped behind their necks.'

'Do exactly as you're told,' Neufeld ordered.

The sergeant did exactly what he was told and so did the three guards who had been resting in the inner room, who walked out as they had been instructed, with obviously no thought of any resistance in their minds. Mallory turned to the guard with the key who had by this time picked himself up somewhat shakily from the floor, and nodded to the barred door.

'Open it.'

The guard opened it and pushed the door wide. Four British officers moved out slowly and uncertainly into the outer room. Long confinement indoors had made them very pale, but apart from this prison pallor and the fact that they were rather thin they were obviously unharmed. The man in the lead, with a major's insignia and a Sandhurst moustache – and, when he spoke, a Sandhurst accent – stopped abruptly and stared in disbelief at Mallory and his men.

'Good God above! What on earth are you chaps –'

'Please.' Mallory cut him short. 'I'm sorry, but later. Collect your coats, whatever warm gear you have, and wait outside.'

'But – but where are you taking us?'

'Home. Italy. Tonight. Please hurry!'

'Italy. You're talking –'

'Hurry!' Mallory glanced in some exasperation at his watch. 'We're late already.'

As quickly as their dazed condition would allow, the four officers collected what warm clothing they had and filed outside. Mallory turned to the sergeant again. 'You must have ponies here, a stable.'

'Round the back of the block-house,' the sergeant said promptly. He had obviously made a rapid readjustment to the new facts of life.

'Good lad,' Mallory said approvingly. He looked at Groves and Reynolds. 'We'll need two more ponies. Saddle them up, will you?'

The two sergeants left. Under the watchful guns of Mallory and Miller, Andrea searched each of the six guards in turn, found nothing, and ushered them all into the cell, turning the heavy key and hanging it up on the wall. Then, just as carefully, Andrea searched Neufeld and Droshny: Droshny's face, as Andrea carelessly flung his knives into a corner of the room, was thunderous.

Mallory looked at the two men and said: 'I'd shoot you if necessary. It's not. You won't be missed before morning.'

'They might not be missed for a good few mornings,' Miller pointed out.

'So they're over-weight anyway,' Mallory said indifferently. He smiled. 'I can't resist leaving you with a last little pleasant thought, Hauptmann Neufeld. Something to think about until someone comes and finds you.' He looked consideringly at Neufeld, who said nothing, then went on: 'About that information I gave you this morning, I mean.'

Neufeld looked at him guardedly. 'What about the information you gave me this morning?'

'Just this. It wasn't, I'm afraid, quite accurate. Vukalovic expects the attack from the *north*, through the Zenica Gap, not across the bridge at Neretva from the south. There are, we know, close on two hundred of your tanks massed in the woods just to the north of the Zenica Gap – but there won't be at two a.m. this morning when your attack is due to start. Not after I've got through to our Lancaster squadrons in Italy. Think of it, think of the target. Two hundred tanks bunched in a tiny trap a hundred and fifty yards wide and not more than three hundred yards long. The RAF will be there at 1.30. By two this morning there won't be a single tank left in commission.'

Neufeld looked at him for a long moment, his face very still, then said, slowly and softly: 'Damn you! Damn you! Damn you!'

'Damning is all you'll have for it,' Mallory said agreeably. 'By the time you are released – hopefully assuming that you will be released – it will all be over. See you after the war.'

Andrea locked the two men in a side room and hung the key up by the one to the cell. Then they went outside, locked the outer door, hung the key on a nail by the door, mounted their ponies – Groves and Reynolds had already two additional ones saddled – and started climbing once again, Mallory, map in hand, studying in the fading light of dusk the route they had to take.

Their route took them up alongside the perimeter of a pine forest. Not more than half a mile after leaving the block-house, Andrea reined in his pony, dismounted, lifted the pony's right foreleg and examined it carefully. He looked up at the others who had also reined in their ponies.

'There's a stone wedged under the hoof,' he announced. 'Looks bad – but not too bad. I'll have to cut it out. Don't wait for me – I'll catch you up in a few minutes.'

Mallory nodded, gave the signal to move on. Andrea produced a knife, lifted the hoof and made a great play of excavating the wedged stone. After a minute or so, he glanced up and saw that the rest of the party had vanished round a corner of the pine wood. Andrea put away his knife and led the pony, which quite obviously had no limp whatsoever, into the shelter of the wood and tethered it there, then moved on foot some way down the hill towards the block-house. He sat down behind the bole of a convenient pine and removed his binoculars from their case.

He hadn't long to wait. The head and shoulders of a figure appeared in the clearing below peering out cautiously from behind the trunk of a tree. Andrea flat in the snow now and with the icy rims of the binoculars clamped hard against his eyes, had no difficulty at all in making an immediate identification: Sergeant Baer, moonfaced, rotund and about seventy pounds overweight for his unimpressive height, had an unmistakable physical presence which only the mentally incapacitated could easily forget.

Baer withdrew into the woods, then reappeared shortly afterwards leading a string of ponies, one of which carried a bulky covered object strapped to a pannier bag. Two of the following ponies had riders, both of whom had their hands tied to the pommels of their saddles. Petar and Maria, without a doubt. Behind them appeared four mounted soldiers. Sergeant Baer beckoned them to follow him across the clearing and within moments all had disappeared from sight behind the block-house. Andrea regarded the now empty clearing thoughtfully, lit a fresh cigar and made his way uphill towards his tethered pony.

Sergeant Baer dismounted, produced a key from his pocket, caught sight of the key suspended from the nail beside the door, replaced his own, took down the other, opened the door with it and passed inside. He glanced around, took down one of the keys hanging on the wall and opened a side door with it. Hauptmann Neufeld emerged, glanced at his watch and smiled.

'You have been very punctual, Sergeant Baer. You have the radio?'

'I have the radio. It's outside.'

'Good, good, good.' Neufeld looked at Droshny and smiled again. 'I think it's time for us to make our rendezvous with the Ivenici plateau.'

Sergeant Baer said respectfully: 'How can you be so sure that it is the Ivenici plateau, Hauptmann Neufeld?'

'How can I be so sure? Simple, my dear Baer. Because Maria – you have her with you?'

'But of course, Hauptmann Neufeld.'

'Because Maria told me. The Ivenici plateau it is.'

Night had fallen on the Ivenici plateau, but still the phalanx of exhausted soldiers was trudging out the landing-strip for the plane. The work was not by this time so cruelly and physically exacting, for the snow was now almost trampled and beaten hard and flat: but, even allowing for the rejuvenation given by the influx of another five hundred fresh soldiers, the overall level of utter weariness was such that the phalanx was in no better condition than its original members who had trudged out the first outline of the airstrip in the virgin snow.

The phalanx, too, had changed its shape. Instead of being fifty wide by twenty deep it was now twenty wide by fifty deep: having achieved a safe clearance for the wings of the aircraft, they were now trudging out what was to be as close as possible an iron-hard surface for the landing wheels.

A three-quarters moon, intensely white and luminous, rode low in the sky, with scattered bands of cloud coming drifting down slowly from the north. As the successive bands moved across the face of the moon, the black shadows swept lazily across the surface of the plateau: the phalanx, at one moment bathed in silvery moonlight, was at the next almost lost to sight in the darkness. It was a fantastic scene with a remarkably faery-like quality of eeriness and foreboding about it. In fact it was, as Colonel Vis had just unromantically mentioned to Captain Vlanovich, like something out of Dante's *Inferno*, only a hundred degrees colder. At least a hundred degrees, Vis had amended: he wasn't sure how hot it was in hell.

It was this scene which, at twenty minutes to nine in the evening, confronted Mallory and his men when they topped the brow of a hill and reined in their ponies just short of the edge of the precipice which abutted on the western edge of the Ivenici plateau. For at least two minutes they sat there on their ponies, not moving, not speaking, mesmerized by the other-world quality of a thousand men with bowed heads and bowed shoulders, shuffling exhaustedly across the level floor of the plain beneath, mesmerized because they all knew they were gazing at a unique spectacle which none of them had ever seen before and would never see again. Mallory finally broke free from the trance-like condition, looked at Miller and Andrea, and slowly shook his head in an expression of profound wonder conveying his disbelief, his refusal to accept the reality of what his own eyes told him was real and actual beyond dispute. Miller and Andrea returned his look with almost identical negative motions of their own heads. Mallory wheeled his pony to the right and led the way along the cliff-face to the point where the cliff ran into the rising ground below.

Ten minutes later they were being greeted by Colonel Vis.

'I did not expect to see you, Captain Mallory.' Vis pumped his hand enthusiastically. 'Before God, I did not expect to see you. You – and your men – must have a remarkable capacity for survival.'

'Say that in a few hours,' Mallory said drily, 'and I would be very happy indeed to hear it.'

'But it's all over now. We expect the plane –' Vis glanced at his watch – 'in exactly eight minutes. We have a bearing surface for it and there should be no difficulty in landing and taking off provided it doesn't hang around too long. You have done all that you came to do and achieved it magnificently. Luck has been on your side.'

'Say that in a few hours,' Mallory repeated.

'I'm sorry.' Vis could not conceal his puzzlement. 'You expect something to happen to the plane?'

'I don't expect anything to happen to the plane. But what's gone, what's past, is – was, rather – only the prologue.'

'The – the prologue?'

'Let me explain.'

Neufeld, Droshny and Sergeant Baer left their ponies tethered inside the woodline and walked up the slight eminence before them, Sergeant Baer making heavy weather of their uphill struggle through the snow because of the weight of the large portable transceiver strapped to his back. Near the summit they dropped to their hands and knees and crawled forward till they were within a few feet of the edge of the cliff overlooking the Ivenici plateau. Neufeld unslung his binoculars and then replaced them: the moon had just moved from behind a dark barred cloud highlighting every aspect of the scene below: the intensely sharp contrast afforded by black shadow and snow so deeply and gleamingly white as to be almost phosphorescent made the use of binoculars superfluous.

Clearly visible and to the right were Vis's command tents and, nearby, some hastily erected soup kitchens. Outside the smallest of the tents could be seen a group of perhaps a dozen people, obviously, even at that distance, engaged in close conversation. Directly beneath where they lay, the three men could see the phalanx turning round at one end of the runway and beginning to trudge back slowly, so terribly slowly, so terribly tiredly, along the wide path already tramped out. As Mallory and his men had been, Neufeld, Droshny and Baer were momentarily caught and held by the weird and other-worldly dark grandeur of the spectacle below. Only by a conscious act of will could Neufeld bring himself to look away and return to the world of normality and reality.

'How very kind,' he murmured, 'of our Yugoslav friends to go to such lengths on our behalf.' He turned to Baer and indicated the transceiver. 'Get through to the General, will you?'

Baer unslung his transceiver, settled it firmly in the snow, extended the telescopic aerial, pre-set the frequency and cranked the handle. He made contact almost at once, talked briefly then handed the microphone and head-piece to Neufeld, who fitted on the phones and gazed down, still half mesmerized, at the thousand men and women moving antlike across the plain below. The headphones cracked suddenly in his ears and the spell was broken.

'Herr General?'

'Ah. Hauptmann Neufeld.' In the ear-phones the General's voice was faint but very clear, completely free from distortion or static. 'Now then. About my psychological assessment of the English mind?'

'You have mistaken your profession, Herr General. Everything has happened exactly as you forecast. You will be interested to know, sir, that the Royal Air Force is launching a saturation bombing attack on the Zenica Gap at precisely 1.30 a.m. this morning.'

'Well, well, well,' Zimmermann said thoughtfully. 'That is interesting. But hardly surprising.'

'No, sir.' Neufeld looked up as Droshny touched him on the shoulder and pointed to the north. 'One moment, sir.'

Neufeld removed the ear-phones and cocked his head in the direction of Droshny's pointing arm. He lifted his binoculars but there was nothing to be seen. But unquestionably there was something to be heard – the distant clamour of aircraft engines, closing. Neufeld readjusted the ear-phones.

'We have to give the English full marks for punctuality, sir. The plane is coming in now.'

'Excellent, excellent. Keep me informed.'

Neufeld eased off one ear-phone and gazed to the north. Still nothing to be seen, the moon was now temporarily behind a cloud, but the sound of the aircraft engines was unmistakably closer. Suddenly, somewhere down on the plateau, came three sharp blasts on a whistle. Immediately, the marching phalanx broke up, men and women stumbling off the runway into the deep snow on the eastern side of the plateau, leaving behind them, obviously by pre-arrangement, about eighty men who spaced themselves out on either side of the runway.

'They're organized, I'll say that for them,' Neufeld said admiringly.

Droshny smiled his wolf's smile. 'All the better for us, eh?'

'Everybody seems to be doing their best to help us tonight,' Neufeld agreed.

Overhead, the dark and obscuring band of cloud drifted away to the south and the white light of the moon raced across the plateau. Neufeld could immediately see the plane, less than half a mile away, its camouflaged shape sharply etched in the brilliant moonlight as it sank down towards the end of the runway. Another sharp blast of the whistle and at once the men lining both sides of the runway switched on hand lamps – a superfluity, really, in those almost bright as day perfect landing conditions, but essential had the moon been hidden behind cloud.

'Touching down now,' Neufeld said into the microphone. 'It's a Wellington bomber.'

'Let's hope it makes a safe landing,' Zimmermann said.

'Let's hope so indeed, sir.'

The Wellington made a safe landing, a perfect landing considering the extremely difficult conditions. It slowed down quickly, then steadied its speed as it headed towards the end of the runway.

Neufeld said into the microphone: 'Safely down, Herr General, and rolling to rest.'

'Why doesn't it stop?' Droshny wondered.

'You can't accelerate a plane over snow as you can over a concrete runway,' Neufeld said. 'They'll require every yard of the runway for the take-off.'

Quite obviously, the pilot of the Wellington was of the same opinion. He was about fifty yards from the end of the runway when two groups of people broke from the hundreds lining the edge of the runway, one group heading for the already opened door in the side of the bomber, the other heading for the tail of the plane. Both groups reached the plane just as it rolled to a stop at the very end of the runway, a dozen men at once flinging themselves upon the tail unit and beginning to turn the Wellington through 180°.

Droshny was impressed. 'By heavens, they're not wasting much time, are they?'

'They can't afford to. If the plane stays there any time at all it'll start sinking in the snow.' Neufeld lifted his binoculars and spoke into the microphone.

'They're boarding now, Herr General. One, two, three . . . seven, eight, nine. Nine it is.' Neufeld sighed in relief and at the relief of tension. 'My warmest congratulations, Herr General. Nine it is, indeed.'

The plane was already facing the way it had come. The pilot stood on the brakes, revved the engines up to a crescendo, then twenty seconds after it had come to a halt the Wellington was on its way again, accelerating down the runway. The pilot took no chances, he waited till the very far end of the airstrip before lifting the Wellington off, but when he did it rose cleanly and easily and climbed steadily into the night sky.

'Airborne, Herr General,' Neufeld reported. 'Everything perfectly according to plan.' He covered the microphone, looking after the disappearing plane, then smiled at Droshny. 'I think we should wish them *bon voyage*, don't you?'

Mallory, one of the hundreds lining the perimeter of the airstrip, lowered his binoculars. 'And a very pleasant journey to them all.'

Colonel Vis shook his head sadly. 'All this work just to send five of my men on a holiday to Italy.'

'I dare say they needed a break,' Mallory said.

'The hell with them. How about us?' Reynolds demanded. In spite of the words, his face showed no anger, just a dazed and total bafflement. 'We should have been aboard that damned plane.'

'Ah. Well. I changed my mind.'

'Like hell you changed your mind,' Reynolds said bitterly.

Inside the fuselage of the Wellington, the moustached major surveyed his three fellow-escapees and the five Partisan soldiers, shook his head in disbelief and turned to the captain by his side.

'A rum do, what?'

'Very rum, indeed, sir,' said the captain. He looked curiously at the papers the major held in his hand. 'What have you there?'

'A map and papers that I'm to give to some bearded naval type when we land back in Italy. Odd fellow, that Mallory, what?'

'Very odd indeed, sir,' the captain agreed.

* * *

Mallory and his men, together with Vis and Vlanovich, had detached themselves from the crowd and were now standing outside Vis's command tent.

Mallory said to Vis: 'You have arranged for the ropes? We must leave at once.'

'What's all the desperate hurry, sir?' Groves asked. Like Reynolds, much of his resentment seemed to have gone to be replaced by a helpless bewilderment. 'All of a sudden, like, I mean?'

'Petar and Maria,' Mallory said grimly. 'They're the hurry.'

'What about Petar and Maria?' Reynolds asked suspiciously. 'Where do they come into this?'

'They're being held captive in the ammunition block-house. And when Neufeld and Droshny get back there –'

'Get back there,' Groves said dazedly. 'What do you mean, get back there? We – we left them locked up. And how in God's name do you know that Petar and Maria are being held in the block-house? How can they be? I mean, they weren't there when we left there – and that wasn't so long ago.'

'When Andrea's pony had a stone in its hoof on the way up here from the block-house, it didn't have a stone in its hoof. Andrea was keeping watch.'

'You see,' Miller explained, 'Andrea doesn't trust anyone.'

'He saw Sergeant Baer taking Petar and Maria there,' Mallory went on. 'Bound. Baer released Neufeld and Droshny and you can bet your last cent our precious pair were up on the cliff side there checking that we really did fly out.'

'You don't tell us very much, do you, sir?' Reynolds said bitterly.

'I'll tell you this much,' Mallory said with certainty. 'If we don't get there soon, Maria and Petar are for the high jump. Neufeld and Droshny don't *know* yet, but by this time they must be pretty convinced that it was Maria who told me where those four agents were being kept. They've always known who we really were – Maria told them. Now they know who Maria is. Just before Droshny killed Saunders –'

'Droshny?' Reynolds's expression was that of a man who has almost given up all attempt to understand. 'Maria?'

'I made a miscalculation.' Mallory sounded tired. 'We all make miscalculations, but this was a bad one.' He smiled, but the smile didn't touch his eyes. 'You will recall that you had a few harsh words to say about Andrea here when he picked that fight with Droshny outside the dining hut in Neufeld's camp?'

'Sure I remember. It was one of the craziest –'

'You can apologize to Andrea at a later and more convenient time,' Mallory interrupted. 'Andrea provoked Droshny because I asked him to. I knew that Neufeld and Droshny were up to no good in the dining hut after we had left and I wanted a moment to ask Maria what they had been discussing. She told me that they intended to send a couple of Cetniks after us into Broznik's camp – suitably disguised, of course – to report on us. They were two of the men acting as our escort in that wood-burning truck. Andrea and Miller killed them.'

'Now you tell us,' Groves said almost mechanically. 'Andrea and Miller killed them.'

'What I didn't know was that Droshny was also following us. He saw Maria and myself together.' He looked at Reynolds. 'Just as you did. I didn't know at the time that he'd seen us, but I've known for some hours now. Maria has been as good as under sentence of death since this morning. But there was nothing I could do about it. Not until now. If I'd shown my hand, we'd have been finished.'

Reynolds shook his head. 'But you've just said that Maria betrayed us –'

'Maria,' Mallory said, 'is a top-flight British espionage agent. English father, Yugoslav mother. She was in this country even before the Germans came. As a student in Belgrade. She joined the Partisans, who trained her as a radio operator, then arranged for her defection to the Cetniks. The Cetniks had captured a radio operator from one of the first British missions. They – the Germans, rather – trained her to imitate this operator's hand – every radio operator has his own unmistakable style – until their styles were quite indistinguishable. And her English, of course, was perfect. So then she was in direct contact with Allied Intelligence in both North Africa and Italy. The Germans thought they had us completely fooled: it was, in fact, the other way round.'

Miller said complainingly: 'You didn't tell me any of this, either.'

'I've so much on my mind. Anyway, she was notified direct of the arrival of the last four agents to be parachuted in. She, of course, told the Germans. And all those agents carried information reinforcing the German belief that a second front – a full-scale invasion – of Yugoslavia was imminent.'

Reynolds said slowly: 'They knew we were coming too?'

'Of course. They knew everything about us all along, what we really were. What they didn't know, of course, is that we knew they knew and though what they knew of us was true it was only part of the truth.'

Reynolds digested this. He said, hesitating: 'Sir?'

'Yes?'

'I could have been wrong about you, sir.'

'It happens,' Mallory agreed. 'From time to time, it happens. You were wrong, Sergeant, of course you were, but you were wrong from the very best motives. The fault is mine. Mine alone. But my hands were tied.' Mallory touched him on the shoulder. 'One of these days you might get round to forgiving me.'

'Petar?' Groves asked. 'He's not her brother?'

'Petar is Petar. No more. A front.'

'There's still an awful lot –' Reynolds began, but Mallory interrupted him.

'It'll have to wait. Colonel Vis, a map, please.' Captain Vlanovich brought one from the tent and Mallory shone a torch on it. 'Look. Here. The Neretva dam and the Zenica Cage. I told Neufeld that Broznik had told me that the Partisans believe that the attack is coming across the Neretva bridge from the south. But, as I've just said, Neufeld knew – he knew even before we had arrived – who and what we *really* were. So he was convinced I was lying. He was convinced that I was convinced that the attack was coming through the Zenica Gap to the north here. Good reason for believing that, mind you: there are two hundred German tanks up there.'

Vis stared at him. 'Two hundred!'

'One hundred and ninety of them are made of plywood. So the only way Neufeld – and, no doubt, the German High Command – could ensure that this useful information got through to Italy was to allow us to stage this rescue bid. Which, of course, they very gladly did, assisting us in every possible way even to the extent of gladly collaborating with us in permitting themselves to be captured. They *knew*, of course, that we had no option left but to capture them and force them to lead us to the block-house – an arrangement they had ensured by previously seizing and hiding away the only other person who could have helped us in this – Maria. And, of course, knowing this in advance, they had arranged for Sergeant Baer to come and free them.'

'I see.' It was plain to everyone that Colonel Vis did not see at all. 'You mentioned an RAF saturation attack on the Zenica Gap. This, of course, will now be switched to the bridge?'

'No. You wouldn't have us break our word to the Wehrmacht, would you? As promised, the attack comes on the Zenica Gap. As a diversion. To convince them, in case they have any last doubts left in their minds, that we have been fooled. Besides, you know as well as I do that that bridge is immune to high-level air attack. It will have to be destroyed in some other way.'

'In what way?'

'We'll think of something. The night is young. Two last things, Colonel Vis. There'll be another Wellington in at midnight and a second at three a.m. Let them both go. The next in, at six a.m., hold it against our arrival. Well, our possible arrival. With any luck we'll be flying out before dawn.'

'With any luck,' Vis said sombrely.

'And radio General Vukalovic, will you? Tell him what I've told you, the exact situation. And tell him to begin intensive small-arms fire at one o'clock in the morning.'

'What are they supposed to fire at?'

'They can fire at the moon for all I care.' Mallory swung aboard his pony. 'Come on, let's be off.'

'The moon,' General Vukalovic agreed, 'is a fair-sized target, though rather a long way off. However, if that's what our friend wants, that's what he shall have.' Vukalovic paused for a moment, looked at Colonel Janzy, who was sitting beside him on a fallen log in the woods to the south of the Zenica Gap, then spoke again into the radio mouth-piece.

'Anyway, many thanks, Colonel Vis. So the Neretva bridge it is. And you think it will be unhealthy for us to remain in the immediate vicinity of this area after 1 a.m. Don't worry, we won't be here.' Vukalovic removed the head-phones and turned to Janzy. 'We pull out, quietly, at midnight. We leave a few men to make a lot of noise.'

'The ones who are going to fire at the moon?'

'The ones who are going to fire at the moon. Radio Colonel Lazlo at Neretva, will you? Tell him we'll be with him before the attack. Then radio Major Stephan. Tell him to leave just a holding force, pull out of the Western Gap and make his way to Colonel Lazlo's HQ.' Vukalovic paused for a thoughtful moment. 'We should be in for a few very interesting hours, don't you think?'

'Is there any chance in the world for this man Mallory?' Janzy's tone carried with it its own answer.

'Well, look at it this way,' Vukalovic said reasonably. 'Of course there's a chance. There has to be a chance. It is, after all, my dear Janzy, a question of options – and there are no other options left open to us.'

Janzy made no reply but nodded several times in slow succession as if Vukalovic had just said something profound.

NINE

Friday 2115–Saturday 0040

The pony-back ride downhill through the thickly wooded forests from the Ivenici plateau to the block-house took Mallory and his men barely a quarter of the time it had taken them to make the ascent. In the deep snow the going underfoot was treacherous to a degree, collision with the bole of a pine was always an imminent possibility and none of the five riders made any pretence towards being an experienced horseman, with the inevitable result that slips, stumbles and heavy falls were as frequent as they were painful. Not one of them escaped the indignity of involuntarily leaving his saddle and being thrown headlong into the deep snow, but it was the providential cushioning effect of that snow that was the saving of them, that and, more often, the sure-footed agility of their mountain ponies: whatever the reason or combination of reasons, bruises and winded falls there were in plenty, but broken bones, miraculously, there were none.

The block-house came in sight. Mallory raised a warning hand, slowing them down until they were about two hundred yards distant from their objective, where he reined in, dismounted and led his pony into a thick cluster of pines, followed by the others. Mallory tethered his horse and indicated to the others to do the same.

Miller said complainingly: 'I'm sick of this damned pony but I'm sicker still of walking through deep snow. Why don't we just ride on down there?'

'Because they'll have ponies tethered down there. They'll start whinnying if they hear or see or smell other ponies approaching.'

'They might start whinnying anyway.'

'And there'll be guards on watch,' Andrea pointed out. 'I don't think, Corporal Miller, that we could make a very stealthy and unobtrusive approach on pony-back.'

'Guards. Guarding against what? As far as Neufeld and company are concerned, we're halfway over the Adriatic at this time.'

'Andrea's right,' Mallory said. 'Whatever else you may think about Neufeld, he's a first-class officer who takes no chances. There'll be guards.' He glanced up to the night sky where a narrow bar of cloud was just approaching the face of the moon. 'See that?'

'I see it,' Miller said miserably.

'Thirty seconds, I'd say. We make a run for the far gable end of the block-house – there are no embrasures there. And for God's sake, once we get there, keep dead quiet. If they hear anything, if they as much as suspect that we're outside, they'll bar the doors and use Petar and Maria as hostages. Then we'll just have to leave them.'

'You'd do that, sir?' Reynolds asked.

'I'd do that. I'd rather cut a hand off, but I'd do that. I've no choice, Sergeant.'

'Yes, sir. I understand.'

The dark bar of cloud passed over the moon. The five men broke from the concealment of the pines and pounded downhill through the deep clogging snow, heading for the farther gable-wall of the block-house. Thirty yards away, at a signal from Mallory, they slowed down lest the sound of their crunching, running footsteps be heard by any watchers who might be keeping guard by the embrasures and completed the remaining distance by walking as quickly and quietly as possible in single file, each man using the footprints left by the man in front of him.

They reached the blank gable-end undetected, with the moon still behind the cloud. Mallory did not pause to congratulate either himself or any of the others. He at once dropped to his hands and knees and crawled round the corner of the block-house, pressing close into the stone wall.

Four feet from the corner came the first of the embrasures. Mallory did not bother to lower himself any deeper into the snow – the embrasures were so deeply recessed in the massive stone walls that it would have been quite impossible for any watcher to see anything at a lesser distance than six feet from the embrasure. He concentrated, instead, on achieving as minimal a degree of sound as was possible, and did so with success, for he safely passed the embrasure without any alarm being raised. The other four were equally successful even though the moon broke from behind the cloud as the last of them, Groves, was directly under the embrasure. But he, too, remained undetected.

Mallory reached the door. He gestured to Miller, Reynolds and Groves to remain prone where they were: he and Andrea rose silently to their feet and pressed their ears close against the door.

Immediately they heard Droshny's voice, thick with menace, heavy with hatred.

'A traitress! That's what she is. A traitress to our cause. Kill her now!'

'Why did you do it, Maria?' Neufeld's voice, in contrast to Droshny's, was measured, calm, almost gentle.

'Why did she do it?' Droshny snarled. 'Money. That's why she did it. What else?'

'Why?' Neufeld was quietly persistent. 'Did Captain Mallory threaten to kill your brother?'

'Worse than that.' They had to strain to catch Maria's low voice. 'He threatened to kill me. Who would have looked after my blind brother then?'

'We waste time,' Droshny said impatiently. 'Let me take them both outside.'

'No.' Neufeld's voice, still calm, admitted of no argument. 'A blind boy? A terrified girl? What are you, man?'

'A Cetnik!'

'And I'm an officer of the Wehrmacht.'

Andrea whispered in Mallory's ear: 'Any minute now and someone's going to notice our foot-tracks in the snow.'

Mallory nodded, stood aside and made a small gesturing motion of his hand. Mallory was under no illusion as to their respective capabilities when it came to bursting open doors leading into rooms filled with armed men. Andrea was the best in the business – and proceeded to prove it in his usual violent and lethal fashion.

A twist of the door handle, a violent kick with the sole of the right foot and Andrea stood framed in the doorway. The wildly swinging door had still not reached the full limit of travel on its hinges when the room echoed to the flat staccato chatter of Andrea's Schmeisser: Mallory, peering over Andrea's shoulder through the swirling cordite smoke, saw two German soldiers, lethally cursed with over-fast reactions, slumping wearily to the floor. His own machine-pistol levelled, Mallory followed Andrea into the room.

There was no longer any call for Schmeissers. None of the other soldiers in the room was carrying any weapon at all while Neufeld and Droshny, their faces frozen into expressions of total incredulity, were clearly, even if only momentarily, incapable of any movement at all, far less being capable of the idea of offering any suicidal resistance.

Mallory said to Neufeld: 'You've just bought yourself your life.' He turned to Maria, nodded towards the door, waited until she had led her brother outside, then looked again at Neufeld and Droshny and said curtly: 'Your guns.'

Neufeld managed to speak, although his lips moved in a strangely mechanical fashion. 'What in the name of God –'

Mallory was in no mind for small talk. He lifted his Schmeisser. 'Your guns.'

Neufeld and Droshny, like men in a dream, removed their pistols and dropped them to the floor.

'The keys.' Droshny and Neufeld looked at him in almost uncomprehending silence. 'The keys,' Mallory repeated. 'Now. Or the keys won't be necessary.'

For several seconds the room was completely silent, then Neufeld stirred, turned to Droshny and nodded. Droshny scowled – as well as any man can scowl when his face is still overspread with an expression of baffled astonishment and homicidal fury – reached into his pocket and produced the keys. Miller took them, unlocked and opened wide the cell door wordlessly and with a motion of his machine-pistol invited Neufeld, Droshny, Baer and the other soldiers to enter, waited until they had done so, swung shut the door, locked it and pocketed the key. The room echoed again as Andrea squeezed the trigger of his machine-pistol and destroyed the radio beyond any hope of repair. Five seconds later they were all outside, Mallory, the last man to leave, locking the door and sending the key spinning to fall yards away, buried from sight in the deep snow.

Suddenly he caught sight of the number of ponies tethered outside the block-house. Seven. Exactly the right number. He ran across to the embrasure outside the cell window and shouted: 'Our ponies are tethered two hundred yards uphill just inside the pines. Don't forget.' Then he ran quickly back and ordered the other six to mount. Reynolds looked at him in astonishment.

'You think of this, sir? At such a time?'

'I'd think of this at any time.' Mallory turned to Petar, who had just awkwardly mounted his horse, then turned to Maria. 'Tell him to take off his glasses.'

Maria looked at him in surprise, nodded in apparent understanding and spoke to her brother, who looked at her uncomprehendingly, then ducked his head obediently, removed his dark glasses and thrust them deep inside his tunic. Reynolds looked on in astonishment, then turned to Mallory.

'I don't understand, sir.'

Mallory wheeled his pony and said curtly: 'It's not necessary that you do.'

'I'm sorry, sir.'

Mallory turned his pony again and said, almost wearily: 'It's already eleven o'clock, boy, and almost already too late for what we have to do.'

'Sir.' Reynolds was deeply if obscurely pleased that Mallory should call him boy. 'I don't really want to know, sir.'

'You've asked. We'll have to go as quickly as our ponies can take us. A blind man can't see obstructions, can't balance himself according to the level of the terrain, can't anticipate in advance how he should brace himself for an unexpectedly sharp drop, can't lean in the saddle for a corner his pony knows is coming. A blind man, in short, is a hundred times more liable to fall off in a downhill gallop than we are. It's enough that a blind man should be blind for life. It's too much that we should expose him to the risk of a heavy fall with his glasses on, expose him to the risk of not only being blind but of having his eyes gouged out and being in agony for life.'

'I hadn't thought – I mean – I'm sorry, sir.'

'Stop apologizing, boy. It's really my turn, you know – to apologize to you. Keep an eye on him, will you?'

Colonel Lazlo, binoculars to his eyes, gazed down over the moonlit rocky slope below him towards the bridge at Neretva. On the southern bank of the river, in the meadows between the south bank and the beginning of the pine forest beyond, and, as far as Lazlo could ascertain, in the fringes of the pine forest itself, there was a disconcertingly ominous lack of movement, of any sign of life at all. Lazlo was pondering the disturbingly sinister significance of this unnatural peacefulness when a hand touched his shoulder. He twisted, looked up and recognized the figure of Major Stephan, commander of the Western Gap.

'Welcome, welcome. The General has advised me of your arrival. Your battalion with you?'

'What's left of it.' Stephan smiled without really smiling. 'Every man who could walk. And all those who couldn't.'

'God send we don't need them all tonight. The General has spoken to you of this man Mallory?' Major Stephan nodded, and Lazlo went on: 'If he fails? If the Germans cross the Neretva tonight – '

'So?' Stephan shrugged. 'We were all due to die tonight anyway.'

'A well-taken point,' Lazlo said approvingly. He lifted his binoculars and returned to his contemplation of the bridge at Neretva.

So far, and almost incredibly, neither Mallory nor any of the six galloping behind him had parted company with their ponies. Not even Petar. True, the incline of the slope was not nearly as steep as it had been from the Ivenici plateau down to the block-house, but Reynolds suspected it was because Mallory had imperceptibly succeeded in slowing down the pace of their earlier headlong gallop. Perhaps, Reynolds thought vaguely, it was because Mallory was subconsciously trying to protect the blind singer, who was riding almost abreast with him, guitar firmly strapped over his shoulder, reins abandoned and both hands clasped desperately to the pommel of his saddle. Unbidden, almost, Reynolds's thoughts strayed back to that scene inside the block-house. Moments later, he was urging his pony forwards until he had drawn alongside Mallory.

'Sir?'

'What is it?' Mallory sounded irritable.

'A word, sir. It's urgent. Really it is.'

Mallory threw up a hand and brought the company to a halt. He said curtly: 'Be quick.'

'Neufeld and Droshny, sir.' Reynolds paused in a moment's brief uncertainty, then continued. 'Do you reckon they know where you're going?'

'What's that to do with anything?'

'Please.'

'Yes, they do. Unless they're complete morons. And they're not.'

'It's a pity, sir,' Reynolds said reflectively, 'that you hadn't shot them after all.'

'Get to the point,' Mallory said impatiently.

'Yes, sir. You reckoned Sergeant Baer released them earlier on?'

'Of course.' Mallory was exercising all his restraint. 'Andrea saw them arrive. I've explained all this. They – Neufeld and Droshny – had to go up to the Ivenici plateau to check that we'd really gone.'

'I understand that, sir. So you knew that Baer was following us. How did he get into the block-house?'

Mallory's restraint vanished. He said in exasperation: 'Because I left both keys hanging outside.'

'Yes, sir. You were expecting him. But Sergeant Baer didn't know you were expecting him – and even if he did he wouldn't be expecting to find keys so conveniently to hand.'

'Good God in heaven! Duplicates!' In bitter chagrin, Mallory smacked the fist of one hand into the palm of the other. 'Imbecile! Imbecile! Of *course* he would have his own keys.'

'And Droshny,' Miller said thoughtfully, 'may know a short cut.'

'That's not all of it.' Mallory was completely back on balance again, outwardly composed, the relaxed calmness of the face the complete antithesis of his racing mind. 'Worse still, he may make straight for his camp radio and warn Zimmermann to pull his armoured divisions back from the Neretva. You've earned your passage tonight, Reynolds. Thanks, boy. How far to Neufeld's camp, do you think, Andrea?'

'A mile.' The words came over Andrea's shoulder, for Andrea, as always in situations which he knew called for the exercise of his highly specialized talents, was already on his way.

Five minutes later they were crouched at the edge of the forest less than twenty yards from the perimeter of Neufeld's camp. Quite a number of the huts had illuminated windows, music could be heard coming from the dining hut and several Cetnik soldiers were moving about in the compound.

Reynolds whispered to Mallory: 'How do we go about it, sir?'

'We don't do anything at all. We just leave it to Andrea.'

Groves spoke, his voice low. 'One man? Andrea? We leave it to one man?'

Mallory sighed. 'Tell them, Corporal Miller.'

'I'd rather not. Well, if I have to. The fact is,' Miller went on kindly, 'Andrea is rather good at this sort of thing.'

'So are we,' Reynolds said. 'We're commandos. We've been trained for this sort of thing.'

'And very highly trained, no doubt,' said Miller approvingly. 'Another half-dozen years' experience and half a dozen of you might be just about able to cope with him. Although I doubt it very much. Before the night is out, you'll learn – and I don't mean to be insulting, Sergeants – that you are little lambs to Andrea's wolf.' Miller paused and went on sombrely: 'Like whoever happens to be inside that radio hut at this moment.'

'Like whoever happens –' Groves twisted round and looked behind him. 'Andrea? He's gone. I didn't see him go.'

'No one ever does,' Miller said. 'And those poor devils won't ever see him come.' He looked at Mallory. 'Time's a-wasting.'

Mallory glanced at the luminous hands of his watch. 'Eleven-thirty. Time *is* a-wasting.'

For almost a minute there was a silence broken only by the rest-less movements of the ponies tethered deep in the woods behind them, then Groves gave a muffled exclamation as Andrea materi-alized beside him. Mallory looked up and said: 'How many?'

Andrea held up two fingers and moved silently into the woods towards his pony. The others rose and followed him, Groves and Reynolds exchanging glances which indicated more clearly than any words could possibly have done that they could have been even more wrong about Andrea than they had ever been about Mallory.

At precisely the moment that Mallory and his companions were remounting their ponies in the woods fringing Neufeld's camp, a Wellington bomber came sinking down towards a well-lit airfield – the same airfield from which Mallory and his men had taken off less than twenty-four hours previously. Termoli, Italy. It made a perfect touchdown and as it taxied along the runway an army radio truck curved in on an interception course, turning to parallel the last hundred yards of the Wellington's run down. In the left-hand front seat and in the right-hand back seat of the truck sat two immediately recognizable figures: in the front, the piratical splen-didly bearded figure of Captain Jensen, in the back the British lieutenant-general with whom Jensen had recently spent so much time in pacing the Termoli Operations Room.

Plane and truck came to a halt at the same moment. Jensen, dis-playing a surprising agility for one of his very considerable bulk, hopped nimbly to the ground and strode briskly across the tarmac and arrived at the Wellington just as its door opened and the first of the passengers, the moustached major, swung to the ground.

Jensen nodded to the papers clutched in the major's hand and said without preamble: 'Those for me?' The major blinked uncer-tainly, then nodded stiffly in return, clearly irked by this abrupt wel-come for a man just returned from durance vile. Jensen took the papers without a further word, went back to his seat in the jeep, brought out a flashlight and studied the papers briefly. He twisted in his seat and said to the radio operator seated beside the General: 'Flight plan as stated. Target as indicated. Now.' The radio operator began to crank the handle.

* * *

Some fifty miles to the south-east, in the Foggia area, the buildings and runways of the RAF heavy bomber base echoed and
reverberated to the thunder of scores of aircraft engines: at the
dispersal area at the west end of the main runway several
squadrons of Lancaster heavy bombers were lined up ready for
take-off, obviously awaiting the signal to go. The signal was not
long in coming.

Halfway down the airfield, but well to one side of the main runway, was parked a jeep identical to the one in which Jensen was
sitting in Termoli. In the back seat a radio operator was crouched
over a radio, earphones to his head. He listened intently, then
looked up and said matter-of-factly: 'Instructions as stated. Now.
Now. Now.'

'Instructions as stated,' a captain in the front seat repeated.
'Now. Now. Now.' He reached for a wooden box, produced three
Very pistols, aimed directly across the runway and fired each in
turn. The brilliantly arcing flares burst into incandescent life, green,
red and green again, before curving slowly back to earth. The thunder at the far end of the airfield mounted to a rumbling crescendo
and the first of the Lancasters began to move. Within a few minutes the last of them had taken off and was lifting into the darkly
hostile night skies of the Adriatic.

'I did say, I believe,' Jensen remarked conversationally and comfortably to the General in the back seat, 'that they are the best in
the business. Our friends from Foggia are on their way.'

'The best in the business. Maybe. I don't know. What I do know
is that those damned German and Austrian divisions are still in
position in the Gustav Line. Zero hour for the assault on the Gustav
Line is –' he glanced at his watch – 'in exactly thirty hours.'

'Time enough,' Jensen said confidently.

'I wish I shared this blissful confidence.'

Jensen smiled cheerfully at him as the jeep moved off, then
faced forward in his seat again. As he did, the smile vanished completely from his face and his fingers beat a drum tattoo on the seat
beside him.

The moon had broken through again as Neufeld, Droshny and
their men came galloping into camp and reined in ponies so
covered with steam from their heaving flanks and distressed
breathing as to have a weirdly insubstantial appearance in the

pale moonlight. Neufeld swung from his pony and turned to Sergeant Baer.

'How many ponies left in the stables?'

'Twenty. About that.'

'Quickly. And as many men as there are ponies. Saddle up.'

Neufeld gestured to Droshny and together they ran towards the radio hut. The door, ominously enough on that icy night, was standing wide open. They were still ten feet short of the door when Neufeld shouted: 'The Neretva bridge at once. Tell General Zimmermann –'

He halted abruptly in the doorway, Droshny by his shoulder. For the second time that evening the faces of both men reflected their stunned disbelief, their total uncomprehending shock.

Only one small lamp burned in the radio hut, but that one small lamp was enough. Two men lay on the floor in grotesquely huddled positions, the one lying partially across the other: both were quite unmistakably dead. Beside them, with its faceplate ripped off and interior smashed, lay the mangled remains of what had once been a transmitter. Neufeld gazed at the scene for some time before shaking his head violently as if to break the shocked spell and turned to Droshny.

'The big one,' he said quietly. 'The big one did this.'

'The big one,' Droshny agreed. He was almost smiling. 'You will remember what you promised, Hauptmann Neufeld? The big one. He's for me.'

'You shall have him. Come. They can be only minutes ahead.' Both men turned and ran back to the compound where Sergeant Baer and a group of soldiers were already saddling up the ponies.

'Machine-pistols only,' Neufeld shouted. 'No rifles. It will be close-quarter work tonight. And Sergeant Baer?'

'Hauptmann Neufeld?'

'Inform the men that we will not be taking prisoners.'

As those of Neufeld and his men had been, the ponies of Mallory and his six companions were almost invisible in the dense clouds of steam rising from their sweat-soaked bodies: their lurching gait, which could not now even be called a trot, was token enough of the obvious fact that they had reached the limits of exhaustion. Mallory glanced at Andrea, who nodded and said: 'I agree. We'd make faster time on foot now.'

'I must be getting old,' Mallory said, and for a moment he sounded that way. 'I'm not thinking very well tonight, am I?'

'I do not understand.'

'Ponies. Neufeld and his men will have fresh ponies from the stables. We should have killed them – or at least driven them away.'

'Age is not the same thing as lack of sleep. It never occurred to me, either. A man cannot think of everything, my Keith.' Andrea reined in his pony and was about to swing down when something on the slope below caught his attention. He pointed ahead.

A minute later they drew up alongside a very narrow-gauge railway line, of a type common in Central Yugoslavia. At this level the snow had petered out and the track, they could see, was overgrown and rusty, but for all that, apparently in fair enough mechanical condition: undoubtedly, it was the same track that had caught their eye when they had paused to examine the green waters of the Neretva dam on the way back from Major Broznik's camp that morning. But what simultaneously caught and held the attention of both Mallory and Miller was not the track itself, but a little siding leading on to the track – and a diminutive, wood-burning locomotive that stood on the siding. The locomotive was practically a solid block of rust and looked as if it hadn't moved from its present position since the beginning of the war: in all probability, it hadn't.

Mallory produced a large-scale map from his tunic and flashed a torch on it. He said: 'No doubt of it, this is the track we saw this morning. It goes down along the Neretva for at least five miles before bearing off to the south.' He paused and went on thoughtfully: 'I wonder if we could get that thing moving.'

'What?' Miller looked at him in horror. 'It'll fall to pieces if you touch it – it's only the rust that's holding the damn thing together. And that gradient there!' He peered in dismay down the slope. 'What do you think our terminal velocity is going to be when we hit one of those monster pine trees a few miles down the track?'

'The ponies are finished,' Mallory said mildly, 'and you know how much you love walking.'

Miller looked at the locomotive with loathing. 'There must be some other way.'

'Shh!' Andrea cocked his head. 'They're coming. I can hear them coming.'

'Get the chocks away from those front wheels,' Miller shouted. He ran forward and after several violent and well-directed kicks which clearly took into no account the future state of his toes, succeeded in freeing the triangular block which was attached to the front of the locomotive by a chain: Reynolds, no less energetically, did the same for the other chock.

All of them, even Maria and Petar helping, flung all their weight against the rear of the locomotive. The locomotive remained where it was. They tried again, despairingly: the wheels refused to budge even a fraction of an inch. Groves said, with an odd mixture of urgency and diffidence: 'Sir, on a gradient like this, it would have been left with its brakes on.'

'Oh my God!' Mallory said in chagrin. 'Andrea. Quickly. Release the brake lever.'

Andrea swung himself on to the footplate. He said complainingly: 'There are a dozen damned levers up here.'

'Well, open the dozen damned levers, then.' Mallory glanced anxiously back up the track. Maybe Andrea had heard something, maybe not: there was certainly no one in sight yet. But he knew that Neufeld and Droshny, who must have been released from the block-house only minutes after they had left there themselves and who knew those woods and paths better than they did, must be very close indeed by this time.

There was a considerable amount of metallic screeching and swearing coming from the cab and after perhaps half a minute Andrea said: 'That's the lot.'

'Shove,' Mallory ordered.

They shoved, heels jammed in the sleepers and backs to the loco-motive, and this time the locomotive moved off so easily, albeit with a tortured squealing of rusted wheels, that most of those pushing were caught wholly by surprise and fell on their backs on the track. Moments later they were on their feet and running after the loco-motive which was already perceptibly beginning to increase speed. Andrea reached down from the cab, swung Maria and Petar aboard in turn, then lent a helping hand to the others. The last, Groves, was reaching for the footplate when he suddenly braked, swung round, ran back to the ponies, unhitched the climbing ropes, flung them over his shoulder and chased after the locomotive again. Mallory reached down and helped him on to the footplate.

'It's not my day,' Mallory said sadly. 'Evening rather. First, I for-get about Baer's duplicate keys. Then about the ponies. Then about the brakes. Now the ropes. I wonder what I'll forget about next?'

'Perhaps about Neufeld and Droshny.' Reynolds's voice was carefully without expression.

'What about Neufeld and Droshny?'

Reynolds pointed back up the railway track with the barrel of his Schmeisser. 'Permission to fire, sir.'

Mallory swung round. Neufeld, Droshny and an indeterminate number of other pony-mounted soldiers had just appeared around a bend in the track and were hardly more than a hundred yards away.

'Permission to fire,' Mallory agreed. 'The rest of you get down.' He unslung and brought up his own Schmeisser just as Reynolds squeezed the trigger of his. For perhaps five seconds the closed metallic confines of the tiny cabin reverberated deafeningly to the crash of the two machine-pistols, then, at a nudge from Mallory, the two men stopped firing. There was no target left to fire at. Neufeld and his men had loosed off a few preliminary shots but immediately realized that the wildly swaying saddles of their ponies made an impossibly unsteady firing position as compared to the cab of the locomotive and had pulled their ponies off into the woods on either side of the track. But not all of them had pulled off in time: two men lay motionless and face down in the snow while their ponies still galloped down the track in the wake of the loco-motive.

Miller rose, glanced wordlessly at the scene behind, then tapped Mallory on the arm. 'A small point occurs to me, sir. How do we stop this thing.' He gazed apprehensively through the cab window. 'Must be doing sixty already.'

'Well, we're doing at least twenty,' Mallory said agreeably. 'But fast enough to out-distance those ponies. Ask Andrea. He released the brake.'

'He released a dozen levers,' Miller corrected. 'Any one could have been the brake.'

'Well, you're not going to sit around doing nothing, are you?' Mallory asked reasonably. 'Find out how to stop the damn thing.'

Miller looked at him coldly and set about trying to find out how to stop the damn thing. Mallory turned as Reynolds touched him on the arm. 'Well?'

Reynolds had an arm round Maria to steady her on the now swaying platform. He whispered: 'They're going to get us, sir. They're going to get us for sure. Why don't we stop and leave those two, sir? Give them a chance to escape into the woods?'

'Thanks for the thought. But don't be mad. With us they have a chance – a small one to be sure, but a chance. Stay behind and they'll be butchered.'

The locomotive was no longer doing the twenty miles per hour Mallory had mentioned and if it hadn't approached the figure that Miller had so fearfully mentioned it was certainly going quickly enough to make it rattle and sway to what appeared to be the very limits of its stability. By this time the last of the trees to the right of the track had petered out, the darkened waters of the Neretva dam were clearly visible to the west and the railway track was now running very close indeed to the edge of what appeared to be a dangerously steep precipice. Mallory looked back into the cab. With the exception of Andrea, everyone now wore expressions of considerable apprehension on their faces. Mallory said: 'Found out how to stop this damn thing yet?'

'Easy.' Andrea indicated a lever. 'This handle here.'

'Okay, brakeman. I want to have a look.'

To the evident relief of most of the passengers in the cab, Andrea leaned back on the brake-lever. There was an eldritch screeching that set teeth on edge, clouds of sparks flew up past the sides of the cab as some wheels or other locked solid in the lines, then the locomotive eased slowly to a halt, both the intensity of sound from the squealing brakes and the number of sparks diminishing as it did so. Andrea, duty done, leaned out of the side of the cab with all the bored aplomb of the crack loco engineer: one had the feeling that all he really wanted in life that moment was a piece of oily waste and a whistle-cord to pull.

Mallory and Miller climbed down and ran to the edge of the cliff, less than twenty yards away. At least Mallory did. Miller made a much more cautious approach, inching forward the last few feet on hands and knees. He hitched one cautious eye over the edge of the precipice, screwed both eyes shut, looked away and just as cautiously inched his way back from the edge of the cliff: Miller claimed that he couldn't even stand on the bottom step of a ladder without succumbing to the overwhelming compulsion to throw himself into the abyss.

Mallory gazed down thoughtfully into the depths. They were, he saw, directly over the top of the dam wall, which, in the strangely shadowed half-light cast by the moon, seemed almost impossibly far below in the dizzying depths. The broad top of the dam wall was brightly lit by floodlights and patrolled by at least half a dozen German soldiers, jack-booted and helmeted. Beyond the dam, on the lower side, the ladder Maria had spoken of was invisible, but the frail-looking swing bridge, still menaced by the massive bulk of the boulder on the scree on the left bank, and farther down, the white water indicating what might or might not have been a possible – or passable – ford were plainly in sight. Mallory, momentarily abstracted in thought, gazed at the scene below for several moments, recalled that the pursuit must be again coming uncomfortably close and hurriedly made his way back to the locomotive. He said to Andrea: 'About a mile and a half, I should think. No more.' He turned to Maria. 'You know there's a ford – or what seems to be a ford – some way below the dam. Is there a way down?'

'For a mountain goat.'

'Don't insult him,' Miller said reprovingly.

'I don't understand.'

'Ignore him,' Mallory said. 'Just tell us when we get there.'

Some five or six miles below the Neretva dam General Zimmermann paced up and down the fringe of the pine forest bordering the meadow to the south of the bridge at Neretva. Beside him paced a colonel, one of his divisional commanders. To the south of them could just dimly be discerned the shapes of hundreds of men and scores of tanks and other vehicles, vehicles with all their protective camouflage now removed, each tank and vehicle surrounded by its coterie of attendants making last-minute and probably wholly unnecessary adjustments. The time for hiding was over. The waiting was coming to an end. Zimmermann glanced at his watch.

'Twelve-thirty. The first infantry battalions start moving across in fifteen minutes, and spread out along the north bank. The tanks at two o'clock.'

'Yes, sir.' The details had been arranged many hours ago, but somehow one always found it necessary to repeat the instructions and the acknowledgements. The colonel gazed to the north. 'I sometimes wonder if there's *anybody* at all across there.'

'It's not the north I'm worrying about,' Zimmermann said sombrely. 'It's the west.'

'The Allies? You – you think their air armadas will come soon? It's still in your bones, Herr General?'

'Still in my bones. It's coming soon. For me, for you, for all of us.' He shivered, then forced a smile. 'Some ill-mannered lout has just walked over my grave.'

TEN

Saturday
0040–0120

'We're coming up to it now,' Maria said. Blonde hair streaming in the passing wind, she peered out again through the cab window of the clanking, swaying locomotive, withdrew her head and turned to Mallory. 'About three hundred metres.'

Mallory glanced at Andrea. 'You heard, brakeman?'

'I heard.' Andrea leaned hard on the brake–lever. The result was as before, a banshee shrieking of locked wheels on the rusty lines and a pyrotechnical display of sparks. The locomotive came to a juddering halt as Andrea looked out his cab window and observed a V-shaped gap in the edge of the cliff directly opposite where they had come to a stop. 'Within the yard, I should say?'

'Within the yard,' Mallory agreed. 'If you're unemployed after the war, there should always be a place for you in a shunter's yard.' He swung down to the side of the track, lent a helping hand to Maria and Petar, waited until Miller, Reynolds and Groves had jumped down, then said impatiently to Andrea: 'Well, hurry up, then.'

'Coming,' Andrea said peaceably. He pushed the handbrake all the way off, jumped down, and gave the locomotive a shove: the ancient vehicle at once moved off, gathering speed as it went. 'You never know,' Andrea said wistfully. 'It might hit somebody somewhere.'

They ran towards the cut in the edge of the cliff, a cut which obviously represented the beginning of some prehistoric landslide down to the bed of the Neretva, a maelstrom of white water far below, the boiling rapids resulting from scores of huge boulders which had slipped from this landslide in that distant aeon. By some exercise of the imagination, that scar in the side of the cliff-face might just perhaps have been called a gully, but it was in fact an almost perpendicular drop of scree and shale and small boulders, all of it treacherous and unstable to a frightening degree, the whole dangerous sweep broken only by a small ledge of jutting rock about halfway down. Miller took one brief glance at this terrifying prospect, stepped hurriedly back from the edge of the cliff and looked at Mallory in a silently dismayed incredulity.

'I'm afraid so,' Mallory said.

'But this is terrible. Even when I climbed the south cliff in Navarone –'

'You didn't climb the south cliff in Navarone,' Mallory said unkindly. 'Andrea and I pulled you up at the end of a rope.'

'Did you? I forget. But this – this is a climber's nightmare.'

'So we don't have to climb it. Just lower ourselves down. You'll be all right – as long as you don't start rolling.'

'I'll be all right as long as I don't start rolling,' Miller repeated mechanically. He watched Mallory join two ropes together and pass them around the bole of a stunted pine. 'How about Petar and Maria?'

'Petar doesn't have to see to make this descent. All he has to do is to lower himself on this rope – and Petar is as strong as a horse. Somebody will be down there before him to guide his feet on to the ledge. Andrea will look after the young lady here. Now hurry. Neufeld and his men will be up with us any minute here – and if they catch up on this cliff-face, well that's that. Andrea, off you go with Maria.'

Immediately, Andrea and the girl swung over the edge of the gully and began to lower themselves swiftly down the rope. Groves watched them, hesitated, then moved towards Mallory.

'I'll go last, sir, and take the rope with me.'

Miller took his arm and led him some feet away. He said, kindly: 'Generous, son, generous, but it's just not on. Not as long as Dusty Miller's life depends on it. In a situation like this, I must explain, all our lives depend upon the anchorman. The Captain, I am informed, is the best anchorman in the world.'

'He's what?'

'It's one of the non-coincidences why he was chosen to lead this mission. Bosnia is known to have rocks and cliffs and mountains all over it. Mallory was climbing the Himalayas, laddie, before you were climbing out of your cot. Even you are not too young to have heard of him.'

'*Keith* Mallory? The New Zealander?'

'Indeed. Used to chase sheep around, I gather. Come on, your turn.'

The first five made it safely. Even the last but one, Miller, made the descent to the ledge without incident, principally by employing his favourite mountain-climbing technique of keeping his eyes closed all the time. Then Mallory came last, coiling the rope with him as he came, moving quickly and surely and hardly ever seeming to look where he put his feet but at the same time not as much as disturbing the slightest pebble or piece of shale. Groves observed the descent with a look of almost awed disbelief in his eyes.

Mallory peered over the edge of the ledge. Because of a slight bend in the gorge above, there was a sharp cut-off in the moonlight just below where they stood so that while the phosphorescent whiteness of the rapids was in clear moonlight, the lower part of the slope beneath their feet was in deep shadow. Even as he watched, the moon was obscured by a shadow, and all the dimly-seen detail in the slope below vanished. Mallory knew that they could never afford to wait until the moon reappeared, for Neufeld and his men could well have arrived by then. Mallory belayed a rope round an outcrop of rock and said to Andrea and Maria: 'This one's really dangerous. Watch for loose boulders.'

Andrea and Maria took well over a minute to make this invisible descent, a double tug on the rope announcing their safe arrival at the bottom. On the way down they had started several small avalanches, but Mallory had no fears that the next man down would trigger off a fall of rock that would injure or even kill Andrea and Maria; Andrea had lived too long and too dangerously to die in so useless and so foolish a fashion – and he would undoubtedly warn the next man down of the same danger. For the tenth time Mallory glanced up towards the top of the slope they had just descended but if Neufeld, Droshny and his men had just arrived they were keeping very quiet about it and being most circumspect indeed: it was not a difficult conclusion to arrive at that, after the events of the past few hours, circumspection would be the last thing in their minds.

The moon broke through again as Mallory finally made his descent. He cursed the exposure it might offer if any of the enemy suddenly appeared on the clifftop, even although he knew that Andrea would be guarding against precisely that danger; on the other hand it afforded him the opportunity of descending at twice the speed he could have made in the earlier darkness. The watchers below watched tensely as Mallory, without any benefit of rope, made his perilous descent: but he never even looked like making one mistake. He descended safely to the boulder-strewn shore and gazed out over the rapids.

He said to no one in particular: 'You know what's going to happen if they arrive at the top and find us halfway across here and the moon shining down on us?' The ensuing silence left no doubt but they all knew what was going to happen. 'Now is all the time. Reynolds, you think you can make it?' Reynolds nodded. 'Then leave your gun.'

Mallory knotted a bowline round Reynolds's waist, taking the strain, if one were to arise, with Andrea and Groves. Reynolds launched himself bodily into the rapids, heading for the first of the rounded boulders which offered so treacherous a hold in that seething foam. Twice he was knocked off his feet, twice he regained them, reached the rock, but immediately beyond it was washed away off balance and swept down-river. The men on the bank hauled him ashore again, coughing and spluttering and fighting mad. Without a word to or look at anybody Reynolds again hurled himself into the rapids, and this time so determined was the fury of his assault that he succeeded in reaching the far bank without once being knocked off his feet.

He dragged himself on to the stony beach, lay there for some moments recovering from his exhaustion, then rose, crossed to a stunted pine at the base of the cliff rising on the other side, undid the rope round his waist and belayed it securely round the bole of the tree. Mallory, on his side, took two turns round a large rock and gestured to Andrea and the girl.

Mallory glanced upwards again to the top of the gully. There were still no signs of the enemy. Even so, Mallory felt that they could afford to wait no longer, that they had already pushed their luck too far. Andrea and Maria were barely halfway across when he told Groves to give Petar a hand across the rapids. He hoped to God the rope would hold, but hold it did for Andrea and Maria made it safely to the far bank. No sooner had they grounded than Mallory sent Miller on his way, carrying a pile of automatic arms over his left shoulder.

Groves and Petar also made the crossing without incident. Mallory himself had to wait until Miller reached the far bank, for he knew the chances of his being carried away were high and if he were, then Miller too would be precipitated into the water and their guns rendered useless.

Mallory waited until he saw Andrea give Miller a hand into the shallow water on the far bank and waited no longer. He unwound the rope from the rock he had been using as a belay, fastened a bowline round his own waist and plunged into the water. He was swept away at exactly the same point where Reynolds had been on his first attempt and was finally dragged ashore by his friends on the far bank with a fair amount of the waters of the Neretva in his stomach but otherwise unharmed.

'Any injuries, any cracked bones or skulls?' Mallory asked. He himself felt as if he had been over Niagara in a barrel. 'No? Fine.' He looked at Miller. 'You stay here with me. Andrea, take the others up round the first corner there and wait for us.'

'Me?' Andrea objected mildly. He nodded towards the gully. 'We've got friends that might be coming down there at any moment.'

Mallory took him some little way aside. 'We also have friends,' he said quietly, 'who might just possibly be coming down-river from the dam garrison.' He nodded at the two sergeants, Petar and Maria. 'What would happen to them if they ran into an Alpenkorps patrol, do you think?'

'I'll wait for you round the corner.'

Andrea and the four others made their slow way up-river, slipping and stumbling over the wetly slimy rocks and boulders. Mallory and Miller withdrew into the protection and concealment of two large boulders and stared upwards.

Several minutes passed. The moon still shone and the top of the gully was still innocent of any sign of the enemy. Miller said uneasily: 'What do you think has gone wrong? They're taking a damned long time about turning up.'

'No, I think that it's just that they are taking a damned long time in turning back.'

'Turning back?'

'They don't *know* where we've gone.' Mallory pulled out his map, examined it with a carefully hooded pencil-torch. 'About three-quarters of a mile down the railway track, there's a sharp turn to the left. In all probability the locomotive would have left the track there. Last time Neufeld and Droshny saw us we were aboard that locomotive and the logical thing for them to have done would have been to follow the track till they came to where we had abandoned the locomotive, expecting to find us somewhere in the vicinity. When they found the crashed engine, they would know at once what would have happened – but that would have given them another mile and a half to ride – and half of that uphill on tired ponies.'

'That must be it. I wish to God,' Miller went on grumblingly, 'that they'd hurry up.'

'What is this?' Mallory queried. 'Dusty Miller yearning for action?'

'No, I'm not,' Miller said definitely. He glanced at his watch. 'But time is getting very short.'

'Time,' Mallory agreed soberly, 'is getting terribly short.'

And then they came. Miller, glancing upward, saw a faint metallic glint in the moonlight as a head peered cautiously over the edge of the gully. He touched Mallory on the arm.

'I see him,' Mallory murmured. Together both men reached inside their tunics, pulled out their Lugers and removed their waterproof coverings. The helmeted head gradually resolved itself into a figure standing fully silhouetted in the moonlight against the sharply etched skyline. He began what was obviously meant to be a cautious descent, then suddenly flung up both arms and fell backwards and outwards. If he cried out, from where Mallory and Miller were the cry could not have been heard above the rushing of the waters. He struck the ledge halfway down, bounced off and outwards for a quite incredible distance, then landed spread-eagled on the stony river bank below, pulling down a small avalanche behind him.

Miller was grimly philosophical. 'Well, you said it was dangerous.'

Another figure appeared over the lip of the precipice to make the second attempt at a descent, and was followed in short order by several more men. Then, for the space of a few minutes, the moon went behind a cloud, while Mallory and Miller stared across the river until their eyes ached, anxiously and vainly trying to pierce the impenetrable darkness that shrouded the slope on the far side.

The leading climber, when the moon did break through, was just below the ledge, cautiously negotiating the lower slope. Mallory took careful aim with his Luger, the climber stiffened convulsively, toppled backwards and fell to his death. The following figure, clearly oblivious of the fate of his companion, began the descent of the lower slope. Both Mallory and Miller sighted their Lugers but just then the moon was suddenly obscured again and they had to lower their guns. When the moon again reappeared, four men had already reached the safety of the opposite bank, two of whom, linked together by a rope, were just beginning to venture the crossing of the ford.

Mallory and Miller waited until they had safely completed two-thirds of the crossing of the ford. They formed a close and easy target and at that range it was impossible that Mallory and Miller should miss, nor did they. There was a momentary reddening of the white waters of the rapids, as much imagined as seen, then, still lashed together they were swept away down the gorge. So furiously were their bodies tumbled over and over by the rushing waters, so often did cartwheeling arms and legs break surface, that they might well have given the appearance of men who, though without hope, were still desperately struggling for their lives. In any event, the two men left standing on the far bank clearly did not regard the accident as being significant of anything amiss in any sinister way. They stood and watched the vanishing bodies of their companions in perplexity, still unaware of what was happening. A matter of two or three seconds later and they would never have been aware of anything else but once more a wisp of errant dark cloud covered the moon and they still had a little time, a very little time, to live. Mallory and Miller lowered their guns.

Mallory glanced at his watch and said irritably: 'Why the hell don't they start firing? It's five past one.'

'Why don't who start firing?' Miller said cautiously.

'You heard. You were there. I asked Vis to ask Vukalovic to give us sound cover at one. Up by the Zenica Gap there, less than a mile away. Well, we can't wait any longer. It'll take –' He broke off and listened to the sudden outburst of rifle fire, startlingly loud even at that comparatively close distance, and smiled. 'Well, what's five minutes here or there. Come on. I have the feeling that Andrea must be getting a little anxious about us.'

Andrea was. He emerged silently from the shadows as they rounded the first bend in the river. He said reproachfully: 'Where have you two been? You had me worried stiff.'

'I'll explain in an hour's time – if we're all still around in an hour's time,' Mallory amended grimly. 'Our friends the bandits are two minutes behind. I think they'll be coming in force – although they've lost four already – six including the two Reynolds got from the locomotive. You stop at the next bend up-river and hold them off. You'll have to do it by yourself. Think you can manage?'

'This is no time for joking,' Andrea said with dignity. 'And then?'

'Groves and Reynolds and Petar and his sister come with us up-river, Reynolds and Groves as nearly as possible to the dam, Petar and Maria wherever they can find some suitable shelter, possibly in the vicinity of the swing bridge – as long as they're well clear of that damned great boulder perched above it.'

'Swing bridge, sir?' Reynolds asked. 'A boulder?'

'I saw it when we got off the locomotive to reconnoitre.'

'*You* saw it. Andrea didn't.'

'I mentioned it to him,' Mallory went on impatiently. He ignored the disbelief in the sergeant's face and turned to Andrea. 'Dusty and I can't wait any longer. Use your Schmeisser to stop them.' He pointed north-westwards towards the Zenica Gap, where the rattle of musketry was now almost continuous. 'With all that racket going on, they'll never know the difference.'

Andrea nodded, settled himself comfortably behind a pair of large boulders and slid the barrel of his Schmeisser into the V between them. The remainder of the party moved upstream, scrambling awkwardly around and over the slippery boulders and rocks that covered the right-hand bank of the Neretva, until they came to a rudimentary path that had been cleared among the stones. This they followed for perhaps a hundred yards, till they came to a slight bend in the gorge. By mutual consent and without any order being given, all six stopped and gazed upwards.

The towering breath-taking ramparts of the Neretva dam wall had suddenly come into full view. Above the dam on either side precipitous walls of rock soared up into the night sky, at first quite vertical then both leaning out in an immense overhang which seemed to make them almost touch at the top, although this, Mallory knew from the observation he had made from above, was an optical illusion. On top of the dam wall itself the guardhouses and radio huts were clearly visible, as were the pigmy shapes of several patrolling German soldiers. From the top of the eastern side of the dam, where the huts were situated, an iron ladder – Mallory knew it was painted green, but in the half-shadow cast by the dam wall it looked black – fastened by iron supports to the bare rock face, zig-zagged downwards to the foot of the gorge, close by where foaming white jets of water boiled from the outlet pipes at the base of the dam wall. Mallory tried to estimate how many steps there would be in that ladder. Two hundred, perhaps two hundred and fifty, and once you started to climb or descend you just had to keep on going, for nowhere was there any platform or backrest to afford even the means for a temporary respite. Nor did the ladder at any point afford the slightest scrap of cover from watchers on the bridge. As an assault route, Mallory mused, it was scarcely the one he would have chosen: he could not conceive of a more hazardous one.

About halfway between where they stood and the foot of the ladder on the other side, a swing bridge spanned the boiling waters of the gorge. There was little about its ancient, rickety and warped appearance to inspire any confidence: and what little confidence there might have been could hardly have survived the presence of an enormous boulder, directly above the eastern edge of the bridge, which seemed in imminent danger of breaking loose from its obviously insecure footing in the deep scar in the cliff-side.

Reynolds assimilated all of the scene before him, then turned to Mallory. He said quietly: 'We've been very patient, sir.'

'You've been very patient, Sergeant – and I'm grateful. You know, of course, that there is a Yugoslav division trapped in the Zenica Cage – that's just behind the mountains to our left, here. You know, too, that the Germans are going to launch two armoured divisions across the Neretva bridge at two a.m. this morning and that if once they do get across – and normally there would be nothing to stop them – the Yugoslavs, armed with their pop-guns and with hardly any ammunition left, would be cut to pieces. You know the only way to stop them is to destroy the Neretva bridge? You know that this counter-espionage and rescue mission was only a cover for the real thing?'

Reynolds said bitterly: 'I know that – now.' He pointed down the gorge. 'And I also know that the bridge lies that way.'

'And so it does. I also know that even if we could approach it – which would be quite impossible – we couldn't blow that bridge up with a truckload of explosives; steel bridges anchored in reinforced concrete take a great deal of destroying.' He turned and looked at the dam. 'So we do it another way. See that dam wall there – there's thirty million tons of water behind it – enough to carry away the Sydney bridge, far less the one over the Neretva.'

Groves said in a low voice: 'You're crazy,' and then, as an afterthought, 'sir.'

'Don't we know it? But we're going to blow up that dam all the same. Dusty and I.'

'But – but all the explosives we have are a few handgrenades,' Reynolds said, almost desperately. 'And in that dam wall there must be ten- to twenty-feet thicknesses of reinforced concrete. Blow it up? How?'

Mallory shook his head. 'Sorry.'

'Why, you close-mouthed –'

'Be quiet! Dammit, man, will you never, *never* learn. Even up to the very last minute you could be caught and made to tell – and then what would happen to Vukalovic's division trapped in the Zenica Cage? What you don't know, you can't tell.'

'But you know.' Reynolds's voice was thick with resentment. 'You and Dusty and Andrea – Colonel Stavros – *you* know. Groves and I knew all along that you knew, and *you* could be made to talk.'

Mallory said with considerable restraint: 'Get Andrea to talk? Perhaps you might – if you threatened to take away his cigars. Sure, Dusty and I could talk – but *someone* had to know.'

Groves said in the tone of a man reluctantly accepting the inevitable: 'How do you get behind that dam wall – you can't blow it up from the front, can you?'

'Not with the means at present available to us,' Mallory agreed. 'We get behind it. We climb up there.' Mallory pointed to the precipitous gorge wall on the other side.

'We climb up there, eh?' Miller said conversationally. He looked stunned.

'Up the ladder. But not all the way. Three-quarters of the way up the ladder we leave it and climb vertically up the cliff-face till we're about forty feet above the top of the dam wall, just where the cliff begins to overhang there. From there, there's a ledge – well, more of a crack, really –'

'A crack!' Miller said hoarsely. He was horror-stricken.

'A crack. It stretches about a hundred and fifty feet clear across the top of the dam wall at an ascending angle of maybe twenty degrees. We go that way.'

Reynolds looked at Mallory in an almost dazed incredulity. 'It's madness!'

'Madness!' Miller echoed.

'I wouldn't do it from choice,' Mallory admitted. 'Nevertheless, it's the only way in.'

'But you're bound to be seen,' Reynolds protested.

'Not bound to be.' Mallory dug into his rucksack and produced from it a black rubber frogman's suit, while Miller reluctantly did the same from his. As both men started to pull their suits on, Mallory continued: 'We'll be like black flies against a black wall.'

'He hopes,' Miller muttered.

'Then with any luck we expect them to be looking the other way when the RAF start in with the fireworks. And if we do seem in any danger of discovery – well, that's where you and Groves come in. Captain Jensen was right – as things have turned out, we couldn't have done this without you.'

'Compliments?' Groves said to Reynolds. 'Compliments from the Captain? I've a feeling there's something nasty on the way.'

'There is,' Mallory admitted. He had his suit and hood in position now and was fixing into his belt some pitons and a hammer he had extracted from his rucksack. 'If we're in trouble, you two create a diversion.'

'What kind of diversion?' Reynolds asked suspiciously.

'From somewhere near the foot of the dam you start firing up at the guards atop the dam wall.'

'But – but we'll be completely exposed.' Groves gazed across at the rocky scree which composed the left bank at the base of the dam and at the foot of the ladder. 'There's not an ounce of cover. What kind of chance will we have?'

Mallory secured his rucksack and hitched a long coil of rope over his shoulder. 'A very poor one, I'm afraid.' He looked at his luminous watch. 'But then, for the next forty-five minutes you and Groves are expendable. Dusty and I are not.'

'Just like that?' Reynolds said flatly. 'Expendable.'

'Just like that.'

'Want to change places?' Miller said hopefully. There was no reply for Mallory was already on his way. Miller, with a last apprehensive look at the towering rampart of rock above, gave a last hitch to his rucksack and followed. Reynolds made to move off, but Groves caught him by the arm and signed to Maria to go ahead with Petar. He said to her: 'We'll wait a bit and bring up the rear. Just to be sure.'

'What is it?' Reynolds said in a low voice.

'This. Our Captain Mallory admitted that he has already made four mistakes tonight. I think he's making a fifth now.'

'I'm not with you.'

'He's putting all our eggs in one basket and he's overlooked certain things. For instance, asking the two of us to stand by at the base of the dam wall. If we have to start a diversion, one burst of machine-gun fire from the top of the dam wall will get us both in seconds. One man can create as successful a diversion as two – and where's the point in the two of us getting killed? Besides, with one of us left alive, there's always the chance that something can be done to protect Maria and her brother. I'll go to the foot of the dam while you –'

'Why should you be the one to go? Why not –'

'Wait, I haven't finished yet. I also think Mallory's very optimistic if he thinks that Andrea can hold off that lot coming up the gorge. There must be at least twenty of them and they're not out for an evening's fun and games. They're out to kill us. So what happens if they do overwhelm Andrea and come up to the swing bridge and find Maria and Petar there while we are busy being sitting targets at the base of the dam wall? They'll knock them both off before you can bat an eyelid.'

'Or maybe not knock them off,' Reynolds muttered. 'What if Neufeld were to be killed before they reached the swing bridge? What if Droshny were the man in charge – Maria and Petar might take some time in dying.'

'So you'll stay near the bridge and keep our backs covered? With Maria and Petar in shelter somewhere near?'

'You're right, I'm sure you're right. But I don't like it,' Reynolds said uneasily. 'He gave us his orders and he's not a man who likes having his orders disobeyed.'

'He'll never know – even if he ever comes back, which I very much doubt, he'll never know. *And* he's started to make mistakes.'

'Not this kind of mistake.' Reynolds was still more than vaguely uneasy.

'Am I right or not?' Groves demanded.

'I don't think it's going to matter a great deal at the end of the day,' Reynolds said wearily. 'Okay, let's do it your way.'

The two sergeants hurried off after Maria and Petar.

Andrea listened to the scraping of heavy boots on stones, the very occasional metallic chink of a gun striking against a rock, and waited, stretched out flat on his stomach, the barrel of his Schmeisser rock-steady in the cleft between the boulders. The sounds heralding the stealthy approach up the river bank were not more than forty yards away when Andrea raised himself slightly, squinted down the barrel and squeezed the trigger.

The reply was immediate. At once three or four guns, all of them, Andrea realized, machine-pistols, opened up. Andrea stopped firing, ignoring the bullets whistling above his head and ricocheting from the boulders on either side of him, carefully lined up on one of the flashes issuing from a machine-pistol and fired a one-second burst. The man behind the machine-pistol straightened convulsively, his upflung right arm sending his gun spinning, then slowly toppled sideways in the Neretva and was carried away in the whitely swirling waters. Andrea fired again and a second man twisted round and fell heavily among the rocks. There came a suddenly barked order and the firing down-river ceased.

There were eight men in the down-river group and now one of them detached himself from the shelter of a boulder and crawled towards the second man who had been hit: as he moved, Droshny's face revealed his usual wolfish grin, but it was clear that he was feeling very far from smiling. He bent over the huddled figure in the stones, and turned him on his back: it was Neufeld, with blood streaming down from a gash in the side of the head. Droshny straightened, his face vicious in anger, and turned round as one of his Cetniks touched his arm.

'Is he dead?'

'Not quite. Concussed and badly. He'll be unconscious for hours, maybe days. I don't know, only a doctor can tell.' Droshny beckoned to two other men. 'You three – get him across the ford and up to safety. Two stay with him, the other come back. And for God's sake tell the others to hurry up and get here.'

His face still contorted with anger and for the moment oblivious of all danger, Droshny leapt to his feet and fired a long continuous burst upstream, a burst which apparently left Andrea completely unmoved, for he remained motionless where he was, resting peacefully with his back to his protective boulder, watching with mild interest but apparent unconcern as ricochets and splintered fragments of rock flew off in all directions.

The sound of the firing carried clearly to the ears of the guards patrolling the top of the dam. Such was the bedlam of small-arms fire all around and such were the tricks played on the ears by the baffling variety of echoes that reverberated up and down the gorge and over the surface of the dam itself, that it was quite impossible precisely to locate the source of the recent bursts of machine-pistol fire: what was significant, however, was that it *had* been machine-gun fire and up to that moment the sounds of musketry had consisted exclusively of rifle fire. And it *had* seemed to emanate from the south, from the gorge below the dam. One of the guards on the dam went worriedly to the captain in charge, spoke briefly, then walked quickly across to one of the small huts on the raised concrete platform at the eastern end of the dam wall. The hut, which had no front, only a rolled-up canvas protection, held a large radio transceiver manned by a corporal.

'Captain's orders,' the sergeant said. 'Get through to the bridge at Neretva. Pass a message to General Zimmermann that we – the captain, that is – is worried. Tell him that there's a great deal of small-arms fire all around us and that some of it seems to be coming from down-river.'

The sergeant waited impatiently while the operator put the call through and even more impatiently as the earphones crackled two minutes later and the operator started writing down the message. He took the completed message from the operator and handed it to the captain, who read it out aloud.

'General Zimmermann says, "There is no cause at all for anxiety, the noise is being made by our Yugoslav friends up by the Zenica Gap who are whistling in the dark because they are momentarily expecting an all-out assault by units of the 11th Army Corps. And it will be a great deal noisier later on when the RAF starts dropping bombs in all the wrong places. But they won't be dropping them near you, so don't worry."' The captain lowered the paper. 'That's good enough for me. If the General says we are not to worry, then that's good enough for me. You know the General's reputation, Sergeant?'

'I know his reputation, sir.' Some distance away and from some unidentifiable direction, came several more bursts of machine-pistol fire. The sergeant stirred unhappily.

'You are still troubled by something?' the captain asked.

'Yes, sir. I know the general's reputation, of course, and trust him implicitly.' He paused then went on worriedly: 'I could have sworn that that last burst of machine-pistol fire came from down the gorge there.'

'You're becoming just an old woman, Sergeant,' the captain said kindly, 'and you must report to our divisional surgeon soon. Your ears need examining.'

The sergeant, in fact, was not becoming an old woman and his hearing was in considerably better shape than that of the officer who had reproached him. The current burst of machine-pistol firing was, as he'd thought, coming from the gorge, where Droshny and his men, now doubled in numbers, were moving forward, singly or in pairs, but never more than two at a time, in a series of sharp but very short rushes, firing as they went. Their firing, necessarily wildly inaccurate as they stumbled and slipped on the treacherous going underfoot, elicited no response from Andrea, possibly because he felt himself in no great danger, probably because he was conserving his ammunition. The latter supposition seemed the more likely as Andrea had slung his Schmeisser and was now examining with interest a stick-grenade which he had just withdrawn from his belt.

Farther up-river, Sergeant Reynolds, standing at the eastern edge of the rickety wooden bridge which spanned the narrowest part of the gorge where the turbulent, racing, foaming waters beneath would have offered no hope of life at all to any person so unfortunate as to fall in there, looked unhappily down the gorge towards the source of the machine-pistol firing and wondered for the tenth time whether he should take a chance, re-cross the bridge and go to Andrea's aid: even in the light of his vastly revised estimate of Andrea, it seemed impossible, as Groves had said, that one man could for long hold off twenty others bent on vengeance. On the other hand, he had promised Groves to remain there to look after Petar and Maria. There came another burst of firing from down-river. Reynolds made his mind up. He would offer his gun to Maria to afford herself and Petar what protection it might, and leave them for as little time as might be necessary to give Andrea what help he required.

He turned to speak to her, but Maria and Petar were no longer there. Reynolds looked wildly around, his first reaction was that they had both fallen into the rapids, a reaction that he at once dismissed as ridiculous. Instinctively he gazed up the bank towards the base of the dam, and even although the moon was then obscured by a large bank of cloud, he saw them at once, making their way towards the foot of the iron ladder, where Groves was standing. For a brief moment he puzzled why they should have moved upstream without permission, then remembered that neither he nor Groves had, in fact, remembered to give them instructions to remain by the bridge. Not to worry, he thought, Groves will soon send them back down to the bridge again and when they arrived he would tell them of his decision to return to Andrea's

aid. He felt vaguely relieved at the prospect, not because he enter-
tained fears of what might possibly happen to him when he
rejoined Andrea and faced up to Droshny and his men but because
it postponed, if even only briefly, the necessity of implementing a
decision which could be only marginally justifiable in the first
place.

Groves, who had been gazing up the seemingly endless series of
zig-zags of that green iron ladder so precariously, it seemed,
attached to that vertical cliff-face, swung round at the soft grate of
approaching footsteps on the shale and stared at Maria and Petar,
walking, as always, hand in hand. He said angrily: 'What in God's
name are you people doing here? You've no right to be here –
can't you see, the guards have only to look down and you'll be
killed? Go on. Go back and rejoin Sergeant Reynolds at the bridge.
Now!'

Maria said softly: 'You are kind to worry, Sergeant Groves. But
we don't want to go. We want to stay here.'

'And what in hell's name good can you do by staying here?'
Groves asked roughly. He paused, then went on, almost kindly: 'I
know who you are now, Maria. I know what you've done, how
good you are at your own job. But this is not your job. Please.'

'No.' She shook her head. 'And I *can* fire a gun.'

'You haven't got one to fire. And Petar here, what right have you
to speak for him. Does he know where he is?'

Maria spoke rapidly to her brother in incomprehensible Serbo-
Croat: he responded by making his customary odd sounds in his
throat. When he had finished, Maria turned to Groves.

'He says he knows he is going to die tonight. He has what you
people call the second sight and he says there is no future beyond
tonight. He says he is tired of running. He says he will wait here till
the time comes.'

'Of all the stubborn, thick-headed –'

'Please, Sergeant Groves.' The voice, though still low, was
touched by a new note of asperity. 'His mind is made up, and you
can never change it.'

Groves nodded in acceptance. He said: 'Perhaps I can change
yours.'

'I do not understand.'

'Petar cannot help us anyway, no blind man could. But you can.
If you would.'

'Tell me.'

'Andrea is holding off a mixed force of at least twenty Cetniks and German troops.' Groves smiled wryly. 'I have recent reason to believe that Andrea probably has no equal anywhere as a guerilla fighter, but one man cannot hold off twenty for ever. When he goes, then there is only Reynolds left to guard the bridge – and if he goes, then Droshny and his men will be through in time to warn the guards, almost certainly in time to save the dam, certainly in time to send a radio message through to General Zimmermann to pull his tanks back on to high ground. I think, Maria, that Reynolds may require your help. Certainly, you can be of no help here – but if you stand by Andrea you *could* make all the difference between success and failure. And you did say you can fire a gun.'

'And as *you* pointed out, I haven't got a gun.'

'That was then. You have now.' Grove unslung his Schmeisser and handed it to her along with some spare ammunition.

'But –' Maria accepted gun and ammunition reluctantly. 'But now *you* haven't a gun.'

'Oh yes I have.' Groves produced his silenced Luger from his tunic. 'This is all I want tonight. *I* can't afford to make any noise tonight, not so close to the dam as this.'

'But I *can't* leave my brother.'

'Oh, I think you can. In fact, you're going to. No one on earth can help your brother any more. Not now. Please hurry.'

'Very well.' She moved off a few reluctant paces, stopped, turned and said: 'I suppose you think you're very clever, Sergeant Groves?'

'I don't know what you're talking about,' Groves said woodenly. She looked at him steadily for a few moments, then turned and made her way down-river. Groves smiled to himself in the near-darkness.

The smile vanished in the instant of time that it took for the gorge to be suddenly flooded with bright moonlight as a black, sharply-edged cloud moved away from the face of the moon. Groves called softly, urgently to Maria: 'Face down on the rocks and keep still,' saw her at once do what he ordered, then looked up the green ladder, his face registering the strain and anxiety in his mind.

About three-quarters of the way up the ladder, Mallory and Miller, bathed in the brilliant moonlight, clung to the top of one of the angled sections as immobile as if they had been carved from the rock itself. Their unmoving eyes, set in equally unmoving faces, were obviously fixed on – or transfixed by – the same point in space.

That point was a scant fifty feet away, above and to their left, where two obviously jumpy guards were leaning anxiously over the parapet at the top of the dam: they were gazing into the middle distance, down the gorge, towards the location of what seemed to be the sound of firing. They had only to move their eyes downwards and discovery for Groves and Maria was certain: they had only to shift their gaze to the left and discovery for Mallory and Miller would have been equally certain. And death for all inevitable.

ELEVEN

Saturday
0120–0135

Like Mallory and Miller, Groves, too, had caught sight of the two
German sentries leaning out over the parapet at the top of the dam
and staring anxiously down the gorge. As a situation for conveying
a feeling of complete nakedness, exposure and vulnerability, it
would, Groves felt, take a lot of beating. And if he felt like that,
how must Mallory and Miller, clinging to the ladder and less than
a stone's throw from the guards, be feeling? Both men, Groves
knew, carried silenced Lugers, but their Lugers were inside their
tunics and their tunics encased in their zipped-up frogmen's suits,
making them quite inaccessible. At least, making them quite inaccessible without, clinging as they were to the ladder, performing a
variety of contortionist movements to get at them – and it was certain that the least untoward movement would have been immediately spotted by the two guards. How it was that they hadn't
already been seen, even without movement, was incomprehensible to Groves: in that bright moonlight, which cast as much light on
the dam and in the gorge as one would have expected on any reasonably dull afternoon, any normal peripheral vision should have
picked them all up immediately. And it was unlikely that any front-
line troops of the Wehrmacht had less than standard peripheral
vision. Groves could only conclude that the intentness of the
guards' gaze did not necessarily mean that they were looking
intently: it could have been that all their being was at that moment
concentrated on their hearing, straining to locate the source of the
desultory machine-pistol fire down the gorge. With infinite caution
Groves eased his Luger from his tunic and lined it up. At that distance, even allowing for the high muzzle-velocity of the gun, he
reckoned his chances of getting either of the guards to be so remote

as to be hardly worth considering: but at least, as a gesture, it was better than nothing.

Groves was right on two counts. The two sentries on the parapet, far from being reassured by General Zimmermann's encouraging reassurance, were in fact concentrating all their being on listening to the down-river bursts of machine-pistol fire, which were becoming all the more noticeable, not only because they seemed – as they were – to be coming closer, but also because the ammunition of the Partisan defenders of the Zenica Gap was running low and their fire was becoming more sporadic. Groves had been right, too, about the fact that neither Mallory nor Miller had made any attempt to get at their Lugers. For the first few seconds, Mallory, like Groves, had felt sure that any such move would be bound to attract immediate attention, but, almost at once and long before the idea had occurred to Groves, Mallory had realized that the men were in such a trance-like state of listening that a hand could almost have passed before their faces without their being aware of it. And now, Mallory was certain, there would be no need to do anything at all because, from his elevation, he could see something that was quite invisible to Groves from his position at the foot of the dam: another dark band of cloud was almost about to pass across the face of the moon.

Within seconds, a black shadow flitting across the waters of the Neretva dam turned the colour from dark green to the deepest indigo, moved rapidly across the top of the dam wall, blotted out the ladder and the two men clinging to it, then engulfed the gorge in darkness. Groves sighed in soundless relief and lowered his Luger. Maria rose and made her way down-river towards the bridge. Petar moved his unseeing gaze around in the sightless manner of the blind. And, up above, Mallory and Miller at once began to climb again.

Mallory now abandoned the ladder at the top of one of its zigs and struck vertically up the cliff-face. The rockface, providentially, was not completely smooth, but such hand- and footholds as it afforded were few and small and awkwardly situated, making for a climb that was as arduous as it was technically difficult: normally, had he been using the hammer and pitons that were stuck in his belt, Mallory would have regarded it as a climb of no more than moderate difficulty: but the use of pitons was quite out of the question. Mallory was directly opposite the top of the dam wall and no more than 35 feet from the nearest guard: one tiny chink of hammer on metal could not fail to register on the hearing of the most inattentive listener: and, as Mallory had just observed, inattentive listening was the last accusation that could have been levelled against the sentries on the dam. So Mallory had to content himself with the use of his natural talents and the vast experience gathered over many years of rock-climbing and continue the climb as he was doing, sweating profusely inside the hermetic rubber suit, while Miller, now some forty feet below, peered upwards with such tense anxiety on his face that he was momentarily oblivious of his own precarious perch on top of one of the slanted ladders, a predicament which would normally have sent him into a case of mild hysterics.

Andrea, too, was at that moment peering at something about fifty feet away, but it would have required a hyperactive imagination to detect any signs of anxiety in that dark and rugged face. Andrea, as the guards on the dam had so recently been doing, was listening rather than looking. From his point of view all he could see was a dark and shapeless jumble of wetly glistening boulders with the Neretva rushing whitely alongside. There was no sign of life down there, but that only meant that Droshny, Neufeld and his men, having learnt their lessons the hard way – for Andrea could not know at this time that Neufeld had been wounded – were inching their way forward on elbows and knees, not once moving out from one safe cover until they had located another.

A minute passed, then Andrea heard the inevitable: a barely discernible 'click', as two pieces of stone knocked together. It came, Andrea estimated, from about thirty feet away. He nodded as if in satisfaction, armed the grenade, waited two seconds, then gently lobbed it downstream, dropping flat behind his protective boulder as he did so. There was the typically flat crack of a grenade explosion, accompanied by a briefly white flash of light in which two soldiers could be seen being flung bodily sideways.

The sound of the explosion came clearly to Mallory's ear. He remained still, allowing only his head to turn slowly till he was looking down on top of the dam wall, now almost twenty feet beneath him. The same two guards who had been previously listening so intently stopped their patrol a second time, gazed down the gorge again, looked at each other uneasily, shrugged uncertainly, then resumed their patrol. Mallory resumed his climb.

He was making better time now. The former negligible finger and toe holds had given way, occasionally, to small fissures in the rock into which he was able to insert the odd piton to give him a great deal more leverage than would have otherwise been possible.

When next he stopped climbing and looked upwards he was no more than six feet below the longitudinal crack he had been look-ing for – and, as he had said to Miller earlier, it *was* no more than a crack. Mallory made to begin again, then paused, his head cocked towards the sky.

Just barely audible at first above the roaring of the waters of the Neretva and the sporadic smallarms fire from the direction of the Zenica Gap, but swelling in power with the passing of every sec-ond, could be heard a low and distant thunder, a sound unmistak-able to all who had ever heard it during the war, a sound that her-alded the approach of squadrons, of a fleet of heavy bombers. Mallory listened to the rapidly approaching clamour of scores of aero engines and smiled to himself.

Many men smiled to themselves that night when they heard the approach from the west of those squadrons of Lancasters. Miller, still perched on his ladder and still exercising all his available will-power not to look down, managed to smile to himself, as did Groves at the foot of the ladder and Reynolds by the bridge. On the right bank of the Neretva, Andrea smiled to himself, reckoned that the roar of those fast-approaching engines would make an excel-lent cover for any untoward sound and picked another grenade from his belt. Outside a soup tent high up in the biting cold of the Ivenici plateau, Colonel Vis and Captain Vlanovich smiled their delight at each other and solemnly shook hands. Behind the south-ern redoubts of the Zenica Cage, General Vukalovic and his three senior officers, Colonel Janzy, Colonel Lazlo and Major Stephan, for once removed the glasses through which they had been so long peering at the Neretva bridge and the menacing woods beyond and smiled their incredulous relief at one another. And, most strangely of all, already seated in his command truck just inside the woods to the south of the Neretva bridge, General Zimmermann smiled perhaps the most broadly of all.

Mallory resumed his climb, moving even more quickly now, reached the longitudinal crack, worked his way up above it, pressed a piton into a convenient crack in the rock, withdrew his hammer from his belt and prepared to wait. Even now, he was not much more than forty feet above the dam wall, and the piton that Mallory now wanted to anchor would require not one blow but a dozen of them, and powerful ones at that: the idea that, even above the approaching thunder of the Lancasters' engines, the metallic hammering would go unremarked was preposterous. The sound of the heavy aero engines was now deepening by the moment.

Mallory glanced down directly beneath him. Miller was gazing upward, tapping his wristwatch as best a man can when he has both arms wrapped round the same rung of a ladder, and making urgent gestures. Mallory, in turn, shook his head and made a downward restraining motion with his free hand. Miller shook his head in resignation.

The Lancasters were on top of them now. The leader arrowed in diagonally across the dam, lifted slightly as it came to the high mountains on the other side and then the earth shook and ripples of dark waters shivered their erratic way across the surface of the Neretva dam before the first explosion reached their ears, as the first stick of 1,000-pound bombs crashed squarely into the Zenica Gap. From then on the sounds of the explosions of the bombs raining down on the Gap were so close together as to be almost continuous: what little time-lapse there was between some of the explosions was bridged by the constantly rumbling echoes that rumbled through the mountains and valleys of central Bosnia.

Mallory had no longer any need to worry about sound any more, he doubted he could even have heard himself speak, for most of those bombs were landing in a concentrated area less than a mile from where he clung to the side of the cliff, their explosions making an almost constant white glare that showed clearly above the mountains to the west. He hammered home his piton, belayed a rope around it, and dropped the rope to Miller, who immediately seized it and began to climb: he looked, Mallory thought, uncommonly like one of the early Christian martyrs. Miller was no mountaineer, but, no mistake, he knew how to climb a rope: in a remarkably short time he was up beside Mallory, feet firmly wedged into the longitudinal crack, both hands gripping tightly to the piton.

'Think you can hang on that piton?' Mallory asked. He almost had to shout to make himself heard above the still undiminished thunder of the falling bombs.

'Just try to prise me away.'

'I won't,' Mallory grinned.

He coiled up the rope which Miller had used for his ascent, hitched it over his shoulder and started to move quickly along the longitudinal crack. 'I'll take this across the top of the dam, belay it to another piton. Then you can join me. Right?'

Miller looked down into the depths and shuddered. 'If you think I'm going to stay here, you must be mad.'

Mallory grinned again and moved away.

To the south of the Neretva bridge, General Zimmermann, with an aide by his side, was still listening to the sounds of the aerial assault on the Zenica Gap. He glanced at his watch.

'Now,' he said. 'First-line assault troops into position.'

At once heavily armed infantry, bent almost double to keep themselves below parapet level, began to move quickly across the Neretva bridge: once on the other side, they spread out east and west along the northern bank of the river, concealed from the Partisans by the ridge of high ground abutting on the river bank. Or they thought they were concealed: in point of fact a Partisan scout, equipped with night-glasses and field telephone, lay prone in a suicidally positioned slit-trench less than a hundred yards from the bridge itself, sending back a constant series of reports to Vukalovic.

Zimmermann glanced up at the sky and said to his aide: 'Hold them. The moon's coming through again.' Again he looked at his watch. 'Start the tank engines in twenty minutes.'

'They've stopped coming across the bridge, then?' Vukalovic said.

'Yes, sir.' It was the voice of his advance scout. 'I think it's because the moon is about to break through in a minute or two.'

'I think so too,' Vukalovic said. He added grimly: 'And I suggest you start working your way back before it does break through or it will be the last chance you'll ever have.'

Andrea, too, was regarding the night sky with interest. His gradual retreat had now taken him into a particularly unsatisfactory defensive position, practically bereft of all cover: a very unhealthy situation to be caught in, he reflected, when the moon came out from behind the clouds. He paused for a thoughtful moment, then armed another grenade and lobbed it in the direction of a cluster of dimly seen boulders about fifty feet away. He did not wait to see what effect it had, he was already scrambling his way up-river before the grenade exploded. The one certain effect it did have was to galvanize Droshny and his men into immediate and furious retaliation, at least half a dozen machine-pistols loosing off almost simultaneous bursts at the position Andrea had so recently and prudently vacated. One bullet plucked at the sleeve of his tunic, but that was as near as anything came. He reached another cluster of boulders without incident and took up a fresh defensive position behind them: when the moon did break through it would be Droshny and his men who would be faced with the unpalatable prospect of crossing that open stretch of ground.

Reynolds, crouched by the swing bridge with Maria now by his side, heard the flat crack of the exploding grenade and guessed that Andrea was now no more than a hundred yards downstream on the far bank. And like so many people at that precise instant, Reynolds, too, was gazing up at what could be seen of the sky through the narrow north-west gap between the precipitous walls of the gorge.

Reynolds had intended going to Andrea's aid as soon as Groves had sent Petar and Maria back to him, but three factors had inhibited them from taking immediate action. In the first place, Groves had been unsuccessful in sending back Petar: secondly, the frequent bursts of machine-pistol firing down the gorge, coming steadily closer, were indication enough that Andrea was making a very orderly retreat and was still in fine fighting fettle: and thirdly, even if Droshny and his men did get Andrea, Reynolds knew that by taking up position behind the boulder directly above the bridge, he could deny Droshny and his men the crossing of the bridge for an indefinite period.

But the sight of the large expanse of starlit sky coming up behind the dark clouds over the moon made Reynolds forget the tactically sound and cold-blooded reasons for remaining where he was. It was not in Reynolds's nature to regard any other man as an expendable pawn and he suspected strongly that when he was presented with a sufficiently long period of moonlight Droshny would use it to make the final rush that would overwhelm Andrea. He touched Maria on the shoulder.

'Even the Colonel Stavroses of this world need a hand at times. Stay here. We shouldn't be long.' He turned and ran across the swaying swing bridge.

Damn it, Mallory thought bitterly, damn it, damn it and damn it all. Why couldn't there have been heavy dark cloud covering the entire sky? Why couldn't it have been raining? Or snowing? Why hadn't they chosen a moonless night for this operation? But he was, he knew, only kicking against the pricks. No one had had any choice, for tonight was the only time there was. But still, that damnable moon.

Mallory looked to the north, where the northern wind, driving banded cloud across the moon, was leaving behind it a large expanse of starlit sky. Soon the entire dam and gorge would be bathed in moonlight for a considerable period: Mallory thought wryly that he could have wished himself to be in a happier position for that period.

By this time, he had traversed about half the length of the longitudinal crack. He glanced to his left and reckoned he had still between thirty and forty feet to go before he was well clear of the dam wall and above the waters of the dam itself. He glanced to his right and saw, not to his surprise, that Miller was still where he had left him, clinging to the piton with both hands as if it were his dearest friend on earth, which at that moment it probably was. He glanced downwards: he was directly above the dam wall now, some fifty feet above it, forty feet above the roof of the guardhouse. He looked at the sky again: a minute, no more, and the moon would be clear. What was it that he had said to Reynolds that afternoon? Yes, that was it. For now is all the time there may be. He was beginning to wish he hadn't said that. He was a New Zealander, but only a second-generation New Zealander: all his forebears were Scots and everyone knew how the Scots indulged in those heathenish practices of second sight and peering into the future. Mallory briefly indulged in the mental equivalent of a shoulder shrug and continued on his traverse.

At the foot of the iron ladder, Groves, to whom Mallory was now no more than a half-seen, half-imagined dark shape against a black cliff-face, realized that Mallory was soon going to move out of his line of sight altogether, and when that happened he would be in no position to give Mallory any covering fire at all. He touched Petar on the shoulder and with the pressure of his hand indicated that he should sit down at the foot of the ladder. Petar looked at him sightlessly, uncomprehendingly, then suddenly appeared to gather what was expected of him, for he nodded obediently and sat down. Groves thrust his silenced Luger deep inside his tunic and began to climb.

A mile to the west, the Lancasters were still pounding the Zenica Gap. Bomb after bomb crashed down with surprising accuracy into that tiny target area, blasting down trees, throwing great eruptions of earth and stones into the air, starting all over the area scores of small fires which had already incinerated nearly all the German plywood tanks. Seven miles to the south, Zimmermann still listened with interest and still with satisfaction to the continuing bombardment to the north. He turned to the aide seated beside him in the command car.

'You will have to admit that we must give the Royal Air Force full marks for industry, if for nothing else. I hope our troops are well clear of the area?'

'There's not a German soldier within two miles of the Zenica Gap, Herr General.'

'Excellent, excellent.' Zimmermann appeared to have forgotten about his earlier forebodings. 'Well, fifteen minutes. The moon will soon be through, so we'll hold our infantry. The next wave of troops can go across with the tanks.'

Reynolds, making his way down the right bank of the Neretva towards the sound of firing, now very close indeed, suddenly became very still indeed. Most men react the same way when they feel the barrel of a gun grinding into the side of their necks. Very cautiously, so as not to excite any nervous trigger-fingers, Reynolds turned both eyes and head slightly to the right and realized with a profound sense of relief that this was one instance where he need have no concern about jittery nerves.

'You had your orders,' Andrea said mildly. 'What are you doing here?'

'I – I thought you might need some help.' Reynolds rubbed the side of his neck. 'Mind you, I could have been wrong.'

'Come on. It's time we got back and crossed the bridge.' For good measure and in very quick succession, Andrea spun another couple of grenades down-river, then made off quickly up the river bank, closely followed by Reynolds.

The moon broke through. For the second time that night, Mallory became absolutely still, his toes jammed into the longitudinal crack, his hands round the piton which he had thirty seconds earlier driven into the rock and to which he had secured the rope. Less than ten feet from him Miller, who with the aid of the rope had already safely made the first part of the traverse, froze into similar immobility. Both men stared down on to the top of the dam wall.

There were six guards visible, two at the farther or western end, two at the middle and the remaining two almost directly below Mallory and Miller. How many more there might have been inside the guardhouse neither Mallory nor Miller had any means of knowing. All they could know for certain was that their exposed vulnerability was complete, their position desperate.

Three-quarters of the way up the iron ladder, Groves, too, became very still. From where he was, he could see Mallory, Miller and the two guards very clearly indeed. He knew with a sudden conviction that this time there would be no escape, they could never be so lucky again. Mallory, Miller, Petar or himself – who would be the first to be spotted? On balance, he thought he himself was the most likely candidate. Slowly, he wrapped his left arm round the ladder, pushed his right hand inside his tunic, withdrew his Luger and laid the barrel along his left forearm.

The two guards on the eastern end of the dam wall were restless, apprehensive, full of nameless fears. As before, they both leaned out over the parapet and stared down the valley. They can't help but see me, Groves thought, they're *bound* to see me, good God, I'm almost directly in their line of sight. Discovery must be immediate.

It was, but not for Groves. Some strange instinct made one of the guards glance upwards and to his left and his mouth fell open at the astonishing spectacle of two men in rubber suits clinging like limpets to the sheer face of the cliff. It took him several interminable seconds before he could recover himself sufficiently to reach out blindly and grab his companion by the arm. His companion followed the other guard's line of sight, then his jaw, too, dropped in an almost comical fashion. Then, at precisely the same moment, both men broke free from their thrall-like spell and swung their guns, one a Schmeisser, the other a pistol, upwards to line up on the two men pinned helplessly to the cliff-face.

Groves steadied his Luger against both his left arm and the side of the ladder, sighted unhurriedly along the barrel and squeezed the trigger. The guard with the Schmeisser dropped the weapon, swayed briefly on his feet and started to fall outwards. Almost three seconds passed before the other guard, startled and momentarily quite uncomprehending, reached out to grab his companion, but he was far too late, he never even succeeded in touching him. The dead man, moving in an almost grotesquely slow-motion fashion, toppled wearily over the edge of the parapet and tumbled head over heels into the depths of the gorge beneath.

The guard with the pistol leaned far out over the parapet, staring in horror after his falling comrade. It was quite obvious that he was momentarily at a total loss to understand what had happened, for he had heard no sound of a shot. But realization came within the second as a piece of concrete chipped away inches from his left elbow and a spent bullet ricocheted its whistling way into the night sky. The guard's eyes lifted and widened in shock, but this time the shock had no inhibiting effect on the speed of his reactions. More in blind hope than in any real expectation of success, he loosed off two quick snap-shots and bared his teeth in satisfaction as he heard Groves cry out and saw the right hand, the forefinger still holding the Luger by the trigger guard, reach up to clutch the shattered left shoulder.

Groves's face was dazed and twisted with pain, the eyes already clouded by the agony of the wound, but those responsible for making Groves a commando sergeant had not picked him out with a pin and Groves was not quite finished yet. He brought his Luger down again. There was something terribly wrong with his vision now, he dimly realized, he thought he had a vague impression that the guard on the parapet was leaning far out, pistol held in both hands to make sure of his killing shot, but he couldn't be sure. Twice Groves squeezed the trigger of his Luger and then he closed his eyes, for the pain was gone and he suddenly felt very sleepy.

The guard by the parapet pitched forward. He reached out desperately to grab the coaming of the parapet, but to pull himself back to safety he had to swing his legs up to retain his balance and he found he could no longer control his legs, which slid helplessly over the edge of the parapet. His body followed his legs almost of its own volition, for the last vestiges of strength remain for only a few seconds with a man through whose lungs two Luger bullets have just passed. For a moment of time his clawed hands hooked despairingly on to the edge of the parapet and then his fingers opened.

Groves seemed unconscious now, his head lolling on his chest, the left-hand sleeve and left-hand side of his uniform already saturated with blood from the terrible wound in his shoulder. Were it not for the fact that his right arm was jammed between a rung of the ladder and the cliff-face behind it, he must certainly have fallen. Slowly, the fingers of his right hand opened and the Luger fell from his hand.

Seated at the foot of the ladder, Petar started as the Luger struck the shale less than a foot from where he was sitting. He looked up instinctively, then rose, made sure that the inevitable guitar was firmly secured across his back, reached out for the ladder and started climbing.

Mallory and Miller stared down, watching the blind singer climb up towards the wounded and obviously unconscious Groves. After a few moments, as if by telepathic signal, Mallory glanced across at Miller who caught his eyes almost at once. Miller's face was strained, almost haggard. He freed one hand momentarily from the rope and made an almost desperate gesture in the direction of the wounded sergeant. Mallory shook his head.

Miller said hoarsely: 'Expendable, huh?'

'Expendable.'

Both men looked down again. Petar was now not more than ten feet below Groves, and Groves, though Mallory and Miller could not see this, had his eyes closed and his right arm was beginning to slip through the gap between the rung and the rock. Gradually, his right arm began to slip more quickly, until his elbow was free, and then his arm came free altogether and slowly, so very slowly, he began to topple outwards from the wall. But Petar got to him first, standing on the step beneath Groves and reaching out an arm to encircle him and press him back against the ladder. Petar had him and for the moment Petar could hold him. But that was all he could do.

The moon passed behind a cloud.

Miller covered the last ten feet separating him from Mallory. He looked at Mallory and said: 'They're both going to go, you know that?'

'I know that.' Mallory sounded even more tired than he looked. 'Come on. Another thirty feet and we should be in position.' Mallory, leaving Miller where he was, continued his traverse along the crack. He was moving very quickly now, taking risks that no sane cragsman would ever have contemplated, but he had no option now, for time was running out. Within a minute he had reached a spot where he judged that he had gone far enough, hammered home a piton and securely belayed the rope to it.

He signalled to Miller to come and join him. Miller began the last stage of the traverse, and as he was on his way across, Mallory unhitched another rope from his shoulders, a sixty-foot length of climbers' rope, knotted at fifteen-inch intervals. One end of this he fastened to the same piton as held the rope that Miller was using for making his traverse: the other end he let fall down the cliff-side. Miller came up and Mallory touched him on the shoulder and pointed downwards.

The dark waters of the Neretva dam were directly beneath them.

TWELVE

Saturday
0135–0200

Andrea and Reynolds lay crouched among the boulders at the western end of the elderly swing bridge over the gorge. Andrea looked across the length of the bridge, his gaze travelling up the steep gully behind it till it came to rest on the huge boulder perched precariously at the angle where the steep slope met the vertical cliff-face behind it. Andrea rubbed a bristly chin, nodded thoughtfully and turned to Reynolds.

'You cross first. I'll give you covering fire. You do the same for me when you get to the other side. Don't stop, don't look round. Now.'

Reynolds made for the bridge in a crouching run, his footsteps seeming to him abnormally loud as he reached the rotting planking of the bridge itself. The palms of his hands gliding lightly over the hand ropes on either side he continued without check or diminution of speed, obeying Andrea's instructions not to risk a quick backward glance, and feeling a very strange sensation between his shoulderblades. To his mild astonishment he reached the far bank without a shot being fired, headed for the concealment and shelter offered by a large boulder a little way up the bank, was startled momentarily to see Maria hiding behind the same boulder, then whirled round and unslung his Schmeisser.

On the far bank there was no sign of Andrea. For a brief moment Reynolds experienced a quick stab of anger, thinking Andrea had used this ruse merely to get rid of him, then smiled to himself as he heard two flat explosive sounds some little way down the river on the far bank. Andrea, Reynolds remembered, had still had two grenades left and Andrea was not the man to let such handy things rust from disuse. Besides, Reynolds realized, it would provide

413

Andrea with extra valuable seconds to make good his escape, which indeed it did for Andrea appeared on the far bank almost immediately and, like Reynolds, effected the crossing of the bridge entirely without incident. Reynolds called softly and Andrea joined them in the shelter of the boulder.

Reynolds said in a low voice: 'What next?'

'First things first.' Andrea produced a cigar from a waterproof box, a match from another waterproof box, struck the match in his huge cupped hands and puffed in immense satisfaction. When he removed the cigar, Reynolds noticed that he held it with the glowing end safely concealed in the curved palm of his hand. 'What's next? I tell you what's next. Company coming to join us across the bridge, and coming very soon, too. They've taken crazy risks to try to get me – and paid for them – which shows they are pretty desperate. Crazy men don't hang about for long. You and Maria here move fifty or sixty yards nearer the dam and take cover there – and keep your guns on the far side of the bridge.'

'You staying here?' Reynolds asked.

Andrea blew out a noxious cloud of cigar smoke. 'For the moment, yes.'

'Then I'm staying, too.'

'If you want to get killed, it's all right by me,' Andrea said mildly. 'But this beautiful young lady here wouldn't look that way any more with the top of her head blown off.'

Reynolds was startled by the crudeness of the words. He said angrily: 'What the devil do you mean?'

'I mean this.' Andrea's voice was no longer mild. 'This boulder gives you perfect concealment from the bridge. But Droshny and his men can move another thirty or forty yards farther up the bank on their side. What concealment will you have then?'

'I never thought of that,' Reynolds said.

'There'll come a day when you say that once too often,' Andrea said sombrely, 'and then it will be too late to think of anything again.'

A minute later they were in position. Reynolds was hidden behind a huge boulder which afforded perfect concealment both from the far side of the bridge and from the bank on the far side up to the point where it petered out: it did not offer concealment from the dam. Reynolds looked to his left where Maria was crouched farther in behind the rock. She smiled at him, and Reynolds knew he had never seen a braver girl, for the hands that held the

Schmeisser were trembling. He moved out a little and peered down-river, but there appeared to be no signs of life whatsoever at the western edge of the bridge. The only signs of life at all, indeed, were to be seen behind the huge boulder up in the gully, where Andrea, completely screened from anyone at or near the far side of the bridge, was industriously loosening the foundations of rubble and earth round the base of the boulder.

Appearances, as always, were deceptive. Reynolds had judged there to be no life at the western end of the bridge but there was, in fact, life and quite a lot of it, although admittedly there was no action. Concealed in the massive boulders about twenty feet back from the bridge, Droshny, a Cetnik sergeant and perhaps a dozen German soldiers and Cetniks lay in deep concealment among the rocks.

Droshny had binoculars to his eyes. He examined the ground in the neighbourhood of the far side of the swing bridge, then traversed to his left up beyond the boulder where Reynolds and Maria lay hidden until he reached the dam wall. He lifted the glasses, following the dimly-seen zig-zag outline of the iron ladder, checked, adjusted the focus as finely as possible, then stared again. There could be no doubt: there were two men clinging to the ladder, about three-quarters of the way up towards the top of the dam.

'Good God in heaven!' Droshny lowered the binoculars, the gaunt craggy features registering an almost incredulous horror, and turned to the Cetnik sergeant by his side. 'Do you know what they mean to do?'

'The dam!' The thought had not occurred to the sergeant until that instant but the stricken expression on Droshny's face made the realization as immediate as it was inevitable. 'They're going to blow up the dam!' It did not occur to either man to wonder *how* Mallory could possibly blow up the dam: as other men had done before them, both Droshny and the sergeant were beginning to discover in Mallory and his *modus operandi* an extraordinary quality of inevitability that transformed remote possibilities into very likely probabilities.

'General Zimmermann!' Droshny's gravelly voice had become positively hoarse. 'He must be warned! If that dam bursts while his tanks and troops are crossing –'

'Warn him? Warn him? How in God's name can we warn him?'

'There's a radio up on the dam.'

The sergeant stared at him. He said: 'It might as well be on the moon. There'll be a rearguard, they're bound to have left a rearguard. Some of us are going to get killed crossing that bridge, Captain.'

'You think so?' Droshny glanced up sombrely at the dam. 'And just what do you think is going to happen to us all down here if *that* goes?'

Slowly, soundlessly and almost invisibly, Mallory and Miller swam northwards through the dark waters of the Neretva dam, away from the direction of the dam wall. Suddenly Miller, who was slightly in the lead, gave a low exclamation and stopped swimming.

'What's up?' Mallory asked.

'This is up.' With an effort Miller lifted a section of what appeared to be a heavy wire cable just clear of the water. 'Nobody mentioned this little lot.'

'Nobody did,' Mallory agreed. He reached under the water. 'And there's a steel mesh below.'

'An anti-torpedo net?'

'Just that.'

'Why?' Miller gestured to the north where, at a distance of less than two hundred yards, the dam made an abrupt right-angled turn between the towering cliff-faces. 'It's impossible for any torpedo bomber – any bomber – to get a run-in on the dam wall.'

'Someone should have told the Germans. They take no chances – and it makes things a damned sight more difficult for us.' He peered at his watch. 'We'd better start hurrying. We're late.'

They eased themselves over the wire and started swimming again, more quickly this time. Several minutes later, just after they had rounded the corner of the dam and lost sight of the dam wall, Mallory touched Miller on the shoulder. Both men trod water, turned and looked back in the direction from which they had come. To the south, not much more than two miles away, the night sky had suddenly blossomed into an incandescent and multi-coloured beauty as scores of parachute flares, red and green and white and orange, drifted slowly down towards the Neretva river.

'Very pretty, indeed,' Miller conceded. 'And what's all this in aid of?'

'It's in aid of us. Two reasons. First of all, it will take any person who looks at that – and *everyone* will look at it – at least ten minutes to recover his night-sight, which means that any odd goings-on in this part of the dam are all that less likely to be observed: and if everyone is going to be busy looking that way, then they can't be busy looking this way at the same time.'

'Very logical,' Miller approved. 'Our Captain Jensen doesn't miss out on very much, does he?'

'He has, as the saying goes, all his marbles about him.' Mallory turned again and gazed to the east, his head cocked the better to listen. He said: 'You have to hand it to them. Dead on target, dead on schedule. I hear him coming now.'

The Lancaster, no more than five hundred feet above the surface of the dam, came in from the east, its engine throttled back almost to stalling speed. It was still two hundred yards short of where Mallory and Miller were treading water when suddenly huge black silk parachutes bloomed beneath it: almost simultaneously, engine-power was increased to maximum revolutions and the big bomber went into a steeply banking climbing turn to avoid smashing into the mountains on the far side of the dam.

Miller gazed at the slowly descending black parachutes, turned, and looked at the brilliantly burning flares to the south. 'The skies,' he announced, 'are full of things tonight.'

He and Mallory began to swim in the direction of the falling parachutes.

Petar was near to exhaustion. For long minutes now he had been holding Groves's dead weight pinned against the iron ladder and his aching arms were beginning to quiver with the strain. His teeth were clenched hard, his face, down which rivulets of sweat poured, was twisted with the effort and the agony of it all. Plainly, Petar could not hold out much longer.

It was by the light of those flares that Reynolds, still crouched with Maria in hiding behind the big boulder, first saw the predicament of Petar and Groves. He turned to glance at Maria: one look at the stricken face was enough to tell Reynolds that she had seen it, too.

Reynolds said hoarsely: 'Stay here. I must go and help them.'

'No!' She caught his arm, clearly exerting all her will to keep herself under control: her eyes, as they had been when Reynolds had first seen her, had the look of a hunted animal about them. 'Please, Sergeant, no. You must stay here.'

Reynolds said desperately: 'Your brother –'

'There are more important things –'

'Not for you there aren't.' Reynolds made to rise, but she clung to his arm with surprising strength, so that he couldn't release himself without hurting her. He said, almost gently: 'Come on, lass, let me go.'

'No! If Droshny and his men get across –' She broke off as the last of the flares finally fizzled to extinction, casting the entire gorge into what was, by momentary contrast, an almost total darkness. Maria went on simply: 'You'll have to stay now, won't you?'

'I'll have to stay now.' Reynolds moved out from the shelter of the boulder and put his night-glasses to his eyes. The swing bridge, and as far as he could tell, the far bank seemed innocent of any sign of life. He traversed up the gully and could just make out the form of Andrea, his excavations finished, resting peacefully behind the big boulder. Again with a feeling of deep unease, Reynolds trained his glasses on the bridge. He suddenly became very still. He removed the glasses, wiped the lenses very carefully, rubbed his eyes and lifted the glasses again.

His night-sight, momentarily destroyed by the flares, was now almost back to normal and there could be no doubt or any imagination about what he was seeing – seven or eight men, Droshny in the lead, flat on their stomachs, were inching their way on elbows, hands and knees across the wooden slats of the swing bridge.

Reynolds lowered the glasses, stood upright, armed a grenade and threw it as far as he could towards the bridge. It exploded just as it landed, at least forty yards short of the bridge. That it achieved nothing but a flat explosive bang and the harmless scattering of some shale was of no account, for it had never been intended to reach the bridge: it had been intended as a signal for Andrea, and Andrea wasted no time.

He placed the soles of both feet against the boulder, braced his back against the cliff-face and heaved. The boulder moved the merest fraction of an inch. Andrea momentarily relaxed, allowing the boulder to roll back, then repeated the process: this time the forward motion of the boulder was quite perceptible. Andrea relaxed again, then pushed for the third time.

Down below on the bridge, Droshny and his men, uncertain as to the exact significance of the exploding grenade, had frozen into complete immobility. Only their eyes moved, darting almost desperately from side to side to locate the source of a danger that lay so heavily in the air as to be almost palpable.

The boulder was distinctly rocking now. With every additional heave it received from Andrea, it was rocking an additional inch farther forward, an additional inch farther backwards. Andrea had slipped farther and farther down until now he was almost horizontal on his back. He was gasping for breath and sweat was streaming down his face. The boulder rolled back almost as if it were going to fall upon him and crush him. Andrea took a deep breath, then convulsively straightened back and legs in one last titanic heave. For a moment the boulder teetered on the point of imbalance, reached the point of no return and fell away.

Droshny could most certainly have heard nothing and, in that near darkness, it was certain as could be that he had seen nothing. It could only have been an instinctive awareness of impending death that made him glance upwards in sudden conviction that this was where the danger lay. The huge boulder, just rolling gently when Droshny's horror-stricken eyes first caught sight of it, almost at once began to bound in ever-increasing leaps, hurtling down the slope directly towards them, trailing a small avalanche behind it. Droshny screamed a warning. He and his men scrambled desperately to their feet, an instinctive reaction that was no more than a useless and token gesture in the face of death, because, for most of them, it was already far too late and they had no place to go.

With one last great leap the hurtling boulder smashed straight into the centre of the bridge, shattering the flimsy woodwork and slicing the bridge in half. Two men who had been directly in the path of the boulder died instantaneously: five others were catapulted into the torrent below and swept away to almost equally immediate death. The two broken sections of the bridge, still secured to either bank by the suspension ropes, hung down into the rushing waters, their lowermost parts banging furiously against the boulder-strewn banks.

There must have been at least a dozen parachutes attached to the three dark cylindrical objects that now lay floating, though more than half submerged, in the equally dark waters of the Neretva dam. Mallory and Miller sliced those away with their knives, then joined the three cylinders in line astern, using short wire strops that had been provided for that precise purpose. Mallory examined the leading cylinder and gently eased back a lever set in the top. There was a subdued roar as compressed air violently aerated the water astern of the leading cylinder and sent it surging forward, tugging the other two cylinders behind it. Mallory closed the lever and nodded to the other two cylinders.

'These levers on the right-hand side control the flooding valves. Open that one till you just have negative buoyancy and no more. I'll do the same on this one.'

Miller cautiously turned a valve and nodded at the leading cylinder. 'What's that for?'

'Do *you* fancy towing a ton and a half of amatol as far as the dam wall? Propulsion unit of some kind. Looks like a sawn-off section of a twenty-one-inch torpedo tube to me. Compressed air, maybe at a pressure of five thousand pounds a square inch, passing through reduction gear. Should do the job all right.'

'Just so long as Miller doesn't have to do it.' Miller closed the valve on the cylinder. 'About that?'

'About that.' All three cylinders were now just barely submerged. Again Mallory eased back the compressed air lever on the leading cylinder. There was a throaty burble of sound, a sudden flurry of bubbles streaming out astern and then all three cylinders were under way, heading down towards the angled neck of the dam, both men clinging to and guiding the leading cylinder.

When the swing bridge had disintegrated under the impact of the boulder, seven men had died: but two still lived.

Droshny and his sergeant, furiously buffeted and badly bruised by the torrent of water, clung desperately to the broken end of the bridge. At first, they could do no more than hold on, but gradually, and after a most exhausting struggle, they managed to haul themselves clear of the rapids and hang there, arms and legs hooked round broken sections of what remained of the bridge, fighting for breath. Droshny made a signal to some unseen person or persons across the rapids, then pointed upwards in the direction from which the boulder had come.

Crouched among the boulders on the far side of the river, three Cetniks – the fortunate three who had not yet moved on to the bridge when the boulder had fallen – saw the signal and understood. About seventy feet above where Droshny – completely concealed from sight on that side by the high bank of the river – was still clinging grimly to what was left of the bridge, Andrea, now bereft of cover, had begun to make a precarious descent from his previous hiding-place. On the other side of the river, one of the three Cetniks took aim and fired.

Fortunately for Andrea, firing uphill in semi-darkness is a tricky business at the best of times. Bullets smashed into the cliff-face inches from Andrea's left shoulder, the whining ricochets leaving him almost miraculously unscathed. There would be a correction factor for the next burst, Andrea knew: he flung himself to one side, lost his balance and what little precarious purchase he had and slid and tumbled helplessly down the boulder-strewn slope. Bullets, many bullets, struck close by him on his way down, for the three Cetniks on the right bank, convinced now that Andrea was the only person left for them to deal with, had risen, advanced to the edge of the river and were concentrating all their fire on Andrea.

Again fortunately for Andrea, this period of concentration lasted for only a matter of a few seconds. Reynolds and Maria emerged from cover and ran down the bank, stopping momentarily to fire at the Cetniks across the river, who at once forgot all about Andrea to meet this new and unexpected threat. Just as they did so, Andrea, in the midst of a small avalanche, still fighting furiously but hopelessly to arrest his fall, struck the bank of the river with appalling force, struck the side of his head against a large stone and collapsed, his head and shoulders hanging out over the wild torrent below.

Reynolds flung himself flat on the shale of the river bank, forced himself to ignore the bullets striking to left and right of him and whining above him and took a slow and careful aim. He fired a long burst, a very long one, until the magazine of his Schmeisser was empty. All three Cetniks crumpled and died.

Reynolds rose. He was vaguely surprised to notice that his hands were shaking. He looked at Andrea, lying unconscious and danger-ously near the side of the bank, took a couple of paces in his direc-tion, then checked and turned as he heard a low moan behind him. Reynolds broke into a run.

Maria was half-sitting, half-lying on the stony bank. Both hands cradled her leg just above the right knee and the blood was welling between her fingers. Her face, normally pale enough, was ashen and drawn with shock and pain. Reynolds cursed bitterly but soundlessly, produced his knife and began to cut away the cloth around the wound. Gently, he pulled away the material covering the wound and smiled reassuringly at the girl: her lower lip was caught tightly between her teeth and she watched him steadily with eyes dimmed by pain and tears.

It was a nasty enough looking flesh wound, but, Reynolds knew, not dangerous. He reached for his medical pack, gave her a reassur-ing smile and then forgot all about his medical pack. The expres-sion in Maria's eyes had given way to one of shock and fear and she was no longer looking at him.

Reynolds twisted round. Droshny had just hauled himself over the edge of the river bank, had risen to his feet and was now heading purposefully towards Andrea's prostrate body, with the obvious intention of heaving the unconscious man into the gorge.

Reynolds picked up his Schmeisser and pulled the trigger. There was an empty click – he'd forgotten the magazine had been emptied. He glanced around almost wildly in an attempt to locate Maria's gun, but there was no sign of it. He could wait no longer. Droshny was only a matter of feet from where Andrea lay. Reynolds picked up his knife and rushed along the bank. Droshny saw him coming and he saw too that Reynolds was armed with only a knife. He smiled as a wolf would smile, took one of his wickedly-curved knives from his belt and waited.

The two men approached closely and circled warily. Reynolds had never wielded a knife in anger in his life and so had no illusions at all as to his chances: hadn't Neufeld said that Droshny was the best man in the Balkans with a knife? He certainly looked it, Reynolds thought. His mouth felt very dry.

Thirty yards away Maria, dizzy and weak with pain and dragging her wounded leg, crawled towards the spot where she thought her gun had fallen when she had been hit. After what seemed a very long time, but what was probably no more than ten seconds, she found it half-hidden among rocks. Nauseated and faint from the pain of her wounded leg, she forced herself to sit up and brought the gun to her shoulder. Then she lowered it again.

In her present condition, she realized vaguely, it would have been impossible for her to hit Droshny without almost certainly hitting Reynolds at the same time: in fact, she might well have killed Reynolds while missing Droshny entirely. For both men were now locked chest to chest, each man's knife-hand – the right – clamped in the grip of the other's left.

The girl's dark eyes, which had so recently reflected pain and shock and fear, now held only one expression – despair. Like Reynolds, Maria knew of Droshny's reputation – but, unlike Reynolds, she had seen Droshny kill with that knife and knew too well how lethal a combination that man and that knife were. A wolf and a lamb, she thought, a wolf and a lamb. After he kills Reynolds – her mind was dulled now, her thoughts almost incoherent – after he kills Reynolds I shall kill him. But first, Reynolds would have to die, for there could be no help for him. And then the despair left the dark eyes to be replaced by an almost unthinkable hope for she knew with an intuitive certainty that with Andrea by one's side hope need never be abandoned.

Not that Andrea was as yet by anyone's side. He had forced himself up to his hands and knees and was gazing down uncomprehendingly at the rushing white waters below, shaking his leonine head from side to side in an attempt to clear it. And then, still shaking his head, he levered himself painfully to his feet and he wasn't shaking his head any more. In spite of her pain, Maria smiled.

Slowly, inexorably, the Cetnik giant twisted Reynolds's knife-hand away from himself while at the same time bringing the lancet point of his own knife nearer to Reynolds's throat. Reynolds's sweat-sheened face deflected his desperation, his total awareness of impending defeat and death. He cried out with pain as Droshny twisted his right wrist almost to breaking-point, forcing him to open his fingers and drop his knife. Droshny kneed him viciously at the same time, freeing his left hand to give Reynolds a violent shove that sent him staggering to crash on his back against the stones and lie there winded and gasping in agony.

Droshny smiled his smile of wolfish satisfaction. Even although he must have known that the need for haste was paramount he yet had to take time off to carry out the execution in a properly leisurely fashion, to savour to the full every moment of it, to prolong the exquisite joy he always felt at moments like these. Reluctantly, almost, he changed to a throwing grip on his knife and slowly raised it high. The smile was broader than ever, a smile that vanished in an instant of time as he felt a knife being plucked from his own belt. He whirled round. Andrea's face was a mask of stone.

Droshny smiled again. 'The gods have been kind to me.' His voice was low, almost reverent, his tone a caressing whisper. 'I have dreamed of this. It is better that you should die this way. This will teach you, my friend –'

Droshny, hoping to catch Andrea unprepared, broke off in mid-sentence and lunged forward with cat-like speed. The smile vanished again as he looked in almost comical disbelief at his right wrist locked in the vice-like grip of Andrea's left hand.

Within seconds, the tableau was as it had been in the beginning of the earlier struggle, both knife-wrists locked in the opponents' left hands. The two men appeared to be absolutely immobile, Andrea with his face totally impassive, Droshny with his white teeth bared, but no longer in a smile. It was, instead, a vicious snarl compounded of hate and fury and baffled anger – for this time

Droshny, to his evident consternation and disbelief, could make no impression whatsoever on his opponent. The impression, this time, was being made on him.

Maria, the pain in her leg in temporary abeyance, and a slowly recovering Reynolds stared in fascination as Andrea's left hand, in almost millimetric slow-motion, gradually twisted Droshny's right wrist so that the blade moved slowly away and the Cetnik's fingers began, almost imperceptibly at first, to open. Droshny, his face darkening in colour and the veins standing out on forehead and neck, summoned every last reserve of strength to his right hand: Andrea, rightly sensing that all of Droshny's power and will and concentration were centred exclusively upon breaking his crushing grip, suddenly tore his own right hand free and brought his knife scything round and under and upwards with tremendous power: the knife went in under the breastbone, burying itself to the hilt. For a moment or two the giant stood there, lips drawn far back over bared teeth smiling mindlessly in the rictus of death, then, as Andrea stepped away, leaving the knife still embedded, Droshny toppled slowly over the edge of the ravine. The Cetnik sergeant, still clinging to the shattered remains of the bridge, stared in uncomprehending horror as Droshny, the hilt of the knife easily distinguishable, fell head-first into the boiling rapids and was immediately lost to sight.

Reynolds rose painfully and shakily to his feet and smiled at Andrea. He said: 'Maybe I've been wrong about you all along. Thank you, Colonel Stavros.'

Andrea shrugged. 'Just returning a favour, my boy. Maybe I've been wrong about you, too.' He glanced at his watch. 'Two o'clock! *Two* o'clock! Where are the others?'

'God, I'd almost forgotten. Maria there is hurt. Groves and Petar are on the ladder. I'm not sure, but I think Groves is in a pretty bad way.'

'They may need help. Get to them quickly. I'll look after the girl.'

At the southern end of the Neretva bridge, General Zimmermann stood in his command car and watched the sweep-second hand of his watch come up to the top.

'Two o'clock,' Zimmerman said, his tone almost conversational. He brought his right hand down in a cutting gesture. A whistle shrilled and at once tank engines roared and treads clattered as the spearhead of Zimmermann's first armoured division began to cross the bridge at Neretva.

THIRTEEN

Saturday
0200–0215

'Maurer and Schmidt! Maurer and Schmidt!' The captain in charge of the guard on top of the Neretva dam wall came running from the guard-house, looked around almost wildly and grabbed his sergeant by the arm. 'For God's sake, where are Maurer and Schmidt? No one seen them? No one? Get the searchlight.'

Petar, still holding the unconscious Groves pinned against the ladder, heard the sound of the words but did not understand them. Petar, with both arms round Groves, now had his forearms locked at an almost impossible angle between the stanchions and the rock-face behind. In this position, as long as his wrists or forearms didn't break, he could hold Groves almost indefinitely. But Petar's grey and sweat-covered face, the racked and twisted face, was mute testimony enough to the almost unendurable agony he was suffering.

Mallory and Miller also heard the urgently shouted commands, but, like Petar, were unable to understand what it was that was being shouted. It would be something, Mallory thought vaguely, that would bode no good for them, then put the thought from his mind: he had other and more urgently immediate matters to occupy his attention. They had reached the barrier of the torpedo net and he had the supporting cable in one hand, a knife in the other when Miller exclaimed and caught his arm.

'For God's sake, no!' The urgency in Miller's voice had Mallory looking at him in astonishment. 'Jesus, what do I use for brains. That's not a wire.'

'It's not –'

'It's an insulated power cable. Can't you see?'

Mallory peered closely. 'Now I can.'

'Two thousand volts, I'll bet.' Miller still sounded shaken. 'Electric chair power. We'd have been frizzled alive. *And* it would have triggered off an alarm bell.'

'Over the top with them,' Mallory said.

Struggling and pushing, heaving and pulling, for there was only a foot of clear water between the wire and the surface of the water, they managed to ease the compressed air cylinder over and had just succeeded in lifting the nose of the first of the amatol cylinders on to the wire when, less than a hundred yards away, a six-inch searchlight came to life on the top of the dam wall, its beam momentarily horizontal, then dipping sharply to begin a traverse of the water close in to the side of the dam wall.

'That's all we bloody well need,' Mallory said bitterly. He pushed the nose of the amatol block back off the wire, but the wire strop securing it to the compressed air cylinder held it in such a position that it remained with its nose nine inches clear of the water. 'Leave it. Get under. Hang on to the net.'

Both men sank under the water as the sergeant atop the dam wall continued his traverse with the searchlight. The beam passed over the nose of the first of the amatol cylinders, but a black-painted cylinder in dark waters makes a poor subject for identification and the sergeant failed to see it. The light moved on, finished its traverse of the water alongside the dam, then went out.

Mallory and Miller surfaced cautiously and looked swiftly around. For the moment, there was no other sign of immediate danger. Mallory studied the luminous hands of his watch. He said: 'Hurry! For God's sake, hurry! We're almost three minutes behind schedule.'

They hurried. Desperate now, they had the two amatol cylinders over the wire inside twenty seconds, opened the compressed air valve on the leading cylinder and were alongside the massive wall of the dam inside another twenty. At that moment, the clouds parted and the moon broke through again, silvering the dark waters of the dam. Mallory and Miller were now in a helplessly exposed position but there was nothing they could do about it and they knew it. Their time had run out and they had no option other than to secure and arm the amatol cylinders as quickly as ever possible. Whether they were discovered or not could still be all-important: but there was nothing they could do to prevent that discovery.

Miller said softly: 'Forty feet apart and forty feet down, the experts say. We'll be too late.'

'No. Not yet too late. The idea is to let the tanks across first then destroy the bridge before the petrol bowsers and the main infantry battalions cross.'

Atop the dam wall, the sergeant with the searchlight returned from the western end of the dam and reported to the captain.

'Nothing, sir. No sign of anyone.'

'Very good.' The captain nodded towards the gorge. 'Try that side. You might find something there.'

So the sergeant tried the other side and he did find something there, and almost immediately. Ten seconds after he had begun his traverse with the searchlight he picked up the figures of the unconscious Groves and the exhausted Petar and, only feet below them and climbing steadily, Sergeant Reynolds. All three were hopelessly trapped, quite powerless to do anything to defend themselves: Reynolds had no longer even his gun.

On the dam wall, a Wehrmacht soldier, levelling his machine-pistol along the beam of the searchlight, glanced up in astonishment as the captain struck down the barrel of his gun.

'Fool!' The captain sounded savage. 'I want them alive. You two, fetch ropes, get them up here for questioning. We *must* find out what they have been up to.'

His words carried clearly to the two men in the water for, just then, the last of the bombing ceased and the sound of the small-arms fire died away. The contrast was almost too much to be borne, the suddenly hushed silence strangely ominous, deathly, almost, in its sinister foreboding.

'You heard?' Miller whispered.

'I heard.' More cloud, Mallory could see, thinner cloud but still cloud, was about to pass across the face of the moon. 'Fix these float suckers to the wall. I'll do the other charge.' He turned and swam slowly away, towing the second amatol cylinder behind him.

When the beam of the searchlight had reached down from the top of the dam wall Andrea had been prepared for instant discovery, but the prior discovery of Groves, Reynolds and Petar had saved Maria and himself, for the Germans seemed to think that they had caught all there were to be caught and, instead of traversing the rest of the gorge with the searchlights, had concentrated, instead, on bringing up to the top of the wall the three men they had found trapped on the ladder. One man, obviously unconscious – that would be Groves, Andrea thought – was hauled up at the end of a rope: the other two, with one man lending assistance to the other, had completed the journey up the ladder by themselves. All this Andrea had seen while he was bandaging Maria's injured leg, but he had said nothing of it to her.

Andrea secured the bandage and smiled at her. 'Better?'

'Better.' She tried to smile her thanks but the smile wouldn't come.

'Fine. Time we were gone.' Andrea consulted his watch. 'If we stay here any longer I have the feeling that we're going to get very, very wet.'

He straightened to his feet and it was this sudden movement that saved his life. The knife that had been intended for his back passed cleanly through his upper left arm. For a moment, almost as if uncomprehending, Andrea stared down at the tip of the narrow blade emerging from his arm then, apparently oblivious of the agony it must have cost him, turned slowly round, the movement wrenching the hilt of the knife from the hand of the man who held it.

The Cetnik sergeant, the only other man to have survived with Droshny the destruction of the swing bridge, stared at Andrea as if he were petrified, possibly because he couldn't understand how a man could suffer such a wound in silence and, in silence, still be able to tear the knife from his grasp. Andrea had now no weapon left him nor did he require one. In what seemed an almost grotesque slow motion, Andrea lifted his right hand: but there was nothing slow-motion about the dreadful edge-handed chopping blow which caught the Cetnik sergeant on the base of the neck. The man was probably dead before he struck the ground.

Reynolds and Petar sat with their backs to the guard-hut at the eastern end of the dam. Beside them lay the still unconscious Groves, his breathing now stertorous, his face ashen and of a peculiar waxed texture. From overhead, fixed to the roof of the guard-house, a bright light shone down on them, while nearby was a watchful guard with his carbine trained on them. The Wehrmacht captain of the guard stood above them, an almost awestruck expression on his face.

He said incredulously but in immaculate English: 'You hoped to blow up a dam this size with a few sticks of dynamite? You must be mad!'

'No one told us the dam was as big as this,' Reynolds said sullenly.

'No one told you – God in heaven, talk of mad dogs and Englishmen! And where is this dynamite?'

'The wooden bridge broke.' Reynolds's shoulders were slumped in abject defeat. 'We lost all the dynamite – and all our other friends.'

'I wouldn't have believed it, I just wouldn't have believed it.' The captain shook his head and turned away, then checked as Reynolds called him. 'What is it?'

'My friend here.' Reynolds indicated Groves. 'He is very ill, you can see that. He needs medical attention.'

'Later.' The captain turned to the soldier in the open transceiver cabin. 'What news from the south?'

'They have just started to cross the Neretva bridge, sir.'

The words carried clearly to Mallory, at that moment some distance apart from Miller. He had just finished securing his float to the wall and was on the point of rejoining Miller when he caught a flash of light out of the corner of his eye. Mallory remained still and glanced upward and to his right.

There was a guard on the dam wall above, leaning over the parapet as he moved along, flashing a torch downwards. Discovery, Mallory at once realized, was certain. One or both of the supporting floats were bound to be seen. Unhurriedly, and steadying himself against his float, Mallory unzipped the top of his rubber suit, reached under his tunic, brought out his Luger, unwrapped it from its waterproof cover and eased off the safety-catch.

The pool of light from the torch passed over the water, close in to the side of the dam wall. Suddenly, the beam of the torch remained still. Clearly to be seen in the centre of the light was a small, torpedo-shaped object fastened to the dam wall by suckers and, just beside it, a rubber-suited man with a gun in his hand. And the gun – it had, the sentry automatically noticed, a silencer screwed to the end of the barrel – was pointed directly at him. The sentry opened his mouth to shout a warning but the warning never came for a red flower bloomed in the centre of his forehead, and he leaned forward tiredly, the upper half of his body over the edge of the parapet, his arms dangling downwards. The torch slipped from his lifeless hand and tumbled down into the water.

The impact of the torch on the water made a flat, almost cracking sound. In the now deep silence it was bound to be heard by those above, Mallory thought. He waited tensely, the Luger ready in his hand, but after twenty seconds had passed and nothing happened Mallory decided he could wait no longer. He glanced at Miller, who had clearly heard the sound, for he was staring at Mallory, and at the gun in Mallory's hand with a puzzled frown on his face. Mallory pointed up towards the dead guard hanging over the parapet. Miller's face cleared and he nodded his understanding. The moon went behind a cloud.

Andrea, the sleeve of his left arm soaked in blood, more than half carried the hobbling Maria across the shale and through the rocks: she could hardly put her right foot beneath her. Arrived at the foot of the ladder, both of them stared upwards at the forbidding climb, at the seemingly endless zig-zags of the iron ladder reaching up into the night. With a crippled girl and his own damaged arm, Andrea thought, the prospects were poor indeed. And God only knew when the wall of the dam was due to go up. He looked at his watch. If everything was on schedule, it was due to go now: Andrea hoped to God that Mallory, with his passion for punctuality, had for once fallen behind schedule. The girl looked at him and understood.

'Leave me,' she said. 'Please leave me.'

'Out of the question,' Andrea said firmly. 'Maria would never forgive me.'

'Maria?'

'Not you.' Andrea lifted her on to his back and wound her arms round his neck. 'My wife. I think I'm going to be terrified of her.' He reached out for the ladder and started to climb.

The better to see how the final preparations for the attack were developing, General Zimmermann had ordered his command car out on to the Neretva bridge itself and now had it parked exactly in the middle, pulled close in to the right-hand side. Within feet of him clanked and clattered and roared a seemingly endless column of tanks and self-propelled guns and trucks laden with assault troops: as soon as they reached the northern end of the bridge, tanks and guns and trucks fanned out east and west along the banks of the river, to take temporary cover behind the steep escarpment ahead before launching the final concerted attack.

From time to time, Zimmermann raised his binoculars and scanned the skies to the west. A dozen times he imagined he heard the distant thunder of approaching air armadas, a dozen times he deceived himself. Time and again he told himself he was a fool, a prey to useless and fearful imaginings wholly unbecoming to a general in the Wehrmacht: but still this deep feeling of intense unease persisted, still he kept examining the skies to the west. It never once occurred to him, for there was no reason why it should, that he was looking in the wrong direction.

Less than half a mile to the north, General Vukalovic lowered his binoculars and turned to Colonel Janzy.

'That's it, then.' Vukalovic sounded weary and inexpressibly sad. 'They're across – or almost all across. Five more minutes. Then we counterattack.'

'Then we counter-attack,' Janzy said tonelessly. 'We'll lose a thousand men in fifteen minutes.'

'We asked for the impossible,' Vukalovic said. 'We pay for our mistakes.'

Mallory, a long trailing lanyard in his hand, rejoined Miller. He said: 'Fixed?'

'Fixed.' Miller had a lanyard in his own hand. 'We pull those leads to the hydrostatic chemical fuses and take off?'

'Three minutes. You know what happens to us if we're still in this water after three minutes?'

'Don't even talk about it,' Miller begged. He suddenly cocked his head and glanced quickly at Mallory. Mallory, too, had heard it, the sound of running footsteps up above. He nodded at Miller. Both men sank beneath the surface of the water.

The captain of the guard, because of inclination, a certain rotundity of figure and very proper ideas as to how an officer of the Wehrmacht should conduct himself, was not normally given to running. He had, in fact, been walking, quickly and nervously, along the top of the dam wall when he caught sight of one of his guards leaning over the parapet in what he could only consider an unsoldierly and slovenly fashion. It then occurred to him that a man leaning over a parapet would normally use his hands and arms to brace himself and he could not see the guard's hands and arms. He remembered the missing Maurer and Schmidt and broke into a run.

The guard did not seem to hear him coming. The captain caught him roughly by the shoulder, then stood back aghast as the dead man slid back off the parapet and collapsed at his feet, face upwards: the place where his forehead had been was not a pretty sight. Seized by a momentary paralysis, the captain stared for long seconds at the dead man, then, by a conscious effort of will, drew out both his torch and pistol, snapped on the beam of the one and released the safety catch of the other and risked a very quick glance over the dam parapet.

There was nothing to be seen. Rather, there was nobody to be seen, no sign of the enemy who must have killed his guard within the past minute or two. But there *was* something to be seen, additional evidence, as if he ever needed such evidence, that the enemy had been there: a torpedo-shaped object – no, *two* torpedo-shaped objects – clamped to the wall of the dam just at water level. Uncomprehendingly at first, the captain stared at those, then the significance of their presence there struck him with the violence, almost, of a physical blow. He straightened and started running towards the eastern end of the dam, shouting 'Radio! Radio!' at the top of his voice.

Mallory and Miller surfaced. The shouts – they were almost screams – of the running captain to the guard – carried clear over the now silent waters of the dam. Mallory swore.

'Damn and damn and damn again!' His voice was almost vicious in his chagrin and frustration. 'He can give Zimmermann seven, maybe eight minutes' warning. Time to pull the bulk of his tanks on to the high ground.'

'So now?'

'So now we pull those lanyards and get the hell out of here.'

The captain, racing along the wall, was now less than thirty yards from the radio and where Petar and Reynolds sat with their backs to the guard-house.

'General Zimmermann!' he shouted. 'Get through. Tell him to pull his tanks to the high ground. Those damned English have mined the dam!'

'Ah, well.' Petar's voice was almost a sigh. 'All good things come to an end.'

Reynolds stared at him, his face masked in astonishment. Automatically, involuntarily, his hand reached out to take the dark glasses Petar was passing him, automatically his eyes followed Petar's hand moving away again and then, in a state of almost hypnotic trance, he watched the thumb of that hand press a catch in the side of the guitar. The back of the instrument fell open to reveal inside the trigger, magazine and gleamingly-oiled mechanism of a sub-machine gun.

Petar's forefinger closed over the trigger. The sub-machine gun, its first shell shattering the end of the guitar, stuttered and leapt in

Petar's hands. The dark eyes were narrowed, watchful and cool. And Petar had his priorities right.

The soldier guarding the three prisoners doubled over and died, almost cut in half by the first blast of shells. Two seconds later the corporal guard by the radio hut, while still desperately trying to unsling his Schmeisser, went the same way. The captain of the guard, still running, fired his pistol repeatedly at Petar, but Petar still had his priorities right. He ignored the captain, ignored a bullet which struck his right shoulder, and emptied the remainder of the magazine into the radio transceiver, then toppled sideways to the ground, the smashed guitar falling from his nerveless hands, blood pouring from his shoulder and a wound on his head.

The captain replaced his still smoking revolver in his pocket and stared down at the unconscious Petar. There was no anger in the captain's face now, just a peculiar sadness, the dull acceptance of ultimate defeat. His eyes moved and caught Reynolds's: in a moment of rare understanding both men shook their heads in a strange and mutual wonder.

Mallory and Miller, climbing the knotted rope, were almost opposite the top of the dam wall when the last echoes of the firing drifted away across the waters of the dam. Mallory glanced down at Miller, who shrugged as best a man can shrug when hanging on to a rope, and shook his head wordlessly. Both men resumed their climb, moving even more quickly than before.

Andrea, too, had heard the shots, but had no idea what their significance might be. At that moment, he did not particularly care. His left upper arm felt as if it were burning in a fierce bright flame, his sweat-covered face reflected his pain and near-exhaustion. He was not yet, he knew, halfway up the ladder. He paused briefly, aware that the girl's grip around his neck was slipping, eased her carefully in towards the ladder, wrapped his left arm round her waist and continued his painfully slow and dogged climb. He wasn't seeing very much now and he thought vaguely that it must be because of the loss of blood. Oddly enough, his left arm was beginning to become numb and the pain was centring more and more on his right shoulder which all the time took the strain of their combined weights.

'Leave me!' Maria said again. 'For God's sake, leave me. You can save yourself.'

Andrea gave her a smile or what he thought was a smile and said kindly: 'You don't know what you're saying. Besides, Maria would murder me.'

'Leave me! Leave me!' She struggled and exclaimed in pain as Andrea tightened his grip. 'You're hurting me.'

'Then stop struggling,' Andrea said equably. He continued his pain-racked, slow-motion climb.

Mallory and Miller reached the longitudinal crack running across the top of the dam wall and edged swiftly along crack and rope until they were directly above the arc lights on the eaves of the guard-house some fifty feet below: the brilliant illumination from those lights made it very clear indeed just what had happened. The unconscious Groves and Petar, the two dead German guards, the smashed radio transceiver and, above all, the sub-machine gun still lying in the shattered casing of the guitar told a tale that could not be misread. Mallory moved another ten feet along the crack and peered down again: Andrea, with the girl doing her best to help by pulling on the rungs of the ladder, was now almost two-thirds of the way up, but making dreadfully slow progress of it: they'll never make it in time, Mallory thought, it is impossible that they will ever make it in time. It comes to us all, he thought tiredly, some day it's bound to come to us all: but that it should come to the indestructible Andrea pushed fatalistic acceptance beyond its limits. Such a thing was inconceivable: and the inconceivable was about to happen now.

Mallory rejoined Miller. Quickly he unhitched a rope – the knotted rope he and Miller had used to descend to the Neretva dam – secured it to the rope running above the longitudinal crack and lowered it until it touched softly on the roof of the guard-house. He took the Luger in his hand and was about to start sliding down when the dam blew up.

The twin explosions occurred within two seconds of each other: the detonation of 3,000 pounds of high explosive should normally have produced a titanic outburst of sound, but because of the depth at which they took place, the explosions were curiously muffled, felt, almost, rather than heard. Two great columns of water soared up high above the top of the dam wall, but for what seemed an eternity of time but certainly was not more than four or five seconds, nothing appeared to happen. Then, very, very slowly, reluctantly, almost, the entire central section of the dam wall, at least eighty feet in width and right down to its base, toppled outwards into the gorge: the entire section seemed to be all still in one piece.

Andrea stopped climbing. He had heard no sound, but he felt the shuddering vibration of the ladder and he knew what had happened, what was coming. He wrapped both arms around Maria and the stanchions, pressed her close to the ladder and looked over her head. Two vertical cracks made their slow appearance on the outside of the dam wall, then the entire wall fell slowly towards them, almost as if it were hinged on its base, and then was abruptly lost to sight as countless millions of gallons of greenish-dark water came boiling through the shattered dam wall. The sound of the crash of a thousand tons of masonry falling into the gorge below should have been heard miles away: but Andrea could hear nothing above the roaring of the escaping waters. He had time only to notice that the dam wall had vanished and now there was only this mighty green torrent, curiously smooth and calm in its initial stages, then pouring down to strike the gorge beneath in a seething white maelstrom of foam before the awesome torrent was upon them. In a second of time Andrea released one hand, turned the girl's terrified face and buried it against his chest for he knew that if she should impossibly live, then that battering-ram of water, carrying with it sands and pebbles and God only knew what else, would tear the delicate skin from her face and leave her forever scarred. He ducked his own head against the fury of the coming onslaught and locked his hands together behind the ladder.

The impact of the waters drove the breath from his gasping body. Buried in this great falling crushing wall of green, Andrea fought for his life and that of the girl. The strain upon him, battered and already bruising badly from the hammer-blows of this hurtling cascade of water which seemed so venomously bent upon his instant destruction, was, even without the cruel handicap of his badly injured arm, quite fantastic. His arms, it felt, were momentarily about to be torn from their sockets, it would have been the easiest thing in the world to unclasp his hands and let kindly oblivion take the place of the agony that seemed to be tearing limbs and muscles asunder. But Andrea did not let go and Andrea did not break. Other things broke. Several of the ladder supports were torn away from the wall and it seemed that both ladder and climbers must be inevitably swept away. The ladder twisted, buckled and leaned far out from the wall so that Andrea was now as much lying beneath the ladder as hanging on to it: but still Andrea did not let go, still some remaining supports held. Then very gradually, after what seemed to the dazed Andrea an interminable period of time, the dam level dropped, the force of the water weakened, not much but just perceptibly, and Andrea started to climb again. Half a dozen times, as he changed hands on the rungs, his grip loosened and he was almost torn away: half a dozen times his teeth bared in the agony of effort, the great hands clamped tight and he impossibly retained his grip. After almost a minute of this titanic struggle he finally won clear of the worst of the water and could breathe again. He looked at the girl in his arms. The blonde hair was plastered over her ashen cheeks, the incongruously dark eyelashes closed. The ravine seemed almost full to the top of its precipitously-sided walls with this whitely boiling torrent of water sweeping everything before it, its roar, as it thundered down the gorge with a speed faster than that of an express train, a continuous series of explosions, an insane and banshee shrieking of sound.

Almost thirty seconds elapsed from the time of the blowing up of the dam until Mallory could bring himself to move again. He did not know why he should have been held in thrall for so long. He told himself, rationalizing, that it was because of the hypnotic spectacle of the dramatic fall in the level of the dam coupled with the sight of that great gorge filled almost to the top with those whitely seething waters: but, without admitting it to himself, he knew it was more than that, he knew he could not accept the realization that Andrea and Maria had been swept to their deaths, for Mallory did not know that at that instant Andrea, completely spent and no longer knowing what he was doing, was vainly trying to negotiate the last few steps of the ladder to the top of the dam. Mallory seized the rope and slid down recklessly, ignoring or not feeling the burning of the skin on the palms of his hands, his mind irrationally filled with murder – irrationally, because it was he who had triggered the explosion that had taken Andrea to his death.

And then, as his feet touched the roof of the guard-house, he saw the ghost – the ghosts, rather – as the heads of Andrea and a clearly unconscious Maria appeared at the top of the ladder. Andrea, Mallory noticed, did not seem to be able to go any further. He had a hand on the top rung, and was making convulsive, jerking movements, but making no progress at all. Andrea, Mallory knew, was finished.

Mallory was not the only one who had seen Andrea and the girl. The captain of the guard and one of his men were staring in stupefaction over the awesome scene of destruction, but a second guard had whirled round, caught sight of Andrea's head and brought up his machine-pistol. Mallory, still clinging to the rope, had no time to bring his Luger to bear and release the safety catch and Andrea should have assuredly died then: but Reynolds had already catapulted himself forward in a desperate dive and brought down the gun in the precise instant that the guard opened fire. Reynolds died instantaneously. The guard died two seconds later. Mallory lined up the still smoking barrel of his Luger on the captain and the guard.

'Drop those guns,' he said.

They dropped their guns. Mallory and Miller swung down from the guard-house roof, and while Miller covered the Germans with his guns, Mallory ran quickly across to the ladder, reached down a hand and helped the unconscious girl and the swaying Andrea to safety. He looked at Andrea's exhausted, blood-flecked face, at the flayed skin on his hands, at the left sleeve saturated in blood and said severely: 'And where the hell have you been?'

'Where have I been?' Andrea asked vaguely. 'I don't know.' He stood rocking on his feet, barely conscious, rubbed a hand across his eyes and tried to smile. 'I think I must have stopped to admire the view.'

General Zimmermann was still in his command car and his car was still parked in the right centre of the bridge at Neretva. Zimmermann had again his binoculars to his eyes, but for the first time he was gazing neither to the west nor to the north. He was gazing instead to the east, up-river towards the mouth of the Neretva gorge. After a little time he turned to his aide, his face at first uneasy, then the uneasiness giving way to apprehension, then the apprehension to something very like fear.

'You hear it?' he asked.

'I hear it, Herr General.'

'And feel it?'

'And I feel it.'

'What in the name of God almighty can it be?' Zimmermann demanded. He listened as a great and steadily increasing roar filled all the air around them. 'That's not thunder. It's far too loud for thunder. And too continuous. And that wind – that wind coming out of the gorge there.' He could now hardly hear himself speak above the almost deafening roar of sound coming from the east.

'It's the dam! The dam at Neretva! They've blown the dam! Get out of here!' he screamed to the driver. 'For God's sake get out of here!'

The command car jerked and moved forward, but it was too late for General Zimmermann, just as it was too late for his massed echelons of tanks and thousands of assault troops concealed on the banks of the Neretva by the low escarpment to the north of them and waiting to launch the devastating attack that was to annihilate the seven thousand fanatically stubborn defenders of the Zenica Gap. A mighty wall of white water, eighty feet high, carrying with it the irresistible pressure of millions of tons of water and sweeping before it a gigantic battering ram of boulders and trees, burst out of the mouth of the gorge.

Mercifully for most of the men in Zimmermann's armoured corps, the realization of impending death and death itself were only moments apart. The Neretva bridge, and all the vehicles on it, including Zimmermann's command car, were swept away to instant destruction. The giant torrent overspread both banks of the river to a depth of almost twenty feet, sweeping before its all-consuming path tanks, guns, armoured vehicles, thousands of troops and all that stood in its way: when the great flood finally subsided, there was not one blade of grass left growing along the banks of the Neretva. Perhaps a hundred or two of combat troops on both sides of the river succeeded in climbing in terror to higher ground and the most temporary of safety for they too would not have long to live, but for ninety-five per cent of Zimmermann's two armoured divisions destruction was as appallingly sudden as it was terrifyingly complete. In sixty seconds, no more, it was all over. The German armoured corps was totally destroyed. But still that mighty wall of water continued to boil forth from the mouth of the gorge.

'I pray God that I shall never see the like again.' General Vukalovic lowered his glasses and turned to Colonel Janzy, his face registering neither jubilation nor satisfaction, only an awestruck wonder mingled with deep compassion. 'Men should not die like that, even our enemies should not die like that.' He was silent for a few moments, then stirred. 'I think a hundred or two of their infantry escaped to safety on this side, Colonel. You will take care of them?'

'I'll take care of them,' Janzy said sombrely. 'This is a night for prisoners, not killing, for there won't be any fight. It's as well,

General. For the first time in my life I'm not looking forward to a fight.'

'I'll leave you then.' Vukalovic clapped Janzy's shoulder and smiled, a very tired smile. 'I have an appointment. At the Neretva dam – or what's left of it.'

'With a certain Captain Mallory?'

'With Captain Mallory. We leave for Italy tonight. You know, Colonel, we could have been wrong about that man.'

'I never doubted him,' Janzy said firmly.

Vukalovic smiled and turned away.

Captain Neufeld, his head swathed in a bloodstained bandage and supported by two of his men, stood shakily at the top of the gully leading down to the ford in the Neretva and stared down, his face masked in shocked horror and an almost total disbelief, at the whitely boiling maelstrom, its seething surface no more than twenty feet below where he stood, of what had once been the Neretva gorge. He shook his head very, very slowly in unspeakable weariness and final acceptance of defeat, then turned to the soldier on his left, a youngster who looked as stupefied as he, Neufeld, felt.

'Take the two best ponies,' Neufeld said. 'Ride to the nearest Wehrmacht command post north of the Zenica Gap. Tell them that General Zimmermann's armoured divisions have been wiped out – we don't *know*, but they must have been. Tell them the valley of Neretva is a valley of death and that there is no one left to defend it. Tell them the Allies can send in their airborne divisions tomorrow and that there won't be a single shot fired. Tell them to notify Berlin immediately. You understand, Lindemann?'

'I understand, sir.' From the expression on Lindemann's face, Neufeld thought that Lindemann had understood very little of what he had said to him: but Neufeld felt infinitely tired and he did not feel like repeating his instructions. Lindemann mounted a pony, snatched the reins of another and spurred his pony up alongside the railway track.

Neufeld said, almost to himself: 'There's not all that hurry, boy.'

'Herr Hauptmann?' The other soldier was looking at him strangely.

'It's too late now,' Neufeld said.

Mallory gazed down the still foaming gorge, turned and gazed at the Neretva dam whose level had already dropped by at least fifty feet, then turned to look at the men and the girl behind him. He felt weary beyond all words.

Andrea, battered and bruised and bleeding, his left arm now roughly bandaged, was demonstrating once again his quite remarkable powers of recuperation: to look at him it would have been impossible to guess that, only ten minutes ago, he had been swaying on the edge of total collapse. He held Maria cradled in his arms: she was coming to, but very, very slowly. Miller finished dressing the head wound of a now sitting Petar who, though wounded in shoulder and head, seemed more than likely to survive, crossed to Groves and stooped over him. After a moment or two he straightened and stared down at the young sergeant.

'Dead?' Mallory asked.

'Dead.'

'Dead.' Andrea smiled, a smile full of sorrow. 'Dead – and you and I are alive. Because this young lad is dead.'

'He was expendable,' Miller said.

'And young Reynolds.' Andrea was inexpressibly tired. 'He was expendable too. What was it you said to him this afternoon, my Keith – for now is all the time there may be? And that was all the time there was. For young Reynolds. He saved my life tonight – twice. He saved Maria's. He saved Petar's. But he wasn't clever enough to save his own. *We* are the clever ones, the old ones, the wise ones, the knowing ones. And the old ones are alive and the young ones are dead. And so it always is. We mocked them, laughed at them, distrusted them, marvelled at their youth and stupidity and ignorance.' In a curiously tender gesture he smoothed Maria's wet blonde hair back from her face and she smiled at him. 'And in the end they were better men than we were . . .'

'Maybe they were at that,' Mallory said. He looked at Petar sadly and shook his head in wonder. 'And to think that all three of them are dead, Reynolds dead, Groves dead, Saunders dead, and not one of them ever knew that you were the head of British espionage in the Balkans.'

'Ignorant to the end.' Miller drew the back of his sleeve angrily across his eyes. 'Some people never learn. Some people just never learn.'

EPILOGUE

Once again Captain Jensen and the British lieutenant-general were back in the Operations Room in Termoli, but now they were no longer pacing up and down. The days of pacing were over. True, they still looked very tired, their faces probably fractionally more deeply lined than they had been a few days previously: but the faces were no longer haggard, the eyes no longer clouded with anxiety, and, had they been walking instead of sitting deep in comfortable armchairs, it was just conceivable that they might have had a new spring in their steps. Both men had glasses in their hands, large glasses.

Jensen sipped his whisky and said, smiling: 'I thought a general's place was at the head of his troops?'

'Not in these days, Captain,' the General said firmly. 'In 1944 the wise general leads from behind his troops – about twenty miles behind. Besides, the armoured divisions are going so quickly I couldn't possibly hope to catch up with them.'

'They're moving as fast as that?'

'Not quite as fast as the German and Austrian divisions that pulled out of the Gustav Line last night and are now racing for the Yugoslav border. But they're coming along pretty well.' The General permitted himself a large gulp of his drink and a smile of considerable satisfaction. 'Deception complete, break-through complete. On the whole, your men have done a pretty fair job.'

Both men turned in their chairs as a respectful rat-a-tat of knuckles preceded the opening of the heavy leather doors. Mallory entered, followed by Vukalovic, Andrea and Miller. All four were unshaven, all of them looked as if they hadn't slept for a week. Andrea carried his arm in a sling.

Jensen rose, drained his glass, set it on a table, looked at Mallory dispassionately and said: 'Cut it a bit bloody fine, didn't you?'

Mallory, Andrea and Miller exchanged expressionless looks. There was a fairly long silence, then Mallory said: 'Some things take longer than others.'

Petar and Maria were lying side by side, hands clasped, in two regulation army beds in the Termoli military hospital when Jensen entered, followed by Mallory, Miller and Andrea.

'Excellent reports about both of you, I'm glad to hear,' Jensen said briskly. 'Just brought some – ah – friends to say goodbye.'

'What sort of hospital is this, then?' Miller said severely. 'How about the high army moral tone, hey? Don't they have separate quarters for men and women?'

'They've been married for almost two years,' Mallory said mildly. 'Did I forget to tell you?'

'Of course you didn't forget,' Miller said disgustedly. 'It just slipped your mind.'

'Speaking of marriage –' Andrea cleared his throat and tried another tack. 'Captain Jensen may recall that back in Navarone –'

'Yes, yes.' Jensen held up a hand. 'Quite so. Quite. Quite. But I thought perhaps – well, the fact of the matter is – well, it so happens that another little job, just a tiny little job really, has just come up and I thought that seeing you were here anyway . . .'

Andrea stared at Jensen. His face was horror-stricken.

SAM LLEWELLYN

Storm Force
from Navarone

To David Burnett

PROLOGUE

March 1944

The radar operator said, 'Contact. Three bloody contacts. Jesus.'

The Liberator dipped a wing, bucking heavily as it carved through one of the squalls of cloud streaming over the Atlantic towards Cabo Ortegal, at the top left-hand corner of Spain. 'Language,' said the pilot mildly. 'Bomb-aimer?'

Down in the nose the bomb-aimer said, 'Ready.' The pilot's leather-gloved hand went to the throttles. The note of the four Pratt and Whitney engines climbed to a tooth-rattling roar. The pilot eased the yoke forward. Girders creaking, the Liberator bounced down into the clouds.

Vapour streamed past the bomb-aimer's Perspex window, thick and grey as coal smoke. At five hundred feet it became patchy. There was sea down there: grey sea, laced with nets of foam.

The bomb-aimer's mouth was dry. Just looking at the heave of that sea made you feel sick. But there was something else: a wide, smooth road across those rough-backed swells, as if they had been ironed –

'See them yet?' said the pilot.

The bomb-aimer could hear his heart beat, even above the crackle of the intercom and the roar of the engines. 'See them,' he said.

At the end of the smooth road three long, low hulls were tearing chevrons of foam from the sea. The hulls were slim and grey, with streamlined conning towers. Slim, grey sitting ducks.

'They're bloody enormous,' said the radar operator, peering over the pilot's shoulder. 'What the hell are they?'

They were submarines, but submarines twice the size of any British or German craft the pilot had seen in four years of long flights over weary seas that had made him an expert on submarines. They were indeed bloody enormous.

The pilot frowned at the foam-crested waves of their wakes. Hard to tell, of course, but they looked as if they were making at least thirty-five knots. If they were theirs, thought the pilot, they could really do some damage. Hope they're ours –

Glowing red balls rose lazily from the conning towers and flicked past the cockpit canopy.

Theirs,' said the pilot, slamming the plane into a tight 180° turn. The tracers had stripped him of his mildness. 'Commencing run.'

There was a lot of tracer now, pouring past the Liberator's cockpit, mixed with the black puffs of heavier flak. The Liberator bucked, its rivets groaning in the heat-wrenched sky. The bomb-aimer tried not to think about his unprotected belly, and closed his mind to the bad-egg fumes of the shell bursts and the yammer of the nose-gunner's Brownings above his head. It was an easy two miles to bombs away: twenty endless seconds, at a hundred and eighty knots.

'Funny,' said the pilot. 'Why aren't they diving?'

The bomb-aimer stared into his sight. 'Bomb doors open,' he said. He felt the new tremor of the airframe as the doors spoilt the streamlining. The sight filled with grey and wrinkled sea. The submarines swam in V-formation down the stepladder markings towards the release point, innocent as three trout in a stream, except for the lazy red bubbles of the tracer.

The bomb-aimer frowned, pressing his face into the eyepiece of the sight. There was something wrong with the submarine in the middle. The deck forward of the conning tower looked twisted and bent. Christ, thought the bomb-aimer, someone's rammed her. Nearly cut her in half. That's why she's not diving. She's damaged –

Something burst with a clang out on the port side. Icy air was suddenly howling at the bomb-aimer's neck. The little submarines in the bomb-sight drifted off to starboard. 'Right a bit,' said the bomb-aimer, calmly, over the hammer of his heart. 'Right a bit.' The three grey fish slid back onto the line. 'Steady.' His leather thumb found the release button. The tracer was horrible now, thick as a blizzard. The bomb-aimer concentrated on hoping that Pearl in the mess wouldn't overcook his bloody egg again, like cement it was yesterday –

'Steady,' he said. The grey triangle was half an inch from the release point. 'Going,' he said. 'Going –'

A giant hammer smashed into the fuselage somewhere behind him. He felt a terrible agony in his left leg. Hit, he thought. Bastard hit us. His hand clenched on the bomb-release button. He felt the upward bound of the aircraft as the depth charges dropped free.

Too early, he thought.

Then there was no more thinking, because his face was full of smoke and his head was full of the agony of a leg broken in four places, and someone was howling like a dog, and as the grey clouds reached down and closed their hands round the Liberator, he realised that the person making all that racket was him.

Ten minutes later the radar operator finished the dressing and threw the morphine syrette out of one of the rents torn in the fuselage by the shell. He thought the bomb-aimer looked bloody awful, but then compound fractures are not guaranteed to bring a smile to the lips. To cheer him up, the radar operator gave him the thumbs up and mouthed, 'Got one!' Through pink clouds of morphine the bomb-aimer saw his lips move, and tried to look interested.

'Hit one,' said the radar operator. 'Saw smoke. One was damaged already, looked like someone rammed it. And we hit at least one.' But of course he might as well have been talking to himself because you couldn't hear anything, what with the engines and a sodding great hole in the fuselage, and anyway, the bomb-aimer was asleep.

Bloody great U-boats, though, thought the radar operator. Never seen anything like them before. Not that big. Nor that fast.

The Liberator droned north and west across the Bay of Biscay, above the corrugated mat of cloud, towards the Coastal Command base at St-Just. There the crew, nervously preoccupied with the hardness of their eggs, were comprehensively debriefed.

ONE

Sunday
1000–1900

Andrea stared at Jensen. The huge Greek's face was horror-stricken. 'Say again?' he said.

'A job,' said Captain Jensen. He was standing in a shaft of Italian sun that gleamed on his sharp white teeth and the gold braid on the brim of his cap. 'Just a tiny little job, really. And I thought, since the three of you were here anyway . . .'

As always, Jensen was dreadfully crisp, his uniform sparkling white, his stance upright and alert, the expression on his bearded face innocent but slightly piratical. The three men in the chairs looked the reverse of crisp. Their faces were hollow with exhaustion. They sat as if they had been dropped into their seats from a height. The visible parts of their bodies were laced with sticking plaster and red with Mercurochrome. They looked one step away from being stone-dead.

But Jensen knew better.

It had cost him considerable effort to assemble this team. There was Mallory, who before the war had been a mountaineer, world-famous for his Himalayan exploits, and conqueror of most of the unclimbed peaks in the Southern Alps of his native New Zealand. Mallory had spent eighteen months behind enemy lines in Crete with the man sitting next to him: Andrea. The gigantic Andrea, strong as a team of bulls, quiet as a shadow, a full colonel in the Greek army, and one of the deadliest irregular soldiers ever to knife a sentry. And then there was Corporal Dusty Miller from Chicago, member of the Long Range Desert Force, sometime deserter, goldminer, and bootlegger. If it existed, Miller could wreck it. Miller had a genius for sabotage equalled only by his genius for insubordination.

But Jensen valued soldiers for their fighting ability, not their standard of turnout. In Jensen's view these men were very useful indeed.

The gleam of those carnivorous teeth hurt Andrea's eyes. It does not take much to hurt your eyes, when you have not slept for the best part of a fortnight.

'A tiny little job,' said Mallory. His face was gaunt and pouchy. Like Andrea, he was by military standards badly in need of a shave. 'Are you going to tell us about it?'

The grin widened. 'I thought maybe you would be feeling a bit unreceptive.'

Corporal Dusty Miller had been almost horizontal in a leather-buttoned chair, staring with more than academic interest at the frescoed nudes on the ceiling of the villa Jensen had commandeered as his HQ. Now he spoke. 'That never stopped you before,' he said.

Jensen's bushy right eyebrow rose a millimetre. This was not the way that captains in the Royal Navy were accustomed to being addressed by ordinary corporals.

But Dusty Miller was not an ordinary corporal, in the same way that Captain Mallory was not an ordinary captain, or for that matter, Andrea was not an ordinary Greek Resistance fighter. Because of their lack of ordinariness, Jensen knew that he would have to treat them with a certain respect: the same sort of respect you would give three deadly weapons with which you wished to do damage to the enemy.

For in that room full of soldiers who were not ordinary soldiers, Jensen was not an ordinary naval captain. As an eighteen-year-old lieutenant, he had run a successful Q-ship, sinking eight U-boats in the final year of the 14–18 war. Between the wars he had been, frankly, a spy. He had led Shiite risings in Iraq; penetrated a scheme to block the Suez Canal; and as a marine surveyor employed by the Imperial Japanese Navy, perpetrated a set of alarmingly but intentionally inaccurate charts of the Sulu Sea. Now, in the fifth year of the war, he was Chief of Operations of the Subversive Operations Executive. Some said that Allied victory at El Alamein had been partly due to SOE's clandestine substitution of a carborundum paste for grease in a fuel dump. And in the last month he had successfully planned the destruction of the impregnable battery of Navarone, and the diversionary raid in Yugoslavia that had led to the fall of the Gustav Line and the breakout from the Anzio beachhead.

But Jensen had only done the planning. These three men – Mallory, the New Zealander, a taciturn mountaineer, tough as a commando knife; the American Dusty Miller, an Einstein among saboteurs; and Andrea, the two-hundred-and-fifty-pound man-mountain with the quietness of a cat and the strength of a bear – were the weapons he had used.

If there were deadlier weapons in the world Jensen's enquiries had failed to reveal them. And Jensen's enquiries were notoriously very searching indeed.

'So,' he said. 'Any of you gentlemen speak French?'

Mallory frowned. 'German,' he said. 'Greek.'

Andrea yawned and covered his mouth with a gigantic hand, still covered in bandages from the abrasions he had sustained holding onto the iron rungs of a ladder under the flume of water from the bursting Neretva dam.

'I do,' said Dusty Miller.

'Fluent?'

'I had a job in Montreal once,' said Miller, his eyes blue and innocent. 'Doorman in a cathouse.'

Thank you, Corporal,' said Jensen.

'Il n'y a pas de quoi,' said Miller, with old-world courtesy.

'We've found you some interpreters,' said Jensen.

Mallory sighed inwardly. He knew Jensen. When Jensen wanted you aboard, you were aboard, and the only thing to do was to check the location of the life jackets provided, and settle in for the ride. He said, 'If you don't mind me asking, sir, why do we need to speak French?'

Jensen grinned a grin that would have looked impressive on a hungry shark. He walked across the bronze carpet to the huge ormolu desk, bare except for two telephones, one red, one black. He said, 'There is someone I want you to meet.' He picked up the black telephone. 'Sergeant,' he said. 'Please send in the gentlemen in the waiting room.'

Mallory gazed at the veining on a marble pillar. Aircraft were droning overhead, flying air support for the troops advancing north from the wreckage of the Gustav Line. He lit another cigarette, the taste of the last one still bitter in his mouth. He wanted to sleep for a week. Make that a month –

The door opened, and two men came in. One of them was a tall major with a Guards moustache. The other was shorter, stocky and bull-necked, with three pips on his epaulettes.

'Major Dyas. Intelligence,' said Jensen. 'And Captain Killigrew. SAS.'

Major Dyas nodded. Captain Killigrew fixed each man in turn with a searching glare. His face was brick-red from the sun, and something that Mallory decided was anger. Mallory returned his salute. Andrea nodded and, being a foreigner, got away with it. Dusty Miller remained horizontal in his chair, acknowledging Killigrew by opening one eye and raising a bony hand.

Killigrew swelled like a toad. Jensen's ice-blue eyes flicked between the two men. He said quickly, 'Take a seat, Captain. Major, do your stuff.'

Killigrew lowered himself stiffly onto a hard chair, on which he sat bolt upright, not touching the backrest.

'Yah,' said Dyas. 'You may smoke.' Mallory and Miller were already smoking. Dyas ran his hand over his high, intellectual forehead. He could have been a doctor, or a professor of philosophy.

Jensen said, 'Major Dyas has kindly agreed to brief you on the background to this . . . little job.' Mallory leaned back in his chair. He was still tired, but soon there would be something to override the tiredness. The same something he remembered from huts in the Southern Alps, after a gruelling approach march, two hours' sleep, and waking in the dark chill before dawn. Soon there would be no way to go but up and over. Climbing and fighting: plan your campaign, grit your teeth, do the job or die in the attempt. There were similarities.

'Now then,' said Dyas. 'To start with. What you are about to hear is known to only seven men in the world, now ten, including you. Other people have the individual bits and pieces, but what counts is the . . . totality.' He paused to stuff tobacco into a blackened pipe, and applied an oil well-sized Zippo. 'June is going to be an important month of this war,' he said from inside a rolling cloud of smoke. 'Probably the most important yet.' Miller's eyes had opened. Andrea was sitting forward in his chair, massive forearms on his stained khaki knees. 'We are going to take a gamble,' said Dyas. 'A big gamble. And we want you to adjust the odds for us.'

Miller said, 'Trust Captain Jensen to run a crooked game.'

'Sorry?' said Dyas.

Mallory said, 'The corporal was expressing his enthusiasm.'

'Ah.' Another cloud of smoke.

Mallory could feel that jump of excitement in his stomach. 'This gamble,' he said. 'A new front?'

Dyas said, 'Put it like this. What we are going to need is complete control of the seas. We're good in the air, we're fine on the surface. But there's a hitch.' Killigrew's face was darkening. Looks as if he'll burst a blood vessel, thought Mallory. Wonder what he's got to do with this.

'Submarines,' said Dyas. 'U-boats. There has been an idea current that between airborne radar and asdic and huff-duff radio direction finding, we had 'em licked.' Another cloud of smoke. 'An idea we all had. Until a couple of months ago.

'In March we had a bit of trouble with some Atlantic convoys, and their escorts too. Basically, ships started to sink in a way we hadn't seen ships sink for two years now.' The professorial face was grim and hard. 'And it was odd. You'd get a series of explosions in say a two-hundred-mile circle, and you'd think, same old thing, U-boats moving together, wolf pack. But it wasn't a wolf pack, because there was no radio traffic, and the sinkings were too far apart. So then they thought it was possibly mines. But it didn't seem to be mines either, because one day in late March HMS *Frantic,* an escort destroyer, picked up an echo seven hundred miles off Cape Finisterre. There had been two sinkings in the convoy. The destroyer went in pursuit, but lost it.' He returned to his pipe.

'Nothing unusual about that,' said Mallory.

Dyas nodded, mildly. 'Except that the destroyer was steaming full speed ahead at the time, and the submarine just sailed away from her.'

'Sorry?' said Miller.

'The destroyer was steaming at thirty-five knots,' said Dyas. 'The U-boat was doing easily five knots better than that.'

Miller said, 'Why is this guy telling us all this stuff?'

Mallory said, 'I think Corporal Miller would like to know the significance of this fact.'

Jensen said, 'Excuse me, Major Dyas.' His face wore an expression of strained patience. 'For your information, U-boats have to spend most of their time on the surface, running their diesels to make passage and charge their batteries. Submerged, their best speed has so far been under ten knots, and they can't keep it up for long because of the limitations of their batteries.' His face was cold and grim, its deep creases as if carved from stone. 'So what we're faced with is this: the English Channel full of the biggest fleet of ships ever assembled, and these U-boats – big U-boats – carrying a hundred torpedoes each, God knows they're big enough – travelling at forty knots, under water. We know Jerry's got at least three of them. That could mean three hundred ships sunk, and Lord knows how many men lost.'

Miller said, 'So you get one quick echo. Not much of a basis for total panic stations. How fast do whales swim?'

Jensen snapped, 'Try keeping your ears open and your mouth shut.'

It was only then that Mallory saw the strain the man was under. The Jensen he knew was relaxed, with that naval quarterdeck sang-froid. Piratical, yes; aggressive, yes. Those were his stock in trade. But always calm. As long as Mallory had known Jensen, he had never known him lose his temper – not even with Dusty Miller, who did not hold with officers. But this was a Jensen balanced on a razor-honed knife's edge.

Mallory caught Miller's eye, and frowned. Then he said, 'Corporal Miller's got a point, sir.'

'Whales,' said Dyas. 'Actually, we thought of that. But one has been . . . adding up two and two.' His mild voice was balm to the frazzled nerves under the frescoed ceiling. 'Another escort reported ramming a large submarine. Then a Liberator got shot up bombing two U-boats escorting a third that bore signs of having been rammed. They were huge, these boats, steaming at thirty-odd knots on the surface. The Liberator reported them as damaged. But when we sent more aircraft out to search for them, they had vanished.

'They were reckoned to be in no state to dive, so they were presumed sunk. Then there was a message picked up – doesn't matter what sort of message, doesn't matter where, but take it from me, it was a reliable message – to say that the Werwolf pack was refitting after damage caused by enemy action. Said refit to be complete by noon Wednesday of the second week in May.'

It was now Sunday of the second week in May.

The painted vaults of the ceiling filled with silence. Mallory said, 'So these submarines. What are they?'

'Hard to say,' said Dyas, with an academic scrupulousness that would have irritated Mallory, if he had been the sort of man who got irritated about things. 'The Kriegsmarine have maintained pretty good security, but we've been able to patch a couple of ideas together. We know they've got a new battery system for underwater running, which stores a lot of power. A lot of power. But there've been rumours about something else. We think it's more likely to be something new. Development of an idea by a chap called Walter. They've been working on it since the thirties. An internal combustion engine that runs under water. Burns fuel oil.'

Miller's eyes had opened now, and he was sitting in a position that for him was almost upright. He said, 'What in?'

'In?' Dyas frowned.

'You can't burn fuel oil under water. You need oxygen.'

'Ah. Yes. Quite. Good question.' Miller did not look flattered. Engines were his business. He knew how to make them run. He knew even more about destroying them. 'Nothing definite. But they think it's probably something like hydrogen peroxide. On the surface, you'd aspirate your engine with air, of course. As you submerged, you'd have an automatic changeover, a float switch perhaps, that would close the air intake and start up a disintegrator that would get you oxygen out of something like hydrogen peroxide. So you'd get a carbon dioxide exhaust, which would dissolve in sea water. Or so the theory goes.'

Jensen stood up. 'Theory or no theory,' he said, 'they're refitting. They must be destroyed before they can go to sea again. And you're going to do the destroying.'

Mallory said, 'Where are they?'

Dyas unrolled a map that hung on the wall behind him. It showed France and Northern Spain, the brown corrugations of the Pyrenees marching from the Mediterranean to the Atlantic, and snaking down the spine of the mountains the scarlet track of the border. He said, 'They were bombed off Cabo Ortegal. They couldn't dive, so they wouldn't have gone north. We believe that they are here.' He picked up a billiard cue and tapped the long, straight stretch of coast that ran from Bordeaux south through Biarritz and St-Jean-de-Luz to the Spanish border.

Mallory looked at the pointer. There were three ports: Hendaye, St-Jean-de-Luz, and Bayonne. Otherwise, the coast was a straight line that looked as if it probably meant a beach. He said, 'Where?'

Dyas avoided his eye and fumbled at his moustache. Since he had been in the room, he had found himself increasingly unnerved by the stillness of these men, the wary relaxation of their deep-eyed faces. The big one with the black moustache was silent and dangerous, with a horrible sort of power about him. Of the other two, one seemed slovenly and the other insubordinate. They looked like, well, *gangsters*. Dashed unmilitary, thought Dyas. But Jensen knew what he was doing. Famous for it. Still, Mallory's question was not a question he much liked.

He said, 'Well, Spain's a neutral country.' He forced himself not to laugh nervously. 'And we've got good intelligence from Bordeaux, so we know they're not there.' He coughed, more nervously than he had intended. 'In fact, we don't know where they are.'

The three pairs of eyes watched him in silence. Finally, Mallory spoke. 'So we've got until Wednesday noon to find some submarines and destroy them. The only difficulty is that we don't know where they are. And, come to that, we don't actually know if they exist.'

Jensen said, 'Oh yes we do. You'll be dropped to a reception committee –'

'Dropped?' said Miller, his lugubrious face a mask of horror.

'By parachute.'

'Oh my stars,' said Miller, in a high, limp-wristed voice.

'Though if you keep interrupting we might forget the parachute and drop you anyway.' There was a hardness in Jensen's corsair face that made even Miller realise that he had said enough. 'The reception committee, I was saying. They will take you to a man called Jules, who knows a fisherman who knows the whereabouts of these U-boats. This fisherman will sell you the information.'

'Sell?'

'You will be supplied with the money.'

'So where is this fisherman?'

'We are not as yet aware of his whereabouts.'

'Ah,' said Mallory, rolling his eyes at the frescoes. He lit yet another cigarette. 'Well, I suppose we'll have the advantage of surprise.'

Miller pasted an enthusiastic smile to his doleful features. 'Gosh and golly gee,' he said. 'If they're as surprised as we are, they'll be amazed.'

Dyas was looking across at Jensen. Mallory thought he looked like a man in some sort of private agony. Jensen nodded, and smiled his ferocious smile. He seemed to have recovered his composure. 'One would rather hope so,' he said, 'because these submarines have got to be destroyed. No ifs, no buts. I don't care what you have to do. You'll have carte blanche.' He paused. 'As far as is consistent with operating absolutely on your own.' He coughed. If a British Naval officer schooled in Nelsonian duplicities could ever be said to look shifty, Jensen looked shifty now. 'As to the element of surprise . . . Well. Sorry to disappoint,' he said, 'but actually, not quite. Thing is, an SAS team went in last week, and nobody's heard from them since. So we think they've probably been captured.'

Mallory allowed the lids to droop over his gritty eyeballs. He knew what that meant, but he wanted to hear Jensen say it.

'In fact it seems quite possible,' said Jensen, 'that the Germans will, in a manner of speaking, be waiting for you.'

Killigrew seemed to see this as his cue. He was a small man, built like a bull, with a bull's rolling eye. He rose, marched to the centre of the room, planted his feet a good yard apart on the mosaic floor, and sank his head between his mighty shoulders. 'Now listen here, you men,' he barked, in the voice of one used to being the immediate focus of attention.

Jensen looked across at Mallory's lean crusader face. His eyes were closed. Andrea was gently stroking his moustache, gazing out of the window, where the late morning sun shone yellow-green in the leaves of a vine. Dusty Miller had removed his cigarette from his mouth, and was talking to it. 'Special Air Squads,' he said. 'They land with goddamn howitzers and goddamn Jeeps, with a noise like a train wreck. They do not think it necessary to employ guides or interpreters, let alone speak foreign languages. They have skulls made of concrete and no goddamn brains at all – can I help you?'

Killigrew was standing over him with a face of purple fire. 'Say that again,' he said.

Miller yawned. 'No goddamn brains,' he said. 'Bulls in a china shop.'

Mallory's eyes were open now. The veins in Killigrew's neck were standing out like ivy on a tree trunk, and his eyes were suffused with blood. The jaw was out like the ram of an icebreaker. And to Mallory's amazement, he saw that the right fist was pulled back, ready to spread Miller's teeth all over the back of his head.

'Dusty,' he said.

Miller looked at him.

'Miller apologises, sir,' said Mallory.

'Temper,' said Miller.

Killigrew's fist remained clenched.

'You're on a charge, Miller,' said Mallory, mildly.

'Yessir,' said Miller.

Jensen's voice cracked like a whip. 'Captain!'

Killigrew's heels crashed together. His florid face was suddenly grey. He had come within a whisker of assaulting another rank. The consequence would have been, well, a court martial.

Mallory ground out his cigarette in a marble ashtray, his eyes flicking round the room, sizing up the situation. God knew what kind of strain the SAS captain must have been under to come that close to walloping a corporal. Jensen, he saw, was hiding a keen curiosity behind a mask of military indignation. Without apparently taking a step, Andrea had left his chair and moved halfway across the room towards Killigrew. He stood loose and relaxed, his bear-like bulk sagging, hands slack at his sides. Mallory knew that Killigrew was half a second away from violent death. He caught Miller's eye, and shook his head, a millimetre left, a millimetre right.

Miller yawned. He said, 'Why, thank you, Captain Killigrew.' Killigrew stared straight ahead, eyes bulging. 'Seeing that there fly crawling towards my ear,' said Miller, pointing at a bluebottle spiralling towards the chandelier, 'the Captain was about to have the neighbourliness to swat the little sucker.' Jensen's eyebrow had cocked. 'I take full responsibility.'

Jensen did not hesitate. 'No need for that,' he said. 'Or charges. Carry on, Captain.'

Killigrew swallowed. ''Ssir.' His face was regaining its colour. 'Right,' he said, with the air of one wrenching his mind back from an abyss. 'Our men. Five of them. Dropped Tuesday last, with one Jeep, radio, just south of Lourdes. They reported that they'd landed, were leaving in the direction of Hendaye, travelling by night. They were supposed to radio in eight-hourly. But nothing. Absolutely damn all.'

Once again, Miller caught Mallory's eye. Jeep, he was thinking. A Jeep, for pity's sake. Have these people never heard of road blocks?

'Until last night,' said Killigrew. 'Some Resistance johnny came on the air. Said there'd been shooting in some village or other in the mountains twenty miles west of St-Jean-de-Luz. Casualties. So we think it was them. But there was a bit of difficulty with the radio message. Code words not used. Could mean the operator was in a hurry, of course. Or it could mean that the network's been penetrated.'

Mallory found himself lighting another cigarette. How long since he had drawn a breath not loaded with tobacco smoke? He was avoiding Miller's eye. They were brave, these SAS people. But Miller had been right. They went at things like a bull at a gate. That was not Mallory's way.

Mallory believed in making war quietly. There was an old partisan slogan he lived by: if you have a knife you can get a pistol; if you have a pistol, you can get a rifle; if you have a rifle, you can get a machine gun –

'Thank you, gentlemen,' said Jensen. 'I'm grateful for your cooperation.' Dyas and Killigrew left, Killigrew's blood-bloated face looking straight ahead, so as not to catch Miller's sardonic eye.

'So,' said Jensen, grinning his appallingly carnivorous grin. 'Think you can do it?' He did not wait for an answer. 'Look,' he said. 'You may think this is a damn silly scheme. I can't help that. It could be that a million men depend on those submarines not getting to sea. I'm afraid the SAS have made a balls-up. I just want you to find these damn things. If you can't blow them up, radio a position. The RAF'll look after the rest.'

Mallory said, 'Excuse my asking, sir. But what about the Resistance on the ground?'

Jensen frowned. 'Good question. Two things. One, you heard that idiot Killigrew. They may have been penetrated. And two, it may be that these U-boats are tucked up somewhere the RAF won't be able to get at them.' He grinned. 'I told Mr Churchill this morning that as far as I was concerned, you lot were equivalent to a bomber wing. He agreed.' He stood up. 'I'm very grateful to you. You've done two jolly good operations for me. Let's make this a third. Detailed briefing at the airfield later. There's an Albemarle coming in this afternoon for you. Takeoff at 1900.' He looked down at the faces: Mallory, weary but hatchet-sharp; Andrea, solid behind his vast black moustache; and Dusty Miller, scratching his crewcut in a manner prejudicial to discipline. It did not occur to Jensen to worry that in the past fourteen days they had taken a fearsome battering on scarcely any sleep. They were the tool for the job, and that was that.

'Any questions?' he said.

'Yes,' said Mallory, wearily. 'I don't suppose there's a drop of brandy about the house, is there?'

An hour later the sentries on the marble-pillared steps of the villa crashed to attention as the three men trotted down into the square, where a khaki staff car was waiting. The sentries did not like the look of them. They were elderly, by soldier standards – in their forties, and looking older. Their uniforms were dirty, their boots horrible. It was tempting to ask for identification and pay-books. But there was something about them that made the sentries decide that it would on the whole be better to keep quiet. They moved at a weary, purposeful lope that made the sentries think of creatures that ate infrequently, and when they did eat, ate animals they had tracked down patiently over great distances, and killed without fuss or remorse.

Mallory's mind was not, however, on eating. 'Not bad, that brandy,' he said.

'Five-star,' said Miller. 'Nothing but the best for the white-haired boys.'

After Jensen's villa the Termoli airfield lacked style. Typhoons howled overhead, swarming on and off the half-built runway in clouds of dust. Inevitably, there was another briefing room. But this one was in a hut with cardboard walls and a blast-taped window overlooking the propeller-whipped dust-storm and the fighters taxiing in the aircraft park. Among the fighters was a bomber, with the long, lumpy nose of a warthog, refuelling from a khaki bowser. Mallory knew it was an Albemarle. Jensen was making sure that the momentum of events was being maintained.

Evans, one of Jensen's young, smooth-mannered lieutenants, had brought them from the staff car. He said, 'I expect you'll have a shopping list.' He was a pink youth, with an eagerness that made Mallory feel a thousand years old. But Mallory made himself forget the tiredness, and the brandy, and the forty years he had been on the planet. He sat at a table with Andrea and Miller and filled out stores indents in triplicate. Then they rode a three-tonner down to the armoury, where Jensen's handiwork was also to be seen, in the shape of a rack of weapons, and a backpack B2 radio. There were also two brass-bound boxes whose contents Miller studied with interest. One of them was packed with explosives: gelignite, and blocks of something that looked like butter, but was in fact Cyclonite in a plasticising medium – plastic explosive. The other box contained primers and time pencils, colour-coded like children's crayons. Miller sorted through them with practised fingers, making some substitutions. There were also certain other substances, independently quite innocent but, used as he knew how to use them, lethal to enemy vehicles and personnel. Finally, there was a flat tin box containing a thousand pounds in used Bradbury fivers.

Andrea stood at a rack of Schmeissers, his hands moving like the hands of a man reading Braille, his black eyes looking far away. He rejected two of the machine pistols, picked out three more, and a Bren light machine gun. He stripped the Bren down, smacked it together again, nodded, and filled a haversack with grenades.

Mallory checked over two coils of wire-cored rope and a bag of climbing gear. 'Okay,' he said. 'Load it on.'

In the briefing hut, three men were waiting. They sat separately at the schoolroom tables, each of them apparently immersed in his own thoughts. 'Everything all right?' said Lieutenant Evans. 'Oh. Introductions. The team.' The men at the tables looked up, eyeing Mallory, Andrea and Miller with the wariness of men who knew that in a few hours these strangers would have the power of life and death over them.

'No real names, no pack-drill,' said Evans. He indicated the man on the right: small, the flesh bitten away under his cheekbones, his mouth hidden by a black moustache. He had the dour, self-contained look of a man who had lived all his life among mountains. 'This is Jaime,' Evans said. 'Jaime has worked in the Pyrenees. He knows his way around.'

'Worked?' said Mallory.

Jaime's face was sallow and unreadable, his eyes unwilling to trust. He said, 'I have carried goods. Smuggler, you would say. I have escaped Fascists. Spanish Fascists, German Fascists. All die when you shoot them.'

Mallory schooled his face to blankness. Fanatics could be trustworthy comrades; but that was the exception, not the rule.

'And that,' said Evans quietly, 'is Hugues. Hugues is our personnel man. Knows the Resistance on the ground. Practically encyclopaedic. Looks like a German. Don't be fooled. He was at Oxford before the war. Went back to Normandy to take over the family chateau. The SS shot his wife and two children when he went underground.'

Hugues was tall and broad-shouldered, with light brown hair, an affable pink-and-white Northern face, and china-blue eyes. When he shook Mallory's hand his palm was moist with nervous sweat. He said, 'Do you speak French?'

'No.' Mallory caught Miller's eye, and held it.

'None of you?'

'That's right.' Many virtues had combined to keep Mallory, Miller and Andrea alive and fighting these past weeks. But the cardinal virtue was this: reserve your fire, and never trust anyone.

Hugues said, 'I'm glad to meet you. But . . . no French? Jesus.'

Mallory liked his professionalism. 'You can do the talking,' he said.

'Spent any time behind enemy lines?' said Hugues.

'A little.' There was a wild look in Hugues' eye, thought Mallory. He was not sure he liked it.

Evans cleared his throat. 'Word in your ear, Hugues,' he said, and took him aside. Hugues frowned as the Naval officer murmured into his ear. Then he blushed red, and said to Mallory, 'Oh dear. 'Fraid I made a fool of myself, sir.'

'Perfectly reasonable,' said Mallory. Hugues was fine. Pink and eager and bright. But there was still that wild look . . . Not surprising, in the circumstances. A Resistance liaison would be as vital as a guide and a radio operator. Hugues would do.

The last man was nearly as big as Andrea, wearing a ragged, oddly urban straw hat. Evans introduced him as Thierry, an experienced Resistance radio operator. Then he drew the blinds, and pulled a case of what looked like clothing towards him. 'Doesn't matter about the French,' he said, 'you can stick to German.' From the box, he pulled breeches and camouflage smocks of a pattern Mallory had last seen in Crete. 'I hope we've got the size right. And you'd better stay indoors for the next wee while.'

It was true, reflected Mallory wryly, that there would be few better ways of attracting attention on an Allied air base than wandering around wearing the uniform of the Waffen-SS.

'Try 'em on,' said Evans.

The Frenchmen watched without curiosity or humour as Mallory, Miller and Andrea pulled the German smocks and trousers over their khaki battledress. Disguising yourself in enemy uniform left you liable to summary execution. But then so did working for the Resistance, or for that matter operating behind German lines in British uniform. In occupied France, Death would be breathing down your neck without looking at the label inside your collar.

'Okay,' said Evans, contemplating the Feldwebel with Mallory's face, and the two privates. 'Er, Colonel, would you consider shaving off the moustache?'

'No,' said Andrea, without changing expression.

'It's just that –'

'SS men do not wear moustaches,' said Andrea. 'This I know. But I do not intend to mix with SS men. I intend to kill them.'

Jaime was looking at him with new interest. 'Colonel?' he said.

'Slip of the tongue,' said Mallory.

Evans looked for a moment faintly flustered. He strode busily to the dais, and unrolled the familiar relief map of the western part of the Pyrenees. There was a blue bite of Atlantic at the top. Along the spine of the mountains writhed the red serpent of the Spanish border.

'Landing you here,' said Evans, tapping a brisk pointer on what could have been a hanging valley above St-Jean-Pied-du-Port.

'Landing?' said Mallory.

'Well, dropping then.'

Miller said, 'I told Captain Jensen. I can't stand heights.'

'Heights won't be a problem,' said Evans. 'You'll be dropping from five hundred feet.' He smiled, the happy smile of a man who would not be dropping with them, and unrolled another larger-scale map with contours. 'There's a flat spot in this valley. Pretty remote. There's a road in, from Jonzère. Runs on up to the Spanish border. There'll be a border post up there, patrols. We don't want you in Spain. We've got Franco leaning our way at the moment, and we don't want anything to happen that would, er, make it necessary for him to have to show what a beefy sort of chap he is. Plus you'd get yourselves interned and the camps are really not nice at all. So when you leave the drop site go downhill. Jaime'll remind you. Uphill is Spain. Downhill is France.'

Andrea was frowning at the map. The contours on either side of the valley were close together. Very close. In fact, the valley sides looked more like cliffs than slopes. He said, 'It's not a good place to drop.'

Evans said, 'There are no good places to drop just now in France.' There was a silence. 'Anyway,' he said briskly. 'You'll be met by a man called Jules. Hugues knows him.'

The fair-haired Norman nodded. 'Good man,' he said.

'Jules has been making a bit of a speciality of the Werwolf project. He'll brief you and pass you on. After that, you'll be on your own. But I hear you're used to that.' He looked at the grim faces. He thought, with a young man's arrogance: they're old, and they're tired. Does Jensen know what he's doing?

Then he remembered that Jensen always knew what he was doing.

Mallory looked at Evans' pink cheeks and crisp uniform. We all know you have been told to say this, he thought. And we all know that it is not true. We are not on our own at all. We are at the mercy of these three Frenchmen.

Evans said, 'There is a password. When anyone says to you, *"L'Amiral"*, you will reply *"Beaufort"*. And vice versa. We put it out on the BBC. The SAS used it, I'm afraid. No time to put out another one. Use with care.' He handed out bulky brown envelopes. 'Callsigns,' said Evans. 'Orders. Maps. Everything you need. Commit to memory and destroy. Any questions?'

There were no questions. Or rather, there were too many questions for it to be worth asking any of them.

'Storm Force,' said Miller, who had torn open his envelope. 'What's that?'

'That's you. This is Operation Storm,' said Evans. 'You were Force 10 in Yugoslavia. This follows on. Plus . . .' he hesitated.

'Yes?' said Mallory.

'Joke, really,' said Evans, grinning pinkly. 'But, well, Captain Jensen said we might as well call you after the weather forecast.'

'Great,' said Miller. 'Just great. All this and parachutes too.'

TWO

Sunday 1900 – Monday 0900

'Ladies and gentlemen, sorry, *gentlemen,*' said Wing Commander Maurice Hartford. 'We are now one hour from drop. Air Pyrenees hopes you are enjoying the ride. Personally, I think you are all crazy.'

Naturally, nobody could hear him, because the intercom was turned off. But it relieved his feelings. Why, he thought, is it always me?

It had been a nice takeoff. Six men plus the crew, not much equipment: a trivial load for the Albemarle, droning up from Termoli, over the wrinkled peaks of the Apennines, and into the sunset. The red sunset.

Hartford switched on the intercom. 'Captain Mallory,' he said, 'why don't you pop up to the sharp end?'

Mallory stirred in his steel bucket seat. He had slept for a couple of hours this afternoon. So had Andrea and Dusty Miller. An orderly had woken them for a dinner of steak and red wine, upon which they had fallen like wolves. The Frenchmen had picked at the food; nobody had wanted to talk. Jaime had remained dour. Hugues, unless Mallory was much mistaken, had developed a bad case of the jitters. Nothing wrong with that, though. The bravest men were not those who did not know fear, but those who knew it and conquered it. On the aeroplane, the Frenchmen had stayed awake while Andrea made himself a bed with his head on the box of fuses, and Miller sank low in his bucket seat, propped his endless legs on the radio, and began a snore that rivalled the clattering thunder of the Albemarle's Merlins.

Mallory had slept lightly. What he wanted was ten days of unconsciousness, broken only by huge meals at four-hour intervals. But that would have to wait. Among the rockfalls and avalanches of the Southern Alps, and during the long, dangerous months in Crete, he had learned to sleep a couple of inches below the surface, a wild animal's sleep that could give way to complete wakefulness in a fraction of a second.

He clambered out of his seat and went to the cockpit. The pilot gestured to the co-pilot's seat. Mallory sat down and plugged in the intercom.

'Cup of tea?' said the pilot, whose ginger moustache rose four inches above his mask, partially obscuring the goggles he wore to keep it out of his eyes.

Mallory said, 'Please.'

'Co-pilot's having a kip.' The pilot waved a thermos over a mug. 'Sunset,' he said, gesturing ahead.

There was indeed a sunset. The western sky was full of an archipelago of fiery islands, on which the last beams of the sun burst in a surf of gold. Above, the sky was dappled with cirrus. Below, the Mediterranean was darkening through steel to ink.

'Red sky at night,' said the pilot. 'Pilot gets fright.'

The plane bounced. Mallory captured a mouthful of tea and hot enamel. 'Why?' he said.

Quiet sort of chap, thought Hartford. Not bashful. Just quiet. Quiet like a bomb nobody had armed yet. Brown eyes that looked completely at home, completely competent, wherever they found themselves. A lean, tired face, motionless, conserving energy. Dangerous-looking blighter, thought Hartford, cheerfully. Lucky old Jerry.

'Weather,' he said. 'Bloody awful weather up there. Front coming in. All right for shepherds. Shepherds walk. But we're flying straight into the brute. Going to get very bumpy.'

'Okay for a drop?'

Hartford said, 'We'll get you down.' Actually, it was not okay for a drop. But he had orders to get these people onto the ground, okay or not. 'Tell your chaps to strap in, could you?' He pulled a dustbin-sized briar from his flying-suit pocket, stuffed it with tobacco, and lit it. The cockpit filled with acrid smoke. He pulled back the sliding window, admitting the tooth-jarring bellow of the engines. 'Smell that sea,' he said, inhaling deeply. 'Wizard. Yup. We'll go in at five hundred feet. Nice wide valley. All you have to do is jump when the light goes on. All at once.'

'Five hundred feet?'

'Piece of cake.'

'They'll hear us coming.'

The pilot grinned, revealing canines socketed into the holes they had worn in the stem of the pipe. 'Not unless they're Spanish,' he said.

They hit the front over the coast, and flew on, minute after endless minute, until the minutes became hours. The Albemarle swooped and plunged, wings battered by the turbulent up currents. By the dark-grey light that crept through the little windows, Mallory looked at his team. Andrea and Miller he took for granted. But the Frenchmen he was not so sure about. He could see the flash of the whites of Jaime's eyes, the nervous movement of Thierry's mouth as he chewed his lips from inside. And Hugues, contemplating his hands, hands with heavily-bitten fingernails, locked on his knees. Mallory felt suddenly weary. He had been in too many little metal rooms, watched too many people, wondered too many times how they would shape up when the pressure was on and the lid had blown off . . .

The Albemarle banked steeply to port, then starboard. Mallory thought there was a new kind of turbulence out there: not just the moil of air masses in collision, but the upward smack of waves of air breaking on sheer faces of rock. He looked round.

The doorway into the cockpit was open. Beyond the windscreen the flannel-coloured clouds separated and wisped away. Suddenly Mallory was looking down a valley whose steep sides rose out of sight on either side. The upper slopes were white with snow. There was a grey village perched up there – *up* there, above the aeroplane. A couple of yellow lights showed in the gloom. No blackout: Spain, thought Mallory –

A pine tree loomed ahead. It approached at two hundred miles an hour. He saw the pilot's shoulders move as he hauled on the yoke. The tree was higher than the plane. Hey, thought Mallory, we're going to hit that –

But the Albemarle roared up and over. Something slapped the deck under his feet. Then the tree was gone, and the aircraft was banking steeply to port, into the next valley.

Mallory got up and closed the door. There were some things it was not necessary to see. Pine trees were, what? A hundred feet high? Maximum. Mallory decided if he was going to be flown into a mountain, he did not want to see the mountain coming.

It went on: the howl of the wind, the bucket of the airframe, the bellow of the engines. Mallory fell asleep.

Next thing he knew the racket was still there, and someone was shaking his shoulder. He felt terrible: head aching, thoughts slow as cold oil. The Albemarle's bomb-aimer was pushing a cup of tea in his face. Benzedrine, he thought. No. Not yet. This is only the beginning.

He had woken into a different world: the sick-at-the-stomach world of dangerous things about to happen. He badly wanted a cigarette. But there would be no time for cigarettes for a while.

A dim yellow light was burning in the fuselage. Bulky camouflaged forms swore and collided, struggling into their parachutes and rounding up equipment.

'Five minutes,' said the bomb-aimer with repellent cheerfulness, when he had finished checking the harnesses. 'Onto the trench.'

'Trench?' said Miller.

The bomb-aimer indicated a long slot in the floor of the aircraft. 'Get on there,' he said. 'Stand at ease, one foot either side.' He pointed at a pair of light bulbs. 'When the light goes green, *shun!*'

'Gee, thanks,' said Miller, and shuffled into position. The first light bulb flicked on: red.

Hugues was behind him. Hugues' mind would not stay still. It kept flicking back over the past two years, with the weary insistence of a stuck gramophone record. After the SS had done what they had done to his family, he had not cared if he lived or died. Then Lisette had come along. And in Lisette, he had found a new reason for living . . .

On a night like this, a reason for living was the last thing you needed. Remember what they taught you in school, he thought. Keep it buttoned up. Don't let anything show –

Lisette. When shall I see you again?

Fear prised his mind apart and climbed in. Fear became terror. His bowels were water, and icy sweat was pouring down him.

First, there was the parachute descent, and of course it was possible that the parachute would not open. Then, even if the parachute did open, that big thin man Miller had two boxes balanced in front of him – *attached* to him, for the love of God! – full of explosives. So they were all dropping out of this plane, six humans and a land mine, in a lump. Jesus. He would be all over the landscape. He would never see Lisette –

Underfoot, he felt a new vibration, like gears winding. The trench opened. The night howled in, black and full of wind. He felt stuck, trapped, cramped by this damned harness, Schmeisser, pack, equipment.

A hand landed on his shoulder. He looked round so fast he almost overbalanced.

It belonged to the big man who did not speak, the bear with the moustache. The big face was impassive. A reflection of the little red bulb swam in each black eye. One of the eyes winked. *Jesus,* thought Hugues. He knows what I'm thinking. What will he think of me?

But surprisingly, he found that the fear had lessened.

Jaime was not comfortable either, but for different reasons. He had the short legs of the mountaineer. In his mind, he had been tracking their route: up the Valle de Tena, then north, across the Col de Pourtalet. He had walked it himself, first with bales of cigarettes, then with mules bearing arms for the Republican cause in the last days of the Spanish Civil War. He reckoned that now they would be coming down on Colbis. He did not like the feel of the weather out there. Nor did he like the fact that they were flying in cloud down a fifty-degree hillside at two hundred miles an hour. Feet on the ground were safe. Mules were safer. He wanted to get back on the ground, because his legs were aching, straddled over the trench, and he could feel the fear radiating from Thierry, slung about with his radios, straw hat stuffed in his pack, his big face improbably healthy in the red light –

Thierry's face turned suddenly green.

Shun.

Six pairs of heels crashed together. The static lines ran out and tautened. The hold was empty.

Through the bomb doors the bomb-aimer glimpsed points of yellow light forming a tenuous L. He said into the intercom, 'All gone.' The pilot hauled back on the stick, and the clouds intervened. The Albemarle banked steeply and set its nose for Italy.

The ground hit Mallory like a huge, wet hammer. There were lights looping in his eyes as he rolled. A rock made his ears ring. He got rid of the parachute, invisible now in the dark, flattened himself against the ground, and worked the cocking lever of the Schmeisser, taut as an animal at bay. For a moment there was the moan of the wind and the feel of grit on his cheek. Then a voice close at hand said, *'L'Amiral.'*

'Beaufort,' he said.

There was shouting. Then more lights – a lot of lights, a ridiculous number – in his eyes. He levelled the Schmeisser. The lights wavered away, and someone shouted, *'Non! Non! L'Amiral Beaufort.* Welcome to France, *mon officier.'*

Unnecessary hands pulled him to his feet. He said, 'Where are the others?'

'Safe.' A flask found his hand. *'Buvez.* Drink. *Vive la France!'* He drank. It was brandy. It drilled a hole in the cold and the rain. People were lighting cigarettes. There was a lot of unmilitary noise, several bottles. A dark figure materialised at his side, then another.

Miller's voice said, 'Any minute now someone is going to start playing the goddamn accordion.'

'All here?' There were grunts from the darkness. There were too many people, too much noise, not enough discipline. 'Hugues.'

'Sir.'

'Tell these people to put the bloody lights out. Where's Jules?'

There was a conversation in French. Hugues replied, his voice rising, expostulating. *'Merde,'* he said finally.

'What is it?'

'These idiots. These goddamn Trotskyite sons of –'

'Quick.' Mallory's voice brought him up sharp as a choke-chain.

'Jules is held up in Colbis. There was an incident with your forces last week. The Germans are nervous.'

That would have been the SAS, thought Mallory, charging around like bulls in a china shop.

'But Colbis is only in the next valley. We will take you there, when we have transport. There is a problem with the transport. They don't know what. A lorry will come soon, they say. *Franchement,'* said Hugues, his voice rising, 'I do not believe these people. They are like the Spanish, always *mañana –'*

'Ask them how soon.' And calm them down, thought Mallory. Calm them down.

'They say to wait,' said Hugues, not at all calm. 'It is seven miles to the village. There may be patrols. There is a cave they know. It is dry there, and German patrols do not visit it. They say it will be a good place to wait. The lorry will come to collect you, in one hour, maybe two.'

Mallory looked at his watch. Raindrops blurred the glass. Just after midnight. Monday already. And they were being told to wait on a mountain top in the rain, and the Werwolf pack was leaving at noon on Wednesday.

He said, 'Where's this cave?'

'I know it,' said Jaime's voice.

Mallory sighed. Patience. 'Let's go,' he said.

Andrea appeared at his side. Mallory felt the comfort of his gigantic presence. 'This is not good,' said the Greek, under the babble of excited talk from the escort.

'We will make it better,' said Mallory. 'Hugues. Tell these people to be quiet.'

Hugues started shouting. The crowd fell silent. They started to walk in the lashing rain.

Jaime set a cracking pace up the valley, towards Spain, following a track that wound through a field of tea chest-sized boulders which had fallen from the valley's sides. The map had been right; those sides were not so much slopes as cliffs. From the rear, Mallory could hear Hugues' voice, speaking French, raised in violent argument with someone. Mallory was beginning to worry about Hugues. Staying alive behind enemy lines meant staying calm. It was beginning to sound as if Hugues was not a calm person. He called softly, 'Shut up.'

Hugues shut up. The procession became quiet.

Mallory said to Miller, 'What was that about?'

'He was looking for someone. Someone who's not around.'

In ten minutes the valley floor had narrowed to a hundred yards, and the sides had become vertical walls of rock, undermined at their base, hidden in inky shadows. 'Here,' said Jaime's voice from the dark. A flashlight beam illuminated a dark entrance.

Andrea materialised at Mallory's side. 'Bad place,' he said. The cave had no exit except into the valley. And the valley was more a gorge than a valley. It felt bad. It felt like a trap. 'Hugues,' said Mallory, without looking round. 'Tell these people that this is no good.'

Mallory turned. 'Hugues,' he said. 'Tell these people –'

He stopped. There were no people. Hugues was a solitary dark figure against the paler grey of the rocks.

Hugues said, 'They have left.'

'Left?' said Mallory.

'Gone to look for the transport. Also, there was a . . . person I wished to see who did not arrive. That was why I had a discussion – yes – an acrimonious discussion.' His voice was rising. 'These people are frankly peasants –'

Andrea said, 'Enough.'

Hugues stopped talking as if someone had flipped a switch. Mallory said to Andrea and Miller, 'We're stuck with this. We need the transport. If we move, they'll lose us. We'll have to wait. Take cover.'

Andrea and Miller were already fading into the dark, taking up positions not in the cave, but among the rocks on the valley floor.

The night became quiet, except for the sigh of the wind and the swish of the rain, and the drowsy clonk of a goat bell from inside the cave.

This is all wrong, thought Mallory. We have been inadequately briefed, and we are dependent on a Resistance organisation that seems completely disorganised. It sounds as if the SAS have already compromised us. If the enemy comes up the valley there is no way out, except into an internment camp in Spain.

Mallory lay and strained his ears into the wet dark rain, wind, goat bells –

And another sound. A mechanical sound, but not a motor. The sound of metal on metal, gears turning. The sound of a bicycle.

There was a sudden crash. The old sounds returned, with behind them the noise of a back wheel spinning, ticking to a stop.

Mallory waited. Then he heard the brief, otherworldly *bleep* of a Scops owl.

Mallory had as yet heard no Scops owls in the Pyrenees. But there had been plenty in Crete, where he had served his time with Andrea.

Something moved at his shoulder: something huge, blacker than the night. Andrea said, 'I found this,' and dropped something on the gritty ground beside him, something that drew breath and started to croak.

Mallory allowed the muzzle of the Schmeisser to rest gently in the hollow under the something's ear. He said, 'Quiet.'

The something became quiet.

Mallory said, 'I am a British officer. What do you want?'

The something said, 'Hugues.'

'Good God,' said Mallory.

The something was a woman.

The woman got her voice back. She batted at Mallory with her hands. She was strong. She said, *'Laisse-moi,'* in a voice both vigorous and tough.

Out in the dark and the rain, Hugues' voice said, *'Bon Dieu!'* Mallory thought he could hear something new in it: shock, and awe. He heard the uncoordinated stumble of Hugues' boots in the dark. 'Lisette!' cried Hugues.

'Hugues!' cried the woman. *'C'est bien toi?'*

Then Hugues was embracing her. The fear was gone now. All the terrible things were gone. All Hugues' life, people had taken what he loved away from him, for reasons that seemed excellent to them but incomprehensible to him. They had taken away his parents and sent him to a stupid English school. They had taken away Mireille and the children because he was a saboteur. And then he had met Lisette, in the Resistance, and become her lover. When SOE had flown him out in the Lysander, he had thought that that had been the end of Lisette, too.

But here she was. In his arms. As large as life, if not larger.

'My darling,' he said.

She kissed him on the cheek, murmuring what sounded like pet names. Then Mallory heard her tone change. She sounded frantic about something.

'*Merde*,' said Hugues, in his new, firm voice. 'We must leave. Now.'

Mallory said, quietly, 'Who is this?'

'Lisette,' said Hugues. 'A friend. A *résistante*.'

'Is she the person you wanted to see who did not arrive?'

'Yes. She is an old friend. She knows the people on the ground in the region. It is an excellent thing that she has found us. Providential. She says there are sixty Germans coming up the valley.'

'Three lorries,' she said. Her accent was heavy, but comprehensible. 'The ones who reached Jonzère told me they caught two of your reception committee, found them with parachutes.'

'How long ago?'

'Half an hour,' said Lisette. 'At the most. They told me to warn you.'

Mallory's stomach felt shrivelled like a walnut. One and a half hours in France, and the operation was as good as over. He pushed the thought into the back of his mind. 'Jaime!' he said.

Jaime appeared out of the night. 'Lisette,' he said, without surprise.

'*Bonjour*, Jaime.'

Briskly, Mallory explained the position.

Jaime said, 'We must go to Spain. It is over. Finished.'

In his mind Mallory saw a soldier, pack on his back, seasickness in his belly and fear in his soul, squashed against the steel side of a ship by a thousand other soldiers. And suddenly, without warning, something stove in the side of that ship, smashed the soldier like an egg, and the cold green water poured in.

Once Mallory had been in a little steel room on a ship in the Mediterranean, checking grenades. There had been a bang. Someone had said, 'Torpedo.' Then the room had started to fill up with water, and the ship with screams, quickly cut off. Mallory had been one of four survivors. Four out of three hundred.

If the Werwolf pack got out intact, there could be a thousand such ships.

Mallory said, 'No other way?'

'None.' Jaime seemed to hesitate. 'Except the Chemin des Anges.'

'What's that?'

'Nothing. A goat track, no more. It runs from Jonzère, at the bottom of the valley, up the ridge, in the manner of the old roads. The pilgrims used to use it, the men with the cockle shells in their hats, bound for Santiago de Compostela, when there were bandits in the mountains. It is a dangerous road. It killed almost as many pilgrims as the bandits did.'

'Where is it?'

Against the dark sky Jaime's small shoulders appeared to shrug. He pointed upwards. 'On the spine of the hill. Here it runs three hundred metres above the valley. Above the cliff. Then it turns over the mountain and down to Colbis. There were pilgrims' inns in Colbis. But we can't go to Jonzère, to the start of the track. It'll be full of Germans –'

'We'll go up the cliff,' said Mallory, as if he were proposing a walk in the park.

There was a second's silence. Then Jaime said, 'To join the Chemin des Anges here? That is not possible.'

Mallory said, 'It is necessary.'

The chill of his voice silenced Jaime for a moment. Then he said, 'But you do not understand. Nobody can climb those cliffs.'

'That is what the Germans will think. Miller?'

Miller had been sitting on a boulder. He knew what Mallory was going to say, and he found the knowledge depressing. 'Yep?'

'Round up the people. Andrea and I are going up the cliff. We'll do a pitch, belay and drop you a fixed rope. Make sure everyone comes.'

Miller pushed his SS helmet back on his head and looked up. For a moment it was like being in a tunnel. Then, far overhead, clouds shifted, and there appeared between the two cliff-masses a thread-fine crack of sky. The wind was blowing up the valley. He could hear no lorries. The dark bulk that was Mallory slung a coil of wire-cored rope over his shoulder and walked towards the cliff. Wearily, Miller rounded up Hugues and Lisette, and Jaime, and Thierry the radio operator, and assembled the stores, and the radio, and the two wooden boxes of explosives, under the cliff. Mallory and Andrea seemed to vanish into the solid rock. The group at the cliff foot sat huddled against the icy rain. From above came the infrequent sound of a low word spoken, the clink of hammer on spike, the scuff of nailed boot on rock. The sounds receded quickly upwards. Human goddamn flies, thought Miller, gloomily. Personally, he had no suckers on his feet, and no plans to grow any. He stood up, cocked his Schmeisser and moved fifty yards down the valley in the rain. Someone had to stand sentry, and the only person on the valley floor Miller trusted was Miller.

Fall in with bad companions and what do you get?

I tell you what you get, he told himself, settling into a natural embrasure in the rock and preparing for the first of the sixty Germans to come round the corner.

You get problems.

There had been times in Mallory's life when he would have enjoyed a good crack at a limestone cliff in the dark. On a cold morning, perhaps, in a gorge in the Southern Alps, when you had got up at one in the morning, the stars floating silver and unwinking between the ice-white peaks of the range.

This was not one of those times.

This was a vertical slab of rock he could barely see. This was climbing by Braille, running fingers and feet over the smooth surface looking for pockmarks and indentations, tapping spikes into hair-cracks, standing with the tip of a boot-toe balanced on a foothold slim as a goose-quill.

But Mallory knew that there is a greater spur to climbing a cliff in the dark than a wish to dwell in the white Olympus of the high peaks. It is to get you and your comrades away from three lorry loads of Germans.

So Mallory climbed that sopping wall until his fingernails were gone, and the sweat stung his eyes, and the breath rasped in his tobacco-seared throat. And after fifty feet, he found a chimney.

It was a useful chimney, the edge of a huge flake of rock that would in a few hundred years separate from the face of the cliff and slide into the gorge. Mallory made a belay, called down to Andrea, and went up the chimney as if it had been a flight of stairs.

At first the chimney was vertical. After thirty feet it started to trend leftward. Then suddenly there was a chockstone, a great boulder that had rolled down the cliff and jammed in the chimney. It formed a level floor embraced on two sides by buttresses of rock, invisible from the bottom of the valley. It was more than Mallory had dared hope for. Fifty people could have hidden up there while the Germans rumbled up the valley and flattened their noses against the Spanish border. Over which they would assume the Storm Force had fled –

Mallory felt a sensation he hardly recognised.

Hope.

Don't count your chickens.

Jaime was the first to arrive. He was carrying the bulky, square-edged radio pack. Jaime was a useful man on a mountain. There was a pause, and Andrea came up, carrying the second rope. 'All at the base of the chimney,' he said. 'Stores too.'

'Good,' said Mallory, belaying the rope and letting the end go.

Now that there were two ropes, things started to move fast. Thierry came up one, breathing in a high, frightened whimper, his straw hat crammed over his eyebrows. The second rope seemed to be taking a long time. 'It's the woman,' said Andrea. 'She doesn't have the strength in her arms.' Mallory saw his huge back dark against the sky as he bent to the rope. She was a big woman; there were not many fat people in wartime France, but she was one of them. She must have weighed ten stone. But Andrea hauled her up as if she had been a bag of sugar, set her on her feet, and dusted down her bulk.

'Merci,' she said.

Andrea's white teeth flashed under his moustache. He had the smile of a musketeer, this Greek giant. Even now, with the rain lashing down and Germans in the valley, Lisette felt enveloped in a protective cloak of courtesy and understanding. Andrea bowed, as if she had been a lady of Versailles, not a shapeless bundle of overcoats crouched on a cliff ledge. Then he let the rope go again.

Hugues came up, too breathless to complain, and went to Lisette's side. Mallory had a nagging moment of worry. Hugues' priorities had to be with the operation, not his girlfriend. Mallory did not know enough about this woman. And he did not know enough about Hugues. For the moment, if her information was good, she had saved their bacon. But if Mallory's instincts were right, she was going to be a distraction. And distractions had no place on an operation like this. On this operation there was a single priority: find and destroy the Werwolf pack.

Hugues would need watching.

Mallory turned away, and hauled up the boxes of explosives and a couple of packs. The rain was turning even colder, developing a grainy feel. Mallory thought, soon it will be snowing. His hands were cracked and sore, and the plaster had peeled off the reopening wounds. God knew how Andrea must be feeling. But the stores were up, stacked on the edge of the boulder, and Miller was on his way up, but with no rope yet. Must get a rope to him; Miller was no climber.

The wind moaned and died. Andrea said, 'Listen.'

There was a new sound in the raw, snow-laden air. Lorry engines.

All the way up the bottom forty feet of the cliff, Miller had been feeling the void snapping at his heels. The wind was freezing, but inside his uniform a Niagara of hot sweat was running. His knees felt weak, his hands shaky. Miller had been raised on the flatlands of the American Midwest. One hold at a time, he told himself. Don't look down. Don't think of the sheer face down there –

Miller patted the cliff above his head, groping for chinks and crevices. Mallory must have found some. But as far as Miller was concerned he might as well have been trying to climb a plate glass window. Both ropes were in use . . .

Hurry, please, thought Miller politely. For forty feet down, things were happening. On the wind from the valley came the sharp whiff of exhaust. He looked up.

The cold, slushy rain battered his face. What he could see of the cliff was black and shiny, the chimney a dark streak rising to the chockstone. He had seen Mallory in a chimney, his shoulders one side, his heels the other, gliding his way skyward with that weightless fluency of his. Miller's limbs were too lanky for that, and his body wanted to plaster itself against the rock, not sit out over the emptiness as Mallory did, applying weight where it was needed, on fingers and toes –

Without a rope there was no way of getting to the chimney.

He pressed his face into the rock. The earthy smell of wet stone filled his nostrils. There was a lightening of the walls. Headlights down the valley.

He moved his hands again. The rock was rough, but there was nothing you could hold on to. Not unless you were a human fly like Mallory. Can't go up, thought Miller. Can't go down. So you just stand here, and hold on, and try not to follow that voice in your head that is telling you to shout and scream and keel gently out and back and plummet into space.

There were lights under his feet, and the gorge was churning with engines. A voice above him said, 'Rope coming!'

The lorries were directly below him now. By the grind of their engines they were moving at a slow, walking pace. Searching. *Nobody looks up.* It is fine. Nobody ever looks up. Particularly not up sheer cliffs.

Not even Germans. No matter how thorough they may be.

You wish.

The rope nudged his face, cautiously. Miller said a quiet, polite thank you. Then he wound his hands into it and began to climb.

'He's coming up now,' said Andrea, in his soft, imperturbable voice.

They were standing at the back of the ledge formed by the chockstone. Its edge was a horizon now, backlit by the glow of the lorries' headlamps. Against the edge was something hard-edged and square. The radio.

'Move that,' said Mallory to Thierry.

Thierry started forward, shuffling, his great bulk moving against the lights. He was tired, thought Mallory. Tired and frightened, in a wet straw hat.

If he had been less tired himself, he might have prevented what happened next.

Thierry scooped up the radio and slung it over his shoulder. As he turned, his foot hit something that could have been a tuft of grass but was actually a rock. The rock went over the edge.

It whizzed past Dusty Miller's head. At the base of the chimney it bounced, removing a fair-sized boulder. By the time it hit the valley floor it was a junior landslide. It landed with a roar fifteen feet to the right of the second truck in the convoy. Small stones pattered against the passenger door of the cab.

The truck stopped. A searchlight on the roof sent a white disc of light sliding across the black face of the cliff.

Miller was fifteen feet from the top, sweating, his breath coming in gasps. Clamp a hand on the rope. Pull up, shoving with feet. Clamp the other hand. There was shouting down below. Clamp the other hand. The hands like grey spiders against the cliff. They could have belonged to anyone, those hands, except for the pain, and the heavy thump of his heart.

And suddenly the other hand was not grey, but blazing, brilliant flesh-colour, and every fibre of the rope stood out in microscopic detail. And Miller was a moth, kicking on the pin of the searchlight.

A rifle cracked, then another. Chips of rock stung his face. His back crawled with the expectation of bullets. Ten feet to go. It might as well have been ten miles.

But there was a burst of machine-gun fire from above, and the searchlight went out, and suddenly the rope in his hands was alive, moving upwards like the rope of a ski tow. And he looked up and saw a huge shape, dim above the cliff, shoulders working. Andrea.

Andrea pulled him up those last ten feet as if he had weighed two hundred ounces instead of two hundred pounds. Miller hit the dirt in cover, rolled, and unslung his Schmeisser. Trouble, he thought. I am not a goddamn human fly, and as a result we are in it up to our necks, and sinking.

Beyond the boulder the cliffs were brilliant white. In their light he could see Andrea cocking a Bren.

'I'll cover you,' said Andrea, in his unruffled craftsman's voice. 'Grenades?'

Miller and Mallory each took two grenades from their belt pouches and pulled the pins. Two, three,' said Mallory. 'Throw.'

There was a moment of silence, broken only by the metallic clatter of the grenades bouncing down the cliff, two left, two right. The world seemed to hold its breath. They would be setting up a mortar down there; taking up positions, radioing for reinforcements. Though, in a gorge like this, radio reception would be terrible –

Then the night flashed white, and four explosions rang as one, followed by a deeper explosion. Andrea crawled to the edge of the ledge. The lights had gone out. There was a new light, orange and black: a burning lorry. The firing lulled, then began again.

Mallory said, 'Cover us for ten minutes. We'll meet you at the top.'

Andrea's head was a black silhouette against the orange flicker of the gasoline fire. The silhouette nodded. For a moment his huge shoulders showed against the sky, the Bren slung over the right. Then he faded into the rocks. The five other men and Lisette gathered up the packs. Jaime said, in a voice apparently unaffected by fear, 'There is a path. A little higher.'

'Miller,' said Mallory. 'We don't want those trucks to get back. Or anywhere with anything like decent radio reception. Anything you can do?'

Miller shrugged. 'I'll give it the old college try,' he said. His hands were already busy in the first of the brass-bound boxes. He felt for one of the five-pound bricks of plastic explosive, laid it on the ground, latched the first box and unlatched the second. The second box was thickly lined with felt. Unclipping a flashlight from the breast pocket of his smock, he used it to select a green time pencil: thirty seconds' delay. Delicately he pressed the pencil into the primer and looked at the radium-bright numerals on his watch. Then he snapped the time pencil, yawned, and carefully lit a cigarette. By the time he had pocketed his Zippo, twenty-five seconds had elapsed. He took the brick in both hands and heaved it out and over the vehicles in the valley below.

Miller really hated heights. But nice, safe explosives were familiar territory. It felt great to be back.

For the space of a breath, there was darkness and silence in which the sound of Germanic shouting rose from the valley, mixed with the scrape of steel on rock as they set up the mortars.

Then the night turned white, whiter than the searchlights, and Mallory was blasted against the cliff by a huge metallic *clang* that felt as if it would drive his eardrums together in the middle of his head.

'Go,' he said, the sound small and distant behind the ringing in his ears.

They began to file up the cliff: Mallory in the lead, then Jaime, Lisette, and Hugues, with Miller bringing up the rear. Andrea climbed the fifty-degree face behind the chockstone until he found another boulder. There he stopped, unfolded the Bren's bipod, and rested it on the stone.

Fires were still burning on the valley floor. The flames cast a flickering light on torn rock and twisted metal, and many still bodies dressed in field-grey. There were three trucks. Two of them were burning. The other lay like a crushed beetle under a huge slab of rock prised away from the gorge wall by the force of the explosion. At the far side of the gorge, three grey figures were draped over the rocks beside what had once been a mortar.

One of the figures moved.

Andrea pulled the Bren into his shoulder, and fired. The heavy drum of the machine gun echoed in the rocks. The grey figure went over backwards and did not move any more.

Then there was silence, except for the moan of the wind and the patter of sleet on rock.

Andrea watched for another five minutes, patient, not heeding the icy moisture soaking through his smock and into his battle-dress blouse.

Nothing moved. As far as he could tell, the radio sets were wrecked, and there were no survivors. But of course there would be survivors. He had no objection to going down and cutting the survivors' throats. But if he did, it was unlikely that he would be able to rejoin the main party.

Andrea thought about it with the deliberation of a master wine maker deciding on which day he would pick his grapes: perhaps a little light on sugar today, but if he waited a week, there was the risk of rain . . .

Naturally, the Germans would assume that the force that had attacked them had gone on to Spain.

Andrea took a final look at the flames and the metal and the bodies. He felt no emotion. Guerrilla warfare was a job, a job at which he was an expert. His strength and intelligence were weapons in the service of his comrades and his country's allies. He did not like killing German soldiers. But if it was part of the job, then he was prepared to do it, and do it well.

To Andrea, this looked like a decent piece of work.

He slung the Bren over his shoulder and began to lope rapidly up the steep mountain. It had begun to snow.

It was a wet snow that fell in flakes the size of saucers, each flake landing on skin or cloth or metal with an icy slap, beginning imme-diately to melt. They slid into boots and down necks, becoming paradoxically colder as they melted. Within ten minutes the whole party was soaked to the skin. And for what seemed like an eternity, there was only the rasp of breath in throats, the hammer of hearts, and the sodden rub of boots against feet as they marched doggedly up the forty-five-degree slope in the icy blackness. Miller's mind was filled with anxiety.

He said to Andrea, 'What do you think?'

Andrea knew what he was being asked. 'They will think we have gone to Spain.'

'Perhaps.'

'And they will send out patrols. In case we have not gone to Spain.'

'Exactly.'

One foot in front of the other. Hammering hearts. Sore feet. Soon they would have to stop. Food was needed, and warmth. But they were walking away from food and warmth, upwards. Into unknown territory. Where they had been assured Jules would be waiting, somewhere warm and dry. Assured by Lisette.

Mallory was having to rely on people he did not know. And that made Mallory nervous.

Mallory said quietly, 'We'd better watch the rear, in case anyone drops out.'

Andrea stepped to one side. The walkers passed him: Jaime in the lead, Miller, Thierry. Then, a long way behind, too far, Hugues and Lisette: Hugues hunched over Lisette, apparently half-carrying her, their shapes odd and lumpy against the white snow, like a single, awkward animal. Andrea could hear Hugues' breathing.

'You all right?' he said.

'Of course,' said Hugues, in a voice whose cheerfulness even exhaustion could not mar.

Andrea frowned. Then he fell in behind, and kept on upwards.

It felt like an eternity. But in reality it was only a little more than an hour before Jaime emitted a bark of satisfaction, and said, *'Voilà!'*

The ground had for some time been rising less steeply. Between snow flurries, Mallory saw a silvery line of snow lying across the black-lead sky: the ridge. Between the walkers and the ridge was what might have been a narrow ledge, running diagonally upwards, its lines softened by six inches of snow. Jaime kicked at the downhill side with his foot, revealing a coping of roughly-dressed stone. 'The Chemin des Anges,' he said.

The path was easy walking, following the contours, skirting precipices over which Miller did not allow his eyes to stray. They followed it up and onto the ridge.

Lack of effort let them feel the chill of their sodden clothes. They paused to let Lisette and Hugues catch up. Mallory took his oilcloth-wrapped cigarettes from the soaking pocket of his blouse, and gave one to Miller. Their faces were haggard in the Zippo's flare. Hugues and Lisette approached.

Hugues said, 'Lisette needs food. Rest, warmth –'

'Don't be stupid,' said Lisette's voice. She sounded weak, but resolute.

'But my darling –'

'Don't you darling me,' she said. 'Can we go on?'

Mallory said nothing. It was possible to admire this woman's spirit. It was less possible to admire the speed at which she moved.

Too slow, thought Mallory. It was all getting too slow, and there was a hell of a distance to travel before they even got to the start line.

His watch said it was 0200 hours. He said to Jaime, 'How long?'

'Two hours. All downhill. The slope is not so bad now.'

Mallory could hear Hugues' teeth chattering. There was a thin, icy wind up here, and the snow was colder. 'Any shelter before then?'

'In ten minutes. A shepherd's hut. There will be nobody.'

'We'll stop for twenty minutes.'

'Thank God.'

The shepherd's hut had a roof and three walls, facing providentially away from the wind. The floor was covered in dung-matted straw, but it was dry, and after the snow it was as good as a Turkish carpet. They burrowed into the filthy straw, smoking, letting their body heat warm their soaking clothes. Jaime produced a bottle of brandy. Lisette was half-buried in the straw next to Hugues. When Mallory shone his flashlight at her, he saw her face was a dead grey. He took the brandy bottle out of Thierry's hand and carried it over to her. 'Here,' he said.

The neck of the bottle rattled against her teeth. She coughed. 'Thank you,' she said, when she could speak.

Mallory said, 'It was a good thing you found us.'

'Love,' said Hugues. 'It was the power of love. A sixth sense –'

'There was a little more to it than that,' she said, dryly. 'Hugues, you are getting carried away.'

'Yes,' said Mallory, warming to her toughness. 'So how did you do it?'

She shook her head. Her shivering was lending a faint seismic movement to the straw. 'They were talking, the *résistants*. One of them I knew. They said the radio signal arranging your drop mentioned that you were carrying money, I don't know if it's true. They made a deal with a German officer. They are demoralised, some of these Germans in the mountains here. And of course the *résistants* too; some of them are no more than bandits. The German was to kill you. Then he was to give them the money and collect a medal, I guess.' Her teeth gleamed in the pale reflection from the snow outside. 'I saw them come back to warn the officer. I knew where they had come from. So I got on my bicycle, and fell off in the right place. And it didn't work out for those pigs.'

'Thank God,' said Hugues, fervently.

Mallory found he was smiling. 'Thank you,' he said. He got up, his weary knees protesting. It looked as if there was a new addition to the party. A brave addition, but a slow one. He hoped that Hugues would get his ardour under control, and start acting human again. He said, 'We're moving out.'

An hour and a half later Jaime led them down a snowy path and into the trees above the village. There was another barn-like building in the trees.

Jaime opened the door and said, 'Wait in here.'

Mallory said, 'Where are you going?'

'To find some friends.' There was a fireplace. Jaime struck a match, lit the piled kindling, and threw on an armful of logs. 'Be comfortable. Dry yourselves.' His eyes were invisible in the shadows under his heavy eyebrows.

Mallory's eyes met Andrea's. He did not like it. Nor, he could tell, did Andrea. But there was nothing he could do.

Jaime disappeared into the night. Lisette sank down in front of the fire and began to pull her boots off.

'Outside,' said Mallory.

She looked at him as if he was mad.

'What if Jaime comes back with a German patrol?'

'*Mais non,*' said Thierry.

'Jaime?' said Lisette. 'Never. He hates Germans.'

Hugues' face was pink and nervous. 'How do you know?' he said. 'How does anyone know? The Germans arrived at the drop site within half an hour. Someone betrayed us –'

'I told you what happened,' said Lisette. 'Now for God's sake –'

'Outside,' said Hugues.

Something happened to Lisette's face. '*Non,*' she said. '*Non, non, non, non.* I am staying.'

'And I also,' said Thierry, his big face the colour of lard under the straw hat.

'*Women,*' said Hugues.

'I am not *women!*' snapped Lisette. 'I am someone who knows Jaime. And trusts him.'

''*Ah, ça!*' said Hugues. 'Well –'

'But perhaps you trust your friends more,' said Lisette.

And when Hugues looked round, he saw that where Mallory, Miller and Andrea had been standing were only wet footprints.

Out in the woods Miller lay and shivered in a pile of sodden pine needles, and thought longingly of the warm firelight in the barn.

He had watched Hugues storm out, heard the slam of the door. Then nothing, except the icy drip of rainwater on his neck, and the mouldy smell of pine needles under his nose.

After half an hour, the rain stopped. There was silence, with dripping. And behind the dripping, the wheeze and clatter of an engine. Some sort of truck came round the corner, no lights. Miller sighted his Schmeisser on its cab. Three men got out. As far as Miller could see, the truck was small, and not German.

A voice said, *'L'Amiral Beaufort!'*

Another voice said, *'Vive la France!'*

The barn door opened and closed.

Mallory saw Hugues come out of the bush in which he had been hiding, and walk across to the barn. Hugues knew these men, it appeared. That was Hugues' area of speciality. So Mallory got up himself, and went in.

The men Jaime had brought wore sweeping moustaches and huge berets that flopped down over their eyes. They carried shotguns. Two of them were talking to Hugues in rapid French. Mallory thought they looked a damned sight too pleased with themselves.

'There are no Germans in the village,' said Jaime. 'But there is a small problem. It seems that Jules has had an accident. A fatal accident, they tell me. He was shot at Jonzère, last night.'

Mallory stared at him. 'How?' he said.

'A matter of too much enthusiasm,' said Jaime.

Hugues ceased his conversation and turned to Mallory. He said, 'Or to tell the truth, a mess.'

Jaime shrugged. He said, 'The *résistants* heard we had landed. There was an idea that we were a regiment, maybe more, because there were only two survivors from the German patrol in the gorge. So Jules heard all this and went to Jonzère to stop these hotheads getting themselves killed. But he was too late. They were firing on the Germans, and the Germans were firing back, and they got themselves killed, all right. And Jules got himself killed with them.'

Hugues blew air, expressing scorn. 'It is not as it is in the north. These mountain people have too many feelings and too few brains.'

It was Jules who had known the man who knew where the Werwolf pack were being repaired. Without Jules, the chain was broken.

Mallory said, with a mildness he did not feel, 'So how are we to continue with the operation?'

'Ah,' said Jaime. 'Marcel has a surprise for you, in Colbis.' He did not look as if he approved of surprises.

'Marcel the baker?' said Hugues.

'That's the one.'

Hugues nodded approvingly. 'A good man,' he said.

Mallory had the feeling that he was sitting in on gossip about people he did not know. He said, 'I need information about the Werwolf pack, not bread.'

'*Voilà,*' said Jaime. 'Marcel proposes breakfast in the . . . in his café. Then he will provide you with transport to where it is you wish to go. He has another Englishman there, you will be glad to hear, who may have information.'

May, thought Mallory. Only may. He took a deep, resigned breath.

'Oh, good,' said Miller, edging towards the fire. 'And the dancing girls?'

'You may find some dancing girls.'

'Breakfast would be fine,' said Miller.

Mallory beckoned Jaime over. The men with the berets followed him as if glued to his side. 'Why are there no Germans in the village?'

One of the men with the berets grinned, and spoke quickly. Jaime translated. 'Because they are all in Jonzère. First, fighting. Now, trying to catch some bandits before they arrive in Spain.' There was more talk in a language that was not French. Basque, Mallory guessed. 'This man says there has been a battle. Many Germans have been killed. There may be reprisals. It is said there was an Allied army in the mountains. In the next valley.'

Mallory raised his eyebrows. 'An army,' he said. From regiment to army, in the space of three minutes.

'Yes,' said Jaime, solemn-faced in the dim light of the torch. 'And they say it is lucky that we were not involved, being so few, and one of us a woman.'

Mallory looked at Jaime hard. Was that the ghost of a wink? Andrea's face was impassive. He had seen it too. His great head moved, almost imperceptibly. Nodding. Suddenly, Mallory found himself perilously close to trusting Jaime.

Mallory hardened his heart. 'Now you listen,' he said. 'I am grateful for your offers of hospitality. But I don't want to go into the village, breakfast or no breakfast. I want our transport out here, and I want to get up to the coast. The more time we spend in the mountains, the messier it's going to get, the bigger the rumours. We want to do this quick and quiet. I don't like rumours and reprisals, or battles. I want intelligence, and I want transport, and I want them before daylight. Tell these people to tell Marcel.'

Jaime said, 'I don't know –'

Mallory said, 'And make it snappy.'

Jaime looked at the steady burn of the deeply-sunken eyes over the long, unshaven jaw. Jaime thought of the cliff that nobody could climb, that this man had climbed; of three burned-out lorries in the pass; and the pursuit on a wild goose chase towards the Spanish border. This was not a man it was easy to disobey. Perhaps he had underestimated this man.

'*Bon,*' he said.

'And now,' said Mallory, when the men in berets had gone outside, 'Thierry. Time to tell the folks at home we've arrived.'

Thierry nodded. He looked big and pale and exhausted. His head moved slowly, as if his neck was stiff, the big jowls creasing and uncreasing, stray strands of straw waving jauntily over the burst crown of his hat. He began to unpack the radio. Miller was in a corner, stretched out full-length on the straw, humming a Bix Beiderbecke tune. Andrea was relaxed, but close to a knothole in the door, through which he could keep tabs on the sentries. Mallory leaned his head against the wall. He could feel his clothes beginning to steam in the heat from the fire.

He said to Hugues, quietly, 'What do you know about this Marcel?'

'Jules' second-in-command,' said Hugues. 'It is an odd structure, down here. Security is terrible. But they are brave men.'

'And we trust them?'

Hugues smiled. He said, 'Is there any choice?'

Mallory kept hearing Jensen's voice. *It seems quite possible that the Germans will, in a manner of speaking, be waiting for you.*

Damn you, Jensen. What did you know that you did not tell us?

It was raining again, a steady rattle on the roof of the barn. On the mountain it would be snowing on their tracks. Perhaps their tracks would be comprehensively covered, and the Germans would not be waiting for them. Perhaps they would be lucky.

But Mallory did not believe in luck.

Thierry said, 'Contact made and acknowledged.'

'Messages?'

'No messages.'

Mallory closed his eyes. Sleep lapped at him. Despite the fire he was cold. Two hours later, he was going to remember being cold; remember it with nostalgic affection. For the moment, he lay and shivered, dozing.

Then he was awake.

A lorry engine was running outside. He gripped his Schmeisser and rose to his feet, instantly alert. He could see Miller covering the door. Andrea was gone. What –

The door crashed open. A man was standing there. He was short and fat, with a beret the size of a dinner plate, and a moustache that spread beyond it like the wings of a crow. His small black eyes flicked between the Schmeisser barrels covering him. He grinned broadly. 'Gentlemen,' he said. 'Colbis welcomes its allies from beyond the seas. *Allons, 'L' Amiral Beaufort.*

Mallory said, 'Who are you?'

'My name is Marcel,' said the man. 'I am delighted to see you. I am only sorry that you had some little problems last night, of which I have already heard.' He bowed. 'My congratulations. Now, into the lorry. It will soon be light, and there are many eyes connected to many tongues.'

Outside, a steady rain was falling. In the grey half-light black pines rose up the steep hillside into a layer of dirty-grey cloud. The lorry was an old Citroën, converted to wood-gas, panting and fuming in the yard. *'Messieurs,'* said Marcel. 'Dispose yourselves.'

Mallory closed the Storm Force into the canvas back of the lorry, and climbed into the front. Marcel ground the gears, and started to jounce down a narrow track that snaked through the dripping trees. 'Quite a fuss,' said Marcel. 'The Germans have met an army of *maquisards,* it is said. Oh, very good –'

Mallory said, 'I am looking for three submarines.'

'Naturally,' said Marcel. 'And I know a man who will take you to them. We must meet him now. At breakfast.'

'A man?'

'Wait and see,' said Marcel, hauling the lorry round a pig in the road.

The trees had stopped. They were crossing open meadows scattered with small, earth-coloured cottages. Ahead was a huddle of houses, and the arched campanile of a church. Nothing was moving; it was four-thirty in the morning. But Mallory did not like it.

'Where are we going?'

'Breakfast, of course. In the village.'

'Not the village.' Villages were rat-traps. In the past eight hours, Mallory had had enough rat-traps for a lifetime.

Marcel said, 'There are no Germans in Colbis. No collaborators. It is important that we go into the village. To see this person.'

'Who is this person?'

'As I say,' said Marcel, with a winsome smile, 'this will be a surprise.'

Mallory told himself that there was no future in getting angry. He said, 'Excuse me, but there is very little time. I do not wish to commit myself to a position from which there is no retreat.'

Marcel looked at him. Above the jolly cheeks, the eyes were hard and knowing: the eyes of a lieutenant whose commanding officer had been killed in the night. Mallory began to feel better. Marcel said, 'This person you must meet cannot be moved. Believe me.'

Mallory gave up. He pulled his SS helmet over his eyes, checked the magazine of his Schmeisser, and leaned back in the seat. Slowly the lorry wheezed out of the meadows and wound its way through streets designed for pack-mules into the centre of Colbis.

There was a square, flanked on its south side by the long wall of the church. In the middle were two plane trees in which roosting chickens clucked drowsily. There was a *mairie*, and a line of what must have been shops: butcher's, baker's, ironmonger's. And on the corner, a row of tall windows streaming with rain, with a signboard above them bearing the faded inscription *Café Des Sports*.

''Ere we are,' said Marcel, cheerfully. ''Op out.'

Boots clattered on the wet cobbles. The etched-glass windows of the café reflected the group of civilians and the three Waffen-SS with heavy packs and Schmeissers; the civilians might have been prisoners. It was a sight to cause twitched-aside curtains to drop over windows – not that there was any visible twitching. The German Forces of Occupation in the frontier zone were remarkably acute about twitched curtains.

Grinning and puffing, Marcel hustled his charges into the café, and shepherded them up through the beaded fringe covering the mouth of a staircase behind the bar. Miller's nostrils dilated. He said, 'Coffee. Real coffee.'

'Comes from Spain,' said Marcel. 'With the señoritas and the oranges. Particularly the señoritas. Come up, now.'

Miller went up the stairs. Mallory was behind him. Miller stopped, dead. Mallory's finger moved to the trigger of his Schmeisser. At the

top of the stairs was a large landing overlooking the square. The
landing had sofas and chairs. Too many doors opened off it. It smelt
of stale scent and unwashed bodies.

Miller said, 'It's a cathouse.'

Mallory said, 'So you will feel completely at home.'

They had been walking most of the night. Mallory was soaking
wet and shivering. His hands felt raw, his feet rubbed and blistered
inside the jackboots. He wanted to find the objective of the operation, and carry the operation out while there was still an operation
to carry out.

And instead, they were attending a breakfast party in a brothel.

'Village this size?' said Miller. 'With a *cathouse*?'

It should have meant something. But the smell of the coffee had
blunted Mallory's perceptions. All he knew was that he had to get
hold of some, or die.

It was light outside, cold and grey. But inside on the sideboard
there was coffee, and bread, and goat's cheese, and a thin, fiery
brandy for those who wanted it. Mallory drank a cup of coffee. He
said to Marcel, 'You said there was someone here.'

Marcel nodded. 'He will be sleeping. Another croissant? I make
them my own self.'

'We'll wake him.'

Marcel shrugged, and opened one of the doors off the landing.

The smell of sweat and perfume intensified. It was a bedroom,
decorated in dirty pink satin. On the bed was a man in khaki uniform, lying on his back like a crusader on a tomb. Bandages showed
through the unbuttoned waistband of his battledress blouse: bandages with rusty stains. On the chair beside the bed was a beret bearing the winged-dagger badge of the SAS.

Mallory glanced at the pips on the epaulette. He said, 'Morning,
Lieutenant.'

The man on the bed stirred and moaned. His eyes half-opened.
They focused on Mallory. They saw a man in a coal-scuttle helmet
and a Waffen-SS smock, carrying a Schmeisser.

'Hiding up in a brothel,' said Mallory. 'All right for some.'

The man's hand crawled towards his pillow. Mallory's hand beat
him to it. His fingers closed on metal. He came out with the
Browning automatic. 'Relax,' said Mallory.

The Lieutenant glared at him with berserk blue eyes. His face
was white, with grey shadows. Pain. He was badly wounded.
'SOE,' said Mallory. 'We've come to bail you out.' Inwardly, his

heart was sinking. This would be one of Killigrew's men. One of the gung-ho shoot-em-up boys who had been dropped and got themselves lost. Who had probably compromised the operation already. Things were in a bad enough mess without a wounded SAS man to slow them down. A badly wounded SAS man, by the look of him. Perhaps he could be smuggled over the border into Spain.

'How do I know that?' said the Lieutenant.

'Admiral Beaufort will tell you,' said Mallory. 'So did a little man called Captain Killigrew.' He opened the buttons of the SS smock. 'And this is British battledress. Seemed tactless to wear it on the outside, somehow.'

'Who told you I was here? Marcel –'

'Marcel was very discreet,' said Mallory, soothingly.

Slowly, the blue eyes lost their berserk glare. The wariness remained. 'Killigrew,' he said. 'Yes. When did you get in?'

'Albemarle, last night,' said Mallory. There was no time for chitchat. 'I need to know what happened to you.'

'Landed on a bit of a plateau . . . near here,' said the SAS man. He obviously wanted to give as little away as possible. 'Brought a Jeep,' A Jeep, thought Mallory. A full-size actual Jeep. On parachutes. Amazing. But that was the SAS for you. 'Heading for the coast. Ambushed. Other chaps bought it. I took a bang on the head and a bullet in the guts.'

Mallory said, 'How did it happen?'

'Driving down a track,' said the SAS man. 'Next thing we knew, there were two Spandaus. One either side of the road. Don't remember much after that. The Resistance brought me here.' There was a shake in his voice. He was very young.

'So it was a road block?' said Mallory.

'Not much of one.'

Mallory nodded. Give me strength, he thought. Conning your way through a checkpoint behind enemy lines, SAS style. Two grenades and put your foot down. 'Where were you going on the coast?'

'Doesn't really matter,' said the Lieutenant. This was his first operation. It was just like school, on the Rugby XV. You went for it, and sod the consequences. Your own team tactics were your own team tactics, and you kept them to yourself. The only thing different about war was this damned bullet. He did not let his mind stray too close to the bullet, in case the pain made him sick again. It felt the size of a cricket ball, down there. And it hurt.

Was hurting worse, lately . . . He concentrated on his dislike for this old man in the Waffen-SS uniform who had burst in and dropped a few names, and thought that gave him a licence to pump him, take over the operation, grab the glory. Let him find out for himself.

The old man's face was close to his. It had a broad forehead and very young brown eyes; eyes like old Brutus, who taught Latin at Shrewsbury and climbed Alps in the summer hols. The eyes seemed to remove the Lieutenant's reserve the way a tin-opener would take the lid off a tin. The old man said, 'Where were you going and who were you going to see?'

The Lieutenant summoned up his undoubted toughness. 'Doesn't matter.'

The eyes hardened. The old man said, 'Don't be childish. There's very little time.'

The Lieutenant gritted his teeth. He desperately wanted to tell someone. It would be less lonely, for one thing, and he was really, terrifyingly, lonely. But a secret was a secret. 'I'm sorry,' he said. 'I don't . . . I'm not authorised.'

Mallory allowed his eyes to rest on this lieutenant. He really was absurdly young. His was the berserker's bravery, frenzied and unbending. If the Gestapo got their hands on him, he would break like a twig.

Mallory sighed inwardly. He got up, opened the door and put his head out. There seemed to be a party going on. He said, 'Andrea.'

The huge Greek padded across from his seat overlooking the square. His shoulders seemed to blot out the light in the little room. Mallory said, 'If you won't tell me, tell the Colonel.'

The SAS man frowned. He saw no colonel. He saw an unshaven giant with a huge moustache. He saw a pair of black eyes, eyes like the eyes on a Byzantine icon, that understood everything, forgave everything. 'Colonel?' he said.

'Andrea is a full colonel in the Greek army.'

'How do I know that's not another bloody lie?'

Andrea sat down in the pink plush armchair. Suddenly the SAS man felt weak, and ill, and about fourteen years old. 'You are frightened,' said Andrea.

'I bloody well am not,' said the Lieutenant. But even as Andrea spoke, he could feel it draining away, all the team spirit, the gung ho, war-as-a-game-of-rugby. He saw himself as he was: a wounded kid who would die in a dirty little room, alone.

'Not of dying,' said Andrea. 'But of yourself, of failing. I also am frightened, all the time. So it is not possible to let myself fail.'

He did not sound like any colonel the Lieutenant had ever heard. He sounded like a man of warmth and common sense, like a friend. Careful, said a voice in the Lieutenant's head. But it was a small voice, fading fast.

Andrea's eyes alighted on a crude wooden crutch, a section of pole with a pad whittled roughly to the shape of an armpit. 'Yours?' he said.

'I'm going to use it,' said the SAS man. 'I can get around all right.' It was not altogether a lie. He could move. It was just that when he moved, he could feel that bit of metal in his guts twisting, doing him damage. But that was not the point. The point was fighting a war. 'Couple of days,' he said. 'Get into the hills.'

'Why don't you come with us?' said Andrea, tactfully. This boy and his crutch would not last an hour in the mountains. He could see it in his face. 'We will take you with us,' said Andrea. 'And you and I, and Miller and Mallory, will finish this operation.'

The Lieutenant's eyes moved back to the first man, the thin one. 'Mallory?' he said. He saw newspaper front pages pinned to the board behind the fives courts. On the front pages were pictures of this man, with a pyramid of snow-covered rock in the background. *That* Mallory. He came to a decision. He said, 'Jules told me. Guy Jamalartégui. At the Café de L'Océan in St-Jean-de-Luz. We would have told you. But . . . there's been a lot of German activity. Radio silence, except in emergency. Jerry's very quick.'

Mallory nodded. Radio detector vans would not be the only reason. The SAS liked to keep their intelligence to themselves, particularly when it was information that might help Jensen and SOE.

'Thank you,' he said. 'Thank you very much.' Sounds of revelry were percolating through the door. 'Now. Can I get you some breakfast?'

Once the shock had worn off, Miller had almost started to enjoy himself. The coffee was undoubtedly coffee, and the bread was still warm from the oven, and while he was not a goat cheese enthusiast, in his present frame of mind he would have cheerfully eaten the goat, horns and all. And by the time he had finished eating, there had been stirrings behind some of the doors. At the Cognac stage, his glass had been filled by a dark girl in a red silk nightdress, and Miller was beginning to be reminded that while occupied France might be occupied, it was still France.

He lay back in his chair, and listened to the rattle of French and Basque from the *maquisards,* and sipped his Cognac. A corner of his mind was on the girl in the red nightdress. But most of it was out there in the square, patrolling the darkness under the trees and in the corners. Soon the village's eyes would start opening and its tongues would start wagging. It was time they were out of here. The girl in the red nightdress ran her fingers through his crewcut. Miller grinned, a lazy grin that to anyone who did not know him would have looked completely relaxed. Which in a way, he was. Because Mallory thought it was okay to be here. So it was okay. In a life that had contained about ten times more incidents than the average citizen's, Miller had never met a man he trusted more than the New Zealander.

He was not so sure about the Frenchmen. Jaime was sitting in a corner, coffee cup between his hands. Jaime seemed at least to know his way around. Now he was watching Hugues, who was fussing round Lisette. A lifetime spent in places where personality carried more weight than law had made Miller acutely sensitive to the way people got along. Miller had the distinct feeling that Jaime did not have a lot of time for Hugues.

Miller had his own doubts about Hugues. Sure, he knew his way round the Resistance. But he was an excitable guy. Lotta fuss that guy makes, thought Miller. And a lotta noise, too much noise. Lisette, now. They were stuck with Lisette. She was slow; she carried too much weight. But she was one tough cookie –

Jesus.

Lisette had been removing her outer clothing. She had been wearing an overcoat, two shawls, and a couple of peasant smocks of some kind. They had made her look like a football on legs. Dressed up like that, she had bicycled up a steep valley road without lights, climbed a vertical cliff and force-marched fifteen precipitous miles without sleep.

What dropped Miller's jaw on his chest was not what she had done. It was the fact that she was just about the same shape without the winter clothes as with them. Face it, thought Miller.

If you were Hugues, and Lisette was your girl, you would maybe feel a tad over-protective yourself.

Because the reason Lisette looked like a gasometer on legs was that she was at least eight months pregnant.

*   *   *

Somewhere a telephone rang, the tenuous ring of a hand-cranked exchange. Down the hall someone answered it, and started shouting in frantic Basque. Miller became suddenly completely immobile, listening. The voices had stopped. Cocks were crowing. Otherwise there was silence.

But behind the silence were engines. Lorry engines, a lot of them.

In the French frontier zone at this particular time in history, there was only one group of people who had a lot of lorries, and the fuel to run them.

Miller grabbed his Schmeisser and yanked the cocking lever. The girl in the red nightdress seemed suddenly to have vanished. Marcel the baker was standing up, smiling from a face suddenly grey and wooden. The engines were in the square now: four trucks with canvas backs. The trucks stopped. Soldiers were pouring out of the backs, soldiers with coal-scuttle helmets and field-grey uniforms, their jackboots grinding the wet cobbles of the square.

A staff car rolled into the square. A tall, black-uniformed officer got out, said something, and pointed at Marcel's lorry. Two soldiers bayoneted the tyres. The lorry settled on its rims.

As Mallory put his head out of the SAS man's door, Andrea's hand went out and grabbed Marcel by the shoulder. Marcel was a big man, but Andrea held him at arm's length with his feet off the ground. He said, 'What are these troops doing here?'

Marcel's face was a mask of horror. 'I don't know . . . I was assured . . .'

In Mallory's mind, gears rolled smoothly and a conclusion formed. 'It's an SS brothel,' he said. 'Isn't it?'

Marcel's face turned a dull, embarrassed purple. 'It is a cover,' he said. 'A good cover. Now, gentlemen . . .'

Andrea dropped him. Marcel rubbed his shoulder. He said, 'Follow me, please.' His voice was calm and urbane: the voice of the perfect host. Already the girls had cleared away the traces of the breakfast. He pointed into the SAS man's room. One of the girls was holding open the door of the wardrobe. The wardrobe had no back. Instead, a flight of steps led down into darkness.

Mallory trusted Marcel. But someone had betrayed them.

Who?

Andrea went to help the SAS man off the bed. The SAS man pushed him away, reached for his makeshift wooden crutch and hauled himself moaning to his feet. As Miller brought up the rear, he could hear the battering of rifle butts on the cafe's front door.

More rats in more traps, he thought. And all for a cup of coffee and a girl in a red nightdress.

Maybe the coffee had been worth it, at that.

The back of the wardrobe slammed behind them. They went downstairs and out into a small yard, wet and empty under the sky. At the back of the yard was a shed, the lintel of its door blackened by smoke. There was a powerful smell of baking bread.

From over the wall came guttural shouts, and the barking of dogs. 'Vite,' said Marcel, shooing them into the shed.

The shed was a bakehouse. There were two bread ovens. The one on the left was shut. The one on the right was open. In front of the oven door was a big stone slab. On the slab lay a metal tray, six feet long by four feet wide. A small, one-eyed man in a dirty apron did not even glance at them. 'On the tray,' said Marcel. 'Two at a time.'

'Where are the others?' said Mallory.

'In the brothel. They speak French, bien entendu. Their papers are good. Vite.'

Miller jumped up onto the tray, and lay with his boxes on the big wooden paddle. Mallory climbed up beside him. 'When the tray stops, roll off,' said Marcel. 'Cover your faces.'

Mallory could hear German voices. A trap, he thought. Another, smaller trap. After this trap, absolutely no more –

He was lying on the tray with his pack on his stomach. He covered his face with his hands. Someone shoved the paddle. A ferocious heat beat on the backs of his hands. He thought of the parabolic brick roof of the oven, smelt burning hair. *The ammunition,* he thought.

But the heat was gone, and they were shuffling off the paddle and onto a stone surface that was merely warm. Mallory raised his head. It was dark, black as ink. After six inches his forehead hit the roof. There seemed to be air circulating.

The tray returned, bearing Andrea and the SAS man. The SAS man was breathing hard and tremulous as Andrea shoved him off the tray. Somewhere, stones grated. That's it, thought Miller. You've got your bread oven, circular, made out of bricks. And there's a little door in the back of it, and we've been pushed through, and now they've closed the door –

Scraping noises emanated from the oven.

– and now they are going to bake a little bread.

He tried to raise his head, to see where the air was coming from. He hit the ceiling. Eighteen inches high, he thought. And nothing to see. Buried alive.

He put out his hand, touched his brass-bound boxes. On the way, his hand touched Mallory's arm.

The arm was rigid, vibrating with what must have been fear.

No. Not Mallory. Mallory was cool as ice. Mallory had scaled the South Cliff at Navarone, when Miller had been mewing with terror at its base.

All right, thought Miller. But down in the middle of every human being there is a place kept locked tight, and in that place lives the beast a person fears most. But sometimes the locks go, and the beast is out, raging in the mind, taking over all its corners.

Mallory's beast was confined spaces.

Dusty Miller stared at the invisible ceiling six inches above his nose, and listened to the sounds coming through the brick wall of the oven. There was a brisk crackling, and a sharp whiff of smoke. They had lit a fire in there, to heat the oven for the next batch of baking. How long do we have to stay in here? he thought. What if Mallory can't take it?

He began to sing. He sang softly, 'Falling in loaf with loaf is like falling for make-believe –'

'Shut up,' hissed the SAS man.

'This is not well bread of you,' said Miller.

'For Christ's *sake* –'

'I'm oven a lovely time,' said Miller. 'And you're baking the spell –'

Mallory knew it was the torpedoing all over again: the little metal room with four men jammed together, the thunder of the terrible blue Mediterranean pouring into the hull, four faces in six inches of air under the steel ceiling, the air bad, hot, *unbreathable* – and Mallory was going to die, of suffocation, certainly, but first of terror . . .

Someone seemed to be talking. Talking complete drivel, in a soft Chicago drawl. Beyond the drawl, far away, there were other voices. German voices.

Miller.

The terror went. Mallory found himself thinking that there were worse things than small spaces. Dusty Miller's puns, for instance.

Miller felt Mallory's hand prod him sharply in the side. He shut up. Mission accomplished.

Suddenly a dog was barking close at hand. Much closer than the far side of the fire in the oven. The compartment where the four men were hiding filled with the scritch of claws on stone. The air holes, thought Miller. There must be air holes, and the goddamn dog's smelt us through them.

They lay looking up at the ceiling they could not see, in the dark that was full of the clamour of the dog. The little cell behind the oven grew steadily hotter. They began to sweat.

At the front of the ovens, Marcel was sweating too. His apron was smeared with flour and the ash of the bracken stalks he used to fire the oven. But he was not thinking about baking. He was looking at the SS officer who was leaning against the doorpost, slapping the barrel of his Luger into the palm of his black leather glove. The SS officer was smiling with great warmth, but his stone-grey eyes were the coldest thing Marcel had ever seen. 'Where are they?' said the officer.

'*Pardon?*' The yard was full of soldiers. A dog-handler came through, dragged by an Alsatian on a choke-chain. The Alsatian's tongue was hanging out, and it was panting eagerly.

The officer said, with patient friendliness, 'The dog has come from the brothel above the café. It is following the scent of someone who was sitting in one of the chairs in the brothel. The scent leads straight to your oven. Why do you think this would be?'

The oven was burning well now. Smoke was pouring out of the door, crawling along the ceiling of the shed and billowing up at the rainy sky above the yard. Marcel pointed into the oven door at the incandescent glow of the burning bracken. 'What are these imaginary people?' he said. 'Salamanders?'

The smile did not waver. The SS man said, mildly, 'If these people are imaginary, why would the dog be so interested?'

'A mystery.'

The SS man said, 'I have the strong impression that there are people in this village who have no business here.'

Marcel said, 'What gives you this impression?'

The SS man smiled, but did not answer. His eyes slid over the bakehouse. He said, 'And what is inside the other oven?'

Marcel yawned. 'Who knows?'

'It is in my mind,' said the SS man, fingering his long, Aryan chin, 'to pull this oven to pieces.'

'*Non,*' said Marcel, his eyes discs of horror. 'My livelihood. Georges. In the oven. What is in the oven, in the name of God? Tell this gentleman.'

'*Pains Flavigny,*' said the one-eyed man.

'Ah!' said Marcel, his face cracking into a large grin. *'Voilà!'*

'Bitte?'

'Georges is from Alsace,' said Marcel. 'So he bakes from time to time *pains Flavigny,* whose vital ingredient is aniseed, beloved of dogs. They do not sell so well, of course. But you know how it is. One must keep the staff happy. It is so hard, in a war, to find –'

The SS man allowed the barrel of his pistol to swing gently towards Georges. 'Open the oven,' he said.

'But the *pains* –'

'Open it.'

'They will be destroyed.'

The officer's finger moved onto the trigger. Georges shrugged. He said, 'It is a crime. But if you insist.' He flicked up the catch on the door and shoved in a small wooden paddle. When he brought it out there was a cake on the end, round and brown. 'Not yet cooked,' he said. 'See, *nom d'un nom.* Sacrilege. Ruin. It is sinking. They will all be sinking.'

The SS officer took the cake and crumbled it in his glove. The dog jumped up, lathering his hand with its tongue. He kicked it in the stomach with his jackboot. It shrank away, yelping. Delicately, he sniffed the crumbs. They smelt powerfully of aniseed. 'Excellent,' he said, still smiling. He turned, and walked out into the yard. The dogs have led us astray, I fear. But there are other methods of arriving at the truth.'

Marcel had followed, wiping his hands on his apron. *'Pardon, monsieur?'*

'Your countrymen have been very stupid,' said the SS man. 'Stupid as pigs. There are rules. We both know that. Rules have been broken. In Jonzère last night, there was fighting, with deaths. You people must learn that laws are to be obeyed. I fear you will find the lesson painful.' The smile. Marcel stood smiling uncertainly back, his insides congealed with terror, watching the icy eyes. 'There is a way of making it less painful. There are British agents in this village,' said the SS man. 'When I find them, I will leave.' He walked through the baker's shop, and into the square, and rested a negligent hand on the tonneau of the staff car. 'Feldwebel!'

A sergeant crashed to attention.

'Knock on the door of each house in this square,' he said. 'Politely. Whoever answers the door, bring them out into the square, and request them to stand . . .' the cold eyes checked, then settled on the long, blank north wall of the church, 'against that wall. While you are doing that, I want a Spandau set up under the trees.'

Marcel's face had turned as white as his flour. He said, 'What are you doing?'

'Fighting a war,' said the officer. 'When we have these people out here, we shall shoot one every ten minutes until I am told the truth. Your bread will be burning, baker.' He smiled. 'You had better go.'

THREE

Monday
0900–1900

Miller had been with the Long Range Desert Force, so he had been hot all right. But nothing on the parched ergs or the wind-blasted scarps of the Sahara had prepared him for the heat behind that bread oven.

He kept talking. He could feel that Mallory needed to be talked to. It was not easy to talk while being cooked, but it must, he thought, be a lot easier to talk while you were only hot than while you were hot and in a state of flat panic. Andrea talked too, reminiscing in a low rumble about the cave in Crete where he and Mallory had resided. And all the time the heat grew, hotter and hotter, searing the skin. There were smells, too: wood smoke and baking smells, with over it all another baking smell that Miller recognised but did not want to mention. It was the smell of confectioner's almonds; the smell of gelignite cooking in its box.

There was a consolation, thought Miller. A small one. If the gelignite set off the Cyclonite, it was going to take some Germans with it. Not to mention the village of Colbis, and a fair-sized chunk of the northern Pyrenees –

A new sound floated through the wall: a harsh judder, dulled by layers of stone. The sound of a machine gun.

Mallory knew he had won. He had beaten his glands, or whatever it was that weakened the knees and liquefied the guts. The machine gun had taken him into the outside world. He was thinking ahead now. 'We're going to need transport to St-Jean-de-Luz.'

'Transport?'

'It's thirty miles by road. The submarines sail the day after tomorrow, at noon. It's too tight to march.'

'Bicycles?'

There was a silence. They were all thinking the same: a pregnant woman and an SAS man with a bullet in the guts were no good on bicycles. A ruthless man who wanted to move fast would leave such impediments behind. Mallory did not know if he was that ruthless. Luckily, there was no chance of his being tested. The SAS man and Lisette knew too much to be allowed to fall into enemy hands.

Like it or not, they were along for the ride.

The SAS man had been lying very still, conserving energy in the heat, listening to the three men talking. Chattering was for girls and wimps and other classes of humanity despised by the SAS. Now he said, 'There's a Jeep.'

A Jeep. Presumably with Union Jacks all over it, two-way radios, heavy machine guns, mobile cocktail bar and sun lounge. You could not beat the SAS. Not unless you were the enemy.

'Well, well,' said Miller. 'This is excellent news.'

Mallory said, 'Where?'

'In the barn at the back of the bakery. It's the Jeep they dropped with us. Under the bracken. Marcel told me they brought it in.'

Mallory said, 'Thank you, er . . .'

'Wallace.' Miller was surprised to feel a hand reach across him. He shook it. It shook his back. So that's all right, he thought. We've been introduced, and now he's lending us his car. And we're walled up in an oven, cooking.

Goddamn limeys.

There was a new sound outside: a voice, at one of the air holes. Marcel's voice. 'You must come out,' said the voice.

'We'll take the Jeep.'

'Yes.' The voice sounded strained. 'You must go away from here. You know where. Your comrades are by the barn. Go soon.'

'Just open the door.'

'Yes.'

A pause. There were movements, felt in the walls rather than heard. Someone was raking the fuel out of the oven. The door separating them from the oven opened, admitting a scorching blast of air. 'Tray coming in,' said Marcel's voice.

Afterwards, Mallory could not remember how they got out. There was a hellish blast of heat, and a smell of burning hair, and then they were standing in the bakehouse, surrounded by large, beautiful volumes of space.

The barn,' said Marcel. He looked suddenly thinner, and his face was a bad greyish colour. 'Follow me.'

Andrea gave Wallace his shoulder. They went into the yard and through a green door. The barn was half-full of bundles of dry bracken stalks. *'Allons,'* said Marcel, and began tearing with more frenzy than effect at the faggots on the right-hand side. 'Here.'

They began pulling the bundles away. After a couple of minutes the rear bumper of a vehicle emerged from the bracken.

'Hey,' said Miller. 'SAS, we love you.'

The vehicle was a Jeep, but not just any Jeep. There was no cocktail bar, and no sun lounge, but they were about the only amenities missing. Mounted in the rear were a pair of Brownings. There was another pair mounted on the hood in front of the passenger seat. The ammunition belts were still in place.

'Here are the other passengers now,' said Marcel. 'They have been in bed. Perhaps sleeping, perhaps not.' He made a sound that might have been a laugh.

Thierry, Hugues and Jaime lurched into the barn. Thierry's hat had a slept-in look. Hugues' eyes were snapping, and he was chewing his lips. He said, 'Where is Lisette?'

There was a spreading of hands and a shrugging of shoulders. Jaime said, 'She is tired. Sleeping. It is best we leave.' His face was grim. 'She has good false papers. She will be safe there.'

Perhaps he was right, thought Mallory. He had better be. There was no time to dig her out wherever she was resting. It was a hitch, but not a setback.

Hugues said, *'Non, merde –'*

'Jaime is right,' said Marcel. Another burst of Spandau fire sounded from the square. He looked as if he was going to cry. He said, 'Please. Be quick. Someone will talk.'

'Talk?'

'They are shooting people. One every ten minutes.' His face collapsed. He put his hands to his eyes.

Hugues said, 'For God's sake, be a man.'

Marcel looked at him vacantly. His cheeks were wet with tears. He said, 'The first person they shot was my mother.'

Hugues went red as blood, then pale.

'God rest her soul,' mumbled Andrea.

Mallory said, 'She has died that others may live. We thank you for her great courage. And yours.'

Marcel met his eye firmly. He said, *'Vive la France.'* He took a deep breath. 'For her sake, I ask that you complete your mission.'

'It will be done.'

He shook Mallory's hand. Andrea put his great paw on his shoulder.

Hugues said, 'I leave Lisette in your care.'

'I am honoured,' said Marcel. 'Now you must go. Then I can make them stop.'

'How?'

'I will tell the girls to say they saw you.'

'The girls?'

'They are friends with some of the Germans. The Germans who come to this brothel. That is why they leave us alone. Used to leave us alone. The Germans will not hurt the girls.'

Mallory said, 'How do we get out?'

'Drive ahead,' said Marcel. 'The entry is beyond the bracken.'

Hugues said, 'I must say goodbye to Lisette.'

'You must go,' said Marcel. 'Please.' He rummaged in a crate, came back with four bottles of Cognac. 'Take these. Go.'

'Non,' said Hugues, his voice rising. 'The child –'

He did not finish what he was going to say because Andrea had reached out a crane-hook hand and gripped his shoulder. Andrea said, 'Like this brave Marcel, you are a soldier,' and pushed him into the back of the Jeep.

Hugues said, shamefaced, 'Tell her I love her.'

Marcel nodded dumbly.

'Miller,' said Mallory. 'Drive on.'

'By the square?'

Mallory turned upon him his cool brown eyes. 'I think so,' he said. 'Don't you?'

The Jeep's engine started first time. They lifted Wallace into the back and climbed aboard as best they could. The engine sounded very loud in the confined space. It would sound very loud in the village, too; there were no other engines running in Colbis.

Miller slammed the Jeep into four-wheel drive. The engine howled as he stamped on the throttle. He let out the clutch. The Jeep plunged into the dried bracken, and kept on plunging. The brittle fronds piled up against the windscreen and spilled into the back. Miller saw daylight, and aimed for it. Covered in a haystack mound of bracken, the Jeep shot out of the barn doorway and into the lane, turned on two wheels, and turned right again. At the end of the lane was a slice of the square, with plane trees. In the slice of square, three SS men were crouched round a Spandau. 'Civilians keep down,' said Mallory, cocking

the Brownings on the bonnet and flicking off the safety catches.
'Open fire.'

The Spandau gunners did not enjoy shooting innocent civilians. It
was, frankly, a disagreeable duty, only marginally better than cleaning latrines. But *Befehl ist Befehl*. Orders are orders.

They were sitting there, ignoring the two clusters of bloody
pockmarks on the church wall above the crumpled bodies of their
first two victims, and concentrating on the third victim, the priest's
housekeeper, a thin, slope-shouldered old woman, standing stiffly
to attention in a flannel dressing gown. The machine gunners were
looking grim and efficient, because they were dying for a smoke.
The sooner they got this over with, the better –

From the back of the square came a clatter like a giant type-
writer. Something hammered the Spandau into the air and sent
it spinning, tripod and all, across the square. Ricochets whined
into the sky. Two of the machine gunners performed sudden
ragged acrobatics and fell down. The third had enough time to
spin round and think, *machine-gun fire,* and see a haystack with
four wheels howling out of an alleyway, the muzzle-flash of
machine guns dancing in the hay, which seemed to be catching
fire. Then a succession of hammers walloped the last gunner in
the chest and his legs lost their strength and his mouth filled
with blood. And as his head bounced limply on the pavé of the
square he saw his comrades, drawn up in lines, start tumbling like
corn before the scythe, and heard the *whoomp* of a petrol tank
exploding.

Then the machine gunner's eyes grew dim, and he died.

Miller yanked the Jeep's steering wheel to the right. The main road
out of the square gaped in front of him. The clatter of the
Brownings was a mechanical thunder in his ears. Something was
burning, with a smell that reminded him of burning tumbleweeds
when he had worked a summer in the Kansas oil fields. It was not
tumbleweed, of course. It was bracken, set on fire by the muzzle-
flashes of the heavy machine guns. It was dry as tinder, that bracken.
Mallory and Andrea were still firing short sharp bursts. Miller yelled,
'Get it off!'

From the square there came a higher, sharper crackle: rifle fire. A
bullet spanged off the Jeep's suspension and moaned away skyward.

Mallory said, calmly, 'Fire low.'

A patrol of Germans had appeared in the road ahead. The Brownings thundered. More bullets cracked over the Jeep. Then the Germans were down, rolling, and the suspension was jouncing as the wheels went over the bodies. The street behind had vanished in a pall of grey-white smoke. The houses were thinning. The crackle of the bracken was a roar.

'Get rid of it!' yelled Miller.

Hugues' coat was smouldering as he unfolded himself from the bed of the Jeep. He was coughing, his eyes streaming. He began to kick blazing faggots of bracken onto the road. Jaime was doing it too, and Thierry, who was making small, frightened prodding movements, clearing his precious radio first.

'St-Jean-de-Luz,' said Mallory, over the slipstream. 'Which way?'

'Up the road,' said Jaime. 'Then there's a track.' He brushed burning bracken from his sleeve. *'Merde.'*

There were strips of blue sky between heavy squalls of cloud. The last of the bracken lay fuming in the road, receding fast. Ahead the pavé stretched, polished black and gently curving. It was the main road out of the valley. A road crawling with Germans – Germans who would by now have found out by radio that a unit of the British army was on the loose in a Jeep. At least, Mallory hoped they would think they were a unit of the British army. That way, there might be no civilian reprisals.

But how had the Germans known to come to Colbis?

It seems quite possible that the Germans will, in a manner of speaking, be waiting for you.

Mallory said, 'Where were you hiding in the village?'

'They spread us round,' said Jaime. 'Me, I was in the brothel. In bed. In the most innocent way, of course.'

'But they searched the brothel.'

'My papers are in order,' said Jaime. His face was dark and closed. 'What have I to fear?'

Mallory nodded. Unanswered questions buzzed around his ears like flies.

'Left,' said Jaime.

Left was a track that turned off the main road, crept along the side of a mountain and into a wood. The Jeep ground through a deserted farmyard and onto a road of ancient cobbles.

'The back way,' said Jaime. 'Arrives close to St-Jean-de-Luz. The main road goes down the valley and joins the big road to St-Jean-de-Luz at the foot of the mountains. This one takes us over a hill, into a valley, then over another hill, and down to St-Jean. But it is only good for mule or Jeep. It's a small road. It doesn't run over the frontier, so the Germans don't pay much attention to it.'

They sat three in the front, four in the back. The SAS man was white, and his eyes were closed. When the Jeep hit a boulder, the muscles of his jaw tautened with pain. For an hour the Jeep moaned upwards into the mountains. Jaime and Hugues were talking quietly in French.

Suddenly, Hugues started shouting. His face was purple, contorted with rage. He got his fingers round Jaime's neck and his knees on his chest, and he picked the small man's head up and slammed it against the bodywork, and pulled it back, and was going to do it again when Andrea's hands closed, one on each arm, and, without apparent effort, detached his hands. Jaime rolled away, coughing and retching. Hugues struggled futilely in Andrea's grip, still shouting.

Mallory said, 'Shut up,' in a voice that cracked like a rifle bullet.

Hugues shut up.

'What's the problem?'

Hugues' eyes were the size of saucers. 'Lisette,' he said.

'What about her?'

'She's not in the village. She was supposed to be in the village, asleep. But not so. Jaime says he saw her. She was taken away. By a German in a leather overcoat. Gestapo.' He put his face in his hands.

Mallory's stomach was hollow with apprehension. He said, 'Is this true?'

Jaime's face could have been carved from yellowish stone. He said, 'It's true.'

Hugues sat up, suddenly. 'We must go to Bayonne,' he said. 'Immediately. Without delay. With the guns we have, the explosives, we can get into Gestapo HQ –'

Mallory said, 'How much does Lisette know about this operation?'

'She knows we are going to St-Jean,' said Hugues. 'But she will never talk.'

Jaime said, 'Everyone talks.'

'Non!' shouted Hugues, losing control.

'She is pregnant,' said Jaime. 'What do you think they will do to the child?'

Hugues' anger evaporated. He seemed to grow smaller. He covered his face with his hands.

Mallory said, 'How did this happen?'

Jaime looked straight ahead, his face without expression. 'I saw from the window of the *bordel*. She was led out. They put her in a big car, and drove away.'

'Why didn't you tell us earlier?'

'There is a thing we must do. The mother of Marcel has died for this thing. So has Jules, at Jonzère, and others. It is war. I kept quiet so our decision could not be . . . influenced.' He looked at Hugues, then back at Mallory. 'You would have done what I did.'

Hugues said, 'Only a monster –'

'Shut up,' said Mallory.

Of course Jaime was right. The object of the operation was to destroy submarines, not chase Gestapo cars across the northern foothills of the Pyrenees. By pretending that Lisette was in Colbis until she was definitely beyond help, Jaime had prevented a worse crisis.

Not that it could be much worse for Lisette.

Mallory tried not to think about what would be happening to Lisette. He said, 'She'll talk.'

'Not for two days,' said Jaime. 'That is the rule. She will hold out for two days to give us time to get clear.'

Thierry cocked his straw hat over his eye and delivered himself of an offensively cynical chuckle. 'The Germans know this also. They will be very persuasive.'

Hugues said, 'Jesus.' His face was grey and bloodless.

'But relax,' said Thierry. 'If the Gestapo ask the wrong question, they will get the wrong answer. How will they ask the right question?'

Mallory knew that in Gestapo HQ at Bayonne, there would be people who could make you beg to be allowed to tell them everything you knew, without a question being asked. He said to Hugues, 'There is nothing we can do. I really am very sorry.'

Hugues looked at him with haunted eyes. 'Old women have lived their lives,' he said. 'Soldiers protect their country. Who can use my unborn child as a weapon of war? What has this poor child done?'

Andrea said, 'These are questions you must ask a priest.' Mallory did not look at him. The Greek had found the bodies of his parents in the river at Protosami. They had been shot by Bulgarian soldiers, then lashed together and thrown to the fish. Andrea knew about total war. So had his parents' killers, until they had died, very suddenly and all at once. 'But the time for asking such questions is when the war is finished. For now, we must only obey orders and fight, because if we think, we go crazy.'

There was no more talking after that.

The Jeep ground on, up and over the mountain, away from the great hazy prospect of the valley. Hugues had opened one of the bottles of brandy Marcel had loaded into the Jeep. His blue eyes turned pink and glassy. A shoulder of wooded hillside interposed itself between the road and the valley. The sun came out from between the shredded clouds. Flies buzzed round Wallace's bloody tunic. The track left the trees and wound across a marshy saddle between two peaks. High overhead, a pair of vultures hung in the blue. There were no Germans, no sign of the war raging out there in the world. As the road started downhill again, Dusty Miller saw a glittering blue line beyond a notch in the whaleback hills. The sea.

'Progress,' he said. 'And about goddamn time, too.'

But the road dipped down again, into the first rank of the chestnut forests, and the blue line disappeared. As the Jeep ground on downhill, Miller's spirits suffered the small but definite dip that with him passed for extreme gloom. They were nearing the coast at last. There was two-thirds of a tank of gas left in the Jeep. Keep on driving, and whatever happens will happen –

But there was a hell of a way to go, through Indian country, to a destination at best uncertain.

'One kilometre now, a big road,' said Jaime, rising from his gloomy silence like a diver from a lake. 'Road to the frontier. Patrolled, I guess.'

'We'll take it quietly,' said Mallory. 'Go on five hundred yards. Turn off the engine. Freewheel.'

The Jeep rolled down the track, silent except for the twang of its springs and the sniffing of Hugues. A light breeze sighed in the chestnuts. It was a beautiful spring morning, quiet except for the song of birds in the trees.

And the guttural voices that drifted up from the road.

Mallory tapped Andrea on the shoulder. The big Greek nodded. He jumped down from the Jeep and started down the track. His gigantic shoulders seemed to merge into the trees in a way not entirely attributable to the camouflage smock he wore. Watching him Hugues shivered, recalling the warm, padded but horribly powerful hands that had pulled him off Jaime as if he had been a light blanket.

His eyes slid to Jaime, to the stony face of the man who had lost him Lisette. Sometimes, being a soldier was impossible.

He looked away. Looking at Jaime hurt his eyes.

Andrea moved down the track quickly and quietly. When he could see the dark glimmer of the road below him he cut into the trees, placing his feet carefully among the ferns and dry leaves. He passed through the forest with the faintest of rustles, more like a breeze than a twenty-stone human. At the edge of the trees, he stopped.

The road was pavé, the square, polished cobblestones of France. Twenty yards to his left was a sandbagged enclosure with a single embrasure from which projected the muzzle of a machine gun. Beside the enclosure, a bar painted in red-and-white stripes blocked off the road. The machine gun was pointing to the right, north, towards France, and, coincidentally, the stretch of road across which the Jeep would have to travel to rejoin the track on the far side, where it dived into the forests at the foot of a tall mountain plated with grey rock.

Andrea absorbed all of this in perhaps ten seconds, checking off a mental list of options. Then he walked quietly back into the trees and inside the wood along the side of the valley, passing above the checkpoint.

From above, he saw that the machine gun was unmanned. Its three-man crew and two other soldiers were lying on the grassy bank of the road, smoking. One of them was telling what Andrea recognised as a dirty joke he had overheard in the town at Navarone. Swiftly, he walked fifty yards through the wood, parallel to the road, in the general direction of Spain. Then he slung his Schmeisser across his stomach, pulled his helmet down over his eyes, and walked out onto the pavé.

At the sound of his boots, the men on the bank looked up. They saw the biggest Waffen-SS they had ever seen, moving light-footed towards them, eyes invisible under the helmet. They had never seen an SS man with a moustache before. Being honest Wehrmacht foot-sloggers, they did not like the SS, and they did not like moustaches. So the sergeant who had been telling the joke pretended not to see this one until he was on top of them. Then he looked up. 'What the hell do you want?' he said. 'A shave?'

The men in the Jeep on the hillside heard nothing. A thrush was singing. A pigeon crashed out of a chestnut tree. Otherwise, there was silence, a silence that reminded Mallory of the silence on the far side of an operating theatre door. Andrea would be doing his horrible worst. After five minutes, mingled with the thrush's song came the metallic cry of a Scops owl.

Mallory said, 'Drive.'

Miller started to drive. This time he used the engine, because there would be no enemies alive to hear it.

Andrea was waiting by the road, wiping a long, curved knife on a tuft of grass. On a grassy bank nearby, five men in grey uniforms were staring at the sky. There was a lot of red among the yellow and white flowers on which they lay. But it was too early for poppies.

Andrea clambered into the Jeep. Miller gunned the engine.

Up the road, a figure in field-grey stumbled out of the trees, buttoning his trousers. When he saw the Jeep, he shouted, 'Halt!'

Mallory straightened his helmet and gripped his Schmeisser. He said, 'I'll deal with him.' But the brandy Hugues had drunk was heating up his mind. The sky and the trees and the mountains were swimming. It was difficult, being a soldier, obeying orders. When it meant that this woman, the woman you loved, Lisette . . . her fingernails, he thought, her teeth. They pull them out with pliers. And the baby –

In the centre of his vision, something new was moving. Something grey. A German soldier.

Hugues knew he had made himself look foolish in front of these granite-faced soldiers. But in his mind was a newborn baby, and a man with a pair of pliers in his hand. He heard Lisette scream. Because the man was walking, not towards Lisette, but towards the baby –

The man who was a German, like the soldier.

Of course he would have to be killed. And it should be Hugues who killed him, to redeem himself in the eyes of the soldiers.

And suddenly there was a gun in his hand, and his finger was on the trigger, and the gun was jumping, and the air was full of the clatter of the Schmeisser.

The bullets went high. Somebody snatched the weapon out of his hands. The soldier flung himself to the ground and rolled out of sight into the ditch. His rifle fired three times. The last shot smacked into the Jeep. 'Let's go,' said Mallory, quietly.

The Jeep roared across the road and up the track on the far side. After two hundred yards, Andrea said, 'Stop here.'

The Jeep stood at the bottom of a long, steep incline. Andrea swung his legs over the side. He plucked the Bren from the back seat, slung it over his shoulder as if it had been a twenty-bore shotgun, and loped away down the track.

He did not have far to go. This side of the valley was armoured with big, grey plates of limestone on which nothing grew. He found a slab that overlooked the road, cast himself flat behind it, and raised his head in time to see the field-grey figure scuttle like a rabbit into the horseshoe of sandbags that was the machine-gun emplacement. The emplacement was full of shadows, but Andrea knew what the man would be doing as surely as if he could see him. There would be a field telephone in there, and the man would be using it to call for reinforcements.

Carefully, Andrea trained the Bren on that shadow-filled horseshoe and adjusted the backsight one notch up. Then he fired four single shots into the lip of the sandbags, spacing them like the four pips on the four of spades. Then he stood up, quickly.

Down in the machine-gun emplacement, the shadow was punctured by something that might have been a grey tortoise, or a steel helmet. The man interrupted his telephone call to defend his life. Andrea watched the tin helmet move as the eyes searched for him. The eyes found him. The helmet became a human figure, struggling to haul the heavy machine gun round on its mount. Andrea watched clinically, without hatred. Should have stayed on the telephone, he thought, with the detached disapproval of a craftsman watching a bodger. Fatal mistake. The Bren's sight settled on the tin helmet. The huge finger squeezed the trigger.

The burp of the machine gun rolled round the cliffs and precipices of the valley. Down in the emplacement, the little figure flung its arms wide, jerked upright, fell over the sandbag parapet, and lay still. Even before the echoes had died, Andrea was striding back uphill.

He smelt petrol before he saw the Jeep. As he came over the hill the other men were out of the vehicle. 'Problem solved,' said Andrea.

'We've got another problem,' said Mallory. Andrea noticed a curious woodenness in the faces round the Jeep. 'We've got a bullet in the petrol tank. Did your friend have time to contact his headquarters?'

'No way of telling,' said Andrea. 'Gas all gone?'

'All gone.'

Mallory, Miller and Jaime got behind the vehicle. Andrea lent his shoulder. The wheels started to roll. Miller twitched the wheel. The Jeep gathered speed, bounced on a boulder, and disappeared with a metallic crash into a ravine.

Thierry had been squatting by his radio, tinkering with the tuning dial. Mallory said, 'Radio silence from now on, please.'

Thierry nodded. He shouldered the pack. 'How far?'

'Twenty kilometres to the sea,' said Jaime. 'There is one ridge in between. A high ridge.'

Miller yawned and shouldered his brass-bound boxes. 'Nice to stretch your legs after a drive in the country.'

Andrea said, 'I'll help Mr Wallace.'

The SAS man was upright. His face was the colour of wood ash, with dark circles under his eyes. He said, 'I'm all right.'

Andrea said, 'Come,' and walked towards him, hands out.

Wallace raised his crutch and held it against Andrea's breastbone. He said, 'I can manage.'

Andrea said, 'Sometimes it is the bravest man who surrenders.'

But Wallace was in a corner, his eyes hardening, getting that berserk look. He said, 'No SOE bastard tells me what brave men do.' His hand was going to the automatic in the holster at his side.

Andrea shrugged and turned away. For a moment his eyes caught Mallory's. There was no expression in them, but Mallory knew him well enough to see he was worried. They were on an island of limestone in a sea of Germans. There was more to worry about than regimental pride.

'Don't want you holding us up,' said Mallory.

The SAS man snapped, 'Nobody's going to hold you up.' He recollected himself. 'Sir.'

Mallory shrugged. 'Jaime first,' he said. 'March.'

They marched.

Things had improved, Mallory reflected.

There were too many of them, one of them was drunk, another wounded, and they had no transport. But they had a destination. That was the plus side.

On the minus side, there was a trail of dead Germans stretching back across the Pyrenees. But there was nothing to be done about that.

Except keep going.

The track climbed from the valley floor, rising steeply and trending northward. It was a good track, built for mules, with wide steps separated by six-inch copings of stone. The vegetation was sparse. The limestone plates lower in the valley continued, less broken up here, until they were walking up a dry gorge between huge, over-hanging crags. Wallace plodded on, wincing at each grind of his crutch against rock, the flies buzzing and crawling round the black-ened dressing on his belly.

At first it was hot. But the sun grew hazy behind veils of cir-rus, and by eleven the sun had gone in and a black edge of cloud had crept across the sky. The adrenaline of the pursuit was gone, oxidised in the weariness of a night without sleep. Life was the slog against gravity, one foot in front of the other, up the inter-minable mule-steps along the dry valley towards a horizon that always gave way to another, higher horizon. Jaime moved at the steady, straight-legged pace of the mountaineer. Thierry plodded on under the weight of the radio, sweat running down his great jowls, darkening the collar of his shirt and the band of his straw hat. Hugues let his head roll on his neck, stumbled a lot, and would not speak when spoken to. And Wallace kept struggling grimly on, crutch grinding on the stones, face contorted with pain and effort.

By noon it was cold and spitting with rain. Another front was coming in from the Atlantic. Mallory said, 'How far to the top?'

'One hour,' said Jaime. He squinted his small black eyes at the lowering clouds. 'Soon we will need shelter.'

'Why?'

'Snow,' said Jaime. 'I know a cave.'

'No more caves,' said Mallory. 'We must go on.'

'This is a . . . particular cave,' said Jaime. 'Twenty minutes more.'

'Particular?'

'There will be a storm,' said Jaime. 'For now, we should save our breath for the road.'

'On,' said Mallory. 'Twenty minutes.'

There was a crash and a clatter. Wallace had fallen. He was not moving. Andrea squatted by his side, hand on his forehead. He looked up at Mallory. His face, normally unreadable, was worried. 'Fever,' he said.

'Can you carry him?'

'Of course.' Andrea picked the SAS man up, slung him over his shoulder, and began to march. The rain started, then stopped again. The cloud was still high, but patches of dirty mist were hanging in the crags, and the air was damp and raw on their faces.

The floor of the gorge rose until they were walking on a bare slope of limestone. It steepened to forty-five degrees. Mallory could hear Andrea's breathing.

'At the top,' said Jaime.

At the top of the slope was a cliff. In front of the cliff was a little plateau that narrowed into a curious little gully, like a gorge in embryo. The gully went back into the cliff, steep-sided, and ended abruptly in a tangle of boulders.

'In here,' said Jaime. 'Behind the rocks.'

Mallory paused at the top of the slope, listening to the breath in his throat, the pound of the blood in his ears.

And another sound.

'Get into the cave,' he said. 'Quick.'

They began to run, slithering on the loose flakes of limestone that carpeted the ground. They had all heard it: the steady drone of an aeroplane engine.

They were not going to make it to the cave. 'Down!' roared Mallory.

They fell on their faces between the boulders. The droning intensified. The Fieseler Storch observation plane came slowly up the path. Between two boulders, Mallory was close enough to see the glint of the observer's binoculars as the plane circled over the little plateau.

The Storch flew on, down the other side of the mountain. Slowly and with great effort, the Storm Force dragged itself into the cave.

The entrance was little more than a crack in the rock, but inside it became a room-sized chamber, with a floor of broken stones and goat droppings, and a ceiling that faded upwards into shadow. The walls were smooth, as if they had been worn by water. There was no water now, except for a few drips from the roof. A cold draught blew from the inside of the cave, bearing the musty smell of stone.

Thierry said, 'Did they see us?'

Mallory shrugged out of his pack. 'No way of telling,' he said. 'Twenty minutes. Then we move on.'

Andrea caught Mallory's eye, and slipped back out of the entrance.

'If they had seen us, they would have turned back the way they had come, and made their report.' Thierry's eyes were anxious under the brim of the straw hat. 'Do you not think?'

'Sure,' said Mallory, not because he was sure, but to keep him quiet. 'Food.' He began rummaging in his pack, pulling out cans of sardines and blocks of chocolate.

'Brew up?' said Miller.

'Not yet,' said Mallory casually. 'Take a look at Wallace, would you?'

Wallace was lying on the stony floor. Andrea had put a pack under his head. The flesh had fallen away from his face, so the nose and cheekbones looked as if they would burst through the skin. He seemed to radiate a dry heat. His eyes were open, but were dull and glazed. 'Hurts,' he said.

Miller crouched at his side. 'Just a little prick,' he said. 'As the actress said to the bishop.' He pushed a morphine syrette into the ice-white skin of the SAS man's dangling upper arm. Wallace moaned and stirred, and said something in a high, incomprehensible voice. Then his eyes closed. Miller unbuttoned the tunic and started to unwrap the bandages on the stomach.

When he had unwrapped them he sat very still for a moment, face immobile. Then he lit a cigarette and took a deep, soothing drag.

The wound was by no means soothing. It was a crater on the right-hand side of the belly; a crater puffed at the edges to an unhealthy redness that shaded to yellow. A faint odour rose from it, the smell of a meat-safe the morning after a hot night. And that was only the outside. It looked as if the bullet had been travelling from right to left. It had passed behind the abdominal muscles. It was still in there, somewhere. Miller had no means of finding out what damage it had done, and very little inclination to do so.

He rummaged in his first-aid box and pulled out a can of sulfa powder. He sprinkled a heavy dusting on the entrance hole, and applied fresh dressings. While Andrea held Wallace up, he rebound the bandages so it looked neat and white and tidy.

Mallory said, 'How is he?'

Miller lit a new cigarette from the stub of the old one. 'Could be lucky,' he said, without conviction.

'Nothing you can do?'

'You can sit there with your mouth open and wonder how the hell he managed to climb a three-thousand-foot mountain,' he said. 'Otherwise, I've packed it with sulfa. I may also pray a little.'

Mallory nodded. The weeks of effort were telling on Miller. His eyes were sunk deep in his head, and they held a manic gleam. Miller had always had an over-developed sense of humour, but now it was developing an edge colder than bayonet steel.

'But I tell you something,' said Miller. 'If he can climb with a stomach like that, he can probably bloody well fly as well.' He rummaged in his pack, pulled out a can of sardines and ate the fish in concentrated silence, using a knife.

Mallory sat down, let his aching limbs relax, and ate some sardines of his own. He was exhausted. Forty-eight hours from now, the Werwolf pack was due to sail. They were going to have to keep moving.

But if they left Wallace, he would die.

Drowsily, he debated with himself. They had already left Lisette. Why not leave Wallace?

If the Storch had spotted them, they would find him here. And he would talk.

Mallory found himself dozing. He sat up quickly, took a Benzedrine out of his pack and swallowed it.

Hugues was nodding over his bottle of brandy. Mallory leaned over and took it out of his hand. He washed the pill down with a fiery gulp and passed the bottle on to Jaime. Andrea was going to have to carry Wallace.

He looked around the grey, cheerless shadows. Andrea was not there. He would be standing sentry. Mallory climbed stiffly to his feet and went to the mouth of the cave.

The gully stretched away like a corridor roofed with sky. In the ten minutes they had been inside, the roof had become lower, changed from black to soft grey. And from out of the grey, whirling on the eddies of a bitter wind, there floated billions of snowflakes. Already the outlines of boulders in the gully were melting and fusing under the chill, white blanket. Of Andrea there was no sign.

Jaime appeared at his side. He said, 'Now only one small hill to the sea.'

'How far?'

'Twelve kilometres.'

'It's snowing.'

'Not down below. Snow up here, rain down below.' Jaime laughed. The brandy had given his eyes a mischievous glitter. 'We can go the inside way, if you want.'

'What do you mean?'

Jaime took his arm, led him back into the cave, and pointed at its shadowy inner recesses. 'Once this was where a river came out of the cliff. The river is still in there, but it has found new ways out. Now it arrives in the valley close to the Hendaye road. And in other places, they say, it springs from the hill. I once met a man, Norbert Casteret, who told me he had walked inside this mountain.

He was a great bore. In great detail he told me: shafts, waterfalls, and the rest.'

'Fascinating,' said Mallory. The Benzedrine was making his ears ring in the intense, snow-muffled silence. There was only Wallace's stertorous breathing, and the drip of water from the cave roof. And now that Jaime came to mention it, something else, something more a vibration than a sound, as if far away, something hugely powerful was roaring and thundering. A waterfall, for instance.

Mallory's muscles tensed and his palms sweated. Caves and water . . . Not fear, he told himself. Only the Benzedrine. He looked at his watch. They had been here fifteen minutes. Time they were moving on. He said to Jaime, 'Moving out in three minutes. The outside route.'

Hugues and Thierry groaned, stretching their cold-stiffened limbs. Miller gathered his pack and his precious boxes. Mallory shouldered his own pack and his weapons. He went once again to the mouth of the cave and down the gully, and looked onto the little plateau. It was empty, except for snowflakes. Where the hell was Andrea?

Then something moved in the snow: a giant moustache, and a pair of black eyebrows that grew larger. Mallory realised that he was looking at Andrea; Andrea wearing a white snow smock, carrying the Bren.

Andrea said, 'My Keith, we have a German patrol.' He spoke calmly, but he was moving fast.

Mallory's ears sang in the silence. 'How many?'

'Perhaps thirty.'

At the edge of the plateau, a ragged line of dark shapes was materialising in the snow. The shapes of German soldiers. And with the soldiers, other shapes, from which came the sound of whining and baying.

Dogs.

There was no point in trying to draw the men away from the cave: the dogs would not be distracted, even if the handlers were.

Andrea stared at him. He said, 'I'll go up the hill and draw them off.'

'No,' said Mallory. He hated saying it. But the dogs would not be drawn. 'Back to the cave.'

Andrea said, 'But the cave is a trap.'

'There's a back entrance.'

One of the figures in the snow shouted. The line stopped.

Andrea sighed, and took aim with the Bren. The machine gun's stammer fell flat in the soft white world. One of the figures buckled and collapsed.

Mallory slid back into the gully. The Schmeisser chattered in his hands as Andrea fell back past him. Bullets smashed rocks above his head. He felt stone-chips sting his cheek, and the trickle of blood. He was moving back towards the cave mouth, Andrea firing past him, covering him. As he arrived at the cave mouth, four figures in field-grey appeared at the end of the gully.

Suddenly, Mallory and Andrea were inside the cave, and Mallory's Schmeisser was bucking in his hands again. Next to him, Andrea was fumbling in his belt. His arm came over, and a grenade was tumbling through the air like a little dark egg, bursting with a big, flat *slam* in the mouth of the gully. There were screams. But there were a lot of bullets coming in now, spanging off the cave mouth and zipping into the dark interior.

The Benzedrine was chewing away in Mallory's mind. *How did they find us?* Dogs. Or the Storch. It did not matter. Either they broke out now, or the patrol would call up reinforcements. Reinforcements were probably on the way already.

Outside, there was a big, steady hammering, and the entrance droned with stinging shards of stone. Reinforcements or no reinforcements, there was at least one heavy machine gun out there. Mortars next.

Mallory thought about what a mortar bomb would do in the mouth of the cave. He saw the air full of razor-sharp chunks of steel and the shrapnel of blasted rock, the ceiling falling in –

The ceiling falling in.

'Miller,' he said. Miller came. Mallory spoke to him. Miller nodded, trotted back into the shadows.

Mallory called over his shoulder. 'Jaime. The exit?'

'Found it,' said Jaime.

Oh, God.

Andrea was crouching behind a boulder. He caught Mallory's eye. His face was the same old face, large and impassive above the sweeping black moustache. But there was something about the set of the big, unshaven jaw that shocked Mallory. Andrea had walked alone from Greece to Bulgaria, through the heart of occupied *Mitteleuropa*. He was a full colonel in the Greek army, and with that army had suffered defeat. With him, Mallory had spent eighteen months behind German lines in Crete, stared death right between the eyes on Navarone and in the Zenica Cage. But in all that time, Mallory had never seen this expression on his face. Up here, five thousand feet above sea level, in a dank cave near the summit of this tilted sheet of limestone, Andrea's face was . . . *resigned*.

Mallory found that his muscles were tense as boards, and in his mind something was scrambling and scuttling, like a terrified animal. He made himself think of the Channel covered with ships, the ships crammed with men, and among them giant submarines swimming swiftly, undetectable, laden with torpedoes. A Spandau burst punched into the cave wall above his head. He said to Andrea, 'Jaime has found the back way.' Andrea's face relaxed. Resignation gave way to the expression that with Andrea conveyed anything from polite curiosity to frenzied enthusiasm. 'Then we should take it,' he said. 'Soon.'

Four minutes later Miller was alone, standing among the boulders at the back of the cave. The entrance was a narrow white window, pointed at the top. The rest of it was dark, black as ink, in contrast to the glare of the snow outside.

Miller filled his eyes with that glare, and tried for three seconds not to think about anything but daylight, and sky. But his right hand was chilled by the stone-flavoured draught blowing from the crack in the cave floor on his right – the crack down which his companions had vanished, and down which he must vanish himself, now that his preparations were complete –

A sleet of bullets lashed through the entrance, and the air was deafening with ricochets. The snow beyond the entrance was suddenly peopled with grey figures, running, firing as they came. Miller fired a burst of his Schmeisser into that brilliant white lancet. Then he lowered himself into the crack, and started to climb down the doubled rope into the dark.

The first two Germans flattened themselves against the walls outside the entrance. They pulled the string fuses on two stick grenades, and flung them into the cave mouth. There was a hollow *boom*, and smoke rolled out. There was no sign of life from the black interior. They threw in two more grenades, to make sure, and waited for the bang.

They did not get it.

What they got was a thunderous roar, and a sheet of flame that lashed out of the entrance and melted the snow for fifty feet, and picked up the men who had thrown the grenades and fired them like cannonballs out of the gully and onto the plateau, where they lay under a sheet of rock fragments that fell out of the sky like hard rain. Where the cave had been was a raw cleft in the mountainside, half-filled with fuming scree.

'*Gott*,' said the Feldwebel. 'What are they putting in the grenades, nowadays?'

'Whatever it is, it's done the job,' said the Sturmbannführer. 'Now pick up those men and for God's sake let us get out of this snow.'

Miller was twenty feet down the crack when the big explosion came. A blast of hot air frizzled his eyebrows and the doubled rope in his hands became two separate ropes. He thought, in one compressed moment: one kilo of plastic with a thirty-second time pencil will not only blow up a limestone cave, but cut a wire-cored climbing rope.

Then he had landed with a crash on wet stone, and a big pain in his leg was filling the world, and dust was in his lungs, and stone was falling on his head.

He became aware that he was lying in a place lit by yellow torchlight, and that the stones falling on his head were small, and the pain in his leg was ebbing. Bruised, not broken, he thought. He groped for a cigarette in the breast pocket of his blouse, and lit it. The smoke rose vertical in the torchlight. Before, there had been a draught.

He said, 'Looks like the roof fell in.'

'Quite,' said Mallory, in a voice perhaps a shade lighter than usual. 'Thank you, Dusty.'

And now all we have to do is get out of here, thought Miller, and find some submarines.

Mallory lit a cigarette himself. The entrance to the shaft had been narrow – almost too narrow for Andrea. Down here it had widened out. It was better down here, as long as you did not think of all those billions of tons of rock around you, the dynamited entrance –

His heart was going like a rivet gun. He could hardly breathe for all that rock up there, sitting on his chest –

Panic later, he told himself. Once you have done the job. For now, there are six men depending on you. The Benzedrine made that sound like a good thing. He took a deep breath. 'Flashlights off,' he said. 'Use one at a time, only when moving.' The light went out. Darkness descended, thick and suffocating as wet velvet. 'Jaime,' he said. 'Your friend Casteret. What did he tell you?'

'It was two years ago,' said Jaime.

'Try to remember.'

There was a pause, in which he could almost hear the wheels spinning in Jaime's brain. 'He entered the cave,' he said. 'The shaft. A river. He said there are many passages: the river made one way out, then found a way to another, lower down, then another. So the mountain is full of holes like a Gruyère, some blocked, some flooded. There is a route, because Casteret found it. But it took him many days.'

'That's it?'

'That's it.'

Many days. In this darkness. Mallory could hear his own breathing, very loud. 'So if we head downhill, we can't go far wrong.'

'Maybe,' said Jaime.

'Very good,' said Mallory. 'I'll lead. Hugues and Andrea, carry Wallace.'

They made a sort of sedan chair out of a couple of webbing straps and Wallace's crutch. Mallory stood up, flexing his stiff limbs. He turned on his flashlight.

It began.

The beam of the flashlight showed a water-smoothed gallery heading steeply downwards. It was high, the gallery, so high in places that the flashlight failed to touch its roof. Once, it had been a runnel of acid rainwater, dissolving its way through a seam of limestone. The water had gone now, leaving a bed of grey pebbles down which they walked as if down the gravel drive of a house in the suburbs of hell.

They went two hundred yards like this, downwards at an angle of perhaps forty degrees, heading west by Mallory's compass. Then the gallery took a turning to the right.

Mallory was pointing the flashlight down at the ground. Suddenly there were two flashlight beams, one where he was pointing it, and another on the roof of the gallery, which was low here. The reason that it was on the roof was that it was being reflected by the black pool that spanned the gallery from side to side before it sloped down into the water.

Dead end.

Mallory's heart was thumping in his ears. In front of them, the roof ran down into the water. Behind them, the cave was sealed.

Trapped.

Dusty Miller saw the flashlight stop. He heard the drip of water, the rasp of the stretcher-bearers' breath. He remembered the panic-stricken rigidity of Mallory in the bread oven. He fumbled in his breast pocket, and lit a cigarette.

'For Christ's sake,' said Hugues, in a voice a good octave too high. 'You will use up the air.'

'Plenty of air,' said Miller, languidly, for Mallory's benefit. There used to be a howling draught up that shaft, remember?' He heard Mallory grunt, as if he did not trust himself to speak.

'And this is a most commodious cave by cave standards. Did I ever tell you about the time I was working the Go Home Point amethyst mine back in Ontario? Little tiny shaft, and we get a flash flood. So there is me, a half-ton of dynamite, and as it turns out a rabid skunk, one hundred foot under the Canadian Shield, and that sucker is filling up quicker'n a whore's bidet –'

'Some other time,' said Mallory.

Miller could hear his voice was back to normal. 'Sure,' he said. 'Well, seems to me there must be some place above that water for all that air to have been coming from, before we blew the cave.' He took a last drag on his cigarette. It made a bright shower of sparks as he threw it away. 'So it ain't the air we have a problem with, it's the cigarettes, and I guess they need smoking right up, because I have a feeling I am going to get real wet.' He walked forward, eyeing the swim of the flashlight beam in the water and unbuttoning his tunic.

'Take a rope,' said Mallory.

'Sure.'

Miller's body was long and pale, corded with stringy muscle in the dimness. He tied the rope round his waist in a bowline, took the waterproof flashlight in his hand, and stepped into the pool.

The water was so cold it burned. He set his teeth and walked on. The gravel under his feet sloped down sharply, continuing the forty-five degree slope of the cave's floor. Within three paces the water was up to his chest, and he was gasping for breath. Within four, he was swimming, the coldest swimming he had ever done. He swam hard, hoping that he was right, that there was a way through here, between the gallery roof and the water, for the draught to blow –

But perhaps the draught had come from somewhere else, a hole in the rock high in the roof, invisible. Perhaps this was a blind-ended hole, deep as the mountain was high, full of this icy water.

What a way to go, thought Miller. Drowning in mineral water. I promise that if I get out of this, I will never drink anything but brandy again.

He clamped the flashlight between his teeth and dived.

Back on the gravel beach Mallory saw the light fade in the dark water, then vanish. He tried not to think of the cold under there, the pressing down of the roof, the ridges of stone that could catch you and keep you under there while you drowned, in the middle of miles of rock –

But the coils of rope moved slowly through his fingers and into the water. Miller was making progress –

The rope became still.

He's in the air again, Mallory told himself.

But the rope remained still for a minute, then two. Mallory's mind told him that it was normal, there was an explanation. But deep down, that creature was raving at him: he's stuck, he's drowned, for Christ's sake –

Mallory found he had seized the rope and was tugging at it, hauling for all he was worth, and the bight of it was thrashing the black pool. Andrea was at his side, saying something soothing, but he could not hear what –

And suddenly a flashlight clicked on, and a voice said, 'Colder 'n the nipple on a witch's tit in there.' Miller's voice.

For a second, Mallory felt deep shame.

'It's like the bend in your toilet bowl,' said Miller. 'There's a little uphill the far side, stalagmites, stalactites, the whole shebang. I put the rope on a stalactite. Or 'mite, whichever. Anyways, it's cold and wet, but once you get to the other side you can breathe.'

Mallory put the shame behind him. There was a lot to do, and he needed a clear mind to do it with.

Miller wrapped his battledress in his waterproof cape, and went back through the icy water. The rest of them came after him, one by one, dragged under the low roof, breath held, clothes and weapons wrapped against the water, Andrea bringing up the rear. On the far side, they stood and shivered in the tomb-like cold. Wallace was the most worrying. 'Work your arms,' said Mallory. 'Circulation.'

Wallace raised his arms weakly, let them fall again. Miller bent over him, tugging his tunic over his arms. He was too weak to dress himself. 'Physical jerks,' he said, and tried to grin. Even the grin suffered from lack of muscle power.

They sat and drank soup brewed on a pressure stove, and checked their weapons. Miller put his oil can down by the edge of the water, and went over the lock of his Schmeisser with a corner of pullthrough. When he had finished the gun, he looked down again at the oil can.

It had been six inches from the water's edge. Now the water's edge was lapping against its base.

Up in the world, there was wet snow and rain. Down here in the underworld, the waters of the earth were rising.

Best not tell Mallory.

After five minutes, Mallory stood up. 'Okay,' he said. 'We're off.'

The gallery ran downhill again. There were a couple more pools, neither of them more than waist-deep. Hugues marched through the blackness head down, hands in pockets, shoulder aching under the pressure of Wallace's crutch. When he brushed against Wallace's hand it felt cold as marble. It was obvious to Hugues that this man was going to die. Why carry him, when they had abandoned Lisette? It was folly, madness. Hugues was a soldier. He accepted that in war there were sacrifices to be made. But some things were too precious to sacrifice. Like the life of the woman you loved, and your unborn child. Deep under the mountain, Hugues was making promises to himself. If I live, he was thinking, things will be different. From now on, I will take care of the things I can see and touch with my own eyes and hands. From now on, it is not the big causes I will fight for. From now on, it will be the people I love.

If there is a from now on.

The brandy throbbed in his head. He marched on, detesting Mallory and Miller and this Greek killer Andrea, their cold, sunken eyes, the hard jokes they made, the way they did not care about individual people, thought only of their operation –

Andrea's boot trod on his heel. He was out of step, stumbling, panting for breath, the blood roaring in his ears.

Not just the blood.

Ever since they had been inside the mountain, the air had been tremulous with a faint rumble. Now the rumble was gaining in intensity. At first it was a long, uniform growl. Then the growl had become a roar that shook the ground underfoot and vibrated in the still air of the gallery. After perhaps a mile the gravel underfoot had become finer, and the ground had started to rise. At the top of a low mound the gallery was suddenly blocked by a wall of rock.

The beam of Mallory's flashlight wavered up the wall to a crack of darkness at its summit. The crack was a foot wide, the roar as loud as a bomber's engines. He put a foot on the wall and began to climb.

It was only twenty feet high, but running water had smoothed away the footholds. It took him a careful five minutes to get to the top. And when he did, he wished he had not.

When he put his head through the crack, the thunder of falling water was like a hand that grabbed his head and shook it. He shone his torch into the darkness. The beam lanced into emptiness. He put his head into the racket, and looked down.

Once, the wall must have been the sill of a waterfall. Now the river had found a lower channel, and the place where the waterfall had been was now a cliff, smooth as ivory, falling away below beyond the reach of his flashlight beam, plummeting like a gigantic mine shaft into the bowels of the earth. From the depths rose the bellow of falling water, and a fine mist of spray that chilled Mallory's face.

Curiously, this hellish hole in the world made Mallory feel better. It might be underground, and dark as the inside of a bank safe. But it was an open space; a problem that with a small stretch of the imagination could be regarded as a problem in mountaineering.

Mallory called for Miller and Andrea. They looked over the edge, and went back to the bottom of the sill. Miller said, 'Holy cow,' in a voice not altogether steady.

'We've got two ropes,' said Mallory. 'I'm going to put them together, double. If I find anything useful, I'll pull twice. Send Wallace down first. You'll have to show the other three how to rappel.'

'Ideal place to learn,' said Miller.

Mallory knotted the first two ropes together, slung the last coil over his shoulder, and went over the edge.

The wall was as smooth as it looked: no purchase for feet. He kept his weight well out, rope over shoulder and up between his legs, walking down the wall. By the time he came to the first knot he was walking in complete darkness. Miller's flashlight was a faint yellow glow far above. The roar of water surrounded him like a thunderstorm. He unclipped his own flashlight and shone it downwards.

Sixty feet below, the beam met something black and gleaming, muscular as the back of a giant slug. For a moment he could not work out what it was. Finally, the truth filtered through. It was a waterfall. A river, a big river, was pouring out of a ragged hole in the side of the shaft, tumbling down into a blackness too deep for the flashlight to penetrate. The roar numbed his mind. He saw a sudden picture of himself suspended like a spider on a string of gossamer, hung in this dreadful shaft. He blanked it out.

The shaft would have been a pothole: a whirlpool a million years old, a spinning auger of carbonic acid sinking its way slowly into the limestone. After the river had gnawed its way down a hundred and fifty feet, it had joined forces with another seam of water, and adopted its course as its own. The new waterfall emerged to his left, almost at right angles to the wall he was descending.

There should be a ledge. Where the old waterfall had been supplanted by the new, there should definitely be a ledge.

He knew he must be getting to the bottom of the second rope. The wall was still smooth. To his left, he could feel the wind of the down-rushing water, falling God knew where. The spray of it had soaked him to the skin. He felt cold and weak. What if there was no ledge, only this smooth wall falling direct to the bottom?

Something touched his back. He almost shouted with the shock. He was lying on his back on a ledge. He shone his flashlight. The ledge was four feet wide, twenty feet long, piled with boulders, crusted white with limy deposits, and shining with water. When he shone his light over the edge, he still saw nothing. There was only the black water rushing past with its mind-numbing roar.

He pulled the rope twice, hard. Then he sat with his back against the wall, and shivered, and gnawed some chocolate.

Wallace came down first, lowered by Andrea. Then there were two loads of packs and weapons and radios, then Thierry and Hugues. Somehow, Thierry had kept his hat. Hugues had had a bad descent: there was blood on his face. Then there were Jaime and Miller, who Mallory imagined would be swearing vigorously, and finally Andrea, leaping down the wall like a huge cat.

When they were all down, Mallory stood up, flexed his aching fingers, looped the ropes over a lime-cemented boulder, and went over the edge again.

This time it was easier. There were footholds, of a sort. Twenty feet after the halfway mark he entered a place where his flashlight, instead of making a yellow disc on black water, created a sort of white halo, as if in fog. The noise was more like an avalanche than a waterfall. There was wind, too, irregular flumes of draught that splattered limestone-tasting water in his face. And suddenly he was standing on dry land again.

This time it was not a ledge. This time the plunging roar of water told him that he was at the base of the waterfall, standing on a beach.

He tugged the rope twice. Then he flicked the flashlight on again, and began to grope his way round the beach. It was a broad horseshoe of broken boulders surrounding a thrashing pool of water. The waterfall must have been twenty feet across and ten feet thick, a solid column of water plunging down two hundred feet and hammering the pool to froth. The pool itself had a circular motion, like a giant bath plughole –

Mallory's heart thudded unpleasantly in his chest. He walked round the piled boulders to one margin of the waterfall. Then he went all the way back round, as far as the other margin.

If he had expected anything, it had been that the river would turn horizontal at the base of the waterfall, and make its way out through the side of the mountain. But there was no horizontal passage.

The shaft was a tube. The reason the water in the pool was spinning like a bath plughole was because it was finding the way out, as water will . . .

Straight down.

Mallory sat on a boulder. Carefully, he fished in his blouse pocket for the oilcloth bag with his cigarettes and lighter. He put a cigarette in his mouth, and lit it.

The draught blew the lighter out. He relit it, but the cigarette was soaked.

Soon, the others began to land on the beach. Mallory's flashlight was dim yellow, the batteries gone. It went out. He flicked his lighter. The petrol caught.

The draught blew it out again.

He sat down, and concentrated on shivering.

Miller came down third, after Wallace, with his eyes shut, cursing. For a man who loathed and despised heights, it struck him that he had been doing an unfair quantity of mountaineering these past few weeks. When he reached the beach, he moved away from the base of the rope; having avoided death by falling, he had no desire to be flattened by a plummeting Frenchman. A gleam of yellow light showed him where Mallory was sitting. Miller flicked on his own flashlight. He was on his last set of batteries. He saw what Mallory had seen: there were no exits. He shivered, too. The reason he shivered was because of the wind –

The wind.

He flashed his torch at Mallory. Mallory's face looked pinched and white. He looked like a man who had wrestled for a long time with a monster, and had discovered that despite his best efforts the monster was not yet dead.

Two packs arrived down the rope. Miller flicked his torch over them, and onto Wallace. Wallace's face had the corpse-look, grey and sunken, but he raised a hand. Miller let the torch beam slide over his bandages. The wound did not seem to be bleeding any more.

Miller suddenly stopped thinking about Wallace. The beam of his flashlight had touched the margin of the water. Five minutes ago, there had been a brick-sized stone by Wallace's foot. Now there was no stone.

Not that the stone had gone – brick-sized stones do not evaporate. What had happened was that the stone was under water.

The water was still rising.

It was not a military problem. But then Miller was not in any strict sense of the word a military person. In fact, having enlisted in the RAF and been posted to the cookhouse, he had simply walked away from his unit; not out of cowardice, but because he wanted to use his talents somewhere they could damage the enemy, not potatoes. He had been astonished when someone had informed him that this constituted desertion. But by then he had been behind enemy lines, causing Rommel severe headaches as a member of the Long Range Desert Force. And nobody had got round to court-martialling him.

But as he stood on that black and shrinking beach, Miller was thinking of a time before the Long Range Desert Force. It was not a time he was particularly proud of, but it was a time when he had caused the maximum possible mayhem using the minimum possible resources.

It had been during Prohibition. For reasons best left undiscussed, even with himself, Miller had found himself in Orcasville, a small white clapboard town on the southern shore of Lake Ontario. It was into Orcasville's pier that a Canadian bootlegger called Melvin Brassman was wont to bring his cargoes of hooch. None of which would have posed any problems for Miller, except that Brassman's boys were causing a lot of trouble in the town, culminating in the rape of three girls, one of them the minister's daughter, and the burning of the warehouses of two merchants Brassman saw as rivals. Having committed these acts of mayhem, Brassman's men had let it be known that any rival rumrunners would be treated as hostile, rammed, and sunk by the steel ex-tug *Firewater*, in which they plied their trade.

It was Brent Kent, one of the burned-out merchants, who had called in Miller, then dynamiting pine stumps in the Finger Lakes region. Kent had laid his problem before Miller, stressing the need for a swift, untraceable, no-blame vanishment of the *Firewater*. There were no explosives in the town, or at least none that could not be traced.

But Miller was more than a demolitions man. Miller was a practical chemist.

Miller had taken possession of an old but superficially seaworthy steam barge, which he had enigmatically christened *Krakatoa*. He had painted the exterior a pleasing royal blue, and let it be known that he was off to Canada to pick up a cargo of hooch. With great puffings and clankings, he and the *Krakatoa* had set off from the Orcasville quay. Just out of sight of land he had stopped the engine, and waited. After twelve hours, he had attended to the *Krakatoa*'s real cargo.

This consisted not of liquor, but several dozen barrels of tallow, and a similar number of carboys of sulphuric and nitric acids. Descending to the deck of the hold with an axe, Miller staved in the tallow barrels. Then, carefully, he uncorked the acid carboys and let their contents gurgle into the barge's ancient wooden bilges. After that, he rowed clumsily away in a dinghy, and was collected by the mayor in his catboat. When they arrived ashore, Miller was observed to be the worse for liquor, bragging in a foolish manner about the large quantity of Canadian whiskey bobbing at anchor offshore, which, landed at nightfall, would wreck the Brassman booze market for good and all.

These braggings swiftly reached the ears of Brassman's Orcasville lieutenant, who made certain long-distance telephone calls. That night, a night of full moon, the *Firewater*, steaming out of the north, saw the low silhouette of the *Krakatoa* at anchor, and took anticompetitive action. The *Krakatoa* was known to be rotten. The *Firewater* screwed down her regulator, achieved ramming speed, and ran her down.

What the *Firewater*'s master had not bargained for was Dusty Miller. When Dusty had rowed away, the barge had exuded a sour smell and a greenish chemical cloud. Now, twelve hours later, the acids swilling in her hold had compounded with the fatty fractions of the tallow, and formed a new substance.

So the rotting wooden barge into which the *Firewater*'s bow had knifed at twelve knots was not a rum ship. It was a rotting wooden barge that contained ten tons of impure and highly unstable nitroglycerine.

The explosion that vaporised the *Firewater* also broke most of the windows in Orcasville, and woke the Mayor of Toronto eighty miles away. Miller left town the following morning, and the town reglazed. There was no further trouble from Melvin Brassman.

Hugues came down the rope. He saw by the dim and pearly light of a single torch that the American, Miller, had gone off to a section of beach opposite the waterfall, a section where, to judge by the boulders piled up against the face of the cliff, there had been a rockfall of some kind. Hugues shivered in the chill wind that was blowing from the direction of the rockfall: a wind that reminded him of the outside world. *Merde,* thought Hugues, gazing into the dark. This is not a war in which anything will be solved. And certainly not by these stupid old men who have brought me to the bottom of this well to die.

The light at the other side of the pool seemed to become suddenly animated, bobbing like a drunken firefly. He stared at it dully. Someone was walking, running, *racing* towards him. A hard body whacked him off his rock and onto the wet ground, and he was struggling, indignant, his mouth full of limy pebbles, while a voice, Miller's voice, bellowed over the thunder of the fall, 'Cover your ears!'

Suddenly, Hugues was given a vision. The shaft became a vast tube of grey rock, the waterfall a silver column falling out of a sky roofed with more rock, every ridge and ledge and pebble razor-sharp, illuminated by a huge flash of light. The noise of the water was momentarily replaced by a new noise, so loud as hardly to resemble a noise at all.

It was the noise of the five pounds of gelignite that Dusty Miller had packed into the rockfall at the point where the draught had been strongest.

When the rock fragments had ceased to fall Miller walked back across the beach, and examined the scene of the explosion. It was a neat job, though he said it himself. The boulders had separated like a curtain. At the focal point of the explosion was a ragged gap perhaps two feet square, through which the wind howled in a jet like water from a fire hose. Miller sniffed at it hopefully, trying to detect the herbs and aromatic plants of the maquis.

It smelt of damp Norman churches.

Can't win 'em all, thought Miller. He shone his torch through the hole. There were jumbled boulders, and beyond them the hint of space: a previous bed of the river. Quick, now, before the water rose far enough to spill down the channel. He walked along the beach to Mallory, directed his torch at his hand and gave the thumbs-up sign. The stony rigidity of Mallory's face relaxed. They assembled the loads and shared them out. Then Miller led the way into the hole in the rockfall. Andrea was the last in. As he stepped up to the hole he found he was walking in water.

The new passage was another tube of water-smoothed rock. The wind was strong in their faces. Mallory looked at his compass. They were heading north. They must have crossed the mountain by now. Mallory was tired, and hungry, and cold, and his feet had been wet for so long that they felt like raw sponges. But they were heading in the right direction. In the gale that was making him shudder with cold he detected the breath of freedom.

Provided there was an exit.

The passage was flattening out. Hugues stumbled. Andrea trod on his heels again; Andrea, who walked with the stolid regularity of a machine. Hugues was exhausted. He wanted to drop his end of the crutch from which Wallace was hanging, stop, rest his blistered feet, sleep in the dark.

Behind him, Andrea's voice said, 'I'll take him for a while.'

Hugues thought, he understands, this one. He understands exactly how weak I am, the way my mind will not be still, but must keep chewing at these questions that have no answers. There was something almost diabolic about that. Hugues felt naked, exposed.

To prove Andrea wrong, he said, 'I'm fine.'

The stretcher party plodded on in the dark. The last torch was turning yellow. There was no sound but the harsh rasp of breathing, and the rustle of water over rock.

Andrea did not want to say anything, but the water in the passage was definitely getting deeper.

It had started as a wetness on the floor. Now it was shin-deep, and it seemed to be rising faster. He thought of the waterfall. He imagined all that water pouring down here. He imagined it pouring down into a chamber with a small exit, making a pool that spread back into the tunnel, a pool that would fill the tunnel up. That would be a problem for the operation, thought Andrea methodically. If they drowned, the operation would not be completed. It would be best if that did not happen.

Mallory walked on. The water shone under the now orange beam of his flashlight, chuckling merrily downhill.

The flashlight became an orange point, and went out.

Mallory lit his Zippo and held it above his head. The flame flickered in the rush of air.

Ahead, the tunnel broadened and became a flat sheet of water that led to a blank wall of rock. Above, at the height of a cathedral roof, a shaft led upwards. It was down this shaft that the wind was howling. The lighter went out. In the darkness left by its flame it was possible to see at the top of the shaft, bright as a diamond in the cold black velvet of far underground, a speck of light.

An unattainable speck. For as their eyes adjusted to the dim glow they saw that the chamber in which they were standing was roughly the shape of an inverted funnel, with the shaft as the spout.

Mallory's mountaineering exploits had covered the newspapers of the Empire. But even master mountaineers do not have suckers on their feet.

Mallory felt a presence by his side. Miller raised his own lighter. The sheet of water was a pool, fed by the knee-deep torrent underfoot. Stalactites threw angular shadows across the ceiling, and stalagmites stood neck-deep in the pool. Beyond each stalagmite was a little writhing in the water.

'It's flowing,' said Miller. 'Must be going somewhere.'

This time he was so wet that there was no point in taking his clothes off. He tied the rope round his waist and waded in.

The first thirty feet was no more than knee-deep. Then, suddenly, the bottom sank away, and he was swimming, treading water rather, swept along by a fierce current in a narrow trench. At the rock wall ahead.

And he knew he had miscalculated.

He opened his mouth to shout, realised it was too late, and grabbed a deep breath of air instead. Then he went under.

The current was like a hand, grabbing him, tearing him down. He went headfirst, felt himself crash against a big rock. Then his shoulders were in a tight opening, too narrow for him to get through, and the current was forcing water into his nose, trying to get it into his lungs. He wriggled convulsively, got free, hit another rock with a bang that made his ears ring. He was in a pipe, a pipe of rock that was such a tight fit that he could not move his arms or legs. The shove of the water was huge. You goddamn idiot, he told himself. You can get away with it once, twice, ten times. But diving into God's waterworks is asking for trouble.

And trouble is what you got.

His chest was bursting. The blood was hammering in his ears, and his head was roaring and juddering like that waterfall back there. Thirty more seconds of this, and he was going to be dead. And then those other guys would be dead. And then those submarines would go through that invasion fleet like three red-hot pokers through a pound of butter.

Chest full of air, oxygen turning to carbon dioxide. Going to suffocate you.

Make yourself smaller.

Breathe out.

Miller breathed out. The contraction of his chest shrank his girth by a fraction. The tunnel's grip slackened. The water hauled him along the pipe, and slammed him into a hole through which his head only just fitted, and poured into his nostrils and gaping mouth.

Now he was going to die.

He was going to die with his head in daylight.

Daylight?

With the last of his strength, he writhed like an eel. And suddenly, whatever it was that was holding his right shoulder had given way, and he was through, out, beyond it all, flat on his back in a cheery little brook that was gurgling down a wooded valley under the five o'clock sky, from which a little snow was falling, but only a little.

He breathed twice, big breaths, with coughing. He looked back at the hole in the hill, a hole no bigger than a badger sett, as it burst out and expanded into a raw rent big enough for a bear, or even Andrea. The flow of water seemed to have lessened. He had broken the bottleneck. There might even be air in the tunnel now. He gave the two pulls on the rope.

It was cold in the little valley. The snow had not settled, but white skeins drifted in a half-hearted manner from heavy black clouds sailing in on the westerly breeze. They inspected and cleaned the weapons, fumbling with cold, water-wrinkled fingers. Jaime found some dry branches and knocked up a fire that burned with hardly any smoke. Andrea made soup. Thierry crammed his straw hat on his head, unpacked his radio, and began to inspect the parts.

Miller took Wallace a can of soup. None of them looked in the best of health, but Wallace looked terrible. His skin was like grey paper, but burning hot to the touch. His eyes were glazed. When Miller tipped some soup down his throat, he vomited immediately.

His wound looked pale and bloodless because of its perpetual rinsing in water. But the yellow edges looked yellower, and the red puffiness angrier. There was swelling, and a nasty putrid ooze. 'Hurts,' he said.

'Bloody awful mess you are,' said Miller. 'Sooner we get you under a roof the better.'

Wallace opened a dull and rheumy eye. 'Lea' me,' he said.

'Leave you my ass,' said Miller, sticking in the morphine syrette and squeezing the tube. 'We'll get a dressing on that. Still hurt?'

'Can't feel a thing,' said Wallace.

'Sure,' said Miller, as if that was the right answer. 'Just get a new dressing on that for you.' He smeared damp sulfa on the wound, bandaged it up again, and covered Wallace with a more-or-less dry blanket.

Mallory said quickly, 'How is it?'

'Looks like it's going wrong,' said Miller, grim-faced. 'Plus shock, I guess. I don't know why he's still alive.'

Mallory's deep-sunk eyes were bright and distant. It was a mystery to him why any of them were still alive. 'We'll take two hours' rest,' he said. 'Jaime knows where we are. The Germans think we're dead. Andrea, get your head down.'

He watched as Miller spread a groundsheet over Wallace, rolled himself up in his poncho, and went immediately to sleep. Andrea was sitting with his back to a tree, eyes invisible. Asleep, awake, nobody knew, and nobody would ask. Jaime and Hugues were asleep. Only Thierry was awake, a large, crouching figure, fiddling with his radio, testing it after its immersion.

Mallory said, 'That thing working?'

He had moved close to Thierry quietly; Mallory knew no other way of moving. Thierry looked up sharply. His fingers moved a switch. An indicator light went out.

Mallory bent and looked at the set. The light had been the TRANSMIT light. He felt the short hairs bristle on his neck. He said with a new, dangerous quietness, 'Thierry. What are you doing?'

'Testing the equipment,' said Thierry.

Mallory said, 'Just as long as you're not transmitting.'

'I heard what you say,' said Thierry irritably, squashing the straw hat over his face and leaning back against a boulder. Mallory walked to the end of the valley. The snow had stopped. Between the squalls of black cloud deep ravines of blue were appearing. There was real warmth in the gleam of sun that lanced down into the trees. Warmth was what was needed. Particularly, it was what Wallace needed. In four hours it would be dark, and it did not seem likely to Mallory that Wallace would survive a night in the open.

And Wallace was not the only worry. Mallory guessed that they were at best halfway down the mountain. They still had to get down into the valley and walk to the sea, where this Guy Jamalartégui was waiting for them. Whether or not the Germans believed that they had died in the collapsed cave beyond the ridge, the roads to the sea would be heavily patrolled.

Mallory eased his sodden feet in his boots, and squeezed his cracked and abraded hands, to change the nature of the pain. The Benzedrine was wearing off. He felt weary and irritable. What they needed was to get dry. Being dry would change everything.

He was too jumpy to rest. He patrolled the wood, walking downhill until the trees started thinning.

Below him a meadow dropped steeply into the smoky blue deeps of the valley. The sun was out again. He could feel its warmth on his face. This far down the mountain the snow had melted as quickly as it had fallen, and the meadow grass was a brilliant green space in which swam constellations of wild flowers, falling away to a hazy gulf in which a village lay like a group of toys, and beyond it a shoulder of mountain, more heavy black clouds, and the metal sheet of the sea.

But Mallory was not looking at the view. He had faded back into the shadow of a stand of pines. He had his binoculars at his eyes. His grey-brown face was stony under the stubble on cheeks and jaw.

In the disc of the glasses the lower slopes of the meadow were lousy with grey mites. The sun gleamed off windscreens: the windscreens of half-tracks and lorries, and of an odd, boxy van with a steel loop on its roof, like the frame of a giant tennis racket.

A radio-direction-finding van.

It came upon Mallory like a flash of revelation: not a flash of lightning, but the dull, red blink of the TRANSMIT light on Thierry's radio.

Thierry had not been checking the equipment. He had been transmitting.

Things began tumbling into place. That damn silly straw hat that Thierry insisted on wearing, rain or no rain, had nothing to do with vanity. It was an identification mark. *Don't shoot the man in the straw hat,* the orders would have said. *The rest, kill them. Not the man in the hat.*

In a manner of speaking, Jensen had said, they will be waiting for you.

Courtesy first of the SAS. And now Thierry.

A short mile away, at the foot of the meadows, three armoured cars had begun to grind uphill, hub-deep in the lush spring grass, leaving tracks like railway lines. Mallory faded back into the woods.

At the gully, everyone was asleep except Thierry, who was still squatting in front of his radio like a lard Buddha. Mallory did not look at him. Andrea was snoring heavily. Mallory shook him by the shoulder. He said, 'I think you should shave off your moustache.'

Andrea said, 'Wha – '

'Quick.'

Andrea's hand went to his upper lip. For the first time since Mallory had known him there was uncertainty in his eyes. 'No,' he said.

Mallory said, 'The Germans are coming. Five hundred men. Armoured cars. Listen.'

Andrea listened. He hung his head. Then, finally, he nodded. Reluctantly, he pulled a razor from his pack and began hacking at the luxuriant growth on his upper lip. 'Twenty years,' he said.

But Mallory was gone, waking the others.

Within two minutes the upper lip was bare, except for a black stubble that matched the rest of his face. A new Andrea stood up: an Andrea clean-shaven, olive-skinned, with a nose increased and cheeks enlarged by the lack of moustache. And there was something else on his normally impassive countenance. Andrea would shave his moustache in the name of duty, but that did not mean he was going to be happy about the man who had caused his loss.

Andrea was angry.

Up on his rock Thierry was beginning to be nervous. People were stirring in the camp, when there should have been no stirring. He looked at the steep walls of trees on either side of him, the valley, the stream babbling out of the mountain. These people would fight to the death. He could imagine the chug of machine guns, the blast of mortar bombs. He was working for the Germans to keep himself safe, not expose himself to danger. A stupid straw hat would not save him from Spandau rounds or shrapnel.

Thierry found that he was on his feet, and that his feet were moving, sidling away towards the woods. He found he was yearning with his whole being for the anonymous shade of the trees. The sky was a bright, hopeful blue beyond those green leaves. His mission was over; there was no shame in running. He would collect the money Herr Sachs of the Gestapo had promised him, buy a bar, listen to dance music, run a couple of girls upstairs; and the sky would never, ever be anything but blue again.

There was no more sidling, now. He was running in earnest, his great bulk crashing through wild raspberries and chestnut saplings. From the corner of his eye he could see someone coming after him. His bowels were loose with terror. He thought he could hear engines now, and the crash of jackboots in the undergrowth. Holding the identifying straw hat on his head with one hand, he shouted, *'Hilfe! Hilfe!'*

The hat and the shouting must have slowed him down. He knew that something had smacked him hard from behind, on the left-hand side of the rib cage. He pitched forward. A voice in his ear said, 'This is from Lisette, animal.' He thought, surprised, that was Hugues, the stupid Norman. What happens now?

There had been something wrong with the blow on his ribs. It hurt too much. It hurt very badly indeed, as if there was a red-hot iron bar in there. A heart attack? thought Thierry. The doctor had warned him: lose weight. But to die of a heart attack in a war. How stupid, thought Thierry, covered in cold sweat. How very stupid. Perhaps one can recover –

He tried to breathe. But his lungs were full of liquid. He coughed. Something poured out of his mouth.

Blood.

In front of him loomed the blank face of the blond Norman, Hugues. He was doing something to a knife. Cleaning it with a handful of chestnut leaves.

He stabbed me, thought Thierry, in a panic. With a knife. I may die.

He died.

The SS men in the armoured car stopped on the edge of the wood, and waited. The Gestapo were manoeuvring the third detector van into position, so the position of the radio could be pinpointed exactly. The terrorists could then be surrounded, and methodically crushed.

The SS men in the armoured car were ready to wait for as long as it took.

For there were rumours in circulation that made it sound very unwise to take any risks with these people. They had, it appeared, already accounted for almost a hundred men. The logical way of dealing with them was massive force. And massive force, thank God, was what was being applied to the problem.

The SS Obersturmführer was not like other men. He turned and watched scornfully as the grey straggles of soldiers marched doggedly up the mountain, and curled a lip. His men might welcome this great application of force. But it looked to the Obersturmführer like taking a sledgehammer to crack a nut. There were only five or six men, terrorists, Frenchmen, British: mongrels, members of inferior races. In the Obersturmführer's view, it was time to get them out of the way, and get on with the war.

At that point, five men walked out of the edge of the wood; or rather, four men walked, carrying a fifth on an improvised stretcher. Three of the walkers and the man on the stretcher were wearing British battledress. Behind them, walking at a safe distance, was a fat, dark man, holding a Schmeisser trained on his companions, with two more Schmeisser's slung round his neck. As planned, he was wearing a straw hat.

He looked up at the armoured car. His dark eyes took in the Obersturmführer's black uniform with the lightning-flashes on the collar of the tunic. He said, in heavily-accented German, 'Three English and two French bastards.'

The Obersturmführer allowed a clammy blue eye to rest on the man. He was disgustingly unshaven, and his clothes were too small and too wet. His accent sounded French, but not quite French. The Obersturmführer said, 'There were supposed to be six of them.'

'One of them is inside the mountain,' said the man in the straw hat. 'And ever more shall be so.'

'Good,' said the SS man. The chilly eyes flicked across the bedraggled group of Englishmen and their two French companions. He jumped down from the armoured car. 'Werner and Groen. Bring the Spandau. Altmeier, radio Search HQ and tell them that the problem has been dealt with.' He gazed clammily upon the prisoners. Herr Gruber, the Chief of the Gestapo in St-Jean-de-Luz, might want to interrogate them. But Herr Gruber was a civilian, an expert at pulling out women's fingernails; he knew very little about the wars fought between man and man. The Obersturmführer sniffed. There was only one cure for vermin. 'A clean death,' he said. 'It is probably more than you deserve. *Komm.*'

They set up the Spandau twenty-five yards away from the armoured car, pointing at a low cliff of limestone. Thirty or forty Wehrmacht soldiers in field-grey hung around, watching. 'Good,' said the Obersturmführer to the man in the straw hat. 'Now tell them to dig.'

'Dig?'

'Not too deep,' said the Obersturmführer. 'Thirty centimetres will suffice.'

Two SS men unstrapped spades from the back of the armoured car, and threw them at the men. Mallory began to dig. So did Hugues and Miller. Wallace, on his knees, picked feebly at the spongy soil. The Wehrmacht men looked disgusted, and began to drift away.

'Good,' said the Obersturmführer ten minutes later, contemplating the shallow pit. 'Tell them to undress.'

They undressed, slowly. The last of the soldiers in field-grey had gone. They hated the revolting tricks of the SS. A man who was a man could not watch this kind of thing. The execution party and its victims were alone under the birdsong and the dripping green trees by the little cliff at the margin of the wood.

There were the three men round the Spandau: the Obersturmführer, and two more SS. Facing them, white-skinned and goose-pimpled in the low sun, were the prisoners. Mallory said in German, 'What about a cigarette?'

The man in the straw hat said, 'Give them a cigarette.'

The Obersturmführer said, 'For a traitor, you are a generous man.'

The man in the straw hat walked across to Mallory, gave him a cigarette, and lit it for him. The Obersturmführer had a sudden feeling that there was something wrong with the transaction.

It was the last feeling he ever had about anything.

Because as the man in the straw hat lit the cigarette for the man with no clothes on, he must have passed over the Schmeisser as well. And suddenly the Schmeisser was firing a long burst at the Spandau crew, who seemed to make a sitting jump backwards and lay twitching, gazing at the sky with sightless eyes. That left the Obersturmführer, his Luger halfway out of his holster. The Schmeisser turned on him. The firing pin clicked on an empty chamber.

The Obersturmführer started to run.

He ran well for a man wearing breeches and jackboots, but not well enough for a man running for his life. Deliberately, Andrea reached into his belt and pulled out a knife. Silver flashed in the sun. The figure in the black uniform stopped running suddenly and collapsed in an untidy tangle of arms and legs. His cap rolled away and came to rest against a thistle. The breeze fluttered his close-cropped yellow hair.

Andrea pulled his knife from the nape of the Obersturmführer's neck and wiped it on the wet grass, waving away the flies that were buzzing over the wound. Already Mallory and Miller were stripping the uniforms from the bodies of the SS men. The Obersturmführer's uniform more or less fitted Mallory.

They tumbled the corpses into the graves they had dug for themselves. They drove back to the little valley and loaded the gear and Miller's boxes into the armoured car. Mallory sat bolt upright, head out of the turret, face grey and unshaven. 'Go,' he said.

Miller put his foot on the throttle. The armoured car jounced down the hill, through the remnants of the Wehrmacht force. The field-grey soldiers looked away. They knew what those Totenkopf bastards had been up to on the mountain.

Up on the edge of the wood the air was silent, except for the buzz of the flies over certain dark patches on the fresh-turned earth, and the whistle of a griffon vulture wheeling high between two clouds.

Down in the valley, the armoured car turned onto the pavé, and began to clatter officiously towards St-Jean-de-Luz.

FOUR

Monday 1900–Tuesday 0500

The inhabitants of St-Jean-de-Luz paid very little attention to an SS armoured car; they saw too many of them. Mallory stared straight ahead at the thickening houses. He said to Jaime, 'We need a safe place. Not a cave this time.'

Jaime nodded. On the outskirts of the town he said, 'Halt here.'

Miller turned the armoured car down a track, through a rusty iron gate with a chain and a padlock bearing a swastika seal. Jaime cut the chain, let them in, and hooked the broken links closed behind them.

Beyond the gate was a farmyard. It looked as if it had been abandoned in a hurry. The farmhouse windows were open, the remnants of shutters flapping in the breeze from the sea. The cattle-sheds were empty too. 'The Nazis took the people,' said Jaime. 'The men to forced labour. 'Later, the women were sheltering *résistants*. They also went. Nobody has come here since.'

Mallory walked round the place. It had an evil, septic smell. There was mouldy hay in the mangers and dried manure still in the cowshed gutters. In the house, the bedclothes were still on the beds, and in the kitchen a saucepan full of mould stood on the cold stove. It was like a house visited by a plague.

But Mallory was less interested in the house than in the exits. The exits were fine. The house stood in a grove of ilex in open fields, plentifully laced with deep, useful ditches. The nearest house was two hundred yards away; the wall it turned on the farm was blank and windowless. And best of all, they were behind an iron gate with an apparently unbroken Nazi seal.

They drove the armoured car into the barn and heaved the door shut. They sat on the broken chairs round the kitchen table and lit cigarettes, while the fleas from the floor attacked their ankles. The westering sun made yellow shafts in the curling smoke. Mallory could have slept for a year.

Hugues said, 'We must go to the café.'

Mallory nodded. Hugues' face was pouchy with exhaustion. Mallory wished he trusted him more. It would be dangerous in the café. He said, 'What if Lisette has talked?'

'If she has talked, she has talked,' said Hugues. 'That is a risk I will take.'

After Colbis, Mallory had begun to think of Hugues as a weak link. But then he had seen him run down Thierry, a Thierry screaming for help, about to break cover under the eyes of the Germans. It had been a nasty job, a job Mallory had been glad he had not had to do himself. Hugues had done it.

And under the one eye of the SS Spandau, standing by the graves they had dug themselves, it had been the same. Certainly, Hugues was frightened. But he was a man who had the courage to face down his fear. And that, in Mallory's book, was the true bravery.

But Hugues' courage was not the issue. The issue was to find out the whereabouts of Guy Jamalartégui.

I am sorry, thought Mallory. But brave or not, I cannot trust you, not one hundred per cent. Once you are out from under our eyes it will be too tempting to bargain for Lisette's life, and the life of your unborn child.

Mallory looked into the veil of smoke surrounding the head of Miller, sprawled in a chair with his boots on the table, and caught his eye. 'I'll go along,' said Miller. 'I could just about handle a drink.'

Ten minutes later they were walking towards the port of St-Jean-de-Luz. Miller made an improbably tall Frenchman, loping along in a black beret and a blue canvas workman's suit whose trousers flapped round his calves. He had found the clothes in a wardrobe at the farm. They stank of rats. His papers, however, had been supplied by SOE and were in order. Hugues was dressed in the sweater and corduroys in which he had clambered through the mountain, and another beret. They were dirty and unshaven. They were chewing raw garlic, and they had rubbed dirt into the cracks and scrapes on their hands. They were convincing peasants on their way from the fields to the café.

St-Jean-de-Luz could almost have been a town outside the war zone. The golden evening light held the particular sparkle that comes from proximity to large expanses of water. The inhabitants were out enjoying the weather. A dark-haired girl haughtily ignored Miller's wink. Miller sighed, and wished he had a cigarette. But all he had was blond tobacco, and smoking blond tobacco in this town would be like hauling up the Stars and Stripes and running out the guns.

The Café de l'Océan was strategically sited on the crossing of two narrow alleys in the Quartier Barre, north of the harbour. At the end of the alley Miller saw two grey-uniformed Germans with a motorcycle combination parked on the quay under a crowd of squalling gulls. They looked as if they were having a pleasant seaside smoke. Soon, an SS armoured car and six men would have failed to respond to signals enough times for there to be noise and fuss. But not, Miller devoutly hoped, too soon.

Outside the café, Hugues looked up and down the alley with the air of a conspirator in a bad play. 'Get in here,' said Miller, not unkindly, and shoved the door open for him.

The Café de l'Océan was a room twenty feet on a side, with a bar across the inside corner. It contained some thirty men, five women, and a fug of cigarette smoke. Two field-grey Germans were playing draughts at a table in the corner. Seeing them, Hugues stiffened like a pointer at a grouse. Miller knocked his arm and said, 'Camouflage.' He hoped he was right.

Hugues swallowed, his Adam's apple bobbing in his throat above the frayed collar of his shirt. He elbowed his way up to the bar, next to an elderly gentleman with a beret, a large grey moustache and red-and-yellow eyeballs. He said to the fat man behind the bar, 'A Cognac for me, and a Cognac for my friend the Admiral.'

The barman had eyes like sharp currants. *'L'Amiral Beaufort?'*

'That's the one.' A fine sheen of sweat glazed Hugues' pink-and-white features. The BBC had sent the password down the line. But it was always possible that something would have gone astray, that this impenetrable barman, whom he knew to be a *résistant,* would refuse to make the next link in the chain.

But that was all right, now.

The barman gave them the brandy, and scribbled a laborious bill with a stub of pencil. Hugues passed a glass to Miller, said, *'Salut,'* and looked at the bill. Pencilled on the paper were the words *Guy Jamalartégui – 7 Rue du Port, Martigny.* Hugues pulled money from his pocket and passed it to the barman with the bill. The barman put the money in the till, tore the bill into tiny fragments, and dropped the fragments in the wastepaper bin.

'*Bon,*' said Hugues. '*On s'en va?*'

Next to him, a voice said in a hoarse whisper, '*Vive la France!*'

Hugues' heart lurched in his chest. The voice belonged to the man with the grey moustache. He turned away.

'I saw the paper. He is a good man, Guy,' said the man with the moustache. His breath smelt like a distillery. 'A very good man. Permit me to introduce myself. I am Commandant Cendrars. Perhaps,' he said, 'you have heard of me?'

Hugues' eyes flicked to the Germans at their draughts game. He smiled, an agonised smile. 'Alas no,' he said. 'Excuse me –'

'*Croix de Guerre* at the Marne,' said the old man. 'A sword long sheathed, but still bright. And ready to be drawn again.' He put his head close to Hugues. A silence had fallen around him. Cendrars' alcoholic rasp was singularly penetrating, his attitude visibly conspiratorial. 'I am not the only one. There are others like me, waiting the moment. The moment which is arriving. Arriving even now. The great fight for the resurrection of France from under the Nazi heel. We are not Communists, *monsieur*. Nor are we Socialists, like the *résistants*. I trust you are not a Communist. *Non*. We are simple Frenchmen –'

'Excuse me,' said Hugues. 'It will soon be curfew.'

Cendrars said, with a significant narrowing of his orange eyes, 'In the mountains today, it is said that they killed six SS.'

The silence had become intense: a listening silence. Miller drained his glass, grabbed Hugues firmly by the arm, and marched him out into the alley. 'What was he saying?'

'Madness,' said Hugues. 'Stupid old bastard. Stupid old Royalist *con* –'

'No politics,' said Miller. 'Home, James.'

They started to walk.

Miller kept a little behind Hugues. He did not like this Cendrars. He liked even less the fact that the news about the killing of the SS on the mountain was already gossip in the town. Germans did not sit still and mourn dead SS men. There would be searches and reprisals –

In front of him, Hugues stopped dead. He was talking to someone: someone small, in a woollen hat and a big overcoat. He had thrown his arms round the small person, was embracing this person, making an odd baying noise that might have been laughing but sounded a lot more like crying. It was a weird and dreadful noise, the sort of noise guaranteed to attract attention. It caused

Miller to pull the beret down over his eyes and start his feet moving in a new direction.

Suddenly, the person said in French, 'For God's sake, shut up.' Hugues leaped back as if shot. His face was amazed, mouth open.

'Be a man,' said the small figure.

The small figure of Lisette.

Miller said, 'Hugues. We have to go.'

'You have to go,' said Lisette.

This is all we need, thought Miller.

Hugues stared at her. He did not understand the words she was saying. Through his tears of joy, her face looked luminous, like an angel's. He had forgotten he was a soldier. He was a man, and this woman was bearing his child. There was nothing else he needed to know. Now they could be happy for ever.

'Free,' he said.

'Correct,' said Lisette. 'Now for God's sake get moving.'

'Moving?'

Miller cleared his throat. Lisette looked as good as new. Not a mark on her. Eight months pregnant. Blooming with health.

That was bad. That was very bad.

Miller said, 'They told us that you were taken to Gestapo HQ in Bayonne.'

'I was,' said Lisette. She looked up and down the alleyway. It was empty, except for the deepening shadows of evening. 'They let me go. Because of the baby.'

Her face was the same as ever: pale, aquiline, with the dark-shadowed eyes and transparent skin of late pregnancy. This was not a woman who had been tortured.

Miller said, 'What happened, exactly?'

'They asked me what I knew, how I came to be in that village. I said I was visiting, that I knew nothing. They . . . well, they seemed to believe me. They said that a woman in my . . . condition would not tell them lies, out of respect for her unborn child.' Her face split in a white grin that sent the shadows scuttling for cover. 'Of course, I agreed.'

'Sure you did,' said Miller. 'How did you find us here?'

'I knew you were heading for St-Jean-de-Luz. It is a known thing that if you require information in St-Jean, you will find it in the Café de l'Océan.'

'Is it?' Miller did not like this. In fact, he hated it. No Gestapo man had ever been worried about an unborn child, let alone an unborn child whose mother had been apprehended in a raid on a Resistance stronghold. The only reason the Gestapo would have let Lisette out was so they could follow her to her friends.

Miller said, 'I have to go.'

'You?' said Hugues.

Miller said, 'We have a military operation here. It seems to me that this town is going to get real hot, real soon. And we have to be moving right along.'

'So Lisette accompanies us.'

Miller looked at him with a face grey as concrete, 'It is whoever has accompanied Lisette from Bayonne that gives me the problems.' He watched Hugues' face. He saw the frown, the struggle. He knew what the answer was going to be. Hugues had abandoned Lisette once in the name of duty. He would not do it again.

Lisette said, 'You must go.'

Hugues said, 'No.'

Miller turned away and started to walk, hands in pockets, stopping himself from running, keeping to a stolid peasant shuffle, heading towards the farmyard.

He heard footsteps behind him: one pair of short legs, one pair of long. In a pane of glass he saw their reflection. Hugues had his arm round Lisette's shoulders and an agonised expression on his face. The steps slowed and halted. Miller walked on, faster, heading for the edge of town.

God damn it, thought Miller. Hugues had seen the address pencilled on the bill at the Café de l'Océan. And it would not take the Germans long to get it out of him.

It was a mess. A five-star, copper-bottomed, stinking Benghazi nine-hole latrine of a father and mother of a mess.

The houses were thinning. A truck engine clattered on the road ahead. Miller faded gently off the verge and into some bushes. A lorryload of soldiers rolled by, blank-faced under their coal-scuttle helmets. Hugues and Lisette had not jumped into the hedge. The lorry stopped alongside them with a wheeze of brakes. An officer climbed down from the cab. Miller heard him bark, *'Papiers?'*

In Miller's pocket was an identity card, work permit, ration card, tobacco card, frontier zone permit, and a medical certificate signed by a Doctor Lebayon of Pau explaining that chronic lumbago had prevented him from being deported to Germany as a forced labourer. Miller derived a certain sense of security from carrying them, but he knew that a detailed cross-examination about his maternal uncles or the colour of Doctor Lebayon's beard would scupper him, quick.

He hoped that Hugues and Lisette were in the sort of mental state that permitted clear thinking. He doubted it.

Quiet as a shadow, he slid away through the bushes. Ten minutes later, he was back in the farmyard.

Mallory said, 'Where's Hugues?'

Miller told him.

Mallory lit a cigarette. Then he dropped it on the floor and stamped it out, and shouldered into his webbing. 'We're off,' he said.

'Off where?' said Miller.

'Martigny.'

'What if they talk?'

'They talk,' said Mallory. 'The Germans will react. If they don't react, nobody's talked.'

And if they do, thought Miller, gloomily, we're dead.

Again.

There was a peak in the Southern Alps that had done this to him: Mount Capps, a treacherous peak, full of crevasses and rotten rock, its upper slopes decorated with snow fields that in the morning sun fired salvoes of boulders and later in the day became loose on their foundations and came slithering down like tank regiments, roaring and trailing plumes of pulverised rock and ice.

Mallory had left his base camp on the third day of the climb, leaving Beryl and George, his companions, waiting. He had bivouacked in the lee of a huge rock, halfway up an ice field, and spent a cold, restless night among the cracks and booms of the refreezing ice.

He had woken at four, and gone out. The sky had been clear, the peak of Mount Capps a peaceful pyramid of pink-tinged sugar icing over whose slopes Venus hung like a silver ball. It was a beautiful morning.

Mallory had walked ten feet away from the tent, into the cover of the rocks he used as his lavatory. He dropped his trousers.

A rumble came from the mountain. Feathers of snow fluttered away from the rocks. The rumble became a roar. He looked back at his tent.

A fifty-foot wall of snow and ice and rock thundered across his field of vision. It must have been moving at two hundred miles an hour. The icy breath of its passage slammed him against the rocks.

Ears ringing, he dragged himself back on his feet.

In the tent had been his pack, with spare ropes, food, extra clothes, sleeping bag.

The tent was gone. In its place was a deep, rubble-filled scar in the mountainside. All he had left was the rope he had taken to the rocks, his ice axe, and the fact that he had been climbing mountains since his tenth birthday.

Mallory buckled his trousers. Beryl and George were down there, waiting for him. They had spent six weeks planning this expedition. Nobody had ever climbed the southeast face of Mount Capps.

Mallory had thought at four o'clock that December morning, nine thousand feet above sea level: Beryl and George and the rest of the team are counting on you. It is not just your life. You have responsibilities. So you get killed going up. On this mountain you are just as likely to get killed going down. Three hours to the summit, then nine hours to base camp.

If you are going to die, you might as well die advancing as die retreating.

So he had shouldered his single coil of rope and his ice axe, and made it back to base camp in eight hours.

Via the summit.

The papers had said he was a hero. As far as Mallory was concerned, he had done the job, and not let the team down, and that was enough.

And now the team were out there on the south coast of England, hundreds of thousands strong, waiting to embark on the transports.

It was a job with risks. But that did not make it any less of a job.

They left quickly across the fields, Andrea carrying Wallace. There had been very little sleep: enough to make men groggy and dazed, but not enough for anything approaching rest. As they tramped through the orchards and fields of young corn it was raining again, and a blustery wind clattered branch against branch.

The town lay in darkness under the evening sky. Night fell as Jaime led them round its southern fringes, crossing darkened roads, climbing a couple of low ridges and scrambling down terraces. Engines were roaring in St-Jean-de-Luz. On the other side of the bay the Germans were moving, there was no way of telling where, or who against. All they could do was hope that the movements had nothing to do with Hugues and Lisette.

One step at a time.

'Wait here,' said Jaime.

They had arrived on a cobbled lane that headed steeply down-hill. At the bottom of the lane water flexed like a sheet of metal.

Jaime drifted off into the dark.

Mallory said, 'Andrea. Recce?'

Andrea put Wallace down behind a wall, in what might have been a potato patch, and gently pressed a Schmeisser into his hand. Wallace's head was buzzing with fever and morphine. At first, he had thought that these people were SOE bunglers, rank amateurs. Now he had changed his mind, or what was left of it. They were the coolest, most matter-of-factly competent team he had ever met up with. It was something that he would never have admitted to himself if he had been a well man. But frankly, they were a lot better than any SAS he had ever seen.

Think rugby. Think of a team that has trained itself not by run-ning up and down the pitch and practising, but by playing first-class matches, and winning. Team spirit was for children. These men were in a different league.

Wallace wanted to live up to their standards. But it was hard to know how. He knew enough about wounds to know he was bad; really bad. Behind the morphine he was cold, except for the big, throbbing lump in his stomach. The lump seemed to be getting bigger, sending sickly fingers of poison into the rest of his body. Should have rested it, he thought. Should have stayed in the brothel.

But staying in the brothel would have meant a German bullet, probably with torture first.

There had been torture, bouncing along those dark, wet passages underground, metal twisting in his belly, burning up with fever, all those weeks – was it only hours? – ago. But it was a torture you could come through, if you were one of a team of grown men.

Hell of a life. Wallace felt the fever-taut skin of his face stretch in a grin. You think you're doing fine in the children's team, with the bombs and the Jeeps and the old gung ho. Then you get into the men's team, and for a minute or two you feel like a man.

And after that, what?

Andrea went quietly over the back garden walls of the village. Somewhere a dog began to bark. Soon all the dogs were barking. In one of the houses a man flung open a window and swore. A light drizzle fell. At the base of the hill – more a cliff, really – the sea shifted silver under the sky.

But for the lack of lights, it could have been peacetime. Somewhere in Andrea's mind there appeared the memory of a wedding, long tables with bottles, laughter and tobacco smoke rising into the hot Aegean night, the moon coming up out of deep blue water. This place could have been like that. And would be again.

But the memory was small, as if seen through the wrong end of a telescope, shrunk not by lenses, but by years of war. It was suffocated by the picture of his parents' bodies, bloodless on the shingle bank of the river. It was suffocated by a choir of death-grunts, and hundreds of night-stalks on which Andrea had not been a full colonel in the Greek army – had hardly indeed been human; had been a huge, lethal animal with a mind full of death.

Andrea slid over the last of the garden walls, and walked across the field that led to the edge of the low cliff. There was a jetty at the bottom of the village, a crook of stone quay in whose shelter a couple of dinghies shifted uneasily on outhaul moorings.

The rain swished gently down. Andrea watched, patient as stone. And was rewarded.

Down there in the lee of a shed at the root of the quay, a match flared, illuminating a face under the sharp-cut brim of a steel helmet, silhouetting a second helmet.

The rain fell. The dogs were still barking. Andrea returned the way he had come.

Mallory, Miller and Jaime were already under the wall.

'Pillbox on the hill opposite,' said Mallory. 'Covers the harbour.'

'Two sentries,' said Andrea. 'On the quay. No pillbox this side.'

'No soldiers in the village,' said Miller. 'This Guy's house is the third house up from the quay.'

'Bring Wallace,' said Mallory.

The dogs were still barking as the five of them went over three walls and came to the back of a cottage. A dog lunged at Andrea, yelling with rage. Andrea laid a great paw on its head and spoke quietly to it in Greek: soothing, earthy words, the words of a man used to working with animals. The dog fell silent. Very quickly, Mallory opened the back door. Miller and Jaime were well into the room before the man at the table even realised they were there.

He was small and thin, with a bald, brown head, a much-broken nose and crooked yellow teeth. There was a spoon in his right hand, a wedge of bread in his left. He was eating something out of a bowl.

He looked up, mouth hanging open, eyes shifting, looking for ways of escape and finding none. He took a deep breath, and prepared to speak.

'We are friends of Admiral Beaufort,' said Jaime. 'Monsieur Guy Jamalartégui?'

The black eyes narrowed. The mouth closed and recommenced chewing. The head nodded. The mouth said, 'Have you brought the money?'

'We have.'

Jamalartégui said, 'There are a lot of you. Only one person will speak at a time. There are Germans.'

'Four in the pillbox. Two on the quay,' said Mallory. 'Is that all?'

Jamalartégui nodded. 'Unless we get a patrol.' He looked vaguely impressed. Andrea laid Wallace in a chair by the stove. Wallace was breathing badly. His face was bluish-white.

For a moment there was silence, except for the wheeze of the cooking range and the rattle of rain against the windows. There was a smell of garlic and tomatoes, wine and wood smoke.

'Jaime,' said Mallory. 'Interpret.'

Jamalartégui dug thick glass tumblers and bowls out of the cupboard by the range, and spread them on the table. 'The Germans steal the meat,' he said. 'But there are eggs, and many fish in the sea.' He got up, and threw onions, peppers and eggs into a frying pan. The room filled with the smell. *'Piperade,'* he said.

Then there was silence.

Mallory ate until he could eat no more. Then he mopped his plate with bread and refilled his wine glass. He said to Jaime, 'Tell him he has some information for me.'

'I am a poor fisherman,' said Jamalartégui, after Jaime had spoken. 'One does not eat without paying.'

'What is a meal, without conversation?' said Jaime. Mallory did not understand the words, but he understood the tone of voice. He reached into his pack, took out the watertight box, and opened it. In the dim yellow light of the oil lamp it was packed with sheets of white paper, bearing a copperplate inscription and the signature of Mr Peppiatt, Chief Cashier of the Bank of England. 'One thousand pounds,' said Mallory. 'For the information, and transport to the site.'

The old man's eyes rested on the five-pound notes. They glittered. He opened his mouth to haggle. 'Take it or leave it,' said Mallory.

'I take half now,' said Guy, through Jaime.

'No.'

'Perhaps you will not like the information I will give you.'

'We shall see. Now talk.'

'How do I know –'

Mallory stiffened in his chair. 'Tell him that it is the duty of a British officer not to abuse the hospitality of an ally.'

Jaime spoke. Guy shrugged. Mallory watched him. This was the moment: the crucial moment, when they would know whether they were on a military operation or a wild-goose chase. The moment for which many people had died.

There was a silence that seemed to last for hours. Mallory found he was holding his breath.

Finally, Guy said, *'Bien.'* Mallory let his breath out. Guy began to talk.

'It is like this,' said Jaime, when he had finished. 'He has seen these submarines. They are at a place called San Eusebio.'

In his mind, Mallory searched the map. The coast of France south of Bordeaux was straight and low-lying: a hundred and fifty miles of beach, continuously battered by a huge Atlantic surf. The only ports of refuge were Hendaye, St-Jean-de-Luz, Bayonne, Capbreton and Arcachon: all shallow, all unsatisfactory for three gigantic submarines. He did not remember seeing any San Eusebio on the map. So we have been looking in the wrong place, he thought. All those people have died in vain.

He said, 'Where's that?'

'Fifty kilometres from here.' Mallory felt the blood course once again through his veins. All they needed to do was pinpoint the place and call in an air strike. The bombers would do the rest. Even if the submarines were in hardened pens – unlikely, or he would have heard of them – there were the new earthquake bombs –

'In Spain,' said Jaime.

Mallory felt cool air in his mouth. His jaw was hanging open. He said, 'Spain is a neutral country.'

Jaime's dark Basque face was impassive. He shrugged. 'But that is where they are. To be in a neutral country could be a convenience, *hein?* And Franco and Hitler are both of them Fascists, *c'est pareil.'*

Mallory said, 'Neutral is neutral.'

'But submarines are submarines,' said Andrea, quietly.

And as he so often did, Andrea made everything clear in Mallory's mind.

For a moment he was not in this fisherman's cottage, with the gale nudging the tiles, and the stove hissing, and the sentries on the quay and the pillbox on the hill. He was back in that briefing room in the villa on the square at Termoli, hot and cool at the same time, tracing the veins in the marble of the columns. It had sounded like a throw-away line then: *You'll be absolutely on your own,* Jensen had said.

But of course, that was what Jensen had to say. Jensen could not order an operation against a neutral country.

There would be no RAF. No support of any kind. The Storm Force was absolutely on its own.

'What the hell is this about?' said Miller.

'We get to blow up some submarines,' said Mallory. 'Very, very quietly.'

'Oh,' said Miller, with the air of a man saved from a great disappointment. 'Is that right? I thought maybe Spain being nootral and all, you know? Fine.'

Mallory poured himself more wine, and lit a cigarette. It was at times like this that he knew he would never be anything but a simple soldier. Jensen had stuck knives between German ribs, and slipped bromide in the wine of Kapitän Langsdorff of the pocket battleship *Graf Spee* the night before she was scuttled. But he was also a diplomat; it was rumoured that he had been offered the crown of Albania, and to many Bedouin chieftains he was the official voice of the British Empire.

This business bore all the hallmarks of Jensen at his devious best. And perhaps the imprint of another hand, more powerful, normally seen clamped round a huge Havana cigar.

Spain's neutrality was at best idiosyncratic. Twenty thousand Spaniards were fighting for Hitler on the Russian Front. The German consulate in Tangier – a Spanish possession – monitored Allied shipping movements in the Straits of Gibraltar. And Spanish wolfram provided a vital raw material for German steelworks.

But the British ambassador in Madrid, Sir Samuel Hoare, was prepared to ignore all this hostile activity in the name of keeping lines of communication open. He had set his face firmly against SOE operations in Spain, for fear of being compromised.

So Hoare would have been kept in the dark about the Storm Force. This operation was not just to prevent a repaired Werwolf pack carving a terrible swathe through an invasion fleet in the

Channel. It was to send a signal over Hoare's head to Franco. To tell the Spanish dictator that the Allies knew just how far he was bending the rules, and to give him an object lesson as to the kind of thing he could expect if the rule-bending continued.

As long as Storm Force achieved its objectives.

If it failed . . .

Mallory lit another cigarette, and tried not to think of being paraded through the streets of Madrid as a saboteur, an infringer of the rights of a neutral state.

Out of the question.

Damn you, Captain Lord Nelson Jensen.

He ground out his cigarette in his wine glass. He said, 'We'll be needing a map.'

Hugues and Lisette had been having a difficult evening. The inspection of their papers by the roadside had passed off well enough: the Germans seemed to be in too much of a hurry for more than a perfunctory cross-examination of an obviously pregnant woman and her lover. There was, after all, a dead SS patrol in the mountains, and justice to be done.

But Hugues was rattled. Was it possible that Lisette was a traitor? Knowingly, no. Unknowingly . . . yes, it was possible.

Hugues made his decision. The operation must continue without them. He took Lisette by the arm. They turned back, towards the middle of town. They had been a pair of lovers out for a stroll, and had been overtaken by the rain and the approaching curfew. What could be more natural than that they should now head home?

'Where do we go?' said Lisette.

Hugues forced a smile. 'To make contact with our other friends,' he said.

So they walked back to the Café de L'Océan, and Lisette sat gratefully at a table while Hugues ordered two *coups de rouge*, and wondered what the hell they did next.

The café had emptied out. It was blowing half a gale now, and flurries of wind agitated the puddles in the road leading down to the port. But the Commandant was still at the bar, speaking in a low, warlike voice to the barman, who was looking sceptical. He glanced round at Hugues, caressed his strawberry nose at Lisette, and returned to his conversation.

A hundred metres away, on the quay, two men in raincoats were talking quietly in German. 'She went in,' one of them said. 'The man with her.'

'Did she make any other contacts?'

'Not that I saw. I lost her for twenty minutes.'

'Scheisse,' said the taller of the two men. 'It'll be curfew in a moment, and we'll lose her completely. I think it is time to start our hare.'

'Pardon?'

'Flush her out, and see where she runs.'

'Ah.'

They walked into the house of M. Walvis, the undertaker, who was a nark for the Milice, the Vichy police. The taller of the two picked up the telephone and jiggled the cradle. When the operator answered, the man said in his heavily-accented French, 'Give me the garrison commander.'

There was a pause while the switchboard operator plugged him in on her board. Then a harsh German voice said, *'Wer da?'*

'Café de l'Océan,' said the man. 'Immediately.' He hung up.

The garrison commander hung up too. At the telephone exchange, the operator released the breath she had been holding while she listened to the conversation, and reached for her plugs.

Two minutes later, the telephone at the Café de l'Océan rang. A woman's voice said, 'Fire at the Mairie.'

'Merde,' said the man behind the bar. *'Les boches arrivent.'*

Hugues had been expecting this moment, he realised. But now that it was upon him, he was paralysed. Being with those soldiers had taken away his willpower.

Not that willpower was any help, in a situation like this.

He stood irresolute, sweating. 'Lisette,' he said. 'Hide yourself.'

'No need,' said the barman, wiping his fat hands on his gigantic apron. 'Our friend in the telephone exchange gives us ten minutes' warning.' He poured himself a small Cognac. 'Drink?'

The Commandant twirled his moustache, and accepted a Cognac for himself. 'At moments like this,' he said, 'it is vital to steady the nerves.'

Hugues was beside himself. *'Non,'* he said. Was this walrus-faced cretin seriously proposing to sit here and wait to be shot? These were *résistants*. If Lisette was found in their company, she would be arrested again. And there was the matter of his papers. His papers would never stand up under detailed scrutiny –

A roaring and clanging sounded in the street outside. With a squeal of tyres, an ancient fire engine skidded to a halt on the cobbles. The Commandant finished his drink and said, 'All aboard!' Leaping into the passenger seat, he clapped a huge brass helmet on his head.

'*Allez-y,*' said the barman.

Hugues stared at him. The barman made shooing movements with his fat hands. '*Vite,*' he said. Lisette's hand grasped Hugues'. 'Come,' she said. The Commandant was beckoning with arthritic sweeps of his arm. She hustled Hugues out and into the cab. The fire engine took off.

There seemed to be seven or eight other men on the engine, all elderly. 'Where are we going?' said Hugues to the Commandant.

'The hour has come,' said the Commandant. 'We go to assist our friends the English.'

'No,' said Hugues. 'You must not.'

'And why?' roared the Commandant, alcoholically. 'Every man on this engine has fought for *la patrie* at the Marne. We are ready to fight and die. For the glory of France. Not for your damned Lenin, *nom d'un nom –*'

Hugues said, 'It must be said that I am not a Leninist.' Stupid old man, he was thinking. Café firebrand –

'Sir,' said the Commandant, drawing himself up. 'I am a soldier. We are all soldiers, and we are fighting an honest war, face to face with the enemy, honourably, not hole-in-corner. Seventy men, hand-picked, will at dawn be rallying to the house of Guy Jamalartégui. The time has come.'

Hugues opened his mouth to tell him that he should keep his childish fantasies to himself. But Lisette got there before him. She said in a conciliatory voice, 'You cannot do this.'

The Commandant raised a hoary eyebrow that fluttered with the speed of the hurtling engine. 'Cannot? Madame, I must tell you that at the Marne, I and thirty of my comrades held our redoubt for three days against a regiment of Boches. Nothing has changed.'

'*Mon Commandant,*' said Lisette. 'I will place confidence in you. What I am about to tell you is of the highest importance, a great secret.' The parts of the Commandant's face not concealed by the slipstream-whipped expanses of his moustache were pinkening with pleasure. 'You will endanger an important Allied mission.'

'My little cabbage, I thank you,' said the Commandant. 'I accept your secret. Do not bother your pretty head with it further. And if you please, Mademoiselle, do not speak to me of fighting and other things you do not understand. A woman's place is in the bedroom and the kitchen.' He pinched her cheek. 'Leave this to the men.'

The crack of Lisette's palm on his ear was audible even over the sound of the bell. '*Vieux con!*' she said. 'Buffoon! At least do not arrive in your stupid fire engine.'

'*Monsieur,*' said Hugues. 'This lady has only this morning escaped the clutches of the Gestapo, while you have been in the café since lunchtime.'

The fire engine was bowling along the southern side of the port. It was raining. From some secret locker in the back, one of the ex-*poilus* had hauled out rifles of ancient design. 'We also fight, who sit in the café,' said the Commandant sulkily, rubbing his ear. On the far side of the harbour, a few fishing boats were tied up at the town quay. Behind them, two large grey trucks were moving through the twilight.

'Look,' said Hugues, pointing. 'They are following us. I beg you. You are endangering this British operation. Secrecy is vital –'

The Commandant said, as if scoring a debating point, 'It is you that they are following.'

Lisette said, '*Mon Commandant*, the end result will be the same.'

'I will not skulk,' said the Commandant. 'I am not listening to you.'

The road left the shore and began to wind uphill between small houses. '*Bien,*' said Lisette, between clenched teeth. 'In that case, there is only one solution.' She reached forward, twitched the key from the fire engine's ignition, and flung it as far as she could into the bushes that lined the road.

'Now run,' said Lisette.

She jumped from the cab. Hugues went after her. She ran well, for a woman who was eight months pregnant. My God, thought Hugues, this is certainly a remarkable woman. He had never loved her as much as he loved her then.

For they were free, she and he. She had left the Commandant, that old fool of a Commandant, to divert the pursuit. The Commandant would get himself killed, and the knowledge of Guy Jamalartégui's address would die with him. And he and Lisette and their child could go to Rue du Port in Martigny, safe from pursuit, and reunite themselves with the English. And Lisette and the child would be safe again.

War was war. But Lisette was what mattered.

It was getting dark; it was after curfew, and the port of Martigny would certainly be guarded. But what other option was there?

At the top of the hill he paused and looked back the way they had come. Three broad-bottomed veterans of the Marne were head down in the bushes, looking for the keys. Beside him, Lisette was making a peculiar sound, as if she was weeping.

But she was not weeping. She was laughing.

Hugues took her hand and started walking uphill at a brisk clip. After five minutes there was firing behind them. Good, thought Hugues. So far, so good.

'Nice place,' said Dusty Miller. 'Sea views. Sheltered bathing.'

They were looking at an Admiralty chart spread out on the scrubbed pine planks of the kitchen table of Guy Jamalartégui. It showed a coastline, steep-to, indented with small, stony coves exposed to the huge bight of the Bay of Biscay. But in the centre of that stretch of coast was something different.

In the times when the world was molten and rocks flowed like water, a huge geyser of liquid stone had forced itself through and at an angle to the other strata. Now, that great irruption of granite formed a peninsula that flung a protecting arm round the bay of San Eusebio. The arm was marked Cabo de la Calavera.

At its entrance, the bay was not more than a hundred yards wide; but inside, it broadened into a two-mile oval of water, deepening to twenty fathoms. The village of San Eusebio was on the landward side of the bay. On the tip of the peninsula, the chart said FORTALEZA: fortress. Below the fortress were buildings, with a note that said CHIMNEY CONSPIC.

'There is a fort overlooking the entrance to the harbour,' said Guy, through Jaime. 'The Germans have put new guns. There is a magazine in the fort, well defended, *vous voyez*, I suppose for the ammunition of the guns and the torpedoes of the U-boats. Also, there is a line of fortifications here.' He put a cracked and filthy thumb across the neck of the peninsula at its narrowest point. 'This is the only way onto the Cabo. There are ancient fortifications, originally against the Arabs, and now also new ones from the Germans, I think. To seaward, the cliffs are high. The land slopes from the seaward side towards the harbour, so that there is a beach of sand looking across towards the town. On this beach there is much barbed wire, and a quantity of mines. These defences run from the inland end of the fortifications along to the buildings of the old sardine factory. There are also two merchant ships in the harbour, which arrived with supplies, ostensibly from Uruguay. These ships discharged their cargo at the fish factory quays. Now they are anchored off the factory. They have many machine guns on their decks, to cover the waters of the harbour.'

'So where are the U-boats?'

Guy shrugged. 'This is a very big fish factory,' he said. 'There was an American, a Basque who made a lot of money in the Pacific salmon fishing, and wanted to help his home town. He built four quays, with a dry dock, and many boats, and wanted to make a big sardine fishery. Naturally, it failed. There were not enough sardines in those years, or ever, on that scale: this was a madman, an American, need one say more? But the buildings are there still. It is a perfect place to make repairs on a ship, or a submarine, *bien entendu.*' He drew with a matchstick, extending a puddle of red wine on the table. He drew four quays like the tines of a fork, forming three bays parallel to the shore. The innermost quay ran along the base of the rock. On the crosspiece connecting the tines, he hatched in a group of sheds. 'There are the quays, the buildings, even the cranes. And it is an easy place to defend.'

Mallory's eyes rested on the chart and the spidery puddle of wine beside it. It was indeed an easy place to defend; and a difficult one to attack. But there were glimmers of light. The brightest was the fact that it was in a neutral country. He said, 'What size is the garrison?'

Guy shrugged. 'It is not a good place to visit, to count soldiers. Perhaps five hundred. Some Wehrmacht. A certain number of SS. The crew from the U-boats. And the technicians, the dockyard people who make the repairs. They came in from Germany, they say, on these so-called Uruguayan ships in the harbour. Perhaps two thousand men in total. They are under the command of a man of importance. A man with a black uniform, I am told. A general, I think; or an admiral. SS or Kriegsmarine, nobody could tell me.'

'They get their supplies from the ships,' said Mallory. 'Where do they get their power?'

'They brought it with them,' said Guy. 'Behind the *fortaleza* is a little town of wooden huts where the men live. Between the huts and the *fortaleza* is a building that was once the laundry. Now they have installed many diesels, with generators. Naturally, it is heavily guarded. There is also a magazine, in a cave in the rock.'

Andrea had been sitting back in his chair, eyes closed, as if asleep. Now he said, 'You know a lot about this place, *monsieur.* How?'

'My friends work on the fishing boats out of San Eusebio. They tell me.'

'There is still fishing at San Eusebio?'

'But naturally,' said Guy. 'It is a port in a neutral country. There is a railway, to take the fish to San Sebastian. The town, it was destroyed by the Fascists. But the quay is a good quay. And the customs . . . well, there is always a need for money, so close to the border.'

Andrea said, 'What does that mean?'

'There are those who have business with the inhabitants. Business not strictly legal, and for which the cooperation of the customs is important.'

Jaime cleared his throat. 'This I know to be true,' he said.

'You know this place?' said Andrea.

'In the course of business,' said Jaime. 'I did not know about these submarines, of course. For me, it was only a useful harbour for cigarettes, wine, commodities of this kind. There was only a little of the town left standing, after these Fascist bastards had finished with it. I have business contacts there.'

'Had,' said Guy.

'*Pardon?*'

'You are speaking of Juanito,' said Guy. 'It was Juanito who told me all these things. Two months ago.'

'I was last at San Eusebio four months ago,' said Jaime, his eyes on Andrea. He was deeply conscious of what Andrea could do to a traitor. He wished passionately for Andrea to be quite certain that he was not holding out on him.

Andrea nodded. He said, 'This knowledge will be useful.'

'*Bon,*' said Guy. 'So Juanito was found on the Cabo. He had been there two, three times before. This time he was selling Cognac to the troops. The Germans caught him. They hanged him from the top of the *fortaleza*. He is still there, what the gulls have left of him. On the flagpole. *Pour encourager les autres.*' His eyes strayed to the tin of bank notes. 'So this is a dangerous game.'

Andrea nodded, his great neck creasing and uncreasing like a seal's. 'In war,' he said, 'there is unfortunately a great deal of danger.'

There was silence, except for the sough of the wind in the tiles. The Frenchmen seemed improbably interested in their hands. Andrea's presence occupied the room like a ticking bomb. Mallory waited. This was the crucial moment: the moment when the running stopped, and the troops had a chance to draw breath and reflect; reflect on the fact that now they had deliberately and with their eyes open to walk out over the abyss, and jump. The time for hot blood was passing. The time for cold blood had begun.

Mallory let Andrea's presence sink in for a moment, as he had done so many times in so many small, hushed rooms these last eighteen months. When the silence had gone on long enough, he said, 'And the seaward defences?'

The change of subject earthed the tension in the room like a lightning rod. Guy laughed, a short, scornful laugh. 'Round the quays they have put anti-submarine nets. Beyond the nets are the cliffs,' he said. 'Eighty metres. And at the bottom of the cliffs, the sea, with waves that come all the way from America.'

'No fortifications?'

Guy's eyebrows rose under his beret. He smiled, the smile of a man who has the welcome sensation that he is once more on familiar ground. *'Mon Capitaine,'* he said. 'With such cliffs and such seas, fortifications are not necessary. Only four months ago, Didier Jaulerry was blown onto the base of the cliff, under the fortifications. He drowned, with his crew. His boat is still there, what is left of it. You can see it at half-tide.'

Mallory nodded. He said, 'What time of tide was it when he went ashore?'

'High water. A spring tide.'

'And the boat is still there, you say.'

Guy's mouth opened and closed again. *'Monsieur.* You are not –'

Mallory did not seem to hear him. He was looking at the chart, rubbing the stubble on his chin with a meditative thumb. At its narrowest, the neck of the peninsula was no more than a hundred yards wide. It would unquestionably be fortified.

'What are the cliffs made of?' he said.

'Granite,' said Guy. 'But rotten granite. Many birds nest there.'

'And at the bottom of the cliff?'

Guy looked at him as if he was mad. 'Rocks. The sea. A big sea, with big waves. Listen,' he said. 'If I were you, I would think about the town. It is destroyed, this town. I told you. In the Civil War, the Republicans held out there. The Fascists burned everything. So there are not too many people, and those who remain live like rats in the ruins. No food, no water. Now that would be your place to land. If you could pass the fortifications in the harbour, you could make an attack . . .'

Guy fell into an uncomfortable silence. These men gave him the idea that he said too much, too lightly; that he was a child in the presence of his elders, babbling. 'So,' said Mallory, finally. 'Your boat.'

Guy's eyes moved to the flat tin box of bank notes under Mallory's hand.

'You will be paid as we land,' said Mallory.

'But, *monsieur* –'

'These are the conditions. And of course, you will be inspired by the idea that you are helping make a world in which it will be possible to spend this money.'

'*Ah, ça,*' said Guy, shrugging with a smuggler's realism. War was part of politics. Money was money; money was different.

'Agreed?'

'Agreed.'

'When can we leave?' Mallory watched him with his cool, steady brown eyes.

Guy was not an impressionable man. But he found himself thinking, thank God this one is not my enemy. 'There will be water in the harbour at four o'clock,' he said. 'The sentries do not pay big attention then. The hour will be too early, the port too small. They will be half-asleep. Be in hiding near the quay. When it is time for you to come aboard, I will show lights for five seconds, by accident.'

'And if there are Germans watching?' said Andrea.

Guy smiled, a weary smile, the smile of a man who has already gone further than he intended and sees no way of getting back to safety. 'I am sure you will know what to do with them,' he said. 'And once you are aboard . . . well, we are a fishing boat. We are one hour from the border here. I shall fly the Spanish ensign. The Germans will respect a neutral flag on the high seas, in territorial waters. It is not the same as the things that happen in secret on the Cabo de la Calavera.'

Andrea nodded. Guy was glad he had nodded.

'Thank you,' said Mallory, and reached for the bottle of wine. From the direction of St-Jean-de-Luz there came the sound of gunfire, mingled with explosions. Mallory lay back in his chair and listened to the clatter of the rain on the roof, the bluster of the gale at the windows, and closed his eyes. Miller and Jaime were already snoring; Wallace was quiet. The gusts seemed to be losing their force, becoming more widely separated. Miller will be happy about that, thought Mallory. And so will I. Miller hated the sea as much as Mallory hated confined spaces. Mallory did not hate it, but he did not understand it, and did not want to –

Then he was asleep.

When he woke up, it was dark. He had been asleep for no longer than four hours, by the taste in his mouth and the ache of his head. There was a voice in the darkness near him: Andrea's voice.

Andrea said, 'There are people outside.'

Knuckles rapped the door. A voice said, *'L'Amiral Beaufort.'* Hugues' voice.

Guy said, *'Entrez.'*

Hugues came in. Lisette was with him. She looked round at the grey, fleshless faces, pouched and deep-shadowed in the yellow lamplight. She said, *'Bonjour.'*

'Bonjour,' said Mallory, urbane and polite.

There was a silence.

Finally Hugues said, 'Miller has told you, I think. Lisette was released. We have evaded pursuit. For some hours we have been hiding in a barn above the village. I kept watch. You can see the road from there. Nobody approached. The Germans have lost sight of us.'

Mallory rested his head on the back of the chair. Hugues looked pale and nervous. Lisette was holding his hand. 'There was shooting,' said Mallory.

'The Commandant and his men,' Hugues explained. 'They are clever, those ones; clever and stupid, at the same time. They will occupy the Germans.'

Mallory nodded. Once again, he had the feeling that events were moving beyond his control. But at least Guy's boat was a means of getting them back in hand.

The wind had become a series of squalls now. Between the squalls there was calm, except for the distant rustle of the sea.

'Guy,' he said, as if he were proposing a game of tennis. 'I think it is time you went to fetch your boat. And the rest of us should move out of here. How long?'

Guy said, 'I could be alongside in half an hour. There will not be much water. But maybe there will be enough.' He pulled a large, tarnished watch from the pocket of his greasy waistcoat. 'At four-thirty.' He cleared his throat. 'As I said, it will be important for you to be discreet.'

'Zat right?' said Miller.

'Monsieur,' said Guy. 'I assure you. The sentries may be sleepy, but they make reports at five minutes to every hour, via a field telephone. I suggest you be very careful.' Guy smiled, a nervous, perfunctory smile. He slid out of the back door and into the night.

Mallory looked at his watch. It was half-past two. Once again he was in a room, with his back to the sea, relying on other people to get him out of trouble. He hoped it would be the last time. He said to Andrea, 'Bring Wallace. We'll get out of here.'

Hugues said, 'What will you do about the Commandant?'

Mallory had the sensation that he had not slept enough. He said, 'The Commandant?'

'The Commandant will be arriving before dawn, he said. With seventy men.'

'The Commandant was drunk,' said Lisette.

Hugues sighed. 'I know this Commandant,' he said. 'He will arrive at dawn.'

Wallace said, 'You'll have a rearguard then.'

Lisette said, 'Commanded by the Commandant? You're crazy.'

Wallace said, 'The Commandant is retired. I am a serving officer. I'll take command.'

Mallory turned his head, and looked at the papery face, the glassy, fever-bright eyes.

'I'm not up to a ride in a boat, sir,' said Wallace. 'Maybe one of these chaps can get me to Spain when the fuss dies down.'

Jaime said, 'It is possible. Certainly, these old fools need orders. But *monsieur* cannot stay in Guy's house. The Boche will destroy it.'

'Hold on,' said Mallory. 'Seventy men arriving at dawn?'

'Commanded by a drunk,' said Hugues.

Mallory looked at Wallace. He would be no good in a boat. His only hope was to rest, and get over the border later, in discreet silence.

Mallory said, 'We will send you the Commandant. We will tell him that you are his commanding officer. You will tell him to go home, and collect you when the fuss has died down.'

'Yes, sir,' said Wallace.

Hugues looked at him, then at Mallory. 'The barn where we stayed is quiet. There is a loft. You can see the road, the harbour. It's a good command post.'

Mallory looked at the transparent face, the cracked lips, the glittering eyes. He walked across the room and shook Wallace by the hand. 'Best of luck, Lieutenant,' he said. 'It's been good having the SAS along. We wouldn't have got this far without you.'

Wallace grinned. 'I think you probably would,' he said.

Mallory said, 'I'll send up the Commandant.' Then he beckoned Miller, and said, 'Help Lieutenant Wallace up to the barn.'

They separated, leaving Mallory with the memory of a handshake that had been no more than a touch of icy bones.

'Brave man,' said Andrea.

Lisette was watching them. She nodded. There were tears on her face.

Miller's steps faded on the path.

Wallace was gone.

Miller threaded across the dark vines and potato-ridges. He carried his burden up the road, into the barn and up the stairs. In the loft, he propped Wallace on the dusty, sweetish-smelling mow. 'No smoking,' said Miller.

'Sure,' said Wallace. 'Thanks.'

'Good luck,' said Miller, arranging three canteens of water within reach.

In the yellow light of the lantern, Wallace looked like an Old Master painting: wounded soldier, with pack, Bren, Schmeisser, grenades and sulfa powder. His face wore a faint smile; a weird, faraway smile, Miller thought. 'Give my regards to England,' he said.

'You'll be there before us,' said Miller, cheerily. 'You can buy me a bourbon at the Ritz.' He went down the stairs in two strides of his beanpole legs, and paused by the door. The view from the barn was excellent. The village lay spread out at the end of its road. Nothing moved in the potato-ridges. The night was still: the wind had dropped flat, and the stars were out. In the loft, Miller heard Wallace stir, a stifled moan of pain. Then hinges creaked.

Miller walked onto the road and down towards the houses. After fifty yards he glanced back. When he had carried Wallace up, the shutters of the loft had been closed. Now, a shutter stood open. From that open shutter Wallace would command a view of the road leading down to the quay.

Miller raised a hand in salute, and walked quietly down to the village.

Hugues said to Mallory, 'Lisette will come on the boat.' Mallory watched him from under his heavy brows. The eyes were tired, but they seemed to Hugues to see everything. 'If we leave her, she may talk,' said Hugues. 'And there are often women on fishing boats. She will be . . . camouflage.'

A pregnant woman, thought Mallory. A hell of a member of a penetrate-and-sabotage expedition.

Lisette did not know where they were going, or why. But if she was picked up, she would talk, all right. This time, the Gestapo would make sure of that.

If she had not talked already.

He said, 'Bring her along.'

* * *

It was twenty to four by the time Miller got back to Guy's house.
There was one dirty glass and one plate on the table. There was no
sign that seven men and a woman had spent part of the night
there. Mallory was waiting, pack on back, Schmeisser in hand.
Miller shouldered his boxes. The Storm Force filed out of the back
door, across the garden walls, until they came out onto the field at
the top of the cliff from which Andrea had watched the sentries.
The wind had dropped flat. The water was smooth as satin, the
swells slopping against the jetty with a small roar. One of the rowing boats was gone from the outhaul. From out of the hazy darkness of the bay there came the pop and thump of ancient diesels
as the fishing fleet got ready for the tide. Of the sentries there was
no sign.

Mallory said to Andrea, 'We'll wait till the sentries give their all-
clear at 0355. Then we'll take care of them. That'll give us half an
hour to get clear.'

'Half an hour?' said a voice at his side. *'Monsieur,* you have my
personal guarantee that you will have all the time in the world.'

Mallory spun round.

'Mon Capitaine,' said the figure, in a gale of old Cognac. 'Permit
me to introduce myself. Le Commandant Cendrars. At your
service.'

'I was telling you about the Commandant,' said Hugues. 'A valuable *résistant.'*

'Pardon me,' hissed the Commandant, shirtily, in French. *'Chef
de la Résistance* of the region –'

'Ah, ça!' said Hugues, scornfully.

Mallory cut off whatever it was he was going to say next.
'Commandant,' he said, 'I am most grateful to you. Hugues, please
interpret. Tell the Commandant that his arrival is most timely. I am
exceedingly grateful to him for his assistance. I am putting him
under the command of Lieutenant Wallace, Commander of His
Majesty's rearguard. Rearguard HQ is the barn above the village.
He is to report there immediately for orders. I would remind him
that stealth and silence are of the essence.'

The Commandant became still. Down on the rain-blackened
quay, a figure was marching slowly: one of the German sentries.
The other sentry would be in the command post, standing by the
field telephone for the 0355 report. The Commandant said, 'A
rearguard action, *hein?* Under the command of a lieutenant? I
must say –'

'Hey!' said Miller. 'Get out of there!' Dark figures were crouching over the pile of equipment on the ground. 'Mind your own damn business –'

Next to his head, something exploded, shockingly loud in the still, starlit predawn. It took him several heartbeats to work out that it had been a rifle going off. 'In the army of the Marne, we do not sneak past the Boche,' bellowed Cendrars. 'We shoot him.' And he fired again.

The German sentry, surprised by the bullet that had smacked into the granite coping of the quay three metres from his right foot, had dived from view. The second shot hit the empty quay.

Miller found that he was on the ground, his Schmeisser cocked and ready in his hands, his heart thumping. You goddamn maniacs, he was thinking.

Mallory saw the Frenchmen still standing against the sky, obvious targets for the machine gunners in the pillbox on the hill opposite. Wallace, he thought, you are on your own.

Perhaps that is what you wanted.

Miller and Andrea had disappeared, as he would have expected. He said, 'Andrea?'

'I'll organize the pillbox,' said Andrea's voice from the darkness.

'Good. Miller?'

'Here.'

'Sentries.'

He looked at his watch. The hands were at five to three. The wires would be humming with the sentries' yelps: *we are under fire, send reinforcements*. The Commandant could not have chosen a worse moment if he had tried.

There was a moment's eerie silence, in which it was possible to imagine that nothing had happened. Then, on the summit of the hill that rose on the other side of the valley in which the village lay, a stabbing flame began to flicker. The Germans in the pillbox were taking an interest.

The sound of the machine gun came a split second later, with the whip of large-calibre bullets. One of the Commandant's men went over like a skittle. The rest of them lay down, old bones creaking. *'Merde!'* said the Commandant. 'What is that?'

Hugues was lying beside Lisette, clutching her hand. He said, wearily, 'You foolish old men, why will you not obey orders?'

Jaime felt something that might have been a breeze pass by him, except that it was no breeze, because breezes do not talk; and this breeze said, 'Come down in five minutes. Bring the equipment,' in the unmistakable voice of Captain Mallory.

Andrea went down through the village and up the hill the other side at a steady jog, conserving energy. The pillbox was directly above him now, its tracers flicking across the top of his vision. He paid them no attention. He had seen the pillbox before night had fallen. This far south, and next to a friendly neutral neighbour, invasion was not a serious fear. So it was not one of the impregnable strongpoints that you found in Crete, designed to stand days of siege. It was merely a concrete box with a steel door and a slit from which the machine gun could enfilade the bay and the quay.

Something was moving out at sea: something that might have been a fishing boat. Its exact outline was hard to determine, because there was a haziness at sea level, a pale vapour like kettle-steam on the dark face of the waters.

Andrea slowed to a walk. There would be a sentry. He put his face close to the ground and saw the silhouette of a man crouching against the hillside. The silhouette looked nervous, flinching at the occasional bullet that whizzed raggedly overhead from the heroes of the Marne on the hilltop opposite.

The sentry was indeed watching that hilltop. It had taken a lot of wangling to get down here onto the Spanish border, where nothing ever happened. He had no idea what had got into these Resistance idiots. Reinforcements would soon be arriving from St-Jean. There would be shootings and burnings in the morning. Meanwhile, this was annoying.

Or perhaps something worse. Rumours of invasion from England were growing in force, no matter how savagely the SS and Gestapo suppressed such defeatist talk. The sentry felt a dull foreboding. Still, if you were going to survive this damned war, Martigny was the place to be stationed –

A forearm like a steel bar clamped across the sentry's windpipe. The knife went in and out once, fast as a snake's tongue. Andrea lowered the body to the ground, put the helmet on his own head, and walked softly to the pillbox door. He took three grenades from his blouse, cradling them like eggs in his vast hand. He pulled the pins from the grenades. He held two of them, levers closed, in his left hand. The other he held in his right hand. He waited for a pause between bursts of fire. Then he banged on the steel door with the grenade.

'Hey!' he shouted, in his fluent German. 'Where is your damned sentry?'

Muffled voices came from within.

'This is Sturmbannführer Wilp!' roared Andrea in a voice hoarse with Teutonic rage. 'This is an exercise. Open up!'

The door opened. The man who opened it saw a large shape topped with a coal-scuttle helmet silhouetted against the stars. He said, *'Was?'*

Andrea kicked him down the stairs and threw the grenades after him. He was already fifty yards down the hill by the time the gun-slits spouted flame and the flat, heavy explosion rolled across the bay.

The sentries were not the Third Reich's finest. By the time Mallory and Miller arrived on the quay, they were in the guard post with the door shut, yelling at each other and into their field telephone, and someone was yelling back.

Mallory hoped Guy would be quick. There were a lot of German soldiers within five miles, and they would all be here in a very short time.

The guard post had once been a net shed. It had a stable door, in two parts. Mallory kicked both parts open. The Germans by the telephone looked round. They had wide, flabby faces, and looked well over fifty. They made no movement towards their rifles. Instead, their hands went up in the air.

'Key,' said Mallory.

The elder of the two handed him the key.

'Rifles on the ground,' said Mallory. The weapons clattered to the flagstones. 'Kick them over here.' He picked up the rifles. Then he smashed the telephone and closed the door. If by some miracle the Commandant of the St-Jean-de-Luz garrison had not been informed of his sentries' screams down the telephone, he could hardly fail to ignore an exploding pillbox. The lorries would already be on the road.

'Now listen,' said Mallory. 'This is a British army operation. It has nothing to do with the Resistance. We are about to board one of our submarines and withdraw. The civilian population have not been involved. Do you understand?'

The sentries nodded, dazed, their eyes shifting from the lean and haggard face, down the SS smock to the Schmeisser, unwavering in the hard, battered hands.

'You will inform your commanding officer,' said Mallory. 'This has been a commando raid, to demonstrate our capabilities. Tell him to remember what we can do.'

The sentries nodded. Their minds would be full of the icy winds of the Russian Front. But the message would have got across.

Mallory and Miller went out onto the empty quay. Mallory padlocked the door.

There was a dampness in the air, mixed with the faint, industrial reek of high explosive from the pillbox. It was quiet, except for the sploosh of the waves and the nearby thud of the fishing boat's engine.

And in the far background, on the edge of hearing, the sound of lorry engines.

The reinforcements were arriving.

Hugues scrambled down the cliff onto the quay, with Jaime and Lisette and Miller's boxes. Andrea was back, too. The fishing boat was coming out of the horizon, masts moving across the stars in the handle of the Plough.

Mallory noticed that the lower stars of the Plough's share had disappeared. He checked it off on a mental list. In the middle of all these disasters, that was something that could be useful.

He said to Jaime, 'Where are those old men?'

'Preparing for a final stand.'

'Go and tell them that for every German they kill, ten Frenchmen will be shot in reprisal. Tell them that this is a British army operation, and that the British army is withdrawing. Tell them that I have informed the sentries accordingly. Make it quick.'

Jaime nodded, and trotted up the cliff. Hugues said, 'For God's sake, where is this fishing boat?'

A dark shape came out of the murk. The fishing boat glided alongside. Andrea said, 'We won't get far without air support.'

It was a joke. It was a joke that was too true to be good. If lorry loads of Germans soldiers arrived on the quay now, they would have no trouble sinking Guy's boat. Machine guns, grenades, mortars, they would do the job.

If they arrived on the quay now.

Mallory thought of Wallace, the look in those china-blue eyes. Wallace was a berserker.

Good luck, Wallace, thought Mallory.

The fishing boat was a dark hulk alongside the quay now, the sound of its engine a clanging thump like the beat of a metal heart.

The lorry engines were nearly as loud, approaching the top houses of the village.

'*Bon*,' said a small figure in Guy's voice, but higher than usual. 'All on boat. Quick, quick.'

Jaime had materialised out of the night, panting. 'I told them,' he said. They went aboard. The propeller churned water under the transom. The bow swung out and steadied on the strip of absolute blackness between the sea and the stars. For a moment the land astern lay dark and quiet, the houses of the sleeping village draped across their valley under the stars.

Then the valley erupted like the crater of a volcano.

In the cab of the lead lorry, the Hauptmann had been tired and bored. The bloody Resistance were having one of their fits. Whoever had knocked off the SS patrol in the mountains had in the Hauptmann's opinion done a good job. It was just that the Hauptmann wished that, having shot the bastards up, they had gone to ground, instead of making a bloody nuisance of themselves in the suburbs of St-Jean-de-Luz and scaring the wits out of his sentries in hopeless little shallow-water ports like Martigny. Until someone had hammered on his door, the Hauptmann had been entertaining Big Suzette in his billet. Suzette might be large, but she was a person of surprising skill. And instead of testing those skills to the limit, the Hauptmann was sitting half-drunk, very tired, and in a state of aggravated coitus interruptus in a truck at the head of a column of three other trucks, one hundred men in all, on the way to sort out a bit of local difficulty in Martigny, on pain of transfer to the Russian Front.

Sod it, thought the Hauptmann.

The lead truck rounded a corner in the lane and started down-hill, into the beginning of the valley, where the houses began. There was an old barn a hundred metres down the road on the right. The Hauptmann paid it no attention, because he was peering at the southern side of the valley, where the pillbox stood. The pill-box should have been heavily engaged, if there was real trouble. But the pillbox was silent. As the truck drew level with the barn it seemed to the Hauptmann that the gun-slits of the pillbox were illuminated by a dull orange glow that waxed and waned. But the brandy was playing monkey's tricks with his eyesight –

A tight cluster of Bren rounds blew the windscreen in with a hellish jangle of broken glass. The driver went halfway out of the window and collapsed like a wet rag. The lorry slewed sideways across the lane, demolishing a wall and coming to rest against a boulder. One of the men in the back saw a jabbing flicker of flame in the open shutter under the roof of the barn by the roadside. As he opened his mouth to point it out, a line of bullets stitched across his abdomen. The last bullet hit one of the stick grenades at his belt. The explosion that followed set fire to the lorry's gas tank. Men spilled out of the three lorries following, and took up positions in ditches and behind potato-ridges. There was obviously a considerable force in the barn. A machine gunner slammed his weapon on the ground in the lee of a ruined pigsty and fumbled for the trigger. He was a badly shaken man, partially blinded by the flames of the burning lorry. His first long burst went wild, the tracers striking sparks from the coping of the quay and whipping out over the water of the harbour. For a moment, half the weapons in the squad fired after his tracers, and the black water of the port was churned to foam. Then a Feldwebel who had been invalided home from the Eastern Front and knew what he was doing started screaming orders, and the squad turned its attention to the shutter under the barn roof.

There must be at least a company in there, thought the squad, hugging the ground and pouring in fire. The black opening became silent. The squad's firing lulled. A man got up and scuttled in with a grenade. A hoarse, agonised bellowing came from the shutter, followed by the burp of two sub-machine guns. The streams of bullets started low and went high, almost as if the men firing them were too weak to hold the muzzles down. The man with the grenade ran into the first burst, and fell down. The Germans opened up again.

This time, the machine gunner put an accurate stream of bullets through the open shutter, one in three of them tracer. A light was then seen inside, yellow and blue, and volumes of smoke obscured the sky. The hay was on fire. And suddenly against that light there appeared the figure of a man; a man crawling on one hand and two knees. In the hand he was not using to support himself he held a Schmeisser, which he fired until it was empty.

Now they could see him, they shot him quickly, and he fell to the ground in front of the barn, which was burning well now as the last year's hay rose in the draughts. The flames spread quickly to the rafters.

The Germans kept on shooting. They had killed one man, sure. But there was no possibility that only one man could have done so much damage.

So they poured lead into the burning barn, the flames dazzling their eyes, until the ridge went and the roof fell in, and a fountain of orange sparks rose at the cold and hazy stars. And when the place was merely a heap of glowing ashes and there was no possibility of anyone being left alive, someone went and looked at the body that had come out of the shutter.

He was lying on his back. His face was peaceful, pale, with a trickle of blood from the corner of the mouth. He was wearing a beret, with the flying dagger of the SAS. The two privates next to the body were almost too frightened to touch it.

'Doesn't look very healthy,' said one of them.

'That's because he's dead,' said the other one.

The battledress blouse was open. The bandages round the belly shone black and wet in the flames. 'Ach,' said one of them. 'Stinks.'

'Brave man,' said the first German. 'To fight like that with his guts hanging out.'

'Bloody idiot,' said the second. He bent and closed the eyes, which were blue, and berserk, and open.

It was four o'clock by the time they got the burning truck out of the lane and moved on down to the quay. This time, nobody was taking any chances.

But when they got down to the sea, there was only the sloosh of the ripples against the quay, and the smooth expanse of the harbour at high water, lightening now with the dawn.

Guy Jamalartégui did not see the huge bloom of flame at the top of the valley. From the wheelhouse window, he was saying, in broken English, *'Messieurs,' 'dames,* welcome to the *Stella Maris.* And now, *Capitaine* Mallory, it is a question of my money –'

Then the guns started up, and Jamalartégui stopped.

One moment the water was dark and smooth. Then it was churning with tracers from the fusillade following the first wild burst the German machine gunner had fired after Wallace had shot up the lorry. The air was whining like injured dogs, and a flock of hammers slammed into the wheelhouse. Guy said, 'Oh,' a curious, breathy sound, as if the air was coming out of more places than his throat. He fell on the deck with a crash like a bag of coal. There were more tracers, but random, whizzing into the air like fireworks, passing over the spidery masts of the *Stella Maris,* dimming and vanishing.

Miller knelt by the body and felt for the pulse in the scrawny neck. He said, 'He's dead.'

Mallory looked down at them through eyes sore with sleeplessness. He realised that it was getting light. He could see Miller, crouched on the deck, his bony knees by his ears. And down there beside him in a pool of something that looked black but was not black, was Guy. A Guy who was no longer breathing; whom that random burst of fire from the hill had caught fair and square across the rib cage.

Mallory stepped over the body. He took the wheel. From the chart he recalled that the shore of the bay ran southwest. So he steered southwest, aiming at the horizon, as the light grew.

The engine thumped on. The sea was black like an asphalt parade ground, the horizon clogged with pale haze.

Andrea fingered the upper lip where his moustache was meant to be, and reached for the bottle of Cognac, and took a long swig. 'No rocks, my Keith, if you please,' he said. 'Only peace and quiet.' Then he lay down in the lee of the wheelhouse.

Mallory kept the bow southwest and motored for the horizon, waiting for the drone of engines, aircraft or marine, that would mean that after all this time, it was all over.

After three or four minutes, he realised that there was something wrong with that horizon. It should have been a knife-sharp line. Instead it looked lumpy and ragged, as if it was made of grey wool. And suddenly the grey skein ahead rose and touched the sky, and the air was wet on his face, and he realised the truth. The *Stella Maris* had sailed into thick fog.

The world was a round room, with walls of grey vapour. It was a room that moved with the *Stella Maris,* southwest. It was a room impenetrable by ships and aircraft, except by accident. A most fortunate room.

As long as you did not mind being off a rocky shore in tides of unknown strength, not knowing where you were going.

FIVE

Tuesday
0500–2300

The sun rolled up, a blood-coloured disc above the ramparts of vapour. From somewhere – astern, possibly, it was hard to tell – heavy explosions thumped across the water. They sounded to Mallory like blasting charges.

Andrea said, 'Wallace was a good man, my Keith.'

Mallory nodded. His eyes hurt with peering into the fog. Wallace had done his duty; more than his duty. Now he was another offering on the altar of war. Unlike most such offerings, his death had not been in vain. Mallory felt sadness, and gratitude.

And puzzlement.

Wallace had not had any high explosives with him. It was unlikely the Germans would have used such explosives to winkle one man out of a hayloft.

It must be Cendrars and his men. They must have got their hands on some quarry explosive, and be slugging it out with the Germans. Mallory profoundly hoped that he was wrong. A pitched battle between the Germans and the heroes of the Marne would only bring down horrors on the civilian population. But he turned his face resolutely away from such speculations. What mattered was what lay ahead, in San Eusebio.

The light grew. They wrapped Guy in a tarpaulin and weighted his feet with a chunk of old scrap iron from the *Stella Maris'* noxious bilges. Jaime took off his beret and said a couple of Basque prayers. Hugues said, *'Vive la France!'* The body pierced the black surface of the sea with scarcely a ripple, and was gone.

The sea was getting to Mallory. In the globe of fog it was quiet, and grey, and solitary: an oasis in the desert of battle and violence that he wandered like a Tuareg. But Mallory disliked the peace of

the sea in the same way a Tuareg might find an oasis cloying. It produced in him a nervous sickness, the sickness that the Tuareg might
feel under green palms among people he did not know, as he
watered his camels and longed to return to the real life of furnace
winds and red-hot sands. Mallory experienced a moment of longing for the rock and ice of mountains: hard mountains whose
habits he understood. Mountains in which he was not the hunter
and the destroyer; mountains in which the only enemies were the
failure of finger and foot to cling to hold, or human will to continue
upwards.

He looked down at Andrea. The Greek was lying by the wheelhouse, smoking, watching the oily heave of the sea. He felt
Mallory's eyes on him. He looked up. 'This is a most disgusting
ocean,' he said.

Mallory nodded.

'These tides,' said Andrea. They are a thing of barbarians. How
can men make ideas when the world they inhabit is being dragged
here and there by the moon? It is for this that you are so restless,
you of the North.'

Mallory laughed. They had escaped from a burning village and
were on their way to attack a fortified rock. And Andrea was complaining about the tides.

But when he looked again at Andrea's face, he saw something
that stopped his laughing. Despite his claims to the contrary,
Andrea was not afraid of men or bullets, night or war. But unless
Mallory was very much mistaken, Andrea was afraid of the cold
black waters of the Atlantic.

He lit a cigarette. There was a breeze now, enough to whip the
smoke away. The sun had gone, and the sky was a leaden grey.
Mallory wedged himself into the corner of the wheelhouse. Twelve
hours, he thought. He took inventory.

The *Stella Maris* was forty-five feet long. She had a tall mast at the
front end and a short mast at the back end, which probably made
her a ketch. There were what looked like sails on the booms, which
Mallory devoutly hoped they would not have to use. There was a
big fish-hold amidships, a dirty little fo'c'sle, and an engine room
abaft the wheelhouse. The engine was a single-cylinder Bolander
hot-bulb diesel, with a rust-caked flywheel the size and weight of a
millstone. In the bullet-shattered wheelhouse was a compass of
unknown accuracy, and the bloodstained Admiralty chart Guy had
spread on his kitchen table all those weeks – hours – ago. The *Stella*

Maris was thumping southwest through the fog at something like five knots, Mallory estimated. They should have moved out of French waters into Spanish. There would be patrol boats.

He offered a cigarette to Andrea. Andrea took it and lit it, scowling from under his black brows at the grey and sunless sea. 'A cold hell,' he said. He began to rummage restlessly in lockers. He found a new bottle of brandy, sniffed it, took a swig, and passed it to Mallory. One of the lockers was full of flags. He pulled out a yellow one. 'Quarantine,' he said. 'For when you have disease on board.' His white teeth showed in his black and bristly jaw. 'Or when you have goods to declare. This flag has never been used, I think.'

He's beaten it, thought Mallory. Andrea was not one to let irrational fears occupy space more profitably reserved for rational fears, like fear of failure in the face of the enemy. 'Guy said there was a Spanish flag,' he said.

Andrea rummaged some more, and came up with a red-and-yellow ensign. It was big, for easy visibility, and looked as if it had done long, solid service. Mallory gave Andrea the wheel, walked out of the wheelhouse and ran the ensign up to the top of the mizzen mast.

So now the *Stella Maris* was a Spanish boat, and all they had to worry about was motoring full ahead into the cliffs of Northern Spain.

The wind was definitely freshening. Ahead, the fog was becoming pale and ragged, and the slow Atlantic heave of the waves was taking on a sharper, more urgent feel.

Behind the wheelhouse, Miller stirred and opened his eyes. He lay for a moment, watching the Spanish flag snapping in the crisp breeze. Then he sat up and lit a cigarette. '*Buenos dias,*' he said. 'Coffee?'

'If you please,' said Mallory.

Miller stumbled down a flight of steps into the grease-varnished galley. From its door there emerged the smell first of paraffin, and then of coffee. He brought Mallory and Andrea mugs, well dosed with condensed milk and brandy. 'Nice as this is,' said Miller, eyeing the sea with scorn and dislike, 'how long does it last?'

'At least till nightfall.'

The *Stella Maris* thumped on, rolling heavily in the swell from the west. The fog was thinning in the breeze, piling into banks. One particularly heavy bank hung to the south, a heap of grey vapour that should, if Mallory's dead reckoning was right, hide the land. Miller drank another cup of coffee and smoked two cigarettes in quick succession. His bony face, already pale with exhaustion, was turning greenish under the eyes. Mallory said to Andrea, 'Better let him steer,' and lay down on the bench at the back of the wheelhouse.

Sleep came immediately, deep as a lake. It all went: the submarines, fog, the approaching cliffs of Spain.

It was a peaceful sleep: not the two-inches-below-the-surface doze of action, but a deep, heavy coma, a sleep of the interregnum between the confusions of the Pyrenees and the task waiting on the Cabo de la Calavera. Watching him, Andrea saw the broad forehead smoothed of the tensions of the last three days, saw the knots at the hinges of the jaw relax. Rest well, my Keith, he thought. You have brought us a long way, but you have only brought us to the beginning.

Mallory dreamed. He dreamed he was in a place in the mountains, in a valley of grey stone through which a glacier inched. He dreamed that there were great birds wheeling in the sky that were not birds, but aeroplanes: Stukas. The Stukas were diving, dropping their bombs, which were bursting around him in red flowers of flame. But Mallory felt nothing, heard nothing, because he was separate from it all. A voice told him, 'You are in the ice.' Wallace's voice. And Mallory realised that it was true. He was encased in a huge block of clear ice, which was saving him from the bombs. But at the same time it was preventing him from feeling anything, and that was bad –

Then someone was shaking him, and he was coming up out of that ice, his mind clicking into awareness that something had changed. The engine was still panting, the boat still rolling. But he seemed to be wet, and there was a new sound: a shrill wailing, an ululation, the sound of the Stukas –

He swung his feet to the deck, eyes searching the sky. There were no Stukas. There were only clouds, arranged in long squalls, their bellies trailing rain. Against them, the *Stella Maris'* masts described jerky loops. Her stub nose rose and fell like a blunt wooden hammer, walloping the troughs into spray that came back down the deck in bucketfuls. The wailing was the wind in the rigging.

'Land, er, ho,' said Miller.

As Mallory stood up he saw the fog bank, smaller and lighter now, shift and writhe. Then a great hand of air seemed to grab it and wrench it aside.

Five miles away, across a grey and gnarled sea, the black cliffs of Spain stood high and clear. Through his glasses Mallory could see a bay, with a cluster of grey houses, and on one of the headlands, the ruins of what might have been a fortress. He took a bearing and checked the chart. 'Forty miles to go,' he said. Miller nodded, without enthusiasm. Miller did not like the sea. As far as he was concerned, four miles would have been better; a lot better, even if there were two SS regiments at the end of it. 'Get Jaime on deck,' said Mallory.

Miller went below. Mallory kept the boat's head to the sea, blinking the spray out of his eyes. It had almost been better in the fog. He felt horribly exposed, out here in the clear grey breeze. And by the feel of it, they would be here all day; the *Stella Maris* was making four knots at best, labouring over these humpbacked seas like a weak-hearted charwoman climbing a flight of stairs.

Jaime appeared on deck, bleary-eyed. He squinted around him, said, 'That's Cabo del Lobo. Long way to go.'

'What about patrol boats?' said Mallory.

Jaime shrugged. 'They make big trouble on the border. This far down the coast, maybe they don't bother. Either way, they like money.'

'Stay on deck,' said Mallory.

Jaime nodded. He said, 'One thing. If you stay out here, people will be suspicious. You're a fishing boat. So we go in under the cliffs, no? That way, you are fishing. And nobody can see you from the land. And if we do get a problem, we throw some lobster pots in the sea.'

Mallory said, 'You know a lot about this.'

Jaime grinned, the grin of a man in his element. 'Frontiers are my business,' he said.

Mallory nodded. Without Jaime, they would not have found the Chemin des Anges, or the cave system. Without Jaime, they would have been dead.

The *Stella Maris* closed the shore. Across two hundred yards of grey and lumpy sea the cliffs reared three hundred feet into the grubby sky swept by the white motes of innumerable seabirds. Miller did not like the look of them at all. At least when their caïque had blown into the south cliff at Navarone it had been decently dark. If Miller was going to get smashed to bits, he would rather not get smashed to bits in broad daylight.

Hugues was on deck, looking as nervous as Miller felt. 'Is okay,' said Lisette, showing her white teeth. 'Jaime has sailed this route many times.'

'I didn't know you were a fisherman,' said Miller.

Jaime grinned, his dark eyes glinting under his beret. 'There are many people in the cigarette fishery,' he said. 'Sometimes you fish from a mule, sometimes from a boat.'

'It is not only lobsters you find in the pots here,' said Lisette.

Through the horrid queasiness of his belly, Miller thought that he saw in her something new, a confidence that she had not had in France. Of course, getting away from the Gestapo and into neutral territory would tend to improve your confidence, particularly if your guide in neutral territory was Jaime.

A sharp-crested hill of water swept under the *Stella Maris'* bow and dropped her into a trough. For a moment, Miller was once again weightless. To seaward a great hole had appeared in the sea, floored with weedy rock. 'Caja del Muerto,' said Jaime. 'Dead man's chest.' The waters closed over the rock with a boom, sending a depth-charge burst of ice-white spray a hundred feet into the wind.

For the next two hours the *Stella Maris* ground on down the inshore channel, invisible from the land. Mallory began to regain confidence. He went to Miller, who was lying in the scuppers alongside the wheelhouse, and said, 'Four hours' sleep. Then check your gear, and I'll brief the team.'

Miller groaned and dragged himself to the fo'c'sle, where Hugues was snoring on his bunk. He rolled into the bunk underneath, and passed out.

Mallory leaned against the wheelhouse, apparently watching the gulls on the cliffs. He had been thinking about Guy's chart of the Cabo de la Calavera and the harbour of San Eusebio. The approach was from the town quay, across the harbour, through the beach defences onto the Cape and into the U-boat repair docks. That was obvious.

Far too obvious.

The tide would be low, just after dark. The beach would be exposed and easy.

Far too easy.

Mallory lit a cigarette, and rested his head against the wheel-house doorpost. There were features of the San Eusebio chart that had been making him think hard about cliffs; particularly if, as seemed likely, the wind fixed itself in the west.

'*Capitaine,*' said Jaime in a new, sharp voice, and pointed.

Mallory followed his finger.

Halfway to the horizon was the silhouette of a grey launch. As Mallory watched, the silhouette foreshortened until he could see the moustache of foam on either side of the bow.

He felt the muscles of his stomach clench and become rigid. San Eusebio seemed suddenly a long way away.

'Well,' he said, calm as a goldfish pond. 'I suppose it's time we hauled the pots.'

El Teniente Diego Menendez y Zurbaran was in a vile mood. It was not being posted to this wet green corner of Spain; he had fought hard for the Nationalists in the Civil War, so he had no objection to the sight of Basque towns in ruins and Basque children starving. It was worse than rain and Basques. A week ago, he had been told in an unpleasant interview with Almirante Juan de Sanlucar, his cousin and commanding officer, that he was to double his patrols and increase his vigilance generally. The Teniente had pointed out that his vigilance was as always at maximum, and that the patrol boat, known to its crew as the *Cacafuego*, was operating all the hours its ancient engine and weary rivets could stand. Sanlucar had assumed a dour, bellicose look, and told him that instructions from above did not take account of such objections. It was the will of . . . someone very exalted (here Sanlucar's lips framed the words *el Caudillo*) that patrols on the stretch of coast for which the Teniente was responsible should be greatly increased.

At the framing of the Dictator's august title, never lightly spoken aloud, the Teniente's heart had started to bang nastily in his chest. At first he had interpreted it as a general rebuke for his laxity; the pay of a Naval officer was scarcely a living wage in this dreary province of surly people and expensive food, so he had fallen into the habit of accepting the voluntary contributions of the smuggling fraternity. But he realised that there was more to it than that after a conversation with Jorge, his bosun. Jorge had observed military activity on the Cabo de la Calavera, and had approached the sentries on the gate, who were dressed in the uniforms of the First Zaragoza Regiment, to offer them the services of certain Basque women he maintained in the Calle Brujo in Bilbao. The soldiers had chased Jorge away, cursing him in a language that was not Spanish. Jorge had expressed to the Teniente the opinion, based on certain military vehicles and black uniforms he had half-glimpsed through the heavily-fortified gate that cut off the neck of the peninsula, that the garrison on the Cabo de la Calavera was German.

And thirty-six hours ago, just before this patrol, the Teniente had been notified that his bow gun crew was to be replaced, as were the port and starboard machine gunners. When the replacements had turned up, they had been German.

The Teniente had nothing against Germans. He disliked them only insofar as he disliked everyone except himself. But their presence on Cabo de la Calavera made him nervous, and their presence at his guns insulted his pride. He valued Spain's neutrality, because it meant his life was not in danger. He needed his bribes. And he had not taken kindly to standing on that worn patch of carpet in front of the Almirante's desk in Santander, being subjected by the Almirante to a diatribe on the importance of duty under the cold grey eyes of an obvious homosexual from the German Embassy in Madrid. This coast was the Teniente's personal patch. The fact that his superior officers' new jumpiness was obviously German-inspired made him feel, insofar as such a feeling was possible for a Fascist, frankly bolshy.

So it was with no great sense of mission that he bore down on the familiar black hull of the *Stella Maris*, hauling lobster pots under the cliff.

He paused a hundred feet away, snarling at Paco the coxswain to keep the boat steady. The *Stella Maris* was head to wind, fat and black as ever. There were a couple of unfamiliar faces: two men who might have been northern Portuguese or even German, tall and lean, wearing singlets despite the cut of the west wind. They lurched uneasily on the *Stella Maris'* splintery deck; it looked to the Teniente as if they were not used to hauling lobster pots. But they were hauling all right. And back in the wheelhouse – it looked as if something had happened to the wheelhouse – Jaime Baragwanath was waving and grinning from under his beret. There seemed to be a woman with him.

The Teniente knew Jaime of old, as a fixer and a smuggler. He brought coffee out of Spain to France, and in the other direction the wines of Bordeaux, to alleviate the suffering caused by *vino negro*. If Jaime was personally on board the *Stella*, she would be carrying a high bulk, high value cargo, like wine.

The Teniente was partial to a few bottles of claret of an evening. Normally, he would have taken his cut at the landing. But he saw in the *Stella Maris* a way to impress his new gunners – and thus, he suspected, the Almirante – with his zeal.

The Teniente lit a thin black cigar and tilted his cap rakishly over his right eye. Plucking the brass megaphone from its clips on the bridge, he put its oxide-green business end to his mouth. 'Halt,' he shouted. 'I am boarding you.' On the foredeck, the crew of the 75-mm gun swivelled their piece to cover the *Stella*.

Mallory put a couple of loops of tail-line round a Samson post, and tied it off with a knot that had more to do with rock faces than boats. He shuffled aft at a fisherman's slouch. He said to Jaime, 'What is this?'

'Routine inspection,' said Jaime, his dark face still, avoiding Mallory's eye. 'This officer takes bribes. He's used to seeing the *Stella* under the Spanish flag, as long as he get money. He maybe want some money. Or maybe some tobacco, drink, who knows?'

'Jaime knows,' said Hugues.

Mallory ignored him. He said, 'Does he normally point guns?'

'Not normally.' Jaime frowned at the men on the *Cacafuego's* foredeck. 'He's got new gunners.'

Mallory nodded and grinned, a simple fisherman's grin, full of salty good nature, for the benefit of anyone watching from the gunboat. His eyes were not good-natured. They checked off the rusting grey paint of the bow, the two blond men balancing easily on the deck by the breech of the 75-mm gun. The Captain was on the bridge. Aft of the bridge, another two men stood at machine guns. Spandaus. Spandaus were light guns, but they could still unzip a boat the size of the *Stella*. A 75-mm gun could blow her right out of the water.

But the guns were not the main problem. The main problem was the array of radio aerials between the two masts.

In his mind, he followed the trail of wreckage back into the Pyrenees. If the *guarda-costa* sent out a signal about unusual occurrences off the Vizcayan coast, any German with a map and eyes to see would be able to grasp the general direction of this dotted line of mayhem.

There was only one solution.

Mallory trotted forward and shouted down the main hatch. Jaime started yelling at the patrol boat in Spanish. The patrol boat was yelling back. Mallory cast off the tail-line of the lobster pots. Then he went aft to the wheelhouse. He said to Lisette, 'Get down, please.' He politely took the wheel from Jaime, spun it hard-a-starboard, and drove the *Stella Maris* straight at the patrol boat's mid point.

The teniente started screaming into the megaphone. That was a mistake. By the time he had realised screaming was no good, the *Stella Maris* was twenty feet away. The 75-mm gun banged once. The shell screamed past the *Stella's* wheelhouse and burst on the black cliff face two hundred yards behind. The Spandaus opened up, bullets fanning across the sky as the gunboat rolled. Then Andrea and Miller came out of the *Stella's* forehatch like jack-in-the-boxes. Andrea hosed the gun's crew with Bren bullets. They disappeared. Hit or not, it did not matter, as long as they were away from the gun. Miller took the Spandau crews. By the time he had finished his burst, the *Stella Maris* was in a trough, the gunboat on a wave. The patrol boat's grey side came down with a rending crash on the *Stella's* stem, and stuck there. The gunners on the patrol boat could not depress their sights far enough to bear on the *Stella*. Andrea had the Bren going by now, hammering a tight pattern of bullets into the patrol boat's hull, at the place where the radios might be. Miller pulled the pins out of four grenades. He tossed them up the patrol boat's side, heard them rattle down her decks, and heard the *blat* of their explosions in the wind. The two boats hung together in the form of a T, bashed and wrenched by the short inshore chop, the *Stella's* bow borne down by the patrol boat's side. There was a hole in that side. The *Cacafuego's* plates were no thicker than a tin can: a rusty tin can –

A wave came under. The *Stella* pitched away from the gunboat at the same time as the gunboat rolled away from the *Stella*. The gunboat's plates gave with a wrenching groan. The two boats came apart, the *Stella's* bow rearing high as Mallory took her round and away.

'Fire!' screamed the Teniente. His ears were ringing from the grenade explosions. The radio aerials were gone, streaming in the breeze. The Teniente heard the bullets clang and whizz, and felt an odd sogginess in his ship's movements. 'Fire!' he screamed again. The *Stella Maris* was twenty yards away now. He saw the Spandau crews sprawled over their guns, and the foredeck by the 75-mm swept clean of men. He found that his feet were wet, and realised that his ship was sinking. He had been sunk by the *Stella Maris*. He opened his mouth to scream for help.

Then he thought of what his cousin would say when he told him that his armed patrol boat had been sunk by a bunch of smugglers.

The Teniente realised that the time had come to die.

He stood to attention, and shut his mouth.

The patrol boat rolled and sank in the space of twenty seconds. There was a tremendous eructation of bubbles. An oar came to the surface. Then nothing.

'*Jesus,*' said Jaime, pale to the lips.

Mallory turned his eyes away from the satiny patch of water where the patrol boat had been. Andrea's eyes were blank. The blankness had very little to do with shock, or the violent sinking of a *guarda-costa* with half a dozen crew. He and Mallory were both calculating whether the *guarda-costa* had announced its attentions on the radio before it had tried to come alongside the *Stella Maris*.

Mallory said, 'Full ahead, I think.'

Andrea nodded, and lowered his great bulk into the engine room.

The Bolander took on a more urgent thump. Mallory cut the tail-lines free from the bow. The *Stella Maris* heaved on westward, the wind cold in Mallory's face.

Jaime came on deck with Lisette. She looked pale. She had reason to look pale. Jaime said, '*Capitaine*, I need a word.'

Lisette watched them walk to the wheelhouse, watched Mallory's straight back, the precise step. Even on this filthy boat, that one walked like a soldier.

Jaime said, 'That was not normal.'

'Sorry?'

'I know this man,' said Jaime. 'The officer commanding the *guarda-costa*. He is a bastard, but a careful bastard. He would never stop the *Stella*. He takes money from smugglers, but not on the sea. Only in the bar, after they have gone ashore. The only reason he stopped us is because someone told him stop any ship.'

'So the Werwolf pack hasn't left,' said Mallory. 'Good.'

Jaime said, 'Was it necessary to kill those people?'

Mallory was not interested. 'There's a war on.'

'So you kill these men. Life into death. Like a mule turning food into shit.'

'War is nasty like that,' said Mallory. 'The reason we are here is to destroy submarines.'

Jaime grinned, a grin that held a horrible irony. 'Perhaps it is just that I do not like to destroy a useful trading partner.'

'There will be better trading after we have won the war,' said Mallory. 'Now, there are some things I need to know about the Cabo de la Calavera.'

* * *

By the middle of the day the sky was whitening under a veil of cirrus, and Miller had been sick fourteen times. Andrea was taking his spell at the pump; Andrea never got tired. Mallory came down into the fish-hold.

'Briefing,' he said. 'Ready for this?'

Andrea nodded, impassive behind his three days' growth of beard. Miller would have done the same, but nodding required energy, and he was saving his energy for when he really needed it.

Mallory said, 'There's a cliff on the seaward side of this Calavera place. Guy said it's not climbable. So the Germans won't be watching it. With luck.'

There was a silence, filled with the pant of the engine and the distant boom of waves on rock.

Miller said, 'If it's climbable, what do we do?'

Mallory lit his sixtieth cigarette since dawn. 'Climb it,' he said.

Miller shook his head weakly. 'Ask a silly question,' he said.

'We'll go over the side after dark,' said Mallory. 'In the dinghy. Jaime and Hugues and Lisette will take the *Stella* on into the harbour. They'll look like fishermen in to make repairs. The Germans have put big defences on the harbour side of the Cabo. As far as I can see, there's very little on the seaward side, because they've decided the cliffs will do the job. We'll go up in the dark, get ourselves some uniforms. Dusty, you'll want to check your equipment. We'll all need to shave. Questions?'

Miller listened to the boom of waves on rock. He said, 'How do we get from the dinghy onto the cliff? Seems to me that the sea has all these waves on it.'

Mallory flattened the chart on the filleting table. 'The sea's coming from the west.' He pointed to the northerly bulge of the shore. 'In behind here there's a wreck; Guy's friend Didier Jaulerry's fishing boat went up the beach four months ago. Jaime says that with the sea from the west, you sometimes get a smooth patch in the lee of the wreck.'

'Sometimes.'

'During the bottom half of the tide. Till about 2100 hours tonight.'

Andrea said, 'It's not full dark at 2100.'

'It is at 2130.'

Miller said, 'But what if the waves are breaking clear over that wreck at 2130?'

Mallory folded the chart briskly, and stuck it in the pocket of his battledress blouse. 'Oh, I expect we'll manage,' he said.

There was more silence. There was a lot to hope for. They had to hope that the *guarda-costa* had not got a radio message off, and that the dinghy would not be spotted by the Germans or smash against the cliff, and that the *Stella Maris'* remaining complement would escape notice in San Eusebio.

The wind went up, and so did the waves. Lisette put her swollen ankles out of her bunk, and moved towards the filthy galley. Hugues stopped her. 'I'll cook,' he said. 'You rest.'

She looked at him with the dark-shadowed eyes of late pregnancy. He saw hostility and frustration. He said, 'What is it?' and tried to put his arm round her.

She pulled away. 'You're right,' she said. 'I'm tired.' She turned her face to the wall. Hugues went grim-faced into the galley and rummaged in the boxes that lined the bulkhead. Half an hour later, smoke was issuing from the chimney, and the smell of frying onions mingled horribly with the stench of the *Stella's* fish-hold. And in an hour, a stew of tomatoes, hard chorizo, onions and potatoes was steaming in a blackened tureen. Jaime pulled a bottle of suspiciously good red wine out of a locker. Mallory, Andrea and Miller sat themselves at the table in the saloon. Mallory and Andrea ate hard and long. There was no talk. This was the grim refuelling of war machines. At the end, Andrea poured another tumbler of wine, lit a cigarette and leaned back against the fishing boat's side, eyes closed, humming a Greek tune full of Oriental runs and quarter-tones. Mallory looked across at him, the massive neck running into the colossal shoulders, the face peaceful in repose. He looked at Miller, smoking, pale-green under the eyes, in front of his largely untouched plate of stew. They looked like fishermen: tired fishermen, who smoked too much and drank too much when they could get hold of it. They looked like the kind of fishermen you would expect to find aboard this leaky boat with no bloody fish in the hold, and a smuggler, and an eight-months-pregnant woman, and the man who had got her pregnant.

They did not look like the cutting edge of a Storm Force whose task it was to climb a two-hundred-and-fifty-foot cliff in the dark, penetrate a strong and watchful garrison, and destroy the submarines of the Werwolf squadron.

Still, thought Mallory. Nobody would have believed the distance they had come to arrive at this point. But here they were. It was just a matter of carrying on: dividing the big problem into small, manageable problems, and solving them, one by one, with the tools at his disposal.

And a hell of a lot of luck.

Miller said, 'I guess I'll go turn in.' He shambled forward to the bunks.

When they were alone, Andrea said, 'What do you think about this?'

Mallory had known the Greek long enough to realise that he did not want an opinion, but a discussion. Mallory was in command of the expedition – there was no argument about that. But Andrea was a full colonel in the Greek army as well as one of the most dangerous and experienced guerrilla fighters in the Mediterranean. To fight at his most lethally efficient, Andrea needed to understand the situation.

Mallory said, 'It's a good place to keep some submarines.'

'Some hidden submarines.'

'That's right.'

'Good security.'

'That's right.'

'And that patrol boat. That was part of the security?'

'The gun crews looked German.'

'True.' Andrea stroked the place where his moustache should have been. 'And that was a routine patrol.'

'Sorry?'

'Not based on specific information.'

Mallory shrugged. 'No way of knowing,' he said.

'Quite.'

'Do we trust all these people?'

Mallory had been wondering the same thing. Jaime had a smuggler's capacity for double-dealing. Hugues was brave, but he had an irrational streak a mile wide. And Lisette . . . well, Lisette under Storm Force control was safer than Lisette at large.

'We've got to,' he said.

Andrea nodded. There was a pause. Then he said, 'It seems to me that the Germans will have problems of their own.'

That had also occurred to Mallory. Spain was full of spies. To keep the occupation of Cabo de la Calavera secret, the garrison would be manned and supplied from the sea, or across the Pyrenees, by night. Either way, it would be a smuggling operation, with all the inconveniences attendant on such operations. And German efficiency or no German efficiency, it seemed likely that a garrison hastily convened and furtively supplied would be a less well-organised garrison than the garrison of, say, Navarone. Confusion would be to the Storm Force's advantage.

Andrea poured the last of the wine into the two glasses, and raised his to Mallory. 'My Keith,' he said. 'Victory, or a clean death.'

'And two days' kip to follow,' said Mallory.

He thought, in five hours, we will be on hard rock again, climbing. He raised his own glass and drank. Andrea swung his boots up onto the bench, put his head on his pack, and closed his eyes.

The door opened. Miller came in.

At first, Mallory thought he had been shot. His face was bloodless, his lips the colour of ashes. But he was walking well, braced against the heave of the *Stella Maris'* deck. In his hands he was carrying the big, brass-bound boxes that held his explosives and his fuses.

Mallory said, 'Sleep first. Check gear later.'

Miller shook his head. He did not speak: it was as if something had happened that had removed his voice. He lifted the boxes and placed them side by side on the gutting table. He unlatched them, opened the lids, and gestured at the contents.

If the Storm Force was a bomb, the personnel were the fuse and the casing and the fins. What was inside those two brass-bound mahogany boxes was the charge: the stuff that would do the job, blast those three Werwolf submarines into water-filled hulks and save the lives of all those men crammed into transports on the Channel.

Mallory looked into the boxes. His mouth became dry. His mind went back six hours, to the bay of St-Jean-de-Luz, the red ball of the sun hauling itself up through the fog, the heavy explosions coming from the land. He had thought that Commandant Cendrars' old soldiers had got their hands on some quarry explosive.

He had been wrong.

They had been fifteen minutes on the cliff at Martigny, while Andrea disposed of the pillbox and Mallory and Miller had explained their wishes to the sentries. During that fifteen minutes, the boxes had been in the care of Commandant Cendrars' enthusiastic veterans.

The veterans had profited from those fifteen minutes. Possibly their arsenal had been running low, or possibly they merely suffered from an enthusiastic lightness of finger. Whichever the case, the outcome was the same.

The brass-bound boxes that had contained the explosives and detonators that were going to blow the Werwolf pack to hell now contained, besides a few blades of wet grass and a couple of small stones, half a hundredweight of best Martigny mud.

There was a silence that seemed to last five years. It was Andrea who broke it. He yawned. 'Oh, dear,' he said. 'Now I must sleep.'

'Take the bunk,' said Miller, through lips numb with shock.

'Thank you,' said Andrea, and shuffled bear-like into the sleeping cabin. It was as if he understood Miller's sense of failure, and attached to it little enough weight to accept the offer of the bunk as full reparation.

Miller said, 'I let it out of my sight.' Never let your tools out of your sight. If you carry a gun, carry it at all times. Keep your knife strapped on, even in the bathtub. And never, ever, leave your Cyclonite and your detonators to be guarded by heroes of the Marne with the wind under their tails. 'We have grenades.'

'Ten grenades,' said Mallory. His knees felt weak. He was sweating. So this is how it ends, he thought.

Miller said, 'Four. We used eight on the patrol boat.' He was thinking again. 'Anyway, grenades won't work on U-boat pressure hulls.' But he did not say it nervously. He said it in a measured, judicious voice, like a prosecution lawyer assessing the chances of convicting a known murderer on circumstantial evidence. If grenades would not work, the voice implied, it would be necessary to find something else that would.

Mallory heard that new voice.

For a moment, he had felt it all slipping away from him. That was because in his exhaustion he had forgotten that this was Dusty Miller, who had destroyed the guns at Navarone and the dam at Zenica, not to mention an Afrika Korps ammunition dump with a Cairo tart's hairpins. Confidence began to tiptoe back into Mallory's thoughts.

'So I guess they'll have a magazine there,' said Miller. 'And they'll have to load the torpedoes some time. Your torpedoes take up most of the space on a U-boat. You couldn't refit with torpedoes on board, could you?' He folded his hands. 'So there's that. And then there's the engines. Those Walter engines. Hydrogen peroxide, you said. Fuel oil. Water. Interesting stuff, hydrogen peroxide.' He leaned his long back against the bulkhead, hands folded across his concave stomach, boots propped on the opposite bench, eyes closed. He seemed to be thinking.

Finally, Mallory could stand it no longer. 'What about hydrogen peroxide?' he said.

But Miller was asleep.

Mallory thought about waking him, then decided against it. If the Werwolf pack was sailing tomorrow at noon, would they not already have loaded the torpedoes? And what was so interesting about hydrogen peroxide?

He lit another cigarette. Relax, he told himself. Miller and Andrea were of the opinion that the operation was possible. So the operation was possible. Easy as that.

Within thirty seconds, Mallory, too, was asleep.

It was the gulls that were the first sign. All afternoon, after the turn of the tide, they had been thickening in the sky. When Mallory went on deck, groggy in the mind after too little and too shallow sleep, their cries filled the air.

The *Stella Maris* had moved out to sea again. A stiffish breeze was blowing from the northwest, and on it the gulls slid and balanced with frantic voices and perfect self-possession. The wind seemed to be blowing out of the sun, which had appeared pale and brilliant below the roof of grey cloud. It was twenty minutes before sunset, but there was no red in that sun. It glared like a big metal eye across the water, draining the colour from everything its rays touched, making the *Stella Maris* black and the seas grey, and the cliffs the dull non-colour of slate. And shining into the eyes of anyone watching from the land.

Mallory lit a cigarette, stuck it between the nicotine-stained fingers of his left hand, and pulled his Zeiss glasses out of their case. He panned the disc of vision across the crawling waves until he found the black line of the land: a flat black line, a continuous cliff, marred here and there by pillars of rock over which a mist of spray hung, silvering the towers of gulls. He moved the glasses to the west.

The line of the cliff suddenly rose into a rounded hump, sheer-sided. The sides plunged straight down into the sea. The structure looked like a steel helmet, or a skull. Cabo de la Calavera. The cape of the skull.

Mallory breathed smoke, and made a fine adjustment to the focus wheel.

On the crown of the skull, at the apex, a stubby white pencil jutted skyward: the lighthouse. The lighthouse was not showing a light. To the right of the lighthouse, on what might have been the skull's forehead, were square-edged masses, topped by a tower. The fortress: an efficient fortress, dug into the cliff to cover the entrance to the harbour of San Eusebio. He moved the disc of the glasses eastward, along the spine of the ridge.

There was a structure of some kind slung across what must have been the throat of the peninsula, but they were too far away for Mallory to see what it was. He could guess, though. It looked like a stone wall, probably with battlements and a moat. The Germans would have supplemented it with a line of fences and trenches. As far as he could tell, it stopped abruptly some distance above the sea – where the cliff became vertical, he guessed. The base of the cliff was a continuous line of white water.

Mallory walked aft. Jaime was at the wheel. Mallory said, 'You have come out of some port. You are in trouble. You are making repairs to the engine. Do you know anybody in San Eusebio?'

'Only professionally.'

'That will do. Get estimates for repairs.' Mallory pointed at the radio set in the wheelhouse. 'That work?'

Jaime grinned. 'A smuggler's radio always works.'

'Keep it switched on. Now let's go ashore.'

'How are you getting ashore?' said Jaime.

Mallory said, 'We'll manage.' At this stage in the expedition, there was no sense in telling anyone on the *Stella Maris* any more than he needed to know. He looked at his watch. It said 2015. 'We'll get to you before 1500 tomorrow. Be alongside the fish quay. We'll sail immediately we're on board.'

'For where?'

Mallory looked pious. 'The Lord will provide,' he said.

Jaime looked at the black rock skull of the Cabo, with its cloud of gulls, tinted by the now-pinkening sun. 'A-okay,' he said. *'Bonne chance.'*

The *Stella Maris'* nose turned and settled on the brow of the skull. The sun was sinking fast now, and as it sank its pink turned to blood, dabbling the cloud-roof with crimson. 'Looks like hell,' said Jaime.

'Sorry?' said Mallory. To him it looked like a sunset, followed by a hard climb in the dark.

'No importa,' said Jaime.

Darkness fell.

An hour later, Mallory, Miller and Andrea were in the *Stella Maris'* dinghy, heaving up and down on the seven-foot swell rolling out of the Atlantic wastes. The pant of the *Stella*'s engine was receding eastward. In the dinghy with the three men were the two coils of wire-cored climbing rope, three Schmeissers with five spare magazines each, and the grenades. They were dressed in Waffen-SS smocks, camouflage trousers and steel helmets. In the breast pocket of his smock, Mallory carried the special pitons Jonas Schenck had made for him in 1938, out of the rear springs of a Model A Ford. Anything else they needed they would have to find on the Cabo.

At least, that was the idea.

Miller sat in the bow of the boat, his knees close to his ears, clutching the lock of his machine pistol to keep out the wet. Miller was fairly sure that this was it: the end. He would not have minded, except that he did not wish the end, when it came, to have anything to do with the sea. Miller had had enough of the sea.

The dinghy rose and sank again, vertiginously, on a glossy black wave like the back of a man-eating animal. Andrea dug in the oars and took a couple of strokes towards the darkness above the booming white line that separated vertical rock from Atlantic ocean.

There,' said Mallory.

In the line of white there was a break; the merest hint of a break, the sort of paling that would come of a wave whose force was spent before it hit the wall. Spent, for instance, by the wreck of a fishing boat once the property of a M. Jaulerry, impaled on the boulders at the base of the cliff.

Miller thought, we will at any rate have the advantage of surprise. And if we live, nobody will be as surprised as me.

Then Andrea gave a final heave and the dinghy went up on the back of another wave, as huge and black as the last. Only this one did not stay huge and black, but while the dinghy was on its crest turned white and foaming, insufficiently substantial to support the dinghy, which was falling, with the whole of the rest of the world, stern-first, in a cataclysm of water that made a sound like an earthquake, and had no bottom –

They found the bottom. They found it with a sudden splintering crash that knocked the seat from under Miller. He discovered that things previously available for holding on to were no longer available for that purpose. Then the wave had him, and he was rolling away somewhere, he could not tell where, except that he had a Schmeisser slung round him, a couple of kilos of negative buoyancy that were going to drag him to a watery grave among the boulders at the base of the cliff, and he thought, so this is it.

But then something had him by the collar of his smock, and was dragging him in the opposite direction from the direction in which the water wanted to take him. And he was out of that black whirl, and on something hard and slimy that he realised must be the deck of the wrecked fishing boat. And Andrea's voice was saying into his ear, 'When we get ashore, check your weapon.' And things were back to normal.

Or what passed for normal, on the seaward side of the Cabo de la Calavera.

At the base of the cliff was a beach of boulders which had fallen from the crags above, forming a sort of glacis on which the waves beat themselves to white tatters. The fishing boat had hit this beach, been driven up to its summit, and landed wedged with a northeast-southwest orientation, its bow rammed against the main face of the cliff, which ran east-west.

Mallory, Andrea and Miller crouched for a moment on the slimy deck, tilted away from the hammer of the seas, feeling the concussion of the rollers in their bones. Then Mallory handed his Schmeisser to Andrea, slung one of the coils of rope over his shoulder, and stepped on nailed soles down the deck towards the ink-black rise of the cliff.

The first ten feet were boulders, slippery with bladder wrack, treacherous in the complete blackness, but by no means steep. Mallory went up carefully but fast, until his hands met something that was not seaweed. Lichen. Then a cushion of vegetation set in sand and peat that crumbled under his fingers. His fingers crawled above it, looking for a hold. They found loose rock. The cliffs of Cabo de la Calavera were not as solid as they looked.

He glanced downwards. The backwash of the breaking waves was a broad white road, cut aslant by the hull of the fishing boat. He felt wet on his face as a big wave hit.

He started to climb.

It was a bad climb. The rock down here was as rotten as cheese, and a sparse vegetation of moss and sea-thrift had taken hold in the cracks. Each hold meant a sweep with the fingers to remove loose soil, a gradual increase of pressure from the fingers until they bore his full weight, resting on at least two firm points while he tested a third, slow and sure, never committing himself. He went up the cliff inch by inch, chest sore from the cigarettes of the past three days, finger muscles burning, horribly aware of the clatter of loose stone down the cliff below him.

After five minutes the climbing became mechanical, as it always did: a delicate shifting of balance from hold to hold, working from the hips, so he seemed to float rather than crawl. And the part of his mind not filled with testing holds and balancing on rock went ahead, onto the Cabo. There were Totenkopf-SS up here, from what Guy had said. There would be Wehrmacht too. And Kriegsmarine, and dockyard workers. A force hastily assembled, wearing a diversity of uniforms, strangers to each other, probably in the final stages of preparing for departure. There would be confusion. Mallory devoutly hoped it would be a confusion he could exploit.

He was seventy feet up now. The wind was battering his ears, and the rumble of the seas had receded until it had become a dull, continuous roar. He reached out his hand for the next hold, fumbling like a blind man.

Suddenly he was no longer blind. Suddenly his hand emerged from the darkness, a pale spider groping its way across quartz and matrix towards the dark shadow of a hold. The cliff face had come into an odd, shadowed relief, a landscape of vertical hills and vales stretching down to a sea whose waves now looked not so much black as silver-grey.

And above the horizon of the cliff, where the sky had been a matt emptiness of squally cloud, there had taken place the change that had brought about all the other changes. The squalls had turned and separated. Between them fingers of deep black sky had appeared, specked with the needle-tips of stars. And into one of those bottomless chasms of darkness swam like a silver lamp a brilliant quarter moon.

Mallory froze, clinging to the face of the cliff. Far below, he saw white surf and the wreck of the fishing boat sheltering its tiny eddy of black water. He could distinctly see shattered wreckage from the dinghy spinning in the vortex. This was bad. Potentially, this was very bad. All it needed was a casual glance down the moonlit cliff. The Storm Force would be pinned down, brushed off the rock face like flies. And the Werwolf pack would sail at noon tomorrow, unmolested.

The wind blew, eddied, became for a second still.

Directly above Mallory's head, someone coughed.

Mallory's stillness intensified until it was like the stillness of the rock face itself. He turned his eyes upwards. The moon was sliding towards a lip of cloud. But before it went and darkness swept back over the cliff, he saw something he had not noticed before.

Up there on the cliff face was an overhang of rock too regular to be natural.

The coughing came again. There was a brief splash of yellow light. A little spark dropped past Mallory's head. A spent match.

Mallory eased his feet on their minute ledges, and leaned in against the cliff. He turned his face upwards and watched.

To his dark-accustomed eyes, the regular glow of the cigarette was as bright as a lighthouse. Against it, he analysed the little bulge of masonry projecting from the cliff. It was a half-moon of stone or concrete, a demilune, a strongpoint built out from a narrow ledge of the cliff. Mallory rested, recreating in his mind the fortifications of the Cabo. This would be the seaward end of the line of fortifications running across the neck of the peninsula.

The moon slid out again. By its light he could see the joins in the masonry. Not German, he thought. Older than this war.

Something gleamed in the moonlight: something shaped like a small funnel. The flash eliminator on the muzzle of a light machine gun. The old Spanish defences had new tenants.

For the blink of an eye, Mallory took stock.

To his right, the cliff was sheer, but climbable. But the moon was painting it a brilliant grey. Figures climbing over there would be plainly visible from the demilune. To the left, the cliff looked even easier, the summit concealed behind a shoulder of rock. There was no way of telling what was on that summit. There was only one thing you could be sure of: even if the top was undefended, and you could arrive there without being seen, you would be the wrong side of the fortifications at the top, and there would still be the gates to get through.

So there was only one way.

Straight up.

He eased the commando knife in the sheath on his right hip, and began once again to climb.

The moon was swimming in a wider gulf now. But Mallory climbed fast and efficiently, knowing that he was directly underneath the demilune, invisible. It took him ten minutes to cover the hundred feet: ten quiet minutes, choosing holds with a surgeon's delicacy, breathing slow and deep through his nose. This was the Mallory who had moved remorselessly up the southeast face of Mount Cook, above the Caroline Glacier. A crumbling Atlantic cliff was a stroll in the park to this Mallory.

The base of the demilune was a bulge of masonry rooted in the natural rock. Mallory paused on an exiguous ridge ten feet underneath it. He collected his breath, then took off his boots and socks and hung them round his neck. The sea was a dull mutter two hundred feet below. Above, he could hear a pair of boots walking four steps left, pause, four steps right, pause. He stood for a moment, fingers and toes gripping their holds, balancing like a man on springs, waiting for the four steps left, two steps right –

He took a deep breath, and went up the final ten feet like a spider up a wall.

If you had asked him then or afterwards what holds he had used or what route he had followed, he would not have been able to say. It seemed to him that one moment he was poised below the emplacement, and the next he was alongside it, looking over a waist-high wall at the silhouette of a figure in German uniform. The figure had its back to him, at the far end of the four steps left. And there was a bonus, because the figure stayed there, shoulders bowed, helmet brim lit flickering yellow from below. Lighting another cigarette. Very soon after the last one –

Mallory loosened the knife in its sheath, put his left hand on the parapet of the demilune, his right on the ledge at its side –

Two things happened.

Mallory's right hand landed in a pile of twigs and dry seaweed and something warm and feathery that suddenly came alive and started to shriek in a high, furious voice. And the moon came out from behind its cloud.

For a split second, Mallory hung by his left hand on the wall, staring into the slack-jawed faces of not one, but two young German soldiers. Then he realised that he had no foothold, and fell, feet kicking air, to the full extent of his left arm. *Fool,* he told himself, feeling the crack of muscle and sinew, gritting his teeth against the agony of his clawed fingers on the rock of the parapet. He waited a split second that felt like a year, waited for the rifle butt to smash his fingers, waited for the Germans to start yelling, alert the garrison –

His right hand was on the cliff face now, clawing for a hold, finding one. Somewhere he could hear the squawking of a frightened gull, the harsh breathing of young, panic-stricken Germans trying to work out a way of getting rid of this *thing* from the cliff, and forgetting that the easiest way of doing it was to yell and let their five hundred comrades do it for them.

Mallory had an idea.

He said, *'Hilfe.'*

He had learned his German at Heidelberg University before the war, and on the high crags of the Bavarian Alps in the sunlit middle years of the 1930s. His accent was perfect; so perfect that the Germans hesitated.

'Get a hold of me,' said Mallory, in German. 'I fell.'

The soldiers were bamboozled with relief. This was not an enemy but a victim, a comrade in need –

The hesitation lasted the fraction of a second. That was enough for Mallory. He heaved himself up and halfway over the parapet. The Germans looked undecided. This was a Mallory undisturbed by seagulls. This was a Mallory who for eighteen months had lived wild as an animal in the White Mountains of Crete.

The Germans did not stand a chance.

Mallory drove his dagger through the first one's eye and into his brain. The second one opened his mouth to shout. Mallory drove his fist into his throat. He tugged the knife from the eye socket. As the body hit the ground the second German came at him, gasping. The man's momentum carried him on, over Mallory's shoulders and the parapet. Then he was hanging face down, caught by the toe of his boot, hooked on a small projection of the stone. If his vocal cords had been functioning, he would have been screaming.

Mallory felt an odd tugging sensation. He saw the German's boot slip, millimetre by millimetre, in the moonlight. Some part of the German had gone through the spare coil of rope Mallory carried on his shoulder. When he fell, he was going to take Mallory with him.

Mallory dived inside the parapet. The German emitted a quiet, rasping croak. The boot went over the edge. A crushing load came suddenly on the rope. It lifted Mallory. But the friction of the parapet stopped it dragging him over the edge.

Cautiously, Mallory found an end of the coil and belayed it to the iron steps set in the rock above the demilune. Then he wriggled out of the toils.

The rope ran out. He looked over the edge.

The part of the German that had caught the coil had been his neck. Mallory left him to hang while he tipped the first German over the edge. Then he began to untangle the rope.

'Okay, Schlegel?' yelled a voice in German from above.

'Fine,' shouted Mallory. Thirty feet below the demilune, the corpse of the second German swung like a clock pendulum over the dizzy swoop of the cliff and the rock-smashed waves at its base.

The moon went in. Mallory let an end of the rope go. The hanging German became a patch of darkness falling through greater darkness to the ribbon of white below. He thought he saw a little splash. Then he finished untangling the rope, and let it drop to where Miller and Andrea were waiting. While they climbed, he put his boots and socks back on.

Five minutes later, Miller and Andrea were with him in the demilune, breathing heavily. He pulled up the rope, coiled it, clambered over the parapet and hung it in the branches of a stunted juniper in the cliff, out of sight below the base. By the time he got back, he could no longer hear their breathing.

'Ready?' he said.

The silhouettes of the two coal-scuttle helmets nodded.

Mallory looked at his watch. The radium-bright hands said 2215. He said, 'I'll meet you by the generators at midnight. Check the sentries on the repair sheds. Look at rotas, timings. And Dusty. Your department. Bangs and so on.'

'Sir,' said Miller.

'And if you could avoid getting caught?'

Andrea's teeth gleamed suddenly in the moonlight. 'But without my moustache, where shall I hide?'

Mallory laughed quietly. 'See you at midnight,' he said. He stepped lightly onto the parapet of the demilune, reached out a hand and a foot, and stepped onto the naked cliff.

For a moment, he hung there in the moonlight, poised easily on the apparently sheer rock wall. Miller closed his eyes and held onto the first of the iron rungs leading upwards from the demilune, his stomach weightless with vertigo. Climbing a rope was one thing. This human-fly business was another altogether.

When he opened his eyes again, the little cloud was passing away from the moon, and the face of the cliff was once more covered with light. But of Mallory there was no sign.

'Off we jolly well go,' said Andrea.

Andrea led the way up the iron rungs in the cliff face. It was a fifty-foot climb. At the top was a sort of stile in the parapet. Before he reached it, Andrea hooked an arm through the rung, brushed the worst of the cliff-dirt from his SS smock, and pulled back the cocking lever of his Schmeisser. This was easier than thrashing around in the Pyrenees. Here, you knew whom you could trust. It was the old team, without distractions: a well-oiled machine.

He stepped up onto the parapet, keeping his shoulders hunched to reduce his mighty bulk. He probably looked nothing like either

of the men Mallory had killed. But it was elementary to suppose
that if two men had clambered down a set of iron rungs to a stone
gull's nest, below which was a precipice and some sea, then the two
men who came back up the rungs were the same two men, even if
they looked different.

He said, in his perfect German, 'Hell, it's cold down there.'

The parapet formed the edge of a sort of terrace ten yards wide,
down a flight of stone steps from another fortified level. A line of
ancient cannons stood rotting at their embrasures. At the end of
the line of cannons were the silhouettes of two men with a
machine gun. One of the men said, 'Bloody cold up here, too.'

Private soldiers, thought Andrea. No problem. 'Coffee,' he said.

'There's over an hour to midnight,' said one of the shadows.
'Befehl ist Befehl.'

Andrea shrugged. He looked down over the edge. The moonlit
precipice fell away sheer to the sea. No sign of Mallory. 'Hurry up,
you.'

Miller came up and onto the terrace.

Andrea said, 'We'll get the coffee and take it down.' The note of
authority in Andrea's voice had not escaped them. An officer.
Officers had their reasons.

'Marsch,' said Andrea.

Miller in the lead, they stamped up the stone steps from the terrace to the summit level.

'Right turn,' said Andrea.

The two of them were marching along a flat plain, paved with
stone, silvery under the moon. To their right, the parapet marked
the edge of the cliff. Ahead and to the left, the ground sloped away
and downwards into the black pit, beyond which guttered the few
yellow lights of San Eusebio. Immediately to the left, cracks of light
showed round the poorly blacked-out panes of what must be a
guardhouse. Immediately behind them was an ancient battlement,
topped with modern barbed wire, that looked as if it stretched from
the cliffs to the beach facing the town.

They were in. In, but horribly in the open.

Somewhere in the guardhouse a bell rang and a man's voice began
screaming: a parade-ground scream, a scream of military emergency
requiring immediate action. Lights jumped on. The surface on which
Andrea and Miller were standing was suddenly a harshly illuminated
plain on which each was the focus of an asterisk of shadows. Men in
jackboots were pouring out of doors, lining up shoulder to shoulder,

distancing off, shuffling jackboot heels on the granite stones. Miller could feel the sweat now, not climbing sweat, but the sweat of being in the middle of five hundred Germans.

Andrea yelled, *'Shun!'* Miller crashed to a halt.

They were in, all right. But not all the way.

What they had not been able to see without the floodlights was straight: a second fence, running parallel with the wall, fifteen feet tall, topped with barbed wire strung between insulators, stretching from the rim of the cliff down to the black waters of the harbour. The area between the fences was a no-man's land, bathed in a pitiless grey-white light that limned every speck of grit, every button and buckle on the hundred-and-twenty German soldiers fallen in between the guardhouse and the sandbagged machine-gun posts on either side of the main gate.

Miller could feel a trickle of sweat on his forehead. Andrea was massive and silent at his side.

In the middle of the inner fence was another gate. The gate stood open. On either side were more machine-gun emplacements. The floodlights gleamed off the steel helmets by the guns.

Andrea's eyes flicked round the yard. The soldiers were Wehrmacht, not SS. His shoulders squared. In a voice of brass, he said, *'Marsch!'* Holding their Schmeissers rigidly across their chests, the two men tramped steadily across the paving. The gate loomed up ahead, a goal of darkness in the palisade of the fence. Miller could feel the mouths of the machine guns pouting at him from their emplacements. At his side, he could see that Andrea's helmet was tilted a fraction, and there was dirt on his camouflage smock. Must have been when he went up the cliff. Wehrmacht hated dirt. Almost as much as they hated SS . . .

Someone, thought Miller, had raised the alarm. It must have been those guys down by the cannons. They had waited for the intruders to walk right into the hornet's nest, and then stirred it up with a pole. They would be looking for two men in SS uniforms. And here were these two men, in wet, dirty SS uniforms, marching across the killing floor under the floodlights.

Miller marched on. A small seed of hope took root and began to grow. Nobody was doing anything about it. Maybe, thought Miller, this is an exercise. Or maybe they are so frightened of the SS that they will not even screw with the uniform. Maybe this is just a regular night in a major military installation, and you have been skulking in the mountains so long you have forgotten.

Pace by pace, the sandbags reached out and funnelled them towards the black gate. Behind them, someone was bellowing orders. On the right, three privates and a Feldwebel were standing rigidly to attention. Miller could feel the Feldwebel's eyes flicking up and down: the eyes of a stickler, used to cataloguing a minute smear on the surface of a boot, a tiny flaw in the polish of a leather strap. And these SS guys were marching through his gate squelching with Atlantic and covered in half a cliff.

Andrea marched on, regular as a metronome, out of the gate area and away from the eyes and into the darkness beyond. The darkness that held the docks and those U-boats, waiting to slide out of the harbour and back into their black underwater world –

They were through. The lights were dimming, shaded by the brim of Miller's helmet. Made it, he thought. We have goddamn well made it –

The darkness was suddenly full of metallic noises. Ahead and to the left, brilliant suns of light came into being. A voice said, in English, 'Do not touch your guns. The hands out to the sides, if you please. You are completely surrounded.'

Miller squinted to one side of the light, but saw nothing. There could be one man or a hundred men back there. A hundred seemed more likely.

Slowly and reluctantly, he spread his arms out in an attitude of crucifixion.

So this is how it really ends, thought Miller.

Figures emerged from the dark, figures in SS uniform. The figures looped the Schmeisser straps over Miller's head and stood on tiptoe to disarm Andrea.

'Welcome, gentlemen,' said the SS Hauptsturmführer. His accent was very good. 'We have been expecting you.'

Then they marched them away.

SIX

Tuesday 2300–Wednesday 0400

They marched them through a little village of wooden huts, past a wire-fenced concrete building that throbbed with diesels. Living quarters, thought Miller, collecting information he would never use. Generator shed. Down on the left, the jackhammer rattle of riveting guns sounded, and the tame lightnings of arc welders flashed blue in the dark. Dockyard stuff. A privileged overview of the whole layout.

'*Halt!*' yelled the Hauptsturmführer in charge of their escort.

They were standing on a bridge in front of a gateway in a tall, windowless granite wall. The gate was studded with iron bolts. Above it were battlements. The sweat was cold on Miller's body, and his body ached. He was exhausted.

A wicket opened in the gate. The Hauptsturmführer stepped forward and showed a pass to the gatekeeper. There was a pause, with the sound of telephoning. Then the double gates opened, and a machine pistol jabbed Miller in the kidney. The squad marched in. The gates clashed to behind them.

They were in a yard, paved with granite, surveyed by the barrels of three machine guns sited on the battlements. Same old thing, thought Miller. 'No imagination,' he said.

'But very competent,' said Andrea, his eyes moving, mapping the yard. 'Thorough.'

'That's Germans for you,' said Miller. 'Thorough.'

The gun muzzle behind him jabbed him painfully in the kidney. 'Silence!' barked the Hauptsturmführer.

'Don't understand,' said Andrea.

'Don't speak German,' said Miller.

And for a second there was a small warmth in the notion that although they were in the hands of the enemy, mission not accomplished and never to be so, they had something up their sleeves.

Two things. There was also Mallory, still at large.

A door opened in the wall opposite. This was not your studded oak, medieval style. This was your basic twentieth-century armour plate, four good inches of Nazi steel. It gaped wide, exhaling a stink of damp stone and sewage. Then it swallowed them in, and the door clashed to at their backs.

They went down granite stairs, through corridors with bombproof roofs and whitewash blistered with mildew. There was a spiral staircase like the entrance to a tomb. At the bottom, a corridor lit glaring white was lined with steel doors. One of the steel doors was open.

'In there,' said the Hauptsturmführer.

'We will take a look,' said Miller. 'If we don't like the linen, we will speak to the manager about –'

The soldier behind him smashed him on the ear with the barrel of his Schmeisser. Miller's head rang with pain. A jackboot shot him through the door. Andrea followed. The steel door clashed shut. Outside, jackboots tramped off down the corridor.

There was brilliant white light, and dirt, and silence.

The warmth had gone. They were in the stone bowels of the earth, and it was cold.

The silence was the worst part.

The room might have been designed as a magazine, or a cell. It had a domed roof, and no window. The floor was of granite flagstones, patched with concrete. There was a grating in one corner, presumably for use as a lavatory. From it there came a vile smell.

The silence was the silence of a place buried beneath tons of masonry and rock. It was the silence of a place with no secret passages, no hope of overpowering guards, no hope of escape. The silence of the tomb.

Mallory, reflected Miller, would have hated it.

Andrea yawned. He said, 'This is really most unpleasant.' Then, with the massive grace of an animal that refuses to be concerned about the future because it inhabits the perpetual present, he located a cleanish patch of floor, lay down, and closed his eyes.

They had left Miller his cigarettes. He pulled out the packet, found a dry one, and lit it.

Then he waited.

The hands on his watch ticked along to eleven-thirty. At eleven-thirty-one, a key clashed in the door, and five men came in.

Four of them were big Waffen-SS whose torsos strained at their camouflage smocks. The fifth was a man of about twenty-five, wearing civilian clothes: a blue double-breasted suit, with a stiff collar and a dark-blue tie. His hair was blond, with a wave. His mouth was a little red rosebud, his eyes blue slugs that crawled over the prisoners' faces.

He waved a handkerchief under his nose. 'Really,' he said, in prissy, faintly-accented English. 'They should do something about the smell.' He smiled, a cherubic smile. 'Gentlemen,' he said, 'I am Herr Gruber.' He snapped his fingers. 'Chair.'

One of the burly SS men trotted into the corridor, and returned with a hard chair. Herr Gruber flicked the seat with his handkerchief and sat down.

Miller and Andrea sat side by side, slouched against the wall. Miller yawned. Andrea watched Gruber with eyes that managed to be simultaneously hostile and condescending. In their travels in occupied Greece, both of them had had experience of the Gestapo. Neither of them understood why they were still alive. Herr Gruber was going to provide the answers.

Miller said, 'So can we help you? Only I am kinda sleepy, and –'

Gruber had made a gesture to one of the SS men. The barrel of the man's gun came round quickly, slamming into Miller's already bruised ear. The pain of the cartilage trapped between metal and skull was ferocious. Miller's eyes watered. He kept his anger down. Save it for later.

If there was a later.

'So,' said Herr Gruber. 'I understand that now you would like to kill me and these soldiers.' He smiled, his cherubic smile. 'And the SS is not what it used to be. So I expect you could probably do it. But I would point out that the odds against you are most impressive. Even if you were to escape this cell, you would quickly lose your own lives. Which if you listen to me may not be necessary.'

Gruber watched the two men closely. Normally, when he told prisoners that there was a road to survival, they could not wait to get onto it and start running, jostling each other off the edge if necessary.

Not these two.

Their faces were haggard under the weatherbeaten glow. They were old: forty at least, and looking older. Herr Gruber could hardly believe that these people had done what they were reputed to have done: evaded a regiment of Panzerjäger, murdered a platoon of SS, found this place. But they had done it. And Herr Gruber was absolutely delighted with their success, which had turned a run-of-the-mill secret weapon into something much more important. They had played, as the saying went, into his hands.

But as they sat there, the big one with the flat, black-eyed stare of a Byzantine icon, and the thin American with the blood running red from his ear into the collar of his tunic, they did not look like men who were playing into anyone's hands at all.

'You have come here to destroy certain weapons,' said Herr Gruber. 'Which of course we cannot permit, not only because we value these weapons, but because of the diplomatic problems this would cause for our friends in Madrid.' The smile did not falter. 'Soon we shall be leaving. And I think that we shall leave you behind us. You seem quite comfortable here. A rest will do you good after your busy time. After which I suspect the Guardia Civil will receive an anonymous call to say that some Allied soldiers have become . . . locked in what will certainly be perceived as an embarrassing position. I hope you will still be alive then.' The smile left his face. The lips were wet and shiny, the eyes icy. 'Though I doubt you will last long in a Spanish internment camp. The guards are trigger-happy. Also the food is neither wholesome nor plentiful, and there is much typhus.' The smile returned. 'And I doubt that anyone at the British Embassy will be too keen to see you again, after the embarrassment you will have caused them. Spain is, after all, a neutral country, and your presence will be held to constitute a most cynical violation of this neutrality.' He licked his lips. In his future he saw sunlit vistas of promotion, victory, universal success. 'Your diplomats are bringing pressure to bear on the Spanish government just now to stop our wolfram exports, and to withdraw Spanish troops from the Russian Front. Your visit here will I think change all that. In fact, it seems to me not unlikely that at the end of this little . . . adventure, Germany will have a new ally.' He sighed. There is only one disappointment, of course. That is that politics prevents me from having you shot out of hand.'

Andrea spat in the general direction of the grating. The Gestapo man tutted. 'Keep your spit,' he said. 'I think you will need it. Now. There is one thing. Your comrade. Where is he?'

Andrea said, 'Comrade?'

Miller looked across at him. In the American's posture the Gestapo man read the bitterness of defeat. Miller said to Andrea, 'What are you trying to prove?'

Andrea said, 'We have no comrade.'

Miller seemed to have developed a nasty twitch in his right cheek. His tongue ran round his dry lips. The Gestapo man spotted the signs of fear, an emotion he had had much practice recognising.

Miller said, 'There's no point.' He turned to the Gestapo man. 'Listen,' he said. 'He's –'

Andrea moved. He moved suddenly, but with the lumbering slowness of a bear, across the filthy floor to Miller. He grabbed Miller round the neck and pulled his head away from the wall, and the Gestapo man knew that next this big man was going to bash this thin man's brains out. That would have been a thing he would have enjoyed watching.

But it was important that it did not happen.

So he gestured to the guards. The guards grabbed one of Andrea's arms each, and pulled him off. It was not as difficult as the Gestapo man had feared. He might be big, but he was weak. These Mediterranean types. Hot blood, but no sinews.

Miller was rubbing his neck. 'Hey!' he whined. 'Ain't no call to beat up on a guy –'

'Insect!' hissed Andrea. 'Reptile!'

'Silence,' said Gruber. The Greek subsided.

The American said, 'The third guy. He's dead.'

'Come,' said the Gestapo man. 'Can you not do better than that?'

'It's the truth.'

The wet blue eyes were as blank as the indicator lights on a wrecked tank. 'How did he die?'

'He fell down the cliff.'

'What was he doing on the cliff?'

'Hiding.' Steady, thought Miller. The *Stella Maris* was in the harbour. No sense involving them. 'He'd led us round from the mainland. He placed the rope. He fell, poor bastard. Strangled himself. Take a look at the bottom of the cliff, you'll find his body. Then you caught us.'

The Gestapo man fingered his chin. Certainly it would be possible to fall on those cliffs. He said, 'It was not a clever thing to do, to enter by the cliffs. You made much noise. Naturally, you were caught.'

Miller hung his head. That was not what the Hauptsturmführer had said. The Hauptsturmführer had said they were expected, and Miller was inclined to believe him. 'Shucks,' he said.

'Quite so,' said Gruber. He stood up. 'Well. I cannot say it has been a pleasure meeting you.' He snapped his fingers. 'Chair.'

One of his SS men took the chair away. Herr Gruber walked across to Andrea, who was propped against the wall. 'Goodbye, Greek,' he said. The cane in his hand lashed out like a striking adder. It caught Andrea across the eyes.

Muscles swelled at the corners of the Greek's jaw. Then he smiled, a happy, white-toothed smile of anticipation. Blood ran from his heavy black eyebrows into the smile. 'For that,' he said, 'you will die.'

Herr Gruber smiled a superior smile, and strode out of the cell.

The door slammed. The lock clashed. The light went out. They were in darkness.

Miller said, 'Colonel?'

'Miller.' The voice sounded strangled.

'Can you see?'

'I can see.'

'More 'n I can,' said Miller. A peculiar noise rattled in the vaulting of the cell.

They might be locked up in the dark, facing the imminent failure of their mission, the decimation of the invasion fleet, and a diplomatic disaster in Madrid.

But Mallory was out there somewhere. And Miller was laughing.

For Mallory, being alone on the cliff had been a sort of liberation. After all those days and weeks of little rest and occasional food, the feel of rock under feet and fingers and the freedom of the great vertical spaces acted like a tonic. He trusted the other two to reconnoitre the landward side and the submarine sheds. But he trusted only himself to reconnoitre from the seaward. There were some things he needed to look at on his own. Mallory was a team player, but Andrea was too big, and Miller got vertigo. There were times when solo climbing was what you had to do.

The moon slid behind a cloud. In the darkness, he began to move swiftly sideways across the face of the cliff. He had gone a hundred yards when he heard the commotion up above: a bell, a voice screaming, the clatter of boots on granite; then the faraway double tramp of jackboots, and a voice, Andrea's, yelling *Marsch!*

The boots stopped.

Mallory could hear nothing after that. But he did not need ears to tell him that this was trouble. He waited for the shooting to start. The shooting did not start.

He hung for a moment, waiting for a patch of moonlight to pass. The cloud returned.

Before he had been climbing diagonally upwards towards the parapet. But the sky above the parapet was glowing with a nimbus of ice-grey floodlights. So he headed low, towards the sea, acquiring the grammar of the crumbling stone through fingers and toes, keeping the bulge of an overhang between him and the parapet.

Soon the floodlights went out, and the Cabo de la Calavera was once again a domed and sinister lump of darkness against the sky. Whatever had happened had happened. Mallory took a deep breath. He knew that nobody would be there to meet him at the rendezvous by the generator sheds.

He was on his own.

Steady.

Worrying about Miller and Andrea was a waste of time. He kept his mind on the operation. One man needed to operate differently from three. Time spent on reconnaissance was time wasted now. He needed to penetrate the Cabo. He needed a weak spot.

He had one in mind.

He began to climb upwards.

Whatever Moor-hating grandee had built the *fortaleza* on the tip of the Cabo de la Calavera had chosen his spot well. The cliffs came sheer out of the sea – more than sheer, on some of the pitches. Mallory concentrated on the rock. Here on the sheer cliffs, it was less friable, and grass and sea-pink had failed to find a foothold. There were little cracks and corrugations that would have given pause to a fly with common sense. But Mallory was desperate. So Mallory went up the face, slow but sure, moving from the hips, gracefully, almost without effort. He worked his way steadily westwards, towards the point on which the *fortaleza* stood, working his way steadily higher. The clouds were thickening again, and the moon had gone. That was useful, even if it meant climbing by feel. The sea was a heavy murmur far below, the wind a tenuous hand pressing on his back.

After perhaps an hour, the wind brought him the stench of drains. When he next looked up, he saw the cliff above him had changed nature. It was no longer natural granite. It had become the outer wall of the *fortaleza*.

Mallory paused, standing on the sheer precipice connecting sky and sea. Cliffs were no problem, and masonry walls he could deal with. It was the transition between the living rock of the cliff and the cut stone of the fortress wall that would be the difficulty.

For where masonry met rock face, a heavy black line crossed the darkness of the wall. The outer face of the masonry was cantilevered out over the rock: machicolated, Mallory seemed to remember. Machicolation or cantilever, it boiled down to the same thing. What he had up there was a bloody great overhang. Mallory was solo, no rope, four spikes. Normally, he would have looked for another route to avoid an overhang. But this time, there was no going round.

Suddenly, Mallory was horribly tired.

He hung there for a moment. The smell of sewage was powerful in his nostrils. When he reached for the next hold, his right hand landed in a foul slime.

A foul slime that must have come from somewhere.

Suddenly, Mallory's weariness was gone. Thank God for Spanish sanitation, he thought. For medieval Spanish sanitation, invented by Arabs, bringers of civilisation to the European world.

And with a bit of luck, bringer of Mallory onto the walls of the Fortaleza de la Calavera.

He started to climb again, keeping to the left, out of the stream of sewage. In two minutes, he was up against the bottom course of the machicolations.

He could see the detail of the overhang now. It was like an inverted flight of seven steps, a foot each, angled outwards at forty-five degrees. Impassable without a rope.

But ten feet to Mallory's right, a vertical line of darkness broke the steps: a line perhaps two feet wide that was not a line, but a crevasse. To the designers of the *fortaleza's* sanitation, it was the outlet from the castle garderobes. To a climber like Mallory, it was a practicable chimney in an impracticable overhang. The tiredness left him. There was a route here. In the face of a route, it was not possible to feel tired.

He crouched on a nearly invisible ledge and checked his spikes. He took his boots and socks off. He put his boots back on his bare feet, and pulled the socks over the boots. Then he swung himself round, face to the cliff, and started to move crabwise towards the chimney.

He knew he was under it from the stinging reek of urine and ammonia. He looked up, sighting against the sky with watering eyes. The slot in the machicolations reached out as far as the last two steps. If he could reach those last two steps, he would be able to get a hand up and onto the masonry of the vertical wall, and find a place to get a spike in.

Garderobe or no garderobe, it was a hideously difficult place. But the thought did not even occur to Mallory. It was a climbing problem, and climbing problems were there to be solved.

He reached in the pocket of his smock, checking his spikes and the leather-wrapped lead mallet he used as a hammer. Then he moved into the dreadful recesses of the chimney.

As he had suspected, it was a chimney of cut stone built out from the living rock. At first, he was climbing the slippery natural rock. When the rock gave way to masonry, he put his shoulders against one side, his feet against the other, and pushed.

The socks over his boots gave him a grip through the slime. The slime lubricated his shoulders as they slid up the cut stone blocks. Easy chimneying, if you could cut out the stench. He was moving outwards now, away from the face of the cliff, following the line of the machicolations. Once, the cliff's sheerness had been daunting. Any minute now, it was going to seem almost like home.

As long as he ignored the black hole above his head, and what might come down it.

Brace the shoulders. Keep the feet against the far wall, hard, so the socks bite through the film of filth and the boot-nails grind into the solid rock. Do it again. And again –

Mallory's helmet clanked against stone. He had run out of chimney.

He stood there, wedged shoulders and feet in that slot in the masonry, his breathing shallow. Two hundred feet below, white tongues of foam curled round jagged rocks and licked up the cliff wall.

Mallory fumbled in his pocket for a spike. Before the war, he would not have considered using spikes. Spikes were for Germans, during the assaults on the north face of the Eiger, the attempts on Kanchenjunga for the greater glory of the Third Reich. Mallory had on one occasion climbed the Big Wall on Mount Cook, removing the spikes left there by an unsportsmanlike German expedition. But in Zermatt he had met Schenck, an American blacksmith and climber who ran a forge in the back of his pickup truck. Schenck had seen a war coming, and foreseen the kind of things that some- one would ask Mallory to do. He had forced on Mallory half a dozen of his specials: three-inch blades of steel cut from the rear springs of a Model A Ford, pierced to hold a loop of rope. When Mallory had demurred, Schenck had pointed out that whatever he thought about using a spike to beat a mountain, using a spike to beat a German was fine.

God bless you, Schenck, wherever you are, thought Mallory in his stinking chimney. He looped a spike's cord round his wrist. Then he reached up and out and round the last two steps of the overhang, running the spike's point across the stones like the point of a pencil until he felt the check that would mean a seam of mortar. Then, gingerly, one-handed, he began to tap it in.

He tapped slowly, with infinite caution, partly for the sake of quietness, but mostly because he had only four of those three-inch splinters of metal left, survivors of the original half-dozen. And much depended on these four: his life, Andrea's and Miller's, the lives of the invasion fleet. He tapped for a full two minutes, until he was sure. Then he put in another spike inside the chimney, level with his eyes. This one went in more easily; he was not working at arm's length, and the mortar in the gully, attacked by hundreds of years of carbonic acid from the rain and uric acid from the garrison, was softer than the mortar on the outside of the wall.

When it was in, he tugged at it stealthily. It held firm. Reaching up, he found the loop of rope on the head of the first spike, shoved his hand through, and applied weight, without loosening his grip on the walls of the chimney.

The spike held firm.

He took a deep breath. Then he gripped that loop of rope and swung his weight out over the abyss. For a moment he was dangling free, a spider hanging from a cornice, a little creature of flesh suspended by a metal spike and a loop of quarter-inch cord two hundred feet above the sullen moil of white surf in sharp black rock. Then he put his left leg up, searching for the spike he had driven into the side of the chimney.

He put the sole of his boot onto that spike, applied his weight like a man applying weight to the pedal of a bicycle, and straightened his leg until he was standing, his leg in under the overhang, his torso vertical, parallel with the wall of masonry that went up, up, into the black sky. His left hand went to his pocket, found another spike, placed it above the first, made the pencil-like scribbling movements until the point caught, burrowed it in the first millimetres until it held, brought up the hammer, and began to tap. The muscles of his right arm and left leg were yelling that they could not be expected to keep this up, that they were going to cause pain, and cramp, until Mallory bloody well stopped this abuse. Mallory forced himself to pay no attention. Tap the spike gently, take your time –

There was the smallest of small movements under the sole of his left boot.

And suddenly he was falling, the full extent of his right arm, until the loop brought him up with a crunch of armpit sinews, and he was dangling once again from the edge of the cornice above the hungry rocks below.

The spike under his foot had fallen out.

Falling, the reflex is to open the hands, make the fingers a feeble approximation of feathers of flesh, spread the limbs, try to turn a solid body into a gliding thing that will fly away from danger.

Mallory knew about reflexes. He knew that the only direction humans fly is vertically downwards. Even as he swung, he kept his left hand clamped around the hammer.

After what felt like ten hours but was more like ten seconds, the swinging stopped. Mallory hung there. *Rest,* his body told him. But he knew that as he hung, the strength would be draining out of him, the blood leaving that arm. The muscles of the right arm needed all the blood they could get. Even if using them meant that the spike up there would pull out of the wall, and drop him through all that air onto all those rocks.

Damned if you hang. Not necessarily damned if you don't.

Carefully, Mallory put the hammer into his pocket. Then he reached his left hand up to join his right, and pulled himself up like a gymnast chinning the bar.

The muscles crunched in his arms. His teeth bared in a rictus of effort. The blood roared in his skull.

But there were his hands, and the spike, and the blessed stones, level with his eyes.

He held on with his right hand, pulled a fold of his smock over the projection of the spike, and lowered himself until he was hanging by the methodical German canvas. Then, very carefully, he teased the last spike out of his pocket, and the hammer, and raised his arms above his head, and began to tap.

Two minutes later he was up, left hand holding the upper spike, right boot on the lower, right hand putting in the next spike. The overhang was a full two feet below: out of sight, out of mind. The wall of the fortress stretched above him, eighty-five feet of sheer masonry to the top of the tower. Mallory kept tapping the spike, not letting himself stop, because stopping meant reaction, and reaction meant the shakes, and the shakes were no good when you were balanced on two little stubs of steel, with no spares.

So Mallory did not stop. Mallory went on up.

It became a rhythm. Tap the spike. Test the spike. New hand. New foot. Shake out the bottom spike, move it to the top . . .

Keep climbing.

To the observer, Mallory would have seemed to drift up that wall in defiance of gravity. But of course there were no observers. The murmur of the sea receded. Small, thick-walled windows passed by to the left and right. Mallory ignored them. He heard the breath in his throat, the blood in his ears, mingled with the roar of the sea. *Tap the spike. Test the spike.* It had started to rain, a thin, persistent Atlantic rain, coming in with the wind on his back. The rain was a help. The reason he was climbing this stone oil drum was that anybody standing sentry on top of a tower rising three hundred feet above the sea would be watching half-heartedly at best. And this was the kind of rain that would turn half-heartedness into actual neglect of duty. *New hand. New foot.* Mallory had an idea that depended on the neglect of duty. *Tap the spike. Test the spike.*

Above, the tower was no longer a cliff losing itself in the dark. It was a wall, a sharp-cut semicircle of stone. Mallory was nearly at the top.

He paused, stuck to the wall like a fly, listening. The wind rushed round his ears, and the rain pulled a flat, mouldy smell from the stone. Above the drizzle of the rain he heard another noise: the tramp of booted feet.

Mallory waited.

The feet marched to and fro. The rain eased, then returned, harder now. A voice above his head said, *'Scheisse.'* The footsteps changed sound, became muffled. There was the metallic click of a latch, a groan of heavy iron hinges. The sentry was taking shelter from the rain.

Mallory started climbing again. He was in a hurry now, but he did not let it alter the steady rhythm of his movements. The rain was becoming heavier, driving in hard and steady on the wind. After the sixth spike he found he could hook his fingers over the parapet. Then he was up, standing on the stone deck inside the battlements in his boots and socks, flexing his stiff fingers.

The top of the tower was flat, except for the turret with the staircase. Its door faced inland, away from the prevailing wind. On the roof of the turret were chimneys, emitting wood smoke, and a group of radio aerials. There were four aerials: three whips and a big shortwave array, and a flagpole. At the top of the flagpole something waved and bumped in the wind – something that was not a flag: a vaguely man-shaped mass against the clouds, but with a disgusting raggedness about the outline. Something that had once been Juanito the smuggler.

Mallory was cold and stiff from a dangerous hour crawling up a vertical wall. Now he felt an angry warmth spread through him, against a lunatic enemy who wanted to rip the world back into the Middle Ages.

His wool-padded boots thudded softly on the stones as he walked across the roof of the tower and flattened himself against the wall of the turret. He could hear a man coughing inside the door. Cigarette smoke wafted out through the keyhole. The sentry was alone.

Mallory waited with the patience of a hunting animal. The rain slackened.

The door opened.

The sentry never saw what hit him. There was a sudden, agonising pain in the left-hand side of his chest. Then there were no more thoughts.

Carefully Mallory wiped the blade of his knife on the dead man's tunic. He unstrapped the man's Schmeisser, and took the two spare clips from his bandolier. He went through the pockets and found the man's paybook. Then he dragged the corpse across the wet roof to the parapet he had climbed, and rolled it over.

It fell with no sound, the way Mallory would have fallen, if he had fallen. Mallory did not stay to watch it.

He took the rags of his socks off his boots. The rain had washed a certain amount of the sewage from his tunic. He squared his shoulders, and checked the Schmeisser with his rope-raw hands. Then he went through the door, closed it silently behind him, and started down the spiral stone stairs inside.

He smelt cigarette smoke, and old stone, and sewage on his tunic. After fourteen steps there was a Gothic-arched doorway, closed with an iron-studded door. A cardboard notice on the door said, in Gothic script, WACHSTUBE: guardroom. God bless the orderly German mind, thought Mallory, with renewed hope. It may yet be the saving of us all.

Beneath the guardroom was another door. From behind it came voices, and the clatter of Morse keys. Radio room. A new noise was coming from below, a busy, many-voiced buzz of ringing telephones and scurrying feet and shouted instructions; the noise of a human anthill, bustling. If the submarines were moving out at noon, this would be the sound of last-minute arrangements being made, repairs finished, evacuations planned. Mallory permitted himself a small, grim smile. It was the kind of bustle that could with a little thought be turned into confusion, and taken advantage of.

He rounded the last turn in the stairs.

Ahead of him was a corridor lined on one side with doors, and on the other with windows looking out onto a darkened court-yard. The corridor was lit with dim yellow bulbs. Mallory began to walk down the corridor at a measured sentry's tread, towards the stone balustrading round the stairway at its end. Cardboard signs labelled a navy office, a dock office, stores. Inside, men leaned over desks tottering with piles of papers, smoking and talking into telephones, and scribbling in the pools of light from their lamps. A German machine: dotting the last i, crossing the last t, before it closed itself down.

Two soldiers, pale men, clerkish, passed him. One of them wrinkled his nose and said, 'What a stink.' Mallory kept his face blank. The clerks accelerated away. Mallory tramped on, slow and steady, towards the stairs at the far end of the corridor, hiding in his measured tread the fact that he did not know where he was, or how to find what he was looking for. What Mallory needed was a clue, any clue. And in an operation like this, strolling tired and sore through the heart of an enemy installation, clues were not easy to come by.

Mallory arrived at the top of the stairs at the end of the corridor. A Kapitän of the Kriegsmarine was coming up. Mallory waited, crashed his heels together, extended a stiff right arm. *'Heil Hitler,'* he said.

The Kriegsmarine Kapitän touched a negligent hand to the peak of his cap, frowning at the wall, not looking at him. To a German, the uniform signified more than the man. And of course, there was the stink.

Mallory offered silent thanks to the *fortaleza*'s sewage, which had let him in and was now keeping people away from him. He started to go down the stairs.

Then he was vouchsafed his clue.

Into the smell of sweat, and smoke, and sewage, and cold stone, had come another smell; a smell that transported Mallory for a split second back to Cairo three years ago, with the tinkle of fountains in marble patios, the murmur of staff officers with creased trousers and soft handshakes making assignations for drinks at Shepherd's

Hotel while the frontline troops died hot, flyblown deaths under the desert sky.

The smell of expensive Turkish tobacco.

It was rising up the stairs, a mere hint of it in the column of cold, wet air. Mallory followed it like a hound.

He went down the stone-balustraded steps, and found himself on a corridor identical to the one above, except that this one was blocked off halfway by a door; not studded, this door, but made of black oak, with elaborate wrought-iron hinges, their strapwork in the form of stylised olive branches. It was an elegant door, built to please the eye as well as turn aside weapons of war. From the orientation of the corridor, Mallory guessed that the rooms beyond would look south, over the harbour. Once, these would have been the Commandant's quarters.

The smell of Turkish cigarettes was stronger here.

These were still the Commandant's quarters.

As Mallory walked up to the door, it opened. An Obersturmführer in the black uniform of the Totenkopf-SS marched quickly out, glanced at Mallory without curiosity, closed the door behind him, and marched on. In his hand was a sheet of paper, and on his face an expression of sulky haste. An odd, harsh voice pursued him. 'Within one hour!' it barked. It sounded as if there was something wrong with the speaker's throat.

'*Jawohl, Herr General,*' muttered the ADC, and disappeared down the stairs.

Mallory pushed the door open.

The smell of Turkish cigarettes rolled out to meet him. Ahead, the corridor continued to a Gothic window full of night. Moroccan rugs covered the flagstones. The air was warm, and the smell of damp stone had disappeared. The light came from a gilt chandelier. Pictures of Spanish saints adorned the walls: male saints, stripped to the waist, bearing the marks of torture.

Mallory was not concerned with the interior appointments. There were two doors each side of the corridor. Three of them were closed; it was inconceivable that they would contain anything as vulgar and tasteless as a sentry. The fourth was open.

It was a huge room, forty feet on a side, with a sofa, two arm-chairs, a coffee table. There was a vast fireplace, surmounted by the carved arms of a Spanish duke. At the far end was a Gothic solar window. In front of the window was a desk with two telephones, a green onyx desk set, a bell-push and an ashtray from which the smoke of a Turkish cigarette rose vertically into the still, warm air. Behind the desk was a man with a pointed head, bald on top but fringed with close-clipped grey-blond hair.

No sentries. How could there be no sentries?

If nobody could get into the castle, there was no need of sentries inside the castle. That was logical.

Mallory walked into the room and shut the door. The man at the desk did not look up. The lights of the room moved in the silver insignia of an SS General, the lightning-flash runes on the collar, the silver skull-and-bones below the eagle on the high-crowned cap on the desk. The thin fingers reached out for the cigarette. The sausage lips sucked, blew smoke. The eyes came up to meet Mallory's.

The eyes were the colour of water, set above high cheekbones in a fleshless face with a cleft chin. The Adam's apple moved in the neck. There was something wrong with the Adam's apple: a dent in the right-hand side, a groove the thickness and depth of a finger. An old wound, perhaps. Striated webs of muscle shifted in the wasted areas where the cheeks should have been. 'What?' said the General, in his thin, harsh croak. He clipped his cigarette into his right hand. Mallory saw the hand was artificial, an unlifelike imitation of hard orange rubber.

Mallory reached in his pocket for the paybook he had taken from the dead sentry, stepped forward to the desk and held it out to the General. The General waved it away impatiently, wrinkling his nose at the smell. Private soldiers did not roll in sewage, then burst into Generals' rooms and identify themselves. What on earth did this *Dummkopf* think he was doing? The orange rubber fingers of the prosthesis strayed to the bell-push.

Mallory plastered a foolish grin on his face, and swatted the artificial hand away from the bell. The General was looking up at him now. A ropy vein was swelling on either side of his neck. He ignored the hand with the paybook. He opened his mouth to shout.

The hand holding the paybook kept moving. The General ignored it. He was watching Mallory's face. The anger was turning to something else, something like puzzlement, or even fear. But the hand with the paybook had gone further than a hand with a paybook need go, and it had dropped the paybook and folded the fingers under a hard ridge of knuckle and accelerated until it was an axehead aimed at the ruined Adam's apple in that stringy neck.

Mallory put his whole weight behind that punch. It was designed to smash the larynx. But whatever the General saw in the brown eyes above Mallory's foolish grin made him move his head at the final split instant, so the knuckles caught him on the side of the neck, bruising the larynx instead of smashing it, and he went backwards out of the carved-gilt chair and into the bow of the window, groping for the flap of his holster as he fell.

Mallory scrambled over the desk after him, his boot-nails leaving tears in the red Morocco top. The General was halfway up to his feet, his back against the stone tracery of the window. Mallory covered him with his Schmeisser. He said, 'Put your hands in the air.'

The General said in a rasping whisper, 'Have you gone mad?'

'Do as you are told,' said Mallory.

'You are not a German soldier,' said the General.

Mallory said, 'No.'

The General's Adam's apple bobbed in his throat. Self-possession returned to the cold-water eyes. He said, 'If you shoot me there will be ten of my men in here before you can take your finger off the trigger.'

'And you will be dead,' said Mallory. 'What good will that do you?' He saw the flicker of calculation in the colourless eyes, and knew that this was not an argument that would work. It might have cut some ice with a junior officer. But for one of Heinrich Himmler's inner circle, there were more frightening things than death.

'So,' whispered the General, with a smile that was no more than a stretch of the lips over the teeth. 'We have been expecting you.'

'That was clever of you,' said Mallory. 'How?'

The General said, 'You will die wondering, I think.'

Mallory yawned. 'Pardon,' he said. It was the old chess game of lies and evasions. 'You captured two men,' he said. 'Where are they?'

The General's face had relaxed. Mallory had shown weakness. He was in control. His orange artificial hand rested on the red leather desk. 'Where you will shortly be,' said the General. The bell-push was six inches away. 'What are you trying to achieve?' This one will hang from piano wire, his brain hissed furiously. From a meathook. He has no idea of the extent of his presumption. But he will learn, kicking his life out on the hook with the cut of thin steel at his damned impudent neck.

'My objectives,' said Mallory. The barrel of the Schmeisser moved like a snake's tongue, and smashed into the General's good arm above the elbow.

The General pulled his hand back. The pain was abominable. The arm was definitely broken. He said, in a whisper unstable with agony, 'For this you will die.'

'Oh, quite,' said Mallory. 'Where are your prisoners?'

The General stood there, cradling his good hand with his orange rubber fingers to take the weight off the upper arm. Nobody had spoken to him like this since the SA purge in 1934. The pain was terrible. He wanted to shout, but his vocal cords were paralysed. He wanted to push the bell, but he was frightened that some other part of him would be broken. When would von Kratow the aide-de-camp be back? An hour. He had told von Kratow to leave him alone for an hour.

He was alone and helpless under those pitiless brown eyes. And he knew, with the sure instinct of the merciless, that the man behind those eyes had as little mercy as himself.

In that moment, he recognised him. The Abwehr had circulated the name, the description, holograph cuttings from the London *Times* and the *Frankfurter Zeitung*, from before the war. Cuttings with pictures of this face, those eyes, fixed without mercy on the next peak to be conquered.

He said in his rasping whisper, 'Mallory.' He breathed hard. 'You will all die together. It will not be an easy death.'

Mallory felt the sweat of relief flow under his stinking uniform. Andrea and Miller were still alive. He said to the General, 'Please. Take your clothes off.'

The General's brain felt starved of blood. He knew the things this man had done. He knew that he was in trouble. He said, 'No.'

Then he dived for the bell-push.

Mallory saw him go, as if in slow motion. He lashed out again with the barrel of the Schmeisser. It caught the General on his bone-white temple. His eyes rolled up. His body went limp and dropped to the Turkish carpet. His head hit the flagstones at the carpet's fringe with a loud, wet *crunch*. He lay still.

Mallory laid the Schmeisser on the desk. He stubbed out the cigarette in the ashtray, took another from the silver box, lit it, and inhaled deeply. He walked across to the door and quietly shot the big bolt. Then he crouched by the body on the floor, and took the pulse in the neck.

There was no pulse.

Mallory began to remove the uniform.

He pulled off the boots, the tunic, the breeches. He paused a moment, face immobile, eyebrow cocked. The uniform was bigger than the body. The General's corpse was white and fleshless, little better than a skeleton. Under the dead-black uniform, the man was wearing ivory silk French knickers.

Mallory began to unbutton his tunic. He thew his sewage-stained clothes behind the curtain, and climbed into the General's uniform.

It had been oversized for the General, but was about the right size for Mallory. He had climbed the castle tower without socks, and large areas of skin had come away from his feet. The General's socks were clean and made of silk, which was soothing; the General's mirror-polished jackboots were a size too tight, which was not. But Mallory's own boots were not the elegant boots of a General, so there was no help for it.

When he had finished dressing Mallory transferred the contents of his battledress pockets to the General's tunic and breeches. He caught sight of himself reflected in the glass of the window. He saw a tall, thin SS General, the hollow-cheeked face shadowed by the cap that came down far over the eyes, the unscarred neck hidden by the shirt collar. Unless he got too close to someone who knew the General well, he would pass. The Cabo de la Calavera force would be a scratch team. They would not know each other well.

You hope.

Stay in the shadows.

He took the cap off, and began to walk round the office. A door led to a room with a shortwave radio on a table.

Mallory went into the bathroom. He washed his hands and face. He changed the blade in the dead man's razor for a new one. He shaved: SS Generals do not have twelve hours' growth of stubble. As he shaved he thought about the way that the lights had come on after the landing, the instantaneous capture of Andrea and Miller. And what the General had said: *we have been expecting you.*

Mallory wiped the remains of the lather from his face, and decided that, disguise or no disguise, he could not face the General's violet-scented eau de Cologne. He walked back to the radio room, stiff-legged because of the pinch of the boots. Jensen had made sure his men were trained in the use of German equipment. He flicked on the power, and tuned the dial to the *Stella Maris'* frequency. *'Ici l'Amiral Beaufort,'* he said.

There was a wave of static. Then a little voice said, *'Monsieur l'Amiral.'* Even across the static it was recognisable as Hugues.

Mallory said, 'I have laid large explosive charges at the main gate. Am expecting reinforcements from the landward.'

Hugues said, 'What –'

Mallory hit his press-to-talk switch. 'Stay where you are,' he said. 'Ignore all further radio communications. Await arrival of main force, one hour. Acknowledge.' He lifted his thumb from the switch.

Static washed through the earphones. For a moment he thought Hugues had not received him. Then he realised that the silence would be the silence of confusion.

Or treachery.

'Acknowledge,' he said again.

'I acknowledge,' said Hugues.

'Out,' said Mallory, and disconnected.

Mallory hobbled back into the office. Very quietly he unbolted the door, walked back to the desk and pulled the body behind the curtain. Then he lit another Turkish cigarette from the box on the desk, and turned away from the door to face the window. It was dark out there. He waited five minutes. Suddenly, the night to the left whitened, as if many lights had come on. Mallory pressed the button on the desk. The door opened behind him. A voice said, 'Herr General?'

Mallory could see in the rain-flecked glass the reflection of a young SS officer, standing to attention with tremulous rigidity, eyes front. The officer would not be able to see Mallory's reflection. Mallory was standing too close to the glass. And of course, the officer was German, so he would notice uniforms, not faces.

At least, that was the theory Mallory was backing with his life. And Andrea's, and Miller's.

He said, in what he hoped was a replica of the General's harsh croak, 'There seems to be a problem by the gate. The lights are on. What is happening?'

'We have reports of enemy action.'

'What do you mean?'

'Intelligence,' said the voice.

Mallory said, 'Investigate this. Personally. Come back only when you have established the nature of this action, and neutralized it. Take all forces at your disposal. The whole garrison, if necessary.'

'But Herr General, the administration . . . we depart at dawn . . .'

Mallory's heart seemed to stop beating. 'At what time?' he said.

'At dawn,' said the SS man, worried. 'The Herr General will remember . . . it was the Herr General who issued the order . . .'

'The time of dawn, idiot,' snapped Mallory.

'Of course.' The SS man sounded flustered. 'My apologies. 0500, Herr General.'

'So you will raise the general alarm,' said Mallory. 'And you will proceed to the gate.'

'But Herr General –'

'With all the men you can find.'

'But the work –'

'Silence!' barked Mallory. 'Leave only the sentries, and one man. I need to interview the prisoners. I shall require an escort. The rest to the gate. I hold you personally responsible.'

'But–'

'You will go out in the rain,' said Mallory, 'and confront the enemy! There is worse than rain on the *Ostfront*!'

He heard boot heels crash together. The officer said, *'Jawohl, Herr General,'* in a tight, offended voice. The uniform would be occupying the whole of his vision.

'Send the escort in five minutes,' said Mallory. 'Dismiss!'

The boot heels crashed again. The door slammed. Alarm bells started ringing, rackety and imperious. Mallory turned, stubbed out the cigarette, and lit another.

Five o'clock. The U-boats were sailing seven hours early. And the Storm Force had not even begun.

There was the stamp of many feet in the corridor outside: the General's staff, trotting off to the gate, scared witless by the prospect of the Russian Front. The footsteps faded. A double knock sounded on the door. Mallory turned back to the window. *'Komm!'* he cried.

A nervous voice said, 'Herr General.'

'We will visit the prisoners,' said Mallory. 'Lead the way.'

'The way?'

'You lead,' rasped Mallory. 'I will follow you. About *turn.*'

The soldier about turned. Mallory clasped his hands behind his back and hobbled out from behind the desk.

In the corridor, he sank his chin into his collar and strode stiffly after the private. Anyone watching would have seen the General, cap pulled low over his eyes, deep in thought, doing his rounds. But there were only clerks to watch. The alarm bells had sent the garrison clattering for the assembly points, and from the assembly points the Feldwebels had bellowed them to the ramparts on the peninsula.

The escort's boots rang in the vaulting and crunched grit on the stone stairs. The pain in Mallory's feet and the aches of his body were small, distant inconveniences.

He had radioed the *Stella Maris* with false information. Within five minutes, that false information had been relayed to the garrison.

Someone on the *Stella Maris* was a traitor.

Lisette was out of France, away from the long arm of the Gestapo. Hugues had his girlfriend and his child safe alongside him; if he betrayed the *Stella Maris* party, Lisette would be separated from him, and probably killed. Which left Jaime: Jaime the dark and silent, the smuggler, connoisseur of secret paths and byways.

Not that it mattered just now.

The soldier halted, with a stamp of his feet. 'Herr General,' he said.

They were in a long corridor lined with steel doors. White lights glared harshly from the ceiling. There was a smell of damp and mould. The sentry standing rigidly at attention outside the nearest door coughed. Mallory said, 'Key.'

The sentry was still coughing.

'Key!' rasped Mallory, holding out his hand.

The sentry said, 'Herr General,' and fumbled at his belt. He looked at Mallory's hand.

And Mallory's skin turned suddenly to ice.

For the sentry was frowning at that outstretched hand. The right hand. The hand of flesh and blood.

The hand that on the real General had been an artificial hand of orange rubber.

'Herr General,' said the sentry, with the face of one undergoing a nervous breakdown. 'This is . . . you are not the General.'

'The key,' rasped Mallory.

But under the brim of his cap he saw the man's hands going for the Schmeisser.

The cell had not changed. It was still cold, and it still stank, and it was still dark, dark with the absolute blackness of a pocket hewn from living rock. Midnight in the goddamn dungeons, thought Miller. Ghosts would be walking, witches doing whatever the hell witches do when it rains. As far as Miller was concerned, the ghosts and the witches could get on with it. Right here, midnight meant time for a cigarette.

He gave one to Andrea, put one in his own mouth, and lit them. The hot little coals began to glow in the dark, and for a couple of minutes there were warm points in this cold, evil-smelling universe.

But cigarettes end. And when they were finished, it was colder again, and lonelier, and worst of all, quieter.

What felt like two hours later, Andrea said, 'What time is it?'

Andrea would be thinking about the operation. Miller was thinking about it too. Miller wanted to get finished up.

Some chance.

He looked at the radium-bright hands of his watch. 'Five past twelve,' he said.

'Any minute now,' said the rumble of Andrea's voice. And although Miller knew it was a packet of bullshit, he felt for a moment that, any minute now, something might happen.

But nothing did.

Not for thirty seconds, anyway. After thirty seconds, the silence was broken by an odd noise.

It sounded like a jackhammer. It was not a jackhammer.

Someone was firing a machine pistol outside the cell door.

The door swung open. Brilliant light exploded into the darkness. A figure stood against the light, a black, angular silhouette. Andrea stared at it, dazzled. From the monochrome blur there emerged a spidery figure, jackboots set well apart, hands on hips, face invisible under the high-fronted black cap. It was the silhouette that stalked Andrea's dreams: the rusty-black silhouette that had stood against the sun on the low hill in Greece, with the blue Aegean twinkling like sapphires under the sky.

Under the hill had been the house of Andrea's brother, Iannis. It had been a small house, with a vine growing over a little terrace of red tiles, fanned by the small thyme-scented breeze that blew up from the sea.

By the time Andrea had got there, the damage had been done. His brother had been suspected of partisan activities, and captured in possession of British weapons. Under the pleasant green shade of the vine, the General had opened a bottle of Iannis' retsina and poured himself a glass. Then he had perched elegantly on the wall, gleaming boots crossed at the ankles, and watched the show.

The show had consisted of lighting the fire of charcoal on which the family had from time to time cooked an alfresco meal. Three Croatian SS had then brought Iannis' three daughters – Athene, six, Eirene, eight, and Helen, nine – out of the house. In the fire of charcoal they had burned off the girls' hands. When Iannis' wife had begun to scream, the General had had her hanged before the eyes of her husband and her still living children. Iannis they had left alive, nailing his hands to the house door against his attempts

to claw out the eyeballs that had seen this thing, and wrench out
the heart that was broken.

It was only after they had hanged the children beside their
mother that Iannis had managed to tear his hands free and run,
run like a maniac, eyes blinded with tears, to the brink of the high
white cliff, and keep running, though his feet were no longer running on ground, but running on air, and he was falling down the
glistening face of that cliff, falling happily, because he would see his
children again, and his wife, and his parents, murdered by
Bulgarians –

Five minutes later, Andrea had arrived, slowly, wearing a straw
hat and leading a donkey in whose panniers were more weapons.
Andrea had stood a moment, blank-eyed, watching. He saw the
woman and the three children hanging from the vine that used to
shade the evening drinking of ouzo. He saw the black-uniformed
SS men, their thick red faces pouring rivers of sweat under the sun,
laughing. The flames began to pour out of the roof of the house. He
saw the silhouette of the General standing on the cliff, admiring a
distant ruin, smiling complacently at the liquid-agate of the sun in
the glass of retsina. He smelt burned flesh.

Then Andrea had seen nothing else.

When he could see again, there were five SS men dead at his
feet. Them he fed to Iannis' pigs. The General he shot in the knees
and threw into the privy to drown. He heard later from the people
of the village that it had taken three days; not that he was interested.
For Andrea had not waited. He had gathered together the bodies of
his brother and his sister-in-law and his nieces, and given them to
the priest for burial. Then he had left, to fight for his country on
other fronts.

Andrea did not like SS officers.

He growled, and started forward, his gigantic hands unclenching.

The SS General dropped the Turkish cigarette he was smoking,
and ground it out with a fastidious toe. He said, 'Unless you really
like it here, I think we should leave.' And his voice was the voice
of Mallory.

There was a moment's stunned silence, broken only by the
sound of moaning from the corridor. Then Miller said, 'Personally,
I find it damp.'

Andrea's eyes were pits of darkness. They moved from Mallory
to Miller and back again. Then his teeth showed in a smile that was
like the sun among thunderclouds. 'You should be careful about

second-hand clothes,' he said. 'You could catch something really nasty. Like a knife in the guts.'

Mallory said, 'It is true that the owner wasn't very well when I left him.'

There were two bodies in the corridor. 'Get their clothes and their paybooks,' said Mallory. Andrea dragged them into the cell, and shut the door. 'And now?' he said.

Mallory looked at Miller. 'What do you need?'

What Miller really needed was his explosives back. But there was no use crying over spilt Cyclonite. 'Whatever,' said Miller. 'These guys will be carrying torpedoes. You can have a nasty accident with a torpedo. I guess I'd like to see the magazine.'

Andrea nodded gravely. During the weeks he had known Miller, he had learned to take this languid, flippant American very seriously indeed.

'I have a feeling,' said Mallory, 'that there might be a certain amount of confusion out there. So the sooner we get dressed, the better.'

Five minutes later, the SS General left the *fortaleza* by the main gate, escorted by two men in grubby Waffen-SS uniforms, one tall and wide, one tall and lanky, marching eyes front, with Schmeissers strapped across their chests. The sentries on the gate saluted. The General returned their salute with his left hand; the right, being artificial, he held rigidly at his side.

Once across the bridge over the moat, the party turned right, down a flight of wide, shallow stairs that led to a sort of crater in the shoulder of the headland. In the centre of the crater was a squat concrete bunker surrounded with barbed wire.

At a slow and stately pace, Mallory and his escort started down the stairs. There were few other people about. The welding torches still flickered their lightnings at the sky by the harbour, and riveters still rattled in the night. Somewhere, truck engines were rumbling; the evacuation was getting under way. But the armed men of the garrison were still apparently up by the main gate.

The garrison would not stay by the main gate for ever. Sooner or later, someone would decide that the threat might be based on faulty intelligence, or that it was not wise to leave the rest of the Cabo unguarded. Before that happened, there would be fifteen minutes, at best.

They were approaching the gate to the bunker. Seen close up, it was not so much a bunker as a fortified entrance, a steel door set behind a system of concrete baffles giving admittance to a low, tumulus-like mound, covered in salt-blasted turf. The entrance to the magazine.

The soldier at the gate stared straight ahead. 'Pass?' he said.

Mallory said, in the General's harsh whisper, 'Open the gate.'

'But Herr General –'

Mallory said, 'The weather in Russia is terrible at this time of year.'

The man's face paled under the floodlights. 'Herr General?'

'Perhaps when you get there you will send me a postcard,' rasped Mallory. 'Now if you would kindly open the gate?'

There was a split second of inner struggle. Then the sentry hauled open the gate in the wire, and Mallory walked through at his cramped, mincing hobble. The sentry must have pressed some sort of switch, because the steel door swung open with a hiss of hydraulics. Mallory and his escorts walked in without pausing. The steel door swung shut behind them. Ahead was a flight of spiral stairs, with at its centre the hoists that fed ammunition to the guns in the fort. Mallory looked at the faces of his companions. They were pale and expressionless, tired, but with a tension to their tiredness that was new. It came from the closing of that steel door.

They were inside now. There were no sandbags to hide behind, no shadows to skulk in. Their only protection against five hundred enemy soldiers was the thin cloth of their uniforms and the shape of the badges they wore. They were small, fragile machines of flesh and blood, armed with small guns. With those small guns and their bare hands, they had to destroy huge machines of steel. It was a nasty feeling; a naked feeling. A feeling from a nightmare.

But this was real. And this was the way it was going to be, from now on.

Down those stairs, Mallory told himself, were the tools for the job. Put Miller near explosives, and his bare hands could shatter an army. Everything was going to be fine.

Except my feet, thought Mallory, hobbling on. His feet felt as if they would never be the same again.

The shaft with the staircase descended into the bowels of the hill. Shells could be carried by hoist. But torpedoes were big, and heavy, and needed to travel horizontally. The floor of the magazine would be on the same level as the floor of the quay.

Miller stamped down the stairs at what he hoped was a convincing Wehrmacht stamp. It was costing him some effort to keep his appearance military. He was a fighter, Miller, but he would have been the first to admit that he was not much of a soldier. As they rounded the last twist of the spiral staircase, he felt a pleasurable anticipation. Once again, it was time to improvise.

At the base of the stairs was a flashproof door. Miller pushed the door open. They were in the magazine.

It was a big magazine. It stretched away in front of them, lit harshly by white bulkhead lights, a devil's wine cellar of grey concrete compartments, bins for shells, and bays for the trolleys that would roll the torpedoes down to the quays where the submarines waited, black and evil, crouching in the cold Atlantic.

Mallory looked at his watch. It was three forty-five.

Christ.

They went through the door, all three of them, and looked down the stark concrete perspective that was the magazine's central aisle. This was where they would find the wherewithal to sink three submarines and scupper the Nazis' last defence against the invading Allies.

But there was a problem.

The concrete bays and alcoves of the magazine contained a few crates. The dollies for the shells lay on their rails, and the torpedo racks, five hundred of them, stood padded with felt. But the crates were cracked open, the dollies burdenless, the torpedo racks bare. A gang of men was dismantling an electric motor.

But apart from the men, the magazine was empty.

They stood there, and watched, and let it sink in. The job was waiting. The tools were missing.

After a minute, Mallory began to hobble down the floor of the magazine, heading for the rails that would have taken the torpedoes to the quay.

The *Stella Maris* was lying on the outside of a raft of fishing boats against the quay wall of San Eusebio. Among the ruined buildings behind the quay, yellow dogs with feathered tails barked maddeningly in the rain. Hugues and Lisette were out of sight below. Jaime was on deck, propped in the splintered remnants of the wheelhouse, smoking. At his side a radio hummed gently to itself. There had been no signals. Jaime was not expecting any more signals.

Across the black water of the harbour, the sheds and quays of the old sardine factory on Cabo de la Calavera, which earlier had flickered with angle-grinder sparks and welder lightnings, were almost dark. It looked as if the work was complete. Now and then, a crane-jib caught the light as it swung. Loading up, thought Jaime. Not long now.

There was activity on the harbour too; the murmur of launches and lighters, moving out to the two five-thousand-ton merchantmen anchored in the deep water half a mile from the quay. On the move, thought Jaime. And who knew where it would all end?

'Slow,' said Mallory. 'Your work is very, very slow. Work faster.'

The Leutnant in charge of the embarkation of the magazine stores felt a hot anger at the injustice of it all. But it was not helpful to be angry with SS Generals. So he clicked his heels and ducked his head and said, 'As the Herr General wishes.'

'The Herr General does,' said Mallory. 'Now I wish to inspect the magazine.'

'Herr General?'

Mallory frowned. 'You speak German, do you not?'

'Herr General.' The man had just been rated for slowness. Leading a tour of inspection for some damned Nazi with a skull-and-bones hat was not going to speed things up. But a General was a General.

'Here were the shells,' said the Leutnant. 'All gone now, as per your orders. Here were the torpedoes. They are also gone, naturally.' He waved a hand at the tunnel leading down to the quay, and walked to another bin lined with empty racks. A pile of grey boxes stood on the floor. 'And in here, the small arms. A few only remaining. Grenades, mortar bombs. The last consignment will be leaving when the barge comes back alongside.' He clashed his heels together again, thumbs nailed to the seams of his breeches. 'I trust the Herr General is satisfied.'

Mallory eyed the three grey wooden boxes the officer had indicated. 'Quite satisfied,' he said. He looked round. Nobody was in sight. 'Andrea?'

The huge Greek took one step forward and crashed his jackboots on the concrete. His shoulders moved. There was a sound like a felling axe hitting a tree trunk. The German officer sighed, and fell down.

'Hide him,' said Mallory. 'Miller, boxes of grenades.'

Miller piled two boxes of grenades one on top of the other: ten grenades to the box, rope handles on either end.

'We'll go to the quay,' said Mallory. His face was the colour of dirty ivory. Exhausted, thought Miller.

Mallory fumbled in his pocket. There were three Benzedrine left in the little foil packet. He gave them out, one each. Benzedrine was not good for you, thought Miller, stooping to pick up the grenades. But then, nor was trying to climb aboard a U-boat to blow it up.

It was a long time since Miller had eaten anything. The pill worked fast. He could feel the strength pouring through him. These pills, thought Miller, dry-mouthed and sweating. You will feel terrible later.

Except that later was hardly worth worrying about, under the circumstances.

Miller laughed. Then he walked with his two companions into the throat of the tunnel that led to the quay.

SEVEN

Wednesday
0400–0500

The tunnel was fifty yards long, lit with the harsh white bulkhead lights installed all over the Cabo. Rails ran down each side, for the torpedo dollies. Down the middle was the walkway. There were men moving up and down the tunnel, moving at a fast clip. When they saw Mallory's uniform their eyes skidded away. Popular guy, thought Miller.

The three men began to march down the walkways, boots echoing. They had gone twenty yards when a voice behind said, *'Halt!'*

Mallory's heart walloped heavily. He thrust his all-too-real right hand into his tunic. Andrea's hands stole to the grips of his Schmeisser. Miller's hands were sweating into the rope handles of the grenade boxes. Mallory spun on the heel of his agonising jackboot.

He was looking at a small, bald man with rimless glasses and a prissy mouth, bulging out of a badgeless uniform. The small man was holding a book.

'Was?' said Mallory.

The small man was not impressed by the death's-head cap badge, the black uniform, the harsh croak of the voice. He pursed his lips. 'It is necessary to fill out the requisite forms,' he said. 'For the withdrawal of these weapons from the magazine. Otherwise, correct systems cannot be maintained.'

Mallory said, 'And you are the inventory clerk.'

'Jawohl.'

'Well, Herr Corporal,' said Mallory. 'Give me your book, and I will sign it.'

The clerk made tutting noises. 'Signature alone is not enough,' he said. 'You will naturally need a requisition form signed by the garrison duty officer.'

Mallory said, in a voice crammed with broken glass, 'Do you know who I am?'

The clerk moistened his small mouth with a grey tongue. 'Yess, Herr General. You are the garrison commander, Herr General.'

'And who signs the requisitions?'

'The duty officer.'

'By whose orders?'

'By your orders, Herr General.'

'So,' said Mallory.

The clerk said, 'I have my orders. The duty officer must sign the requisition.'

Mallory checked his watch. It said 0405. In fifty-five minutes the submarines were due to sail.

In fifty-five minutes, they could still be arguing with this clerk. The only thing stronger than the uniform was the system.

He said, 'Corporal, I compliment you on your attachment to duty. The duty officer is on the quay. You will accompany us there, please.'

'But –'

'*Schnell,*' Mallory's voice was a bark that admitted no contradiction.

The clerk, he had decided, was a blessing. An officious little blessing with rimless glasses, but a blessing nonetheless.

'Lead on, Corporal,' said Mallory, in a harsh purr.

The clerk led on.

The mouth of the tunnel was walled off. On one side was an opening for the torpedo dolly track. On the other was a sort of wicket gate for the pedestrian walkway. By the wicket gate was a species of sentry box. In the sentry box were two figures like black paper silhouettes: SS.

From the corner of his eye, Mallory saw that Andrea's hands had not moved from the grips of his Schmeisser. He wished he had a Schmeisser of his own. But he had a Luger, and the insignia of his uniform. That should be enough –

Except that the face above the uniform was not the right face.

He tugged down the peak of his cap.

The heels rang on. The SS sentries in the box had blank faces the colour of dirty suet. Their uniforms were rusty, their belts grainy, the folds of their jackboots cracking with salt. Their eyes were cold, and vicious, and restless. When they settled on Mallory's uniform, something happened to them, something that was not the other ranks' usual reaction to an officer's uniform. It was a look

compounded of furtiveness and pride. Esprit de corps, thought
Mallory. Oh, dear.

There were fifty SS men on the Cabo de la Calavera: the élite,
keeping an eye on things for Himmler. They would know each
other, all right.

But the only way onto the quay was through that night-black
wicket by the sentry box.

Mallory shouted, 'Attention!'

The SS faces became blank and automatic. The General's uniform was doing its job. The boot heels ground concrete as Mallory,
Miller, Andrea, and the magazine clerk marched on. The magazine clerk looked pleased with himself, proud to be part of something important and official. Mallory was profoundly grateful to
him. The magazine clerk was credibility. The SS knew the magazine clerk.

They were close now: ten feet away. Mallory walked with his
supposedly artificial hand in his breast, head bowed, as if in deep
thought. Through the wicket came the smells of the sea, stirring
the chill, leaden air of the magazine. The smell of the endgame.

The eyes were on them now, peripherally at least. In the corner
of his vision Mallory could see the white, large-pored skin, the
brown eyes seamed below with the marks of arrogance and cruelty.
He could smell the uniforms, the sour smell of rain-wet black serge
badly dried, leather on which polish was fighting a losing battle
with mildew. He could smell the oil on the Schmeissers, the tobacco
smoke, and garlic on their breath.

Then they were past, and Mallory was sweating –

'Herr General?' said a voice, a hard voice, cold, a little tentative:
the voice of one of the black-clad sentries.

Mallory took another step.

'The Herr General will please stop,' said the voice.

'Quiet,' murmured Mallory, in English. Then he said, in his
approximation of the General's bust-larynx rasp, 'What do you
want?'

'If the Herr General would show us his pass?'

Mallory made a small, exasperated noise. 'Clerk,' he said. 'Show
them your pass.'

The clerk's face was pink and shiny behind the rimless spectacles. He fumbled in his pocket.

'Quickly,' grated Mallory. 'Time is wasting.'

The SS man's eyes flicked at the clerk's pass. He handed it back.

'And now,' he said, 'the Herr General's pass.'

Something seemed to have removed the bottom of Mallory's stomach. There was a sort of icy purr in the voice, the sound of a cat about to stab a claw into a rat.

Miller put down the boxes of grenades. His hands were wet on the grips of his Schmeisser. He moved it casually, negligently, until it was covering the guard who was not doing the talking. The guard who was doing the talking had an odd expression on his face. Miller understood it.

It was the expression of a man who knew the General well, but who had been conditioned to respond to uniforms, not faces.

Miller knew that something bad was going to happen.

The SS man wet his lips with a grey tongue. He said to Mallory, 'Herr General, what is the Herr General's name?' His right hand was under the level of the desk. There would be an alarm button down there.

Miller thumbed the selector on the Schmeisser to single shot, and took up the first pressure on the trigger. Andrea, he noticed, had his hands off his gun. Andrea said, with a wide, despairing gesture of both spread palms, 'For God's sake, who do you think you are talking to?'

The SS sentry opened his mouth to reply. But he never got the words out, because Andrea's gesture had become something else, and his huge right had gone into the sentry's face, the heel up and under the nose, driving the bone into the brain, while the other hand, the left, had sprouted a knife that went in and out of the other sentry's chest, and in and out again. The two helmets clanged on the concrete.

There was a long, dreadful silence that lasted perhaps a second. Then something small scuttled past Miller. The clerk.

He stuck out a foot. The little man went flat on his face. His spectacles skittered away on the concrete. The face he turned to Miller was the face of a blind mole. He said, 'Please.'

Miller looked at him. This was not an SS man. This man had all the malice of a ticket office clerk in Grand Central Station.

But this man could stop the operation dead.

Miller looked away.

There was a sound like a well-hit baseball. When Miller looked back, the magazine clerk was silent, face down, but breathing.

Andrea sighted along the barrel of his Schmeisser. 'Thought I'd bent it,' he said.

They dragged the clerk and the SS men out of sight behind the desk of the sentry box. The clerk was still breathing.

Then they walked onto the quay.

They were standing on the inshore end of the map the late Guy Jamalartégui had drawn beside the chart on his kitchen table with a matchstick and a puddle of wine.

The Basque-American who had donated the port to his sardine-fishing compatriots had not stinted. The quay was built of cut granite, on a scale that would have excited the respectful envy of a Pharaoh. The magazine entrance was set in the low cliff halfway down the long side of the innermost quay. Three more quays ran parallel to the first. There were rails set into the paving of the quays, designed presumably to carry waggonloads of sardines, first to the long sheds at the base of the quays for canning, and then to the sardines-on-toast enthusiasts of Europe.

Now, the black lanes of water between the granite fingers of the quay held no fishing boats; probably they never had. Instead, the long, sleek hulls and oddly streamlined conning towers of three great U-boats lay under the cranes.

Three men walked past, smoking, splashing in the puddles left by the night's rain. They were wearing baggy blue overalls, and had the hell-with-you air of dockyard mateys the world over. They paid no attention to Mallory and his two guards. Their task was finished. On the nearest submarine – presumably the one that had been reported rammed – a small gang of men was packing up what looked like oxy-acetylene welding gear. For the rest, what was going up and down on the cranes was definitely stores.

Mallory watched a tray of green vegetables and milk cans. Last-minute stores, at that.

More men in blue overalls drifted up the quay. There was a building up there, a green clapboard facade on a tunnel in the cliff. From it there drifted a smell of frying onions. The canteen, thought Mallory. The men going towards the canteen carried tool boxes. The men coming back had bags and bundles as well as the tool boxes. They had gone for a final meal up there, and picked up their possessions. At the far side of the harbour, launch engines puttered in the dawn; the engines of the launches ferrying the dockyard mateys out to the merchant ships waiting in the harbour, Uruguayan flags fluttering on their ensign staffs.

Mallory waited for another pair of workmen to walk past. They studiously avoided his eye, the way a skilled civilian technician of any nationality would avoid the eye of a murderer and torturer. The next pair came. One of them was a huge man, as big as Andrea.

That was what Mallory had been waiting for.

He said, 'You and you.'

The two men gave him the looks of schoolboys with permanently guilty consciences. One of them dropped his cigarette and stamped on it. The big man's cigarette dangled, unlit.

'Don't worry,' croaked Mallory. 'You have committed no crime.'

Their faces remained wooden.

'Smoke if you wish,' said Mallory. Another man was walking towards them, by himself. Mallory pulled out the General's lighter and lit the big man's cigarette with his left hand. 'There is one little job,' he said. 'Hey! You!'

The solitary man halted. Mallory pointed back at the magazine tunnel. *'Komm!'*

He marched into the tunnel. The lights were very bright after the grey predawn outside. The dockyard men were yawning and sullen. It had been a long night shift, and they wanted to get some food and climb aboard a merchant ship and go to sleep. They did not want to do any more jobs, particularly jobs for this whispering child murderer and his nasty-looking bodyguards. The big one said, 'What is it then?'

'Further,' said the SS General.

They were in the magazine tunnel. There were steel doors let into the wall, and a smell of new blood. The General pointed at one of the doors. 'In there,' he said.

The big man turned round. 'Why?' he said.

It was then he saw the bodyguards' guns, foreshortened, looking between his own eyes with their own deadly little black eyes.

'Take off your overalls,' said Mallory.

The big man was a bully. He was tired, and hung over, and hungry. Being told to undress had the effect on his temper of a well-flung brick on a wasps' nest. Nobody talked to him like that, SS General or no SS General. And word was that this SS General was a poof. 'Take 'em off yourself,' said the big man, and took a swing at the General's jaw.

He never saw what hit him. He merely had the dim impression that someone had loaded his head into a cannon, fired it at a sheet of armour plate, and dropped the resulting mess into a black velvet bag.

His two companions watched with their mouths open as Andrea dusted his hands, stripped the overalls off the big man's prone body, and loaded the tools back into their box.

'Strip,' said Mallory.

They stripped at a speed that would have won them first prize in an undressing contest.

'The door,' said Mallory.

Miller went to the steel door. It closed from the outside, with a latch. Inside was a locker with tins of paint, ten feet on a side.

'In,' said Mallory.

One of the men said, 'How will we ever get out?' He looked frightened; he was a civilian, caught up in something not his quarrel.

Mallory did not believe that a grown man could stand back from a war. As far as Mallory was concerned, you were on his side, or you were the enemy. He said, 'How do you get on those U-boats?'

'With a pass.'

'What pass?'

The man produced a much-folded card, seamed with oil.

'Anything else?'

'No. Who are you?'

Mallory went and stood so that his face was two inches from the German's. 'That is for me to know and you to wonder,' he said. 'I am going out there. I wish to move freely. If I am captured, I will not say a word about you, and that door is soundproof. So you have a choice.' He could feel the sweat running down inside his uniform, see the impassive faces of Miller and Andrea. Not much more than half an hour now. 'If you are telling me the truth, you have nothing to fear. If not, this locker will be your tomb.'

The man's throat moved violently as he swallowed. He said, 'There is . . . in fact . . . something else. A word.'

'Ah,' said Mallory.

'*Ritter,*' said the man. 'You must say *Ritter* to the gangway sentry.'

Mallory said, 'If you are not telling the truth, you will die in your underpants.'

'It is the truth.'

'Your overalls,' said Mallory, 'and what size are your boots?'

'Forty-two.'

Thank God, thought Mallory. 'Also your boots,' he said.

Five minutes later, three dockyard mateys were wandering down the quay towards the ferry. They were carrying much-chipped blue enamel toolboxes and smoking cigarettes. Their faces were surprisingly grim for men bound for Lisbon, home and beauty. But perhaps that would be because of the danger of submarines.

Outside the sheds at the root of the quay, the three men stopped.

Andrea looked up. The clouds had rolled away. The sky was duck-egg blue. Dawn was coming up, a beautiful dawn, above this press of people and their deadly machines.

Mallory said to Andrea in a quiet, level voice, 'We'll want the *Stella Maris* standing by.'

'I'll arrange that,' said Andrea.

Mallory looked down the first finger of granite. On either side were foreshortened alleys of water, with the bulbous grey pressure hulls and narrow steel decks of the submarines. There were two gangplanks down there, one leading left, the other right, a crossroads of quay and gangplanks. This was the access to two submarines. If you could get past the sailor at the base of each gangplank, rifle on his shoulder, cap ribbons fluttering at his nape in the small dawn breeze.

Mallory took a deep breath of the morning air, and tried not to think about the little steel rooms inside those pressure hulls, into which he must go with his grenades.

'Peroxide,' said Miller, sniffing.

'Sorry?'

'Hydrogen peroxide. Smells like a hairdressing parlour. Hunnert per cent, by the smell of it. Don't get it on you. Corrosive.'

Mallory said, 'What do you recommend?'

Miller told him.

'Fascinating,' said Mallory, taking a deep breath. 'I'll do the right-hand one. You do the left.'

Andrea said, 'Good luck.'

Mallory nodded. There was such a thing as luck, but to acknowledge its existence was to hold two fingers up to fate. What Andrea had to do was potentially even more dangerous than climbing around U-boats with a toolbox full of hand grenades.

Not that there was much to choose between the jobs. Dead was dead, never mind how you got there.

Mallory was not wasting time thinking about death. He was planning the next phase.

Andrea slipped away into the crowds heading for the ferries. Mallory and Miller started to walk down the quay towards the sentries. Miller had his hands in his pockets, and he was whistling.

Good lad, thought Mallory. What would it take to get you really worried?

Miller's thoughts were less elevated. The smell of peroxide had taken him back to Mme Renard's house in Montreal, to Minette, a French-Canadian girl with an educated tongue and bright yellow curls. There had been something about Minette, something she had shown him with two goldfish and a bag of cement –

Concentrate.

Down in his saboteur's treasure-house of a memory, he knew that the catalyst for hydrogen peroxide was manganese dioxide. Manganese dioxide would separate the hydrogen from the oxygen, and make a bang next to which a hand grenade would look stupid.

Manganese dioxide was the obvious stuff.

Unfortunately, it was not the kind of stuff people left lying around.

He was at the bottom of the gangway. He grinned at the sentry and showed him his pass. '*Ritter,*' he said, rattling his toolbox. 'Problem with lavatory. Two minutes only.'

The sentry said, 'Thank God you've arrived, then.'

Miller walked up the gangplank.

Andrea shouldered his way through the thickening crowd on the quay. There was a sense of urgency, now, and very little Teutonic efficiency about the milling scrum of men and soldiers. He made his way to the quay's lip.

And stopped.

The queue might be inefficient, but the embarkation procedures were well up to standard. There were four iron ladders down the quay. At the bottom of each ladder was a launch. At the top of each ladder was an SS officer with a clipboard. As each man arrived at the front of the queue, the SS man scrutinised his identity card, compared the photograph minutely with his face, and checked his name off the list. Only then was he allowed down the ladder.

Once the launches themselves had left the quays they did not hang about. They went straight alongside the two merchant ships anchored in the harbour; merchant ships on whose decks were un-naval but nonetheless efficient sandbag emplacements from which peered the snouts of machine guns.

Even in the evacuation, the Werwolf facility was leaving nothing to chance.

Andrea's overalls and identity card had belonged to Wulf Tietmeyer. No amount of oily thumbprints could obscure the fact that Tietmeyer, though roughly Andrea's size, had red hair and pale blue eyes. Furthermore, Andrea had no desire to end up on a Germany-bound merchant ship.

Muttering a curse for the benefit of his neighbours, he turned back into the crowd, forging his way through the press with shoulders the size and hardness of a bank safe, a dockyard matey who had left something behind and was on his way to fetch it.

As he reached the root of the quays one of the submarines emitted a black cloud of exhaust, and the morning filled with the blaring rattle of a cold diesel. Start engines meant that they would be sailing at any minute. He looked at his watch. In eighteen minutes, to be precise. And precise was what they would be.

He looked across the mouth of the harbour at the town of San Eusebio, glowing now in the pale dawn. The windows of its houses were smoke-blackened, empty as dead men's eyes, the campaniles of its two churches jagged as smashed teeth. But alongside the quays, in front of the blind warehouses lining the harbour, the fishing fleet was anchored two deep. And among them, on the outside near the front, were the tar-black hull and ill-furled red sails of the *Stella Maris*.

Four hundred yards away. A short swim in the Mediterranean. But the four-hundred-yard neck here had a roiling turbulence, with little strips of inexplicable ripples. The tide was going out, sucking at the base of the quay. It looked to Andrea as if there was a very large amount of water trying to get out of a very small exit. Andrea guessed that this might be a long swim indeed.

But Andrea had been brought up on the shores of the Aegean. Among his recent ancestors he numbered divers for sponges, and he himself had spent his childhood as much in as out of the water. Andrea swam like a fish –

A Mediterranean fish.

Slowly and deliberately, Andrea pulled a pencil and notebook from his overall pocket and walked to the seaward end of the outermost quay. Nobody paid him any attention as he passed the sentry at the foot of the gangway of the outermost U-boat. Why should they? He was a large inspector in blue overalls, frowning with his thick black eyebrows at the state of the quay. The Germans were a nation of inspectors. It was natural, in this little German world on the edge of Spain, that even in the final stages of an evacuation someone should be making notes on the condition of the quay.

At the end of the quay, iron rungs led down the granite. For the benefit of anyone watching, Andrea stuck his pencil behind his ear, pursed his lips and shook his head. Then he began to climb down the iron rungs.

As he sank below the level of the quay, he was out of sight of anyone except the sentries in the *fortaleza*, and he was hoping that with sixteen minutes to sailing, the sentries would have been withdrawn. From the bottom rung he let notebook and pencil whisk away on the current. He struggled out of his overalls, kicked off his boots, and removed the rest of his clothes. They hovered a moment in the eddy at the foot of the wall, then sailed off down the tide.

Naked, Andrea was brown and hairy as a bear. He touched the gold crucifix round his neck, and lowered himself into the green swirl at the foot of the rungs. He thought, it is freezing, this Atlantic.

Then he launched himself into the tide.

'Ritter,' said Mallory to the sentry at the foot of the gangway opposite the one up which Miller had disappeared.

The sentry was wearing leather trousers and a jersey coming unravelled at the hem. His face as he glanced at Mallory's identity card and handed it back was pale, with a greasy film of sweat. Scared, thought Mallory, as he walked up the gangplank. These may be secret weapons, but they are still U-boats, and U-boat crews do not live long. To drown in a steel box, inch by inch . . .

Mallory had tried that once. It was not something he ever wanted to try again.

But he was standing on the U-boat's grey steel deck, the worn enamel handles of the toolbox slippery in his hand, and there was a hatch forward, standing open. The torpedo room was forward. On a submarine this size, a grenade would do little damage. Unless, Miller had said, you used it as a fuse, a primer, stuck to the tons of Amatol or Torpex or whatever they used. Then you would get a result –

Mallory made himself walk towards the hatch. It would be easier to stay on deck, not go below, into that little steel space that might at any moment go under the water –

Easy or not, it had to be done.

The hatch was a double steel door in the deck. A steel ladder plunged into a yellow-lit gloom. At the bottom of the ladder a face looked up, sallow and bearded, blue bags under the eyes. A Petty Officer.

'What the hell do you want?' said the Petty Officer.

'Check toilets,' said Mallory, dumb as an ox.

'I don't know anything about any toilets,' said the Petty Officer. 'Go and see the Kapitän.'

'Where's the Kapitän?' Mallory could feel the minutes ticking.

'Conning tower. You'd better be quick.'

Mallory went back down the deck, and up the metal rungs on the side of the conning tower. He took a deep breath and let himself down into the tower itself.

The smell was oil and sweat, and something else. Peroxide. A man in a grubby white polo-neck jersey with an Iron Cross was arguing with another man. Both had pale faces and beards.

Mallory cleared his throat. 'Come to fix the toilet,' he said.

The man with the Iron Cross was wearing a Kapitän's cap. 'Now?' he said. 'I didn't know it was broken. Get off my boat.'

'Orders,' said Mallory. The morning was a disc of daylight seen through the hatchway.

'I'm Kapitän –'

'The Herr General was most insistent.'

'I shit on the Herr General,' said the Kapitän. 'Hell. Go and look at the toilet, then. But I warn you, we are sailing in ten minutes, and if you're still on board I'll put you out through a torpedo tube.'

Mallory said, stolidly, 'That will not be necessary.' But the Kapitän was back at his argument, with no time for dockyard mateys.

Engine at the back. Torpedoes at the front. Front it is.

Mallory hefted his toolbox, shinned down the ladder under the periscope and started along the corridor leading forward.

There was a crew messroom, racked torpedoes, bunks everywhere. The lights were yellow. There seemed to be scores of men, packed dense as sardines in a tin; but this was worse, because it was a tin in which the sardines had somehow suddenly come alive. Mallory shoved his way through. There are no windows, said the voice in his mind. You are below the level of the water –

Shut up, he told himself. You are still alongside.

He walked under the open hatch. The Petty Officer glanced at him and glanced away. Ahead, the passage ran through an oval doorway and ended. On the other side of the bulkhead he saw a long chamber lined left and right with fat tubes. The torpedo room.

And on his right, a tiny compartment: a lavatory. Head.

He looked round. The Petty Officer was watching him. Mallory winked, went into the lavatory and closed the door. His hand was sweating on the handles of his toolbox. Count to five, he thought.

There was a new sound, a vibration. The engines had started. Some-where, a klaxon began to moan. Now or never, thought Mallory.

He walked quickly into the corridor, scratching his head, and turned right into the torpedo room.

There were two men in there, securing torpedoes to the racks. They were like horizontal organ pipes, those torpedoes. Both the men were ratings.

'Shit,' said one of them. 'You'd better hurry.'

'Checking seals,' said Mallory. 'Couple of minutes. Which one of these things do you fire first?'

'Those,' said the rating, pointing. 'Now if you would be so good, go away and shut up and let us get on with getting ready to load those damn fish into those damn tubes.'

The torpedoes the rating had pointed at were the first rack, up by one of the ranks of oval doors that must lead into the tubes. Mallory wedged himself in behind the torpedoes, out of sight of the men. He found a stanchion on the steel wall of the submarine and looped the string lanyard on the grenade's handle over it. Then he unscrewed the grenade's cap, gently pulled out the porcelain button on the end of the string fuse, and tied it to the shaft of the tor-pedo's propeller.

First one.

He took out a spanner and crossed the compartment. The rating did not look up. He attached a second grenade to the port side lower torpedo, where the shadows were thickest. The third and fourth he attached to the next row up.

There were feet moving on steel somewhere above his head. The vibrations of the engine were louder now.

'That's okay,' said Mallory. 'Don't want sewage everywhere, do we?'

The ratings ignored him. He walked out of the torpedo compart-ment, down the corridor. The hatch was still open. He could smell the blessed air. He pushed past a couple of men, put his foot on the bottom rung of the ladder.

A hard hand took his arm above the elbow. A quiet voice said, 'If you're here to mend the toilets, what were you doing in the tor-pedo room?'

Mallory looked round.

The voice belonged to the bearded petty officer.

'Cast off!' roared a voice on deck.

Above his head, the hatch slammed shut.

* * *

Twenty yards away, Dusty Miller was in a different world. Miller was a trained demolitions man. He reckoned he had seven minutes. He had gone straight for the conning tower, checked out the Kapitän and the navigating officer bent over the charts. 'Come to look at the lavs,' he said.

The navigating officer gave him the not-interested look of a man ten minutes away from an important feat of underwater navigation. 'What lavs?'

'They just said the lavs.'

'You know where they are.'

Miller shrugged, feeling the weight of his toolbox, the hammer, the spanners, the four stick grenades in the bottom compartment. 'Yeah,' he said.

Mallory had gone forward, looking for the torpedoes. Miller went aft.

On most U-boats, the engine room consisted of a big diesel for surface running and to charge huge banks of lead-acid batteries, and an electric motor for underwater running. The Walter process was different. The diesel did all the work. When the U-boat was under water, the engine drew the oxygen for its combustion from disintegrated hydrogen peroxide, and vented the carbon dioxide it produced as a waste gas directly into the water, where it dissolved.

Miller went down the hatch in the control-room deck and crept along the low steel corridor. Men shoved past him. He took no notice. He wandered along, apparently tracing one of the parallel ranks of grey-painted pipes leading aft along the bulkhead.

And after not many steps, he was in the engine room.

It was as it should have been: the thick tubes coming from the fuel tanks, each with its stopcock: oils, water, hydrogen peroxide. There were men working in there, working hard, oiling, establishing settings on the banks of valve wheels. The big diesel was running with a clattering roar too loud to hear. Miller caught an oiler's eye, winked, nodded. The oiler nodded back. Nobody would be in a submarine's engine room at a time like this unless he had business there. And at a time like this, the business would certainly be legitimate.

So Miller stooped, apparently examining the pipes, and ran his professional eye over the maze of tubes and chambers.

And made his decision; or rather, confirmed the decision he had made already.

On the surface, the Walter engine was a naturally aspirated diesel. The changeover from air to peroxide was activated by a float switch on the conning tower. It was a simple device; when the water reached a certain level, the switch closed, opening the valve from the peroxide tank to the disintegrator. In Miller's view, the destruction of the valve would release a lot of inflammable stuff into a space full of nasty sparks.

There was a very real danger of explosions, thought Miller happily, opening his toolbox.

His fingers worked quickly. The float switch controlled a simple gate valve. Tape the grenade to the pipe. Tie the string fuse to one of the struts of the gate valve wheel. When the wheel turned, the string would pull out of the grenade. Five seconds later . . . well, thought Miller; ladies and gentlemen are requested to extinguish all smoking materials.

He arranged two more grenades, using the length of the string fuses to make for slightly greater delays, one on the water intake and one on the throttle linkage where it passed a dark corner.

Then he walked back, climbed into the conning tower, and said, 'All done.'

The navigating officer did not look up. Piss off,' he said.

'Oh, all right,' said Miller. He went up the ladder and into the chill, diesel-smelling dawn, and trotted down the gangplank and onto the quay.

He knew something was wrong as soon as his boots hit the stone. Two men were hauling the gangway of the boat opposite back onto the quay. Men were moving on the foredeck, waiting to haul in the lines when the stevedores let them go. Miller saw one of them bend and slam shut an open hatch. To left and right the quay was a desert of granite paving, dotted with a few figures in uniform, a few in overalls. Miller had worked with Mallory for long enough to recognise him, never mind what he was wearing.

None of the figures was Mallory.

So Mallory was still on the boat, and the boat was sailing.

On the boat opposite, a couple of heads showed on the conning tower. One of them wore the cap of a Kapitän.

'Oi!' yelled Miller, above the pop and rattle of the diesels. 'You've got my mate on board.'

The Kapitän looked round, frowning. The springs were off. They were down to one-and-one, a bow line and a stern line. They were sailing in two minutes. The Kapitän looked at the scarecrow figure on the dock, the chipped blue toolbox, the lanky arms and legs protruding from the too-short overalls. He shouted to one of the hands on the narrow deck.

The hand shrugged, scratching his head under his grey watch cap. He bent. He caught hold of the handles of the hatch, and pulled.

Mallory's whole body was covered in sweat. His mind did not seem to be working. Drowned in a steel room, he was thinking. No. Not that –

'What were you doing in the torpedo room?' said the Petty Officer.

'Pipes,' said Mallory. 'Checking pipes.'

'Like hell,' said the Petty Officer.

And at that moment, there fell from heaven a beam of pure grey light that pierced the reeking yellow gloom of the submarine like the arrow of God.

The hatch was open.

Mallory knew that a miracle had happened. It was a miracle that would take away the death by drowning in a metal room, and let him die under the sky, where he did not mind dying in a just cause.

He also knew that the Petty Officer could not live.

Mallory looked up the hatch. There was a head up there. 'Now coming,' he shouted. The head vanished. His hand was in the small of his back, closing round the handle of his dagger in the sheath there. It came round his body low and hard, and thumped into the Petty Officer's chest, up and under the ribs. He kept the momentum going, shoved the man back onto a bunk, and pulled a blanket over him. Then he went back up the ladder.

The man on deck kicked the hatch shut. A stevedore had cast off the lines. Green water widened between the submarine and the quay. From the conning tower, a voice roared, 'Jump!'

Mallory looked round. He saw the Kapitän, a cold, vindictive face above the grey armour plate.

'Doesn't like dockyard people,' said the man on the bow line. 'Nor do I.' And he put up a seaboot, and shoved.

Mallory could have dodged, broken the man's leg, saved his dignity. But what he wanted now had nothing to do with dignity. It was to get off this submarine, quick.

He jumped.

He heard the toolbox clatter on the submarine's pressure hull. He saw the blue wink of it disappear into deep water.

It, and its three grenades.

Then the water was in his mouth and eyes, and he was swimming for the quay. He could hear the Kapitän laughing. He paid no attention.

He was thinking, five minutes to destroy the third U-boat.

How?

Andrea was swimming too. In fact, he was swimming for his life.

The waters of Greece were warm sapphires, blown by the meltemi certainly, but tideless, unmoving.

The waters of Vizcaya were different. The waters of Vizcaya were dark emeralds, cold as a cat's eye.

And they moved.

When Andrea had lowered his shrinking body into the water and let go of the iron rung, the eddy had taken him and spun him, so that the quays and the harbour whirled around his head. The cold had stolen his breath at first, so he trod water, and watched the harbour wheel a second time. Then he had fixed his eyes on the distant, ill-kempt masts of the *Stella Maris*, and started to swim.

On the face of it, things were fine. But he knew as soon as he entered the channel that this was all wrong.

He could breathe now. He was swimming, the great muscles of his shoulders knotting and bunching, driving his body through the cold salt water. He was swimming breaststroke. If they saw him, they would see only a head, a small head, that they would think was a seal. There had been anti-submarine nets off the end of the quays. But those nets were down now, folded away in the holds of the merchant ships, because the submarines were coming out.

So it was just a four-hundred-yard swim to the *Stella Maris*. Ten minutes. Fine.

Except that it was not working out that way.

The tide was like a river, sweeping him out of the narrows and into the sea. The *Stella Maris'* masts were sliding away upstream, fast, terrifyingly fast.

This was new. And it was unpleasant, not because it was frightening, because nothing physical, not even death – especially not death – frightened Andrea. But Andrea's life was based on not letting people down, and allowing the things that had been planned to come to pass. He had perfect faith that Mallory and Miller would accomplish their part of the job.

He was beginning to have less faith that he could do the same.

In spite of the Benzedrine, he was growing tired. Even he, even Andrea, was growing tired. He knew his reserves of strength were finite. There was no point in trying to swim straight at his objective.

Brains, not brawn.

He turned until he was looking at the tall black bows of the merchant ships anchored in the harbour. He could hear the clank of their windlasses as they came up over their anchors, could see a couple of launches crawling across the glossy shield of the water. He began to swim, facing directly into the current and about ten degrees to the right.

For anyone else, it would have been instant exhaustion, suicide.

For Andrea, it was possible.

He swam with short, powerful strokes into the current, building a bow-wave of water on his nose. The quay where he had started had fallen away as he had been washed out to sea. But after five minutes of hard swimming, it had also fallen away to the left.

And the inner of the two merchant ships, which had been stern-on, was now showing its starboard side.

He did not let himself hope that he was making progress. He swam on doggedly, another two hundred strokes. He crossed a spine of white-tipped standing waves. A couple of waves smacked his face. He inhaled salt water, choked. He was really tired now. Now he had to look.

He looked.

The *Stella Maris* was a long way ahead, up-tide. But she was only some twenty degrees to the right.

He was getting across.

But his troubles were by no means over.

There was a bigger lift to the waves now, a regular roll. When he looked ninety degrees left and ninety degrees right, he saw not the quays of the town or the cliffs of the Cabo beneath the walls of the *fortaleza*. He saw open sea.

Andrea swam on. He was holding steady now. There was less tide out here. But he could feel in the screaming muscles of his legs and shoulders and the hammer of his heart that he was approaching the limit of his strength.

In Andrea's book, it was the mark of a man that he did not admit that there were limits.

Somewhere, Andrea found a reserve. With that reserve he started to move forwards. Progress heated his blood, and the heat of his blood helped progress. He found that he was moving up the slack water off the beach on the San Eusebio side of the channel, and that the quays, with their double ranks of fishing boats end-on, were coming closer.

He trod water for a moment.

His feet touched bottom. He looked back the way he had come. Except for a strip of deep green in the middle of the passage, the water on either side of the channel was paling. It looked as if it dried out at low tide. Ahead, the water was also pale, darkening only where the channel swept in under the quay where the fishing fleet was moored.

It had been a big swim.

But if he had waited another five minutes, he could probably have walked most of it.

Another man might have laughed, or cried, or felt relief. As far as Andrea was concerned, none of that was necessary. An exhausting set of conditions had ceased to apply, and a less exhausting set now obtained. The objective remained: to get aboard the *Stella Maris* within the next – he glanced at his waterproof watch – four minutes.

He began to wade.

Hauptsturmführer von Kratow did not like Spain. Latins were a slovenly bunch, racially suspect and entirely lacking in culture. But von Kratow did realise that to an operation such as Project Werwolf, they had their uses. It was just, he mused, trotting up the stone stairs of the *fortaleza* to report to the Herr General, that there seemed to be something in the air. Organising an embarkation should not be difficult. But there was a spirit of . . . well, *mañana* . . . that made even SS order and system show a tendency to buckle.

Still, everything was in order now. The attack at the main gate seemed to have been a false alarm. The embarkation was almost complete. All that remained was to report to the General, who would be highly delighted. A bastard, the General, with his Turkish tobacco and what his troops reckoned was the limpest artificial wrist in the Reich. But an appreciative bastard, particularly if, like von Kratow, you were a cleancut Junker with a nice leg for a jackboot, and you did your work correctly. Von Kratow was pretty sure that three repaired submarines and a smooth embarkation would mean promotion.

He pushed open the elaborate door of the General's quarters, and sniffed for the Turkish tobacco.

There was no Turkish tobacco.

Von Kratow frowned.

For as long as he had been the General's ADC, there had been a cigarette smouldering between the General's artificial fingers. The only time he was not smoking was when he was asleep. He would not be asleep now, not with the evacuation nearly finished.

Von Kratow opened the door.

A buttery morning light was pouring through the part of the Gothic window not covered by the curtains. The tobacco smell hung stale in the air, and last night's fire had died to bitter ashes. Von Kratow walked across to the desk, and collected himself a handful of Turkish cigarettes from the box. The General would never notice. The Luftwaffe brought him new supplies weekly; God knew where they found them nowadays.

Von Kratow yawned and stretched. It had been a long night, in a long series of long nights. But now it was over.

Beyond the stone fretwork of the windows the harbour was a sheet of green glass lit by a heavy yellow sun glaring just above the mountains to the east. The merchant ships were up over their anchors, the launches heading back on what must be almost the last of their journeys to pick up the now diminished clods of men from the quay. Down in the repair facility, the Werwolf boats were emitting a blue mist of exhaust. The inshore boat had dropped her shore lines and seemed to be nosing towards the exit.

So that's it, thought von Kratow. Mission accomplished. Time to catch the boat. Time to make sure the Herr General caught the boat.

Von Kratow was a tidy-minded man. Before he went to knock on the bedroom door, he drew back the heavy brocade curtain that was half-obscuring the window.

That was when he found the General.

For perhaps ten seconds von Kratow stared stony-faced at the oyster silk underwear, the ivory-white skin of the face, the black flow of dried blood from the right ear. Then his hand went to the cigarette box on the desk. He lit one of the General's cigarettes and thought, silk underclothes.

Then he put out a deliberate finger, and pressed the button behind the curtain.

The general alarm button.

Suddenly, the Cabo de la Calavera was full of bells.

Mallory crawled up the iron rungs on the granite wall, coughing water. The quays opened in front of his eyes: a sheet of granite paving and drying puddles, studded with cranes, riven by the three great crevasses of the submarine docks. The innermost submarine was moving. From behind him there came the clatter of diesels, and the churn of water blowing from ducted screws over rudders. That submarine – his submarine – was on the way out too.

The top of the conning tower of the last submarine was stationary. It stayed in his eye as he rested at the top of the ladder. He was tired now, Benzedrine or no Benzedrine, so tired that he could hardly drag himself up a set of rungs in the quay.

He saw a terrible thing.

He saw Dusty Miller on the conning tower of that submarine. Miller was arguing with a man in a cap, demanding admission, by the look of it. The man in the cap, the Kapitän, presumably, was telling him you are cluttering up the joint, and I am sailing now, so get off, before you get stuck.

Dusty Miller won. He vanished from view.

Quick, thought Mallory. *For God's sake, be quick.*

He looked at his watch. It was three minutes to five. Early, he thought. They're leaving early.

Too late.

Mallory began to crawl away from the submarine he had visited, the submarine with the dead Petty Officer in the head –

It was then he noticed that the harbour was full of bells.

The conning tower into which Miller had vanished began to slide along the quay.

Mallory could almost hear the orders: *in the event of problems, move out.*

So three minutes early, the U-boats were moving out.

And one of them had Miller on board.

Something snapped in Mallory. He clambered to his feet, exhaustion forgotten. He stumbled along the quay after that conning tower, yelling hoarsely with rage. But the conning tower slid away faster than he could chase it down the quay.

The three great U-boats gathered in the turning basin at the end of the quays, stemming the tide: huge grey metal whales the length of destroyers, solid as rocks with their squat, streamlined conning towers, white water churning from their propellers. Men scuttled on their decks, making the final preparations for sea. Their Kapitäns conferred, conning tower to conning tower, with the casualness of men who knew that a hundred metres of water made them untouchable.

Mallory looked over the edge of the quay, made frantic by the bells.

He saw a rowing boat.

It was a small, filthy rowing boat, a quarter full of water. But it held oars and rowlocks, and it was more or less afloat.

Mallory grabbed the painter that tied it to the bollard on the quay. He wound his ruined hands into that rope, climbed down it and cut it with his knife. The boat floated free. There was an idea in his mind, a crazy idea, born out of exhaustion. Go to that U-boat. Hammer on the hull. Tell them there had been a mistake. Dockyard matey inside. Needs taking off. Quick. Then they could go on, aboard the *Stella Maris*, and have at least some chance –

He pulled with the oars. The dinghy shot across the eddy at the end of the quay.

The tide caught it.

Four knots of tide.

Mallory could row at two knots, flat out.

The U-boats were gliding past at horrifying speed. Mallory turned, tried to get back.

Not a hope. The U-boats might as well have been in Berlin.

With a great sickness in his heart, Mallory began to crab across the channel towards the *Stella Maris*. Soon the air was full of whipping sounds, and little explosions, like fireworks. Someone was shooting at him. In fact a lot of people were shooting at him, from the merchant ships. Dully, he remembered the rings of sandbags on their hatch covers, the snouts of machine guns, other guns too. They would probably hit him.

Mallory found that he did not care. Something had gone wrong, he did not care what. They had lost Miller. A voice in his head, a voice like Jensen's, said: if Miller had to die, this was how he would have wanted to die.

Mallory's own voice answered: *rubbish*.

'Orders,' shouted Dusty Miller to the Kapitän of the last U-boat. 'From the General. I have to check the officers' head. You do not sail for five minutes.'

The Kapitän had a cropped bullet head and a broken nose, and a look of extreme exhaustion.

He said to the coxswain at his side, 'Take this man below. Make sure that he is on the quay when we sail. This is your responsibility.'

'Aye, aye,' said the coxswain. He was a small, pale man, and he did not look pleased to be sent off the conning tower. 'What is it you want?'

'Engine room head,' said Miller, rattling his toolbox.

'There isn't an engine room head.'

'I got my orders,' said Miller.

The coxswain said, 'I'll show you, then.' He started down the ladder, and headed towards the back end of the boat.

The conning tower hatch was a disc of daylight above the control room. As Miller started down the ladder, he thought he heard bells, and shouting. But he knew he had five minutes in hand. The bells must be meaningless. What was in the forefront of his mind was how he was going to get rid of this damned coxswain.

The central alleyway of the U-boat was familiar territory to Miller now: yellow lights, heat, sweaty faces. What was not familiar was the sound of the engine. It was still a huge, clattering roar. But now it was a roar that changed pitch, went on and up, held steady, and went up again.

The coxswain stopped. He looked at Miller. His lips moved. It was not possible to hear what he said over the racket of the diesel. But it was easy enough to read his lips.

Miller's heart thumped once, painfully, in his chest.

The words the coxswain's lips were framing were, 'We've sailed.'

For a second, Miller's face felt wooden with shock. Then he grinned. 'Well, then,' he said, though he knew the other man would not hear him. 'We've got a load of time.'

The coxswain arrived at the engine room. 'Look,' he said. 'No head.'

Miller grinned, his wide, starry-eyed idiot's grin. 'Oh, yeah,' he said.

The coxswain pointed back along the corridor towards the ladder. Miller could almost see the thoughts running through the man's mind: *this is not my fault, it's because we sailed early. All I have to do is get this fool back to the Kapitän. The Kapitän has forgotten him in the heat of the moment. I will be in the clear –*

Miller stared at the coxswain, still grinning, as the coxswain made pointing gestures back towards the ladder. Miller craved that ladder like a fiend craves dope. The coxswain came back to him and shoved him towards the ladder.

Miller hit him.

He hit him hard in the stomach. If it had been Andrea, the punch would have killed the man. But Miller was a demolition expert, not a bare-hands killer. The coxswain whooped and doubled up onto the deck. Miller looked round.

There were three men in the alleyway. They were all watching.

Miller stepped over the body on the deck, and walked smartly aft. The roar of the engines had steadied now. He walked through the watertight door into the engine room. He slammed it, and dogged the handles quickly behind him. Ahead of him, hanging from a stanchion in the deckhead, was a chain hoist. Just like a mine, thought Miller, grabbing the chain. Miller had spent thousands of hours in mines, some of them very happy. As he wrapped the chain round the door handles, he felt right at home.

Someone was trying to undog the door now. When bare hands did not work, they started to hit the handles with what sounded like a sledge hammer. Bash away, thought Miller. We are talking good German chain here, and submarines are not built to resist the enemy within.

In fact, enemies within were virtually unknown on submarines.

Because when a submarine went down it went down, enemy within and all.

Miller told himself: it had to happen, one day.

It did not help.

He bent and opened the toolbox, and took out the two grenades.

Suddenly, he smelt tobacco smoke.

Round the end of the diesel block came a pale, oil-stained man in a singlet, with an undoubtedly illicit cigarette in his mouth. He glanced at Miller's face, the glance of a crew member who knows his shipmates and is baffled by the emergence of a new face from their midst. Then his eyes moved to Miller's hands.

Miller grinned at him, and put the grenades stealthily back in the box.

The man's eyes stayed glued to the grenades.

He went white as an oily rag. Then he picked up a wrench, dropped his cigarette, and came at Miller.

He was a short man, almost dwarfish, as wide as he was high. The coxswain had been out of shape because he only did whatever they did in the control room. This man was an engine room artificer, with big muscles under the white skin of his shoulders. He got both hands on his wrench, and he hefted it like a baseball bat, and he came down the aisle at Miller like an oil-stained Nibelung. Miller swung the toolbox at the man. It was an overconfident swing, inspired by too much Benzedrine and not enough judgement. It missed by a mile. The Nibelung smacked at the toolbox with his wrench. The toolbox flew out of Miller's hand, skidding down the gratings, bursting open as it slid. Tools and grenades spilled out. Miller caught a glimpse of the grenades, unarmed, useless, skittering into the tunnel where the propeller shaft ran. Then he threw himself to one side, and the wrench whacked into the steel bulkhead where his head had been.

Miller stood there, back to the door, panting, heart hammering. The yellow lights shone in the short man's sweat. His face was a flat mask of anger. Then Miller saw it flicker, and he knew why. There was a new note to the engine: a high-pitched whine. The deck was tilting underfoot, gently.

The whine was the disintegrator. The engine had switched from fuel–air to fuel–decomposed hydrogen peroxide.

The submarine was diving.

The squat man came at Miller again. Miller kicked him in the stomach. It was like kicking corrugated iron. The man came on regardless.

Away from the door, thought Miller. Can't move away from the door, or he'll take the chains off, and the rest of the crew will get in –

The spanner crashed against the metal. Miller skipped out of the way. Door or no door, he was no good with his head caved in.

Miller knew that he was losing.

But the squat man had forgotten the door even existed. He was a submarine engineer, and when people bring grenades into their engine rooms, submarine engineers lose the power of rational thought. He swung again.

Miller dodged clumsily. The wrench caught him on the shoulder, numbing his arm. He stumbled back against the engine, head between the clashing tappets, and rolled down to the grating.

He saw another wrench. Picked it up. Too heavy to swing. Better than nothing.

The Nibelung came at him again. Miller scuttled round the far side of the engine. Retreating, always retreating. This was a man who knew his patch, and what he was going to do was hound Miller into a corner, and kill him, and that would be that. A Werwolf on the loose, and all that work in vain.

It was the thought of the wasted effort that really upset Miller. Energy stormed through his veins. As the man came in again, he swung his wrench. The man jumped back. The heavy steel head whacked a pipe in the wall, just under the thread of a joint.

And suddenly the engine room smelt like a hairdresser's salon.

The Nibelung's face had changed, too. He was staring at that pipe that Miller had hit. And he did not look angry any more. He looked frightened out of his wits.

Miller felt the weight of the wrench in his hand. He knew he did not have many more swings left in him. One more.

The man still had half his mind on the pipe.

Miller swung the wrench at the pipe, then again, into the side of the man's head.

There was a solid *chunk* that Miller felt rather than heard. The man's eyes rolled back, and he went down like a bag of cement.

Dead, thought Miller. Dead.

Quick.

Peroxide was roaring out of the pipe, gurgling over the body of the engineer. As it hit the engineer's body, it foamed.

There was another catalyst that broke down hydrogen peroxide into hydrogen and oxygen. It was called peroxidase, and it was found in human blood.

Miller ran to the aft end of the engine room. There was a sort of cupboard next to the propeller shaft gland, a steel-doored locker that bore the words *Siebe-Gorman*.

The engine room was filling with free oxygen and hydrogen.

On the deck, the Nibelung's cigarette ceased to glow and began to burn with a hard, bright flame.

Quick, thought Miller.

It was all feeling very slow to Mallory, as if the world had started moving through a new kind of time, viscous and syrupy. He saw the flat green mirror of the water, the red and green tracers rising from the merchant ships, slow as little balloons, queuing up to accelerate round his head and kick the water to foam. Under the rocky brow of the Cabo de la Calavera he saw the U-boats moving, hovering, arranging themselves into line ahead. Miller was on the lead boat. Then came the other boat Miller had visited. Mallory's was last.

The rowing boat rocked in the little waves of a tide-rip. The sun was warm on his face. Something smashed into the transom of the rowing boat. He shielded his eyes from the splinters, felt the rip of flesh on his cheek, the run of liquid that must be blood. The rowing boat spun in an eddy. He saw the San Eusebio town quay, the fishing boats tied up alongside. The movement of the rowing boat in the eddy made the masts of the boats appear to be moving –

One set of masts was moving. The masts of the *Stella Maris*.

They were moving slowly, crawling against the spars of the other boats and the blank shutters of the quayside warehouses. They were accelerating, the black hull narrowing, the masts coming into line as whoever was at the wheel pointed the nose straight at Mallory. Coming to pick him up.

But not Miller.

The U-boats were moving out from the quays now, gliding slowly across the peaceful green satin of the water. The first was already in the channel, the green water rumpling over its deck, diving. Diving quickly, so as not to be seen leaving a neutral harbour. Diving with Miller on board.

Metal smashed into the rowing boat by Mallory's feet. Suddenly there was water where there had once been planking, water pouring in through three holes the size of fists. Mallory tried to stem the water with his foot, but his foot was too small, and suddenly the rowing boat was part of the harbour, and cold water was up around Mallory's neck.

An engine was thumping close at hand. The tar-black nose of the *Stella Maris* swept up, pushing a white moustache of foam. A head leaning over the bow said, *'Bonjour, mon Capitaine.'* The head of Andrea.

Andrea's hand came down. It grasped Mallory's wrist. Mallory felt himself plucked skyward, grabbed a wooden rail, and landed face down on the *Stella*'s filthy deck.

'Welcome aboard,' said Andrea. 'Where's Miller?'

A burst of machine-gun fire smacked into the *Stella*'s stern. Mallory pointed.

The lead U-boat was halfway down the channel. All that was showing was its conning tower.

Andrea's Byzantine eyes were without expression. Only the great stillness of the man gave a clue to his emotion. The *Stella Maris* turned, and headed down the channel. Mallory lurched aft and took the wheel from Jaime. He steered the *Stella* right up to the flank of the last U-boat. There were still heads on the U-boat's conning tower. One of the heads was yelling, a hand waving at this dirty little fishing boat to keep clear, keep out of the way. The fire from the merchant ships was slackening now, for fear of hitting the U-boat.

And down below, thought Mallory, down in the torpedo room the hands would be manoeuvring the hoists over to the first torpedo, opening the tube, loading up, ready for an enemy waiting out there in the Bay. The hoists would be lifting, stretching the string fuse of the grenade, scratching the primer, starting the five-second delay.

Mallory stood there in the cool morning breeze, watching the two conning towers ahead, one half-submerged, the other with its base awash. Sixty yards away, the water began to creep up the deck of the last U-boat. The heads were gone from the conning tower.

There was no explosion.

They have found the grenades, thought Mallory. How can you expect to destroy a U-boat with grenades and string? He wound the wheel to port, to keep the *Stella* in the narrow strip of turquoise separating the pale green of the shallows from the ink-blue of the deep-water channel. The U-boat's hull was under now.

It was getting away.

Mallory groped for a cigarette, put it in his mouth, and watched the channel.

The channel blew up in his face.

It blew up in a jet of searing white flame that went all the way up into the sky, taking with it millions of tons of water that climbed and climbed until it looked as if it would never stop climbing, a reverse waterfall that made a noise loud enough to make a thunderclap sound like the dropping of a pin on a Persian rug. A wall of water smashed into the *Stella Maris*, walloped her onto her beam ends and broke over her. When she lurched upright again, her mainmast was gone. But somehow her Bolander was still thumping away, and Andrea was up among the rigging with an axe, chopping at shrouds and stays, kicking the tangle overboard where it lay wallowing like a sea monster, mingling with the oil and mattresses and other less identifiable bits of flotsam emanating from the still-boiling patch of sand and water that had once been one-third of the Werwolf pack.

Must have been right down in the channel, thought Mallory. Otherwise it would have blown us up with it –

Further out to sea there was another rumble, followed by an eruption of bubbles on the surface. The bubbles were full of smoke. When they burst, they left a film of oil on the surface.

Hugues said, 'What was that?'

'Another U-boat,' said Mallory. The bubbles rose for thirty seconds: a lot of bubbles, big ones. No bodies. No mattresses. A machine of steel had become air and oil.

'*Bon Dieu,*' said Hugues, appalled.

Jaime said, 'The ships.' He was looking backwards, over his shoulder.

The merchant ships had their anchors up. Magnified and indistinct beyond the pall of smoke and spray still descending from the first U-boat, they looked huge. From the machine guns on their decks the tracers were rising again.

'*Merde,*' said Jaime.

The ships were faster than the *Stella Maris*. They would catch her up and sink her. At best, they would sink her. Well, Dusty, thought Mallory, with a new and surprising cheerfulness. We are all in this together. Andrea had pulled the Bren out of the hold, and was lying on the *Stella*'s afterdeck, taking aim at the lead merchant ship. Flame danced at the muzzle. A Bren against ships. Not fair, thought Mallory –

From seaward there came a rumble that made the *Stella* shudder under Mallory's feet. When he looked round, he saw a white alp of water rise offshore. And he forgot about the merchant ships, forgot about everything. For that alp, collapsing as soon as it had risen, was a watery headstone for Dusty Miller.

Three out of three. One hundred per cent success.

But Dusty Miller was dead.

Bullets from the merchant ship lashed the air beside his head, and whacked into the *Stella*'s crapulous timbers. Mallory paid them no heed. He turned the fishing boat's nose for the open sea.

It was calm, that sea, its emerald smoothness marred only by patches of oil and debris. The old fishing boat laboured towards the northern horizon, reeking of hot metal from the engine room hatch, rolling heavily with the volume of water in her belly.

And on her heels, gaining ground, Uruguayan flags limp on their halyards, spitting a blizzard of tracer, came the merchantmen.

Hugues said, 'What now?'

Mallory grinned, a grin that had no humour in it. His eyes were shining with a brilliance that Hugues found completely horrible.

'We take cover,' said Mallory. 'They sink us, or catch us, or both.'

Bullets were slamming into the *Stella*'s deck. The air whined with splinters. 'She will fall apart,' said Hugues.

'Very probably,' said Mallory. 'They were out of the harbour now. The leading merchant ship was entering the narrows, spewing black oil-smoke from its funnel, heading steadily down the dark-blue water of the channel. Once it was through the channel, it would speed up. And that would be the end of the *Stella Maris*.

They did not bother to take cover. They watched the bow of the merchant ship: the high bow, with the moustache of water under its nose, heading busily along the channel. Above its nose was the bridge, the thin blue smoke of the machine guns on its wings, and the heads of men, pin-sized, watching. It would be that moustache of water that would be the last movement. The *Stella Maris* would rise on it just before the merchant ship's nose came down and rolled her under, crushed her into the cold green sea –

Suddenly, Mallory stopped breathing. Hugues was by his side, gripping his arm with fingers like steel bars.

For the moustache of white water at the stem of the merchant ship had disappeared. The steel knife-edge had risen in the water, and stopped.

The ship had run aground on the U-boat that had blown up in the channel five minutes previously.

As they watched, the tide caught the ship's stern, slewing it until the freighter was a great steel wall blocking the channel: the only channel out of the harbour.

For a moment, the gunfire stilled, and a huge sound rolled over that windless frying pan of water.

The sound of Andrea, laughing.

Then the machine guns opened up again.

This time they opened up with a new venom, bred of fury and impotence. The bullets lashed the sea to a white froth, and the fishing boat's hull shuddered under their impact. Mallory crouched inside the wheelhouse. Another five minutes, he thought. Then we are out of range. The noise was deafening. The air howled with flying metal. And mixed with it, another sound.

Hugues. Hugues, shouting. Hugues was standing on the deck, yelling, pointing at something in the water. Something orange. Something that moved, raised an arm and waved, a feeble wave, but a wave nonetheless. Something that was a hand, holding a fuming orange smoke flare.

And when the orange smoke rolled clear of the face, the face, though coughing and distorted, was unmistakably the face of Dusty Miller.

Mallory spun the wheel. The *Stella* turned broadside onto the merchant ships' torrent of bullets. Hugues stood upright, insanely conspicuous, out of cover. Miller came floating down the side. 'Grab him!' yelled Mallory.

Hugues leaned over the side. As they passed Miller, he stuck his hand down, and Miller put his up, and the hands met and gripped. Now the *Stella* was towing Miller along, and Hugues' arm was the tow line. Hugues suddenly shuddered, and four dark blotches appeared on his vest. But by then Andrea was there, grasping Miller with his great hand. He gave one heave. And then they were all lying on the deck: Andrea, Hugues and Miller, Miller gasping like a gaffed salmon, leaking water.

Mallory turned the wheel away from the harbour entrance. The orange smoke faded astern. Soon they were out of range, and there were no more bullets.

Miller lit a cigarette. His face was grey and white, the bags under his eyes big enough to hold the equipment of a fair-sized expeditionary force. He said, 'Good morning. Do we have a drink?'

Mallory handed him the miraculously undamaged bottle of brandy from the riddled locker in the wheelhouse. 'How did you get out?' he said.

Miller raised the bottle. 'I would like to drink to the health of two Krauts,' he said. 'Mr Siebe and Mr Gorman. And the cutest little submarine escape apparatus known to science.' He drank deeply.

Andrea came aft. He said, 'Hugues needs to talk.'

Hugues was lying on the deck in a red pond. Mallory could hear his chest bubble as he breathed. Hugues said, 'I am sorry.' He could speak no more.

Andrea said, 'This man is a traitor.'

Mallory looked at the blue-white face, the suffocated eyes. He said, 'Why?'

Hugues' eyes swivelled from Andrea to Mallory. Andrea said, 'To save Lisette, and his child. The Gestapo followed her to St-Jean. When they tried to pick her up with Hugues, he made a deal. They did not arrest us there, because it would have been more interesting for them to catch us in the act of sabotage. So when Hugues knew we were on the Cabo, he fed them information.'

Hugues shrugged. 'I did it for my child,' he said. Then blood came from his mouth, and he died.

Lisette was standing half-out of the hatch. She looked pale and tired, the shadows under her eyes dark and enormous. The eyes themselves had the thick lustre of tears.

'He was a man who had lost everything he loved,' she said. 'When he was in the Pyrenees the first time, he told me what had happened to his wife, his children. He was a lonely man. I can't describe to you how lonely. He was a good man.' The tears were running now. 'A man of passion. For his country. For me. In war, these things can happen, and they are not so strange.'

'*Enfin*, he was a traitor,' said Jaime. Mallory looked at the dark, starved face, the heavy black moustache, the impenetrable eyes. Jaime shrugged, the shrug of a smuggler, of a man who would walk through mountains if he could not walk over them, of a man whose hand was against all other men. Nobody would ever know whether Jaime was fighting because of what he believed in, or because he wanted to survive. Probably, Jaime did not know himself.

Mallory looked at Andrea's face, dark and closed, and at Miller's haggard countenance, the oil and salt drying in his crewcut. Perhaps none of them knew why they did these things.

Perhaps, in the end, it was not important, as long as it was necessary to do these things, and these things got done. He clambered to his feet and put his arm around Lisette's shoulders.

She said, 'I did not love him. But he is the father of my child. And that is worth something, *hein?*'

It was not the sort of question Mallory knew how to answer.

EPILOGUE

Wednesday
1400

The *Stella Maris* was heading north on a broad navy-blue sea. Cabo de la Calavera had dropped below the southern horizon an hour ago. A radio message had been sent. Now there was nothing but the blue and cloudless dome of the sky, and dead ahead of the *Stella,* a tenuous black wisp no bigger than an eyelash stuck above the smooth curve of the world.

The eyelash became an eyebrow, then a heavy black plume. The base of the plume resolved itself into the Tribal class destroyer *Masai,* thundering over the low Atlantic swell at thirty-five knots, trailing an oily cloud of black smoke, her boiler pressures trembling on the edge of the red.

The Lieutenant-Commander who was her captain looked down at the filthy black fishing boat, stroked his beard, and hoped he was not going to get any of that rubbish on his nice paint. He walked down to the rail and said, 'Captain Mallory?'

The villain at the fishing boat's wheel said, 'That's right.'

There were two other villains on deck: red-eyed, sun-scorched, bleeding, unshaven. But the Lieutenant-Commander's eye had moved over the bullet-scarred decks and gunwales, and caught the glint of a lot of water through the open hatch of what was presumably the fish-hold. The Lieutenant-Commander said, 'I wonder if you would care for a spot of lunch?'

Mallory looked as if lunch was not a word he understood. He said, 'Could we have a stretcher party?'

'You've got wounded?'

'Not exactly wounded,' said Mallory.

The stretcher party trotted onto the *Stella*'s splintered decks. Mallory pointed them towards the bunkroom. A curious noise came into being, a high, keening wail. The Petty Officer in charge of the stretcher party looked nervously over his shoulder. He had been on the Malta convoys, and he knew about Stukas.

Mallory shook his head.

'Five for lunch?' said the Lieutenant-Commander.

'Six,' said Mallory.

The Lieutenant-Commander frowned. 'I thought you lost someone.'

'You lose some,' said Miller. 'You win some.'

The stretcher came up on deck. Behind it was Jaime. Strapped to it was Lisette. And in her arms, wrapped in a red sickbay blanket, was a small bundle that wailed.

The Lieutenant-Commander gripped the rail. 'See what you mean,' he said.

'I was a little more pregnant than the Captain thought,' said Lisette. 'I hope I cause no trouble.'

'Quite the reverse,' said the Lieutenant-Commander.

They walked onto the destroyer's beautifully painted deck. A Lieutenant took them to the tiny but spotless wardroom, and poured them gigantic pink gins. 'I expect you chaps have had quite a party,' he said.

They stared at him, bleary-eyed, until he went as pink as his gin. A signalman trotted in, flimsy in hand. The Lieutenant read it. 'Captain Mallory,' he said. 'For you.'

Mallory's eyes were closed. 'Read it,' he said.

This was a horrid breach of etiquette. The Lieutenant said, 'But –'

'Read it.'

The Lieutenant squared his shoulders. 'Reads as follows,

CONGRATULATIONS SUCCESSFUL COMPLETION OF STORM FORCE. TIMING PROVIDENTIAL. HAVE ANOTHER LITTLE JOB FOR YOU. REPORT SOONEST. JENSEN.

Mallory looked at Andrea and Miller. Their eyes were bloodshot and horrified. So, presumably, were his.

He said: 'SIGNAL TO CAPTAIN JENSEN. MESSAGE NOT UNDERSTOOD, BAFFLED, STORM FORCE.' He held out his glass. 'Now before we all die of thirst, could we have a spot more gin?'

SAM LLEWELLYN

Thunderbolt
from Navarone

To Hex, Bert and Garlinda

PROLOGUE

Kapitän Helmholz looked at his watch. It was ten fifty-four and thirty-three seconds. Twenty-seven seconds until coffee time on the bridge of the armed merchantman *Kormoran*. At *Kapitän* Helmholz's insistence, coffee time was ten fifty-five precisely. A precise man, Helmholz, which was perhaps why he had been appointed to the command that had put him here in this steel room with big windows, below the red and black *Kriegsmarine* ensign with its iron cross and swastika board-stiff in the meltemi, the afternoon wind of the Aegean. Outside the windows were numbers one and two hatches, and under the hatches the cargo, and forward of the hatches the bow gun on the fo'c'sle and the bow itself, kicking through the short, steep chop. Beyond the rusty iron bow the sea sparkled, a dazzling sheet of sapphire all the way to the horizon. Beyond the horizon lay his destination, hanging like a cloud: a solid cloud – the mountains of Kynthos, blue with distance. It was all going well; neat, tidy, perfectly on schedule. Helmholz looked at his watch again.

With fifteen seconds to go until the time appointed, there it was: the faint jingle of the coffee tray. It always jingled when Spiro carried it. Spiro was Greek and suffered from bad nerves. *Kapitän* Helmholz raised his clean-cut jaw, directed his ice-blue eyes down his long straight nose, and watched the fat little Greek pour the coffee into the cups and hand them round. The man's body odour was pungent, his apron less than scrupulously clean. His face was filmed with sweat, or possibly grease. Still, thought Helmholz with unusual tolerance, degenerate Southerner he might be, but his coffee was good, and punctual. He picked up the cup, enjoying the smell of the coffee and the tension on the bridge as his junior officers waited for the *Herr Kapitän* to drink so they could drink too. Helmholz pretended interest in the blue smudge of Kynthos, feeling the tension rise, enjoying the sensation that in small ways as well as in large, he was the man in control.

A mile away, in an iron tube jammed with men and machinery, a bearded man called Smith, with even worse body odour than Spiro, crammed his eyes against the rubber eyepieces of his attack periscope and said, 'Usual shambles up forward, Derek?'

'Probably,' said Derek, who was similarly bearded and smelt worse. 'Blue touchpaper lit and burning.'

'Jolly good. Fire one, then.'

From the spider's eyes of the torpedo tubes at the bow of His Majesty's submarine *Sea Leopard*, a drift of bubbles emerged, followed by the lean and purposeful Mark 8 torpedo. Tracking the deflection scale across the merchantman's rust-brown hull, Smith stifled a nervous yawn, and wished he could smoke. Three-island ship. Next fish under the bridge. That would do it. 'Fire two,' he said. It was not every day you bumped into a German armed merchantman swanning around on her own in the middle of nowhere. Sitting duck, really. 'We'll hang around a bit,' he said. 'Maybe they'll have some Schnapps.'

'Can but hope,' said the Number Two.

Helmholz's feeling of control did not survive even as long as it took to put his cup to his lips. It was one of the great ironies of his life that while at sea he was an automaton, as soon as he came in sight of land he was racked with an intellectually unjustifiable impatience. Suddenly his mind flooded with pictures of the *Kormoran* alongside the Kynthos jetty, unloading. The sweat of impatience slimed his palms. It was crazy to be out here with no escort; against reason. But there was such a shortage of aircraft for the direct defence of the Reich that the maintenance fitters had mostly been called back to Germany. So most of the air escort was out of action. The E-boats were not much better. Which left the *Kormoran* alone on the windy blue Aegean, with an important cargo and a pick-up crew . . .

He put his coffee cup to his lips.

Over the white china rim, he saw something terrible.

He saw a gout of orange flame leap up on the starboard side, level with number one hatch. He saw number one hatch itself bulge upward and burst in a huge bubble of fire that came roaring back at him and caved in the bridge windows. That was the last thing he saw, because that same blast drove the coffee cup right through his face and out of the back of his head. His junior officers suffered similar lethal trauma, but their good manners ensured that this was to the ribcage, not the skull. Perhaps Helmholz would have been consoled that things had been in order right until the moment of oblivion.

'Bullseye,' said Lieutenant Smith. 'Oh, bloody hell, she's burning.'

Burning was not good. Even if there was no escort waiting in the sun, the plume of black smoke crawling into the sky was as good as a distress flare. His thoughts locked into familiar patterns. The *Sea Leopard* had been submerged a long time. If there was to be a pursuit, now was the moment to prepare for it.

'Breath of fresh air, I think,' said Smith. 'Up she goes.'

And with a whine of pumps and electric engines, HMS *Sea Leopard* began to rise through the gin-clear sea.

They were not more than half a mile from the *Kormoran*. Great creakings came to them, the sound of collapsing bulkheads. Poor devils, thought Smith, in a vague sort of way; they were all poor devils in this war. They were all men stuck in little metal rooms into which water might at any minute start pouring.

'She's going,' said Braithwaite, the Number Two.

Sea Leopard broke surface, shrugging tons of Aegean from her decks. Smith was up the conning tower ladder and on deck with the speed of a human cannonball. The sea was steep and blue, the wavecrests blown ice-white by the meltemi. The black smoke of the burning ship leaped from the pale flame at its roots and tumbled away towards Kynthos. She was settling fast by the bow. One torpedo in her forward hold, one under her bridge. Nice shooting, thought Smith, wrinkling his nostrils against the sharp, volatile smell of the air. Not petrol. An altogether homelier smell; the aroma of stoves in the cabins of the little yachts Smith had sailed in the North Sea before the war. Alcohol. Not Schnapps: fuel alcohol.

The submarine began to move ahead, towards the wreck. In the crust of floating debris that covered the water were shoals of long cylindrical objects. Smith's heart jumped. They looked like torpedoes. But they were too small. Gas bottles, they were; cylinders. He put his heavy rubber-armoured glasses on them. O2, said the stencilled letters. Oxygen. No bloody good to anyone.

There was a flash and an ear-splitting bang. When Smith could take notice again, he saw a great boil of bubbles. The ship was in half. Both halves sank quickly and without fuss.

The black cloud of smoke blew away. Except for the flotsam, the sea was empty, as far as you could see from a ten-foot conning tower among eight-foot waves. Petty Officer Jordan and a couple of ratings hooked a crate and hauled it aboard. 'Aircraft parts,' said Jordan.

Smith was disappointed. He really had been hoping for Schnapps. 'Better get going, what?' he said.

Jordan went below. *Sea Leopard* turned her nose west, for the friendlier waters of Sicily, away from the threatening smudge of German-held Kynthos. No survivors, thought Smith, raking the waves with his glasses. Pity. Couldn't be helped –

He paused. A couple of miles downwind, something rolled on the top of a wave, and what might have been an arm lifted. He opened his mouth to say, steer ninety degrees. A human? Wreckage? Worth a look.

But at that point his eye went up, climbing the vaults of the blue blue sky. And in that sky, he saw a little square of black dots. Aircraft.

He hit the klaxon and went down the conning tower and spun the hatch wheel. *Sea Leopard* sank into the deeps. *Kormoran* had been just another merchant ship in just another attack. Now it was time for *Sea Leopard* to take measures to ensure her own survival, to do more damage.

'Tea,' said Smith. They usually had a cup of tea sometime between eleven and half-past. Just now, he saw, looking at his watch before he wrote up the log, it was eleven minutes past.

ONE

Monday 1800–Tuesday 1000

It was raining in Plymouth, a warmish Atlantic rain that blanketed the Hoe and blurred the MTBs and MLs sliding in the Roads. In the early hours of their captivity the three men in the top-floor suite of the Hotel Majestic had spent time looking out of the window. They had long ago given up. Now they sprawled in armchairs round a low table on which were two empty brandy bottles and three overflowing ashtrays: men past their first youth and even their second, faces burned dark by the sun, eye-sockets hollow with the corrosive exhaustion of battle. They were in khaki battledress, without insignia. One was huge and black-haired. Another was tall and lean, with the hard jaw and steady eyes of a climber. The third was a rangy individual with a lugubrious face, glass of brandy in one hand, cigarette in mouth.

It was the third man who spoke. 'This is not,' he said, 'what I call a vacation.'

The third man's name was Miller. In so far as he had a rank, he was a corporal in the RAF. He was also the greatest demolition expert in the Allied armies.

The man who looked like a climber nodded, and lit a cigarette, and returned to his thoughts. This was a man you could imagine waiting for ever, if necessary; a man completely in control of himself. This was Captain Mallory, the New Zealander who before the war had been a world-famous mountaineer, and who had since done more damage to Hitler's armies than the entire Brigade of Guards. 'It's better than being machine-gunned,' he said.

Miller thought about that. 'I guess,' he said. He did not look sure.

'Soon,' said the big man, 'there will be work to do.' His accent was Greek, his voice soft but heavy, spreading a blanket of silence through the room. Andrea was a sleepy-eyed bear of a man, dark enough to look perpetually in need of a shave, his upper lip infested with a black stubble of regrowing moustache. He looked like the less respectable type of bandit, a mountain of sloth and debauchery. This impression had misled many of his enemies, most of them fatally. In fact, Andrea was a full colonel in the Greek army. Furthermore, he was as strong as a mobile crane, as fast and light on his feet as a cat, and as level-headed as an Edinburgh lawyer. When he spoke, which was not often, people gave him their full attention.

Miller and Mallory closed their minds to the soft rain on the window.

'They think we are spies,' said Andrea. 'They think we have made a deal with somebody and run away. It is not an unreasonable suspicion. Do you blame them?'

Miller took a swig out of his glass. 'They asked us to blow the guns on Navarone,' he said. 'We blew 'em. They asked us to destroy the Neretva Dam. Up goes the Neretva Dam. They sent us after the Werwolf subs. The Werwolf submarines get broken.' His long face was lugubrious. 'And now they tell us they have another job for us, and they pick us up in the Bay of Biscay and bring us all the way to Plymouth, and to demonstrate their everlasting admiration they lock us up in a fleabag hotel and put sentries on the door.' He coughed, long and loose and nasty. 'Sure, I blame them.'

'They've had ten-tenths cloud since the Werwolf raid,' said Mallory. 'They haven't been able to do a photographic recce, and there's no independent confirmation. And if you remember, it wasn't an easy job.'

'I remember,' said Miller, grimly.

'So look at it like this,' said Mallory. 'They locked us up here because they don't believe we could have achieved our objective. But we know we did. So we're right and they're wrong, and when they find out they are going to be very sorry. So it is all a very nice compliment, really.'

'I don't want compliments,' said Miller. 'I want a few drinks and some decent food and a little feminine society. For Chrissakes, Jensen knows what we can do. Why doesn't he tell them?'

Andrea put his hands together. 'Who can tell what Jensen knows?'

There was a small silence. Then Mallory said, 'I think we should go and talk to him.'

'Oh, yeah,' said Miller. 'Very amusing. There are thirty commandos on the landing.'

'I did not,' said Mallory, 'notice any commandos on the windowsill.'

Miller's face was suddenly a mask of horror. 'Oh, no,' he said.

Andrea smiled, a pure, innocent smile of great sweetness. 'Captain Jensen takes cocktails in the mess at ten minutes past six. The mess is in the basement of this hotel. It is now five past.'

'How did you know that?'

'I looked at my watch.'

'About the cocktail hour.'

'There is a chambermaid here from Roumeli,' purred Andrea. 'I talked to the poor girl. She was very pleased – are we ready?'

The room had filled with damp air. Mallory had raised the window. He was standing with his hands on the sill, looking down the sheer face of the hotel. 'Child could do it,' he said. 'We're off.'

The cocktail bar of the Hotel Majestic in Plymouth had been a fashionable West Country rendezvous in the 1930s, largely because it was the only cocktail bar in Plymouth, a town which otherwise found its entertainment in the more violent type of public house. It was eminently suited to wartime use. For one thing, it was mostly below ground, a comforting feature for those wishing their business to be undisturbed by the Nazi bombs that had all but obliterated large areas of the city. For another, its proximity to the naval dockyard gave the barman, an alert Devonian called Enrico, privileged access to the bottomless wells of gin which were as indispensable a fuel for His Majesty's warships as the more conventional bunker crude.

At six, the usual crowd were in: seven-eighths male, eight-eighths in uniform, talking in low voices from faces haggard with overwork and lack of exercise. At five past, Captain Jensen walked to his usual table: a small man in naval uniform with a captain's gold rings on the sleeve, a sardonic smile, and eyes of an astonishing mildness, except when no one was looking, at which point they might have belonged to one of the hungrier species of shark. With him was a stout man with a florid face and the heavy braid of an admiral.

'Submarines,' the Admiral was saying. 'Damn cowardly, hugely overrated in my opinion.' He gulped his pink gin and called for another.

'Yes?' said Jensen, taking a microscopic sip of his own gin. 'Interesting point of view.'

'Not fashionable, I grant you,' said the Admiral, whose name was Dixon. 'But fashion is a fickle jade, what? Capital ships, I can tell you. The rest of it, well . . . Submarines, aircraft carriers, here today, gone tomorrow.'

Jensen raised a polite eyebrow. The Admiral's face was mottled with drink. He had recently arrived as OC Special Operations, Mediterranean, having been booted sideways from duties in the narrow seas before he could do any real damage. Jensen was interested in the Mediterranean himself – had, indeed, conceived and commanded some Special Operations of his own. It would have been reasonable to assume that he would have resented the arrival of a desk-bound blimp like Dixon as his superior officer. But if he did feel resentment, he showed no sign. Jensen was a subtle man, as his enemies had found out to their cost. Acting on Jensen's information, two Japanese infantry divisions had fought each other for three bloody days, each under the impression that the other was commanded by Orde Wingate. A German Panzer division had vanished without trace in the Pripet Marshes, following a road on a map drawn from cartographic information supplied by Jensen's agents. Since early in the war, others of his agents had been the unfailing fountainhead of the cigars smoked by the most important man in Britain. Jensen had a finger in all pies. He had paid close attention to the development of his own career, but even closer attention to the question of winning the war. In the second as well as the first, he was known to be completely ruthless – a fact that might have given a more intelligent man than Dixon cause for worry.

But Dixon could not see over the mountain of his self-importance. Dixon had room in his mind for only one thing at a time. Just at the moment, that thing was gin.

'Lovely thing, drink after hard day at office,' said the Admiral, waving for his third pinkers.

'The Werwolf reconnaissance photographs,' said Jensen. I've seen them. Total success.'

'Yes,' said the Admiral. 'Where's that damn waitress?'

'Can I have your order to release my men?'

'Men?'

'The men you had confined to quarters.'

'Tomorrow, for God's sake. During office hours.'

'They might value a little liberty before the mission.'

'They'll do as they're damn well ordered. Waitress!'

Jensen's small, hard face did not lose its mildness, but he was conscious of a little twitch of anticipation. He knew Mallory, Miller and Andrea well; had indeed hand-picked them from a pool of the hardest of hard men. He knew them for excellent soldiers. But he also knew that they were not the kind of troops the Admiral was accustomed to. Locking them in a hotel room under heavy guard because you did not have the imagination to understand the stupendous success of their last mission was not a tactful move. Mallory, Miller and Andrea were not used to the close proximity of superior officers. They obeyed orders to the letter, of course. Still, Jensen had a distinct feeling that there would be trouble –

There was a small commotion by the entrance.

The Majestic was the kind of hotel whose frontage is criss-crossed with string-courses, cornices and swags of stone fruit. Mallory had sniffed the wet sea air, sighted on the fire-escape two windows along. Then he had lowered himself from the windowsill on to the bunch of limestone plums that decorated the lintel of the window below. Here he had paused, then hopped on to its neighbour. Miller, cursing inwardly, took a deep breath and followed him. Six storeys below, a cat the size of a flea prowled in a yard of trash cans. Miller got his feet on the fruit. He took another breath, and jumped for the next lintel. It was not more than six inches wide. Mallory had landed on it soft and quiet and confident as if it had been the flight deck of an aircraft carrier. To Miller, it looked about as accommodating as a child's eyebrow. His mouth dried out in midair. He felt his boot make contact, the toe bite, then slither. His stomach shrank, and as he teetered and began to fall his mind had room for one thought and one thought only. Navarone, Yugoslavia, the Pyrenees, and it ends here at the Hotel Majestic, Plymouth. How stupid –

Then a steely hand grabbed his wrist and Mallory's voice said, 'Hold up, there.' Then he was standing on the lintel, breathing deep to slow the thumping of his heart. Suddenly the fumes of the brandy and the cigarettes were blowing away and he had the sense that something had started again, like a machine that was winding up, moving on to the road for which it had been designed. The hesitancy was gone. Thought and action were the same thing.

He took the next two lintels in his stride. On the fire-escape landing he looked back. Andrea was drifting across the face of the hotel like a gigantic shadow. The Greek landed light as a feather next to them. They trotted down the iron stairs, spread out, automatically, with the discipline that had established itself these last weeks. Covering each other, covering themselves . . . Going out for a drink.

They flitted off the fire-escape, trotted through the alley to the front of the hotel, and up the grand stone steps into the lobby. The man behind the desk saw three men in khaki battledress without insignia. He had been a hall porter on civvy street, and he knew trouble when he saw it. Among the immaculate officers walking through the lobby, these men stuck out like wolves at a poodle show. Their boots were dirty, their eyes bloodshot, and they moved at a murderous lope that made him wish he could leave, fast, and become far away. Alarm bells started ringing in his head. Deserters, he thought, and dangerous ones. It did not occur to him that deserters were unlikely to be hanging around in smart hotels. These men made him too nervous to think. His hand went for the telephone. He knew the number of the Military Police by heart.

He told the operator what he wanted. But when he looked up, the men had gone. For good, he imagined, dabbing sweat from his pale brow with a clean handkerchief. There had been no time for them to cause any trouble, and they would not get past the sentries on the cocktail bar. He cancelled the call.

But the men had not gone; and they had indeed got past the sentries.

It had happened like this: three men in battledress without insignia had attempted to gain entrance to the mess bar. Challenged, one of them had barked the sentries to attention, an order the sentries had (for reasons they did not properly understand) found themselves obeying. Another, a very big man with black curly hair, had taken away their rifles with the confidence of a kind father removing a dangerous toy from a fractious child. The third, having passed remarks uncomplimentary to their personal turnout and the cleanliness of their weapons, which he had inspected, had followed his two companions into the hallowed portals.

As they gazed upon the shut door, the sentries became aware that they had failed in their duty. There had been no chance of their succeeding, of course; the situation had been out of their hands. But that was not going to make matters any easier to explain to the sergeant. They were on a fizzer, for sure. As one, both sentries went through the door.

Through the fog of smoke, they saw their quarry. All three of them were with a small naval captain. They were standing rigidly to attention. The small captain caught the sentries' eyes, and waved them away. 'Really,' he said, mildly, to the three men. 'You'll frighten the horses.'

'Thought we'd pop out for a drink,' said Mallory.

Jensen raised an eyebrow. Thirty commandos, said the eyebrow, and I hope you haven't bent any of them.

'We came down the fire-escape,' said Mallory. 'We were very thirsty.'

Into Admiral Dixon's brain there had sunk the idea that something untoward was happening. He did not expect his evenings to be interrupted by soldiers, particularly soldiers as scruffy and badgeless as this lot. He was further amazed when he heard Captain Jensen say, 'Oh, well. While you're here, I can tell you we've got the snapshots. Total success. Well done. Briefing scheduled for 2300 hours.'

Admiral Dixon said, in a voice like a glacier calving, 'Who are these men?'

'Sorry,' said Jensen. 'Captain Mallory. Corporal Miller. Colonel Andrea, Greek Army, 19th Motorized Division. Admiral Dixon, OC Special Operations, Mediterranean.'

The Admiral rested his gooseberry eyes on the three men. Miller watched the veins in his neck and wondered idly how much pressure a blood vessel could take before it burst. 'Why,' said the Admiral, 'are they improperly dressed?'

'Disgraceful,' said Jensen, with severity. 'But as you will remember, they have just completed a mission. They were confined to quarters on suspicion of collusion with the enemy, so they haven't had a chance to pop up to Savile Row. I think that in view of reconnaissance reports on the outcome of their mission, we can give them the benefit of the doubt. Unless you feel an Inquiry is necessary?'

'Hrmph,' said the Admiral, mauve-faced. 'Mission or no mission, can't have this sort of nonsense –'

'Walls have ears,' said Jensen smoothly. 'You have called a briefing for 2300 hours. That will be the moment to discuss this. Now, gentlemen. Refreshment?'

'I thought you'd never ask,' said Miller. There was a waitress. Jensen ordered. The three men raised their glasses to Jensen, then the Admiral. 'Mud in your eye,' said Miller.

'Here's how,' said Jensen.

The Admiral grunted ungraciously. He swallowed his gin and left.

'Well, gentlemen,' said Jensen. 'We're very pleased with you; most of us, anyway.' He smiled, that gleaming, carnivorous smile. 'You will be collected at 2245 hours. Till then, I bid you sweet dreams.'

'Dreams?' said Miller. It was not yet seven o'clock.

'I always think a little nap can be most refreshing before a lot of hard work.'

'Work?' said Mallory.

But Jensen was gone.

'Sleep?' said Mallory. 'Or drinks?'

Andrea pushed his glass forward. 'You can sleep on aeroplanes,' he said.

'Drinks it is,' said Mallory.

A car with a sub-lieutenant raced them through the blacked-out streets of Plymouth. The city was stirring like a huge, secret animal. The tyres kicked fans of water from deep puddles as they skirted piles of rubble and came to a set of high wire gates with naval sentries in greatcoats and bell-bottomed trousers. Beyond the gate was the dark bulk of a squat building with a sand-bagged entrance. The sentry led them through a heavy steel door into a disinfectant-smelling hall and down a flight of cement stairs, then another and another. Mallory felt the depth and silence pressing in on him. Suddenly he was tired, achingly tired, with the tiredness of two months of Special Operations, and the months before that . . .

But there was no time for being tired, because another steel door had sighed open, and they were in a windowless room painted green and cream. There were chairs, and a blackboard. Everything was anonymous. There was no clue as to where they were bound. There were three naval officers in the room, fresh-faced and wind-burned. Sitting apart was a willowy man in a Sam Browne over a tunic of excessively perfect cut. He was smoking a fat cigarette that smelt Turkish, gazing from under unnecessarily long eyelashes at the fire instructions behind the dais, and fingering a thin moustache. Mallory found himself thinking of Hollywood. It was an odd mixture of people to find a hundred or so feet under Plymouth.

Admiral Dixon and Captain Jensen walked into the room. With a scuffing of chair legs, the men stood to attention. 'Good evening,' said Jensen. 'Stand easy. You may smoke.' Dixon ignored them. He sat down heavily in a chair. His eyes were glassy and he was breathing hard, presumably from the effort of walking down all those stairs. Mallory reflected that if coming down had been that bad, someone would have to carry him up. Jensen, on the other hand, looked fresh as the morning dew. He stood on the balls of his feet, perky as a bantamweight boxer, while an orderly unrolled maps on the board.

Mallory knew that in the coastlines and contours of those maps their fates were written. There were the three fingers of the Peloponnese, blue sea, Crete, the island-splatter of the Dodecanese. And larger-scale maps: an island. Not an island he recognized, though when he glanced across at Andrea he saw him straight-backed and frowning.

'Very good,' said Jensen, when the orderly had finished. 'Now I said I had a job for you, a tiny little job, really. It's a bit of a rush, I suppose, but there it is, can't be helped.'

'Rush?' said Mallory.

'All in good time,' said Jensen. 'First things first. Admiral Dixon you already know. Gentlemen –' here he turned to Mallory, Miller and Andrea '– certain people are very pleased with what you achieved last week.' Admiral Dixon shook his head and sighed. 'So pleased, in fact,' said Jensen, 'that they want you to do something else. Probably much easier, actually.' He turned to the map at his back. Miller listened to the hum of the ventilation fans. It was all very well Jensen saying things were easy. He was not the one getting shot at. Miller doubted that he knew the meaning of the word.

The central map showed plenty of blue sea, and an island. It was the shape of a child's drawing of a beetle, this island: a fat body dark with close-set contours and a head attached to its north-eastern end by a narrower neck. 'Kynthos,' said Jensen. 'Lovely place. Delightful beaches. Very few Germans, but the ones there are particularly interesting, we think.'

Mallory and Miller slumped in their chairs. As far as they were concerned the only interesting German was a German they were a couple of hundred miles away from. But Andrea was still upright in his chair, his black eyes gleaming. Andrea was a Greek. The things the Germans had done to his country were bad, but they were much, much better than the things the Germans had done to his family. Andrea found Germans very interesting indeed.

'I'll start at the beginning,' said Jensen. 'Last year we bombed a place called Peenemunde, on the Baltic. Seems the Germans were building some sort of rocket bomb there; doodlebugs first, bloody awful things, but there was supposed to be something else. Germans called it the A3. Goes into outer space, if you can believe this, and comes back, wallop, faster than the speed of sound. Blows a hole in you before you've even heard it coming. Good weapon against civilians.' Mallory searched Jensen's face for signs of irony, and found none. 'We're expecting it any day now. And there's something else; bigger version, larger, longer range, more dangerous, good for use against troops. Questions so far?'

'Why bother with outer space?' said Miller.

'Think of a shell. Longer the range, higher the trajectory.'

'You'd need a hell of a bang to get it up there.'

Jensen smiled. 'Very good, Miller,' he said. 'Now what we believe is this. These A3 things are rockets. Thing about outer space, there's no air to burn your fuel. So your rocket needs to take its own air with it. These A3 things are supposed to burn a mixture of alcohol and liquid oxygen. One of our submarines sank a ship off Kynthos the other day, surfaced to look for, er, survivors. All they found was oxygen bottles. And a stink of alcohol.'

'Schnapps,' said Miller.

Jensen smiled, and this time even the artificial warmth was gone from the ice-white display of teeth. 'Thank you, Corporal,' he said. 'If that is all, I shall hand you over to Lieutenant, er, Robinson.'

Lieutenant Robinson was a tall, stooping man with round tortoise-shell spectacles and a donnish air. 'Thank you,' he said. 'Hmmyes. Kynthos. Typical Vesuvian post-volcanic structure, Santorini series, basalts, pumice, tufa, with an asymmetric central deposition zone –'

'Lieutenant Robinson used to teach geology at Cambridge,' said Jensen. 'Once more, this time in English, if you please, Lieutenant.'

Robinson blushed to the tops of his spectacles. 'Hmmyes,' he said. 'Kynthos is, er, mountainous. Very mountainous. There's a town at the south-western end, Parmatia, more a village really, on a small alluvial plain. The road from the town transits a raised beach –' he caught Jensen's eye – 'follows the coast, that is, mostly on a sort of shelf in the cliffs. There is no road across the interior suitable for motor transport. To the north-east of the mountain massif is another island, smaller, Antikynthos, connected to the main massif by a plain of eroded debris and alluvium –' here Jensen coughed '– a stretch of flat land and marshes. This smaller island is itself rocky, taking the form of a volcanic plug with associated basalt and tufa masses, and on this there stands an old Turkish fort and the remains of a village: the Acropolis, they call it, the High Town. There has always been a jetty on Antikynthos. Recently this has been greatly improved, and the aerodrome upgraded. In the view of, er, contacts on the island, some sort of factory is being established.' He took a photograph out of a file and laid it in an overhead projector. A man's face appeared on the screen: a round face, mild, heavy-lidded eyes behind wire-rimmed spectacles. 'Sigismund von Heydrich,' he said. 'Injured during the bombing of Peenemunde. Highly talented ballistician —' Jensen's eye again '— rocket scientist. He was spotted boarding a plane at Trieste, and we know the plane landed on Kynthos. They've built workshops in the caves under the Acropolis. But there's only a light military presence. Couple of platoons of *Wehrmacht*, nothing worse, as far as we know.'

Jensen stood up. Thank you, Lieutenant,' he said. The Lieutenant looked disappointed, as if he had planned to go on for some time. 'Well, there you are. Simple little operation, really. We want you to land on Kynthos and make a recce of this Acropolis. You'll be briefed on the development of the V4, which is what they're calling this one. Any sign of it, and we'd like it disposed of: air strikes will be available, but if they've got it a long way underground, well, Miller, we have the greatest confidence in your ability to wreck the happy home. Questions so far?'

'Yessir,' said Mallory. 'You say we've got someone on the island already?'

'In a manner of speaking,' said Jensen. 'There was a transmitter.'

'Was?'

'Transmissions ceased a week ago. It may be that the Germans found it. Or it may equally be that someone dropped it. Frightfully stony place, as you know.'

Mallory caught Miller's eye, and saw the wary resignation he felt himself. Jensen did not pick them for the easy ones.

'And of course there'll be Carstairs in case you need help. Now if you've got any questions, ask them now, and we'll get into the detail.'

Miller said, 'Who's Carstairs?'

'Good Lord,' said Jensen. 'Hasn't anybody introduced you? Very remiss. Perhaps Admiral Dixon will do the honours. Admiral?'

Dixon heaved himself to his feet. 'Captain Carstairs, make yourself known,' he said, and there was something in his face that much resembled smugness.

The man in the beautiful uniform stood up and saluted. His hair was brown and wavy, his moustache clipped into a perfect eyebrow. 'Gentlemen, how d'ye do?' he said.

'Captain Carstairs is a rocket expert,' said the Admiral. 'He is also experienced in special operations. Before the war he led expeditions up the Niger and in the Matto Grosso. He has overflown the North and South Poles, and climbed the north face of Nanga Parbat.'

Andrea caught Mallory's eye. Mallory's head moved almost imperceptibly from side to side. Never heard of him, he was saying.

'Wow,' said Miller. The Admiral looked at him sharply, but the American's eyes were shining with honest reverence.

'So I am very happy to say,' said the Admiral, 'that Captain Carstairs will make an ideal commanding officer for this expedition.'

There was a deep silence, full of the hum of the fans. Mallory looked at Jensen. Jensen was gazing at the place where the ceiling met the wall.

'Any questions?' said the Admiral.

'Yessir,' said Mallory. 'When do we start training, sir?'

The Admiral frowned. 'Training?'

'It'll take a month. Six weeks, maybe.'

Blood swelled the Admiral's neck. 'You're out of here on a Liberator at 0200 hours. You will transfer to an MTB near Benghazi. You'll be ashore and operating by 0300 tomorrow. There will be no training.'

'MTB?' said Mallory.

'Motor Torpedo Boat,' said Dixon.

'Bit indiscreet,' said Mallory, who knew what an MTB was. 'Noisy.'

'Can't be helped,' said Jensen. 'Sorry about the training, sorry about the MTB. But it's a matter of . . . well, put it like this. There's a bit of a flap on. These damned rockets are a menace to our rear and our flank in Italy. They can deliver three tons of HE with an accuracy of fifty yards. They need disposing of before they're operational, and we think that will be soon. We'd fly you in, but Staff say it's the wrong place for a parachute drop. So MTB it'll have to be. Time is of the essence.'

'Can't be done,' said Mallory. Suddenly he felt Jensen's eyes upon him like rods of ice.

The Admiral's neck veins swelled. 'Look here,' he said, in a sort of muted bellow. 'It is against my better judgement that I am using an insubordinate shower like you to perform a delicate operation. But Captain Jensen assures me that you know what you are doing, and takes responsibility for you. Well, let me make myself clear. If you do not obey my orders and the orders of Captain Carstairs in this matter, you will be charged with mutiny so fast your feet will not touch the ground – what are you doing?'

Mallory was on his feet, and so were Miller and Andrea. They were standing rigidly to attention. 'Permission to speak, sah,' said Mallory. 'You can get your court martial ready, sah.'

The Admiral stared, flabby-faced. 'By God,' he said. 'By God, I'll have you –'

Jensen cleared his throat. 'Excuse me, Admiral,' he said. 'Might I make a suggestion?' The Admiral seemed to be beyond speech. These men work as a unit. Their record is good. Might I suggest that rather than operating as a top-down command structure they be attached to Captain Carstairs as a force of observers, leaving Captain Carstairs in command of his own unit but without specific responsibility for these men, who would, as it were, be attached yet separate? This would obviate the need for special training, and establish the possibility of cross-unit liaison and cooperation rather than intraunit response to *ad hoc* and *de facto* command structures.'

The Admiral's jaw had dropped. 'What?' he said.

'Mallory's the senior captain,' said Jensen. 'And of course there is a colonel in the force.'

'Who's a colonel?'

'I am,' said Andrea.

Now it was Carstairs' turn to stare. Andrea needed a haircut, and his second shave of the day. His uniform needed a laundry. Carstairs raised an eyebrow. 'Colonel?' he said, and Miller could hear his lip curl even if he could not see it.

The air in the briefing room was thick and ugly. 'Greek army,' said Andrea. 'Under Captain Mallory's command, for operational purposes.'

'Uh,' said the Admiral, looking like a man who had just trodden on a fair-sized mine.

Jensen said, 'Come out here, all of you,' and marched into the corridor. Out there, he said, 'You've got Carstairs whether you like him or not. I want you on this mission. I'm ordering you to take him along.'

'And wipe his nose.'

'Also his shoes, if necessary.' Jensen's eyes were bright chips of steel.

'Under my command,' said Mallory.

'I know about rockets,' said Miller. 'I know as much about rockets as anyone. We don't need this guy. He'll get in the way. We'll wind up carrying him, he'll –'

'We would be fascinated to hear your views,' said Jensen in a freezing voice. 'Some other time, though, I think.'

'So who needs this guy?'

'If you mean Captain Carstairs, the Admiral wants him. And that, gentlemen, is that. Now get back in there.'

They knew Jensen.

They got back in there.

The Admiral said, 'Captain Carstairs will be a separate unit, taking his orders directly from me.'

Carstairs smiled a smooth, inward-looking smile. Technically, Mallory was his superior officer. All the Admiral was doing was muddying waters already troubled. They stood wooden-faced, potential disasters playing like newsreels in their minds.

'Last but not least,' said Jensen. 'Local support. Lieutenant.'

Robinson stood up, spectacles gleaming. 'There is Resistance activity on the island,' he said. 'But we want your operation kept separate. Civilian reprisals, er, do not help anyone.' Andrea's face was dark as a thundercloud. He had found the bodies of his parents on a sandbank in the River Drava. They had been lashed together and thrown in to drown. He knew about reprisals: and so did the Germans who had done the deed, once he had finished with them. Robinson continued, 'We will be landing you in Parmatia. There is a gentleman called Achilles at three, Mavrocordato Street in Parmatia. He will provide you with motor transport up the island to the Acropolis. We'll have a submarine standing by at a position you will be given at midnight on Thursday, Friday and Saturday. If you're there, hang up a yellow fishing lantern as a signal. If not . . . well, he'll wait until 0030 on Saturday, then you're on your own. Got it?'

'Got it.'

'But avoid all other contact. We'd like you to be a surprise. A thunderbolt of a surprise. That's what this Operation is called, by the way. Operation Thunderbolt.'

'After the weather forecast?' said Miller.

'How did you guess?' said Jensen.

'You did it last time,' said Miller.

Jensen did not seem to hear. 'Now,' he said. 'The detail.'

For the next two hours, in the company of the geologist and a man from SOE, they studied the detail.

'All right,' said Jensen, as they folded away their maps. 'Armoury next.'

The armoury was the usual harshly-lit room with racks of Lee Enfields. The Armourer was a Royal Marine with a bad limp and verbal diarrhoea. 'Schmeissers, 'e said you wanted,' said the Marine, pulling out boxes. 'Quite right, quite right, don't want those bloody Stens, blow up on you as soon as Jerry, go on, 'ave a look, yes, Corporal? Oh, I see you are the more discriminating type of customer, grenades, was it?' But even his flow of talk could not hold up over the grim silence that filled that little room. Mallory and Andrea sat down on the bench and disassembled a Schmeisser each, craftsmen assessing the tools of a deadly trade. The hush filled with small, metallic noises. Andrea rejected two of the machine-pistols before he found one to his liking, then another. Miller, meanwhile, was in a corner of the room, by a cupboard the size of a cigar humidor. He had a special pack, lined with wood and padded. Into this he was stowing, with a surgeon's delicacy of touch, buff-coloured bricks of plastic explosives, brightly-coloured time pencils, and a whole hardware store of other little packets and bottles.

Mallory reassembled his second Schmeisser. For you, Carstairs,' he said.

Carstairs looked languidly up from the sights of a Mauser. 'Never touch 'em, old boy.'

'You'll need one.'

'I'll be the judge of that,' said Carstairs, tapping a Turkish cigarette on a gold case. A silenced Browning automatic lay across his knees. 'Stand off is my motto. Works with impala. Works with Germans. Now look here, Sergeant, have you got a hard case for this?' He held up the Mauser carbine and a Zeiss 4X sniperscope. Several Mausers would be going to Kynthos – they were rugged carbines essential for long-range work. But the sniperscope was delicate as a prima ballerina's tutu – nothing to do with the kind of knockabout you could expect if you were storming a hollow mountain full of rockets.

As they left the armoury, Andrea fell in beside Mallory. 'What do you think?' he said.

'I think we should keep our eyes open.'

'Exactly, my Keith.' They walked on in silence. 'And what is this Nanga Parbat?'

'A mountain. In the Himalayas. There was an expedition to climb it in 1938.' Mallory paused. He hated what came next. 'A German expedition.'

'There was no war in 1938.'

'No.'

But all of a sudden Mallory's stomach was a tight ball. There was something wrong with this. It was the same feeling he had had on the south icefield of Mount Cook, watching his right boot go up and forward, watching the weight go on, but because of that feeling, not committing himself. Which had been just as well. Because when it felt the weight of that boot – brownish-black leather, new-greased, criss-cross laces in the lugs, that boot – the world crumbled and slid away, and what had been smooth ice had turned into a cornice over a ravine, a cornice that had crumbled under him and was swallowing him up.

Except that he had taken warning from that knot in the stomach, and kept his weight back, and walloped his ice axe behind him at the full reach of his arm, felt it bite, and hauled himself out of the jaws of death and back on to clean ice. And climbed the mountain.

The knot in the stomach was not fear, or at least not only fear. It was a warning. It needed listening to.

TWO

Tuesday 1000–Wednesday 0200

Al-Gubiya Bay is a small notch in the coast west of Benghazi. That morning, it contained a group of khaki tents, a concrete jetty, and one and a half billion flies. Alongside the jetty an MTB crouched like a grey shark. Her commander, Lieutenant Bob Wills, was sitting on the forward port-hand torpedo tube. The sun balanced on his head like a hot iron bar, and the flies were driving him crazy, but not as crazy as the orders he had received. He wondered what the hell they were dropping him in this time.

A three-ton lorry clattered on to the quay, stopped, and stood snorting in its cloud of Libyan dust. The canvas back of the lorry twitched and parted. Four men got down.

Three of them walked together, silent, closed-faced. Their faces were gaunt and sunburned. They looked at the same time exhausted and relaxed, and under their heavy equipment they walked with a steady, mile-devouring lope. Ahead of the three was a slenderer man. He was dressed like them in battledress without badges of rank. But his walk had more of a strut in it, as if he thought someone might be watching, and at the same time he moved uneasily in the straps of his pack. This and a certain finicky neatness in his uniform made the Lieutenant think that he was not completely at home.

The neat man had quick brown eyes that checked the MTB and the cuff-rings of the Lieutenant's tunic, hung from the barrel of the five-pounder. He said, 'Good morning. I'm Captain Carstairs.' The man smiled, a white, film-star sort of a smile. Wills was tired from months of night operations, and the smile was too dazzling.

He said, 'How d'ye do?' Carstairs' handshake was a bonecrusher. Wills' feeling of tiredness increased. 'Good flight?'

'Dreadful,' said Carstairs. 'Bloody Liberators. Can't hear a thing. Bring back Imperial. The Cairo run, what?'

'Yes,' said Wills. Himself, he had never been able to afford to fly in the Sunderlands of Imperial Airways. Lot of side, this Carstairs, he thought. He raised a hand to Chief Petty Officer Smith, who was loading stores down the quay. 'Chiefy. Help Captain Carstairs with his stuff, there's a good chap.'

During his brief chat with Carstairs, the other three men had climbed aboard the MTB and stowed their equipment. Without appearing to move very much they seemed to get a surprising amount done. The shortest of the three introduced himself as Mallory in a voice with a faint New Zealand twang.

'Morning,' said Wills.

Mallory saw a square youth with sun-bleached curly hair and a sunburned nose.

'Made yourself at home, I hope,' said Wills.

'Hope that's all right.'

Wills grinned. 'Top-hole,' he said. 'We don't stand on ceremony here.' He embraced with a sweep of his arm the blue bay, the parched dunes, the concrete jetty. 'You get out of the habit, in a tropical paradise.'

'Very attractive,' said Mallory, brushing away a couple of thousand flies.

'Wait till we get to sea,' said Wills. He was older than he looked, Mallory realized. From a distance, he might have been your standard British sixth-former. Close up, you could see the eyes. The eyes were a thousand years old.

'Been here long?' said Mallory.

'Long enough. Stooging around causing trouble on the island. Yachting with big bangs, really. Speak a bit of the lingo. Do what we can to make a nuisance of ourselves.'

'Quite,' said Mallory. He liked this youth. There was something in his eye that said he could really cause the Germans some trouble, if he put his mind to it, and putting his mind to it was what he was good at.

'We ready?' said Wills.

Mallory nodded.

'Top-hole,' said Wills. Carstairs was not his cup of tea, but these men were different. They spoke quietly, and looked at him steady-eyed, and when they shook his hand their grip was firm but economical, as if in this, as in anything else they did, they would use just enough force to get the job done properly, no more, no less. This fitted neatly with Wills' view of life, and he found himself favourably impressed. There was also another sensation lurking on the fringes of his conscious mind, and for a moment he did not know what it was. But ten minutes later, pouring the gin in the cupboard-sized wardroom, it came to him.

He was very glad they were on the same side as him.

'Excuse me,' he said. 'Couple of things to organize.'

The heavy throb of the MTB's engines came through the wardroom bulkheads, and the stink of high-octane gasoline. The sleek grey boat scrawled a white question mark on the blue bay, roared out to sea and turned east.

It was a calm and beautiful day. Carstairs went on deck, thrusting his chiselled profile into the twenty-knot slipstream. Mallory, Miller and Andrea found plywood bunks, rolled on to them, and closed their eyes: except Mallory. Mallory lay and felt the bound of the MTB over the swell, and the tremor of the Merlin engines, and rested his eyes on the plywood deck above him. There were matters he needed to ponder before he slept.

As they had left the armoury, a runner had caught him by the arm. Telephone, sir,' he had said.

The voice on the telephone had been light but hard: Jensen.

'No names,' it had said. 'Something I wanted to say, between us two, really.'

'Yessir.'

'I wanted to say the best of luck, and all that.'

'Yessir.' Jensen would not have rung his mother to wish her luck. Mallory waited.

'Our new friend,' said Jensen. 'The expert. He's okay, but you might like to keep your eye on him.'

'Eye?'

'Just a thought,' said Jensen. I've got a feeling he might be on a sort of treasure hunt.'

'Treasure hunt? What sort of treasure hunt?'

'If I knew, I wouldn't be telling you to keep an eye on him, would I? Well, I expect you'll be wanting to get on your way.'

Mallory lay and watched the deckhead. There were undoubtedly problems on Kynthos. But Mallory strongly suspected there was also a problem on the MTB, a problem called Carstairs. Mallory did not trust the man. Nor, it seemed, did Jensen. So why did Jensen insist that Carstairs be part of the mission? Of course, it had not been Jensen who had insisted. It had been Admiral Dixon. Mallory found himself thinking that a spell on the bridge of a destroyer would do Dixon a lot of good: or on an MTB, a floating fuel-tank, a bladder of aviation fuel with two Merlin engines . . .

But Dixon was safe behind his desk, and that was a law of nature. Just like the fact that Carstairs was along for the duration.

Railing against the laws of nature was entirely pointless. Mallory was not given to doing pointless things.

A new vibration added itself to the bone-jarring roar of the twin Merlins. Mallory was snoring.

He awoke much later, prised a cup of coffee out of the galley, and climbed on to the bridge. The sun was sinking towards the western horizon, North Africa a low dun line to the south. As far as any German aircraft were concerned they were heading east, for somewhere in the Allied territory in the gathering shadows ahead.

A rating brought up a plate of corned beef sandwiches and more coffee. It was quieter on the bridge. Mallory wedged a deck chair in a corner. As he ate his mind kept coming back to Carstairs. Why would an experienced guerrilla fighter have chosen a sniper rifle with a notoriously delicate sight? If they were all on the same operation, why were they notionally two separate units? Why –

A shadow fell across him. It was Carstairs, slender fingers in the pocket of his battledress blouse: like Clark Gable, thought Mallory. His hand came out with the gold cigarette case. He opened it, offered it to Mallory. 'Turkish this side, Virginian that,' he said.

'Just put one out,' said Mallory. 'Tell me something. What are you doing on this trip?'

'Same as you,' said Carstairs.

'So what . . . qualifies you?'

Carstairs smiled. 'I've knocked about a bit.'

'And you're a rocket expert.'

'So I am.'

'Where did you pick that up?'

'Here and there,' said Carstairs, vaguely. 'Here and there.'

You got used to vagueness on Special Operations. It was a mistake to know more than you needed to know. So why did Mallory have the feeling that Carstairs was using this fact for his own purposes?

'Ever done armed insurgency work?' he said.

'Not exactly. But there have been . . . parallel episodes in my life.'

'What's a parallel episode?' said a new voice: Miller's.

'A not dissimilar operation.'

'I had one of those, but the wheels dropped off.'

'I beg your pardon?' Carstairs' face was stiffening.

'All right,' said Mallory. Carstairs, it seemed, was too important to have a sense of humour. 'You're good in mountains. You can shoot.'

Carstairs yawned. 'So they told me on Nanga Parbat.'

'I thought that was a German expedition.'

'It was.' They stared at him. 'The Duke of Windsor asked me to go. Rather a chum of mine, actually, so one couldn't refuse. I speak pretty good German. I'm a climber. What's wrong with that?'

Mallory said nothing. The Nanga Parbat expedition had been supervised by Himmler in person. It had conquered the peak, but only by cementing in spikes and installing fixed ladders and ropes. They might as well have put scaffolding up the face. It was not what Mallory called climbing.

Carstairs said, 'The idea was to get to the top.'

Well, that was true.

'And the rockets,' said Miller, doggedly. 'Where did you find out all this stuff you know about rockets?'

Carstairs was not smiling any more. He said, 'We have all led complicated lives I am sure, and a lot of the things we have done we would not necessarily have told our mummies about. You can take it from me that I know what I know, and I am under orders from Admiral Dixon, Corporal. Now if you will excuse me I could do with forty winks.' And he went below.

'Temper,' said Miller, mildly.

Mallory lit a cigarette. He did not look at the American. 'I would remind you,' he said, 'that Captain Carstairs is a superior officer, and as such is entitled to respect. I would like you to give this thought your earnest attention.' His eyes came up and locked with Miller's. 'Your very close attention,' he said.

Miller smiled. 'My pleasure,' he said.

The MTB churned on down the coast. The sun sank below the horizon. Miller lay on the wing of the bridge, watching the last light of day leave the sky, and the sky fade to black, and upon it a huge field of silver stars come into being. Wills murmured an order to the man at the helm. Over Miller's head, the stars began to wheel until the Big Dipper lay across the horizon, the last two stars in its rhomboidal end pointing across an empty expanse to a single star riding over the MTB's bow.

They had turned north.

* * *

It was eight hours' hard steaming from Al-Gubiya to Kynthos. Rafts of cloud began to drift across the sky, blotting out patches of stars. The breeze was up, ruffling the sea into long ridges of swell. *M-109* made heavy weather, jolting and banging and shuddering as she jumped from bank of water to bank of water. Nobody slept, any more than they would have slept in an oil drum rolling down a flight of concrete steps.

Up on the bridge, Wills peered into the black and tried not to dwell upon the fact that *M-109* was the tip of a huge phosphorescent arrowhead of wake that shouted to anyone in an aeroplane 'Here we are, here we are'. This was not a subtle operation. 'Weave her,' he shouted into the helmsman's ear. The helmsman began to weave her port and starboard, panning the beam of the fixed radar scanner across the sea ahead.

'What you got?' said Wills to the man with his head in the radar's rubber eyepiece.

'Clutter,' said the man. 'Bloody waves –'

The MTB hit a wave, shot off into the air, and came down with a slam that blasted spray sixty feet in the air and buckled Wills' knees. His coffee cup shot across the bridge and exploded in a corner. Somewhere, probably in the galley, a lot of glass broke.

'Shite,' said the radar operator, and twiddled knobs. 'Dead,' he said.

'What do you mean, dead?' said Wills, though he knew perfectly well, because this always happened with radar. But they were deep in bandit country here, and the MTB was his first command, and this was his first Special Ops run, and he wanted things to go right, not cock up –

'Valve gone,' said the radar operator. 'Two, three valves.'

'How long?'

'Twenty minutes.'

Could be worse, thought Wills, lighting his sixty-third cigarette of the day. Could be better. Half an hour without radar, well, you can survive that.

So the MTB swept on blind under the stars: blind, but not unseen. Far down on the horizon, a dirty fishing caïque was hauling nets. In her wheelhouse, a man trained German-issue binoculars on the pale streak of water to the westward. Then he picked up the microphone of a military radio, and began to speak, giving first a call sign, then a course and speed that corresponded to the MTB's.

*   *   *

'Done, sir,' said the radar operator. 'No contacts.'

'Nice work,' said Wills, looking at his watch, then at the chart on the table under the red night-lights. 'Top-hole.' He rang for port engine shutdown, half-ahead starboard. *M-109*'s nose settled into her bow wave. One engine burbling heavily, she crept towards Kynthos, twenty miles away now. The breeze had dropped: the sea was like black glass.

'Still clear?' said Wills to the radar operator.

'Clear,' said the operator.

'Top-hole,' said Wills.

But of course the radar could not see astern.

As the engine note faded smoothly, Miller fell just as smoothly from a doze into a deep sleep. After what seemed like a couple of seconds he was awakened by somebody shaking him. 'Morning, sir,' said a voice, and an enamel mug was shoved into his hand, a mug hot enough to wake him up and make him curse and hear Mallory and Andrea and Carstairs stirring, too. When they had drunk the sweet, scalding tea, they went on deck.

There was no moon, but the Milky Way hung in a heavy swathe across the sky. By its light he could see a crumpled heap of rubberized canvas on the deck on the forward face of the wheelhouse. He groped for a foot pump, found one, plugged in the hose and started tramping away. The crumpled heap swelled and unfolded like a night-blooming flower, and became a rubber dinghy; an aircrew dinghy, actually, because unlike the naval dinghies it was boat-shaped instead of circular, and thus rowable; but unlike the dinghies used by the SAS, it was yellow instead of black, and would, if discovered by the enemy, be taken for the relic of a crashed aircraft instead of the transport of a raiding party. Andrea drifted up, silent as a wraith, and Mallory. Carstairs made more noise, his nailed boots squinching on the deck, grunting as he dumped his pack and his rifle.

'Three minutes to drop,' said a voice from the bridge.

Here we go again, thought Miller.

Then the night became day.

For a moment there was just stark blue-white light, the faces of the men on the bridge frozen, every pore mercilessly limned, the dinghy and the landing party in the slice of black shadow behind the superstructure. Then, very rapidly, things began to change.

The light blazed from a source as bright as the sun, behind them, low on the water. Someone was shouting on the bridge: Wills' voice. From behind the light came the heavy chug of a large-calibre machine gun. The bridge windows exploded. Glass splinters hissed around the dinghy, and someone somewhere let out a bubbling howl. Then more guns started firing, some from the MTB now.

'Stay where you are,' said Mallory, calm as if he were walking down the Strand. 'Two minutes to landing.'

'Shoot that bloody light out!' roared Wills, from the bridge.

They huddled in the shadow of the superstructure. Suddenly the blue-white glare vanished. The blackness that followed it was no longer black, but criss-crossed with ice-blue and hot-poker-red tracers. The MTB's deck jumped underfoot like the skin of a well-thrashed drum. Whatever was attacking was big, and heavily armed. They heard Wills' voice shout, 'Full ahead both!' The MTB started to surge forward.

But the tracers were homing in now. There was something like an Oerlikon or a Bofors out there. Into Miller's mind there popped the picture of the back end of the MTB: a huge tank of aviation gas, contained in a thin skin of aluminium and plywood. One Oerlikon round in there: well, two, one to puncture it, one to light it . . .

Miller found himself longing passionately for a row in a rubber dinghy on the night-black sea –

Crash, went something on the aft deck. Then there was a jack-hammer succession of further crashes. The MTB's machine guns fell silent. The engine note faltered and died, and she slowed, wallowing. An ominous red glow came from her after hatches.

Mallory's mind was clicking like an adding machine. Options: stay on board and get blown to hell; go over the side, with at least a chance that they would get ashore and on with the mission. No contest.

'Go,' he said.

The MTB had slewed port-side on to the tracers whipping out of the dark. They manhandled the rubber boat over the starboard rail and into the dark water. Miller climbed down, and stowed the packs and the oilcloth weapon bags as Mallory and Andrea lowered them. The orange glow was heavier now, beginning to jump and flicker, so Mallory could see Miller and Andrea working, and Carstairs, eyes flicking left and right, nervous for himself, not for anybody else. Not a team player, Carstairs. Hard to blame him, on top of a burning bladder of petrol in enemy waters –

Whump, said something the other side of the bridge, and the shock wave blew Mallory on to the deck. Then there was another explosion, bigger, and a blast of air, dreadfully hot, that carried with it a smell of burning eyebrows and more glass. Something crashed on to the deck alongside. By the light of the flames, Mallory saw it was Wills, blown, presumably, out of the glassless windows of the bridge. Unconscious at least, thought Mallory, ears ringing. If not dead –

Wills opened his eyes. His face was coppery with burns, his expression that of a sleepwalker. He started to crawl aft. Another explosion blew him backwards into Mallory's legs. The flames were very bright now, the air vibrating with heat. 'Into the dinghy,' said Mallory.

Carstairs went over the rail at a hard scramble, followed more sedately by Andrea. Aft of the bridge, the MTB was a sheet of flame. A man emerged, blazing, and fell back into the inferno. 'Come,' said Mallory to Wills. He half-saw other figures going over the rail, heard the splash of bodies.

Wills looked at him without seeing him, and started to walk into the wall of flame. Mallory grabbed his arm. Wills turned and took a swing at him. Mallory went under the punch, grabbed him by the shirt and trousers, and heaved him overboard. The deck was swelling underfoot like a balloon. Mallory went to the rail and jumped.

It was only when he hit the water that he realized how hot the air had been. He found himself holding the rope on the rubber flanks of the dinghy. 'Row,' he said. They already were rowing. There was another head beside him in the water: Wills, eyes wide and rolling. He scrambled into the dinghy and pulled Wills after him. Wills showed a tendency to struggle. He wanted to be with his ship –

The night split in two. There was a blinding flash. A shock wave like a brick wall hurtled across the water and walloped into the dinghy. Torpedoes, thought Mallory, against the ringing in his ears. Torpedoes gone up.

Then a thick chemical smoke rolled down on them. Under its black and reeking blanket they rowed and coughed and rowed again, squinting at the radium-lit north on Mallory's compass, for what felt like hours. 'Clearing,' said Miller at last. Overhead, the sky was lightening. They sat still as the fumes thinned around them, leaving them naked and exposed on the surface of the sea. But there was no one to see them. As the last of the smoke eddied away, it was plain that under its cover they had got clear. All around them was black night, with stars. The best part of a mile to the westward, the dark shape of some sort of coastal patrol boat lay half-wrapped in smoke, moving to and fro in the water, shining lights, looking for survivors.

And in that confusing patchwork of light and smoke, not finding any.

To the eastwards, the sky stopped well short of the horizon, cut out by the jagged tops of mountains: the mountains of Kynthos.

Mallory called the roll.

'Carstairs.'

'Here.'

'Andrea.'

'Here.'

'Miller.'

'Sure.'

'Anyone else?'

'Wills,' said Wills, in a strange, faraway voice.

'Nelson,' said another. 'And Dawkins. 'E's unconscious. I've 'urt me arm.'

'Okay,' said Mallory, level-voiced, though inwardly he was worried. There was work to do, and not the sort of work you could do if you were carrying maimed and unconscious sailors about with you. They had hardly started Operation Thunderbolt, and already it was in serious trouble.

Save it, he told himself. They were on the deep sea, with three extra people and a job to do. What was necessary now was to get ashore.

'Row,' he said.

They rowed.

After a while, a voice said, 'I'm getting wet.' A sailor's voice: Nelson.

It was true. The side of the rubber dinghy, which had been hard, was becoming flaccid. 'Probably the air inside cooling,' said Carstairs. 'The water's colder than the air, isn't it? So it'd shrink –'

'Got a leak,' said Miller. He found the pump and plugged it into the side. There was no chance of using his feet, so he squeezed the concertina bag between his hands. After two hundred, his arms felt as if they were on fire. But the tube was not deflating any more. 'Here,' he said to Carstairs.

'Sorry, Corporal?' said the drawling voice in the dark.

'Your go, sir,' said Miller.

Carstairs laughed, a light, dangerous laugh. 'I'm sorry, Corporal,' he said. 'I don't think I'm with you.'

Miller gave a couple more squeezes to the pump. The sweat was running into his eyes. 'Yessir,' he said. 'Yessir, Cap'n, sure thing.' Carstairs was only a dark shape against the stars, but Miller was sure he was smiling a small, superior smile –

'Give it to me,' said Andrea. Miller felt it plucked from his hands, heard the steady, monotonous pant.

'Carstairs,' said Mallory. 'You can row now.'

Carstairs' shadow froze. But Mallory's voice had an edge like a hacksaw. 'Delighted,' said Carstairs. 'Jolly boating weather, eh?'

For two endless hours, the oars dipped, and the pump panted, and the black mass of Kynthos crawled slowly up the stars. At 0155, Wills, who had been sitting slumped on the side, suddenly raised his head. 'Port twenty,' he said, in a weird, cracked voice.

'What?' said Miller, who was rowing.

'Left a bit.'

'Why?'

'There's a beach.'

'How do you know?' said Carstairs.

'Pilot book. Recognize the horizon.' Wills made a loose gesture of his hand at the saw-backed ridge plunging towards the sea ahead and to the right.

Carstairs said, 'You're in no condition to recognize anything.'

'So what do you suggest?' said Mallory, mildly.

'Straight for the shore,' said Carstairs. 'Up the cliffs.'

'Listen,' said Wills.

Miller stopped rowing, and Andrea stopped pumping. They listened.

There was the drip of the oars, and the tiny gurgle of the dinghy moving through the water, and something else: the long, low mutter of swell on stone. 'Cliffs,' said Wills. 'Doesn't feel like much out here, but there'll be a heave. Lava rock. Like a cross-cut saw. Two foot of swell, bang goes your gear, bang goes you.'

It was a lucid speech, and convincing. Carstairs could find no objection to it. He lapsed into a sulk.

Mallory had seen the beaches on the map, all that time ago in the briefing room under Plymouth. There were half-a-dozen of them at this end of the island, little crescents of sand among writhing contours and hatchings of precipitous cliffs. If it had been him in command of the Kynthos garrison, he would have watched them like a hawk.

The muttering grew.

"Scuse me,' said the voice of the sailor Nelson. 'It's Dawkins, sir. I think 'e's dead.'

'For Christ's sake,' said Carstairs, high and sharp. 'Save it for later. We'll –'

But Mallory had moved past him, and had his fingers on Dawkins' neck. The skin was warm, but not as warm as it should have been. There was no pulse. I'm afraid you're right,' he said.

'Throw him overboard,' said Carstairs. 'He's just dead weight.'

'No,' said Mallory, pumping.

'You –'

I'm taking operational responsibility for Able Seaman Dawkins,' said Mallory.

There were cliffs on either side and ahead, now, not more than fifty yards away. The dinghy lifted spongily in the swell. They were in a sort of cove.

Andrea said, 'Wait here.'

'What are you doing?' said Carstairs.

Andrea did not answer. He seemed to be taking off his battle-dress. A pair of huge, furry shoulders gleamed for a moment under the stars. Then he was gone, quiet as a seal in a small roil of water.

'Reconnaissance,' said Mallory. 'Hold her here, Miller.'

Cradled in the bosom of the sea, protected on three sides by a small, jagged alcove of the cliffs, they waited.

THREE

Wednesday 0200–0600

Private Gottfried Schenck was not in favour of Greek islands. The beer was terrible, the food oily and the women hostile, particularly in the last couple of days. Still, it was better than the Russian Front, he supposed. He had thought it a place completely without danger, until the unpleasantness on Saturday. Tonight he had seen the flick of tracer and the flash of a big explosion out at sea. It looked as if things were getting worse. He had commandeered a bottle of wine from a peasant he had met with a flock of goats; vile stuff, tasted like disinfectant, but at least it stopped the jitters. He looked at his watch. Two o'clock. Four hours till his relief at dawn. Time to have a look in the next cove, perhaps have a crafty fag with his mate Willi.

He turned and walked along the edge of the sea, his boots making only the faintest of crunches on the sand.

From his vantage point by a rock thirty yards to seaward, Andrea watched him go, waited, counting; saw the sudden flare of a match beyond the headland . . .

Not that anybody normal would have seen this. But Andrea's eyes were used to weighing matters of life and death in thick darkness. He waited in the milk-warm water, counting, watched the sentry come back on to the beach, throw away the glowing butt. Then, with no fuss or turbulence, he sank below the surface.

The cigarette had not done Private Schenck any good. He felt sleepy, and there was a filthy taste in his mouth. What he really needed was a swim, but if anyone caught him swimming on duty there would be hell to pay –

He had arrived at the end of the beach. He turned round and started back, moving smartly to wake himself up, shoulders square,

eyes on the tip of his nose, trying as he often did to feel the way
he had felt all those years ago at Nuremberg in the temple of
searchlights, when he had believed in all this damned Nazi
nonsense –

Behind him, something rose from the water beyond the small
waves that broke on the shore: something impossibly huge that
gleamed with water in the starlight and took two loping steps
towards him, clapped a vast hard hand over his mouth and hauled
him through the breakers and bent him creaking towards the
water, as he tried to shout, but managed no sound at all, like a child
in the hands of this terrible thing from the sea. Schenck had given
up even before his face hit the water, gently, oh so gently, and
stayed there, under those huge, remorseless hands, until his mouth
opened and the bad taste of cigarettes and old wine became the
taste of salt, and he breathed.

Andrea waited until the bubbles ceased to rise. Then he swam
back to the dinghy, and talked low and short to Mallory. A minute
later, the dinghy was heading for the beach.

Things now began to move very fast for the still-dazed Wills. As
soon as the dinghy's nose touched the sand, they were out, dragging the packs on to their backs, hustling him and Nelson up the
beach and into the low scrub of thorn and oleander at its back.
'Watch them,' said Mallory to Carstairs. Carstairs looked as if he
was going to protest, but suddenly Mallory and Miller were gone,
and there was nowhere else to go, so Carstairs had no option.

Dimly in the starlight they saw Andrea drag Dawkins' body from
the dinghy, and tow him out through the little breakers and into
deep water. Nelson started forward, but Wills put a hand on his
arm. They heard the hiss as Miller enlarged the hole in the dinghy
and left it in the surf, watched Mallory and Miller brush out the
footprints on the beach, reversing up into the bushes.

Wills' head was buzzing like a hive full of bees. He was streaming sweat, and he felt sick, or rather he felt as if someone else a lot
like him felt sick, because he was somewhere else. Nearby, Andrea
was climbing back into his fatigues. Wills heard himself say, 'All
right, Nelson?'

'Shouldn't have done that to poor Dawks,' said Nelson.

'He's dead,' said Wills. 'He doesn't know. He's being useful.'

'It ain't right,' said Nelson. He sounded aggrieved: bit of a bar-
rack-room lawyer, Nelson. "E needs burying. There's no call to
chuck 'im in the sea.'

'There was a guard,' said Andrea. I killed him. Now the Germans will think he found poor Dawkins, and they fought, and both drowned.'

'You 'ope,' said Nelson, who did not hold with foreigners.

'Yes,' said the foreigner, in that lion-like purr of his. 'And so should you, if you do not want to die.'

Hearing the voice, Nelson realized that he desperately and passionately wanted to live.

'Miller,' said Andrea. 'Have a look at Nelson's arm.'

Miller pulled out a pencil light, lodged it between his teeth, and unwrapped the strip of rag from the seaman's right forearm. The cut gaped long and red against the white skin. 'You'll live,' said Miller. 'Sew you up later.'

'Jesus,' said Nelson weakly. 'It's really bad. Oh Jesus. It feels bloody terrible.'

'You won't die,' said Miller. 'Not of a cut arm, anyway. No bleeding, and all nice and clean and tidy with seawater.' He sprinkled sulfa into the wound, bound it swiftly and expertly with a bandage from the first-aid kit, and made a sling out of the rag. 'Good as new,' he said.

But as he tied the sling, he could feel that despite the warmth of the night, Nelson was shivering.

Mallory said, very quiet, 'Put out that light and let's go.'

They crossed a stony track along the back of the beach. Inland, the ground rose steeply. Mallory halted them in a grove of oleanders. 'Wait here,' he said. Nelson sat down with a heavy thump.

'Shut up,' said Carstairs, too loud.

Silence fell: a silence full of the rustle of the breeze in the oleanders, and the trill of the cicadas, and the small crunch of the surf on the shore.

And German voices, talking, from the next beach.

It was just the chatting of sentries bored by a long night duty. But it ran a bristle of small hairs up Nelson's spine. And suddenly the silence of the group was not just six people keeping quiet, but a sort of frozen hole in the middle of the night noises. He felt sick, with burning petrol, and his shipmates gone, and a nauseating pain in his arm, and poor old Dawks chucked in the sea. And now he was mixed up in God knew what with a bunch of bandits, in enemy territory. He had signed up for the Navy, not the bleeding Commandos. What he wanted now was a nice POW camp, not to get shot out of hand for raiding enemy territory with the skipper and these four hard nuts . . .

These two hard nuts.

As Nelson counted the heads against the sky, he saw that in the middle of the silence – quieter than the silence itself, in fact – the big one and the thin one had vanished.

Mallory and Andrea went quickly down the track, one either side. They moved quiet as shadows, stooping to avoid the tell-tale flick of a silhouette against the sky. Their packs were with Miller in the oleanders. They carried knives and Schmeissers, and the knowledge that if they used either they were dead, and the mission was finished.

As he trotted on, part of Mallory's mind was chewing at the problems of the mission. There were several ways of adding up a fire at sea, a cut-up rubber dinghy, a dead British matlow and a drowned German sentry. Some of them were innocent – a survivor of the wreck, a fight in the shallows. Others were not. The rubber boat was a type used in aircraft, not MTBs. Why would a guard drown, having fractured a British seaman's skull? Anyone with any brains was going to bump into these questions, particularly on an island as sleepy as Kynthos. Perhaps in a couple of *Wehrmacht* platoons, there would not be too many brains.

But from Mallory's experience, there would be brains in plenty: thorough, inquisitive, fine-slicing brains . . .

Speed was what was needed.

They had rounded a headland. There was a low, regular lump that might have been an observation post. They skirted it to the rear, and found the road improving, running round the back of a half-mile beach of pale sand washed with the drowsy roar of the small surf. Behind the beach, an untidy huddle of rectilinear blocks gleamed white in the starlight. Houses. Parmatia.

They moved inland, through a belt of scrub and onto a valley floor tiled with little gardens and lemon groves. A couple of dogs barked lazily as they passed. The air was warm and still.

Mavrocordato Street was a long jumble of small farms and sheds. Number three was shuttered up tight against the sickly influences of the night air. Round the back, a shutter stood open. Andrea and Mallory took a last look over the dark plain. Then Andrea went in through the window.

If Miller had not been Miller, he would have been getting bored. Instead, once he had closed the cut in Nelson's forearm with a neat line of stitches, he had propped his head on his pack, felt a large regret that in their present circumstances it was not possible to light a cigarette, and closed his eyes. Not that he was asleep. It was merely that Miller was a man who hated unnecessary effort. In the darkness of the rocks, the only thing you got from a visual inspection of your surroundings was eye-ache. Also, by closing your eyes you gave your ears the best possible chance. He lay there, and sorted the sounds of the night: breeze in the leaves, the rustle of the sea, cicadas, the small click of a beetle rolling a pebble, the breathing of Wills and Nelson and Carstairs –

No breathing from Carstairs.

Carstairs had gone.

Carstairs had gone God knew where.

Miller was a gambler. Before the war, he had spent much of his life in the weighing of odds. Since he had been mixed up with Mallory and Andrea, not much had changed, except that the consequences of losing a bet had become more deadly. And even in the old days, the kind of people Miller had played poker with were not the kind of people you welshed on and lived.

So Miller weighed up the odds. Carstairs was reputed to know what he was doing. Miller was a corporal, Carstairs was a captain, running his own show under the Admiral.

Carstairs was on his own.

Mallory waited outside the window in a horrible silence, the dreary silence of the hours before the dawn, when nature is at its lowest ebb and sleep most closely approximates to death. His finger rested on the trigger of his Schmeisser. He tested the night sounds, found nothing amiss. He was a soldier, Mallory, and a mountaineer, a man not given to fantasy or speculation. But once again he felt the tightness in his stomach he had felt on the way out of the armoury in Plymouth. This warm world that smelt of farms lay under the shadow of death –

The shutter creaked faintly. Andrea's voice said, 'Come.'

Mallory found himself in a cool room that smelt of scrubbed floors and old wine. The shutter closed, and there were fumbling sounds, as if someone was draping the window with a cloth. A match scraped, and a mantle flared and began to glow. The person who had lit it was small, with a hood over his head and a long, Bedouin sort of robe. 'Achilles?' said Mallory.

'Achilles is dead,' said Andrea. 'The partisans have blown up the road. The Germans took reprisals. One hundred and thirty-one people were killed in the square on Saturday. Achilles was one of them.'

Mallory said nothing. If there was no road, it would be hard to get the Thunderbolt force across the mountains even if there were no wounded. With wounded, it would be next to impossible –

'I will take you,' said their host, and swept back the hood of the robe. Swept it back from a tangled mass of black hair, and a smooth face with a straight nose and big, black eyes that glowed with tears and fury.

This,' said Andrea, 'is Clytemnestra. She was the sister of Achilles.'

'For twenty-three years,' said the woman. 'Twenty-three years, and two months, and three days, and four hours, before those pigs . . . those worse than pigs' – here she plunged into a machine-gun rattle of abuse in a dialect that Mallory recognized from his months in the White Mountains in Crete – 'saw fit to take him away and murder him.' She pulled a wine bottle and some glasses out of a worm-eaten cupboard. 'But we are together,' she said. 'We will be together again. Together, we will take you across the mountains.' She sloshed wine into the glasses.

'You know the paths,' said Andrea.

'Of course I know,' she said. 'And if I do not know, then my brother Achilles will walk at my side, and show me.'

They drank in silence. Mallory heard the glass rattle against her teeth. Too wild, thought Mallory. He made his voice calm and level, the voice of a policeman at the scene of an accident. 'Could you bear to tell me what's been going on, this past week?'

She did not look up. 'The more people who know, the better,' she said. 'It should be carved in letters four feet high on the cliff of the Acropolis, so people can see –' She caught Andrea's eye. Then her head bowed again, and she took his mighty hand, and for some time could not speak.

After a little while, she dried her eyes on her rusty black shirt and took a deep breath. 'Forgive me,' she said.

'There is nothing to forgive,' said Andrea, and the slow fire in his eyes kindled hers, and she nodded. 'Tell us, and we will avenge your brother.'

'Achilles was a farmer,' she said. 'A farmer and a policeman. There were half-a-dozen men in the mountains, klephts, thieves, what have you. We all on this island hate the Germans, we do what we can to make their lives awkward, in small ways, you understand. But these klephts in the mountains, they were always causing trouble. For their own pleasure, not Greece's freedom. They stole Iannis's wine, and Spiro's sheep, and they raped poor Athene, and every man's hand was against them, because they were bandits, not fighters. Then last Monday they tried to steal a German patrol truck, and they were drunk, so they made a mess of it and one of them got killed.' Her head dropped.

'Steady,' said Andrea, squeezing her hand.

She nodded, pushing the hair out of her eyes. 'So on Tuesday there arrived many aeroplanes at the aerodrome, with many soldiers. And the word went round the island that from now on it was a new world, with no mercy. But these klephts either did not hear or did not want to hear. So in revenge for the killing of their man they planted a big charge of explosive at a place where the cliff overhangs the road to Antikynthos and the Acropolis, the only road, you understand.' Mallory nodded. He understood all too well. 'And they blew the cliff down on to the road. Nobody was passing, of course.' Here she looked disappointed. 'But these new soldiers came, and they climbed over the rubble. They had a new kind of uniform, mottled-looking, like the sun in an olive grove. There was one man, with a crooked face and very pale eyes, the officer. He took one person for every metre of road destroyed, he said.' The tears were running again. 'One hundred and thirty-one people, men, women, children, it didn't matter. The women and children he machine-gunned. The men he hanged.' She fell silent.

Mallory left her in peace for a couple of minutes. Then he said, 'And the partisans?'

'They left the island the night before the hangings. Saturday. They stole Kallikratides' boat, and went away, who knows where, who cares? They left a note saying it was a tactical withdrawal. But we know that they were frightened that someone would catch them, us or that man Wolf, it didn't matter –'

'Wolf?' said Mallory.

'That's this officer's name. Dieter Wolf, they call him, may he rot in hell. He hanged Kallikratides, too. With his own hands.'

'The same Dieter Wolf?' said Andrea.

'Sounds like it.'

Andrea nodded, heavily. In his mind he could see a village in the white mountains of Crete, dry mountains, full of the song of grasshoppers and the smell of the herbs the peasants plucked from the wild plants to eat with their lamb. But today there was another smell wafting across the ravine. The smell of smoke, the black plume that rose from the caved-in roof of the village church. The church into which a *Sonderkommando* had driven the women and children of the village; the church to which they had then set fire. All this because one of the patriarchs of the village had shot with his old shotgun one of the *Sonderkommando* he had found in the act of raping his daughter . . .

Andrea and Mallory had lain in cover across the unbridged ravine that separated them from the village. They had arrived too late. In the shaking disc of his field glasses an officer stood: a man in scuffed jackboots, with a white, crooked face and no hair, cleaning a knife. Later, they discovered why the knife had needed cleaning, when they found a grandfather disembowelled by the roadside. Even at this range, the officer's eyes caught the sun pale and opaque, like slits of brushed aluminium. Then he and his troops had boarded their armoured personnel carriers and roared away down the road to Iraklion.

Andrea had found out that this man was Dieter Wolf, and promised himself and the dead of that village that he would have his revenge.

'Sometimes,' he said, 'God is very good.' He looked at his watch. 'It will be getting light,' he said.

'I will get dressed,' said Clytemnestra. 'Then I will show you across the mountains.'

She went. Doors slammed. Mallory poured Andrea a glass of wine, drank one himself, lit a cigarette.

According to Lieutenant Robinson in the bunker at Plymouth, Kynthos was a soft target. But if Dieter Wolf was here taking reprisals, that meant only one thing. Cambridge don or not, Robinson had been wrong.

He ground out his cigarette and tossed the butt into the stove. The door opened. Clytemnestra was wearing baggy black breeches, soft leather boots, a fringed shawl at her waist, a worn embroidered waistcoat lined with sheepskin over her black shirt. Her hair was bound into a black silk scarf. She looked dull, crow-black, a thing of the shadows. Only her eyes were alive, burning –

There was a thunderous knocking at the door. She shooed Andrea and Mallory on to the stairs. 'Coming, coming,' she said, and opened up.

Andrea's world was keyhole-shaped. He could see very little, and his breathing was deafening in his ears. The kitchen seemed to

have filled with people. There was silence, except for the shuffle of
boots on tiles: not jackboots, though; boots with unnailed soles.
The talk broke like a wave; a Greek wave. Despite all the noise,
there were only two visitors.

'Be quiet, be quiet!' cried Clytemnestra. 'Please!' She seemed to
be a woman people listened to. Silence fell. 'Now. Ladas, what is it?'

'There was this man,' said Ladas. 'Iannis the Nose saw him. He
was snooping in the square, looking into cars, windows, you name
it. Dressed in a soldier's uniform. Not a German uniform: British,
maybe, Greek, who knows? Straight away we thought, the partisans are back. And you may call us cowards, but you know yourself they were no better than thieves, and my poor Olympia that
they shot . . . for a victory perhaps it might be worth losing a sister,
but for those damned thieves of partisans, those *Kommunisti* bastards, never, God's curse on –'

'You are right,' said Clytemnestra, soothingly, without impatience. 'Tell me more about this man, in whom I must tell you I do
not believe.'

'He has curly hair and a thin moustache, so thin, like a worm on
his lip. He carries a rifle, many grenades. When he saw me I
thought he would shoot. But he vanished only, into the dark, like
a ghost.'

'Perhaps he is a ghost.'

Ladas scowled so that his mighty eyebrows nearly met his
mighty moustache. He did not look like a man who believed in
ghosts. 'You know this town,' he said. 'It is full of spies. If a spy says
to this German pig, "I have seen a ghost", this German pig will kill
people until the ghost comes to life. What can we do?'

'Watch and pray until the ghost goes away.'

'How can you know?'

'This can only be a ghost. This is the way you deal with ghosts.'

There was a silence. The man with Ladas had a heavy, stupid
face with small, suspicious eyes. He looked like a man who might
believe in ghosts. He said, 'She is wearing her clothes.'

'Yes,' said Ladas. 'You are wearing your clothes.'

Clytemnestra looked drawn and weary. 'When you have no man
in the house,' she said, 'you must take the sheep to the mountain
yourself. And it will soon be dawn. Now back to your beds. Some
of us have work to do, even if you want to run around in the dark
squeaking of ghosts.'

They left.

Clytemnestra opened the stairs door. 'What is this?' she said. 'Who is in the village?'

'Hard to say,' said Mallory. But he knew. It was Carstairs, of course. There were things he needed to say to Carstairs. 'It will soon be light,' he said.

Outside, the air smelt sharp and fresh. The sky over the mountains was still deep blue and thick with stars, but low down, towards the peaks, the blue was paling.

'This man,' said Andrea to Clytemnestra. 'He is one of our people.'

She walked fast through a maze of paths that wound among the gardens. 'Then you should control him,' she said. 'Why is he wandering in the village like a madman? He will get people killed.' They walked on in silence.

Something was worrying Mallory. 'And you,' he said. 'You shouldn't be with us. We are soldiers, in uniform. We have no connection with you. There will be no reprisals. But if they find you with us –'

'If I don't come with you, how will you find your way across the mountains?'

'We have maps.'

She laughed, a large, scornful laugh that sent a couple of doves flapping from their roost. 'Use them to roll cigarettes,' she said. 'If you use the tracks you will see on them, the Germans will find you. They have the same maps –'

'Hush,' said Mallory.

They were on the road through the dunes, approaching the southern end of the beach.

'Down!' said Andrea. A figure stood suddenly outlined against the paling sky. Its head was blocky with a coal-scuttle helmet, its shoulders tense over its rifle. '*Wer da?*' it said.

Mallory's breath was loud in his ears as he lay face down in the dunes. Andrea was at his side. Mallory knew what he would be thinking, because he was thinking it himself. The pre-dawn was quiet. The cocking lever of the Schmeisser would sound like a train crash. One shot, and it would all be over . . .

Clytemnestra walked forward, hips swaying insolently. 'Who wants to know?' she said, in Greek. 'What murdering son of a whore comes to my home and gets between me and my work?'

'*Vas?*' said the soldier.

'I looking for my sheeps,' said Clytemnestra, in terrible German.

The soldier stood undecided. Mallory could not work out whether he had seen them. Beside him, Andrea sighted on the place under the man's left shoulder blade where he would drive the knife. He put one mighty palm on the gritty soil, tensed his legs to spring –

'Go on, then,' said the soldier.

'I evacuate my bowels on your mother's grave,' said Clytemnestra, in Greek. 'I dig up her remains and feed them to my pigs, who vomit.'

'Nice meeting you,' said the German, in German, and stamped back down the beach.

Mallory took his hand away from the cocking lever. The palm was wet with sweat. He and Andrea rose from cover. After that, they marched in silence.

As they turned up the track behind the beach, Andrea said, 'Wait.'

They waited.

Ahead, over the noise of the cicadas, there came the sound of a stone rolling under a boot.

'Three minutes,' said Andrea's huge, purring whisper by Mallory's ear. Then, silent as a shadow, he was gone.

The path unreeled under Andrea's boots as he ran. He could feel the blood taking the power around his body, the thing that made him not a man in the grey pre-dawn, but a hunting animal closing with its prey. He saw the figure ahead, clambering up the path. He was alone, moving probably quite fast, but to Andrea slow and clumsy.

Andrea looked around him with that special radar of his. He sensed the town, Mallory and Clytemnestra behind him, the German soldiers on the beach, the two corpses in the surf, the little party ahead.

He sprang.

A great hard hand went over the mouth. The other hand went to the nape of the neck. He began the pull sideways to dislocate the vertebrae.

It was the smell that stopped him.

It was the smell of hair oil; a hair oil that Andrea had smelt before, on the MTB, in the dinghy, tonight. A powerful smell, sickly even by Greek standards. Expensive.

The smell of Captain Carstairs.

Andrea decided not to break the neck, after all. Instead he kept a hand over the mouth, and said, 'No noise, or you die.' Then he waited for Mallory.

So Miller lay with his eyes closed, devoting himself to analysis of the night sounds.

He heard Carstairs coming up the path, and rolled to his feet, Schmeisser in hand. Then he heard Andrea's attack. After the brief scuffle came the brief bleep of a Scops owl. Mallory's signal. Miller let out a long breath as three dark figures arrived in the camp.

'All right,' said Mallory's voice. 'Moving out.'

'Where to?' said Miller.

'Germans on the beach,' said Mallory. 'Silence.'

Wills was already upright. Nelson's cut had stiffened, and he needed some persuading. 'Hurts,' he said, whining.

'Up,' said Wills. 'Show a leg.'

Grumbling, Nelson got up. Then they were slinging packs and weapons, starting up a steep, stony path among the bushes. And very soon the path was so steep that there was no spare energy even for wondering, or indeed doing anything except keeping the feet moving and the breath rasping and the heart beating. All the time, the sky in the east grew lighter.

FOUR

Wednesday 0600–1800

Just after six o'clock, the sun hauled itself over the mountain. 'Stop now,' said Clytemnestra. 'We eat.'

They slumped to the hot, stony ground and started fumbling for cigarettes and chocolate. They were on a ledge, a bare shelf of rock made by a crack that ran across a great cliff that seemed to rise sheer from the sea. Nelson said, 'Water.' Miller passed him his canteen. The seaman drank avidly, water spilling down his face and on to his shirt. Miller twitched the water bottle out of his hand.

'Sod that,' said Nelson. 'I've got a mouf like a bleeding lime kiln.'

'We all have,' said Miller. He pulled a cigarette from his packet and lit it with a Zippo. He had been a Long Range Desert Group man, doing damage behind enemy lines in the Western Desert. Water was more important than petrol, which was more important than motherhood, religion and the gold standard. 'You drink in the morning and at night. Drink in the day, you just sweat it right out again. Now let's have a look at your arm.'

Nelson would not let him. His face was bluish and hostile under his sweat-matted red hair. "S all right,' he said, and fell back into a sullen silence.

Wills said, in his odd, marble-mouthed voice, 'Pull yourself together, man.' But Nelson would not meet his eye.

In daylight, Wills was a mess. He had no eyebrows, and no hair on the front part of his head. His skin shone with tannic acid jelly, and there was a great bruise on his right temple. As he looked out over the blue void of the sea, his eyes were glassy and his hand trembled. Mallory guessed that he was thinking about his ship. He offered him a slab of chocolate and a wedge of the bread they had brought from Mavrocordato Street. Wills shook his head.

'Sorry about your ship,' said Mallory.

Wills made a face that made him look ridiculously young. 'Poor chaps,' he said.

'First command?' said Mallory.

Wills nodded. There were tears in his eyes.

'Can you go on?'

'Of course.'

'Good man.'

'Don't worry about Nelson,' said Wills. 'Top-hole chap.'

Mallory nodded. Loyalty to your men was a good thing. He just hoped that it was a two-way process.

Carstairs was sitting off to one side, by himself. There was dust in his greasy curls, and his eyebrow moustache was distorted by a wet red graze. 'How are you doing?' said Mallory.

'Fine,' he said, very curt.

'I want you to stay close,' said Mallory. 'You could get hurt.'

'Now you look here,' said Carstairs, as if he was talking to a taxi driver who had taken him to the wrong street in Mayfair. 'This is not the first time I've been behind enemy lines. Believe it or not, I am capable of looking after myself. And if you have any worries on that score, I suggest you cast your mind back to Admiral Dixon and the briefing. It is none of your damn business whether I get hurt or not.'

Mallory smiled, a peaceful white smile. 'How's your neck?' he said.

Carstairs' face filled with sullen blood.

'Listen,' said Mallory, 'it's my job to look after my men, and avoid reprisals against the islanders. So any time you want to do a little freelance snooping around the civilian population, I should be grateful if you would talk to me first.'

'Ask your permission?' he said. 'Go to hell.'

'Liaise,' said Mallory.

'Go to hell.'

Mallory was not smiling any more. He said, 'Admiral Dixon is a long way away. You nearly had a nasty accident with Colonel Andrea. You are lucky to be alive. Think about it.'

Carstairs thought about it. 'Where is Andrea?' he said.

'Sentry duty,' said Mallory.

'A colonel's work is never done,' said Carstairs, and smiled a superior smile.

'So what were you doing in the village?'

'I was looking for transport,' said Carstairs. 'Not that it's any affair of yours.'

'Transport where?'

'To the Acropolis.'

Mallory pointed to his boots. 'You're looking at it.'

'Sorry?'

'The partisans blew up the road.'

'Fine,' said Carstairs. He grinned, suddenly. 'I should have asked. Saved myself a stiff neck.'

Mallory nodded. It was nearly an apology. 'All comes out in the wash,' he said, getting to his feet. 'Five more minutes, gentlemen. Make the most of them.'

The ledge where they had paused was in dead ground. But from Andrea's vantage point above and to the side, he could see the beach where they had landed, and the bay of Parmatia, and the white town spread out like a map below.

Things were happening down there.

As he watched, three field-grey lorries moved out of the town and along the road behind the bay. For a moment they were hidden from view. When they came out, there were only two lorries. They halted at the landing beach. Ant-like figures spilled out, clotted into groups at the waterside.

It looked very much as if someone had found the bodies of Dawkins and the sentry. And the third lorryload of soldiers might have stopped to look for seashells.

Then again, they might have decided to start up the track into the mountains.

That might or might not be dangerous. As an army the *Wehrmacht* were fine soldiers. As individuals, a lot of them were conscripts, and a lot of them were going through the motions, waiting till it was time to go home, win or lose.

The *Sonderkommando* were different. The *Wehrmacht* felt a sort of horrified scorn for Dieter Wolf and his men. They were volunteers, hand-picked for fitness, ruthlessness and cunning – soldiers who loved killing for killing's sake, particularly when it was seasoned with plenty of rape, loot and torture. Dieter Wolf was the nearest thing the Nazis had to a special forces leader. He was a known intimate of the lengendary Otto Skorzeny. The presence of his *Sonderkommando* on the island meant two things.

One, the Germans had no desire to be interrupted in whatever they were doing in the Acropolis.

And two, these mountains would soon be swarming with soldiers.

When Andrea went back to the ledge, the rest of the party was already upright. Wills put out a hand to steady himself, missed the rock, and sprawled in the dust. Carstairs raised an eyebrow. Miller helped him back on to his feet. His eyes seemed to be looking in different directions. 'Sorry,' he said, in that voice that sounded as if there were marbles in his mouth. Concussion, thought Miller. How would you understand an Englishman with concussion?

'Up,' said Clytemnestra. She kicked her boot-toe on to a small ledge, hoisted herself upwards and disappeared. The party followed; all except Nelson.

Nelson stayed at the bottom, shaking his head, shoulders bowed. He had a mop of red hair, white skin, a face flushed and sulky. Andrea, the rearguard, said, 'You want help?'

'My arm hurts,' said Nelson.

'Everybody hurts,' said Andrea. 'If we don't walk, we get hurt worse.'

'I'm not a commando,' said Nelson. 'I'm a bleeding matlow. What am I doing running around on cliffs like a poxy goat?'

'Your duty,' said Andrea. Gentle as a mother with a child he picked him up, and put him on the first step of the path. Nelson looked white-faced over his shoulder and downwards. Then he started climbing, using both feet and both hands. It struck Andrea that a man who could climb with such vigour might not have very much wrong with his arm at all.

All morning they climbed, at first on steep sea-cliffs, and then in a tangle of ridges and small valleys grown with scrub. By eleven o'clock they were five thousand feet above sea level, in a little valley of juniper and holm oak. Goats wandered among the boulders, their bells clonking mournfully. The men walked heavily, mouths parched, tormented by the small gurgle of the stream in the valley's bed. Too hot,' said Clytemnestra, wiping sweat from her forehead. 'We'll rest here three hours.' She led them on to a ledge overlooking the valley, and pushed aside a huge old rosemary bush. Behind the bush was the dark entrance of a cave.

Mallory was impatient to be pushing on. But he could see that Wills was just about done up. All of them could do with a rest: eight hours, never mind three.

Patience.

Carstairs had the map out. The mountains here formed ridges that spread from the central plateau like the fingers of a right hand.

They had climbed from the beach between the first and second fingers, and crossed the ridge to the valley between the second and the ring fingers. Beyond the next ridge, between the ring finger and the little finger, the road ran. It was here (Clytemnestra said, pointing) that the partisans had blown the cliff down on to the road and blocked it solid.

Carstairs offered to stand sentry. Mallory settled down in the corner of the cave next to Miller and lit a cigarette to drive off the stink of goat dung.

'Nice place,' said Miller. 'Reminds me of a boarding house I used to use in San Francisco.'

'The carpet, you mean?' said Mallory.

'That and the fleas.' Mallory's eyes were closing. 'I'll do it,' said Miller.

'Yes.' Mallory was asleep.

They both knew that what Miller had been talking about was keeping an eye on Carstairs.

So Miller sat and smoked. Andrea and Mallory snored, Wills fell into a sort of twitching stupor, and Nelson curled into a ball. As for Clytemnestra, she had gone into another compartment of the cave, and it was impossible to tell whether she was asleep or awake, though now he came to think of it, Miller could not imagine her asleep.

After about half an hour, Miller got quietly to his feet and crept to the mouth of the cave.

Carstairs had taken up position in the ruined walls of a hut further up the ledge, commanding a view of the entrance to the valley and the ridge opposite. It was a good place to see without being seen. Miller walked up to it quietly. The valley shimmered in the heat, and a lizard scuttled away over a stone. Inside the shadows of the ruin, Carstairs made no sound. Miller went to the door, and looked in.

Carstairs was gone.

Miller stood quite still, thinking. There could be reasons. Went behind a rock, Miller told himself; call of nature. But even as he had those thoughts his binoculars were out, and he was scanning the valley, rocks, trees, a goat dragging at a branch with its teeth –

There.

High on the ridge opposite, a small, khaki figure was toiling towards the crest, rifle over its shoulder. Miller lowered the glasses. For a moment he considered giving chase. But the ridge was

steep, and God knew what lay beyond, and Miller was no mountaineer.

He went back to the cave and pressed Mallory's hand. The New
Zealander's eyes snapped open.

'Sorry, sir,' said Miller. 'Carstairs gone.'

Mallory said, 'Take guard.' Then he slung over his shoulder his
Schmeisser and a coil of silk rope, and went out at a fast lope.

Miller watched the rangy khaki figure jog into the bottom of the
valley, step from boulder to rickety boulder with the casual stride of
a man taking a morning stroll. A speck in the air caught Miller's eye;
an eagle soaring on a column of hot air. He watched it idly for a
minute or so. When his eye returned to Mallory, he was surprised
to see him already at the far side of the valley. Miller put the glasses
on him, saw him come to the bottom of a cliff that anyone short of
a fly would have walked around. But Mallory put his hands on it
and went up it without fuss or difficulty, as if lighter than air. Miller
propped himself against a rock, checked his weapon and lit a cigarette. As befits one who understands demolition, beneath his leath-
ery exterior he was a sensitive man. He felt a sort of distant pity for
anyone on the wrong end of that pursuit.

Even Carstairs.

Out of the shadow of the cave, it was hot; hot enough to swell
Mallory's tongue in his head and bring the sweat rolling down the
creases at the corners of his eyes and down his hollow cheeks. The
air in the valley hung still and heavy, full of the smell of thyme and
baking stone, and the cigarettes Mallory had smoked all these days
and nights and weeks of bad food and snatched sleep.

At first his head felt sore and out of step with the world. But after
a couple of minutes he got his mind fixed on Carstairs. Carstairs
taking off on his own, with a long-range weapon. Carstairs was a
dirty little mystery who needed solving before he blew the mission.

So Mallory hitched up his Schmeisser and trotted across the bottom of the valley, and went straight up the cliff on the far side, feeling the life return to his fingers and back and legs as he shifted from
hold to hold on the firm, warm rock. Within half an hour he was
standing on the crest of the ridge: not on top, where someone
could see him, but below the skyline, in the little puddle of shade
at the foot of a boulder. Here he pulled out his binoculars.

It took ten patient minutes of searching that wilderness of rock
and scrub before he saw the little flicker of movement: a man,

moving at a steady, plodding walk towards a range of low ridges in the distance. Khaki battledress, slung rifle. Carstairs.

Mallory started after him.

The Englishman was not more than twenty minutes ahead. Not even a mile, in this terrain. Steadily, Mallory wore down his lead.

They crossed a couple of low spurs of hill. Mallory checked his compass, and pulled the map out of his blouse pocket. After an hour and a quarter, the ground dipped sharply. Ahead, Carstairs flicked into shadow, and became invisible. Mallory was not worried. He knew where his man was heading.

What he did not know was why. He brushed through a fringe of scrub, and stopped dead.

In front of him there was no more ground. Beyond the lip of the cliff was a deep gulf of air, in which swallows hawked and swooped, and beyond that, the vast blue void of the sea. He lay down, and peered over the edge. He was looking down a three-thousand-foot precipice. Somewhere far below, hidden by overhangs, the sea muttered at the island's rocky skirts. A thousand feet below, the swoop of the cliff was interrupted by a flat platform of rock that ran along it like a step. It was fifty yards wide, this step, its outside edge scattered with wind-blasted shrubs, its inside blurred with the rock falls of centuries.

Vertically below Mallory's eyes, a green fur of trees grew on a glacis of rubble. To his right, the glacis was huge, extending most of the way up the thousand-odd feet of the cliff, new and raw, blocking the shelf completely.

Along the shelf there snaked the white ribbon of the road, vanishing into the great cone of rubble. This must be what was left of the overhang the partisans had blasted down to cut the island in half.

It was not going to stay cut long. The sound of diesel engines clattered up to Mallory's ears. Round the bulge of the landslide, there ran a pale band of levelled and compacted rock. As Mallory watched, a mechanical digger trundled round and deposited a load of rubble into what might have been a hole. It looked very much as if the road was nearly open again.

And Mallory was not the only one who thought that way. At the foot of the slide stood a little queue of vehicles: a horse and cart, three German army trucks, and a field ambulance, the red cross on its roof shimmering in the heat. A small knot of men sat in the shade of a little stand of pines.

And a couple of hundred feet down the cliff, masked from the vehicles by a buttress the size of a cathedral tower, a little khaki figure dangling like a spider on a thread.

Carstairs, descending.

Mallory watched him for a moment, weighing the odds. Let him go, catch him. Shoot him. Shooting him was the option he would have preferred, just now. But the Admiral was Jensen's superior officer. Shooting involved noise, which would attract attention, and besides, he was well out of Schmeisser range. Shooting was just a beautiful dream.

Mallory moved in dead ground to the top of the buttress. Carstairs had doubled his rope around a natural fin of rock. Mallory pinched the ropes together and tied a constrictor knot around the pair. If Carstairs wanted to pull the rope down so he could descend further, he was in for a disappointment.

Mallory looked down. The rope was a white line ruled down the cliff, disappearing at an overhang. Mallory measured out enough of his own rope to reach the overhang. Then he belayed it on a knob of rock, turned his back to the void, and leaped out and down. The pyramid nails of his boots bit once, twice. Then he was by the overhang, holding, looking down.

There was a ledge below, thirty feet wide, running diagonally downwards to the slide area. It was broad enough to have trees on it, and an undergrowth of juniper and caper bushes. The doubled rope terminated in a small area of broken stone. Carstairs was nowhere to be seen.

Mallory went down Carstairs' rope, braking just before he reached the bottom to avoid the tell-tale crunch of boots. Carstairs had left a flattened trail in the scorched grass by the bushes. Very quietly, Mallory pulled out his knife and followed it.

The ledge followed the curve of the cliff face for fifty yards, wide as a road, sloping towards the ravine floor at an angle of forty-five degrees. Through the head-high scrub Mallory could see grey vehicles, men moving, the red cross on the field ambulance's roof. He moved on, very stealthy –

'Don't move,' said a voice in his left ear. Something pushed into his left kidney. He knew without looking that it was the barrel of a silenced Browning.

'What the hell do you think you're doing?' he said.

'Minding my own business,' said Carstairs. His immaculate hair was disarranged, and sweat was rolling into his silly moustache. His eyes had a wild, dangerous look.

Mallory said, 'If you shoot me, you'll have fifty Germans after us.'

The gun in his kidney did not waver. 'Why are you following me about?' he said.

'Because you were standing sentry and deserted your post.'

'Don't be damn silly –'

'You listen here,' said Mallory. 'I don't care how many admirals you are taking your orders from, I am your superior officer by seniority and I would remind you that you are subject to my orders even if you are not directly under my command.'

There was a very faint lessening of pressure. Seventy-five feet below, the red cross on the ambulance roof glowed in the sun.

'You won't get through this alone,' said Mallory. 'It's team work, or nothing.'

The pressure of the Browning faded. Mallory watched as Carstairs holstered it and half-turned, performing some operation that made a small, metallic sound, putting something in his pocket. Carstairs nodded, smoothed his hair, gave a rueful film-star smile slightly marred by the scabbing graze on his upper lip. 'Just thought I'd pop and have a look,' he said. 'When I was in the town they said the road would be opening soon. So I thought, well, it'd shorten the journey, know what I mean?'

Mallory had a very good idea of what he meant. But what Carstairs meant had nothing to do with what Carstairs said. 'We'll carry on over the mountains,' he said.

Carstairs shrugged. He bent and picked up his sniper rifle, and started back up the path towards the rope. A dove, disturbed by his passing, clattered out of a holm oak tree. Three more, disturbed by the first, zigzagged away over the road in a kerfuffle of wings. Carstairs and Mallory stood still, holding their breath. For a moment, a thick, pregnant silence hung over the gorge. Then there broke into that silence a voice, giving orders, steady and professional, in German. 'Schmidt,' it said. 'Take two men and get on to that ledge and see what's going on.'

Mallory and Carstairs turned and ran. 'Go,' said Mallory, when they reached the bottom of the rope.

Carstairs grabbed hold and went up, kicking his feet into the rock, making a lot of noise about it, Mallory thought as he unslung his Schmeisser, but travelling at commendable speed. When Carstairs got to the overhang, Mallory shouted, 'Cover me!' turned and gripped the rope, and started to walk up the wall.

The rock was coarse and pitted, so it took no more than a couple of minutes to reach the base of the overhang. German shouts came from below. Mallory decided that this was one of those occasions when speed was more important than technique. He went over the overhang hands only, expecting to find Carstairs waiting, covering the cliff base, ready to open fire. But Carstairs had not bothered to wait: look after number one was Carstairs' motto. He was a pair of bootsoles half-way up the cliff. Even as Mallory glanced up, a rifle banged down below, and a bullet kicked chips from the wall by Carstairs' shoulder. The fixed rope was taut over the overhang. A German was coming up. Mallory pulled the pin from a grenade, let the lever spring back and counted to three, listening to the fizz of the internal fuse. On four, he tossed the grenade over the edge.

The sound of the airburst rolled around the hard faces of the cliff. The rope slackened suddenly. There were screams. Mallory tossed another grenade, five seconds this time, and started up his own rope. By the time he heard the flat bang from the ledge, he was half-way up. Someone was firing down there. He could hear the bullets strike, wild and far away. He found a perch, pulled another grenade out of his pouch, hauled the pin out with his teeth, and let it rattle down behind him. There was traffic manoeuvring in front of the landslip. They would be trying to get some vehicle-mounted weapons to bear. *Bang*, said the grenade. No sound from above. He was at the top.

Carstairs was hauling in his rope, coiling it. He glanced at Mallory, completed his coil, and started away uphill. Mallory caught him.

'I said cover me,' he said.

Carstairs cocked an eyebrow. 'Didn't hear,' he said.

'We've got to show ourselves.'

'Don't be silly.'

Mallory found that his Schmeisser was in his hands, pointed at the ground between him and Carstairs. 'We need to show them it's an Allied operation. Not partisans. In case of reprisals.'

'Oh for God's sake –'

'If you disobey a direct order I shall regard it as a mutinous act.'

Carstairs saw in Mallory's face what that meant. He flinched as if he had received a smack in the teeth. He laughed, a weak laugh. 'Christ,' he said. 'I . . . oh, if you say so.'

Mallory took him along the clifftop in dead ground. Above the slide, he went to the edge of the cliff. The vehicles were still below. The men had gone: taking cover. Mallory stood up, dragging Carstairs with him. 'Allied regular troops!' he roared, in English and German. Then he threw his last grenade into the void and stepped back. A storm of machine-gun fire tore the air where they had been standing.

'Now move,' said Mallory, and started back the way they had come.

They were in trouble. The element of surprise was gone. If that had been *Wehrmacht* down there, it was big trouble. If it was Dieter Wolf's *Sonderkommando*, it was big, big trouble.

Whatever shape the trouble came in, there was no doubt who lay at the root of it.

Carstairs.

They got over the top of the first ridge without being shot at, trotted into the valley beyond and scaled the far side. As Mallory went up the last low cliff to the summit, a bullet cracked by his ear. A rock by his right hand exploded into stinging chips. The ridge was there, knife-sharp against the blue sky. He jumped for it and hauled himself over. As he lay in cover to calm his breath, a burst of machine-gun fire pulverized the top six inches of the rock plates behind which he lay. Carstairs was beside him, spitting out powdered stone.

'Give me the rifle,' said Mallory. 'Go and tell the rest of them.'

Carstairs said, 'Oh, really.' Then perhaps he remembered the conversation in the dead ground above the cliff, or perhaps he saw the look in Mallory's eye. Whichever the case, he handed over the rifle and ran.

Mallory moved fifty yards below the skyline, resurfacing in a notch between two boulders, and rested the fore end of the Mauser on the ground in front of him. He snapped the guards off the telescopic sight, took a couple of deep breaths, and cuddled the butt to his shoulder. Into the disc of the sight floated rocks, low, dark-green bushes. The disc settled. And across it jogged a figure in field-grey uniform, coal-scuttle helmet, Schmeisser held across the body.

Mallory put the cross hairs on the centre of the chest and squeezed the trigger. The Mauser bucked. The grey figure flung its arms out and slammed backwards into the rocks. Behind it, Mallory saw the quick, dancing flicker of a machine-gun's muzzle flash, heard the crash and whine of the rounds smacking rock. He paid no attention. His eye was back on the sight, and he was searching among the rocks, finding the grey cobblestones of the Spandau crew's helmets. The machine gun opened up again.

Mallory could just see the dark upright of the loader's jackboot as he knelt by the weapon. He raised the sight a couple of clicks. Then he shot the man just below the knee. The gunner turned his face. Mallory shot him in the side of the head, and transferred his attention to the men advancing across the notched and rock-strewn plain –

There were no men. On the grey, ridged valley floor nothing moved but the bushes, fretted by the small wind from the sea.

Mallory began to crawl backwards, knees and elbows, behind the cover of the ridge. Once in cover, he doubled under the lee of the rocks. A *Wehrmacht* garrison would have been ragged and dull-edged. The men in cover looked sharp and well-disciplined. Behind the smell of thyme and rosemary and his own sweat, he seemed to detect the keen, ugly whiff of Dieter Wolf.

He went back to the ridge. A figure moved over to the right, out of the ground, over a rock, back into cover, fast as a rabbit. He sent a Mauser round after it, heard the whine of the ricochet. Missed. He slung the rifle and ran down the ridge, from stone to stone across the valley floor, hurdled the stream, went up the other side and into the cave.

Carstairs was back. He and the others were waiting, loaded up, ready to go. Mallory glanced in his direction. 'You're under arrest,' he said.

Carstairs' face turned blank, fish-white. 'You can't –'

'Disarm him,' said Mallory to Miller. Mallory's Schmeisser just happened to be pointing at Carstairs' stomach.

Stiff-faced, Miller removed Carstairs' Browning and knife.

Carstairs said, 'I didn't mean –'

'You have jeopardized the operation,' said Mallory. 'You will be dealt with later.' He pulled out a map, beckoned Clytemnestra. 'We've got thirty men after us,' he said. 'Where do we go?' He gave her a pencil.

She drew a line: a tenuous line that zigzagged on to a tight bunch of contours until the contours ceased, giving way to the hatchings of rock faces. 'We'll mark the path with piled stones,' she said.

He put his finger on a narrow white stripe among the contours and hatchings. 'What's this?' he asked.

She told him. Then they made a rendezvous, and she led the party out and along the ridge: Wills and Nelson, Wills still dazed-looking and rubber-legged, Nelson scared, sunburned under his carroty thatch, hugging his arm, grey-faced with pain or fear or both, and Miller with his big pack, and Carstairs somewhere between hangdog and arrogant.

'Get up in those hills,' said Mallory, handing Miller a copy of the map reference. 'See you later.'

Miller tilted his head back, looking at the hills. If they were hills, so were the Goddamned Himalayas, he thought. And soon he was going to be up there, making like the abominable snowman or an eagle or something. Miller was a creature of the American Midwest. His idea of the ideal landscape was a billiard table, flattened out a little.

'Take it easy,' he said to Mallory.

'We'll do our best.' Mallory's face was set, his eyes remote. He was loading rounds into a Schmeisser magazine, already working on the problem of thirty Germans against two Allied troops who had first to fight a rearguard action and then to complete an operation.

'We'll be with you in two hours, maximum,' he said. 'If we're not, you go on.'

Miller turned away, grim-faced. He shouldered his big pack, and set off in the wake of Carstairs, Clytemnestra and the two sailors.

The path led upwards: over the ridge, down the other side, along a little ribbon of flat ground that wove through a great field of boulders, and on to the face of a mountain – hill, Miller told himself, remember it's only a hill – that if it had been by the seaside you would have called it a cliff.

The sweat ran into Miller's eyes. The pack straps dug into his shoulders. From below came the hammer and crack of small-arms fire. Mallory and Andrea were busy.

Ahead, Wills stumbled and crashed into a rock. 'All right,' he mumbled. 'All right.'

'Help him,' said Miller.

Clytemnestra pulled at his arm. She said, 'He is too big for me, poor man.'

'Cap'n Carstairs?' said Miller.

Carstairs scowled at him. Then, grudgingly, he hauled the sailor's arm around his neck. 'Move it,' he said.

Haltingly, the procession climbed on.

Back by the cave, things were getting complicated.

The *Sonderkommando* had sneaked up behind the ridge, making maximum use of cover. It had done them very little good. There was always a moment when they were going to be silhouetted against the skyline. They were superior in numbers. But they had no artillery and no mortars, and it did not look as if they ran to air support. While it was small arms against small arms, there was not a lot of progress that could be made against two determined defenders.

So Andrea and Mallory moved from the cave towards the ruined hut, keeping in cover, stopping to snipe at the matchhead-sized helmets that popped over the skyline, but never stopping in the same place twice. The sun was moving across the sky, but it was still hot.

At four thirty-one, there was a pause in the firing on the ridge opposite the cave. Mallory and Andrea were only ten yards apart. They looked at each other, then at the ridge opposite. Nothing moved. For a moment, birds sang, and the breeze blew, and there might have been no war at all. Then something a long way away made a small, flat explosion, and Mallory and Andrea grovelled on the ground, because they knew what that meant.

High in the air, a fleeting black dot came into being, hung for a moment, and fell to the ground thirty yards in front of them. There was a sharp, ear-damaging *crump,* and shattered stone flew past their ears. Mortar. When Mallory ran between two rocks, a gun opened up with a low, heavy clatter. They had brought up a mortar and re-manned the Spandau, and they were both on the other side of the ridge.

Mallory wiped away the blood that the stinging chips of stone had brought to his forehead. The idea of fighting a pitched battle against a numerically superior enemy with mortars and heavy machine guns was not appealing. But fight they must, to give the rest of the party time to get clear. He crawled to the other end of his line of rocks and fired. The machine gun opened up again. Under cover of its sheet of lead, five field-grey figures bounced out of cover, scuttled across five yards of open ground, and dived out of sight. Another mortar round pitched into the rocks, closer this time.

Andrea shouted. 'Going, my Keith!' he roared. It could have been a cry of pain: but Mallory knew it was precisely the opposite. Andrea was out to even the odds.

Andrea went up and over the ridge behind Mallory's position, ran along it in dead ground for two hundred yards, recrossed the spine, and began to worm his way across the valley floor like a giant lizard.

He heard firing and explosions up to his right; Schmeisser fire from Mallory now, the sound of battle, several defenders working hard; or of one man, moving around, making noise and fuss. They were a team, Andrea and Keith Mallory. So far, it was all satisfactory.

The ground had begun to slope uphill. There would be men posted to protect the flanks. Andrea lay still as a stone, moving his head up inch by inch.

Twenty feet to his right, a German soldier was sitting behind a stone, scanning the rocks down the valley.

Andrea allowed his head to sink away. He moved over the ground like a giant shadow, seeking the strips of darkness along the sides of bushes, the lee of small stones. He moved not like a man moving over ground, but like a huge ripple of the ground itself. In four steady minutes, he completed a semicircle. He was looking at the back of a helmet, a tunic with a leather harness, corrugated canisters at the waist, tense shoulders . . .

Andrea moved forward, silent as a shadow, knife in front of him. There was a brief struggle, without sound. The German made a sharp exhalation. No inhalation followed. Andrea laid the body in the dust, wiped his knife on its tunic, and went with great caution forward over the ridge.

Here he crouched behind a boulder and waited. He heard the *whap* of the mortar, the explosion on the other side of the valley. He saw the heads of the men around the mortar, the gleam of the sun on the tube of the weapon. And further up, in a nest of rocks on the reverse slope of the ridge, the machine-gunners. He noticed that the arc of fire from the Spandau pit was ahead only, and that apart from the man he had killed, there was nobody protecting the flanks. This must be a hastily-assembled squad, sent up the cliffs in hot pursuit, undermanned and under-equipped . . .

All this went through his mind in the blink of an eye. During this blink he had wormed through the rocks to the machine-gun pit. The gunner fired a burst at the hill opposite. In Andrea's mind, the field-grey figures facing Mallory got up, ran forward, flopped down again: advancing.

From cover, Andrea threw three grenades into the mortar pit. Then he unslung his Schmeisser and stood up.

Mallory knew he was in trouble. The *Sonderkommando* were in Schmeisser range now. The mortar fire had ceased, presumably for fear of scoring own goals. He had laid aside the rifle, and was trying to look three ways at once. Under cover of the last burst of machine-gun fire, the enemy had come within a hundred and twenty feet. He had seen one scuttling away to the right, and up to the left he thought he had seen movement, though he could not swear to it. He was going to find out, though. He settled himself grimly behind the rock, and waited for the Spandau to open up: short burst, to get his head down and signal to the men. Then the longer bursts, the blizzard of metal that would keep his head down while the *Sonderkommando* swarmed aboard –

The Spandau burped; the short burp. Then there was a huge explosion: bigger than a grenade. It sounded like a lot of mortar bombs going off at once. Hot on the heels of the explosion was a long burst of Schmeisser fire, with screams.

In the silence that followed, he sighted through the crack in the stone wall. He saw the grey helmets rise, squeezed a short burst over the rock. Then the machine gun opened up again, and through the crack he saw the men rise from cover. He waited for the metal rain to start pelting around his ears. The machine gun started its deadly hammer. But the rain did not come.

He put his eye to the sighting cranny.

Down below him, the field-grey figures were up and advancing, but not under a curtain of friendly fire. They had risen into the open at the first burst of the machine gun. And the second burst had whipped not over their heads, but into the thick of them. The rocks below Mallory were strewn with field-grey corpses. To the right, a man was groaning. To the left, movement caught Mallory's eye. He turned. A camouflage uniform, much stained with new blood, was lurching at him through the rocks. He put a short Schmeisser burst into the helmet. The man went over with a crash.

On the far side of the valley, a figure stood up. Acting on reflex, Mallory went for the rifle. Then he stopped.

It was Andrea.

Andrea walked quickly across the valley and up to the cave. By the time he got there, Mallory had his feet up on a rock and was smoking a cigarette. 'That was useful,' he said.

Andrea nodded. He was a superlative craftsman in the art of war, and he had done his job. Mallory gave him a cigarette. He lit it, shouldered his pack, and loped off up the hill. Mallory went after him.

At the top, he looked back at the valley where thirty men had died or run away. The shadows were lengthening towards evening.

Evening of the first day. There was nothing to feel good about. The Germans knew there was a British force in the mountains. They did not know it contained two wounded sailors and a man who did not know how to obey orders. They would come looking, and soon.

What had happened in the valley had been a victory. But it had been only one battle in what looked like a very long campaign.

FIVE

Wednesday 1800–Thursday 0300

After the field of stones, the path led on and up. It was not much of a path: more a strip of bare mountainside, marked with stones placed one on another like the little men children put up on beaches to knock down with more stones. As they passed the markers, Mallory kicked them down. It was six o'clock, and the sun was heading for the rock-masses of the western horizon when they reached the top of the slope and found themselves at the base of a cliff.

'What are we,' said Andrea. 'Flies?'

Mallory shook his head. He took a mouthful from his water bottle, and cast left into deep shadow, to a place where the cliff seemed less than vertical. At the base of the slope was one of Clytemnestra's little stone men.

The slope was not a hill. It was more like the leading edge of the dorsal fin of a fish – a dorsal fin a thousand feet high and three feet wide, made of rotten rock, tapering away into the far distance. Mallory pointed at the map.

'It's a ramp,' he said. 'A stepladder. Up there, it gets wider.'

'And then,' said Andrea, sighing, 'it gets narrower again.'

He had a point. But the sun was sinking, and this was no time for debates.

They went up.

It was easy climbing. Andrea plodded away, keeping his eyes in front of him, not thinking about the void on either side of the blade of rock – keeping his mind on the far side of the mountains; on the marshes, the Acropolis, how to cross the one and get into the other . . .

The path was broadening. It became a sort of plateau. Mallory came up behind him, and went ahead to reconnoitre.

From somewhere far away there came a small, remote buzzing.

Andrea found himself a ledge with a bush growing off it, squeezed himself in, and watched, cursing, as evening fell over his beloved country.

To the west, the island fell ridge on ridge to the mottled blue sheet of the sea. The valleys below were blurred with veils of haze, veils tinged faintly with flame-colour and blood-colour, prophesying the sunset. And above it all, flying out from the high blind cliffs ahead, gleaming silver in that low sun, was an aeroplane.

Mallory watched that plane, too. Ahead of him the ridge threaded across to a maze of cliffs and canyons, cliffs piled on cliffs, and above them the summit of Mount Skaphos. And above the summit cliffs a sky of purest blue, and in that blue the aeroplane. A Fieseler Storch; a slow-flying aeroplane, with an observer. Looking for them.

The Storch banked gently, and began to spiral downwards. It came lower and lower, until from his position in the rocks Mallory could see the pilot's head, catch the glint of binoculars in the observer's seat . . .

He turned his face to the ground, and hoped the bloody thing would go away.

On the mountain shoulder at the far end of the ridge, Miller heard the engines, too. The rendezvous map reference was a cave – no more than an overhang of the cliff, really. Clytemnestra was dozing, Wills muttering in a half-sleep, Nelson sitting with his back against the cliff, hugging his slashed arm, staring bug-eyed at a boulder, as if it was showing him a film about things he did not find pleasing. As for Carstairs, he was in a clump of bushes in front of the cave, unarmed still, watching the ridge and the valley below.

'What's that?' said Nelson.

'Plane.'

'What do they want?'

'If I was a bird, I'd ask them.'

Nelson shook his head, an odd, feverish shake. Miller reckoned he was a nasty mixture of ill and frightened. Miller was a demolition man, not a nursemaid. But his good nature made him say, reassuring, 'We'll keep still and not show our faces, and we'll be fine.' And then what? he thought. All the way over the mountains to storm some huge Goddamned bunker, and we say, listen, you wounded and you crazy, hang loose in the mountains till you hear a great big bang, and then Poppa will make sure you get home . . .

Sure.

He took out a cigarette and stuck it in his mouth. He did not light it: on an evening like this, a spotter plane could see the flash of a buckle, the white of an eye, a puff of cigarette smoke.

In the back of the cave, Wills said in a loud, definite voice, 'Henry!'

There were no Henries. 'Back to sleep,' said Miller. 'There's a good lootenant.'

'Damned plane's late,' said Wills. 'Got to be in Paris for lunch. Camilla's waiting.' He got to his feet, stood swaying. 'For God's sake,' he said.

'Sit down,' said Miller, alarmed now.

'You,' said Wills. 'You, that man. Siddown and shaddup.' He came to the front of the cave. Miller stood up, to stop him going out on to the ledge. 'Honestly,' said Wills.

'Please,' said Miller. 'Sir.' The Storch was at the outer edge of its spiral, turning back towards them.

Wills said, 'Stand away. She's my fiancée y'know. We're lunching in Paris. Top-hole. Special treat.' His eyes were glassy, looking at things in a different world; customs at Croydon aerodrome, perhaps. He rummaged in the pocket of his filthy, sweat-stained jacket. 'Here y'are.' He might have thought he was pulling out his passport.

What he actually pulled out was his cigarette case. His silver cigarette case, highly polished. He waved it in Miller's face.

'Put it away,' said Miller.

But Wills kept waving it. A flash of westering sun bounced off it and into Miller's eyes. Horrified, Miller grabbed it out of his hand.

Behind them, the Storch's engine-note changed from a drone to an angry buzz. The pilot opened the throttle wide, banked steeply, and flew straight as an arrow over Mount Skaphos, heading east.

It looked very much as if the pilot had seen it too.

Mallory watched the change of course, heard a second later the new roar of the engine. He knew what it meant, and so, judging by the way he came loping across the rocks, did Andrea.

They hit the ridge at a dead run, pebbles scattering under their feet and looping out and into the void below. Ten minutes later they were climbing a steep, near-invisible path among genista bushes, and Miller was materializing out of the rock face ahead.

'Moving out,' said Mallory. 'Where's Carstairs?'

Carstairs stood up in his bush. 'Cigarette?' he said, producing his case. 'Turkish this side, Virginian that.'

'Put it away,' said Andrea. 'Captain Carstairs, I have something to say to you. Atten-shun!'

Carstairs dropped his cigarette and came to attention. His face was like the face of a man who, walking down the street in the dark, has just realized that what he has trodden on is not a paving stone but an open manhole.

'Captain Carstairs,' said Mallory. 'I am changing our operational basis.' His voice quiet and level, as always. But there was a cold power to it that made the hair rise on Carstairs' scalp. 'For the remainder of this operation you will consider yourself under my command and the command of Colonel Andrea. When the occasion presents, you will face court martial for desertion in the face of the enemy. Is that clear?'

Carstairs said, white-lipped, 'That is not –'

'Any complaints should be set out in writing and submitted after the conclusion of the operation,' said Mallory. 'Meanwhile continue to consider yourself under arrest. Your conduct under arrest will be taken into your account at your court martial.'

There was a silence. Carstairs stood pale and numb. The penalty for desertion in the face of the enemy was death. The message was clear and simple: behave or die.

Andrea said, 'Corporal, return this man's weapons.'

'Pleasure,' said Miller.

Carstairs found himself sweating. For a moment, this loose array of bandits had turned into a sharp, formal military unit. Carstairs realized that he had underestimated them; underestimated them badly.

From now on, he would have to use new tactics.

Mallory said, 'Clytemnestra. We'll need to go on into the mountains. Hide till dawn.'

'Of course.'

Mallory drank water, shouldered his pack. 'We'll move out,' he said. Clytemnestra took the lead. He walked beside her. 'What are the chances of the Germans getting ahead of us?' he said. 'Cutting us off?'

'Not tonight,' she said. 'The other sides of the island are very steep. It is bad country up there.'

Miller was trudging behind them, cigarette hanging out of his mouth. 'You wanna know what I'd do?' he said. 'I'd put some guys in a plane, maybe two lots, one ahead of us, one behind. And I'd fly them up here and I'd make them jump out, and they could chase us the hell and gone and their legs wouldn't even ache.'

They toiled on up the thread of a path that zigzagged towards the summit of the steep slope above the cave. The breath rasped loud in Mallory's ears. He was tired, but not yet tired enough for Benzedrine. There was a strange buzzing in his head . . .

There was a strange buzzing in the air. It grew, became a drone, then a roar.

He looked up.

Three aeroplanes rumbled across the sky: Tante Jus, Junkers Trimotors, lit gold by the sun like squat, ungainly millionaires' toys. The doors in their sides were open.

Not toys.

Mallory's head felt dry and empty, filled with the sound of his breathing. He made himself walk more quickly.

The rest of the group knew death when they heard the beating of its wings. They began to walk more quickly too.

Under Wills' nose, the Gieves sheepskin-lined seaboots went trudge, trudge in the shale. It seemed to Wills that he had been walking for ever; up and up and up, with his feet boiling and his brain banging around in his skull like a turnip in a dixie. It hurt like hell, he would grant it that. It hurt like hell and tasted blue and smelt like aluminium and it felt sad as velvet. But he could remember his own name, now, so he supposed he was getting better. He also remembered that at some point in some world or other he had had a ship, and there had been a bang, and now he had no ship any more.

There was a slope up, and after the slope some rocks. And now there was a wall on his port-hand shoulder and to starboard a great deep swoop of nothing, and in his head the roaring, whining, zinging hum of blood, or aeroplanes, or something. He looked to the right, out over the void, even though the sun hurt his eyes. It was red, the sun, blood-colour. It shone on sea and land and jellyfish.

Jellyfish? Jellyfish in the sky, floating down into the deep shadows of the ground.

Something wrong with the above statement. Check details.

Details of what?

Under Wills' nose, the Gieves sheepskin-lined seaboots went trudge, trudge in the shale.

* * *

Down below, the white silk parachutes of the *Sonderkommando* drifted earthward, each one pink as a baby's fingernail in the warm glow of the sunset, on to the flat patch at the foot of the steep ridge Andrea and Mallory had climbed after their defence of the cave.

'How long till dark?' said Mallory.

Clytemnestra shrugged. 'Forty minutes,' she said.

Mallory looked at the slow laborious trudge of Wills, the agonized hobble of Nelson. The men on the parachutes were fresh. The people on this cliff path had climbed five thousand feet, and had not slept for twenty-four hours.

The path they were on was a narrow ledge running across the face of a sheer cliff. Ten minutes later, the ledge joined another ledge. The main path went off to the left. Another, scarcely visible, snaked away to the right. Andrea spoke at length with Clytemnestra, in Greek, then to Mallory. They bent their heads over the map. Then Mallory said, 'Carstairs. You go with Clytemnestra and the wounded. Andrea, Miller, come with me.'

'Smashing,' said Carstairs, with a frank Boy Scout grin.

Mallory did not smile back. He said, 'The Germans will be here in twenty minutes. Get a move on.'

Carstairs got a move on. The small, shuffling file disappeared up the thready path to the right.

Miller sat on a boulder. Twelve hundred feet below his boots, stunted olives rocked in the small evening wind. Beyond them, a file of tiny grey figures trotted towards the base of the slope. Miller lit a cigarette.

'Okay,' said Mallory. 'Now listen.'

Miller listened. When Mallory had finished, he said, 'Are you serious?'

Mallory looked him in the eye, hard and steely. He said, 'What do you think, Corporal?'

Miller sighed. He reached above his head and stubbed his cigarette on the left-hand fork of the track, wide, obvious, well-used by men and goats. He said, 'I guess you're serious.'

'Thank you,' said Mallory. 'Now, shall we get on with it?'

Averting his eyes from the frightful emptiness below, Miller began to scramble along the left-hand path.

It did not take long to find what he was looking for: a place where the ledge bulged out from the cliff face on a cornice of rock, with a little pile of debris at its inner edge. Miller dropped to his knees and began scuffling in the dirt on the inside of the ledge. He found what he was looking for: a letter-box-sized crack in the rock. Reverently, he opened his pack, took out four sticks of gelignite, and taped to them a time pencil. He snapped the glass ampoule in the time pencil, tamped the bomb into the letter box, wedged rocks over the top, and replanted the rosemary and spurge he had disturbed with his digging.

'Done,' he said.

Andrea nodded. The lower limb of the sun was kissing the horizon, drawing a road of fire across the sea. He was watching the place where he and Mallory had been hiding when they first heard the Storch. It lay empty under the sky, pink in the sunset.

Then it was not empty any more.

Suddenly, the empty area was striped with the shadows of men; one shadow, then two, shadows that dispersed quickly into the rough ground, taking cover. Andrea had counted sixty parachutes. He waited until he had lost count of the men on the outcrop. Then he took his Mauser, settled the sight on one of the helmets down below, and took up the first pressure on the trigger.

'Ready?' he said to Miller.

Miller was never ready for this kind of thing. But he nodded anyway. Andrea fired.

A quarter of a mile up the path, Mallory had found a narrow chimney; a seam between two plates of rock, polished smooth by the action of winter rains. He settled the two coils of silk climbing rope around his shoulders. Then he put in a boot, turned his foot to wedge the sole, stepped up, and raised his hand. He heard the crash of Andrea's rifle, and the clatter of a Schmeisser. He kept climbing. The crack got narrower up here. He jammed in his right forefinger, and bent it to enlarge the knuckle. With his free boot, he groped the wall until he found a hold, no more than a pimple of rock. The pyramid nail of his boot bit home. He moved the first foot, got a new hold in the crack with the knuckle of his other hand. If he had looked down, he would have seen that he was already a man's height above the ledge with the path, that the precipice was opening out below him. He did not look down. Instead, he concentrated on the rock-sheets in front of him, climbing from the hips, body out from the wall. Before the war, they had called it the Mallory Float; a perfectly balanced stance on the face that took him drifting up, defying gravity. One of the great rock climbers, they called him: and one of the great mountaineers. A man who could walk for thirty-six hours, and climb five thousand vertical feet at the end of it.

As long as nobody shot him.

After a couple of hundred feet the crack petered out. Mallory paused, drove in a spike with the leather-bound lead hammer in his belt, belayed to it the first of the two silk climbing ropes around his shoulders, and paid out the coil. The rope fell away into the shadows below. Then he went on up, climbing on hammered-in spikes until he came to a zone of rougher rock; rock about as rough as an old brick wall. To any climber except Mallory, it would have looked smooth and impossible. To Mallory, it might as well have been a stepladder. He went on up, slow and steady, not bothering with spikes. At three hundred and thirty feet, he came upon an area of rotten rock that gave way to soil. He had arrived at the top.

He belayed the second rope to a boulder, and dropped the free end down the face of the cliff. Then he lit a cigarette and told the weary ache in his limbs to be still, and settled down to wait.

Andrea and Miller were sitting down too; but not for reasons of repose. The inside of the path represented dead ground, so on the inside of the path they were sitting, backs to the wall, while a steady covering fire from the German troops below whanged up into the cliff face above their heads. Every now and then, Andrea stuck the barrel of his Schmeisser over the edge and squeezed off a short burst.

'Go,' said Andrea, after ten minutes.

They went.

As they belly-crawled along the ledge, the sun was a small red glow on the western horizon, and the stars were coming out. Andrea leaned over the path edge, blasted half-a-dozen rounds into the void, ducked quickly back, and carried on up the path. The space below suddenly crackled with blue-red muzzle flashes, the bullets splashing against the rocks safely to the rear. On the hook, thought Miller, with a solemn cheerfulness. Bless your innocent hearts.

On they crawled, the full quarter-mile, until Miller's hand brushed the rope. He took a deep breath, and swallowed whatever it is that you swallow when your mouth is as dry as a Saharan cave floor. Then he grasped the rope and started to climb.

Down on the ledge, Andrea took the clip from his Schmeisser and groped for one he had reserved in a special pocket of his pack. His fingers found the two tapes he had wrapped around the magazine

to identify it as tracer. He slapped it into the machine pistol, and
fired: fired along the line of the ledge this time, back the way he
and Miller had come, five rounds, tracer. The bullets smacked rock,
tumbled in a firework display that said: up here; we went this-a-
way. Then he fired another burst off to the right. From below, on
the plain where the parachutists had landed, and where a radio
operator might be sitting, it would look as if a battle was starting on
the path.

Andrea slung his Schmeisser, gripped the rope and started to
climb. When he reached the spike, he coiled the first rope and
worked the spring-steel piton out of the rock. Then, light as a
feather, he went up the second rope and over the cliff edge.

Mallory and Miller were sitting with their backs against boulders, dim, looming figures against the stars. From three hundred
feet below, there came the clink of metal and the crunch of jackboots on shale: men, running in silence, chasing an enemy.

An enemy who was no longer there.

When the sound of pursuit had died away, Mallory, Miller and
Andrea turned their faces east, for the precipices of Mount Skaphos
and the plains beyond.

Private Emmanuel Gruber was a proud man and a good soldier. He
was proud to be in the *Sonderkommando*: proud that *Hauptmann*
Wolf had singled him out, proud that he had achieved the objectives of the training course, proud to have received a hint that he
was in line for promotion to *Feldwebel*. And proud that tonight he
had been ordered to bring up the rear of the pursuit squad; forty
men, another twenty waiting at base as reinforcements. It was safe
back here, too; though of course (Gruber told himself hastily) if
Hauptmann Wolf ordered him into the jaws of death he would leap
in without hesitation.

So on went Gruber at the double, supremely fit, right shoulder
to the cliff, left shoulder to the void. He could have run all night.

Except that on the inside of the widening in the path he had
passed a second previously, the time pencil of Miller's blasting
charge had come to the end of its sixty-minute career.

A gout of flame blasted straight out of the cliff face, and a clap of
thunder drove Gruber's eardrums together in the middle of his head.
He staggered, head ringing. A flying chunk of stone caught him in
the small of the back, and he would have staggered again, except
that the foot meant to take his weight found not ground but space.

He fell with a long, depressed cry, bounced twice, and had time to regain terminal velocity before he went into the olive trees below.

So he was not in a position to see what his comrades in the pursuit squad of the Wolf commando saw: that in the area of the blast the path they had been following no longer existed, and in its place was a cliff face as clear and lacking in footholds as a billiard table stood on its end.

Not that there was any point worrying about it. As the *Leutnant* lost no time in explaining, nobody was going back anyway. The order of the night was hot pursuit. The enemy had attempted to mine the path. Poor Gruber had taken what had been meant for all of them. Meanwhile, there was no time for hanging around.

The *Sonderkommando* turned and resumed the chase.

They trotted up the path, along the cliff, into a steep-sided valley. It was dark, and the radio did not work in this place of cliffs and ravines. After three hours' running, they found themselves on a bare mountainside, in a steep-canted field of boulders that stood silent and ominous on the starlit rock. Here the *Leutnant* rejected with fury a suggestion that they should bivouac, the better to continue the search at dawn. *'Vorwärts!'* he cried. 'Onward!'

At that precise moment, seven miles, three gorges and two thousand five hundred vertical feet away, Able Seaman Nelson was reaching the end of his tether.

They were still walking. Nelson had difficulty remembering a time when he had not been walking. His feet were sliding in his boots, whether in blood or the fluid of burst blisters he did not dare look. The cut in his arm had always been painful. Now it had set up a deep, deadly throb that travelled up the inside of his bicep and into his armpit. It would have been at the centre of his world, that throbbing, had there been room for it.

But all there was room for at the centre of Nelson's world was terror.

Not that he was a coward. You could not be an AB on an MTB, and fight your way through nights full of tracer bullets and high-octane petrol, and be a coward. Ashore in Portsmouth, after an air raid, he had come close to a George Cross, burrowing into the teetering pile of rubble that had once been a house, ARP and fire brigade shouting at him, don't be a bloody fool, come back, she'll collapse; but Nelson had kept going, found the middle-aged woman in the flowery housecoat, dragged her back out into the rain and the searchlights and the metallic clink of falling shrapnel.

But the MTB and Portsmouth had been with his mates. Now, Nelson had a hole in his arm the size of a slit trench, and he was blundering around some mountains with the Old Man, who had gone barmy, four bandits in uniforms without insignia, and a Greek bint with rolling eyes and grinding teeth who gave him the willies. It was the people and the mountains that were getting to Nelson. At sea, you fought your gun and took your chance with your mates, and while you did not like it unless you were bloody cracked, you could put up with it, like. The dry land was too bloody dry, and the people were too bloody violent, and you could see the look in their eye while they tried to kill you, and that was just not bloody on. A couple of hours ago there had been all that shooting down the hill, and a hell of a bang, God knew what that had been about. And now they were on this terrible path, black as the inside of a cow, and any minute now some Jerry might pop out from behind a rock and say, boo, you're dead –

For the seventy-third time since sunset, Nelson caught his boot on a rock, stumbled, jolted his arm, and bit his lip to stop himself whimpering. Because this was not going to end. You had to face it. Things were going to get worse, not better. It gave him the willies, and that was bleeding that.

Ahead, Clytemnestra's voice said something in Greek. Nelson followed the dim hulk of the person in front up a steep slope towards a small light that had somehow started to shine. Another bloody cave.

But it was not a cave. The walls were too smooth, the angles too perfect. In the middle of the floor was a sort of raised stone plinth. On the plinth, the big Greek man – he must have joined the file in the dark, though Nelson could not remember seeing it happen – was spreading the little tins of compo rations, a bottle of brandy, a radio.

Nelson slumped to the ground, propped his back against the wall, and let his head loll on his breast. The lanky American spoke, in Greek. Clytemnestra replied. Nelson did not like not understanding. 'What does she say?' he said, querulous.

Miller looked at him, saw a blue-white face, black circles under haunted eyes. 'I said what is this place. She said it's a tomb.' He gestured at the plinth. 'The dining table there is where they laid the stiff. Eat something.' He waved a hand at the compo and the brandy.

But Nelson's stomach was a small, clenched fist. He could not eat. He could only sit there and strain his ears at the night, at the thousand miniature nights contained in the shadows of this house of the dead. This house of the soon-to-be-dead . . .

He tried to get up. The muscles of his legs were too stiff. He toppled sideways. Someone was shouting, frantic, in his voice. Hands grabbed him, laid him out, tipped brandy down his throat.

He fell into a sort of coma. He was dimly aware of someone doing something to his bad arm, of a pinprick. Then there was a deep, buzzing silence.

They sat around the stove. The little blue flames cast fluttering shadows on the tomb's ceiling. Nelson and Wills sprawled along a wall, Nelson's arm new-dressed, half a syrette of morphine running in his blood; Wills snoring in a heavy, exhausted drone. Clytemnestra had folded her hands over her stomach and put her head on her pack, and was sleeping quietly as the tomb's original tenant.

The remaining four men did not sleep; not yet. Their cigarettes pulsed and glowed. They were resting, but it was the rest of a hunting animal, or a latched spring, ready to leap from repose into violence with no intervening period of acceleration. Carstairs sat a little apart from the others, cleaning his machine pistol.

Mallory said, 'Captain Carstairs, the court martial is in session.'

Carstairs raised an eyebrow, not lifting his eyes from the breech mechanism.

Mallory said, 'By your actions this afternoon you have endangered the lives of your comrades and the success of the operation.'

'Operational necessity,' said Carstairs. He yawned, and lay back on the musty floor.

Andrea spoke. His voice had a note in it that Mallory had never heard before, and in the flicker of the stove-flames his bear-like shoulders seemed to fill the vault of the tomb. 'Captain Carstairs,' he said. 'The charge is that today, having been posted sentry, you did desert your post in the face of the enemy. The penalty is death. You may speak in your defence.'

Under the cold lash of that voice, Carstairs seemed for a moment to freeze. Then he laughed, a thin, nervous laugh. 'I don't think Admiral Dixon will agree,' he said.

'I am not interested in Admiral Dixon.' Andrea's hands moved. There was the metallic sound of a Schmeisser cocking lever.

Carstairs looked at his own weapon, in pieces on the groundsheet. He looked at Mallory and Miller, and found no comfort. His face was impassive, faintly quizzical, but there was a little sheen of sweat on the upper lip. He said, 'If you put it like that.' He took out the gold case, and selected a cigarette with deliberation.

There is an explanation,' he said, eventually. 'I have orders of
my own, from Admiral Dixon. Who incidentally will not be very
pleased to hear that you see fit to override his authority and haul
me in front of a kangaroo court –'

The Schmeisser in Andrea's hand moved upwards an inch, so
Carstairs could see all the way down the barrel. Carstairs did his
best to look bored. 'But since you want an explanation, you can
have one. There was a survivor.'

'A survivor?'

'After the *Kormoran* was torpedoed. Before she went down.
Apparently someone hopped on to a life raft, bit of driftwood, God
knows, and paddled off downwind and landed on Kynthos. This
person was picked up by the Germans, in a very bad way, in a
coma, actually, just before the partisans blocked the road.'

'How do we know this?' said Andrea.

'Agent in Parmatia radioed in,' said Carstairs. 'That's who I was
looking for in town last night.' He made it sound as if he had been
doing the rounds of the night spots. 'But apparently they got
themselves killed shortly after they sent the signal.' Andrea's face
was like stone. 'Anyway, they told me in the village that this
survivor was in the ambulance, in the convoy heading over the
road as soon as it opened. Like today. He's still unconscious, apparently. Important fellow in ways I am not at liberty to disclose. I
have orders to debrief him. If you don't like that, you can always
check with Admiral Dixon, or your Captain, what d'ye call him,
Jensen.'

Andrea said, 'That's it?'

Carstairs shrugged, nonchalant as his voice. His eyes were not
nonchalant, though. They shifted between Mallory and Miller.
'Just about,' he said. He put his hands on his knees, and composed
his features into something like manly frankness. 'Look here. I
can't say I liked sliding off into the blue. But I thought, well, an
hour and a half, make a recce, and it would be just my neck, not
everyone else's. How was I to know that Captain Mallory would
come bumbling in and queer my pitch, what?'

Miller was watching Mallory. The New Zealander's face was still
and mild, but he was watching Carstairs closely. 'You wanted to
talk to this . . . survivor,' said Mallory.

'That's it.'

'And how were you planning to do that?'

'I told you,' said Carstairs, with the exasperation of a teacher
repeating a lesson to a small child. 'It was a recce. I wanted to see

if the road was open. How am I meant to talk to an unconscious man in a military ambulance?'

Mallory said, 'Why do you need to debrief this man?'

Carstairs smiled, all teeth and superiority. 'Sorry, old boy,' he said. 'Love to help. But, well, Admiral's orders. No can do.'

Silence fell, except for Wills' snores and the bluster of the wind in the tomb's entrance.

Finally, Mallory said, 'He's got a point.'

Miller said, 'Has he hell.'

Andrea's black eyes snapped at him. 'Thank you, Corporal,' he said. That will be enough.' The Schmeisser moved away from Carstairs' eye. 'Captain Carstairs, you are a member of this force, and will in future communicate your operational intentions to its field commander. The record will show that you have been reprimanded without loss of pay.'

Carstairs nodded, as if at a waiter who had brought him his change. He said, 'I knew you'd see sense. Now if you'll excuse me, I'll get forty winks.'

Mallory took first watch, sitting outside the tomb under the thick mat of the stars. The night was quiet, except for the sigh and bluster of the breeze in the rocks.

There was a faint movement at his side. When he looked round, he saw Andrea, blotting out a sizeable patch of sky.

'What do you think?' said Andrea.

'Jensen says he's okay.'

'Jensen's in England.'

'Quite.'

There was a silence. Andrea and Mallory had worked together for a year; the kind of year that contains more than most lifetimes. They knew each other well. 'So,' said Andrea. 'There is a problem, my Keith?'

Mallory lit a cigarette. 'He says he was on a recce,' he said. 'So when I caught up with him, he was standing on the cliff directly above the ambulance, with a grenade in his hand and the pin out. And I thought, strange kind of recce. That's the problem.'

'I see,' said Andrea. 'Truly, I see.' There was another pause. 'But we must keep this man, because these are the orders of Jensen. Mouth shut and eyes open, I think.'

'Of course,' said Mallory. Andrea was right. But it was the last thing you needed, on an operation like this.

'I'll do the dawn patrol,' said Mallory. Andrea nodded, and went in to sleep.

SIX

Thursday
0300–1200

Miller woke Mallory three hours after midnight. He tumbled out thumping-headed, dry-mouthed, to stand his guard. It came hard to some soldiers, this wakefulness in the dead time before dawn, when the metabolism was at its slowest. But Mallory was used to early mornings. He had spent his life in mountains where you could not climb after eleven a.m. because of the deadly rain of rock let go by melting ice fields. So he lay a second, his eyes wide open. Then he put his hand to where he knew his weapon would be, swung on his pack and went out into the air.

The stars still hung in the sky. He went up a slope of rocks and stationed himself above the tomb entrance, in a niche of the boulders. There was nothing but the rock, and the stars, and the clean night air. His mind flew back to other mornings on the shoulders of Mount Cook, the white peaks of the Southern Alps all around, waiting in frozen stillness for the first pink touch of the sun.

He pulled out a slab of chocolate and a round of flat Greek bread, ate until he did not want to eat any more, then kept on eating. It was going to be the sort of day when a body needed all the fuel that could be crammed into it.

He analysed the possibilities. The two sailors would have to be parked somewhere; here, perhaps. Must ask Clytemnestra. There was Clytemnestra herself. Clytemnestra needed to be kept out of sight, or there would be reprisals.

And Carstairs. Carstairs was a climber. Carstairs could fight. But Carstairs was the most dangerous of the lot. Mallory had never seen the Greek as angry as he had been last night. The Schmeisser-point court martial might have looked theatrical, but Carstairs had been within seconds of having his brains on the tomb roof –

Mallory stiffened.

The sky was lightening now, turning a darker-than-battleship-grey that cast the jagged peaks around him into sharp relief. But that was not what had made Mallory sit up and very quietly work the cocking lever of his machine pistol.

Down among the ravines and gulches they had travelled the night before, he had heard the short, sharp yip of a hunting dog.

He got up, and slid down the slope and into the tomb. It smelt of sleep. He passed among the supine forms like a cold wind, Miller and Andrea first, then Carstairs and Clytemnestra. 'They've got bloodhounds,' he said. 'We must leave.'

'We go on,' said Clytemnestra. 'It is downhill. Not so difficult.'

Mallory left her to wake the others, and tumbled outside again. He, Miller and Andrea faded into the rocks. The dog yipped again, very close. Five men in SS camouflage smocks came round the corner. The one in the middle had a lead in his hand. On the end of the lead, straining, was a black-and-tan dog. A Doberman, actually, thought Mallory, with the inconsequence that comes of extreme stress. Not a bloodhound.

The dog started a continuous strangled baying, and turned up the hill towards the tomb mouth. Mallory put his Schmeisser to his shoulder and opened fire.

Nelson had slept badly. It was more like a coma than a sleep, a sort of delirium in which the dreams writhed below the surface like maggots in a wound. Everything was burning: the terraced house in Coventry where he had been brought up, the BSA motor bike he rode to work, the house where he had gone to rescue the woman in the housecoat, the MTB's bow gun crew: all solid and living one minute, the next stripped by the flames to rafter and bone, brick and tile and flesh melting away like wax. And the noise: the throbbing of his arm like an engine in the armpit, across to the heart, and with every heartbeat the engine accelerating in the horror of the dream, until the noise was continuous and Nelson knew he could not stand any more of this –

Then the real noise started, and Nelson slammed awake.

The roof was flickering with a hard blue-white light, and it was difficult to breathe because the tomb was full of fumes; the fumes of gunsmoke. In the blue-white flicker bodies were moving, made jerky by the flashes. There was the American running towards the door, and the big Greek in the entrance itself, rolling over and over, rising on one knee to squirt bullets into the dark, then rolling on and out beyond the light. Even Wills was up, dazed-looking, fumbling with the bolt of a big rifle.

Nelson hugged his arm, thirsty, head bloated with fever. He understood that there was nothing he could do. He could not shoot. He could not run. All that remained was to sit here and wait for the Germans to come barrelling in through the entrance – there would be a lot of them, he was sure of that, and the skipper and the Greek and the rest of them would be flattened by sheer weight of numbers. And when the Germans came in they would first look him in the eye and then blow him into little bits.

Nelson cringed at the thought.

Then he had an idea.

He was no good for fighting, not in this state. He was no bloody good to anyone. He would get himself out of the way, nice and safe.

Suddenly everything seemed radiantly simple.

But Nelson was leaving one thing out of account. In his veins there ran not only blood, and the throb of his wound, but also a considerable amount of morphine.

Andrea and Miller had had the same idea as Mallory. The rocks chattered with gunfire. The five Germans rolled over and were still. The dog, his handler dead, slunk whining into the boulders. Mallory lowered his gun.

Twenty-five more Germans came round the corner.

Mallory slammed a new clip into his Schmeisser and cursed. The new men were not in formation, like their late comrades in the dog squad. They had heard the gunfire. They were spread out among the boulders, bad targets for the Mauser, too distant for the Schmeissers. Normally, Andrea and Mallory and Miller would have faded into the landscape. But Clytemnestra and Carstairs and the sailors were still inside the cave.

Mallory began to sweat. This was the guerrilla's nightmare: an assault by superior enemy forces on a fixed position. Either you faded, or the operation was finished. It was an evil decision to have to make.

Then all thoughts of the decision went out of his mind, and he was frozen by a strange and terrible sight.

A figure had walked out of the tomb; a strange figure, dressed in rags, with a blue-white face and red hair in a halo round his head. Nelson. Nelson with his good hand in the air, and his bad hand in its sling, and his eyes spinning in his head with terror and morphine.

'Oi!' he yelled in a high, cracked voice. 'Me sailor. Me not soldier. Me non-combatant, prisoner of war, you savvy, cock? You no shoot, got that?' He stumbled down the little path towards the rocks where the Germans lay hidden. The silence was so intense that Mallory could hear the squinch of a pebble under his foot.

There is a German behind that rock, thought Mallory, as Nelson approached a tall, pyramid-shaped slab. And I can't cover Nelson because he won't know what to do if I open fire . . .

Nelson was nearly at the pyramid rock, still waving his good arm and yelling. As he passed the rock, a camouflaged arm shot out and grabbed his collar, and a black boot kicked him behind the knees so they collapsed and he was suddenly kneeling on the path, sideways-on to the observers above the tomb. As Mallory watched, a hand with a Luger came out and dug into the nape of Nelson's neck. The dull *whap* of the shot floated up the hill.

Nelson smashed forward on to his face and lay twitching.

Mallory had seen a lot of life, and a lot of death, too. But this cold assassination of an unarmed man in the process of surrender froze him to the spot. And that split second he stood frozen he heard a soft, metallic sound, and a voice behind him said in heavily-accented English, 'Drop your gun.'

He dropped it. There was no chance of doing anything else. The order had only been an order, but the sound had been a rifle bolt. He waited for the bullet in the back of the neck, his mind clear of thoughts, his eyes on the mountains, rank on serried rank under the pink dawn sky.

The shot did not come.

The voice behind him said, *'Marsch.'*

Mallory marched.

He saw Miller walking towards him, a rifle at his nape. He saw the tomb mouth full of camouflage smocks, heard shouting, saw Carstairs come out, hands in the air, Wills, stumbling, eyes screwed up against the painful light of dawn.

A German strutted up to Miller, a *Leutnant*, sharp-faced under a grey peaked cap. 'Is this all?' he said, in English.

'All what?' said Miller.

'All your people,' said the German.

'Nope,' said Miller.

Mallory's eyes rested on him with some curiosity. He trusted Miller. But he trusted Andrea too. And Andrea had disappeared, and so had Clytemnestra. He and his fellow-prisoners might be in considerable danger. But with Andrea on the loose, so were the Germans. What was Miller playing at?

'Where are they?' said the German.

'As a citizen of the United States of America,' said Miller, 'I see all people as my people. Like it says, "Bring me your poor, your huddled millions" –'

'Masses,' said Mallory.

'I thought it was millions,' said Miller.

'Silence!' yelled the *Leutnant*, 'Kneel!'

Miller looked at him, then at Mallory. They knelt.

'What is your mission on Kynthos?' snapped the *Leutnant*.

'Name, rank and number,' said Mallory. 'I will give them to your superior officer.'

The Germans behind the rocks were coming out of cover, drifting towards them, curious now they had caught up with their quarry. Bunch up, said Mallory in his head. That's good.

'Together,' said Wills, who sounded stronger and more definite, 'with an official protest. How dare you.' He was angry to the point of incoherence. 'How dare you in contravention of the Geneva Convention summarily execute one of my –'

The *Leutnant*'s jackboot sent him sprawling among the rocks.

'Now,' said the *Leutnant*. 'Tell me now, or I will shoot you, this man first.' Mallory could hear the shuffle of boots on rock as the men gathered round. *Sonderkommando* behaviour, he thought. Not *Wehrmacht*. *Wehrmacht* were soldiers. This lot were murderers.

'Noo!' cried Miller. 'Please!' He cast himself on the ground. Mallory cast himself down too, abasing himself.

And incidentally taking cover.

A sleet of lead blasted out of the rocks and the tomb mouth. The *Leutnant* screamed and fell across Mallory. Mallory grabbed the man's Schmeisser. A German saw him move and brought his machine pistol round. Mallory saw the muzzle flash, felt the officer's body shake as the rounds meant for him thumped into the *Leutnant*'s torso. Then his own Schmeisser was hammering, and the German's machine pistol was firing in a great arc in the sky as his dead finger tightened on the trigger.

After that everything was quiet, except for a voice, shouting. At first it shouted in German. 'Hands up!' it said. 'You are covered!'

The three Germans left standing raised their hands. 'Keep hidden!' roared the voice, in Greek. Talking to Clytemnestra. Mallory climbed to his feet. Miller was already up.

Somewhere, a radio said, in German, 'A Force, A Force, come in.'

Mallory found the set under a body, rolled it aside, lifted the mike to his mouth. 'A Force,' he said. 'Mission complete.'

'Please give me a code word with that,' said the voice.

Mallory took his thumb off the transmit switch. 'What is the code word?' he said to the nearest living German.

'Schultz, *Feldwebel* 175609 –'

Something moved at the corner of Mallory's eye. It was Carstairs, with a Luger. He knocked the German to the ground with the barrel and jammed it into the man's mouth. Mallory heard the pop as a tooth broke. 'The man said, code word,' said Carstairs. He pulled the gun out of the man's mouth. 'One. Two –'

The German had no way of telling whether Carstairs was going to count to three or fifty, but with a gun muzzle half an inch from his eye socket he was not going to hang around to find out. 'Wild Hunt,' he said.

Mallory thumbed the transmit switch. 'Wild Hunt,' he said, and released it.

The set hissed an empty wash of static. There was no reply.

The German with no front teeth laughed. 'You are out of time. They are looking for you already.'

'Bastard,' said Carstairs, and cocked the Luger. The German turned grey. Sweat stood on his forehead as he stared at death.

'Leave him,' said Mallory.

Carstairs raised an eyebrow.

Mallory said, 'Take their clothes.'

'Clothes?' said Carstairs, looking down at his own immaculately-tailored tunic. 'They won't fit.'

'Best-dressed corpse in the mountains, right?' said Miller, who was already taking off his trousers. 'Change everything but your boots.'

'Why?'

'So your feet don't get sore,' said Miller, struggling into the camouflage smock and hanging the radio on his belt. 'Move it.' He grinned at Carstairs, a grin not at all sincere. 'Pardon me. Move it, Captain.'

Carstairs moved it.

They rolled the bodies over a cliff. They took away weapons and ammunition, and the survivors' boots and socks. Then they bound and blindfolded them, and left them barefoot and helpless in a field of razor-edged lava rock. Nelson they buried as best they could. Then they resumed the march, Mallory first, Wills after him, then Carstairs and Clytemnestra, with Andrea bringing up the rear.

They were on a sort of plateau now, a high, windswept place without cover, still cold with the morning chill, but brilliantly lit by the low sun. They marched on, towing long shadows from their boot heels, squinting against the sun in their eyes. Mallory hoped nobody would put any aeroplanes up. It was a forlorn hope, he was pretty sure. German uniforms or no German uniforms, German radio procedures were cast in stone. A dud procedure meant trouble. And these were not the kind of people who closed their eyes to trouble –

Someone stumbled into Mallory's back. He looked round in time to see Wills plough off to the right, trip over a stone and fall flat on his face.

'Leave him,' said Carstairs.

Mallory ignored him. He went and crouched beside Wills. For the first time, he saw the damage the *Leutnant*'s boot had done. The man's face was a mask of blood, the bruise on his temple the colour of blue-black ink.

'Leave me,' mumbled Wills.

Miller came up, squatted and took out the first-aid kit. He said, 'Hold up,' and trickled drinking water between his cracked lips. 'Think you can walk?'

'Course,' croaked Wills. 'Dizzy spell.' He got half-way to his feet, then toppled sideways in the dust.

Andrea said, 'Come.' He lifted Wills like a child, and hauled him on to his back. 'We'll find some shade.'

'Quickly.' Clytemnestra was chewing her lower lip. 'We must cross this part. Then the ground is broken. Safer –'

Mallory held up his hand.

The breeze sighed in the rocks. Above the breeze, another sound: the small, faint drone of an aeroplane's engine.

It was the Storch again; the same Storch. It saw them straight away, circled lazily in the deep blue morning.

'Wave,' said Mallory.

They all waved, even Wills, on Andrea's back, raised a lethargic hand: a patrol of *Waffen-SS* saluting their comrades in the wilderness.

But Mallory was thinking radio. The observer would have been talking. Either the ground patrols had a listening schedule, to which they should have responded. Or he was talking to his base station, reporting five men and a Greek heading east, and the base station would be checking where the Greek fitted in . . .

After another half-hour's march they were in broken ground, sloping away to the eastward. Clytemnestra walked out ahead now, moving fast and light among the hillocks and boulders like a hound making a cast. After ten minutes, she stopped and beckoned. They walked over to her.

She was standing at the head of a seam of the ground, deepened by running water into a groove no more than three feet wide. She led them down the groove. After a hundred yards it was already a ravine, plunging steeply downwards, disappearing from view round a colossal buttress of rotten stone. There was a path along the right-hand side of the ravine; a narrow ribbon of flat ground. This path Clytemnestra took. Another Goddamned goat path, thought Miller gloomily, trudging along. The German who had originally owned the smock he was wearing had been an eater of raw onions, by the smell of it –

'Here,' said Clytemnestra.

They had arrived at the end of the gorge, on a ledge balanced like an epaulette on a vast shoulder of rock. The ledge was perhaps thirty feet wide. On it were a couple of walls that might once have been part of dwellings. On its inside edge the cliff was patched with the stone fronts of cave-houses. 'Very hard place to find,' said Clytemnestra. 'Once, klephts live here, bandits. Now, nobody.' She walked across to a patch of green moss and ferns between two of the walled caves. A trickle of water fell from a projecting rock into a bowl roughly carved from the stone. 'Everything you need,' she said. Mallory was looking east.

Beyond the ledge, the ground dropped away three thousand feet in a series of precipices over a vast and hazy gulf. The bottom of the gulf was flat and green, marked into rectangular fields. At the southern end of the fields, a dark line, presumably a fence, separated out what looked like a group of huts and a brown-and-yellow expanse of baked earth and dry grass that must be an aerodrome, its eastern and northern sides formed by the sea.

Mallory raised his glasses to his eyes.

Beyond the fields was a stretch of reeds and whitish flats in which water glittered under the sun. It must have been the best part of a mile wide. On the far side the ground rose again, steep and black; the remains of a plug of magma, Lieutenant Robinson's volcano, remnants of a cone of pumice and ash washed away by time. There were buildings up there, some white and gleaming, others ruined; and some, as Mallory focused his glasses, trailing a faint plume of dust.

'Aerial,' said Carstairs.

Mallory panned his glasses up an apparently endless face of bare black cliff. At the cliff's summit, he saw the spider-like tracery of wires and pylons. An aerial array, all right.

'They are building something,' said Clytemnestra. 'They take stone across, from the place down there.'

Three thousand feet below, a ruler-straight line ran from the base of the cliff, across the marshes, to a group of huts at the base of the Acropolis. 'What is it?' said Carstairs.

'Railway line,' said Clytemnestra. 'For stone and gravel.'

'Where's the quarry?' said Mallory.

She pointed straight down.

I'm a guy, not a fly,' said Miller.

Mallory was not listening. He said, 'Ropes. Weapons. Anything not vital, leave it up here. Clytemnestra, can you stay here for twenty-four hours? We'll be back.'

She pointed down the ledge, to a place where the path narrowed, and there were the hard outlines of more ruined buildings. 'There is the Swallow's Nest,' she said.

'Password,' said Mallory. 'You'll need one.'

'Jolly boating weather,' said Wills.

'Shoot anyone who doesn't use it.'

'Jolly what?' said Clytemnestra.

'Never mind –'

'Quiet,' said Andrea. Over the dim rumour of humanity from the vale below there came once again the sound of an aeroplane engine.

They were standing on a wide part of the ledge, smooth as a parade ground, without cover. Standing up or lying down, they would stick out like a poached egg on a black table.

'Wave,' said Mallory.

The Storch came round the escarpment at eighty knots, not more than a hundred feet out. The people in SS uniform waved, the way they had waved last time. Mallory could see the faces of the pilot and the observer, curious, blank behind their goggles, not waving back. It went past once. 'That's it,' said Carstairs.

The Storch dropped a wing and turned, so slow and low it almost seemed to hover. Mallory could see the observer's lips moving as he spoke into his microphone. They were being checked up on. The carnage by the tomb would have been discovered by now.

'Wave,' said Mallory. Bluff, and bluff again, and hope like hell it worked, though hope grew harder to sustain –

But Carstairs had his Schmeisser at his shoulder, and its clatter was ringing in the cliffs, and the Storch was banking away, and a long line of pock marks appeared in the Storch's unarmoured belly. The plane's bank became a roll, a staggering roll that turned into a sideslip that would have been a spin except that half-way through the first turn the face of the escarpment came out to meet the aircraft. A wing touched delicately, crumpled like the foil from a cigarette packet. The propeller churned into the rock, the nose telescoped, a tiny spark of flame flicked back on the cowling, and among the noise of buckled and cracking metal came the big, solid whoomp of the fuel tank blowing. The Storch came momentarily to rest, perched nose-up on a sixty-degree slope, blazing from propeller boss to tailskid. Mallory could see the observer beating at the cockpit cover, jammed because of the heat. Then the plane began to slide tail-first into the abyss, gathering speed, leaving a long plume of black smoke, bouncing out from the cliff, over and over, breaking up as it fell.

Then it was gone, and all that remained was the smoke, tangled in the crags and bushes in the morning calm.

If you wanted a pointer to this place, thought Miller, you could not have done much better unless you had picked up a dirty great paintbrush and made an arrow on the cliff and marked it SHOOT HERE.

'Good show,' said Carstairs, stroking his silly moustache.

'Excellent,' said Miller, wearily.

Mallory felt tired to the marrow of his bones. And it had not yet begun. There would be men up here. A lot of men.

'All right,' he said. 'As I was saying before we were so rudely interrupted. We'll get down there. Clytemnestra. Situation's changed. You'd better come too.'

Clytemnestra said, 'No.'

'Oh?'

'Wills cannot move, not just now. The hiding places up here are very good. There will be no trouble. If we came, we would be in the way.' She smiled, a ferocious flash of teeth in her face. 'I think you are good fighters, you three.' She turned to Carstairs. 'But you will get yourself killed.' She said in Greek, 'And these other people, too. You are like a barnyard cock. A lot of noise and fuss, but that is all. No patience. A child, not a man.'

'What does she say?' said Carstairs.

'She admires you intensely,' said Miller, who had learned good Greek in the process of blowing up targets in Crete and the Peloponnese.

'Objectives,' said Mallory, hurriedly. 'Listen.'

'Permission to, er, speak,' said Carstairs.

Mallory grinned at him, a grin without humour. 'No,' he said. 'You will for the purposes of the next phase of this operation consider yourself under my orders, and keep quiet. Do I make myself clear?'

Behind its mask of sweat and grime Carstairs' face was smooth, his eyes remote and distant. 'Perfectly,' he said.

'Our objective is to destroy the rocket factory,' said Mallory. 'Yours is different. I authorize you to disclose it, to avoid confusion.'

'It would be a great pity if we . . . interfered with one another,' said Andrea. His big hands were resting on the Schmeisser, light and casual. The ledge was full of a studied politeness; but under the politeness lay a wire-taut thread of violence.

Carstairs was not stupid. He knew that for the third time, he had made life complicated and dangerous for the rest of the Thunderbolt Force. He knew that these men were used to achieving their objectives, and did not let anyone or anything stand in their way. The time had come for a dose of frankness – carefully measured, but a dose none the less. 'I'll go after the aerials,' he said.

Mallory had been sitting apart, binoculars on the plain and the Acropolis. 'It's a bad climb to solo,' he said.

'I'll manage,' said Carstairs. He had his own glasses out. Things were moving on the airfield. A Trimotor was taxiing, and a group of vehicles was parked at the root of the causeway that took the road across the marsh to the Acropolis. There was an ambulance among them. 'I'm off,' he said.

'Your objectives,' said Andrea. This time, the hands on the Schmeisser looked firmer. 'The aerials. Then this person you have to . . . debrief?'

'For Christ's sake,' said Carstairs. 'This is need-to-know information.'

'We need to know,' said Andrea flatly.

Far below, the Trimotor was taxiing to the downwind end of the runway.

'Very well,' said Carstairs. 'If you insist. The *Kormoran* was boarded before she sank. She was carrying new German code books. Maybe this . . . survivor saw the boarding party. Highly likely, actually. In

Parmatia they said he was unconscious. I'm hoping he still is. If he has woken up and told the Germans what he saw and they transmit the news back to Berlin, or Italy, or anywhere else, then bang goes a very useful intelligence source. A vital intelligence source, you might say. So I don't care what you men are doing, I'm going after those aerials to shut them up. And then I'm going to find the man who was in the ambulance, awake or asleep.'

'And then?' said Mallory.

Carstairs' face was hard as stone. 'Use your imagination, Captain,' he said.

So now they were assassins, thought Mallory. Not soldiers. There was a difference.

'Over there,' said Mallory, pointing at the dark massif opposite. 'Northern end. There's a village.'

'Once a village,' said Clytemnestra. 'Now a prison. For slaves.'

'Slaves?'

'The men of the island. The Germans make them work in their factory.'

'Well, well,' said Mallory. 'We rendezvous there at midnight.'

'Where?'

'There is a little street by the church,' said Clytemnestra. 'Athenai Street. It is dark. There are no guards.'

'How do you know?'

'We go there.'

'I thought it was a prison.'

'It is. But we are Greeks. We will wait from midnight here.' She pointed to a spot on the map in her hand. 'Then if you have not found us we will come to find you at dawn.'

Far below, the Trimotor was up and off the runway, a minute grey cross chasing its shadow over the dim marshes. Soon, the plateau above would be full of paratroops.

'Moving out,' said Mallory.

How come I always say never again, thought Miller, and every time I say it I am doing it again within twenty minutes?

'Go,' said Mallory.

Miller did not look down. He knew what was underneath him: three hundred feet of cliff, with a slope of sharp scree to bounce on, then another precipice –

He braced the doubled rope over his shoulder and up between his legs, and started to walk backwards down the cliff. His packful of explosives wanted to unbalance him. His knees wanted to shake him loose. His breakfast wanted to fling itself into the glad light of day –

'Hold up,' said Carstairs' voice. Miller found himself teetering on something that Mallory would probably have called a ledge, but as far as Miller was concerned was no bigger than a bookshelf, and a shelf for small books at that.

'Between the legs,' said Carstairs, with his oily smile. 'Up the back. Round the –'

But Miller had gone, bounding out into space, half a hundredweight of explosives on his back. He did not like heights, but he liked Carstairs even less.

When Miller hit the scree slope, Andrea was already there. Carstairs and Mallory followed, pulled the ropes down and belayed again. Andrea and Carstairs, then Miller and Mallory went down again, and again, until they were standing on a scrubby shoulder of rock, a stratum that had stood up to rain and wind and sun better than the rest of the cliff. Mallory and Carstairs were coiling the ropes, making the coils fast, slinging them on their small packs.

Once Miller's knees had stopped shaking, he had time to recognize a change in Carstairs. Miller on a cliff was a fish out of water. But as he watched Carstairs coil the rope and run his eye over the next pitch, he recognized that this was a man in his element.

The hard stratum made a broad, rubbly road along the cliff face, inaccessible from above and below. They had already lost two thousand feet in height. The valley floor was closer now, and from somewhere ahead and downhill came the pant and clank of heavy machinery.

The Tante Ju had gone overhead twenty minutes previously. If the Germans had dogs, they would be on the ledge by now. Miller wondered how Wills would be doing. Okay, as long as he had Clytemnestra there.

Miller frowned.

Clytemnestra reminded him of someone, for a moment he could not think who. As he scrambled through the dense and thorny underbrush, he remembered. Those eyes, that jaw, that figure; Darling Miss Daisy.

Darling Miss Daisy had been a good friend of his in Chicago during the Dirty Thirties. Darling Miss Daisy's speciality had been removing all her clothes except a garter in front of the patrons of the El Cairo Tearooms, a rendezvous whose definition of tea was loose at best. As a token of their appreciation, the tea drinkers would stuff high-denomination banknotes into Miss Daisy's garter. Miss Daisy had been a good friend of Miller's, and had one night asked him along to witness the performance. This he had done with much appreciation. By the close of her act Darling Miss Daisy, nude except for the garter and a pair of high-heeled pumps, had collected some eight hundred dollars, in those days a most considerable sum.

At this point, a citizen called Moose Michael had jumped out of the crowd, grabbed Miss Daisy from behind, and pushed a gun into her swan-like neck. Miss Daisy was no stranger to this sort of carry-on, and relaxed. Guys with what this guy had on his mind on their minds always made a bad move sometime, and that was when you set the dogs on them.

But Moose Michael's hand was not groping for Darling Miss Daisy's outstanding assets. It was groping for the money in the garter. This was not in the rules. Miss Daisy clenched her perfectly-formed fist, rolled her flashing black eyes, and gun in her neck or not, broke Moose Michael's jaw in four places.

Miller could see a lot of Darling Miss Daisy in Clytemnestra. Trudging on through the scrub, he crossed her and Wills off the worry-list.

Ahead, the clank of machinery was getting louder.

SEVEN

Thursday
1200–2000

Leutnant Priem had been in North Africa, and at the invasion of Crete, and most recently in Yugoslavia. As he skirted the shoulder of the ravine (they could have done with a dog; but the dogs had disappeared) he thought: this could be a great posting, this island, if the commanding officer used his brains. One stupid Storch crashes, observer's been drinking Metaxa, screaming down the radio, and Wolf panics, and here we are pretending to be mountain goats, heading for his bloody map reference as if we were doing a security sweep for a Führer visit . . .

The path came out on the ledge. Cicadas trilled in the noonday sun, and the air was heavy with the whiff of thyme and rue. Priem cast a scornful eye over the ruined buildings. How could you believe in the glories of Greek culture when the people lived in such hovels? Degenerate scum. No better than animals. Of course, nobody had been here for years . . .

'Search the place!' he barked. He lit a cigarette and sat in the shade. A lizard lay on a slab of rock, bringing itself up to temperature for the next hunting trip. Lucky damned lizard. Nothing to do but sit around in the sun all day. While Priem had to make a pretence of searching these places where nobody had been, ever. That was Wolf for you. Savage, but *gründlich*. Thorough –

'*Herr Leutnant?*' yelled a voice.

Priem stamped out his cigarette and went to interview the sergeant.

'Buildings empty,' said the sergeant. 'Found this here, sir.' He pointed with the tip of his jackboot at a little pile of golden cylinders. Cartridge cases.

Priem was suddenly not relaxed any more. 'Good,' he said. They were Schmeisser cases. 'And the aeroplane?' he said.

'Over here,' said the sergeant. 'One hundred and three metres down.'

'Rope,' said Priem.

'Rope in place,' said the NCO.

The wreckage of the Storch was draped over a crag. Priem climbed round it, scrutinized the burned remains of the pilot and the observer, frowning slightly. He paused to examine the line of bullet-holes starting at the wing-root and vanishing under the belly.

He climbed back to the ledge in silence. 'Sergeant,' he said. 'We will establish a field HQ here. Search again, particularly down the cliffs. And give me that radio.'

Higher on the mountain, in what would once have been the uppermost street of the bandit village, Clytemnestra and Wills lay in darkness. It was a cool darkness, smelling slightly of mould, but that was not surprising, since their hiding place was situated under the ruins of the washing-copper in the corner of four walls that had once served as a laundry.

This village of bandits was a village for which searches and razzias were no novelty. The crusaders had rummaged it, then the Turks, then the Greeks. The Germans were merely the latest in line.

Just as long (Clytemnestra reflected, listening to the concussed muttering of Wills) as they did not bring their dogs.

It was a tidy enough quarry, as quarries went; a big horseshoe cut in the cliff, fans of fallen stone at the base, a couple of diggers moving across a white floor trailing clouds of dust. There was a crusher, a big machine with a hopper and a black funnel that belched smoke, panting and grinding, discharging crushed stone into another, larger hopper. Under the larger hopper ran a railway track. As the men on the quarry lip watched, a train reversed into the quarry and positioned the first of its four trucks under the hopper. The hopper-release opened. A dose of crushed stone roared into the truck. The locomotive moved on. Another dose roared into the second truck. Move. Roar. Move. Roar. The locomotive hissed steam and began to pull out, gathering speed.

'Well?' said Carstairs.

'Wait,' said Mallory, eyes down on his watch.

The train bustled off across the plain, shrinking on its converging lines, speeding on to a causeway across the marsh, shrinking still. At the far end a cloud of white dust rose, then whipped away on the breeze. The breeze was up, now. A long edge of grey was travelling down the sky from the north. 'Twelve minutes,' said Mallory. 'Down we go.'

'Why?' said Carstairs.

The other men were slinging their packs. Miller pointed behind them, up the cliff, where little figures were descending on ropes, rummaging every ledge and hollow. 'They're still looking,' said Mallory. 'If we don't keep moving, they'll spot us.' Carstairs' mouth went dry. He scrambled to his feet, and down the flank of the quarry.

Far away, a long steam-whistle blew. The stone train had emptied its trucks. Now it was on its way back.

The four men went down the big fan of rubble on the quarry's northern side. The sun beat hot on the white stone as they ran, jumping from stone to stone, slithering in the small gravel, dust trailing from their heels. Men below looked up; labourers, mostly, in dusty overalls, trailing shovels, smoking cigarettes. They saw four men in camouflage smocks and *Wehrmacht* caps sliding down a pile of rubble. They were used to seeing soldiers; too many soldiers.

A sentry walked over, *Wehrmacht*, a *Feldwebel*, bored and dusty. The *Sonderkommando* had only been on the island three days. Mallory was betting that between the *Wehrmacht* guards and the *Sonderkommando* there would be no love lost. 'What do you want?' said the *Feldwebel*.

Mallory said, 'Mind your own damned business.'

The *Feldwebel* blinked. 'It is my business.'

'Perhaps you would like to explain that to *Hauptmann* Wolf.'

It did not work. 'I have my own officers,' said the *Feldwebel*. 'I do not need to talk to your nasty little *Hauptmann*.'

Mallory said, 'Very wise,' and started to walk past him towards the rock crusher.

'One moment,' said the sentry. 'Papers.'

'Don't be bloody stupid,' said Mallory. They were all walking now, towards the shade of the crusher, the sentry nearly running alongside them. The cloud had covered the sun. The air felt thick and moist.

The sentry got in front of them and unslung his rifle. 'Papers,' he said, and in his eye there was a meticulous glint, the legendary obstinacy of the German NCO. Mallory's heart sank.

'All right,' said Mallory. 'Shall we go and see your commanding officer?' Andrea was standing close behind him. Above them, the stilts of the rock crusher towered like the legs of an enormous insect. Mallory could feel Andrea moving. The guard's life was hanging by a thread. He looked Mallory up and down . . .

And saw his boots.

They were caked with dust, scuffed and battered. They were variations on a theme of British paratrooper's boots, manufactured for Mallory by Lobb of St James' Street, London, in collaboration and discussion with Black's of Holborn, expedition outfitters, fitted on his personal last, studded with pyramid nails hand-sharpened with the file Mallory carried in his pocket.

They should have been regulation German army jackboots.

There was no way of knowing what was in the *Feldwebel*'s mind, but Mallory could guess. The *Feldwebel* was a high priest of order and regulation, and the boots were heresy and sacrilege. The rifle came up. The eyes went round. The mouth opened to shout.

Mallory caught hold of the rifle barrel and pushed it sharply aside, stepping aside himself as he did so. Something very big and very fast came past him. The *Feldwebel* made a loud whooshing sigh, and crumpled forward over Andrea's fist. Andrea heaved him upright. He whipped out the knife he had driven up and under the man's ribs and into his heart, and in the same movement pushed the body back into the shadows under the crusher. The air was thick and still. A couple of big raindrops made dark blots in the dust.

Mallory lit a cigarette. Nobody said anything. Mallory blew smoke and said, 'Listen.'

They listened. Thunder rumbled. The rails were humming. Three minutes later, the train came in.

In the cab, the driver yawned. He was German, and so was his fireman. Give a Greek this job, and nothing would get done. The soldiers were as bad. They were meant to sign each load in and out as the train went through the gate in the fence by the guard-house. But they were *Wehrmacht*, not railwaymen. They had made him do all the signing at the beginning of his shift, so he could come and go as he liked –

The hopper roared. He pulled forward to the second red post, applied the brakes, turned to tell the fireman to chuck a bit more coal on. The fireman was blond, with blue eyes in a sooty face. The engine driver's mouth fell open.

This was not him. This was a man with a lean brown face and the coldest grey eyes the driver had ever seen.

The engine driver was about to shout when he felt something press against his leather jerkin. Something sharp. He felt the sting of cold steel in the fat on his belly. He closed his mouth. Fill up,' said the man. 'Then drive.'

The engine driver did not ask what had happened to his fireman. He said, 'The pressure is down.'

There were two men in the cab with him now: the lean-faced man and another with an eyebrow moustache. The man with the eyebrow moustache opened the firebox, and shovelled in coal. 'All right,' he said. 'Off we go, what?'

The driver blew out his oil-stained moustache. 'No,' he said. The thing in his belly moved a couple of inches. Skin broke. Blood rolled. It was raining now, hot, steamy rain, but the driver was suddenly bathed in cold sweat. 'Sorry,' he said. 'Yes. Of course. Very well.' His hand went to the regulator.

The leg of the hopper started to move. The train gathered speed. The quarry face faded into a grey curtain of rain. The gate loomed, guard post beside it. Mallory crouched on the footplate, and Carstairs bent, shovelling. The driver stared straight ahead, not acknowledging the wave of the crop-headed sentry drinking coffee in the wooden hut. And the train was travelling on an embankment over green fields. To the right was young corn and rain-grey sea. To the left was more young corn, terminated abruptly by a tall fence of mesh and barbed wire, with sheds and what looked like a fuel dump. Tailplanes stood like blunt sharks' fins beyond the sheds. Ahead, down the cylinder of the ancient locomotive, the fields fell away. The train rattled through a belt of reeds. Then there were rain-pocked pools of water on either side, dead-looking, dotted with clumps of sickly vegetation. The margins of the pools were crusted with white deposits. The place had a flat, washing-soda stink. When Mallory licked his lips, his tongue was dry with lime.

Over to the left was another causeway, carrying a road. At its landward side it passed between high fences, with red-and-white-striped barriers, huts for a platoon of soldiers, and a machine-gun post on either side, one to cover the approach, the other to cover the causeway itself. Mallory was glad he had decided to come by train.

The far shore was upon them: first a glacis of new stone, then a flat area that looked as if it had been reclaimed from the marsh. Beyond the flat area, the basalt colossus of the Acropolis rose like a wall. On the far side of the reclaimed area, behind a chainlink fence, was a vehicle park. As Mallory watched, an ambulance rolled in. The doors opened. A pair of orderlies lifted out a stretcher and ran with it through the rain and into a steel door set in the face of the cliff.

Mallory glanced at Carstairs. Carstairs was watching the ambulance too.

The tracks ran across the reclaimed area on a trestled viaduct ending in a set of buffers. Below the viaduct was a pile of crushed stone. Two huge concrete mixers churned alongside the rock piles.

The train slowed to a crawl. The driver raised his hand to another lever and pulled it. The train shuddered. Looking back over the tender, Mallory saw the hopper of the first wagon tilt sideways, and dump its cargo over the side of the trestle with a roar. An explosion of dust mingled with the rain and spread over the cab.

'Out,' said Mallory into the fog.

When the dust settled, Carstairs was gone.

The driver reversed the engine and opened the throttle. The train shuttled back across the marshes and the fields, past the bored sentry and into the quarry. Men were still moving on the escarpment, searching. They were lower down, now.

It was only a matter of time, thought Mallory. The clock had been ticking. And now it was about to strike.

The train slowed. The locomotive came to a halt by the first red post. The driver pointed. On the steel staging beside the cab was a lever. Mallory stepped off the footplate and hauled. The hopper opened with a roar. The truck filled. Miller and Andrea appeared out of the shadows. 'In,' said Mallory.

Up ahead in the sentry box, there was turbulent movement. The sweaty guard came out of the door into the rain, cramming a steel helmet on to his cropped head with one hand, waving a rifle in the other. He was shouting, his words drowned by the roar of the diggers and the huge metallic pant and grind of the crusher.

It was time to leave.

The sentry had slung his rifle and was dragging the gates shut across the railway line, boots slipping in the big puddles. The train picked up speed. Mallory saw his face, red-eyed. Then the locomotive hit the gates with a crash, and there was a squeal of tortured metal, and the train was through. When Mallory looked back, he saw a wisp of smoke coming from the guardhouse window. His eyes fell on Miller. 'I guess he sat in his ashtray,' said Miller, returning his gaze with great innocence.

The wisp of smoke became billows, turning orange at the roots as the Thermite bomb Miller had tossed through the window burned its way through the desk and into the floor, consuming paper and timber and the sentry's lunch, and most importantly the Bakelite of the telephone system.

'Now listen to me,' said Mallory.

They all listened. Even the train driver listened. He did not understand, but he trained his ears with maximum concentration on the string of incomprehensible syllables that came from the New Zealander's lips. All of them knew that what was about to happen in the next five minutes was a matter of life and death. The train driver thought it would probably be death.

As it turned out, the train driver did not need to understand. The train thundered through dense curtains of rain into the marshes. As he stood trembling with terror, he felt himself seized by strong arms and flung like a human cannonball at the swamp. He landed in a pool of foul-smelling water that stung his eyes like caustic. When he could breathe again, he struggled on to a mud bank and lay there coughing. After a while, he heard a terrible noise.

The engine driver was a railwayman, not a soldier. He decided that discretion was the better part of valour. He still was not seeing too well. But he could locate the noise, all right. He began to crawl, swim and flounder as fast as he could in the opposite direction.

Andrea threw the engine driver out of the right-hand side of the cab, away from the greatest number of prying eyes. Then Mallory hit the throttle and jammed it right forward. Even with a full quota of trucks, the locomotive was over powered for the job. Now it was only half-loaded. As steam blasted into its cylinders it leaped forward, belching smoke, and shot across the last of the embankment. By the time it hit the trestled dumping section, it was travelling at forty miles an hour, all thirty-five tons of it.

'Go,' said Mallory.

As Miller jumped, he could see a steam-shovel working, hazy and grey in the rain, but he was not thinking about witnesses, because he had fifty pounds of high explosive in his pack, and besides, Mallory and Andrea were beside him in mid-air. Then they were hitting the side of a pile of crushed stone a terrible whack, rolling over and over in a soup of falling water and wet stone dust.

The train thundered through the buffers, corkscrewed into mid-air, drive-wheels spinning. It lost momentum, crashed on to the rubble bed of the reclaimed ground, and tobogganed forward into the cliff. The basalt face crumpled its nose like a cardboard mailing tube and drove its boiler back into its firebox. There was a mighty roar and a thunderclap detonation. The reclaimed ground was suddenly obliterated by a scalding fog of escaping steam and rain and stone dust.

In that fog, a voice close to Miller's ear said, 'Go now.' Mallory's voice. In the background was shouting, and the churn of the concrete mixers, and a klaxon.

Miller got up, and ran behind Andrea in what he assumed was the right direction. Somewhere, the klaxon was still screaming.

Andrea was bleeding. Miller imagined he was probably bleeding himself. There was an entrance ahead, a hole in the cliff. The klaxon noise was coming out of the horn above the hole. Andrea said, in German, *'Herein.'* In. Somewhere a sergeant was shouting, a *Feldwebel* telling people to take cover. Wait a minute, thought the rational part of Miller, that is a German secret weapon factory, you can't go in there. Besides, where's Mallory?

But by that time he was inside the mountain, and with a steady hum of hydraulics the steel door was easing to . . .

Was shut.

In the cellar of the ruined house above the ledge, Clytemnestra woke suddenly from a fitful sleep. Next to her she could hear the breathing of Wills: regular breathing, shallow. He was improving, she thought. Men do improve after a few days, unless they die . . . Her thoughts strayed towards Achilles: her own dear brother Achilles, tall and strong and quick to laugh, his falcon's beak of a nose above the moustache, his eyes glittering with kindness and amusement. The whacking of rifle-butts on the door. The dragging away of Achilles, and her next – her last – sight of him, on the cart in the square, the Nazi swine yanking the noose taut over his head; the look in his poor eyes, that said this is really happening, to me . . .

Clytemnestra dragged her thoughts back from that thing too dreadful to contemplate. It had filled her mind with a turbulence that broke against the edge of her consciousness in waves of rage. She reached out her hand for her gun. She closed her fingers on the cool metal. It had a grounding effect, drew her back to the here and now.

To what it was that had woken her up.

When she remembered what that had been, she drew in her breath and did not let it out. And in the silence, that thing came again: half-way between a howl and a yelp, the distant sound of a

dog. Not the sheepdogs they used in the mountains: a more purposeful sound. The sound of a dog hunting. One of the black-and-
tan dogs the *Sonderkommando* used for hunting people.

She reached out and squeezed Wills' hand. The feel of his warm
flesh gave her encouragement. 'What is it?' he said.

She told him.

'Well,' he said. 'We'd better do something about it, eh?' As he
said it, he felt a sense of wonder: his head was clear, his thoughts
sharp. He remembered very little about the past twenty-four hours,
except a blurred procession of images, feet walking over rock,
Nelson, terrible dreams . . .

But that was all over now. He groped for his Schmeisser and
snapped in a new magazine. Clytemnestra had her eye to the spy-
hole in the wall. 'How many?' he said.

'Four. And the dog.'

'One feels they may be in for a bit of a shock.'

Clytemnestra said, 'A very big shock.' She did not go in for his
English understatement. After all, there was no shock like dying.

'Good dog, Mutzi,' said Tietmeyer, the handler.

Marsdorff did not agree. This damned animal had dragged him
and Schmidt and Kohl up a cliff in the noonday sun. It had relieved
itself on a handhold, which he had then put his hand on, and of
course everyone had found that very amusing. Marsdorff was a
pudgy, maggot-coloured man, who owed his place in the
Sonderkommando more to a lack of scruple than to any positive military talent. Basically, Marsdorff was very good at hanging people,
an accomplished hand with a red-hot iron and a pair of pliers, and
no beginner when it came to the process of gang rape – a business
that in Marsdorff's view was often approached crudely and without
thought. A really well-handled woman could keep a squad amused
for some days –

'Good dog,' said the handler. The Doberman on the choke lead
growled and slavered, claws scritching on the bare rock as it hauled
Tietmeyer up the path towards the ruined house. It had needed
some persuasion to come out of the rocks by the tomb, into which
it had fled after the death of its previous handler. Now it was back
at work, though, it seemed enthusiastic to make amends. 'There's
been someone in there, all right. Gone now.'

'Oh, good,' said Marsdorff, with sarcasm. 'Eagles, are they? Or
mountain goats?'

'Let's hope they're goats,' said Kohl, who disliked Marsdorff. 'I don't mind shagging a goat, but eagles are right out.'

'You have to draw the line somewhere,' said Marsdorff, sagely. He was not joking. 'On a bit.'

Negligently, the four men approached the next group of ruins. They did not believe anyone was on this island who was not supposed to be. Apparently there had been shooting. Well, they would believe it when they saw it.

The path had come to a narrow place, a defile dug out between a blade of rock and the cliff. The defile ended in a sort of groove, shoulder-deep in bare rock, leading to another group of ruined houses, the first of them a massive stone building, with loopholes staring blankly at the defile and the groove. They entered the groove, Tietmeyer in the lead. In one of the loopholes, something moved; a short, slender pipe. The barrel of a machine pistol. Tietmeyer said, nervously, 'I don't –' There was a large and dreadful noise, and the groove filled up with bullets. All of them jumped. None of them hit the ground alive.

Wills walked up to the bodies. He was pale again. 'Christ,' he said.

Clytemnestra squatted by Tietmeyer's body and liberated his Schmeisser, half-a-dozen magazines and a bunch of stick grenades. Then she spat in the dead face, and moved on to the next corpse. Wills watched the place where the path came round the bend in the rocks. 'They'll be back,' he said. 'Unless they're deaf.'

Clytemnestra raised a scornful eyebrow. 'So let them come,' she said. She pointed upwards, to where the cliff bulged out in an overhang like the brow of a stone genius. 'If they come there, we swat them like spiders.' She pointed over the lip of the path. 'There, they will not come unless they are birds. From this way' – she pointed to where the path ended among the houses – 'also, you will need to be a bird. And up the path, all must pass between the narrow rocks. It is like the path at Thermopylae. But you have never heard of Thermopylae, I expect.'

'Battle in ancient Greece,' said Wills. 'Played in a mountain pass. Three hundred Spartans v. a hundred thousand Persians. Home team triumphant. Leonidas played centre forward.'

'So now help me with these bodies, and we should get back to the houses.'

'Quite,' said Wills. It would have been bad taste to point out that the heroes of Thermopylae had died while achieving their victory.

He helped Clytemnestra topple the bodies over the cliff. Then he gathered up an armful of guns and bombs and scrambled after Clytemnestra back to the Swallow's Nest.

They were not the first people to have had the idea of defending this eyrie. The Swallow's Nest was the fortress-like building commanding the defile, a tower that overhung the abyss like a swallow's nest in the eaves of a roof. Wills' boots rang in the thick-walled rooms. He put his head into something that might have been a waterspout, or a nozzle for boiling oil. The valley was full of rain and the mutter of thunder. Far below, the path was a faint zigzag rising to the base of the cliff. And on the path, little creatures crawled: German soldiers.

It occurred to Wills that while the Swallow's Nest might be an impregnable redoubt, on an island crawling with German soldiers it was also a blind alley.

For a very small moment after the steel door hissed shut, Miller and Andrea stood quite still, listening. There was in all conscience plenty to listen to.

They were standing in a corridor hewn from the basalt. The corridor was lined with doors, full of voices echoing from the hard surfaces of the rock, and the steel plate of the door, and the girders that supported the staircases and the lighting and forced-draught units, and the loudspeakers that at this very moment were squawking klaxon noises into the babel below.

There were men everywhere. There seemed to be a lot of *Wehrmacht*, and a sprinkling of camouflage-smocked *SS*, and civilian workers, some mechanical-looking, in blue overalls, and one man in a white lab coat with pen-clips showing in the breast pocket, and rimless glasses below a head like a pumpkin. A squad of Greeks marched past, dressed in the rags of peasant field clothes, under the guard of four *Waffen-SS*. Everybody was too busy scuttling to and fro to spend any time staring at a couple of filthy, bloodstained men in ripped camouflage smocks.

For the moment.

The moment did not last long. A *Wehrmacht* NCO came marching past. He stopped, stared up at Andrea, and said, 'What the hell do you think you've been doing, killer?'

Andrea stood to attention, eyes front, chin out.

'How tall are you?' barked the NCO. The man's eyes were small and evil. Any minute now, thought Miller, they were going to slide down Andrea's body to his boots, his British army-issue boots, and that would be that –

Two metres, *Feldwebel*,' said Andrea.

'Never seen shit piled so high in my life,' said the NCO. Andrea's eyes had slid down the corridor. A door had opened. A wisp of steam floated into the corridor. A man with a drawstring bag came out, fumbling with his tunic buttons. 'You *Sonderkommando* cutthroats think you can march about the place with your arses filthy, you can –'

'Permission to take a shower, *Feldwebel?*' roared Andrea.

'Permission to take a shower, *Feldwebel?*' roared Miller.

Andrea turned left, cracked his boots on the concrete, and headed for the door. The *Feldwebel* turned away. If these Nazi animals wanted to take a shower during a general alert, then a shower they would take, *Herr Gott*. They were above the law, these brutes. The best you could hope was that they refrained from cooking and eating your men, and robbing the dead. God knew what the army was coming to. All mixed up with this *Sonderkommando*, and civilian labourers, and boffins, and God alone knew what other riffraff. Apparently some fool had crashed a train in the quarry, too. Beer, thought the *Feldwebel*. That was what you needed in a climate like this, at a time like this. He stumped off in the direction of the Sergeants' Mess.

The klaxons had stopped. *ALLES KLAR*, said the big metal voice in the corridor. ALL CLEAR. STAND DOWN.

Andrea shoved open the door of the shower room.

It was a big shower room, full of steam and the cursing of men who had stopped their showers and hauled their uniforms on over soapy bodies only to be told that the whole business had been in vain.

So now they stood under the showers, brown heads and arms and legs and milk-white German torsos, and washed. Miller and Andrea found a steamy corner, took off their tell-tale boots, and buried them and their battledress under the camouflage smocks. Then they stepped under the water.

'Most refreshing,' said Miller.

'Exactly so,' said Andrea.

'Murderers,' said a small man, presumably *Wehrmacht*, under the next nozzle.

Andrea reached out a huge hand, picked him up by the chin, and said, 'What exactly do you mean by that?'

The *Wehrmacht* man was very small and very frightened, but also very brave. 'What I said.'

Andrea gazed at him. Finally he said, 'You're quite right.' He grinned horribly. The little man ran away.

'Don't like each other, do they?' said Miller, in German.

'Sometimes,' said Andrea, grimly, 'life can be very beautiful.'

He looked around in the steam, scowling, a hairy giant with someone else's towel wrapped round his waist. Miller had a sudden mental glimpse of this shower room in a few hours: red gouts of flame shooting through the doors, the ceiling bulging in, dust and screams where the steam now hung . . .

If everything went according to plan.

Meanwhile, he knew what Andrea was looking for. Andrea was looking for someone in the shower with the same size feet as him.

Three hundred yards away, Mallory was thinking boots, too.

After he had jumped out of the train, he had hit the ground with his feet, cradling his Schmeisser. He had rolled, the paratrooper's roll, come back on his feet like a cat, and started running through the rain and steam and dust for the cliff face. There had been shouts. He paid no attention. Carstairs was up the face of the cliff, heading for the aerials. He did not trust Carstairs. Carstairs needed watching. So Mallory was going up the cliff towards the aerials, to keep an eye on him. He knew the face of that cliff, had summed it up in his mind the way a yachtsman sums up a chart or a fisherman a stretch of river.

He arrived at the locomotive, a crushed barrel issuing jets of scalding steam. He ran up the iron side, avoiding the geysers. The white fog was thick here. Suddenly he was at the rock wall.

Once, it would have dropped straight into the marsh. Since the reclamation of the land it now dropped straight into the platform where the railway and the road causeways arrived at the Acropolis. But there had been building inside the cliff, and ten feet above the platform, a drainpipe had been cemented in. Now, Mallory ran along the locomotive's boiler, jumped, locked his fingers round the drainpipe, drew up his legs, drove his bootnails into the rock, and straightened his knees. He got a foot to the top of the drainpipe, stood there a moment, perfectly in balance. The rain and steam were thick as porridge up here. Somewhere thunder roared, or perhaps it was the locomotive's boiler, mingled with the sound of the big concrete mixers.

He reached up. At fingertip height, an electric cable ran across the sheer face. He flexed his knees, and jumped. The cable came into his hands, fat and solid, anchored to the wall with good German steel. He drove his boots into the rock and walked his feet up. Tenderly, so as not to pierce the insulation, he got a sole to the cable. Then he shifted his weight, bending his knee. In a couple of seconds he was standing on the cable, walking to the right, northwards, twenty feet off the ground.

From his vantage point he saw grey rain thickening into a solid mat of vapour, from which rose a confused roar of noise. The hiss of escaping steam was fading. The sound of voices was louder; raucous voices, bellowing orders, and the churn of the big concrete mixers. He did not have long. He walked on along the cable, one foot delicately in front of the other, water streaming down the cliff to his left. He was concentrating on his balance, tiptoeing along behind the curtain of the rain.

The concrete mixers were still grinding away below him. You did not stop concrete mixers. You kept them turning, or they went solid. From high above there descended on a cable an angel of mercy in the form of a great steel bucket.

There now began one of the longest minutes of Mallory's life. He moved along the cable until he was standing on a concrete cornice directly above the concrete mixer. The cornice was eighteen inches wide. He lay along it, face averted from the yard.

Down below, men shouted and milled. The rain sheeted down, soaking Mallory to the skin. The bucket dropped, five feet from his right ear, clanked down into the enclosure in front of the mixer. He heard the flop of the concrete as the operator shot it down the pipe and into the bucket, the groan of the wire as it took the strain. Then the bucket was rising again.

Mallory got back on his feet. He saw the grease-black cable rise before him, no handhold there. He saw the battered steel rim of the big bucket. He knew it was now or not at all.

As the rim came up to eye level, he jumped.

His clawed fingers hit concrete-splattered steel, hung on. His toes found the flange at the top of the bucket.

Down below, someone started shouting. It was a new kind of shouting. It meant only one thing. Trouble.

He looked down. The reclaimed area was a mass of men, swarming around the wreck of the stone train like worker ants around a queen. Mallory scrambled on top of the bucket. His final glimpse stayed with him. Heads, helmeted or capped or just hairy, milling to and fro. And in the middle of all those heads, one face turned upwards into the rain, eyes wide, open-mouthed. *Wehrmacht-grey* shoulders. An expression of total shock.

Mallory sat on the handle of the bucket out of sight of the ground, and hoped that nobody would pay any attention to one man who had spotted something wrong with the concrete lifting gear. The cliff moved past fifteen feet away, sheer and black. Carstairs was up there somewhere; either that, or dead. Mallory would rather have been climbing. The bucket was a trap. There was no way off it –

The bucket stopped with a jerk, and hung swinging. Seven hundred and fifty feet below, little figures milled. Seven hundred and fifty feet is two hundred and fifty yards. At two hundred and fifty yards a human face is invisible, even if it is staring at you, or looking at you through binoculars, or aiming a rifle at you. Mallory drew his head back sharply. Then he looked up.

Some distance above – it was impossible to tell exactly how far, but it could have been a hundred feet – was a projection in the cliff face. A jetty or platform, crusted, by the look of it, with spilt concrete, and a crane jib. Not a crane, perhaps; a windlass. Call it what you liked, there were people up there. And the odds were that they had been warned by telephone that there was someone on the concrete bucket. So why would they halt the bucket in mid-ascent?

There were a lot of answers. The one that made the most sense to Mallory was that they were waiting for reinforcements.

Mallory looked at the cliff face. It had sloped gradually away from the bucket. Now it was a good twenty-five feet off through the rain, a wall of black basalt, but weathered up here, unsmoothed, pockmarked . . .

Only twenty-five feet. Too far to jump.

For a moment, Mallory watched that wall with the intensity of a falcon watching a pigeon. Then he unstrapped the lightweight rope from his pack, took a deep breath, and began.

He looped an end of the rope through the handle of the bucket, and hauled in until the two ends were equalized. He grasped the doubled rope, spat on his hands, and went over the side.

It was flimsy stuff, this silk rope, only one up from parachute cord. Harder to grip than the wire-cored Manila they had used on Navarone and in the Pyrenees; but lighter. Infinitely lighter. You could carry twice, three times the length for the same weight –

Comforting things, technicalities. They had brought him down hand over painful hand until he was hanging seventy-five feet below the bucket, like a spider on a thread, turning slowly.

He wound his left hand into the rope above his head, let go with his right. The horizon wheeled around him: clouds, the mountains on the far side of the valley, the sea, a ray of sunlight striking through the clouds making a sudden dazzling path; then the slopes and faces of the Acropolis, the cliff, twenty-five feet away, not far at all. His left hand was agony now, the rope biting like a cheese wire. His right fumbled with the rope, tying a double figure-of-eight as the world turned another forty-five degrees, ninety, to the lengthening shadows of the aeroplanes and the fuel dumps on the dim sward of the airfield. And directly below, spinning with wonderful slowness, the little corpse of the wrecked train.

The knot was finished. The two strands of the rope were tied together. Mallory jammed his right boot into the loop, and put his weight on it, and flexed his left hand to get the blood circulating again. He hung there and let the world turn another two hundred and seventy degrees. Nobody seemed to be shooting at him. When the spin had brought him face to the cliff again, he let his weight drop back.

Seven hundred feet above the wrecked train, seventy-five feet below the bucket, a hundred and seventy feet below the crane, he started to swing.

He swung like a child on a rope hung from a tree branch, except that he was a soldier an eighth of a mile from the ground. The arc grew. He could feel the air dividing in front of his face, smell, as he approached the cliff, that odd smell of hot wet rock, half clammy, half aromatic.

He started to analyse the place where he would land. His present arc would leave him somewhere too smooth. Over to the right, erosion had left a little hook, a semi-detached plate of rock with a tuft of sun-dried grass sprouting from the crevice above. It swept towards him. He reached out his hand, measuring. Just short. The next swing, he moved the axis, gave the rope a little extra pull, gained that extra ounce of speed; so that on the next swing he found himself at the top of the arc, weightless, standing for a split second on nothing, stationary at the apex of his swing. He put out his hand and grasped the little hook of rock, jamming his fingers into the crevice behind it. His weight came on to the flake. He heard his finger joints crack. His boot hit the rock. The nails found a hold. He stood for a second like a starfish, his right hand and right boot holding the cliff, his left arm and left boot engaged with the doubled rope. He shifted the foot. Now he had two boots on the face, his right hand on the flake, his left holding the rope. He would need the rope again –

The flake under his right hand gave way.

There was no warning. One second he was on the wall, getting balanced. The next he was out, falling, no holds anywhere except in his left hand, where the thin rope was sliding through his palm, and the ground far below was coming up to meet him.

He clamped his teeth and his fist at the same time. His fist slid to the knot he had tied in the end of the rope, the bulky double figure-of-eight. He stopped with a crack that tried to tear his arm out by the roots. Each swing tried to shake him off. He held on grimly. As the oscillations grew smaller, the centrifugal force was not so tormenting. He got his right hand on to the rope, then his foot. He manoeuvred himself into a standing position. He thought his knees into not shaking.

Then he started all over again.

This time, he left nothing to chance. He found a new handhold, and went for it. But this time, he committed himself only when he was quite sure. He found himself a place to stand, and he stood there, and methodically untied the figure-of-eight, and coiled the rope, and slung it, and started to climb up and to the left, into a sort of shallow gully or couloir, where he would be out of sight from below and above.

He went up hard and steady, climbing from the hips, his mind fixed on the next hold, never mind the top; the top was just another rest, and would look after itself. It was not until he got into the couloir that he started to shake.

Up in the Swallow's Nest, Wills' head was getting clearer by the minute. One of the things becoming clearest was that he was in a tightish spot, with a woman. He opened a tin of sardines, and looked at Clytemnestra, the olive curve of her cheek against the black fringe of her shawl; hard as a steel spring, light on her feet as a feather. The other thing he had noticed, now that his brain was working again, was that she was extremely beautiful. In Wills' experience of women, which was limited to a few devoted hours spent carrying the golf clubs of his cousin Cynthia, they were not to be counted on in tight spots. Well, not not counted on, exactly; but their place was not in the line of fire, but on the . . . well . . . home front. Clytemnestra seemed to be different. This had come as a shock to Wills, though not a disagreeable one. He ate another sardine.

Clytemnestra was peering down one of the spouts of the Swallow's Nest. As Wills watched, she took a German stick grenade, pulled the toggle, and dropped it through the spout.

Well, thought Wills, fitting her into a known structure. For Clytemnestra and the islanders of Kynthos, this is the home front. He watched the grenade fall, wobbling in the air. The little figures on the zigzag were bigger now, five hundred feet below. They did not look up.

It was a nicely calculated drop. The grenade burst in the air, at about waist height. Wills heard nothing that he could class as an explosion; a flash and a puff of smoke, and a split-second later a flat, ineffectual-sounding *whap*. Three of the little figures on the path were not on the path any more. The rest stopped and lay down; fifteen of them at the most, with more coming up behind. A lot more. They faltered, all of them. It must be unnerving to find yourself under fire from a place you could not see, on an island of which you were supposed to be in control.

After a while, small voices floated up from below, mingled with birdsong. The men below started to move in little rushes. If they had been on a plain or a hillside, they would undoubtedly have spread out. But this was a cliff, and the path was the only means of access. They were bunching again, directly below the Swallow's Nest . . .

Thermopylae!' yelled Wills, and pulled the strings on two bombs, and let them go.

Again the flash and the puff and the *whap*. Again the little figures, flung off the path and vanishing over the horizon. Again the silence.

But in that silence, a Single word. *Hoch*. Up. And all of a sudden, in that huddle of figures, a series of pale discs: faces. And after the faces, the small flicker of muzzle flashes, and the sting and whine of bullets beyond the Swallow's Nest walls.

Clytemnestra sat back, her legs out in front of her, and took a sip of water, and smiled at Wills, showing those white teeth and those fierce eyes, slapping the dirty floor-slabs as you might pat a horse. What she was saying was that there were six feet of good solid masonry between them and those bullets. Nothing was going to shift them, short of artillery.

Wills grinned back at her, feeling the stretch of burned skin on his face.

A shadow flitted across his thoughts. There were a lot of Germans out there. Up here in the Swallow's Nest there was food and ammunition for a couple of days, no more. Maybe they would be relieved. The men in the Acropolis were good men, they had proved that already. Four men, said the small, dark voice in Wills' head. Against a thousand or so.

He heard the scritch of grenade fuses, the *blat* of the explosions, Clytemnestra hiss a curse. A file of soldiers was running up the last zigzag and into the shelter of the cliff. The grenades knocked three of them down, but that left a dozen. Clytemnestra grabbed for her Schmeisser. The Swallow's Nest filled with its jackhammer clatter. She swore again, stopped firing. The range was too big. Wills found himself a loophole that covered the mouth of the path, and waited, sighting down the groove in the stone. Clytemnestra had shot the first lot. It was Wills' turn.

For twenty minutes, nothing moved out there except a lizard, hunting flies on the plates of rock at the mouth of the defile. Then the lizard became suddenly still, as if listening. A fly landed within six inches of it. It paid no attention. Fast as an eye blinking, it was gone.

After it there came, first of all, a boot. Wills rested the foresight of the Schmeisser on the place where the knee would be, and moved the v of the backsight up to cradle it.

A man came out, helmet down, like a rabbit with a ferret on its tail, slap into the sights. Wills fired a four-round burst. The man straightened up and fell backwards into the soldier who was following, stopping him. While he was stopped, Wills shot him in the head. He slammed back. Another man was behind him, and another. Wills fired a longer burst. Hands went up and legs buckled and somebody somewhere began shouting, whether from pain or shock he could not tell. The main thing was that nobody else came through the gap. Like pheasants, he thought. Like pheasants that you take out in front, one, two, except with a machine pistol you could take three, four, five. His head was light, and he thought that he might be going to laugh or cry, he could not tell which. 'Like pheasants,' he said.

'Like Nazi swine,' said Clytemnestra.

Suddenly, Wills was shaking. Clytemnestra put her hand on his shoulder, and made small, soothing noises. I'm sorry,' he said, when he could speak. 'I was in the Navy. It's a new way of . . . seeing men die.'

She smiled and nodded. She did not understand, though. She had seen her brother hanged for no reason except that he had been in the wrong place at the wrong time. She was not thinking about the way she felt. She was thinking about the enemy, hoping one of them would show himself and she would have a chance to kill him. Kill or be killed, thought Wills, a little wildly: that is the whole of the Law –

Outside, a machine gun started hammering. The bullets whanged off the stones. None of them found its way through the loophole. Clytemnestra was firing now, short bursts again. She must have learned from someone, thought Wills. Short bursts don't overheat, and guns that don't overheat don't jam. Andrea might have taught her –

· 'Four more,' she said, snapping out the magazine.

It was lives out there, Wills knew. Not weapons training. Seven men bleeding down that hillside. Five left.

The machine gun opened up again. Clytemnestra was still reloading. Wills popped up, saw two more men running along the groove, squeezed the trigger, tumbled the first one like a rabbit, cut the second one's knees from under him. Don't do it, you bloody fools, he was thinking. Christ, why am I saying this? I want to live. But now he could see these men, he wanted them to live too, to stop bursting out of the slot in the cliff and running down that gutterful of flying lead –

He got his wish. They stopped. Down below, the path zigzagged empty. Wills offered Clytemnestra a cigarette. She refused. He lit one himself. He could feel the pressure of the silence: fifty men, waiting in dead ground for the next thing to happen.

Whatever that was going to be.

'They're getting ready,' he said.

Clytemnestra showed her teeth. 'Soon, we kill them all,' she said; Helen, Medea, the whole vengeful regiment of Greek myth rolled into one and carrying a sub-machine-gun.

They waited.

Nothing happened.

They both watched the slot in the cliff, the things lying in the rock gulley that had once been men, but were now mere bundles of rags drowned in a long gutter of shadow. The sun was going down.

'What do we do when it gets dark?' said Wills.

'Leave,' said Clytemnestra. 'There is a way. A way beyond.'

'So what happens if the Germans find it?' said Wills.

'Nobody will find it who was not born on Kynthos,' she said, with a scorn so magnificent that it drove away the anxieties flocking round Wills, and really made him believe that there were things here invisible to normal eyes, things that only Clytemnestra could see.

'Top-hole,' said Wills.

Something that sounded like an express train roared overhead. There was a huge explosion. The floor of the Swallow's Nest shook as if in an earthquake. 'Christos!' said Clytemnestra. 'What was that?'

'Gun,' said Wills. 'Eighty-eight, probably.' Now that there was actually a military problem to engage his mind, he felt oddly better. 'They'll have them on the airfield, for flak. They'll be spotting it in, I expect. Chaps round the corner'll be on the radio.' His mind rolled on. There would be no radio to the airport gun emplacements. Telephone only. So the chaps round the corner would be transmitting to the big aerials on the top of the Acropolis, and someone up there would be calling the fall of shot to the chaps by the gun. Elaborate, but it seemed to work –

Another express train passed overhead and to the right. Another explosion pummelled their ears. Another earthquake shook the floor. Bracketed. Now all the gunners had to do was dot the i.

The sun was well behind the mountains, now. Far away across the valley, an edge of shadow was creeping up the sunlit crags of the Acropolis.

A great fist smashed Wills to the ground. He found himself lying with his head on Clytemnestra's belly, his ears chiming like a belfry, bits of cement and chips of stone raining down on him. Overhead, where the roof should have been, he could see a patch of blue sky veined with little golden wisps of sunset cloud. There was a strong reek of burned stone and high explosive.

'Wait till they hear about that,' said Wills, in a voice that did not quite shake.

'About what?' Clytemnestra's hand was in his hair. She stroked it absent-mindedly, as if he was a dog.

'They're zeroed in,' said Wills. 'Hang on to your hat.'

EIGHT

Thursday
2000–2300

The rain had passed. From the west face of the Acropolis, the sun was a red-hot cannonball falling into a sea of ink. Mallory climbed hard and fast, staying in gullies, where the shadows lay like a dark liquid. He was not interested in the view. He was looking forward to the falling of night. Things were safer in the dark . . .

He paused, comfortable in his foot- and handholds, and looked about him. He was on a vast, curved face, a sort of oil drum of rock. He had bypassed a couple of vents and entrances; the concrete crane was a thousand feet below him. The oil drum was the final peak on top of which the aerial array stood. He was tired. Fumbling in his pack he found the Benzedrine, popped out a couple of pills, swallowed them.

High on the curved face of the rock, something flickered across Mallory's vision. A mere speck, crawling from one gulley, across a sun-gilded ridge and into the next gulley. It might have been a bird, a bee, even. But Mallory knew that it was his quarry. Carstairs, climbing very fast, solo. He hoped the man's technique was up to it.

There was only one way to be sure.

Mallory went after him. The Benzedrine spread cool energy through him as he drifted up that cliff, keeping just below the line of shadow the sinking sun drove up the cliff from the mountains at his back, relying on the contrast between the light and the darkness to hide him. Ten minutes later, he was in the same chimney as Carstairs, an easy chimney, with a chockstone seventy feet up, and the summit just beyond the chockstone. He looked up, shielding his eyes against the grit coming down off Carstairs' boots. If Carstairs wanted the aerials, two would do the job more easily than one.

Mallory whistled.

* * *

Carstairs had never done such a long solo. He was an expedition climber, a man used to ropes and Sherpas and a glass of cold Champagne at base camp. At first, his knees had shaken, and the loneliness had pressed in on him. But he was a good technical climber, so he had taken it easy, taken it slow, driven himself up all those vertical feet, safe as houses, accelerating as he got the hang of it until he was climbing at a pretty fair speed. Oh yes, he had begun to think, I'm good at this. Now, as far as he could see, he was nearly at the top. There would be guards at the top; after all this climbing, fighting . . .

He was up and under the chockstone now. The boulder jammed into the crack blocked his further progress. He would have to go out on to the lip of the crack, work his way round the boulder, then prepare for the . . . well, final assault. He belayed his rope. Then he reached up a hand, straining round the boulder for a crack, probing with the tip of a spike. Found a place. The spike went in. He worked it in further; worked it in by hand. There would be guards up there. The clink of a hammer on a spike would carry. The guard would look over . . .

That was when he heard the whistle.

His heart leaped in his chest. He glanced down, saw the figure in the *SS* smock. A German. His hands were engaged. He could not get a weapon. He did not know it was Mallory, following him. All he knew was that that figure down there would go for his gun, shoot him out of the sky. He needed to get out of the line of fire. Over the stone. He put his weight on his right hand, swung out of the chimney . . .

He was half-way out when he lost his grip and fell.

He saw the floor of the world turn under his eyes. For a split second he thought, this is it. Then the rope caught him. He swung wildly. Something smote him a wicked bang on the head, and everything went first red, and then black.

Mallory saw the foreshortened figure above reach out, grab, slip, fall, swing. He heard the wet smack of the head on the rock, saw him twitch, then hang limp on the rope.

He waited for the rope to stop swinging, the deadly swing that could work a spike loose. Then he went up, fast, out of the groove in case Carstairs fell, up the right-hand side on holds a fly would have despised. He reached the spike and checked it. It was deep in the crack, holding; a good belay in a difficult spot. Carstairs knew what he was doing, all right.

Once he had checked the belay, Mallory went to the body. There was a good pulse, a lump rising on the back right-hand bulge of the skull under the hair, sticky with brilliantine and stone-grit. The man would live. Mallory hauled the body up into a sitting position, looped the tail of the rope under its armpits and rolling-hitched it on to the standing part. Now Carstairs was sitting on the end of the rope like a drunk on a bar stool, dangling over a thousand feet of nothing. Perfectly safe.

Mallory went through his pockets, found the cigarette case, the knife, the silenced Browning automatic in a shoulder holster; a murderer's weapon. In the waist pouches, he found what he was looking for: two blocks of a substance like putty, wrapped in greasy paper. Plastic explosive. But no time pencils.

Mallory stood wedged in the chimney, sweating. Plastic explosive was funny stuff. You could burn it. You could spread it on bread and eat it, if the worst came to the worst. And of course you could blow a hole in steel with it. But only if you had some fulminate of mercury to start it off, in those little colour-coded pencils, the size of a long cigarette.

Mallory went back to Carstairs' pockets. The gold cigarette case came out. There was lettering on it: 'Darling Billy, from Betty Grable – What a night!' Mallory opened the case one-handed.

Turkish this side. Virginian that. And in the middle, the time pencils.

Mallory shoved the case in his breast pocket and climbed on. The cliff face was curving away from him now, becoming less a precipice, more a slope. He could see the aerial pylons glowing as if red-hot in the last rays of the sun. He stayed low, creeping on his belly until he could see the whole dome of the summit. The pylons stuck out of the naked rock, a hundred feet apart, supporting a web of fine wires. There seemed to be a lot more wire than was required for normal short-wave apparatus. Mallory supposed that if you were shooting things into space, you would need some sort of sophisticated radio to find out what was happening to the machinery. Not that he cared. It was as much part of a weapon as a sight was part of a rifle. His job was to destroy it.

He made a circuit of the mountain top. It had the look of a place untrodden except by maintenance engineers. There was a trap door at the far side, a hefty steel object set in concrete. To the east, the Acropolis continued as a series of lower peaks, a series of plugs like the noses of a clip of giant bullets, a hot wilderness of shale and

sun-scorched shrubs, its declivities filled with the violet shadows of
evening; a hard place, with a sense of pressure underneath it.
Mallory was a New Zealander. He knew the sensation of standing
on a volcano; the feeling that the ground under his feet had once
been a white-hot liquid, pushing to get out into the air, burn and
destroy. No change there . . .

He found himself peering into the deepest of the valleys: more a
hole than a valley, really. And in its bottom, instead of the usual
dried-up pond with a patch of thorny scrub, was something else.
No vegetation: a smooth, dark bowl. It was as if the hole was a deep
one, made shallower with carefully-slung camouflage nets.

Mallory filed the information away in his Benzedrine-sharpened
mind, and trotted up the dome to the base of the aerials.

There was a faint hum up here, a sense that the ether was troubled by invisible forces. Mallory crouched and wrapped a charge of
plastic explosive round the base girders of one of the pylons, making sure it was good and close to the wrist-thick wire that snaked
along the rock from the hole by the trap door. Should bring one
pylon down, break that cobweb of wires. Mending them would take
time – time during which the Acropolis would be dumb and deaf.

He packed on the charges, pushed in two black time pencils,
crushed them and pulled out the safety tags. The electrolyte began
eating away at the corrosion wire that held back the spring-loaded
plunger from the blasting cap. Ten minutes, perhaps less on a warm
evening like this. The sun was balanced on the horizon. Time to get
clear. He went down the slope until the slope became a cliff. He doubled his rope around a projection of the rock, looped it over his shoulder and up between his legs, and walked backwards out and down,
casting left and right for the chimney where he had left Carstairs.

He found it on his left, saw the chockstone coming up, slowed
his descent. He would need to get the Englishman on to a ledge,
keep him warm, get a briefing from him, leave him to recover –

He stopped next to the chockstone. Somewhere behind him and
below, deep in the gulf of shadow that was the marsh and the valley, a gun fired: the peculiar flat crack of an 88. Normally, Mallory
would have pitied the poor devil who was on the receiving end of
that high-velocity, flat-trajectory packet of death. He would also
have asked himself who, on this German-controlled island, was
shooting at whom.

But he did not ask himself any of this, because he had other
things on his mind.

He had left Carstairs unconscious, trussed into a sitting position, hanging from a piton over a thousand-foot drop.

Now, Carstairs was gone.

Mallory looked down. On the floodlit platform three hundred yards below his feet, people were moving, vehicles crawled, a gang was clustered round the engine. (*Crack,* said the 88 again, down in the valley.) There was none of the ants'-nest activity you would expect if the body of a commando with a Clark Gable moustache had plummeted out of the sky and into their midst.

Mallory thought for a moment.

There was no telling where Carstairs had gone. The only certainty was that in (he looked at his watch) four minutes, anywhere near the aerial site was going to be a very unhealthy place to be.

Hauling down his rope from the summit belay, he made it fast again, wrapped it round himself, and slid rapidly into the thickening shadows below.

For Miller, the shower he took in the entrance lobby of the Acropolis V4 complex was not the most refreshing in living memory. The water was hot, the soap plentiful, the hygiene nothing to complain about by the standards of twenty-four hours on a Sporadic mountainside. It was the company Miller objected to. Mixed at best, he thought gloomily, watching a rat-faced *Wehrmacht* private disrobe, pick his nose, and waddle under the showerhead. At worst –

'Scrub my back?' said a voice behind him. He turned to see a large blond individual with no neck and a crew cut smiling upon him tenderly.

'Can't reach,' said Miller. The blond man pouted, and started to lather his vast acreage with violet-scented soap. He was about the same size as Andrea, something (Miller observed) that Andrea had not been slow to notice. Andrea was out of the shower, had dried himself on someone else's towel, and was sidling towards the locker where the blond man's clothes were hanging.

The blond man finished soaping himself. He had a disappointed air. He put himself under the jet of water and rinsed off the lather. There were *SS* lightning-flash runes tattooed on his mighty bicep. Miller could see Andrea struggling into a pair of jackboots. It looked as if he would be some time. The outside door opened. A man came in, lanky, about Miller's height, with a brown engineer's coat and a clipboard. The coat would be useful. The clipboard was a blessing from God. Miller said to the blond man, 'You off, then?'

'Not much happening here,' said the blond man, sulkily.

'Ah,' said Miller. 'Well I think this is your lucky day. See that guy just come in?' He pointed at the man in the engineer's coat. 'Very nice guy,' said Miller. 'Likes a bit of fun.'

'Zat so?' said the blond. 'Thanks, friend.'

'Any time,' said Miller, and sashayed rapidly on to dry land.

As he dried himself, he watched the lanky engineer hang up his overall coat with finicky precision, put his trousers on a hanger, arrange on the floor of the locker a pair of brown suede shoes, become indistinct in the steam, and start soaping himself. Miller saw the large figure of the blond SS man start making his way casually towards him. He tweaked open the locker, removed the engineer's clothes and marched over to his own untidy pile. He put on his own undergarments and the engineer's overalls, slung his pack on his back, and bundled his own clothes up inside the scarf so they looked like washing. When he turned he found himself looking at an SS leutnant with Andrea's face and a washing bundle of his own.

'Come,' said Andrea. 'Quick.'

Some sort of fight seemed to have broken out in the shower. 'Ja, Herr Leutnant,' said Miller. They walked out of the door, an SS man and an engineer, the engineer carrying a load of laundry, the SS man talking to him with earnestness and concentration.

'What now?' said Miller.

'Find out the geography. What's on your clipboard?'

There was a list of bolt sizes, with under it some blank paper. Miller shuffled the blank paper to the top. The pair of them walked off, Andrea chin up and arrogant, Miller trailing behind doing his best to look dazed and acquiescent, struggling under the awkward load of clothes and explosives.

'Hey!' said Andrea. 'You!'

A small Wehrmacht man had been passing. He said, 'Me?'

'None other,' drawled Andrea. 'Take these clothes. Throw them away.'

'Away?' The man's eyes were dull and stupid.

'A tubercular patient in the village,' said Andrea. 'They are to be burned. Now. Where is the hospital?'

'Third level,' said the soldier.

'Remember this,' said Andrea. 'The faster you go, the more likely you are to live. And don't tell anyone, or they'll give you the treatment.'

'Treatment, Herr Leutnant?'

'Paraffin enemas,' said Miller, with a ghastly grin.

The private gulped and scuttled off, holding the bundles as far away from him as possible.

'Now,' said Andrea. 'Let us see to the state of the wiring in this pest hole.'

'Yes indeed,' said Miller, bowing his head over his clipboard and writing diligently. 'After you, *Herr Leutnant.*'

They walked up the steel stairs, slowly, but putting distance between themselves and the crisis that would be developing in the shower. The base level seemed by a thrum in the rock to consist of machinery and shelters. Above were living quarters: they passed rooms in which double-tiered bunks stretched away to impossibly distant vanishing points, a couple of mess rooms wafting the sour smell of boiled sausage and fried onions. A *Wehrmacht* major was marching towards them. 'Two hundred and ten,' said Andrea. Miller scribbled on his clipboard. The *Wehrmacht* major stopped, frowning. Miller felt his stomach hollow out.

'What are you doing?' said the major.

Andrea crashed to attention. '*Heil Hitler!*' he yelled, shooting out his right arm.

'Oh,' said the major, who had a mild, clerkish, non-Nazi sort of face. '*Heil, er, Hitler.*' He gave the army salute. 'What are you doing?' he said again.

'Light bulb audit,' said Andrea, with a face like granite.

'Light bulbs?' said the major, frowning at the *SS* runes on Andrea's smock.

'Those are my orders,' said Andrea.

'*Jawohl,*' said Miller, squinting furiously at the bridge of his nose and trying by willpower to stop the sweat running down his face.

The major sighed. 'So they fly you from the Harz specially to count the light bulbs,' he said. 'Shouldn't you be torturing women or something?'

'*Herr Major?*' Andrea's face was as stiff as a poker.

The major shook his head. There was drink on his breath. 'Oh, hell,' he said. 'I suppose someone's got to do it.'

'*Jawohl Herr Major,*' shouted Andrea.

'Carry on,' said the major. He walked away, muttering.

They carried on. They went up more stairs to something that seemed from the smell of antiseptic to be a hospital level: though there was no hospital to be seen, merely a horizontal corridor with a steel catwalk suspended over a rough floor of volcanic rock. The hospital was an opening off the tunnel. At the tunnel's end was a concrete doorframe with a lift inside it. On the right of the lift was a small wooden structure, like a sentry box, but bigger.

There were fewer people up here. A couple of men walked past, deep in conversation, wearing engineers' coats like Miller's. They looked at him as they passed. He nodded. They nodded back and walked on without altering their step. At the end they paused by the sentry box, fished out passes of some kind. An *SS* man came out of the sentry box. He looked at the passes, the engineers, back at the passes, the engineers again. Then the engineers signed a book, and moved on to the lift.

'They've got keys,' said Andrea.

'You would almost think,' said Miller, 'that they did not want anyone to get in.'

As he spoke, there was a small, distinct bump that seemed to come not down the tunnel but through the rock itself. Miller felt a twinge of significant happiness. He was always suspicious of the ability of anyone but himself to use explosives. But it seemed likely now that Mallory had managed to make the stuff go off. And knowing Mallory, he would have put it in the right place.

All this he thought very fast indeed. There were klaxons moaning again, and he found that he was walking, walking alongside Andrea – not into the great mass of people seething and swirling behind them on the lower levels, but forward; forward towards the sentry box at the foot of the lift shaft.

Up in the Swallow's Nest, Wills lay with his head on Clytemnestra's belly and dust in his eyes and wondered why he was not dead yet.

He did not lie for long. He got up and grabbed at a Schmeisser and went once again to the loophole. The sun was all the way down now; outside, the world lay in deep shadow, deepest over the bodies crumpled in the gulley of the path. The killing ground was quiet, empty of living things. The last ray of sun lit the summit of the mountain above the Acropolis, where the aerials were.

From that summit there came a small, brilliant flash, followed some time later by the tiny thump of an explosion.

He raised his glasses to his eyes.

A black smear of smoke drifted in the light. The aerials had gone.

Down in the valley, the 88 crashed again. The shell smashed into the cliff, miles above their heads. Wills thought for a moment, then went back to Clytemnestra. He wanted to talk; but he found himself grinning too hard.

'What is it?' she said. She was picking herself up now.

'They were talking to the radio room on the mountain,' said Wills. 'Someone was spotting for the 88. The aerials have gone. They're firing blind.'

Clytemnestra got up and reeled to the loophole. She pushed the hair out of her eyes. Wills gave her a water bottle. She spat out the first mouthful, then drank deeply. 'Fine,' she said.

Wills had stopped grinning. The immediate danger was past. Longer-term, the situation had not changed. 'We're still stuck,' he said. 'All they've got to do is wait there till we starve.'

'Oh, no,' said Clytemnestra. 'Not true, my sad English friend. Now it is dark.'

'Can't eat dark,' said Wills.

She laughed. It was a confident laugh, most encouraging. 'Tonight,' she said, 'we eat not dark, but sheep.'

Concussion, thought Wills. Poor girl, what the hell will I do with her now? 'Sit down,' he said. 'More water.'

'I have sat down enough,' she said. 'Also, I have drunk all a woman needs to drink, who is about to take a journey.'

'Journey?' said Wills, fogged.

'We are leaving,' said Clytemnestra, shouldering her pack. 'Follow me.'

'Top-hole,' said Wills. He strapped on his pack and slung his Schmeisser. Once, before he had started skulking in the mountains with beautiful Furies, he had been the commander of an MTB. That had been in another life, over twenty-four hours ago. He squeezed a burst out of the loophole at the slot in the rocks, the muzzle flash making blue lightnings in the dark. Then he was jogging down the stone stairs into the mould-smelling lower room of the Swallow's Nest, out into the warm night, up the alley that did duty as this hamlet's main street, his back crawling with the expectation of bullets, through a passage so narrow he had to turn sideways, following the faint scuff of Clytemnestra's boots in front. The passage became a path. Thick bushes brushed against his legs, and once something that looked like a wall of trees reared up in front of him and whipped his face, and he knew he had gone through a curtain of some kind. Then they were climbing athwart a slope so steep he could touch the ground with his right hand, while on his left he felt the presence of a dark and mighty gulf. At last, the voice in front said, 'Stop.' He groped his way along until he found an opening, and slid in. There was a scrape and a flare of light as Clytemnestra lit a match. She ran her hand along a ledge, and came down with a stub of candle. They were in a cave, square-sided: another tomb. 'They won't find us here,' she said. 'Not without dogs.'

There had been dogs everywhere. But Wills found himself so tired that he would not have batted an eyelid if the whole pack of the hounds of Hell had been baying at his heels. Tired or not, Wills had been decently educated at public school, and he knew how to treat a lady. 'Are you quite comfortable?' he said.

Clytemnestra yawned, the yawn of a sleepy cat. 'I have killed some Germans,' she said. 'I am free in my country. How should I not be comfortable?'

'You might have a nice armchair,' said Wills. 'Dinner at Ciro's. Bottle of Romanée-Conti. Nip along to the Mottled Oyster after-wards –'

'Mottled Oyster?' said Clytemnestra.

'Night club,' said Wills. 'Dancing.'

'And you would need a woman,' said Clytemnestra. 'A beautiful girl.'

There was a short silence. Then Wills said, 'No shortage here,' and lay back, head on pack, so that even in the candlelight there would be no chance of her seeing the crimson in his face. When he glanced furtively across at her, he saw that she was smiling a small, contented smile. It suddenly struck him that he had been manoeu-vred into saying what he had just said. Hello, he thought. Hello . . .

But before his thoughts could develop further, he was asleep.

Mallory welcomed the darkness as if it had been a long-lost brother. What he did not welcome was the fact that he had lost Carstairs. If he had fallen, that was very bad. If he had not fallen, then knowing Carstairs that was probably even worse.

He scrutinized the face of the cliff with a pair of small but powerful Zeisses that he had removed from a Panzer general, the Panzer gener-al being at the time *en route* for a British prison camp having been plucked from the Cretan mountains by Mallory and his comrades. In the disc of his vision, Mallory saw the corrugations of the cliffs, ridge and gulley, boulder and boiler plate, precipice and ledge –

The disc stopped. Mallory balanced on two toes and a hand, and moved the focus wheel as gently as a biologist focusing on a new bacillus.

Across the cliff wall two hundred yards to his right, a shadow was moving – a shadow like a four-legged spider, scuttling and pausing.

Mallory shifted the disc of the glasses ahead, in the direction Carstairs was travelling. He saw a ledge; a ledge too sharp and clearly-defined in construction to be altogether natural. A way into the mountain. A way through to the *Kormoran* survivor. His objective.

But as Mallory started once more to watch him move across the cliff, he frowned. There was something wrong with the way the man was moving. He watched the right hand, a pale crab against the dark rock. It scuttled, then paused, patting the surface as if the mind guiding it was working in short bursts, going numb between bursts of lucidity. The mind, Mallory realized, of a man who had recently hit his head very hard on the side of a mountain.

Something on the ledge caught Mallory's eye: a sudden flare of light, a face and a helmet-brim suddenly glowing sharp and clear as a soldier sheltered a match in cupped hands to light a cigarette.

Carstairs kept struggling on, as if he had not noticed anything. Perhaps he had not. Mallory would have cursed if there had been time for cursing. Instead, he took his boots off and hung them round his neck. Then he stepped across on to the wall and started climbing, fast and smooth.

He was travelling four feet to Carstairs' three, but Carstairs had a long start. As he climbed, Mallory saw with increasing clarity that to Carstairs, the ledge was simply a way in, and that his brain was not working well enough for him to be cautious. What was going to happen was that he was going to blunder straight into the guard, who would have the advantage of surprise, and a clear head. If Carstairs was captured alive, Dieter Wolf would have him answering questions in about ten minutes. If the sentry killed him, the word would be out that the partisans in the mountains were now inside the Acropolis defences. Presumably, the Germans would have been relying on their security at the gates, rather than running checks inside the Acropolis. But that would change in a moment, and life would get very difficult for anyone who was inside.

Perhaps it already was.

Mallory climbed on, eating up the traverse. Holds were plentiful. Many men might have been made nervous by the six hundred feet of nothingness below. But Mallory had slept on the west face of Mount Cook, in a sleeping bag hung from two pitons over five thousand sheer feet. He climbed carefully, but with nerves untroubled by altitude.

What was preying on his mind was Carstairs, now thirty feet below and twenty yards to the right. Mallory could hear him: the scritch of nails on rock, the harsh gasp of his breathing. And if Mallory could hear him, so could the guard . . .

Carstairs was a biscuit toss from the ledge now. With his dark-adjusted eyes, Mallory watched the dreadful story unfold.

The guard had been smoking his cigarette and humming, gazing, no doubt, upon the beauty of the sea, now a silver-paved floor under the vault of the stars. Then suddenly he stopped, dropped his cigarette, unslung his rifle, moved right to the back of the ledge, and plastered himself against the cliff wall.

Carstairs' boots sounded like a marching army. Mallory knew what was going to happen. There was a low parapet around the ledge. As soon as Carstairs' head and shoulders came above it, the sentry would open fire, secure in the knowledge that Carstairs' hands would be fully occupied with climbing.

Mallory as good as ran across the cliff. He could feel the stone tearing at his stockinged feet, but he paid no attention. As the ledge arrived twelve feet below, he began to move slowly. The cliff was gritty up here, and dislodging the smallest pebble could lead to disaster.

Very slowly, he moved across the face until the sentry's steel helmet was a metallic egg below, the barrel of his rifle trained on the right-hand end of the parapet. If only he had had a silenced Browning, thought Mallory, like the one Carstairs carried, and Miller . . .

But all Mallory had was a knife.

He moved the last six inches to the left. Now he was in position directly above the sentry. He took the knife from its sheath and gripped it in his hand. He looked down at that steel helmet, and for a fraction of a second there flitted across his mind pity for this boy who was just doing his duty, and disgust at himself, washed by the current of war against this man, now the agent of his drowning.

He shifted his foot half an inch to give him a purchase, and prepared to jump. He felt the pebble roll, and stopped, knowing it was too late. He felt it escape, saw it fall, a tiny crumb of stone, heard the small *plink* as it hit the brim of the soldier's helmet. The soldier looked up: a young face, shocked, mouth open. The last thing he saw was Mallory, falling like a thunderbolt, hands down, knife out, felt the crushing weight, the terrible sting of the razor-sharp steel.

Then he saw no more. He struggled for a moment, though: the wild, reflex struggle of an organism already fatally wounded, going through the motions of self-defence, to the limit of its dying strength.

Mallory was not prepared for it. The knife had gone in hard and deep, and he had expected the man to collapse. Instead he found the dagger torn from his hand and the man's tunic rent away from his fingers as the spasming muscles jerked the man out of his grip and away, over the parapet.

And the ledge was an empty slice of rock, with a steel door concreted into the cliff at its back.

'Carstairs,' said Mallory, low-voiced.

Carstairs hauled himself over the parapet. He sat down, and let his head hang, and said, 'What the hell happened?'

'You tried to commit suicide,' said Mallory, cold. 'You nearly succeeded.'

'Wha?' said Carstairs, uncomprehending. 'Oh, I see. Joke.' He fumbled in his breast pocket. 'Cigarette? Virginian this side, Turkish tha – Oh, God. Lost me case.'

'Here,' said Mallory, and gave it to him. 'No smoking.'

'Oh, I say,' said Carstairs, frowning. His brain was not working. 'Sentry's gone. Relax, eh? Nobody knows we're here.'

Mallory shook his head. He walked over to the steel door, and shoved it open. 'They will,' he said. 'They will.'

Private Otto Schultz weighed eighteen stone, and this evening every single ounce of him was completely fed up. Some fool had crashed a locomotive, and Schultz had spent a miserably sweaty hour with winches and levers and NCOs screaming at him. Then he had gone for his dinner, and half-way through his fourth sausage all the aerials (someone had said it was the aerials, anyway) had been bombed or shot up, nobody knew which, so they had all had to go and sit in the shelters. And then, before he had had time to finish his food, he had been told to report for duty in the guard-house with two of those *Sonderkommando* thugs. They had spent the last half-hour reminiscing about some place called Treblinka, about which Schultz had no desire to hear. Then one of them, Putzi he seemed to be called, had beaten Schultz at chess. Schultz was pretty sure Putzi had cheated, but that was not the sort of thing you accused a *Sonderkommando* man of, if you wanted to keep your head on your shoulders. Putzi had high cheekbones and hard blue eyes and a smile that never faltered. But sitting there across the table from Schultz, you could see he was just a piece of vicious scum, like all the rest of them. Schultz had been a mathematics teacher, and he did not enjoy being trounced at chess by thugs.

'Your move,' said Putzi, as if Schultz did not already know. Schultz moved. Putzi's grin became more scornful. He moved his bishop. 'Checkmate, fatso.'

'Rubbish,' said Schultz. But Putzi was right. He opened his mouth to concede.

But he never said it.

There was a crash like a bomb going off. Something fell on to Putzi from the sky, and he vanished, the table with him. Splinters of wood flew around the guardhouse. Schultz leaped to his feet and hit the red general alarm button.

Sigmund, the other *Sonderkommando* man, was bending over the mess on the floor. 'Dead,' he said.

Schultz gave the subject ponderous but methodical thought, and arrived at an understanding. A human body, by its uniform a member of the *Wehrmacht*, had fallen through the asbestos roof of the guardhouse with enough force not only to kill Putzi but to drive his corpse some distance into the floorboards. This implied that he had fallen from a considerable height – one of the lookouts on the cliff face above, no doubt. A tragic accident. Schultz wagged his head on its great rolls of neck.

Then Sigmund rolled the sentry's jellified body off the crushed corpse of Putzi. It was at that point that Schultz sat down heavily, and started to shake.

For there was no part of Schultz's imagination that could explain what kind of accident it was that had sent a *Wehrmacht* private plummeting out of the heavens with a British Special Forces-issue dagger driven to the hilt in its right eye.

When the charges on the aerials went off and the air-raid klaxon began to sound, Miller and Andrea had a short discussion. Men were still strolling in the corridor, unmoved by the moaning of the alarm. Presumably, they were far enough into the mountain to be safe from bombs. So they walked briskly down the steel staging to the sentry box in front of the elevator, and came to attention in front of the guardhouse. There was a *Feldwebel* and a private behind an armoured-glass window, wearing camouflage uniforms. They looked at Andrea. The *Feldwebel's* eyes flicked from his dark

Mediterranean features to his badges of rank. Miller saw the man start to frown, then deliberately smooth his face out. There was a fixed number of huge *SS Leutnants* on Kynthos. It looked as if this might be a *Feldwebel* with eyes and a memory. Look out, he thought: trouble.

Andrea said, 'I want to look at your records.'

The Sergeant said, 'Records, *Herr Leutnant?*'

'The pass records. There may have been a breach of security.'

The Sergeant stiffened. 'I can assure the *Herr Leutnant* that –'

'Let us in.'

'The *Herr Leutnant* will excuse me,' said the sergeant. His hand went for the telephone.

Miller started to cough. He coughed very badly, doubling up, out of the vision of the men in the guard hut. He had his knife out, and as he doubled up he hooked the blade under a cable that ran out of the hut and away down the tunnel, and cut.

Inside the hut, the sergeant jiggled the cradle furiously.

'Let me in,' said Andrea, low and dangerous.

The sergeant was looking ruffled now. 'But I do not . . . that is, I am not acquainted with the *Herr Leutnant's* face.'

'This is of no interest to me,' said Andrea. 'You will however remember the *Hauptmann* Wolf, with whom you will renew your acquaintance very speedily unless you open up as instructed, immediately.'

At the mention of Wolf's name, the sergeant's face turned a nasty grey, and his memory apparently lost its influence. 'Open the door,' he said to the private. The door opened. Andrea walked in. 'The books,' he said.

The sergeant handed over a large ledger. Andrea put it on the desk, leafed through the pages. 'Excuse me,' said the sergeant. 'The telephone is *kaput*. I must arrange for repairs. Schmidt –' he looked at the private '– fetch a maintenance crew.'

Andrea slammed the book. 'All seems to be in order,' he said. 'But Schmidt, stay here. There is a general alert. Maximum vigilance. Now, give me the key.'

The sergeant snapped to attention. *'Herr Leutnant?'*

'The key,' said Andrea. 'To the lift.'

'The *Herr Leutnant's* pass?'

Andrea said, patiently, 'My pass is being renewed. Now my duty takes me into that lift.'

The sergeant's face turned to stone. 'I am sorry,' he said. 'No pass, you cannot. It is not permitted.'

'I am sorry too,' said Andrea, in a low, dangerous rumble. 'And you will be sorrier, I promise you.'

The sergeant stared straight ahead of him, the impassive stare of the German NCO who knows he is obeying orders, that the chain of command is complete, that his position is unassailable and his duty done.

Two engineers stopped at the window. 'Carry on,' said Andrea. The engineers signed their names and the time in the book. 'You will please report this telephone out of order,' said Andrea to the engineers. The private escorted them to the lift door. One of them opened it with his key, pulled back the inner door, slid the outer door into place. The lift machinery hummed.

'Very good,' said Andrea. 'You have made a note, *Herr Doktor* Muller?'

'I shall get my notebook,' said Miller. 'One moment.' He crouched, opened the pack he had been carrying. The sergeant moved suddenly, and looked over the lid and inside. His eyes widened and his jaw dropped, and he raised the Schmeisser in his hands.

But Miller had a hand of his own, and in it was a Browning automatic with a long cylindrical snout. The snout coughed flame. The wall behind the *Feldwebel* turned red. He slammed backwards into the wall, eyes blank, a new eye in the middle of his forehead. The private ran out of the shed and started to run, unlimbering his own Schmeisser as he went. Miller went after him. The man turned. Miller raised the Browning two-handed. The private went down.

'Hide the bodies,' said Andrea, dragging the *Feldwebel* out of the shed and round to the back.

Miller nodded. He looked whitish in the face, and his hands were shaking. As he hauled the private back to the shed, the man's heels clattered on the grating. Andrea bent, and retrieved a key from the ring on the man's belt.

'Signature,' said Andrea, pushing the book at Miller. Both men signed the register. 'Key,' said Miller.

Once you had turned the key in the lock, it was a lift like any other lift. The motor hummed. Outside the concertina inner door the wall went by, a rough-hewn shaft that seemed to go on for ever, with iron step-rungs inset. It was an unpleasant sensation,

Miller found, standing in this lattice-sided can with rock all around you, two bodies by the downstairs exit, God knew what waiting upstairs –

The lift stopped.

It did not stop at a floor. It stopped between floors. There was nothing to see except the walls, and the steps, and Andrea. 'I am afraid,' said Andrea, 'that someone has found some bodies.'

'The steps,' said Miller. He hated this elevator. He wanted out as fast as possible.

'They will be expecting that,' said Andrea. 'We will stay here, my friend. More or less.'

Well, thought Miller, what can you do, Andrea being a colonel and all, God damn it.

'Up,' said Andrea, and pointed to the escape hatch in the roof.

Oh, no, thought Miller. Not again. Not standing around waiting to be torn apart by machinery again. Nor waiting for a wire rope to break and the plummeting to start –

But by this time his head and shoulders were already through the trap door, and Andrea was shoving hard from below. Miller found himself standing in darkness on top of the lift, next to an oily cable. Andrea shoved up the pack, then came up himself, and sat on the trap door.

There was a jerk. The lift started upwards. It went up a long way. Miller could hear the engine. He started to sweat. To distract himself he examined as much of the machinery as he could. 'This is a piece of cheap Kraut rubbish,' he said, 'not an Otis.'

'What?'

'Nothing,' said Miller, rummaging in the pack.

Then Andrea said, 'Quiet.'

They froze. The sound of the machinery was very close above. Out of the corner of his eye, Miller could see a streak of light gleaming on the flange of a huge wheel spinning in the obscurity above. The streak of light from the upper door.

The lift rose past the streak, and stopped. The machinery was close overhead; close enough to touch. Many boots crashed into the car. 'The ceiling,' said a German voice. There was a grunting, as if someone was trying to push. Andrea stood on the door, braced against the axle of the winding drum above his head. 'Help me,' said the voice below.

Someone presumably helped him. Tall men, they must be, and big. Sweat rolled down Andrea's face, and the veins in his neck stood out like hawsers. 'Some fool's welded it shut,' said a voice from below. 'Some bloody Greek.'

Which was not, thought Miller, as he worked at what was in his hand, so far off the mark.

'No good,' said a voice with the bark of authority in it. 'They must be on the steps down below.'

Under Miller's feet, the lift lurched, and started downwards. Miller and Andrea just had time to grab the axle overhead. It was turning, the axle, but it was greasy. The lift dropped away below, leaving a shaft like a well. Andrea heaved himself over to the wall and hung on to the first of the steps. Miller reached a hand towards Andrea. The big Greek caught him just as his fingers let go. Miller slammed into the ladder, grabbing the cold metal. 'Out,' he said.

'There'll be a guard—'

'Out. There's no safety lock.'

Andrea heard real urgency in his voice. He did not know what Miller was talking about. But he had worked with Miller long enough to trust his instincts.

Miller was right. The door slid open. Andrea and Miller stepped on to the threshold, blinking in the sudden light.

The eight *Wehrmacht* soldiers outside raised their Schmeissers to belly height. '*Hände hoch*,' said the officer in charge. '*Ausweis, bitte.*'

'For Christ's sake,' said Miller, in his excellent German. 'It's one or the other.'

'*Hände hoch*,' said the officer. He had an efficient look that Miller disliked intensely. The lift was in a sort of lobby, shielded by concrete walls from whatever took place beyond. Andrea and Miller separated, standing one on either side of the door. The officer started rummaging in Miller's pockets. It was evident to Miller, with four Schmeissers trained upon him, that he and Andrea were in big trouble. But then again, the only thing that really amazed him was that they had got this far.

Andrea had a look of great stupidity on his face. He rolled his eyes towards the empty door of the lift shaft, and gave Miller a wink cunningly judged to be both conspiratorial and obvious. 'You bloody idiot,' said Miller, with venom. 'They've had it now.'

The German officer frowned. He said, 'Cover me,' to his men. Four of them went to the lift door, and peered down the shaft.

'Nobody,' said the officer.

Miller glanced at his watch. 'Now, boys!' he said.

From the lift shaft there came the sound of a large, hollow boom, followed by a twang of breaking cable, screams, and a crash. The men at the door were blown backwards by a blast of hot gas. The men covering Andrea and Miller clapped their hands to their scalded eyes. One of them fell into Andrea, who heaved him down the shaft.

Miller felt quietly proud. It was not everyone, he considered, who would, under the kind of pressure he and Andrea had suffered on the lift roof, have noticed that it was a device with neither a safety wire nor a shaft brake. Nor would it have been just anybody who would have taken the time to wrap half a pound of plastique round the cable, with a five-minute time pencil.

Miller flattered himself that it had all gone rather well.

But he did not waste time feeling smug. He pulled a fire extinguisher out of its clips, smashed the button in, and started spraying the men staggering about by the lift gate. *'Hilfe!'* he yelled. *'Feuer!'*

When the first reinforcements came round the corner, they found a huge *SS* man and a lanky engineer in a cloud of evil-smelling smoke, dousing the fuming lift shaft and half-a-dozen smouldering soldiers with foam. The reinforcements started yelling as only German reinforcements can yell. More fire extinguishers started going off. And nobody paid any attention when the *SS* man hefted his pack and vanished into the workshops, accompanied by the engineer.

NINE

Thursday 2300–Friday 0300

Herr Doktor Doktor Professor Gunther Helm was a neat man. His brown overall was sharply pressed, his black shoes polished to a mirror-like sheen, and his dark, narrow moustache trimmed with mathematical exactness below his long, mobile nose. Helm was a specialist in inertial guidance systems. It had been bad enough to be removed from his comfortably ancient rooms above the river at Heidelberg University to a shed on a Baltic sand-flat at Peenemunde. This place, this hideous warren of black rock and bare cable and improvised factory space, was unpleasant. Worse, it was untidy.

Boots were crashing in the tunnel ahead. They belonged (Helm saw, as they rounded the corner) to two SS men. To two of the untidiest SS men he had ever seen. For one thing, neither of them seemed to have shaved for at least twenty-four hours. For another they were filthy dirty, smeared with white clay and blood, and unless he was gravely mistaken, wearing non-regulation boots. In addition, one of them had a moustache not unlike his own, but *(Herr Doktor Doktor Professor* Helm was compelled in all frankness to admit) considerably blonder and more lustrous. They had a wild look, as if they had been outdoors. They took up more room than seemed necessary. Frankly, Helm found them intimidating.

'Where's the hospital?' said the one without the moustache.

'The hospital,' said Helm, flustered. 'You proceed down this corridor. You will see three fire extinguishers on the wall, then a steel staircase. Ignore this. Proceed until you see a sign saying *Ausgang* – no, I am wrong; *Eintritt*, it says –'

'What level?' said the SS man, who was Mallory.

Helm was notoriously a hard man to stop, but there was enough violence in the voice to stop him. 'Third level,' said Helm, and found himself flung back against the wall by the breeze of their passing. Breathing heavily, he returned to his desk, picked up his slide rule, and re-entered the calm, ordered world of numbers. Somewhere at the periphery of his attention, he heard the klaxons going again. The klaxons were always going in the factory. It was part of the general untidiness. Since there was no way of controlling it, it was in the view of *Herr Doktor Doktor Professor* Helm best ignored.

He therefore ignored it.

The klaxons started as Mallory and Carstairs clattered down a steep set of spiral stairs. There was the distant crash of steel doors slamming, the bang of running feet. A squad of men ran up the stairs. Mallory braced himself. The squad ran past. Mallory started running again, full-pelt, down the endless latticed-steel corkscrew of the stairs. Endless stairs, in a vertical tube through the solid rock –

Carstairs was right behind Mallory now. Uniform or no uniform, thought Mallory, it was a nasty naked feeling to be inside this hollow mountain, knowing that one look at your papers –

Something hit him in the small of the back. A boot, he had time to think: whose boot?

Then Mallory was down, off balance, diving forwards, his shoulder driving into the sharp steel edge of the step, steel helmet (thank God for the helmet) ringing like a gong against the stair treads. Mallory bunched up and rolled, the way he had been taught to roll in his parachute training, tucking in his hands, protecting his fingers and his elbows and knees from the hammer of acute-edged metal. He went down twenty steps before he hit the wall. He lay there, ears ringing, winded. Carstairs ran past. Carstairs pushed me, he realized. Carstairs wanted time on his own. What for? To find the survivor of the shipwreck. Mallory remembered the grenade, pin out, above the ambulance in the gorge. Not to debrief the survivor. To do something more final than that . . .

A couple of *Wehrmacht* privates rattled down the stairs. One of them aimed a kick at his *SS* ribs. It hurt. But Mallory grinned. Dissension in the enemy camp was truly a marvellous thing.

Dissension in his own was a different matter. He spat blood, and hurried stiffly down the steps. Three minutes later, he came to a door. On the rock above the door was stencilled a broad black number three. Mallory went through it.

He was at the opposite end of the long, steel-floored corridor from the place where Andrea and Miller had taken the lift.

'Papers!' screamed a voice. It belonged to a *Wehrmacht Leutnant*, white in the face and greasy with sweat. Behind him, at the far end of the corridor where the lift doors had once stood, there was a throng of men, noise and smoke and shouting.

'Papers!' screamed the *Leutnant*, again.

Mallory gazed upon the man with freezing eyes. 'There are wounded men down there,' he said. 'They need you.' Then he walked straight through him. The *Leutnant* reeled back into the wall. His hand went to his holster flap. Mallory allowed his own hand to stray to the grip of his Schmeisser. The *Wehrmacht* officer thought better of his move, and hurried towards the lift door. Mallory walked through the doorway with the red cross above it. An orderly looked up from a desk. 'The man from the shipwreck,' said Mallory.

The orderly looked nervous. There had been too many alarm bells, and he really hated these *SS*. 'Down there,' he said, pointing down the corridor. 'Your friend's already with him.'

'When I want your conversation I'll ask for it,' said Mallory, to pour oil on the flames. Then he crashed off down the corridor.

The door the orderly had indicated was closed. Mallory twisted the handle. It was locked. It was a hospital door, not a military door; a flimsy thing of cheap deal. Mallory hit it with his boot, hard, next to the handle. The orderly had been watching him. When he caught his eye he quickly looked away. The door held. Mallory knew he was on the edge. Never mind how much trouble there was between *Wehrmacht* and *SS* and boffins, there came a time when he would no longer get away with disobeying orders and wrecking government property. But Carstairs was behind that door, with a man Mallory was interested in, and who would not be alive for long, unless –

His boot hit the door again. This time it burst open with a splintering crash.

It was a small, green room, with a smell of cleanliness, a bed and a chair. There were two men on the bed: one lying down, legs thrashing, the other bent over him. The bending man was Carstairs. The reason for his bending was that he had a pillow in his hands, a pillow he was pressing over the face of whoever it was that was lying on the bed. The survivor of the *Kormoran*, at a rough guess.

Mallory could kill, all right. But he was a soldier, not an assassin. There was a difference between killing and murder.

He said, 'Stop that.'

Carstairs did not answer. His face was set and ugly, ridged with muscle, holding the pillow down. Mallory lifted his Schmeisser. 'Stop it now,' he said.

Carstairs raised one hand to swat the barrel aside. 'No noise,' he said. 'Quiet, you idiot.' The assumption that he would not use the weapon fed Mallory's irritation. He jabbed Carstairs on the arm with the barrel. The flapping of the supine figure's legs was weakening. 'All right,' said Carstairs, face twisted with effort. 'So fire.'

Mallory did not fire. Instead, he kicked Carstairs very hard on the bundle of nerves inside his right knee. It was a kick that would hurt like hell, but do no permanent damage.

It worked.

Carstairs crashed to the ground, grabbing for his dagger. Mallory stamped on his hand and let him look down the black tube of the machine pistol's muzzle.

The man on the bed said, 'Jesoos.'

'Shut up!' hissed Carstairs.

'Hold your tongue,' said Mallory.

The man on the bed was small and stout, with curly black hair and a thick black moustache and a very bad colour. 'Don' kill me,' he said. 'Don' kill me. For why you want to kill me?'

Mallory looked at Carstairs, then at the black-haired man. He said, in English, 'What happened to you?'

The small man's eyes narrowed. He said, in German, 'Why are you speaking English?'

Mallory lay wearily back in the chair. Carstairs was spluttering like an unexploded bomb on the floor. 'Because I'm English,' he said. 'Who are you?'

'Shut your bloody mouth,' said Carstairs, frantic. 'I forbid you to speak.'

'So,' said the short man, indignation getting the better of suspicion. 'I answer your damned question, and you tries to suffocate me. And now there is another German *SS* who talk English and want to know. Is it for this that I swim, I paddle, I bring –'

'Start at the beginning,' said Carstairs, wearily. 'Go on.'

'How do I know who you are?' said the Greek.

Mallory offered the man a cigarette, lit one himself, closing his mind to the idea that outside that door was bandit country, crawling with people who would kill him as quick as blow their noses. Carstairs had had orders from Admiral Dixon to assassinate this man. Mallory had countermanded them. There would be trouble in England, too. Wearily, he took off his helmet.

The Greek made a sound half-way between a gasp and a squeak. 'Mallory!' he said. 'Is no possible.'

Mallory looked at him, one eyebrow up.

'Mount Cook,' said the Greek. 'My cousin Latsis he went to New Zealand for the farm. But the farm no work out good so he get work with expedition, because he know how make food in fire far from roof. He cook with you. He send me photograph, newspaper story. You and Latsis. You remember? My cousin Latsis. Sure you remember. Yes, yes, you remember.'

Mallory remembered, all right. He remembered the Mount Cook expedition, the first and last major expedition he had led in the Southern Alps, after his lone climbs. He remembered far too many people, far too much organization: the green New Zealand sky over the white prisms of the mountains, the crisp new air, the sound of too many voices; the taste of burned beans. He remembered a charming Greek with a huge nose, a ready smile, and absolutely no talent in the kitchen.

'Big nose,' said Mallory.

If there had been wine in the little hospital room, someone would have opened it. As it was, the Greek seized Mallory's right hand in both of his and shook it furiously. 'I am Spiro,' he said. 'And I must tell you what I told your . . . this man.' Here he narrowly failed to spit on Carstairs. 'I have got the machine.'

'The machine?'

Carstairs said, 'Now look here –'

'The seven-rotor Enigma,' said Spiro. 'Of course.'

'What is the seven-rotor Enigma?' said Mallory.

'Nothing,' said Carstairs. 'Spiro, I should warn you –'

'Shut the mouth,' said Spiro. 'I am tired. So bloody tired you would not believe. Always I keeps my mouth shut –'

'A little longer,' said Mallory. 'First, we must get you out of here.'

'So let's get out,' said Spiro. 'And then I show you machine.'

'Show us?' said Carstairs. 'You don't really mean you've got it?'

'Yes,' said Spiro. 'What did you think?'

Carstairs' face had gone a nasty shade of grey. 'They told me you knew about it,' he said. 'That you had been sent to steal it. But that there was no hope, what with the shipwreck. I was to . . . silence you before you were tortured. If I'd known . . .'

'Of courses,' said Spiro, nastily. 'First murder, then asking questions. Fool.'

Carstairs gave him a sickly smile. 'Awfully sorry,' he said, 'but I'm sure you understand, what? Now, then. This is marvellous. Exactly where is it?'

Spiro turned upon him a puffed and hostile gaze. 'I tell your friend when we are out,' he said. 'Just for now, it is in a safe place. Okay?'

'Where?'

'Out first,' said Spiro. 'Where later.'

Miller found the workshops most impressive. In the lava bubbles of the cold volcano, the Germans had built a fair-sized factory. There were machine shops and an assembly line staffed by brown-coated engineers, with Greek slave labourers in blue boiler suits wheeling racks of parts and tools. The air was full of the limey reek of wet concrete. Someone somewhere was building something. Miller found an abandoned trolley and loaded in the explosives pack. They trundled it along the lines of benches, through tunnels into new caverns, with curved alloy castings and cylindrical motors of huge complexity with nozzles and no driveshafts, fuel and lubricant tanks, steel doors marked with skull-and-crossbones stencils, until at the end they came to a series of concrete baffles built out across the passage. Standing in front of the baffles was an *SS* man with a Schmeisser. Above his head, a large sign said: *Eingang Verboten*.

'Looks like it,' said Miller. 'Plan?'

Andrea did not answer. But Miller saw from the corner of his eye the huge Greek's right hand go to the place on his belt occupied by his knife. And not before time: from behind, there was the sound of shouting and running feet. The confusion by the lift seemed to have sorted itself out.

Somewhere ahead, a field telephone rang. The *SS* man picked up the receiver and gave what must have been a password. Then his eyes bulged out of their sockets and his mouth opened and no sound came out, because Andrea had walked straight up to him and slammed his knife between his fourth and fifth ribs and into his heart, and as he slid to the ground had plucked the telephone from the dead fingers. *'Bitte?'* said Andrea.

'Intruders,' said the voice. 'Two men.' The voice gave a fair description of Andrea and Miller. 'Shoot on sight,' it said. 'Tell *Hauptmann* Weiss.'

'*Zu Befehl,*' said Andrea. He put the telephone down and tore the wire out of the junction box.

Miller had dragged the corpse out of sight. They walked round the baffles, and found themselves confronted by a huge steel door. Andrea rapped on it with his gun-butt. '*Hauptmann* Weiss!' he said.

A slider on the door went back. 'Who wants him?'

'Wolf. Immediately.'

There was the sound of grumbling. A wicket opened in the steel door. A man in *SS* uniform started through. The silenced Browning jumped in Miller's hand. The *SS* man fell back. The two men ran in, and shut the door behind them. Two *SS* privates were hauling their Schmeissers into firing position. Miller shot both of them.

'Christos,' said Andrea.

It was the first time Miller had ever heard him blaspheme. But he could see why.

They were on the concrete floor of an enormous yard. There were very few people. In the middle of the area, a hundred yards away, stood a cylindrical object painted in a black and white checkerboard pattern that gave it the look of an obscene toy made for the children of giants.

But it was not a toy. It was a rocket – a rocket so much bigger than any other rocket Andrea or Miller had ever seen that it removed the breath from their lungs.

It was standing in a framework of gantries. High above, a roof of camouflage netting billowed gently in the night breeze. From connection points on its bulging flanks, hoses snaked away to doors behind blast-deflection baffles in the sides of the . . . hole, was what it was, thought Miller; not a crater, but a hole left by the parting of the ways of three magma streams in three different directions.

'Most impressive,' he said.

Andrea just shook his head.

Behind them, someone was hammering on the steel door.

Miller rubbed his hands. They had now entered his area of special expertise. The gentle art of destruction, of which Miller was one of the world's great exponents.

'Now listen here,' said Corporal Miller to Colonel Andrea, and opened the big wooden pack. Andrea listened. After a couple of minutes, he stowed four packages in his haversack, walked across the concrete to the gantry. Whistling, he trotted up the steps until he came to the level just below what he presumed was the business end. Here he paused, and moulded the putty-like explosive to the surface, leaving a thickness in the middle. Into the thickness he pushed an eight-hour time cartridge, crushed the tube, and withdrew the tag.

When he turned, a scientist was staring at him. 'Monitoring,' said Andrea. 'Telemetry.'

The man pointed at the charge, mouthing. 'Oh, all right,' said Andrea, and kicked the man off the platform and on to the concrete. Then he started down.

Miller was nowhere to be seen.

He had strolled across to the baffles in front of the place where the pipes came out of the wall. *Brennstoff*, said stencilled letters. Fuel. He unlatched the door. There were no guards: nobody except another engineer in a brown coat, who simply nodded at him as he let himself into the chamber.

It was a squared-off cave, lit with harsh fluorescent lights. On the concrete floor, rank after rank of huge steel tanks lay like sleeping pigs. Half of them were thick-walled, pressurized: liquid oxygen. The rest were of riveted steel. Miller felt a momentary gloom at the thought of all that good alcohol going to waste. Then he sighed, took a little toolkit out of his pocket, and followed the hoses to their starting point. There were two tanks, one of oxygen, one of alcohol, the one next to the other. As he had hoped, their contents were indicated by ordinary *Luftwaffe*-pattern flow gauges downstream of the outlet valve. Humming, Miller pulled a tub of grease from the pocket of his overall. He unscrewed the cover of the valve, scooped some of the tub's contents out with a wooden spatula, and greased the innards heavily.

'*Wer da?*' said a voice at his shoulder.

Miller turned to see an *SS* man pointing a machine pistol at him. 'Maintenance,' he said.

'*Vas?*'

Miller shoved the grease under his nose. 'Slippery stuff, cretin,' he said. 'Feel.'

But the soldier, thinking perhaps about the cleanliness of his uniform, said, '*Nein,*' and pushed the tub away.

'Suit yourself,' said Miller, under whose arms the sweat was falling like rain. 'Only twenty more to do.'

The soldier grunted. The rifle muzzle dropped. 'Get on with it, then,' he said.

'So what's all the fuss about?' said Miller.

'Someone's stolen some uniforms in the showers,' said the *SS* man. 'So they're all going crazy. Now the telephones are dead.' He yawned. 'So they panic, these *Wehrmacht* bastards. Some of us have got work to do. No time to panic.'

Miller grunted, took himself along to the next tank, unscrewed the gauge cover, smeared on the paste from his tub: his own patent paste, compounded of carborundum powder, magnesium, iron oxide and powdered aluminium. When the gauges started to spin, the carborundum would heat up. When it reached the right temperature, the magnesium would ignite and start the aluminium powder reacting with the iron oxide: an exothermic reaction, they called it, meaning that it got hot as hell, hot enough to melt iron and burn concrete. Certainly enough heat to ignite alcohol. And if by any chance an oxygen tank should rupture, well, the structural integrity of the entire V4 plant would be severely compromised. If not destroyed.

Personally, Miller was betting on destruction.

He did a couple more valves, for luck. Then he shoved his hands into his pockets and strolled, whistling, out of the fuel store.

Andrea was standing by the door, Schmeisser at the ready, as if on guard. 'Hey!' said Miller. 'You!'

Andrea snapped to attention.

'Follow me!' Miller started up the wall of the crater. He marched quickly, though his leg muscles were suddenly cracking with weariness, the blood pounding in his skull and his breath rasping in his throat. They scrambled from rock to rock, pushed under the edge of the roof of tarpaulins and camouflage nets. Behind them, the crater glowed under its blue floodlights. They began to scramble over the rocks towards the rendezvous.

Outside the hospital, the corridor was an ants' nest. Nobody paid any attention to two *SS* men with a stretcher. Mallory and Carstairs carried Spiro down two flights of steel stairs. The shift was changing. Greek workers were shuffling down a corridor Mallory had not previously visited. There were few light bulbs, and a smell of cheap rice cooking, and latrines badly cleaned. A hundred yards later they rounded a corner and came to a wire-mesh fence with a gate, beside which stood a bored-looking *SS* man. 'Throw it into the sea,' said the sentry, when he saw the stretcher.

'First, it has work to do,' said Mallory. The sentry laughed. 'We'll be a while.'

'Long as you like,' said the sentry, heaving the gate open. 'Don't touch the women, though. They'll claw it off.'

Mallory could feel Spiro's shivering transmitted along the handles of the stretcher. He walked on.

The camp was no more nor less than the old village of the Acropolis, cordoned off from the rest of the island by a wire fence, so the precipices and fortifications that had once kept out the Turk now served to hold prisoner the Greek. It was a depressed, ruinous place, harshly lit by the floodlights set in the cliff face above. They carried the stretcher into the shadows of Athenai Street, and set it down.

Mallory lit a cigarette, drawing the harsh smoke into his lungs. In the blue-white streets, black-overalled figures came and went. There was no curiosity. A village without curiosity, thought Mallory, is a village that is dead: and for a moment he felt a pure, clear disgust for the men who had killed it.

Then he said, 'This machine.'

'Po!' said Spiro. 'Po, this machina!' The words began to pour out of him in a torrent.

'Steady,' said Mallory.

'Okay,' he said. 'Okay. Only when they have you in this place, you keep your eyes shut one, two days, breathe slow, they say *Ach Gott* he sleeps still, they stick in you pins and needles, you do not twitching, wait for you do not know what, then when you think, well, now I will have to be awake but when I awake I will be fear and tell them all about everythings and they will kill me real slows real slows, the hell with it I will rather die than sleep no more, then sudden you get the angels down flap flap.' Here he cast himself upon Carstairs and began to cover his face with wet kisses.

'Ugh,' said Carstairs.

Mallory watched with some enjoyment as Carstairs disentangled himself. 'So what's the story?' he said.

'The machina –'

'From the beginning.'

'Yais,' said Spiro. 'Give me cigarette.'

'Turkish this side, Virginian that,' said Carstairs automatically, proffering his case.

'I spit on your Turkish,' said Spiro.

'The story,' said Mallory.

'Okay, okay. So I am in Trieste. In Trieste I am cook in café by docks, everything nice, when they tell me, Spiro, go on ship.'

'Who tell you?'

'SIS. Peoples in London. Spying peoples. They say Spiro, the King of Britains, big friend of the Kings of Greece, he need you stop listening to German mens talking in cafés, go to find cooking mans on *Kormoran*, arrange bad things. Then get on *Kormoran* and find out what goings on. So I find cooking man on *Kormoran* and give him accidents with open window and broken leg, and look at Spiro then, cook on this lousy God damned pig bastard ship *Kormoran* God rest his poor soul if his mother could see him now –'

'The story,' said Mallory.

'The story, hokay. So I am working in the café with SIS and this guy, my contact, he say, get on this pig bastard ship *Kormoran*. So I go down to the port and it is a mess, you know, they are bombing him, and all the way down the back end there is this ship, this dirty little ship, and they say sure, the cook's mate has fell down and broked his leg so we needs a cook's mate and Spiro we know you are not a cook – normally,' said Spiro, 'I working as a thief, but the war, you know. So come aboard, they say. Well me I say I must go and kiss my girl goodbye, nice girl, very big moustache, but they say, no, come aboard now, so there I go, and they put me on that ship, slam door. Very strange ship. Outside dirty filthy like a latrine. Inside more tidy, clean, like German ship. And captain and officers stand-to-attention *Heil Hitler* sort of mens, must have all things regular and particular. Then big crateses arrives on an army sort of train, and more, gas bottles, I don't know. Spiro had thinked, oh ho, stupid SIS peoples, false alarm. But then Spiro thinked, oh shits, if it ain't a false alarm what in hells kind of alarm is this? But I carries on washing up, bringing bridge coffees, all that. Then,' said Spiro, his vast black pupils swimming with sincerity, 'come the miracles.' He drew breath. He was panting. He was also, Mallory realized, very frightened.

'It was morning,' he said. 'I took coffee to bridge. Ten fifty-five hours precisely. *Kapitän* Helmholz insist, exactly that time, no seconds before, no seconds after. Stupid bastards, dead now. So I get off bridge fast. And I am a little way down the stairs when bam! Something hit ship, then bam! Something else, and I can tell that all this is turning higgledy turvy and it is hot like hell and peoples screamings. So then I see the man go out of the radio rooms and up to the bridge, then one more bang and more broken glasses and he roll down stairses, head gone. Well I have seen before, bringing coffees to Sparks, that code machina, this seven-rotor Enigma, is in radio room, and SIS always pay good money for code machina. So I go quick double quick into the radio rooms and catches up the machina in his cases and jumps overboard double quick, big wind, everything terrible bright, and the case is a heavy thing and she wants to sink and it try to kill me but I do not let him. Well by the mercy of God the Creator the Redeemer may His name be blessed for ever and ever amen and also His holy saints' – here he caught Mallory's eye – 'I am finding a big broken crate of wood, a hatch, who knows? And there is a great wind blowing. And it blow me far and away, and on to the shore of Kynthos. Now you tellings me, is that or is that not a miracles yes or no?'

'Miracle,' said Mallory. 'Definitely.'

'And the machine,' said Carstairs. 'What about the machine?'

'Hah!' said Spiro. 'Well. I got him on beach. Very ill, I was. Lying with him, sleeping, very thirsty, sand in face, no move. Then a chap I think is there, speaking Greeks, give me drink of water.' He was frowning, as if he did not remember properly. 'Like dreams. Like dreams. Then I hear his voice loud, and other voices, not so loud, further away, and they are speaking Germans. I trying to get up, but no luck, fall on face bang, pass out again. And when I wakes up again I am in some ambulance, on some bed, and there are Germanses everywhere, but no machina.'

'No machine,' said Carstairs. 'Then they've got it.'

'Greeks man got it,' said Spiro. 'I spose. I never seen it no more. But I worry, I worry. I am thinking, if I wakes up, then they ask me questions, so I will be asleep and they will not ask me no questions and I will not be frightened. Because I am weak, you know, when I am tired like this, and I will tell anybody anything. So I make out I am knock out. So there.'

'You pretended to be in a coma for a week?' said Mallory.

'Just about. Yes,' said Spiro, with some smugness. 'Eat, drink when nobody lookings. When you are very very frightens you can be very very brave.'

Carstairs said, 'You are very brave and we admire you like hell, but we will tell you all about that later. Where is the machine?'

'I remembers,' said Spiro. 'This chap who give me drink of water on beach. He said he was hiding this thing in a place that only he know, nobody else, ever. So is okay. He is a good guy, I think: hate Germans scums, fight for us, our side. And he give me his name. So now we go find him, tell him, British armies arrived, hand over, me old cocky. Everything hunky-boo.'

'So what was his name?' said Carstairs.

'Achilles,' said Spiro. Then, by Mallory's computation about a thousand years later, 'What wrong? You get problem?'

'Yes,' said Mallory. 'Just a bit.'

Because Achilles was the name of the brother of Clytemnestra, who had been hanged in the Parmatia razzia. So it seemed very much as if the seven-rotor Enigma machine was somewhat lost.

In the dark very close behind them, someone cleared his throat. Mallory's hand jumped automatically on the cocking lever of his Schmeisser.

'Not today, thanks,' said a voice. And Miller stepped into the lamplight, with Andrea close beside him.

'I'll go and find her,' said Andrea.

'Find who?' said Carstairs.

'Clytemnestra. Achilles' sister.'

'You heard.'

'He wasn't exactly whispering.'

Carstairs laughed, his short, patronizing bark. 'Clytemnestra could be anywhere.'

'We have a rendezvous,' said Andrea. 'The road's open, again. We'll take transport. We'll find this machine.'

Carstairs nodded his head, wincing slightly. 'I expect you will,' he said. Then he swayed and lay down, suddenly.

'What is it?' said Mallory.

'Giddy,' said Carstairs. He tried to sit up, fell down again. 'Christ.'

'Stay there,' said Mallory. You could not expect a man who had smashed himself unconscious on a rock to laugh lightly and carry on as if nothing had happened. 'Andrea, get going. Miller, what's your timing?'

'Eight-hour fuses,' said Miller.

'Yes,' said Mallory. 'And the rest of it?'

'Depends when they start pumping fuel,' said Miller.

'Any sign of anyone doing any rocket firing?'

'Dunno,' said Miller. 'They've got one standing right there, pointed out of the roof. There weren't no action we could see. But I guess they could have that sucker ready to go in, what, two hours, from a standing start?'

Andrea said, 'I'll be at the jetty by sunrise.' There was no sound of movement. One moment he was there; the next, the darkness had flowed in to occupy the place where he had been standing.

'Well,' said Miller. 'This is real nice.' Miller was a man who believed in reconnaissance. On the way to the village, he had checked the place out. Once, it had probably been a thriving little community. Now, by the look of it, the original inhabitants had been displaced, the houses turned into dormitories for the men who worked inside the mountain, the church desecrated, a field kitchen on its mosaic floors turning out coarse bread and a soup whose smell did not inspire Miller to make its further acquaintance.

There was one bonus. The village was a prison, with the guards on the outside. The Germans would be looking for escapers, not intruders.

Miller left Mallory with Carstairs and Spiro, and went scouting. He walked quietly among the little knots of men in the village square. Soon, he observed a man with a disc-shaped loaf of white bread and a bottle of wine. Miller had lived through Prohibition in the States, and his nose for a bootlegger was practically supernatural. So he followed on down a narrow alley, and found a lamplit door and inside it an old man with a white bandit's moustache, who looked at Miller's gold drachmae with a face that did not budge an inch, but was still extremely impressed. 'Where you from?' he said.

'Crete,' said Miller.

'How did you find me?'

'I found you,' said Miller, dour. He did not want to be gossiped about. 'What you got?'

The old man hauled bread, wine and olives from a wormy wooden box. Miller blessed him, and walked out.

At the back of the church was a little house; the priest's house, perhaps, built right up against the wall. It was dusty and cobwebbed, and had an odour suggestive of graveyards, and its floors were connected not by stairs but by a movable ladder, somewhat worm-eaten. But it was dry and secure, and to Miller it looked better than the Waldorf Astoria. He went back for Mallory and Carstairs and Spiro. Inside, he took out sardines and chocolate, and the bread and olives, and the wine. They ate like hungry wolves, tearing great lumps of bread and washing them down with draughts of turpentine-flavoured retsina. It seemed to Miller that for a man suffering from delayed concussion, Carstairs seemed to have a hearty appetite; a very hearty appetite indeed. Miller had taken a good few knocks on the head in his time as gold-miner and bootlegger. As far as he remembered – which was not, admittedly, very far, given the nature of the injury – for some weeks afterwards the very thought of food had been enough to make him spew his guts up . . .

Different strokes for different folks, thought Miller, watching Carstairs tap a cigarette on his gold case and light up. Very different folks. Carstairs was very different indeed.

Soon after this, in fact about ten seconds after this, he left his body behind, the sore eyes and the aching bones, and drifted down and down into a soft void, a place of no pain and total rest –

Then someone had hold of him and was yanking at his shoulder, and the softness was gone and the soreness in his head and his bones was back at double strength, and he was awake, looking at his watch. The watch that said he had been asleep for only ten minutes.

But during that ten minutes, the world had changed completely.

The crack under the door of the house had become a white-hot bar of light. Outside, there was noise; the noise of sirens squawking, of feet running; jackbooted feet. German feet.

Miller grabbed his thoughts by the scruff of the neck and told them to get themselves organized. They resisted, floating in and out of focus. Perhaps Andrea had got himself caught. Perhaps the Greek with the white moustache had reported that a stranger with a Cretan accent had paid him in gold. Perhaps they had found the plastic explosive charges on the rocket . . .

Or perhaps they had discovered all these things.

Mallory's voice came out of the darkness by his ear. 'Look after these two,' it said. 'I'll do the rest.'

Miller opened his mouth to complain. But the words never came out. For at that moment, there was a thunderous knocking on the door.

'The ladder,' said Mallory.

The knocking ceased, then came again. This time, it did not stop.

Andrea had had no trouble so far.

He had left unhindered by the gate. From there he had walked down to the transport compound, drifting through strips of shadow, a darker patch of the general darkness. He watched a truck come in over the causeway, unload, reload, heard the driver receive his orders in the traditional *Wehrmacht* bellow. The truck was returning across the causeway to the aerodrome. Andrea crept up to it, attached two rope slings to the back axle leaf springs, and lay across them as another man might have lain in a hammock. The truck started up and roared across the causeway. The driver showed his pass, and was allowed into the aerodrome. The truck rolled to a halt by a group of sheds; by the sound of voices and crockery, a mess room.

Andrea waited for the driver to get out, then dropped to the ground. Two pairs of boots were walking away towards the Acropolis. Otherwise there was nobody in sight.

Staying in the shadows, Andrea walked quickly into the open darkness of the airfield, heading for the far side of the perimeter. Once the runway lights flicked on, and he lay flat as a twin-engined plane landed and taxied to the dispersal area. Otherwise the world seemed quiet, out here in the warm breeze and the smell of dust and bruised dry grass. He accelerated to a trot, came to the fence, took out the little wire-cutters from his pack, and made himself a small trap door in the mesh, a door just big enough to squeeze through, its lower edge camouflaged in the dirt. Against the sky he could see the leggy alien form of a guard tower. There would be sentries –

There was a sentry.

The man strolled by. Andrea smelt the smoke of the cigarette in his cupped hand. This was not a sentry on lookout; this was a sentry going through the motions. If he was looking for anybody, he would be looking for people trying to break in, not out. The sentry passed. Andrea moved on, keeping very low.

Suddenly the night turned white.

Andrea saw his hand in front of him, a great brown spider on the bare, gravelly soil. He saw the guard tower, every plank and strut lit in remorseless detail; he saw the sentry, half-turned, mouth open, eyes round with fear.

For a moment, Andrea thought they had turned on the searchlights, and braced himself grimly for the shouts, the thwack of bullets. Then he realized that the light was not coming from close at hand, but from behind him, beyond the marshes. He turned his head, glanced over his shoulder. The Acropolis was lit up like a wedding cake. Klaxons whooped in the night. Whatever was happening, it seemed unlikely to be an air raid.

In the tower a telephone started ringing. The sound broke the sentry's trance. He trotted up the ladder. By the time Andrea heard his voice he was already moving on hands and knees across that flat gravelly stretch.

Then he was on his feet, loping away into the darkness. Behind him the perimeter lights jumped into life. But by then, he was far into the dark fringes of the night, less than a shadow against the loom of the mountains.

He was running across a checkerboard of fields, splashing through little irrigation gulleys, his feet brushing wheat and carrots, clogging with the rich volcanic soil of the plain. After a while, the ground began to rise. He was approaching the mountains.

Wills was in a churchyard. He seemed to be spending most of his time among the dead, nowadays. He hoped it was not an omen.

He had woken two hours ago, in the tomb above the Swallow's Nest. There had been something on his face: Clytemnestra's hand. 'Come,' she said. 'We must go.'

He was groggy with sleeplessness. For a moment he did not want to go anywhere, except back into the comfortable dark. Then he remembered about Clytemnestra, and he got his feet under him, and told himself that there was a reason for moving, and that was to go wherever Clytemnestra was going . . .

Then he was out again in the soft night, climbing something that he knew in daylight would have scared the wits out of him, but which at this hour was merely a near-vertical wall of rock with foot and handholds at strategic intervals; a path, in fact; a vertical path.

They went up it and on to a flat place. Clytemnestra took his hand and squeezed it, signalling silence. They walked past the dark shape of a German sentry, all the way past until he realized that she was still holding his hand and he hers, which he put down to forgetting to let go. Then they were off, heading north, as far as he could tell, over a dizzy and bewildering series of paths and precipices, tending gently downhill. After perhaps two hours they burst from a maze of boulders on to a ledge or cornice of rock, spiked with black cypresses. They walked through a small area of grass, on which daisies glittered faintly under the stars, and into a plain white building. Nailed double doors swung open as they approached a church. A small figure, black as the sky and wearing a hat like a pygmy oil drum, flitted away into the night without speaking.

'What was that?' said Wills, unnerved.

'The Patriarch,' said Clytemnestra, and drew him in through the door, and closed it.

At first, there was darkness, musty with incense. Then there was the little yellow glow of a sanctuary lamp. Clytemnestra had taken her hand away from his. As his eyes got used to the gold-tinged gloom, Wills saw that she was kneeling, head bowed in prayer.

Wills had done a bit of praying himself, in chapel at school with the other chaps, and then less formally but more sincerely on lonely nights at sea with the E-boat tracers floating out of the dark at him. But up here in this strange, musty place, he felt there were more important things to do than pray.

He opened the door and slipped out.

There was a low parapet around the churchyard. Below it, the valley lay spread like a dark map. There were lights down there: runway markers flicking on, the roar of a plane landing, the markers flicking off again. The village on the Acropolis was lit, too, with the smaller yellow lights of candles. Then suddenly the airfield had become a blue-white square, dazzling in its intensity, and all over the Acropolis floodlights had leaped into being. And floating across the intervening gulf of air there came the sound of klaxons.

Something was happening.

Wills checked the clip in his Schmeisser. Then he hunkered down in the black pit of shadow between a wall and a cypress tree, and waited.

Time passed. There was only the thyme-scented breeze, and the night, and whatever devilry they were hatching on the other side of the marshes. Earlier, in his dazed wanderings, Wills had not cared whether he lived or died. He had lost his ship, and his men, and he was far, far out on the most precarious of limbs.

But since he had recovered enough to notice Clytemnestra, he was interested in living again. Of course it was never easy to work out how women thought, not if you had gone straight from Wellington to Dartmouth and then active service. But he did have the definite impression that she was not . . . well, averse to his company. She was a remarkable girl. A really spiffing girl –

Something descended on his mouth like a huge, soft leather cushion. A hand. Another hand came on the nape of his neck, and his chin was lifted until it would lift no further, and it dawned on Wills in a spasm of absolute horror that these hands did not care that this was as far as the chin went, they were going to go on lifting until his neck broke, and that would be the end of him –

'Hands up!' said a voice in Greek. A woman's voice. There was the metallic sound of a cocking lever. The hands relaxed.

Wills fell forward on to the parapet, groping for his Schmeisser. 'Back off,' he said. Then, remembering, 'Jolly boating –'

'Captain Wills,' said a voice he recognized: a soft voice that might have been a purr or a growl, there was no way of being sure. Andrea's voice. 'Captain Wills, you should not sit in a place where you can be seen against the sky.'

'Go away,' said the woman's voice. Clytemnestra's voice. 'Leave him alone, you great stupid ox.' She was beside Wills now, cradling his head in her hands. 'Can't you tell who is on your side and who isn't? Are you blind?'

'Understandable error,' said Wills, checking that his head was still there. 'Bit of luck you were coming out of the church, though.'

Clytemnestra snorted. 'Do you think I would leave you alone in the night?' she said. 'I have been watching you for the past two hours.' She put an arm around his waist. 'If you can't look after yourself, someone else will have to.'

Andrea cleared his throat. 'I hate to interrupt,' he said. 'But tell me, how much did you know about the life and habits of your late brother?'

In the view of Josef Koch, this island was a filthy place. Only a week ago, he had been pleased. After a winter chasing partisans around Yugoslavia the prospect of a little sun, sand and sea had been very enticing. But once he was actually here it had all gone wrong, thought Koch, hauling at the wheel, dragging the lorry's bonnet round yet another hairpin bend. The people on this island had the temperament of angry hornets, and most of the women had moustaches. If they were not fighting you, they were fighting each other. The *Wehrmacht* were bloody useless. The boffins were boffins: bloody useless too. Josef Koch's mind floated back to happier times: Bosnia, a wood with half-a-dozen partisans wired to the trees, him and a couple of privates slinging a rope over a branch, setting up the seesaw: a novelty, the seesaw, a thing of Josef's own invention. The idea was that the terrorist stood on one end of the seesaw, and Josef stood on the other. Josef was a big man: fat, some called him, if they dared. The terrorist, of course, had a noose round his neck tied to the branch above. The idea was that the private soldiers would tell Josef jokes, and try to make him laugh so he lost his balance, and the terrorist's end of the plank went down, leaving the terrorist kicking, but not alive, not after five minutes, anyway. The other thing Josef liked to do was walk towards the terrorist, so the terrorist's weight brought the plank down slowly, slowly, tightened the noose round the neck, while all the while Josef explained the error of the terrorist's ways, and the terrorist died, twisting and jerking on the rope, looking into Josef's thick-lipped grin and bulging, pink-veined eyes. It was fantastic, the fun you could have with a simple plank. Though obviously the terrorists did not enjoy it so much.

Josef sighed. He liked hanging people. He had had a goodish time in Parmatia last week, but that had been a small-scale operation. It sounded like there would be more such work soon, though. There had been fighting in the mountains, and trouble at the works, and . . . well, the Boss was severely ticked off, and when the Boss was ticked off, the best place to be was far away. So it was absolutely no hardship for Josef Koch to be driving this truck, on the Boss's orders, down the coast road to Parmatia to bring back some suspected partisan sympathizers from the lockup.

Next bend. Haul the wheel, change down a gear, foot flat on throttle –

There was a stone in the road. More a boulder, really. Josef stamped on the brake. The lorry halted. That was another thing you got, on this island. Lumps of mountain all over the road. There was a crowbar in the back. Sighing, Josef opened the door, swung his legs out, and slid down from the cab.

That was when the peculiar thing happened.

As his boots hit the road, he found himself grabbed from behind, scruff of neck and seat of pants. All of a sudden he had no control over his own destiny. A boot landed with shattering violence on his back, and the dark ground was passing at horrid speed under his eyes as he headed for the verge.

Not that there was a verge.

At the edge of the road was a strip of loose stones, on which the *Feldwebel* bounced once, face first. Beyond the strip of stones was silence, moving air, and far below, the shift of the sea.

The *Feldwebel* found that he was falling down a cliff. He screamed. The scream lasted exactly the time it took to fall two hundred feet on to sharp rocks.

On the road, the lorry stood, engine purring. Andrea helped Wills drag the driver's mate to the side of the road and roll him over into the dark, while Clytemnestra wiped the blade of her long knife on a tuft of dry grass. The driver's mate had bled surprisingly little. Wills possessed himself of the man's camouflage smock and took the wheel. Clytemnestra climbed into the middle, and Andrea squeezed his mighty bulk in next to her, lit a cigarette, and slumped back, hands on the grips of his machine pistol. 'Parmatia,' he said.

Beyond the windscreen, the world began to move, white stone, pine and juniper, cliff and gorge, gleaming in the light of the blacked-out headlights. The dark puddle on the road behind faded into the blackness of the night.

They headed for Parmatia.

* * *

From the top of the ladder in the house by the Acropolis church, Miller could see Mallory at the door. The knocking persisted. Carstairs was up through the hole in the ceiling now. Miller hauled up the ladder, fast. As he pulled its foot through the hole, the door opened, loosing a flood of blue-white light into the squalid ground floor. It picked out straw, rubbish, and Mallory. Mallory with his hands on his hips, glaring at the three soldiers outside, Schmeissers levelled: Mallory shouting in German, walking towards them, out into the light . . .

And that was the last Miller saw of him, because the ladder was up and he was lifting it to the next ceiling, where there was another hole. The floor creaked alarmingly as Spiro headed for the ladder. Miller picked out the joists with a pencil flashlight, shooed Carstairs to the ladder foot, then went after him. Spiro was already climbing, at a speed truly remarkable in one so recently bedridden. Carstairs went after him, more groggily.

At the top, they were in a low attic, whose ceiling was the underside of the roof tiles. 'Leave the ladder,' said Miller, and started to push aside the heavy clay half-cylinders. After five minutes' steady work, his head broke through, and he was spitting worm-eaten beam and ancient bamboo lining into the night air.

In front of him was a low white parapet. Beyond the parapet was the roof of the church, sweeping at one end up to the cupola, and at the other to a belfry, open to the air, with a three-foot parapet running around its edge. The belfry would be accessible from the church, as well as over the roof.

Miller very much liked the look of the belfry.

He took off more tiles, scrambled through the roof, and pulled the other men after him. Then he replaced the tiles, and led them across the parapet to the dark slope of the church roof.

'Shit,' said Spiro. 'I don' likes highness.'

'It's not high,' said Miller.

'Looks high to me,' said Spiro.

'Go,' said Miller.

'No,' said Spiro.

It was quite obvious to Miller that the Greek meant what he said. Hard to blame the guy, really. He had done plenty already, and everyone drew the line somewhere.

Pity it was right here, though.

Something barged Miller aside. It was Carstairs: Carstairs with something held out in front of him, something with a faint sheen under the stars. A very faint sheen: the sheen of the blued-steel blade of a killing knife, nine inches of razor-sharp unpleasantness. 'Ow!' said Spiro.

Carstairs said, 'Listen, greasy boy. You heard what he said.' His arm moved slightly.

'Ow!' said Spiro again.

'We don't really need you any more,' said Carstairs. 'So you give me one good reason to stop me carving out your nasty yellow liver.'

Miller was shocked. He did not, however, intervene.

Spiro became lost in deep thought for about three and a half seconds. Then he started to scuttle up the church roof like an overweight monkey.

Carstairs went after him. Miller followed, moving slow and careful. The roof seemed to be in doubtful condition. There was a nasty springiness to it, a suggestion of sag. Mindful of the fifty-foot drop to a hard stone floor that lay below it, Miller found himself holding his breath.

The belfry parapet loomed invitingly ahead. But they were moving out of the shadow now, and between them and the parapet lay a brilliant wedge of floodlit tiles. Spiro did not like the look of it. His pace was slowing perceptibly. He had chosen a bad place to slow down, because they had moved some distance along the roof, and below the eaves of the church was no longer the crumbling shelter of the priest's house, but the village square. And in the village square, a squad of German soldiers was standing. All it took was for one of them to look up –

'Go!' said Carstairs.

Spiro froze.

Carstairs pulled out his dreadful knife and prodded the Greek's foot. Spiro squeaked, scuttled like lightning up the roof and hauled himself over the parapet. His short legs waved for a moment in the air. Then he vanished. Safe.

Not safe.

In his last frantic scuffle, Spiro had dislodged a tile. It started slowly. It accelerated, rattling down the floodlit section of the roof. Miller stuck out a hand and made a grab for it. For a moment he thought he had it. But Greek roof tiles are heavy affairs, made with plenty of good solid clay, and no human fingertips can restrain one once it has got the bit of gravity between its teeth.

Miller watched that tile loop out into space and fall, tumbling over and over, towards the cobbles of the square where the squad of soldiers stood, only needing to look up.

* * *

When Mallory opened the door, light flooded in. There were three soldiers outside, rifles at the ready. Mallory looked them scornfully up and down. 'What the bloody hell is all the noise about?' he said, in a German pregnant with the accents of Heidelberg University, where in his pre-war climbing days he had indeed spent six months.

'Orders to search the house,' said one of the privates, squinting at this nasty-looking *SS Leutnant*, with shadowy hollows on his face and a rifle slung negligently over his shoulder.

'I've already searched it,' said Mallory. One of the soldiers opened his mouth to speak. 'Give me that gun,' said Mallory.

The man handed over his rifle without hesitation. Mallory looked it over with the scorn of an epicure who has found a dead rat in his soup. He pulled the bolt out of the rifle and threw it on to the ground. 'It stinks!' he said. 'Clean it! Now get out of my way!' He marched into the square.

There were a lot of soldiers: a terrible lot of soldiers. Mallory found himself seriously worried. A good search would certainly land them all in trouble. Carstairs he had little confidence in, besides which the man was woozy from his bang on the head. Spiro was a charming personality, but not what you would call a natural athlete. Miller would look after himself. But with that much dead weight round his neck, he was going to need all the help he could get.

Mallory marched briskly across the square, up the street towards the village gates, and turned sharply into Athenai Street where they had made rendezvous. The houses were dark and ruinous. At the end, the cliff face was a pit of blackness in the night. Settling the rifle firmly on his back, Mallory started to climb.

The cliff was steep but pocked with steps and holds where stone had been cut to build the village. Mallory went up until he was looking down on the rooftops illuminated by the blue-white lights mounted on the cliff face. He considered getting above those lights, sixty feet above him now. But he had a feeling that just for the minute, he might be better off below them. He moved along a ledge – a ledge to him, anyway; to anyone else, it was no more than a thread-fine irregularity in the face of the rock – until he came to a broad crack, sunk in black shadow. Into this he fitted himself, and stood invisible.

Below, the roofs of the village shone livid in the floodlights. The streets were stripes of violet-black, except for the square, a handkerchief of naked white under the stars.

In that white rectangle little black shapes moved, precise, mechanical movements, pairs attaching to other pairs to make bigger blocks, which in turn fragmented . . .

Mallory knew that what he was watching was a search of the town. And what was being searched for was him, Spiro, Carstairs, and Miller –

Something caught his eye. Behind the church was the priest's house, leaning against the bigger building like a small, drunken man holding on to a fat wife. There was movement on the church roof.

Mallory watched the little figures wait by the parapet, saw the first of them – Spiro, it was – move haltingly towards the triangle of light that lay over the tiles. He unslung the Mauser and put it to his shoulder. Spiro swam into the sight's circle; Spiro hesitant, Carstairs at his heel, jabbing. Mallory saw the tiles rock as Spiro pressed on. He saw the tile come free, accelerate, check as Miller got his fingers to it, carry on. The palms of his hands were suddenly damp with sweat. He panned the sight down. A line of German soldiers stood under the eaves of the church, at attention, listening to some officer or other, barking orders. The cross-hairs of the sight settled on the helmet of the soldier closest to the church wall. Mallory squeezed the trigger.

All hell broke loose.

The steel helmet flew off the head and smacked into the church wall. The soldier slammed flat on the cobbles, a dark patch of blood spreading around his ruined head. The report of the rifle rolled like thunder on the flat, hard faces of the buildings. Even before the echoes died, Mallory had his Schmeisser in the firing position and was hosing the square with bullets, the stabbing spear of flame from the gun's muzzle saying here I am, here I am, up here on this cliff.

Down in the square grey bodies rolled and crawled and shouted, taking cover. There was fire coming up from the square now, sporadic bursts, ill-directed, but focused loosely on the crevice in which Mallory was hiding.

But Mallory was no longer there. He had moved away, upwards, in the shadows. Now he was approaching the lights. Below, the village seethed and muttered like a cauldron. Seventy feet above the place he had fired from, he paused and looked down. In the belfry of the church, he glimpsed three heads; visible only from above, those heads.

And what with one thing and another, nobody had noticed anything as trivial as the fall of a tile from a church roof.

Mallory moved on, shoulders and feet, up the crack in the rock. Above him the cliff soared for ever into the wild, cool dark. Below him, the village swarmed like an ants' nest stirred with a stick. Someone was firing tracer, the rounds smacking the rock face and spinning away into the dark until it must have seemed that there were forty men up here, so more men opened fire from the town . . .

Really, thought Mallory, climbing fast and steady, it was a deplorable lapse of discipline. But he had no illusions. Soon the brilliant organization of the German army would reassert itself, and life would become even more difficult and dangerous than it was at the moment.

For him, anyway. The men in the village should be left alone: the Germans would assume that the whole squad was on the cliffs of the Acropolis. All he had to do was keep moving, draw away the pursuit.

Keep moving.

For a moment he hung on the face of the cliff and thought of the precipice above him, crag on crag, a couple of thousand feet to be conquered against gravity. He could taste the old cigarettes in his throat, feel the grit of sleeplessness in his eyes, feel the weary ache of continuous action in his bones. The Benzedrine had worn off. If he took any more, he would be seeing things . . .

Better to see things than to fall off.

Mallory took two of the pills out of the foil and swallowed them. Then, wearily, he began to haul himself up the wall. Forty feet above, he found what he was looking for.

He was on a level with the lights. Bullets still whined and spanged around him, but nobody was aiming. Between the spots of brilliance was only darkness, and it was in that darkness that he existed, anonymous.

He paused, eyeing the face. He could already feel the jump of the Benzedrine at his stomach, his blood beginning to fizz.

Just above his head ran a heavy cable: the cable that brought the power to the floodlights. Mallory pulled the clasp knife from his pocket and wrapped around its handle the rubberized bag in which he kept his shaving kit. He wished he had his commando knife, but the commando knife was gone. He had no idea of the clasp knife's insulating properties, but rubber was supposed to be all right. Go on, the Benzedrine was telling him, it will be fine, you are immortal, if things don't work out you can spread your wings and jump clear over the village and into the cool sea –

Steady.

He reached his right hand up, and positioned the blade on the outside of the thick insulation. Then he began to saw.

The edge of the knife sank into the rubber as if it had been butter. He felt the touch of some kind of armour. Then the blade went through the armour, and shorted out the live and the neutral.

The night suddenly turned blue, as if it had been struck by lightning. Then, just as suddenly, it turned black, as the lights went out. Pitch black: black as the inside of a coal hole.

Mallory left the knife wedged in the wire, and looped his silk rope over the cable. He whipped a new tracer magazine from his ammunition pouch and clapped it into his Schmeisser. He went back along the wire twenty feet, until the rope came taut. Then he fired a burst into the square, and let go of the cable.

The rope took him in a great swinging arc across the cliff face. He felt the scrape of rock at his hands and knees, felt himself rise again towards the cable, reached up a hand, gripped the rubber, and found a hold. In the same movement he fired again, another burst into the square, and swung back the way he had come. From the corner of his eye he could see tracers still spinning and ricocheting down there. He fired another burst, swung back. This time he did not shoot. The enemy would have seen three bursts of tracer virtually simultaneously, from places forty feet apart. There would be at least two men up here, they would assume; possibly more. Two men covering the retreat of a whole squad.

Diversion established, thought Mallory. Now it is time to get away from here. Up; gain height.

He hauled himself up on the cable.

The cable came out of the wall.

All of a sudden he was falling, hanging on to the rubber insulation, trying to remember what the hell happened further down the cliff: a wall to smash into, or merely a long drop . . . He clamped his hands and closed his forearms against the scrape of the rock. He could feel the staples popping up there one by one, the wild rush of the night on his face. It occurred to him that his knife would have fallen out of the wound in the rubber. The circuit would be open again.

Two things happened.

One, a staple held. Mallory found himself hanging there in the night, far above the village, heart pounding, the weight of his two weapons and equipment doing its best to pop his arms from their sockets.

Two, the lights came on. Mallory's over-brightened brain saw quite clearly the cliff as visible from the square: a towering sheet of rock, with a dotted line of brilliant lights, dislodged from their moorings, dangling down its surface, saying: look here, this direction. And on the end, wriggling like a frog on a hook, a small human figure.

For a second, a great silence hung over village and cliff.

Miller had taken advantage of the darkness to stand in the belfry and assess the situation, secure in the knowledge that nobody could see him. When the lights came on, he had experienced the mild flicker of interest that in Dusty Miller passed for surprise. It had passed through his mind that Mallory, suspended on a bit of wire over about a hundred and twenty heavily-armed Germans, seemed likely to be in some trouble. Miller had already noticed with admiration the streams of tracer that had come pouring from various different spots on the darkened cliff. It had seemed exactly as if a fair-sized body of men was up there. So it would not be amazing if Mallory's colleagues did a little something to cover him.

All this he thought in the time it took to unclip four grenades from his belt, two for each hand, pull the pins, and heave them over the belfry roof and into the square. All eyes in the square had been on the cliff, raising guns for the fusillade that would blow Mallory to kingdom come. The arrival of the grenades in their midst came as something of a shock.

Miller ducked down, saw the flashes light up the night, heard the crash of the explosions, the whine of shrapnel, the screams of the wounded. There was a sputter of gunfire, sporadic and disconnected. It said to Miller that the troops in the square had realized that they were disagreeably exposed where they stood on that brightly-lit rectangle of paving, and had decided to take cover.

But this was of only passing interest to Miller. What got his immediate attention was that the lighting cable, glaring up there on the cliff, now bore only its light fittings.

Mallory was gone.

'Here,' said Clytemnestra.

Wills stamped on the brakes. The lorry halted. Round the corner were the quarry and the landward end of the rail causeway. They were back.

Out in the dark, something moved. Wills cursed gently to himself. There were not supposed to be any sentries until the quarry fence. He flicked on the headlights, feeling a stealthy shift of weight as Andrea, who had been riding on the rear step of the truck, took his departure into the night.

There was a sentry in the lorry's windscreen; a fat sentry with a sullen expression, blinking in the headlight beams that illuminated the rolls of fat at his belt and the spidery outlines of the quarry machinery and the shed Miller had burned, vanishing into the dark behind him. Wills put his elbow on the window and said, 'Morning.'

The fat sentry frowned. He said, 'Where's Koch?'

Wills' grin stiffened. His German was not up to deep conversation. Presumably, this man was a friend of the driver. The plan had been to drop Andrea off a mile short of the quarry. But they had overshot.

'Went flying,' said Wills, trying to hide his atrocious accent by mumbling.

'Where?'

'Back home,' said Wills.

The sentry frowned again, and switched on his torch. Wills could feel Clytemnestra rigid in the seat beside him. This is bloody stupid, he thought. All the way across the island, no worries. Into Clytemnestra's brother's favourite cave for the machine. Grab machine, drive back towards rendezvous, everything tickety-boo.

And now one fat sentry was going to sugar the whole shooting-match.

The torch came closer to the driver's side window. 'What the hell do you think you're doing out here, this time of night?'

'Minding my own business,' said Wills.

'Papers,' said the sentry. Then he said something else – something with no words, that was the sound of all the air being driven out of his body for the last time ever – and slumped with a crash against the lorry door. Behind where he had been standing, a figure that might have been a bear stooped and cleaned what might have been a knife on a tuft of dry grass by the roadside. Andrea swung his pack into the cab. Where he was going, he would need to travel light. 'Go,' he said. 'Till dawn, at the airfield jetty.' He paused, slapped the mahogany box on the passenger seat. 'And look after this thing, yes?'

'With my life,' said Clytemnestra.

Andrea watched the lorry turn in the road and rattle off the way it had come. He looked across at the Acropolis. There were lights;

too many lights for his liking. Silent as the night itself, he padded along the road to the quarry gates.

He heard the sound of voices, saw the glow of a cigarette where a couple of sentries were finding courage in conversation. Down the chainlink fence a little, he found a place where the base of the wire was loose. He wormed his way under. The root of the causeway lay just ahead and to the left. Andrea clapped a German steel helmet on his head, straightened up, and began to march steadily along the sleepers towards the Acropolis.

Mallory hung three hundred feet above the village, and wished he could smoke. He had almost forgotten what it was to walk upright on level ground. His bones felt the pull of gravity, and groaned.

As he stood wedged into a crevice, he had the sense that things had gone badly wrong. Below, the village was heaving with German soldiery. Andrea was out there in the night, on an errand that had only the smallest chance of succeeding. Miller, Spiro and Carstairs were treed in the belfry. Benzedrine or not, he was too tired. He needed four hours' sleep. But in four hours it would be getting light. The enemy were waiting for the light, so they could find the scattered elements of the Thunderbolt Force and pick them off one by one. Command and control were what was needed. Command and control. Big words. Words for men who were not so tired that they could hardly move.

Mallory looked down. The church was below him. He needed to regain the belfry: establish rotas, stand watches, organize a way out, make the second rendezvous at dawn. He needed a way down to the church.

There was no way down that did not go straight through five hundred Germans.

In the square below, sentries had been posted. The world had settled. Hot pursuit had cooled. All the Germans had to do was wait. There had been too many operations, too much action, too little sleep. The Thunderbolt Force was fragmented like quicksilver. This looked very like The End –

Above Mallory's head, something made a small noise. To his right, a pale streak had come into being on the dark rock. To his left, another. Ropes.

There was a new noise: a clinking and grinding. Boots.

Mallory knew then that he had been wrong about the waiting. The Germans were on the front foot; someone somewhere had argued his case, and argued it well. They were searching the Acropolis, pebble by pebble. The *Wehrmacht* garrison would not be combing cliff faces with ropes. This was *Sonderkommando* work. The work of Dieter Wolf, highly professional, utterly deadly.

Mallory unslung his own rope and looked down into the square. There were half-a-dozen men there, no more. The architectural and human debris of Miller's grenades had been cleared away. There were the men descending from above, and the men waiting below. And Mallory in the middle.

From the movements of the ropes on either side, the men were quartering the cliff, poking their noses into every little nook and cranny, methodical at last. It was the least you expected of an élite German unit.

The men down below, possibly over confident, were not in cover.

Mallory made his plan.

Reaching out, he grabbed the nearest rope and sawed it off short with a razor blade from his shaving kit. Then he hauled in the other rope. In its middle he tied a marlinespike hitch and placed the knot around a hand grenade. Finally, he took the rope he had cut, coiled it, and belayed it to a little post of rock.

Mallory fitted the flash eliminator to the Mauser, and wished he had a silencer. But silencers cut the muzzle velocity, and their steel-wool baffles only worked for half a dozen shots. He filled the magazine and slotted it silently into the rifle. The scuffling noises from above were louder now. He ran the telescopic sight over the square. Two men in the open. Two behind the buttresses of the church. The gleam of a helmet in the alley.

Mallory made a list in his mind, measuring the necessary movements of the carbine. Then he took a deep breath, sighted on the gleam in the alley, and pulled the trigger.

The gun roared. He moved to the men by the church, one, two; one dead, one winged, but the heavy bullet would do him no good, and the men in the middle of the square were diving for cover as Mallory worked the bolt and pulled the trigger. One of them was down, not moving, the other one a pair of heels vanishing behind the buttress, damn, and the cat was properly among the pigeons now.

Mallory pulled the pin on the hand grenade he had looped into the searcher's rope and let it swing away. He kicked the rope he had cut out into space, grabbed it, and went down as close to free fall as made no difference. There were shots from below, but the bullets went wide. Mallory's boots hit the cliff, and he bounced out, a wide arc, descending. There was a scream from above. One of the searchers had discovered that his rope had shrunk. A body whistled past, bounced once, and crashed into the buildings at the cliff's foot. Mallory was slowing now, crabbing sideways for the roof of a building. The bullets were getting closer. Then there was a heavy explosion overhead, and another body whizzed past, preceded this time by a length of rope. The grenade had done its stuff –

Mallory landed on a roof, let go of the rope and rolled, unhitching his Schmeisser. He was breathing hard, his heart hammering at his ribs. Above him in the lights he saw three men descending, foreshortened. He loosed off a burst at them, saw two of them let go, heard the crash of their bodies coming down. The third stopped in a crease of black shadow. Mallory saw the muzzle flash. Rounds whacked into the roof around him, and grit stung his face. He felt naked on this roasting-pan of a roof. There was no cover. He squeezed off another burst at the cliff face and scuttled to the edge of the roof. Bullets cracked past his head, whipping across the cobbles from the direction of the church. He could feel the breath rasping, the sweat running. Another burst of bullets from on high kicked chips out of the parapet by his head. He took another look at the square, squeezed off a burst, rolled over the parapet and dropped to the cobbles.

It was a long drop, longer than it had appeared. Mallory landed awkwardly, felt his ankle turn as far as his boot would let it, sharp prongs of pain jab up towards his knee. No more climbing, he thought, rolling and firing at the same time, heading for the patch of shadow, ankle hurting like hell and going to hurt worse later, if anything was going to be hurting at all –

He was across the alley and in the shadow. His helmet crashed into stone. A mounting block. He was invisible, in cover. Safe as houses.

For as long as it took someone to unhook a grenade. Say, twenty seconds. There was no way out. Mallory fought the Benzedrine, and the pain, and the weariness, scrabbling for an answer. Miller was up in the tower. Wills was off with Clytemnestra. Andrea was . . . well, God knew where Andrea was. The important thing was not to give Miller away. If they found Miller, they found Spiro, and if they found Spiro, Spiro could be expected to tell them everything he knew.

As far as Mallory was concerned, there were no answers.

A great hush fell over the square. Mallory lay, ears pricked, waiting for the fizz of the grenade fuse, the rattle of metal on stone that would signal the finish.

But instead, he heard a voice.

'Herr Kapitän Mallory,' it said. It was a military voice, with an odd, bubbling hiss in it. How the hell does he know my name? thought Mallory.

'We have recognized you,' said the voice, as if it had heard his thoughts, 'by your skill, at first, it must be said. *Kapitän* Mallory, there are things I should like to know.'

Of course there are, said Mallory to himself. 'Who the hell are you?' he said, aloud. He was surprised he still had a voice, let alone a voice that sounded clear and normal as it bounced from the surface of the buildings.

'Hauptmann Dieter Wolf,' said the voice. And to Mallory's astonishment, a man walked out into the light. He wore a high-crowned cap, whose peak hid his eyes. Someone at some time had smashed his jaw, and whoever had mended it had not been a master of his craft, not by a long chalk. The lower mandible was horribly skewed; it looked as if it would not shut properly. Spit bubbled in the corner as he breathed, giving his voice its nasty liquid hiss. It gave him a permanent crooked grin; a crocodile grin. There was a Luger in his hand. No grenades, though.

'Come out here,' said Wolf.

'Quite comfortable where I am,' said Mallory.

Wolf's twisted jaw writhed. 'Let me put it like this,' he said. 'I have men in position who can drop some things into your hole. This would be a pity, I suppose. I have heard a great deal about you.'

Mallory had to acknowledge that Wolf was right, it would be a pity. He hesitated, his mouth suddenly dry: a dryness he had felt before, high on a Southern Alp without a name, foodless at the top of a couloir, the sun coming on to the ice above, freeing salvos of boulders that swept the gulley clean as a whistle. It was the dryness that came when you had run out of ideas, and you had to put judgement on the shelf, and trust to luck in a place where luck was not in plentiful supply.

Mallory pulled himself to his feet. His ankle hurt, now. Everything hurt. It was most unlikely that *Hauptmann* Wolf wanted to talk to him about the weather. More probably, he would want to cut him in half with a Schmeisser. 'Closer,' said Wolf. He had his Luger pointed at Mallory's stomach. Mallory could feel the presence of Miller in the belfry. He schooled himself not to look up.

'So,' said Wolf. 'We are honoured that you have been able to visit, *Herr Kapitän* Mallory. You and your friends, *Kolonel* Andrea of the defeated rabble once known as the Greek army. And of course Corporal Miller, of the Catering Corps.'

'Who?' said Mallory.

The saurian jaw stretched in something approaching a smile. The grin broadened. A thread of drool hung from the corner of the ruined mouth. 'They are both dead,' he said. 'The *Kolonel* was shot. Miller we hanged.'

'Sorry to hear that,' said Mallory. His ankle was killing him. He told himself he did not believe a word of this. But his stomach was hollow with something worse than hunger.

The weariness flowed over him in a heavy wave. Admit it. There were hundreds of them, four Thunderbolts. Wolf was lying about Miller. But Andrea . . .

'And now,' said Wolf, with horrid affability, 'I am going to kill you.' Delicately, he put the Luger back in its holster and secured the flap. Removing his cap, he skimmed it on to the mounting block. Fumbling behind him, he pulled out a nine-inch dagger. Mallory had heard of this dagger. Wolf liked to use it to disembowel people.

'One thing,' said Mallory. I'm flattered that you recognized me. How did you do it?'

'I should say that I recognized you from the newspapers before the war,' said Wolf. 'But it would not be true. The fact is that your friend Andrea told me, under torture. Just after he had told me where to find the charges you had placed so amateurishly on the Victory weapons.' It was not just his jaw that had been broken. Without his cap, his whole head looked as if it had been crushed and clumsily reformed. The eyes were cold slits under a white-fuzzed cranium that might have been moulded from dough by a child with a taste for the macabre.

Mallory smiled at him, the bright, enthusiastic smile of someone who has just been given a lovely present. Andrea would not have revealed the time of day under torture. This unpleasant specimen was beyond a shadow of doubt telling lies.

'Now,' said Wolf. 'Come here, Captain Mallory.' He beckoned, with the dagger held out in front of him. As he beckoned, he advanced.

Mallory felt for his own knife, then remembered both of them were gone. He tested his ankle. Not good. He stood his ground, watching the knife.

They were two figures standing on that sheet of floodlit cobbles, feet apart, intent at the hub of their radiating shadows. One with pack on back, unmoving; the other stealthy, feline almost. Both of them focused on the little starburst of light on the point of Wolf's dagger.

Wolf was close enough for Mallory to smell his sweat. It was a sour smell, violent, disgusting. Mallory watched the knife wrist sinking for the first upward thrust. He shifted his weight until it was on his good leg. Wolf's eyes betrayed no feeling. His knife hand came round and up, hooking at Mallory's belly. But Mallory was not there any more. He had arched away like a bullfighter from the horns, grabbing at Wolf's wrist as it came past, to transfer the man's momentum into a twist that would dislocate the elbow.

But as his hands locked on Wolf's wrist, he knew it was not going to work. The SS man's arm was thick as a telegraph pole. It was an arm whose owner had slept well and eaten well. Mallory's fingers were worn with cliff and battle, and his reserves were close to rock bottom. He could not hold on. The arm wrenched away. Wolf brought his left hand round, fast, a closed-fist blow that made Mallory's ears ring. He kept his feet with difficulty. Wolf came in again, hooking with the knife. Mallory aimed a kick at his knee, made contact, but he had kicked with his right foot, the bad foot, and pain shot up his leg and he fell over, feeling something burn his ribs, cool air on his side. Wolf had cut him. Not badly: a surface cut to the ribs.

It would get worse.

He struggled to his feet.

Wolf was waiting for him. His breathing was steady and even. Little bubbles of spit formed and burst in the corner of his wrecked mouth. 'Now,' he said. 'I'll give it to you now.' He came in, knife in front of him like a sword. Mallory knew he was in bad trouble. He had lost sight of the fact he was going to die. There was no time for fear, or thinking ahead. The name of the game was survival, every second a bonus wrenched from the crooked jaws of death.

He got inside the knife, trapped the huge arm under his own arm, butted his steel helmet into that disgusting jaw, heard a tooth or two pop, brought his knee up into the groin, found it blocked by a leg that might as well have been made of wood. The arm was coming round behind him. He tried to cringe away from the knife, but the arms were remorseless, and he was exhausted –

The world went mad.

The square filled with a gigantic noise, the noise of a thousand typewriters, the whine of many hornets' nests kicked to hell, two, maybe more huge explosions. Sensing a minute faltering of Wolf's hold, Mallory smashed his helmet once more into the *SS* man's face. This time the nose went, and the man grunted and reeled, and behind Mallory the knife clattered on the cobbles. But then the arms came on Mallory's neck, tilting his head sideways, and Mallory knew that this time he had had it for sure, and for the first time the fear of death showed itself in his mind, a dark and ugly thing –

But only for a split second.

Because suddenly those terrible arms were off his neck and he was lurching back, free, and a voice was saying, 'Get your weapon.' A familiar voice.

Andrea's voice.

It had, Miller reflected, been a bad five minutes.

They had been sitting in the belfry nice and peaceful. Miller had even managed to get a little shuteye – a very little, seeing that he did not trust Carstairs, and that Spiro was trembling like a frightened rabbit and muttering about bulletses and gunses and getting outses of here. Miller was worrying about Mallory, sure, especially after all that stuff with the lights. But when you knew Mallory as well as Miller, you could tell when he was in real trouble and when he was staging a diversionary action. The stuff with the lights, though it had made Miller's flesh creep, was definitely a diversionary action. When Mallory had vanished from the end of the cable, there had been silence. A silence that Miller had very definitely appreciated. Then had come the shooting, and the voice in the square.

The voice in the square had been different.

It had woken Miller up, a thing he held against it. When he put his eye to the waterspout in the belfry floor, he saw the big man in the breeches and jackboots and high-fronted cap, standing tough and arrogant among the sprawled bodies of the Germans. He saw Mallory hobble out to meet him. Miller's stomach became hollow with apprehension.

It was not just that Mallory looked tired, and the monstrous figure in the jackboots looked fresh as paint.

There were other things to be seen: things invisible to Mallory, but visible to Miller in his eminence. It was what staff would call a fluid situation. Staff could call it what they liked. To Miller, it looked like a mess.

Round the corner from Mallory, out of his line of sight, a machine-gun post had been set up. Miller did not know why, but he had a nasty feeling it could have something to do with reprisals on the civilian workers. He was not actually worried about the civilian workers, because when those rockets went up, the Germans were going to need all the manpower they could get.

What really worried him was something else: a shadow he had seen floating from darkness to darkness in the alley on the far side of the square. A big shadow, impossibly big: a shadow with the shoulders of a bear and the lightness of a butterfly.

He dug Carstairs in the ribs. 'Stand by to give covering fire,' he said.

'You're joking,' said Carstairs, huddling into his corner of the bell tower. 'They'll have us in a second.'

'Listen up, Captain,' said Miller. 'If you don't give covering fire, I'll blow your Goddamn head off.'

'Who the hell do you think you're talking to?' said Carstairs.

'I'll blow your head off, sir,' said Miller. Then he gave him his orders.

Down below, there was the sound of a dagger clattering on to cobbles. The man in the breeches had Mallory in a headlock and appeared to be breaking his neck.

'Open fire,' said Miller. He stood up, tossed two grenades, sighted the Schmeisser on the three heads inside the Spandau emplacement, and fired two short bursts. Behind him the belfry trap door slammed open, and Carstairs' boots clattered down the ladder. A man stood up in the Spandau emplacement and fell across his gun. The grenades exploded, blowing him out again, accompanied by the two other men. There was movement in other windows as a squad of Germans took cover, Miller waited for the withering fire that would lash Mallory to the ground –

But while he had been disposing of the machine gun, the shadow had detached itself from the alley and moved in half-a-dozen great strides across the cobbles. The shadow was no longer a shadow, but had become Andrea. And Andrea had put a mighty forearm around the neck of the man with the crooked head, and wrenched him away from Mallory, and tucked Mallory in behind him like a hen protecting its chicks, and reversed towards the church door, using the crooked-headed man, *Hauptmann* Wolf in person, as a human shield, though human was not the word anyone who knew Wolf would have used.

Miller found it all very impressive. He heard the church door below burst open, Carstairs open up. Then he flung himself through the trap door in the belfry floor and went down the ladder into the dark, into the middle of a knot of people that consisted of Carstairs and Spiro, Mallory and Andrea, with Wolf instead of sandbags.

Andrea said, 'Get behind me.' The German had a face that Miller did not like. He seemed to be swearing. Andrea's mighty forearm tensed. The squashed-pumpkin skull turned purple under the thistledown hair. 'Now,' he said.

Miller took Carstairs' Schmeisser gently away from him, and gave it to Mallory, just in case. They moved towards the mouth of the alley, crossing the wide floodlit spaces of the square. It felt horribly exposed out here. But none of the SS would shoot for fear of hitting their commanding officer –

A man flicked into view behind the church, wearing field grey, not camouflage, lifting a rifle to his shoulder. Miller put the bead of the Schmeisser's sight on the man's chest and squeezed off a four-round burst. The man crashed back into the shadows.

'Thank you,' said Mallory.

'Don't mensh,' said Miller. But beneath the grin was something they all knew. Wolf's soldiers might not like to shoot their colonel. But the regular *Wehrmacht* garrison would not be bothered one way or the other. With the amount of noise and fuss coming out of the Greek village, it stood to reason that reinforcements would start arriving soon. And that this time, they would do the job properly.

The mouth of the alley closed around them. Ahead, two lines of houses jostled each other on either side of a strip of cobbles. Then the houses on the left-hand side gave way to a blank wall: a wall with steps of ancient stone rising to battlements.

'Up,' said Andrea.

They went up. Behind them, the village was suddenly quiet as the dead under its lights. Mallory peered down the walkway behind the battlements. There was a guard tower, but as far as he could see, no guards.

'Over,' said Andrea.

Mallory unlimbered his pack, tossed the silk climbing rope over the edge. 'Spiro,' he said.

'No,' said Spiro. 'I no go. I stays. High places, bullets, very bads.'

'You go,' said Mallory. 'Rope round your neck, round your waist, all the same to me.'

'But sea down there,' said Spiro. 'Very bad, wets, no swim good.'

'Fields,' said Andrea. 'Not sea. Get in a ditch. Now go.'

He grabbed the fat man's wrists. Mallory tied a bowline round the barrel chest and tipped him, still struggling, between the battlements. He and Miller lowered him into the dark until a sound floated up, more a squeak than a shout. Spiro had arrived.

Still the village lay quiet.

Wolf said, 'You're crazy. Give up now.'

'Carstairs,' said Mallory. 'Go.'

Carstairs took hold of the rope and launched himself over the edge.

'Miller,' said Mallory.

The lights blazed off the cliff. The houses of the village stood bone-white and still. But the world was changing. Outside the orbit of the lights, the sky seemed paler. And from the gates came the sound of nailed jackboots, running.

TEN

Friday 0300–Saturday 0030

As Miller put his foot over the wall, the first grey uniforms came round the corner. He flung himself to the ground, put the Schmeisser to his shoulder, and squeezed the trigger. Two men went down. The others fell back.

'Go,' said Mallory.

Miller would have hesitated, but he knew that when Mallory spoke in that tone of voice you did what he said. He grasped the rope and went down hand over hand. He could hear a voice shouting in German. Andrea's voice. Shouting something about *Hauptmann* Wolf.

Miller's boots hit the ground. 'Where?' he said.

'Here,' said Spiro, in a terrified squeak. Thank Gods you come.'

'Now hear this!' Andrea shouted, in German. 'I have with me *Hauptmann* Wolf, a name known to you all. The *Hauptmann* is in great danger. Hold your fire.'

The noise of boots had stopped. The alley below the wall was empty. Silence had fallen. But it was not an empty silence. It was the silence of a village full of Greek labourers holding their breath; the silence of a platoon of *Wehrmacht,* waiting for Andrea to blink. A silence like the silence between the last tick of the timer and the detonation of the bomb.

Then a voice from the alley gave a curt order.

'*Nein*!' yelled Wolf.

But the order had been given by a serving officer of the *Wehrmacht,* and was not to be countermanded by an SS man in enemy hands. Half the platoon laid down covering fire. The other half began the advance.

Andrea felt Wolf's body jump in his arms as the first salvo hit. A bullet scorched a track across the skin of his forearm. The body went limp. He dropped it, rolled back, his uniform wet with blood. Mallory was already over the edge. Andrea yanked the pin from a grenade, laid it carefully under the battlement round which the climbing rope hung noosed, grasped the rope and went over the edge.

He slid in silence through the night, rope crooked in his elbow, braking with the sole of one boot on the instep of the other. Against the sky – much paler seen from the thick blackness down here – he saw a head lean over, two heads, heard covering fire from below, finished counting, hoped the ground was close now –

And from above there came the great flat *clang* of the grenade detonating in the angle between wall and stone floor. The rope became immediately slack, the noose cut by the explosion. There were yells from above, yells Andrea scarcely heard because the ground had rushed twenty feet up to meet him and hit him with a bang, and he was rolling, once, twice, away from the wall, and behind him there were two crashes as the bodies blown over the wall hit the ground, but by that time he was on his feet, running away from the dark loom of the wall.

And a voice said, 'Over here.'

Mallory's voice.

Two more steps, and Andrea was in something that from the evil smell of its bottom and the steepness of its sides must be a drainage ditch. Now that his eyes were accustoming themselves to the dark, he saw that his head was on a level with a flat plain, more of the small fields that covered every horizontal square inch of this island.

'Here,' said Mallory again.

Andrea put his head down and began to run. There was tracer overhead. In its lurid flicker he could see reeds, blades of grass, the deep footprints of the rest of the party in the mud ahead. As he ran, his mind went back to a time when he had had a pack, equipment, maps.

Particularly maps.

Andrea was a deadly fighting machine, but fighting ability alone was not enough to make you a colonel. What made you a colonel was tactical sense, the ability to read from a map the features of any given terrain that a force could use to ensure the achieving of an objective.

The objective now was the aerodrome. Between here and the aerodrome, the marsh was at its broadest and stickiest. To the south was the causeway with the road, which would be heavily guarded.

To the north, the fields ran up to the beach, and the jetty. According to the briefing, the jetty was heavily guarded too, but less heavily than the road.

It had been obvious for some time that the jetty was the only option.

He caught up with Mallory, who was limping along, bundling the little Greek Spiro along the bottom of the ditch: good man, Spiro, lot of noise of course, but very brave to have got this far. They paused to take stock.

At the base of the Acropolis cliffs, the high walls of the village stood out stark and black. Every now and then a burst of tracer whipped from the battlements into the fields. The shooting seemed to be directed in a northerly direction, towards the causeway. It looked like the spastic twitchings of a military force without a head – twitchings that both Andrea and Mallory knew would not last long. Soon, the superb military organization would reassert itself, and the marshes would be combed, blade of grass by blade of grass, and there would be no escape, for them or the Enigma machine.

'Well, my Keith,' said Andrea. 'I think we must take up yachting.'

So it was that an intelligent owl would have seen a little straggle of men, heavily camouflaged with mud, deploy across the fields of young corn, and start to jog purposefully towards the bay on the northern shore of the Acropolis. They moved in a loose curve, using cover as and when they found it, a clump of oleanders here, a field-shed there. But the focus of their movement was the expanse of hard-packed gravel and mud with the long pier and deep-water jetty, connected to the water gate of the Acropolis by a mile of road.

An hour later, the sky was turning grey, and the island was emerging from the anonymity of the night. Mist hung caught in the olive groves on the slopes of the western massif, and drooled from the notches of invisible hammocks in the high Acropolis. A smear of peach-coloured cloud hung like a banner past the north-eastern capes. Miller was lying in the rough grass by the edge of the road. To the right, the Acropolis loomed in the half-dark. To the left, the shed by the jetty stood dark against the shifting sea. The road connected the two. 'The morning after the ball,' he said.

Mallory blinked his gritty eyes. 'First,' he said, 'the telephone line. Then we move in.'

Miller looked down the road towards the sheds. There were other shapes. Concrete shapes, squat and bulbous. Machine-gun posts, if they were lucky. Eighty-eights, if they were not.

He sighed, rolled over, and cut the telephone line. Then he bustled around, making his preparations.

Up and about the Germans might be. But to Dusty Miller, there was a feeling almost of homecoming. This was the old life, the Long Range Desert Group life, crouching in a ditch in flat land, waiting for the convoy.

Miller had always been a great believer in subtlety. During Prohibition, when others had run booze across from Canada in heavily-armed trucks with supercharged engines, Miller had been a master bootlegger. Having disposed of his principal competitors by persuading them to ram a bargeful of unstable nitroglycerine, he had bought himself a railroad wagon. This railroad wagon he had attached to various trains. It left Thunder Bay loaded with Canadian rye, was shunted into a siding north of Duluth, and unloaded into a private ambulance, whose uniformed driver did the rounds of his discriminating clientele. While others shot each other to bits for the sake of fancifully-labelled cleaning fluids, Dusty's product had been of impeccable quality, and arrived as regularly as the tide. Miller had made a hundred and ten thousand dollars in very short order. Good business was good business, and nothing to do with fast cars and machine guns. It was not his fault that the gold mine he had bought with the profits contained less gold than the average three-year-old child's teeth. Subtlety, thought Miller, dry grass up his nose. Subtlety was everything –

The first truck of the convoy passed. The second was opposite. Miller clicked the switch in his hand. A sun-bright flash appeared under the truck's fuel tank. The truck slewed sideways, blocking the road. Thick smoke billowed from the wreck, composed partly of burning truck and partly of the smoke powder Miller included in his patent traffic reduction bombs. There was very little wind.

The smoke settled in a pyramid over the road, blocking it. Someone somewhere was shooting, but Miller could hear no bullets. By the sound of it, Andrea and Mallory were making space for themselves in the front. Miller went to his allotted place in the rear of the lead truck, shooing Carstairs and Spiro ahead of him. The truck picked up speed. The pall of smoke dwindled behind, covering the still forms sprawled on the road. By the swerve and judder, at least two of the tyres were blown. Spiro's eyes were spinning in his head. Carstairs was stroking his moustache. 'Nice engines, these trucks,' said Miller, looking at his watch. 'Terrible ride, though. Oh, look. They left us a machine gun.'

The truck entered the jetty compound crab-wise, with a tearing roar and a cloud of dust. Faces behind the windows of the harbourmaster's office hut looked pale and nervous. The telephones were dead, and something had happened on the road, there was no way of telling what. Still, it seemed as if the reinforcements had arrived.

A huge man in a *Wehrmacht* helmet climbed down from the truck. The men in the hut relaxed. This guy was the kind of guy you wanted on your side when things looked doubtful. Thank God, they thought, he's one of ours.

'*Morgen*,' said the big man, smiling a huge white smile; Andrea was famous for the size and whiteness of his smile. 'Telephone's down.'

'Tell me about it,' said the under-harbourmaster. 'What the hell's going on up there?'

'Bit of fuss in the camp,' said Andrea. '*SS* man found fornicating with a goat. The Greeks didn't like it.'

'Poor bloody goat,' said the harbourmaster, wrinkling his nose.

'We're taking a boat,' said Andrea. 'Checking the aerodrome perimeter.'

'Nice day for it,' said the harbourmaster. 'Coffee later?'

'Maybe,' said Andrea, and loped off. The harbourmaster yawned. It was a lonely life out here on the dusty quay, now that the ships had stopped arriving. All you got was the occasional shipload of stores, and fuel, alcohol and oxygen for the factory, and aviation stuff to be barged across the shallow bay to the airfield landing. Otherwise, the gun crews were getting a tan, and everyone was getting hot, fly-mad and bored. They said there was going to be a rocket firing sometime today. Maybe that was what all the fuss was about –

The big man and his four companions were already on the quay. One of the men seemed to be a civilian. There was something wrong with their boots, but that was none of the harbourmaster's business. They already had the harbour launch started up, and were climbing aboard. Someone cast off the shore lines. The boat puttered off the quay and into the ink-blue bay that lay between the jetty and the aerodrome. It shrank, heading for the aerodrome fuel jetty. Goodness, thought the harbourmaster, yawning, again. They're in a hurry.

That was when the motor cycle and sidecar combination clattered out of the smoke. The man in the sidecar hung limp over his machine gun. The rider climbed off and started banging on the harbourmaster's door, shouting. It took the harbourmaster a good three minutes to get any sense out of him. When he did, he almost wished he had not bothered.

'Awfully sorry,' said Carstairs, 'but how exactly do you propose to get through the fence?'

'I guess we'll think of something,' said Miller. Miller was sitting in the bottom of the boat, the wooden pack open beside him, pushing time pencils into his little buff bricks of plastic explosive. Spiro was looking away, like a child, knowing life was horribly dangerous, but not wanting to admit to himself the full scale of the horror.

'Get us a plane,' said Mallory.

'Of course,' said Carstairs.

'What?' said Spiro, no longer able to deny the evidence of his own ears. 'You steals plane?'

'Steal one. Buy one. Borrow one. Who can tell?' He held out his cigarette case to Spiro. 'Turkish this side, Virginian that.'

'I spits on your Turkish,' said Spiro, mechanically. 'No smoke. Much explodibles here.'

'Oh, for God's sake,' said Carstairs, applying the gold Ronson to a Muratti. 'You can eat that stuff.'

'No!' roared Spiro. 'You want explosion in belly, you eats it! Not Spiro –'

'Quiet,' said Mallory. He was looking back at the shore with his glasses. Men were swarming in the vehicle park by the harbourmaster's shed. There was activity in the 88's gun-pit, too, alongside where they had left the lorry parked. The boat chugged across the quiet blue surface of the bay. They were half-way. Not far enough. 'Left a bit,' he said.

Andrea pushed the tiller with his hip. The boat yawed. In the gun-pit, the muzzle of the 88 flashed. The report came at the same time that the shell kicked water and yellow high explosive smoke in the air eighty feet to the right.

'Right a bit,' said Mallory.

Another bang. This time the shell roared past with a sound like a train, clipped the surface of the bay, ricocheted and blew a hole in the beach. Nobody cheered. They were in a little wooden boat in the middle of a little blue bay, feeling very naked indeed.

'This is it,' said Carstairs. He was pale now. 'The next one. Christ, what are we doing here? Like fish in a barrel –'

'Tchah!' said Spiro. 'Coward! Be a mans!'

The 88 spoke again. This time the shell burst close enough to shower them with chemical-tasting spray. Another shell came, made a smaller splash, skipped, burst on the shore.

'Hah!' said Spiro, who had worked himself into a sort of frenzy. 'Missed again! Bloody square-head fools!'

'Shut up.' Carstairs' composure had cracked. 'We're dead. What the hell possessed me to –'

A huge explosion sounded from beside the harbourmaster's hut. A mighty tree of black smoke grew in the sky.

'Left a bit,' said Mallory.

Carstairs climbed up from the bottom boards, and gaped at the shore. As the smoke cleared it was apparent that the 88 had been blown out of its pit. It now lay on the edge of a vast crater, a mass of twisted metal. As for the lorry, it had vanished clear off the face of the earth.

'What was that?' he said.

Miller gazed at him with blue and innocent eyes. 'I guess,' he said, 'that I must have left a bomb in the truck. Very careless.'

Carstairs swallowed. He did not reply. The boat chugged on. The far shore was coming nearer. Finally, he said, 'Why aren't the machine guns firing?'

Mallory kept his eyes outside the boat. 'It's all that petrol,' he said.

'Petrol?'

Miller pointed a kindly finger at the land ahead. The shore consisted of a strip of white beach with a jetty. Above the jetty was a sun-scorched grass bank. On top of the jetty and the green bank were small, coloured objects. 'Oil drums,' he said. 'Gas cans.' He pointed over the stern, directly behind them.

'There's your guns,' he said. Then he turned, and pointed straight ahead. 'And there's your aerodrome fuel dump. So if they miss us and take a ricochet, up goes the whole caboodle. They have a problem, my man.'

Carstairs thought for a moment of pointing out that it was not only the Germans who would find an aviation fuel dump a problematic place to be in a hail of bullets. Given what he knew of the present company, he kept his mouth shut. It would soon be over.

One way or another.

There were no guard towers along the seaward side of the aerodrome – this far out in the Aegean, the designers of the defences could be forgiven for not expecting shallow-water sea-borne attacks. But as the boat came to within a couple of hundred yards of the shore, a lorry roared down the buff-green strip of vegetation between the security fence and the beach. Andrea gave the tiller to Mallory, sighted down the barrel of the Spandau he had commandeered from the truck, and opened fire. The lorry swerved suddenly and crashed on to the beach. Andrea kept hosing down the little figures that crawled out of the back. Soon none of them was moving. Just to make sure, he loosed a burst at the drums on the jetty. They felt the blast of the flat, oily explosions, smelt the sweetish reek of the black smoke that rolled off the burning drums. Then they were ashore, low, crawling to the fence. There was no time for delicacy. Mallory opened the decompression valve on the boat's engine, unscrewed the lever, and put it in his pocket. Miller shoved a brick of plastic explosive against the bottom of the wire and snapped the time pencil. 'Down!' he yelled.

Thirty seconds later, a roar and a fountain of sand announced that the fence was now metal rain. Odd shots were coming in from the wreckage of the lorry. The Thunderbolt squad used the explosion crater as cover, hauling themselves and the Spandau up the sparse, burned slope of the berm. On the other side, fenced in by a mound of earth, was a half-acre field of oil drums, and a bowser.

'Well,' said Miller. 'They're not going to do a whole lot of shooting in here, I guess.'

Spiro could not speak.

Mallory had sized up the situation. Now he took control. 'They won't do anything to endanger their fuel dump,' he said. 'We'll hold it here. Carstairs, how about you?'

'Transport,' said Carstairs. He was looking white about the lips and pinched about the nose. He took out his cigarette case. 'Turkish this side, Vir –'

'Not here,' said Mallory, mildly. 'Now you get over there with Miller' – he pointed to the dumpy fuel bowser parked by the entrance – 'and he'll hot-wire it for you, and you and I will go and steal an aeroplane, and then we will come back and get everyone.'

'Piece of cake,' said Carstairs.

Five minutes later Carstairs came back in the bowser and Mallory climbed in. They rolled out of the fuel dump and across the aerodrome. Andrea gave quiet orders to Miller, who trotted over to the far end of the dump. When he returned, there were two people with him: Clytemnestra and Wills.

'Good morning,' said Andrea, with old-world courtesy.

'Morning,' said Wills. Clytemnestra was holding his hand.

'You found your way.'

'Been here most of the night,' said Wills. They walked back to an above-ground firefighting pond. Beside it, lying casually in the dirt, was a polished mahogany box with a webbing handle.

'Yais,' said Spiro. 'Yais, this is the damn bloody machine that will make us all killed. I spit on him' – he spat – 'and curse him to hell.'

'Sure,' said Miller.

'Better take cover,' said Andrea, shoving rounds into the magazine of the Mauser. 'Here.' He handed the rifle to Wills, and said to Clytemnestra, 'Do you want one?'

'What do you think?' Her eyes flashed dark fire.

Andrea shrugged. 'Cover me,' he said, and gave his orders.

Miller and Clytemnestra went to the top of the grassy earthwork protecting the fuel. The surface of the aerodrome stretched away under the sun, a yellow-dun billiard table shot with shining patches of wind-flattened grass. And on that billiard table, small figures were advancing.

Andrea had been busy. He had rolled two fifty-gallon drums of aviation fuel to the top of the bank, siting them six feet apart. Between the drums, he set up the Spandau. Miller kept working, rolling the barrels up the slope, placing them along the crest of the earthwork.

'Bloody hell,' said Wills, whitening somewhat beneath the peeling mahogany of his face. 'It's an Aunt Sally.'

'What does that mean?' Clytemnestra was scowling down the sights of her rifle. The nearest soldier was four hundred yards away.

'If the Germans shoot at us,' said Wills in a dazed voice, 'they stand a good chance of hitting one of those drums. If they hit one of those drums, they stand a good chance of knocking it down and setting it on fire, and rolling it down into a lot of other drums, and blowing up their principal fuel dump. Their supply ship has been sunk. This is precious stuff. They won't want to lose it.'

'So?' said Clytemnestra, shrugging her broad shoulders. 'They won't shoot. This is good, no?'

'Of course,' said Wills, weakly. 'It's just not . . . normal, that's all.'

'Nothing is very normal,' said Clytemnestra. A German soldier was walking on top of her rifle's foresight. Her finger tightened on the trigger. Even as she squeezed, Andrea's Spandau started to chug heavily. Out there on the bare brown plain tiny figures began to drop and roll.

Wills sighted and squeezed, worked the bolt, sighted and squeezed again, and felt the barrel grow hot in his left hand. There were a lot of them: a terrible lot of them. They were not shooting back, though. Thus far, the gasoline drums were a success. But there were too many. They would be able to capture the position by sheer weight of numbers. Unless . . .

Wills knew with a sort of gloomy certainty that Andrea would have other plans, featuring the destruction of the fuel dump and everyone in it.

The machine gun jammed. The enemy trotted on over the shimmering grass. Any minute now, thought Wills.

Then from behind the line of attackers and to the left, he heard the cough and roar of an aero engine starting; first one, then another, throttling up, then back into a steady clatter. And from the direction of the huts there taxied a twin-engined Heinkel.

The aircraft stuck its nose on to the yellow-dun grass and swung towards the advancing Germans. A heavy, road-drill clatter added itself to the roar of the engines.

'My God,' said Wills. 'He's machine-gunning them.' And even as he spoke, the front line of the advance began to collapse. The Germans faltered and stopped. The Heinkel swung back towards the fuel dump and taxied, fast. It came to a halt by the dump entrance. Andrea said, 'Go. I'll come.' He had cleared the Spandau jam. There was still movement out there; squads were re-forming on the grass, and NCOs' yells drifted down the breeze. As they ran for the entrance, they heard Andrea's Spandau begin to chug again.

The Heinkel's door opened. Mallory looked out. Beyond him, Carstairs sat at the controls, smiling an odd smile; a smug smile, cat-gets-the-cream.

'All aboard,' said Miller, swinging the mahogany Enigma case in his hand. Mallory jumped down, and went to fetch Andrea. Miller heaved the case up and into the plane. Carstairs reached down and grabbed it. Miller was starting to help Clytemnestra on to the step when Carstairs said, 'I don't think so.' There was a Schmeisser in his hand. The muzzle trembled slightly. It was pointing straight between Miller's eyes.

'What?' said Miller.

'Bit of a load, six people plus pilot,' said Carstairs. 'Not a good idea.'

'What the hell are you talking about?'

'We don't want to take any chances with the machine, do we?' said Carstairs. 'I mean, who can you trust, nowadays?'

'You bastard,' said Wills. 'You absolute bloody –'

Miller stopped him. He said, 'What are you going to do with that thing?'

'Take it to the Allies,' said Carstairs. 'Trouble is, I haven't decided which ones. Everyone wants it. The Yanks have got dollars, the Russians have got gold, and even the poor old Brits have got a couple of bob stowed away in a sock, I shouldn't wonder. And they don't like each other much. I'm going to have a little auction, that's all. Now stand back.'

Miller stood back, pulling Wills and Clytemnestra back with him. His face was completely blank. 'Goodbye,' he said.

The door slammed. The engines throttled up. The Heinkel began to roll. Wills raised his Schmeisser. Miller knocked it down with his hand.

'You can't let him get away,' said Wills. 'He's a bloody thief. A traitor. You –'

'Hush,' said Miller, and Wills observed now that Andrea had come down from his post. 'The Germans think we're all on that plane.'

The Heinkel reached the end of the runway and pivoted on one wheel. The engines crescendoed as the throttles went through the gates. It began to roll. It rolled faster and faster, shrinking with distance, the tail lifting, the wheels rising on their suspension until there was daylight under them and the undercarriage came up. A hand came out of the pilot's window and waved. Then the aircraft turned over the buildings and headed out to sea, chased by the impotent black puffs of a couple of anti-aircraft shells.

'Hell,' said Wills. 'Oh, bloody hell.'

The Heinkel rose steeply into the deep Mediterranean blue. Soon it was no more than a dot, headed north-west, for Italy. Spiro was watching it as if it were a ghost. All his work, said his slack jaw and fishskin jowls; all his massive bravery, his tolerance of Captain Helmholz, his feigning of coma, his sliding around on ropes in the dark; all in vain.

Wills was not so tongue-tied. He was pale and shaking with rage. 'Sir,' he said to Mallory. 'I must protest. I must jolly well tell you that I shall be submitting a report to my superiors about this shameful, pathetic –'

He stopped. The black dot hung high in the blue vault of heaven. And then, shockingly, it changed. There was a brilliant white flash, and a puff of smoke, and comet-tails of falling debris. And later, several seconds later, the small *bap* of an explosion.

'It blew up,' said Wills. 'It just bloody well blew up.'

'Goodness me,' said Miller, mildly. 'So it did.'

'But he had the machine,' said Wills.

'Yeah, well,' said Miller. 'I knew there was something.' He was leaning on the concrete lip of the firefighting pond. He pulled a string that led into the murky deeps. On the end of the string was a chunky oilcloth parcel. 'This here is the Enigma machine,' he said. 'Captain Carstairs only had the case. I guess someone must have put something else in it.'

Wills gaped at him, then at the Enigma machine; the key to the deliberations of German High Command, a window into the enemy's most secret responses to the Allied second front, due to open any day now.

'There is a game you play with three cups and a pea,' said Mallory. 'Corporal Miller is the world champion. Now let us find somewhere to lie up for the day.'

Spiro's face was a miserable bag of sweating lard. 'Lie up?' he said. 'You crazy. They searches everywhere, finds us, catches us. We deads, matey boy.'

'Speak for yourself,' said Miller. 'Personally I am alive. And I have an idea that people in the great wide world are going to think we were on that plane.'

Spiro's face suddenly shone with hope and anticipation. 'My hell!' he cried. 'By the Godsalmighty you are one hunnert per cents!'

Andrea came down from the bank. 'They're coming,' he said.

'Time to leave,' said Miller, looking at his watch. Like ghosts, they flitted over the earthwork and were gone.

Feldwebel Braun approached the fuel dump wall with his usual briskness, his squad well scattered over the ground, as per the tactical manual when advancing in the face of enemy fire. Except that there was now no enemy fire. The defenders of the dump had gone quiet – not surprisingly, since they had all flown away in that Heinkel. There had been a lot of disorganization and general unpleasantness these last few days. Braun looked forward to a more normal life in which regulations would be observed and there would be the minimum of fighting.

Crouching slightly – from habit rather than the expectation of enemy fire – he led his squad to the earthwork and into the fuel dump in a succession of short, textbook rushes.

But the dump was empty. He wandered into the stacked oil drums. There were signs of occupation: spent cartridge cases, a foil wrapper from a bar of chocolate. But they were safely out of the way; out of the sky, too, he thought, chuckling heavily. All that remained were the oil drums, like the stumps of a forest turned to steel.

There was a fungus on one of the stumps. Braun walked closer, to examine it. An odd brown growth, with a pencil-sized object sticking out of it, a pencil with a black stripe on the shaft.

Braun opened his mouth to shout. He never made it.

A black time pencil means a ten-minute delay at twenty-five degrees centigrade. It was a warm spring morning, so the corrosive action of the liquid in the pencil's barrel was accelerated. As Braun ran towards the oil drum, the fuel dump blew up in his face.

They were sitting in a deep creek in a clump of reeds when the explosion came. The dry stems hissed and shook, and a blast of heat passed overhead, a waft of air hot enough to fill their nostrils with the smell of scorched grass. Then the smoke rolled up, and blotted out the sun.

Mallory put his head on his pack, and squinted up at the lip of the creek. Andrea was up there, standing sentry. When you are dead already, thought Mallory, you don't have to die . . .

At which point he fell asleep.

The sun was going down as the four SS men and two civilians wound out of the marshes and started along the fence of the aerodrome where it ran by the sea. The wire was bent, the angle-iron posts melted. The launch was where they had left it. Over on the Acropolis, all was quiet.

Reverently, Mallory laid the Enigma machine on the bottom boards of the boat, lifted the engine cover, and screwed the decompression lever back into place. He wound the starting handle, dropped the decompressor. The engine caught with a big, heavy chug.

'Nice night for a test firing,' said Miller. The sky was a vault of blue velvet pricked with stars. He looked at his watch again. 'They must have found the primary charges,' he said. 'They should have gone eight hours ago, easy.'

'Cast off,' said Mallory.

'*Wer da?*' said a voice from the shore. And suddenly there were figures there: dozens of figures, light gleaming on steel helmets and guns, and Mallory felt a great lurch of the heart, because the Thunderbolt squad were tired and sore and their identification would not stand up to scrutiny, and they had the most secret machine in the world in a sack on the boat's deck.

'Out,' said the voice in the dark.

'What the hell are you talking about?' said Mallory.

The voice said, 'Show us your documents.'

'Go to hell,' said Mallory. 'Refer to *Hauptmann* Wolf.'

'*Hauptmann* Wolf is dead, thank God. Out,' said the shadowy figure.

The not so shadowy figure.

The whole island was suddenly lit by a gigantic white flash. It illuminated with a pale and deadly light the twisted fence. It flung the shadows of the platoon on the shore up the scorched black berm of the fuel dump, and brought the glare of noonday to the black sheet of the water and the sugar-white houses of the Acropolis.

After the flash came a blast wave that raised a four-foot ridge of water and knocked most of the soldiers on the beach off their feet. The boat lurched high, then down again, bounced off the coping of the jetty. The people on the boat had been facing away from the explosion. The men on the shore had been looking into it. Their vision was a series of red blobs, shifting and wavering. 'Must help!' shouted Mallory, ears ringing. 'Quick!'

The boat's engine hammered. Water churned under her counter. She moved away from the jetty, towards the Apocalypse.

The mountain was burning. From tunnels and shafts and galleries there spewed gouts of flame and sparks. And from the top of the mountain, presumably the launching area next to which the fuel tanks had stood, there rose huge and twisting tongues of fire that burned and detached themselves and rose into the smoke that climbed and spread like a roof over land and sea.

'Most impressive, Corporal Miller,' said Mallory.

'I was born on the Fourth of July,' said Miller.

Under the roof of smoke the launch, with Wills at the helm, chugged across the dark water towards the jetty on the opposite shore. Some three cables short of the jetty, anyone watching would have seen the boat turn hard-a-port, run parallel with the eastern shore of the bay, continue its course past the headland and out to sea.

But there was nobody to watch small boats going about their business. All eyes were on the mountain of Antikynthos, erupting for the second time.

The boat's engine became a fading heartbeat, and vanished into the inky shadows offshore.

Two hours later they were at the rendezvous, on the long, glassy corrugations of the sea. Andrea found a bottle of brandy in his pack. They passed it round. There was a fishing line in a locker. Miller dangled it over the side, smoking and dozing. Mallory lay against the engine box with his eyes closed. Spiro sat and shivered, his eyes jerking left and right, his face a jaundiced yellow in the light of the lantern on the stubby mast. And in the shadows, close together, Wills and Clytemnestra sat holding hands. Into Wills' mind had come the certainty that the currents of war that had thrust him and Clytemnestra together would soon start running in new directions. He should have been relieved that the long ordeal was over. Instead, sore, battered and burned though he was, he felt something approaching sadness.

Miller was singing 'Your Feet's Too Big' and hauling in his line, when there was a commotion in the water nearby. A long, dark shape rose against the sky. A voice floated across the water. 'Any of you chaps called Mallory?'

'Yes,' said Mallory.

'Come on, then. Tea's brewing.' Pause. 'Nasty smell of smoke,' said the voice.

Mallory's eyes went back across the water to the hot orange glow that had once been the V4 plant.

There was a clang of boots on a steel pressure hull, the slam of a hatch, the whine of ballast-pumps filling tanks. Then there was silence; silence except for a sound that might have been the fading pant of a single-cylinder diesel, and the great, stirring rumour of the sea.

EPILOGUE

The sun was shining brilliantly on an emerald-green lawn, laid out for croquet. At the end of the lawn stood a small figure in an impeccable tropical uniform: Captain Jensen, a captain no longer, his sleeves and cap incandescent with bullion in the bright noonday. With him were Andrea, Mallory, Miller, and Wills; Wills looking faintly shifty in the presence of so much scrambled egg, the rest gaunt and hollow-eyed, and apprehensive, as if they were waiting for something.

The debriefing was over. The Enigma machine was already in a Hurricane *en route* for Tangmere, with a large and well-armed escort.

'Well,' said Jensen. 'That's that, then.'

Mallory said nothing. It would not have been politic to mention Admiral Dixon. Carstairs' role had already been explained. But Mallory was not feeling politic. Carstairs had been first a liability, then a danger, and finally a traitor. Carstairs had been Admiral Dixon's idea.

So Mallory said, 'We'd expected to find Admiral Dixon here.'

Jensen grinned, his alarming tiger's grin. 'I bet you had,' he said, and Mallory, as so often when he was with Jensen, knew that he had been outplayed and outmanoeuvred by a master. 'By the way,' said Jensen. 'It isn't Admiral Dixon any more. Captain Dixon, RN, Retired.' He looked down at the bullion on his arm. A broad stripe had joined the narrower gold hoops. 'Only room for so many admirals in the Service,' he said.

They looked at him: Andrea, hulking against the sun, Miller with his hands in his pockets, apparently half-asleep, and Mallory, the flesh bitten away from his face by hunger and exhaustion. That was Jensen for you. They had thought they had been playing one game on Kynthos, and they had played it well. But they had been pieces in another game, the game of intrigue and back-stabbing that Jensen had been playing against Dixon –

'Just one of those things,' said Jensen. He nodded at Wills. 'He doesn't mind, even if you do.'

But Wills was not listening. His mind was back on the submarine, standing in the conning tower, feeling the last pressure of Clytemnestra's hand on his, watching her steer the boat into the smokereeking night, heading for Parmatia. The turbulent currents of war had washed them apart, sure enough. In the smoother flow of peace, though, he would be back . . .

Jensen was saying something. 'Well,' he said, briskly. 'All's well that ends well, eh?'

'Yessir,' said Mallory.

'And I am very glad to see you. Very glad. Particularly glad today, as it happens . . .'

'Oh, no,' said Miller, under his breath. 'No, please.' Andrea was staring at Jensen, horrified. Mallory opened his mouth to speak, but Jensen put up his hand.

'. . . because I have a job for you,' he said. 'Just a tiny little job, really. And I thought, since the three of you are here anyway . . .'

Mallory sighed. 'We would be fascinated to hear about it,' he said. 'But we will need brandy.'

'Large amounts of brandy,' said Andrea.

'Five star,' said Miller. 'Roll out the barrel.'

'Of course,' said Jensen. 'And then we will begin.'